MW00826747

The Fourth Realm
Ten Realms Book 4
By: Michael Chatfield

Chapter: Internal Burning Pill

Erik was in one of the private rooms of the Alva Healing House. In one hand, he held the Internal Burning pill. It had red cracks running through it and faint embers seemed to gather around it.

In his other hand, he held a simple looking, curved dagger.

He let out a breath and looked up at the IVs that were hooked up to his arms. He opened the taps on them, allowing the stamina and healing potions to flow through the tubes and into his veins.

Erik took a deep breath. The Mana in the room moved with him as he prepared his Simple Heal spell.

Erik threw the pill into his mouth and stabbed the dagger into his left calf. He had already cleaned the area and covered it in Wraith's Touch.

The pill burned its way down his throat, reaching his stomach, where it unleashed powerful and very concentrated Fire-attribute Mana inside his body.

Fire attribute flames compounded the effect as power was released into his very bones over time, the two of them creating a synergistic effect.

The potions entering his body went to work as Erik used his healing spell, causing the Mana around him to burst into motion with the full might of a Mana King.

His body began to glow red from the Fire-Mana inside him. The blue-concentrated Mana in Alva appeared around him, the blue surrounding the red but not mixing. Erik's Mana channels started to glow with the concentrated power within.

Rugrat was the only other person in the room. Erik sat cross-legged on the stone floor, circulating Mana into his Simple Heal. His face twitched in pain as he was burned from the inside out by the powerful Fire-attribute Mana.

It burned through his body, destroying blood, tissues, and more. It was as if a fire elemental had been created within his body that had no choice but to destroy Erik's body, even as he tried to save himself.

Erik pulled the blade out from his leg, a thread of fear filling his mind. Erik laughed coldly.

Maybe today is the day I die. There was an odd sort of calm that came with that thought. He had no regrets, he had done all he could and wanted to do.

But if I will die this day the reaper better come prepared for a fight!

He forced himself through the ordeal. He was already committed and there was nothing he could do but deal with his decision. He grit his teeth, changing from Simple Heal to Focused Heal. He pulled out a needle filled with a powerful healing potion, gripping it in his hand, ready at a moment's notice.

A rumbling noise came from within Erik's body as the power from the pill and the damage from the destructive Fire-attribute was being overcome by Eriks focused heal. It was like a good burn from working out, only much, much faster.

He cried out as his body was rapidly rebuilt. The Fire-attribute Mana was within his body but it was being forcibly healed, his magic repairing the damage already done.

Another wave of Fire-attribute Mana was pulsed out from the pill in his body, reaching farther than the wave before.

His entire body was suffused with fire mana, slowly it was adapting, instead of acting like oil and water, his body was adapting incorporating the fire mana his very tissues were consumed and infused with the Fire-attribute Mana. His skin took on a red and dry appearance. Where his skin cracked, yellow-looking blood escaped his body.

His eyes seemed to be glowing with a deep-red flame as the heat around him increased.

From his bones, muscles, skin, tissues and down all the way to his marrow, his entire body was bathed in Fire-attribute Mana. The pill continued to send out wave after wave of Fire-attributed destruction while he healed the newly fire tempered flesh and bone.

Erik's body grew with the amount of power within his body, forcibly increasing his height. The Fire Mana seeped into his muscles and bones, changing them irrevocably to be longer, tougher and heavily resistant to fire.

Erik's mind had moved past the pain, it was no longer the focus, it was a drive. The burning was so intense that he felt that if he were to move his body, he would turn to ash.

Rugrat had put his hands on Erik some time ago and was healing him. He took a needle from his storage ring and injected it directly into Erik's body. Then he called in other healers. Seeing Erik's appearance, the other healers couldn't help but pause before they put their thoughts away and used their healing spells.

Erik's mind was fighting against the pain, focusing on breathing and casting his spell. His entire existence focused on these two things; everything else was background noise.

Another round of deep rumbling noises came from within Erik's body. Popping noises could be heard as Erik's bones, which had been refined, impurities burned away looking like polished marble as it's density had only increased with the mutative effects of the Fire-attribute Mana running through his system. The cuts across his skin closed, the red and yellow-looking blood within his veins became a healthier, darker red and his blood grew thicker, as if turning from water to syrup. Erik's heartbeat sounded out in the room, stronger and more powerful than ever. He shed his old skin, his new skin unblemished, with no signs of the damage from before.

His muscles were more defined, packed with explosive power.

Erik let out a breath through his nose, expelling the heat, causing the air to distort, making the healers sweat from being in such close proximity of the hot breath.

The healers continued to heal Erik. The Fire Mana that had ruined his body turned from toxin to tonic, as it purged out impurities that Erik hadn't been able to draw out with poison.

His entire body had been purified by the Fire-attribute Mana.

His Body Like Stone was merely the foundation. The process of tempering his body through flames had further ignited his inner potential and continued his journey to progress into the higher levels of Body Cultivation.

As soon as the strain on his body was relieved, he passed out.

As he rested, the other healers continued to heal him, curing the hidden injuries within his body that had been left after taking the tempering pill.

"Well, looks like that's one way to temper your body," concluded Rugrat. He wiped the sweat from his forehead. He stepped back after putting Erik in his bed. Rugrat's legs shook from the power he had channeled through his body and the stress of knowing his friend's life was in his hands.

As Erik slept, Rugrat noticed Erik's body continued to go through changes. The Fire-attribute Mana that had destroyed his body was no longer the raging Fire Elemental from before. It had been destroying his body but with the help of the healers and Rugrat, Erik's body had been able to withstand the destructive forces of the Fire-attribute Mana. Erik had now taken the power of the Fire attribute for his own.

Erik's Strength had reached new heights. His resistance toward Fire-attribute Mana was now incredible. Normal flames wouldn't be able to harm him anymore. He could exist in places filled with Fire-attribute Mana more easily now as well. Even purifying Fire-attribute Mana and storing it in his body was now possible.

Mana Gathering cultivators looked to purify, compress, and then control Mana of all attributes, increasing the strength of their Mana channels and their mental capabilities so that they could handle different attribute Mana without being destroyed from within. Body cultivators on the other hand didn't manipulate the different types of Mana. They tempered their bodies, taking in different attribute Mana by going to different lands filled with concentrated Mana and phenomena. They walked into volcanoes, into cold tundra, braved places of distorted space, mountains of lightning and skies of tempest winds. Step by step, they walked into lands that would kill others, all in a hope to increase their Strength. One wrong step and they could be crippled or killed.

***

Erik woke up some time later. A nearby healer came over immediately.

"How did it go?" Erik asked, as he used Simple Organic Scan to look through his body. He could see that his body had gone through a powerful change.

"The effects of the pill were resolved," The healer responded. Then they paused, taking time to gain the confidence to ask their question, "Were you able to increase your Body Cultivation?"

Erik opened up his notifications.

==========

Your base stats have increased!

==========
Stamina +1
Strength +1
Agility +1
Stamina Regeneration +1
==========

"So little?" Erik pondered as he opened up his active quests.

==========
Quest: Body Cultivation 2
==========

The path of cultivating one's body is not easy. To stand at the top, one must forge their own path forward.

==========
Requirements:
Reach Body Like Iron Level
==========

Rewards:
+6 to Strength
+6 to Agility
+6 to Stamina
+10 to Stamina Regeneration
+1,000,000 EXP
==========

"Looks like reaching Body Like Iron will not be an easy task," Erik sighed to himself.

Still, he opened up his character sheet and took a look at the changes there.

==========
Name: Erik West
==========

Level: 32
==========

Race: Human

==========

Titles:

From the Grave II

Mana King

Dungeon Master II

Reverse Alchemist

Poison Body

==========

Strength: (Base 27) +39

==========

660

==========

Agility: (Base 20) +41

==========

335

==========

Stamina: (Base 30) +9

==========

585

==========

Mana: (Base 6) +35

==========

410

==========

Mana Regeneration (Base 10) +40

26. 50/s

==========

Stamina Regeneration: (Base 28) +33

13. 20/s

==========

Erik closed his notifications and then closed his eyes, feeling for the changes in his body. When he leveled up, the power of the Ten Realms would enter his body, modifying it. When he was able to temper his own body it wasn't the strength of the Ten Realms but his own personal Strength that increased. It took time getting used to the changes in his stats when he leveled up, as if he were using a new tool but when his base stats increased, it only took a few moments to adjust.

It was like how a marksman could pick up any gun and be decent with it, just as a layman could do the same. Yet a marksman would be able to quickly acclimate to the new weapon, improving their effectiveness with it faster than the layman.

Erik checked himself once more before he started to pull out the IVs.

The healer who was tending to him asked, "Sir?"

"Looks like it works," Erik responded, "but the pill by itself won't be enough." Erik got up, a frown on his face. His next ideas to complete his Fire tempering were a lot more drastic. "How long have I been out for?"

"Just one day," the healer replied.

"Then there's still plenty of work to be done, Thank you for your help." Erik told the healer watching him. He then headed out of the healing house and toward the academy.

Chapter: Sockets

Rugrat was hammering away at a piece of metal. When they had returned from the Third Realm, Rugrat threw himself into smithing but training their troops had taken over and he had needed to put smithing to the side.

As he trained Alva's military, he had mentally worked on new ideas and plans. Sending messages to Tan Xue and Taran, they had taken on different projects he had thought of. After he had seen more of the Ten Realms, he had a number of ideas that they hadn't considered before. He had talked to Julilah and Qin about formations as well. When he had five seconds of free time, he had read through books that he'd borrowed from the library. Then, he helped Erik with increasing his Body Cultivation.

Now *finally*, he was able to get into the smithy once again. Though this time it was not the smithy from before but a tier-three smithy, complete with testing rooms, massive refineries and several different furnaces and smelting areas that people could use to draw out their skill to its fullest. Rugrat's mobile smithy was decent. It was an Apprentice-level smithy and wouldn't reduce one's ability to forge powerful items but it wouldn't help either. Only Journeyman-level smithies and higher had the capability to increase one's smithing ability.

The simplest workspaces were Apprentice-classed. Before, there had been Novice-grade work areas that could slightly decrease a person's smithing ability, leaving them with a worse final product. but, These had been mostly abandoned by the time of the smith's upgrade.

Now, there was an Expert-level smithing room and five Journeyman smithing rooms, along with twenty Apprentice-level smithing rooms.

From the flames, to the tools and flames the different rooms saw a jump in grade. The Journeyman-level smithing rooms had powerful flames that could deal with all Mortal-level metals and a few Earth-grade metals without needing extra help from the smiths.

The Expert-level flames could melt Earth and low-level Sky metals easily, other lower grade flames would need a catalyst or enhancers that might reduce the quality of the flame and the forge later on. The tools that were supplied by the higher level forges could not only deal with these high-octane flames but excel and remain unaffected by the increase in power and hardness of the various metals.

There were also formations in the smiths that concentrated Mana, increasing one's Mana Regeneration rate, as well as passive formations that increased one's smithing ability. These formations helped to remove distractions and put the smith in the best possible mental state while they were working.

The new formations were only located in the Journeyman and higher workshops. If one was an Apprentice, then they would get a ten percent increase in smithing ability in the Journeyman-level smithing rooms and twenty percent when they were in the Expert-level rooms. A person at the Journeyman level would only get a five percent increase in smithing ability in the Journeyman smithing rooms and a ten percent increase in the Expert-level rooms. This didn't sound like much but it increased the ease with which one might reach a state of enlightenment and how long they could maintain it.

With this bonus, people at the cusp of a breakthrough would sell their soul to get even an hour in the Expert-level smithing room.

Clear rules had needed to be put in place to regulate each different forges' schedule. Preference was given to the council members, then the department heads, followed by those with the highest ranked skill level, descending downward through the skill levels so that the time in the Expert-smithing room wouldn't ever be wasted.

Rugrat co-ruled Alva, so he could have demanded use of the Expert-level smithing room but instead he had taken a Journeyman-level room. Tan Xue was trying to break through from Journeyman to Expert. As the department head, she didn't have to care about lessons too much, instead passing on insights to the teachers and focusing on improving her own skills.

Though at the moment, she was nowhere near the forges, spending her time with the formation workshop people. Her problem wasn't her smithing skill; her problem lay in her skill with formations. Journeyman-level weapons or armor were those that had one innate effect and a formation or enchantment. Her enchantments were simple, allowing them to be Journeyman weapons but they were still on the weaker side of Journeyman.

An Expert-class smith needed to pull out two innate effects from their crafted weapon along with the space for two enchantments and the ability to bind to a single person. . She could bring out the two innate effects with difficulty but she wasn't sure how to complete the two enchantments and the binding ability. So, she had turned from smithing to formations and spending her time talking to Qin and Julilah to increase her knowledge. She didn't need to know all of the secrets to formation making but the general knowledge would allow her to alter how she made her weapons, so that they would be able to hold two enchantments.

A person in the First Realm with an Expert-level piece of armor or weapon could rise to power, dominating in the First Realm. Even people from the Fifth and Sixth Realms would be tempted by Expert-level gear.

Rugrat, seeing the struggles that Tan Xue was facing and knowing his own weakness in formations, had come up with a new idea.

Rugrat hammered down on the metal. It hummed with his resonating blow, the red-hot metal singing. Rugrat had a grin on his face at seeing the metal bend to his will, turning from ingot to tool.

It was something he thought he would never see again after his crippling injury. He had been sure he would never feel the heat on his face or the Mana that boiled in the air and rushed through his veins. It was like jumping out of a plane or being a teenager racing around in a car. The rush of creation was definitely Rugrat's drug of choice. Maybe it was a close second, after beer.

Rugrat put his hammer away, picking up the iron bar and forming a Mana blade. Pieces of metal fell from what he was holding, hissing as they touched the floor.

Rugrat didn't notice, completely focused on his work the Journeyman room's higher mana content and the Heart Calming pills that Erik had passed him turned him into a machine as he worked.

His movements were like a work of art. The rough form transformed in his hands, changing from a rigid piece of metal to the back of a gauntlet. It took him less than a minute as he finished that step and quenched the metal.

It was a right hand gauntlet and it looked like the back of a set of fingerless gloves. Adding the enhancer caused red and black veins to trace through the Mortal-iron metal, making it look similar to damascus steel.

Rugrat put the gauntlet on a table and clamped it in place with a vise. He formed his mana blade once again and kept focused on his plan for the gauntlet. Directly in the back of the piece, there was a circular space about one inch in diameter. He started carving inside the circular recess. He put the blade away once he finished that step and took out a file to clean up the metal, smoothing and finishing it.

Rugrat pulled out a notebook that he'd filled with information that he had researched for this project. He found the right page and pulled out a design. He looked it over and checked the metal.

"Well, never easy," Rugrat muttered as he took out a fine pointed writing tool and started copying the lines on the piece of paper to the gauntlets.

It took him a few times to get the lines right. He measured up the lines and traced throughout the metal twice before he took his Mana blade to the lines. He traced them out slowly with fluid movements. Lines flowed back from the fingers and thumb, crossing and weaving through one another before they reached the circular socket.

Rugrat, made some lines deeper before he pulled out another diagram and started to work within the socket. Then, he cut out a locking mechanism into the socket. He moved to the smithy, where there was a pot of blood-looking liquid.

"Well, hopefully the enhancer will increase the conductivity," Rugrat muttered to himself. He had mixed the concoction up earlier. The base was the same enhancer that he had used with the Mortal iron, combined with a few other stabilizing ingredients.

Rugrat grabbed the gauntlet with tongs. As he held the gauntlet over the blood-red concoction, he scooped up the substance and poured it over the gauntlet. It oozed into the grooves he'd created and dripped down into the bucket below. Rugrat poured a few more times as the mixture started to cool until it filled all of the lines he'd carved out.

Even when the mixture dried, it still looked like fresh blood with veins running through the metal hand.

Rugrat set it aside, then picked up the metal he had cut off from the gauntlet and put it into the furnace. He used his tongs to pull out a small piece of metal and repeated the processes all over again, creating the left handed gauntlet.

He compared the two. They were perfectly identical.

Rugrat placed them to the side and then took out yet another piece of already enhanced and red-hot metal.

He hammer tapped this piece out, creating a thin piece of metal. Then, he turned his Mana blade into a circle and, using it like a cookie cutter, he cut down into the metal. He ended up with identical, thin circular coins.

Rugrat quenched, then smoothed and finished the thin-coins. Sitting down at his workbench, he pulled out several sheets from his notebook and placed them in front of him. Once again, he copied out the designs and carved out the lines from the paper onto the metal. He messed up a few times but he had also made extra blank coins.

It took him some time but once he was finished he gathered up his items and then headed out of the smithing room, rushing toward the formation workshop. He burst in, finding Julilah, Qin and Tan Xue in the same room. All three women looked up as Rugrat moved to the middle of the room and dumped his new gauntlets on a table.

"I had a thought and before I knew it, I made it. Let me know what you think," Rugrat blurted. His mind was still under the effects of the calming formation and the pill he had consumed. It gave him laser-like focus but it made him ignore everything else.

Tan Xue reached the tables first and she picked up one of the gauntlets. "High Journeyman-level workmanship. The enhanced metal is powerful. Is this another blank?" Tan Xue asked as she looked at the coins that the other two were picking up.

"Sockets, weapon armor, smithing, sockets," Rugrat said. It seemed as if half of his brain was shut down as he paused and stuttered through the words. "Weapon engraved with necessary components except formation. Formation multi-layered plates lined one over another, fused together into whole." Rugrat grabbed a glove and a coin.

"Put formations into slots." Rugrat stammered as he mimed putting the coin into the circular socket and turning it. "Weapon has formation, can change formation as needed. No longer need to engrave formations into weapons. Two components of one whole. Upgrade formations, or upgrade weapons, increase in power."

Through Rugrat's broken sentences and simple words, the other three's eyes shone, looking between the gauntlet and the coins.

Rugrat pulled out his notes of the different drawings and blueprints he had crafted and put them on the table. His notes and images were rough outlines, scrawled across the pages. He opened it up to a page of circles and different diagrams that he had named 'Sockets'.

Tan Xue looked at the information, having to squint a few times to read through it.

She frowned as she stopped reading, digesting the information and unpacking it.

"If you had a weapon and say two of these sockets, then you could pick and choose the formation plates to place in them. Increased striking speed, cutting strength, Water Affinity attacks, Fire, or Earth," Tan Xue marveled.

"The formations or the armor could be changed as needed. Thus allowing one to increase in Strength and without needing to buy new equipment for every situation. Say you go from a desert to an arctic wasteland, simply change out your formations to increase your fighting ability. You could have your high-grade armor, Expert-level smithed, and get Journeyman-level formations, then replace the plates with Expert formation plates at a later date. These could also save you from ruining the armor from a botched formation. Many times, it is the formation master, not the smith, who breaks the armor if they don't understand it well enough. Doing the formation separately means that you can't ruin the armor!" Qin squeaked.

"Need to work on weapons!" Rugrat announced as he turned and departed as quickly as he had arrived. Now that he had completed one task, his mind had moved to the next. Firearms.

Once Rugrat had made it back to the smithy, he pulled out his M40, Big Momma and his modified rifle.

With quick actions, he broke them down into their component parts. He pulled out barrels and other components that had been made by the other smiths according to the specifications that he had listed, as well as wood furniture and other components.

Rugrat checked the parts against one another, making sure that they were all identical. Anything that didn't meet his standards got a note on them and was put to the side. Well, thrown, with some cursing tossed in.

Rugrat pulled out some Mortal metal he had already enhanced to increase its durability and ability to dissipate heat. He pulled out notes, checked sizing and used his Mana blade on parts and ingots as he went. He cut the ingots down into the manageable metal blanks, then he started off his rough cuts, stripping off excess materials working the blank into his desired shape.

He cut all of the blanks down, fifteen of them in total. Then he did his finishing cuts. . The only noises that could be heard were Rugrat working, his Mana blade cutting through metal, shaping small pins, to cocking handles, firing pins and the other components of a bolt action rifle.

He had no idea of the uproar that he had created in the formation workshop as Julilah and Qin brought in other formation Apprentices to look at what he'd made.

***

The information made sense. The coins were just miniaturized formation plates. He had created two of them that matched the gauntlets to increase their ability.

Tan Xue looked up from the plans some time later. "Socket weapons. If I was able to create a weapon with two innate abilities and incorporate two sockets in it, would I reach the Expert level in smithing?" she asked herself.

Without anyone noticing, she slipped out of the formation workshop and headed to the smithy. She pulled out a few ingots of Earth-grade iron. With Rugrat's help and his notes, she and Taran had figured out how to make their own Earth-grade ingots and further refined the process, requiring less Mortal Mana stone dust. They had kept their Earth-grade iron on them; it was too valuable for them to sell.

Tan Xue stoked the fires in the Expert-level smithy and took one of the focusing pills from the alchemists. She pulled out an array of blueprints, sifting through them before she came to a simple dagger.

"Requires less materials and it isn't that big, so it will be easier to add the required lines needed to transmit the power of the socket. I think I can hide the sockets in the pommel too," Tan Xue muttered to herself. She pulled out a fresh piece of paper and started to draw out a blueprint, first the blade, then the lining that would overlay it, then the lines needed to interface the sockets with the weapon. She worked on her plans a number of times, scrapping them and re-making them, working them until they looked as though they might actually work.

When she left the formation workshop, it had been late afternoon. By the time that she finished her blueprints, it was starting to brighten in Alva. The few birds that lived in the parks and the farmlands were chirping.

Tan Xue looked at her finished designs and turned to her furnace. Her eyes saw nothing other than the flames as she increased the temperature and checked through her storage rings before she found the right enhancer which she added into the Earth-grade iron. Unlike Mortal items and below, higher grade materials had very high Mana content. So, a portion of the metal was consumed when enhancing Earth-grade iron. Mana gathering formations did their best to make sure that there wasn't a large loss but there was always something taken.

It was another reason that increasing one's skill became harder in the higher realms. Lower grade ingredients or materials might be salvageable but as the materials got higher grade, once they were used, they would turn to scrap unless the salvager was highly skilled indeed.

Tan Xue willingly accepted the loss in material as she alloyed the Earth iron.

Chapter: Specialization

Rugrat was still working in the smithy. He hadn't left since entering yesterday after his brief trip to the formation workshop. The smithy and the workshop had gone into an uproar over the new socket type weapons and formations, not that Rugrat noticed a damn thing.

Erik left them to it as the Alva military came back to the barracks after finishing their two days of leave.

Glosil stepped forward and then turned to face Erik, who stood at the front of the formation.

"I, Glosil Bardon, do solemnly swear on the Ten Realms that I will support and defend Alva Dungeon, the dominion of Erik West and Jimmy Rodriguez, against all enemies, foreign and domestic; that I will bear true faith and allegiance to the same and that I will obey their orders and the orders of the officers appointed over me, according to the rules and laws created with their assent. That I take this obligation freely, without any mental reservation or purpose of evasion and that I will well and faithfully discharge the duties of the office to which I am about to enter."

The oath was confirmed by the Ten Realms as a golden light fell over the both of them. The glow of the oaths made the barracks light up as the council members and the officers who had been assigned in the military had the light of oath around them

Behind Glosil, the rest of the soldiers raised their hands and repeated their oaths, inserting their own names. Their families watched as they made their final oath, the one that brought them into the military of Alva, only solidifying what they had already sworn before when they had joined Alva.

"I accept your oath," Erik said. The power around him and the others dissipated, his word overriding them all. He and Rugrat held the primary power to directly order the military to do their bidding if they so desired, as long as it assisted Alva.

Silence fell over the men and women standing there.

"At ease!" Erik said.

They relaxed in place, unlocking their necks and looking at him as he stepped forward and nodded to Glosil. He turned and started walking slowly, pacing in front of the formation.

"For the last three or five months, you have trained. You have left behind your civilian selves and become a true military. It is your mission to protect Alva. To do that, you will need to grow in Strength. It is not a secret that Rugrat and I plan on reaching for the Fourth Realm. What has not been said is that the rest of you will be coming to the Fourth Realm with us to hone your skills, to show you the different realms, to bring you into confrontation with an enemy that is stronger than you. Rugrat and I have gone to the other realms practically alone up to this point but the Fourth Realm is not just another realm. Many of you might have heard of its nickname: the battlefield realm.

"This is because the Fourth Realm is a land of opportunity, a place where people can gain great Strength or falter and paint the ground in their blood. The Fourth Realm's strength and allure doesn't come from mines, or from gardens, from workshops or sects. It comes from dungeons. The Fourth Realm is littered with dungeons that different groups fight over. The more powerful a nation is, the more dungeons they command. There are many kinds of dungeons: some are filled with rare monsters that are reborn over time, others that are filled with rare minerals that can be mined but grow back with time others that are incredible places to cultivate Mana Gathering or Body Cultivation. Finally, they contain dungeon trials like our own battlefield dungeon that allow a person to gain points to use in the prize hall to claim prizes of amazing power.

"Our mission will be to scout the Fourth Realm, to learn more of its secrets and learn of different dungeons. If possible, we will capture those dungeons. If not, we will destroy them. We will also increase our Strength. Below us there are another five floors. In the Metal floor, there are creatures that might reach level forty. Fighting in the battlefield dungeon will increase our Strength but doesn't increase our coordination. If we are to operate as a military, we have to work as a whole, not just in smaller parties." Erik stopped walking and looked at them all.

"What we have done so far is your basic training. For the next two months, we will gather intelligence on the Fourth Realm and we will continue to train. You will all be issued new weapons and trained with them by the best fighters we have. Erik waved his hand and a repeating crossbow appeared.

"This is a repeating crossbow mark one. When you pull the trigger, it will continue to fire until the magazine is empty, much like the repeating ballistas. The old pedal-style ballistas will have a new repeating mechanism like this, allowing you to stay in cover when using the weapon system." Erik put the crossbow away and pulled out his personal rifle.

"This is a rifle. Rugrat and I will be picking sharpshooters, who will be qualified to use these weapons. They have a much longer range than the ballista and their accuracy is higher. With buffs, their firepower is stronger than the heavy repeater ballista and they can fire at a comparable rate.

"Everyone has completed their first aid training. Those who have done schooling with the healing house or with the alchemists will be trained as combat medics. Alchemists will be trained to create poisons, gunpowder, and other materials that we will need. You may also train as chefs, sword fighters, spear fighters, trackers—everyone will at least have one specialization. By the end of this training period, everyone will be assigned a mount. You will know how to ride as naturally as they run. You will all be able to use the repeater crossbow, ballista, and the rifles to a passable degree.

"To reach the Fourth Realm, you will all need to be level thirty, so we will be going to the battlefield dungeon to see what you've learned and put your skills to the test. Check the notice-board to sign up for specialization courses and to see if you have been recommended for a teaching position. Someone who has over three specializations will be allowed to try out to join the special teams."

The three special teams had been slimmed down, turning in-to two special teams with ten members in each. Roska led one and Niemm led the other. Storbon was a good commander but Niemm was a steadier hand. Storbon, who had been feeling the pressure of leadership, took the position of second-in-command well.

There was a hope that, in the future, the special teams would reach the point where they were a company-sized unit with four special teams.

Although they wanted to expand the special teams, they were determined not to sacrifice ability. Earning a position had actually become harder with the new changes in Alva's military. The current members of the special teams had to work hard to retain their positions.

The men and women of the Alva military knew that they were strong but the special teams were on a different level. They threw themselves into anything that could increase their strength, whether that was trials, body cultivation, mana culti-vation, learning from the academy. That information had then been tempered through handling life and death situations and trusting in one another completely. When working together they became much stronger, they might only be able to fight maybe two or three people of the same level but they could go up against three or four other groups of the same size and level and win. Through using their combined skills they understood, overcame, and destroyed their enemy.

"Atten-tion!" Erik called out, causing them all to snap upright. "Dis-missed!"

They turned and marched off before breaking ranks and quickly heading for the information board.

Erik headed up to the office, ready to receive the pre-selected teachers and specialty trainers to give them their standing orders.

***

Storbon looked at the boards of different specializations. He had been picked as one of the teachers for in-field maintenance because of how he used his smithing and tailor skills in the field to make sure that his and the others' gear were in the best condition.

He was also given a course to run on spear techniques and ways to fight, along with Tully from Special Team Two and a potential applicant to the special teams named Domonos,.

Storbon looked at the combat medic classes, the field cooking courses, marksman courses, rifle and repeater courses, bowman courses, Fire mage courses, lightning mage courses, battlefield formation course, sword and shield courses with avid interest. Anything related to war that someone had knowledge of, a course was made around it.

With the changes in Alva's military and their training, they had increased their Strength but more importantly their coordination. Everyone had striven to increase their Strength before as a personal goal. Now, their goal was to improve themselves to help their comrades.

Storbon hadn't thought the two different ideas would have a minimally different effect but he saw he was wrong as people signed up for as many classes as possible.

They didn't want to just push to be a part of the special teams; they wanted to improve upon the strengths that they had and shore up their weaknesses to better serve their units.

Storbon felt his blood boil in excitement. He knew how strong their fighting power was when working together. These courses built upon that basic knowledge that had been burned into their minds and got them to think and react more.

Storbon put his name down on a few sheets for new courses and then headed out of the barracks. One course started later that afternoon. Storbon's classes didn't start until early the next morning after group physical training.

Storbon's feet carried him to the healing house, where he saw a few other military members. "Hello, I'm looking to further temper my body," Storbon said.

"How many temperings have you completed?" the smiling woman at the front desk asked.

"I've done four. I need to temper my organs as part of my next step."

"Okay, I will see if there is someone available." The woman checked a list and then talked into her sound transmission device.

"Sir!" Yao Meng snapped to attention after quickly noticing that Starbon had entered the main door.

"At ease," Storbon waved Yao Meng's actions away.

"Fancy meeting you here, boss," Yao Meng said.

"They still let you in this place?" Storbon replied with a smile.

Yao Meng laughed and winked. "What work you having done?"

"Body Cultivation, organs,reaching for Body Like Stone. You?" Storbon said.

"One more body tempering, brings me up to four, and opening up one more Mana gate," Yao Meng sighed in response.

"That ain't gonna be cheap," Storbon said. The healing house might not have many patients from injuries but they were constantly helping people to temper their bodies, to raise their Body Cultivation or to make the path of Mana Gathering Cultivation a bit smoother.

Erik had forged a path ahead with his Body Cultivation, and he and Rugrat had submitted all they knew on the two subjects. That information, combined with their knowledge of the human body, had led to further refinement of how one could open their Mana gates and temper their body using methods previously unknown in the realms.

Mana gates were pierced and people circulated their Mana for ten minutes in the morning and night. Mana gathering formations and or Alchemy concoctions could both be provided for a price to increase how quickly they were able to open their Mana gates. The body tempering concoctions used to temper the different systems were highly targeted but they did not need to be tailored for each person. However a healer or multiple healers would need to be on staff, watching over them as they tempered their bodies. Stamina and healing potions, as well as healing spells, made sure that the temperings went well. Concoctions that would render the person unconscious while undergoing the temperings were used to make sure that there were no complications.

The cultivations were both time-consuming and resource-intensive practices, so they cost a fair amount to carry out. Otherwise, the healing house would be filled with people all the time.

They were always looking to make it cheaper and faster but there was a lower limit to their costs.

"Tell me about it. My drinking fund is going to be hurting for a bit but thankfully I put all of my money into those new savings accounts. Actually made some money off it," Yao Meng said with a pleased smile.

"Storbon?" A healer asked as she came out into the waiting area.

Storbon raised his hand and made his way over.

"See you on the other side," Storbon said to Yao Meng.

"Catch you on the flip side," Yao Meng said, trying to act suave as he walked up to the receptionist. "So I need to temper my body, open a Mana gate, and even more importantly, could I take you out on a date?" Yao Meng asked the receptionist, who laughed.

Storbon grinned as he followed the healer into the back of the healing house.

Chapter: Gathering

Rugrat finally stumbled out of the smithy and collapsed in his room in the barracks.

The manor had been given over to Delilah since Erik and Rugrat had taken up residence in the barracks.

Erik left him with a few Stamina Regeneration potions, then went to meet with the staff on the different courses he would be leading and summoned Glosil into his office.

"Sir!" Glosil snapped off a salute. Instead of the regular American military salute, Erik and Rugrat had gone with a Roman salute, placing one's right fist over their heart. It was harder to see and if someone forgot on the battlefield, it wouldn't be that noticeable. Also, it looked cool.

Erik tapped his fist against his chest. "I'm going to be heading to the Third Realm for a few days, at most a week. I'll be taking a group of people with me up there and I'll return with those who are finished working on the restaurant. I'll be meeting with Old Hei, my teacher, and gathering information on the Fourth Realm as well as looking over the location there. While I am gone and Rugrat is out of commission working on some kind of project, you are in charge. So, before I leave, are there any questions that you have for me?"

"Not that I can think of, sir," Glosil said.

Erik nodded. Glosil was the direct commander of the Alva army, while Erik and Rugrat commanded all of the military forces of Alva, which included the adventurers, the army, the special teams as well as the rest of Alva. They could take command of individual units if they desired but when it came to the army, they went through Glosil, confirming his position and establishing a solid chain of command.

Glosil dealt with the day-to-day management as Erik and Rugrat dealt with further training, planning for the future, and strategy. That did not mean that Glosil didn't have any say but there was a clear divide between their responsibilities.

"Okay. Look after Alva while I'm gone."

***

Erik looked over the group with him. They were bundled up against the cold. Nearly all of them were traders but there were a few farmers and people from the cookhouse as well.

They had taken the dungeon's teleportation formation to one of the hidden teleportation arrays they'd placed near cities with totems.

It took them a half day to trudge through the snow and then through the mud streets of the city. Reaching the totem, they each paid their one Mana stone and disappeared in a flash of light.

They reappeared in the Third Realm Division Headquarters. The traders and the others, some who'd spent their lives in Alva Village and Alva Dungeon, looked around in clear awe.

They stripped off their heavy outer layers and pushed on, Erik leading the way through the crowds.

"Fifty gold," the woman said as they reached the front of the lines.

Erik opened his coat. His mid-Journeyman Alchemist badge was pinned on his armor.

She cast a verification spell on the badge. "Have a good day, Journeyman." The lady smiled.

Erik smiled back and went on.

The others paid their fifty gold fee to enter the city. The totem was as busy as ever, with people coming through with special massive storage holding caravans, others wearing Alchemist Association symbols on their chests.

Such a scene in the First Realm was unheard of. The sheer amount of money needed to move so many people and items was incredible.

They left the totem and weaved through the streets. It wasn't long until he spotted the Sky Reaching Restaurant.

"Well, it looks like Matt put all of his skills to the test." Erik smiled, looking up at the building. It stood over the other buildings, it was tastefully built and situated so it looked out over the city. With clean lines, the building's stone was white with floor-to-ceiling windows. The underside of the overhanging roofs was made with a lighter wood, creating a striking contrast against the clean gray tiles. It made one study it, looking at its striking details.

As they got to the street, they saw that there was a line through a side door. The main gates were open but the large guards standing there only allowed a few people past. Both of them were from the Alva Adventurer's Guild.

"Well, looks like it has become quite the popular location," Erik said under his breath, looking at the people entering and leaving.

Erik and his group moved toward the entrance.

"Look, another group looking to be tossed out," someone in the passing crowd around the restaurant said.

"I've never seen them before. The seating in the Sky Reaching Restaurant is highly sought after—only the upper echelons of the city can get a reservation! The rest of us have to hope that their store doesn't run out of goods!" someone added.

"It was only last week that the son of the Denang trading group's leader created a ruckus and was not allowed in!"

"I heard his father came personally to express his apologies and has since sent his son out of the city to carry out trade in another of their cities," another added in a low voice.

"The Sky Reaching Restaurant is generous. They made it clear that it was on the son, not on the father. The merchant head even made a reservation on the spot for his trade company to celebrate a large deal!"

"Renting out that much space—it must have cost tens of Mana stones!" someone said in awe.

"Truly, the rich know how to show off their power!" another mocked.

People sneered and looked at the group with disdain, stopping what they were doing to watch the show.

Erik paid them no attention as he strolled up to the entrance and pulled down his hood.

"Mister West." The two guards cupped their fists and bowed at their waist.

"Who is he for the guards to bow that low? They only do that when Pill Head Hei is arriving."

"No need for that," Erik waved off their bow. "Is Matt in?"

"He is in his office, working on some plans or other. Do you want us to let him know you're here?" Instead of the guards' normal stony expressions, they seemed ten years younger with happy smiles on their faces as their eyes darted to the others behind Erik, overjoyed to see some of their friends from back home.

"I'll go bug him myself. Can you see if you can find some room for this lot?" Erik asked with a smile, pointing at the group.

"We can probably find a floor somewhere," One of the guards grinned.

"You'll be tasting the backside of my spoon," one of the cooks warned, putting her hands on her hips.

"No need for that, Agatha." The female guard smiled.

The cook's expression collapsed into a smile as she waved a finger at the guard. "Your mother is worried sick. She sent me to keep an eye on you and make sure you get a boyfriend!"

The female guard's expression fell as her shoulders slumped.

"Come on, one needs a good posture! You take good care of your weapons but not yourself!" Agatha sighed and shook her head.

"Office?" Erik asked the other guard.

"Office." The guard nodded.

Erik and the others looked to escape the chatter between the guard and her family friend. Another guard took her place as they moved toward the restaurant.

There were plants being tended to in various places in the courtyard and around the walls themselves. Erik remembered the smell that had been there before but now it was neutralized by these plants that not only covered the smell but made one feel relaxed.

Looking at the plants, Erik nodded in appreciation. They were ingredients that could be used to make perfumes and con- coctions to calm one's mind.

I never thought that we would start to use ingredients to mask the smell of the neighbors. Erik chuckled to himself, studying the interior of the restaurant.

The side entrance led to a store where prepared meals were sold to the people of the Division Headquarters. Everyone was only allowed to buy one meal to make sure that the greatest num- ber of people were served and that traders didn't buy up all of their stock and drive the price up.

The traders with Erik couldn't help but look at the store with shining eyes. All of them had brought multiple meals from the First Realm, some of them made by Jia Feng herself, her direct apprentices, or the teachers of the cooking department.

They headed through the building, passing through the garden in the middle of the front tower, and continued through to the private areas.

Erik got some directions, heading to the back right hand tower. He walked up the stairs, reaching the top of the building and passed other people working in the restaurant, or others who had come from Alva Dungeon to carry out trade, learn about Alchemy, or simply to explore. Erik reached Matt's room and knocked on the door.

"Give me a minute!" Matt yelled from the other side.

Erik waited before Matt appeared. He wore a baseball hat and Erik had no idea where he had gotten it made. A pen was tucked up in his hat. His hands were covered in ink and graphite from pens and pencils.

"What's up, my dude!" Matt broke into a smile.

"I see that you've been busy," Erik said as the two of them fist bumped and Matt waved Erik into his apartment. It was in the back of the restaurant and it contained a bathroom, a bedroom, and an office that butted up against one of the large windows looking out over the city.

"Yeah, well, one thing led to another and voila. What do you think?" Matt asked nervously.

"I think that you've done better than I ever thought possible. Turning this place into a restaurant, that was a bold move but one that's turning dividends. And it gives the people from the cooking department practical experience. I heard that you even established cooking lines to reduce serving times?"

"Yeah, and storage rings have been useful—allows us to keep things good for months. Only the chefs in the upper levels are making food for the customers. The others are all pumping out food for the people who buy it at the store or for the traders. The Alva trade tax is applied to everything that is sold here and I have been keeping hold of the profits. It cost us seven thousand Mana stones to build this place. The running costs to pay everyone is two hundred Mana stones a month.

"On an average day, we will generate two hundred Mana stones in income. We've been operating for nearly three months now and each month in the Third Realm is forty days. So, with the deductions, the restaurant has turned a profit of 16,400 Mortal Mana stones. With sales to traders and renting space, we have made an additional seven hundred and fifty-six Mana stones' worth. That many stones is rather a pain in the ass to carry around. But Old Hei introduced me to Ebeneezer, who converted it into more manageable amounts. I've got sixteen Earth-grade Mana stones, eleven Mortal cornerstones and fifty-six Mortal Mana stones." Matt waved his hand as several high-grade boxes appeared in front of Erik. Matt grinned.

Even Erik, who was not really affected by money—considering how fast he earned it and then spent it on his different crafts—could not help but look at the boxes with apprehension. "Just two hundred Mana stones in wages per month? Is that enough?" Erik asked.

"Think of it as a paid internship. They are getting paid and they can test out their new ideas, without worrying about the ingredients. We grow ingredients ourselves or get them from Alva at prices that are unheard of here in the Third Realm. Literally, coppers and silvers turned into gold and Mana stones. Demand still outstrips our supply, driving the price up. The cooks also get to put their skills to the test in a high-stress environment, and they don't have to pay for food or sleeping quarters. They also get to see the Third Realm. Most are pleased with just that.

"An initiative started with the chefs, where they will head out to some of the powerful families and cook for them privately and they can earn a dozen or more Mana stones with just one meal. This is not all though. Room and board is ten gold per day, including food and sleeping quarters. This is what the traders, alchemists and architect interns are all paying. There are some twenty people living here right now under those arrangements. This has created another twelve Mortal Mana stones of profit. Then there are the architectural plans that people are asking to purchase. Those can earn hundreds of Mana stones for just one set of plans. The alchemists are actually the ones making the least amount of profit due to the high cost of the resources in the division but it is hard to get these items from anywhere else so they buy them willingly. In secondary income, including the taxes, Alva has earned another one hundred and thirty Mana stones, bringing it to twelve cornerstones and another thirty-one Mortal Mana stones. Oh and six hundred gold." Matt pulled out a bag of gold and passed it to Erik.

The weight made his hand sink.

"Damn," Erik said.

"Right?" Matt laughed, shocked by it all as he looked at the wealth in his room.

Erik took a moment, looking at it all before he took it into two storage rings. "Aren't you interested in this at all?"

"Kind of? Like, don't get me wrong—I like money but this is way more than I would need to live on and I can see what Alva might become. I feel good seeing where it might go. Plus, I'm earning money hand over fist, trading with people and making blueprints for different stuff. I'm getting to do what I want, not what I'm told to do. Money is a big thing back on Earth but with Alva I know that I'll be okay. I think I was trading and trying to make a lot of money before so that I could be stable, you know?" Matt sat down at his seat in front of his drawing table. "Now with Alva, it's the first time I've been able to relax. Like, I just wanted a place to stay, and now that I've got it, I can focus on other things. Things that are important to me and not just money." Matt shrugged.

"Well, seems that you're a good manager to have for all of this." Erik looked out of the windows. "And, dude, this place is bad ass. I'm glad that we finally have an architect. Though do you know how many of the people from the blueprint office are now looking to try to make their way up here now?"

Matt laughed, embarrassed and proud. "I'll make it down to do some lectures. I've been racking my mind for information. You and Rugrat said that once I reach the Journeyman stage of a skill that I'll be able to remember more but I'm still working to get there. I've copied down a bunch of information that I remember but most of it is going to need a calculator and an understanding of math. It's a pain in the ass doing math with just pencil and paper."

Erik smiled at Matt's problems.

Matt's sound transmission device lit up with a message. He replied to it and frowned.

"You need to deal with something?" Erik asked.

"Yeah, some big shot showed up." Matt grabbed his pencil and took off his hat.

"Were you able to get information on the Fourth Realm?" Erik asked.

"This is what I've been able to get so far from conversation or otherwise." Matt pulled out three thick folders.

Erik accepted them and put them into his storage ring. "All right, you deal with the big shot. I'm going to head to the Alchemist Association to meet with Old Hei and then go to the Blue Lotus. I might not be back until later."

"Do you want protection?" Matt asked.

"Nah, I should be fine." Erik pulled his badge off his armor and attached it to his cloak so it could be seen from the outside.

"Very well, sir," Matt said in an exaggerated voice getting a smile from Erik before Matt's smile turned more serious. "You look after yourself."

"You too man," Erik said.

***

Erik made it to the Alchemist Association Division Headquarters after passing several checkpoints and a number of different secretaries and then finally Khasar.

He found Old Hei in his study. His desk was covered in Alchemy books and an assistant was asking him questions off to the side. Old Hei answered them while he continued to research. As one increased in level, there were other changes that happened with their body that weren't reflected in attributes. An increase in mental abilities and an increased lifespan were some of these hidden advantages.

Old Hei continued to note something down as the secretary went silent, seeing Erik enter the room.

Old Hei frowned as he looked at what he had just written down. "I think that works. Erik, what do you think?" Old Hei turned around his notebook.

Erik approached and looked at the information inside. "Using the centrifuge to refine three different substances from a singular ingredient," Erik said. It made him think about how if blood were placed into a centrifuge, the result would not be just one substance. It would be broken down into different components that made up blood; mainly the plasma, platelets, leukocytes and erythrocytes. Together, they were blood but the individual components had vastly different functions.

"It is a good theory but there are some flaws. Do you know the densities of the different substances?"

"Density?" Old Hei asked.

Erik thought about how to explain it and instead got a cup, filling it with water and then another, adding salt to it.

"So the water is the same, but adding in salt." Erik poured salt into one of the cups of water and stirred it up until it was dissolved. He pulled out some coloring and put it into the water, turning it green.

"Now if we *slowly* pour some of that unsalted water ontop." Erik did so and the clear water stayed ontop of the green water. "Now the green salt water hasn't been diluted. The dense salt water remains at the bottom and the less dense normal water rests on top of it.

"Liquids with smaller differences in density will take longer, or higher speeds with the centrifuge will be necessary to separate out. Some components might not separate at all, as they have the same density," Erik said. "It might take heating up or cooling the product in order to get the different parts to separate out, or in reverse combine."

"Density," Old Hei said, marveling at having found a missing piece of information he had never thought of before.

"With heat, the density of an item might change. Think of it like a piece of cloth: as heat is applied, the threads that make up the piece of cloth move apart from one another, which increases the area it takes up but it allows more through the cloth," Erik said.

"Your token," Hei said.

Erik pulled it out and gave it to Hei, who tossed it to his secretary.

"Feng Fen, go and get Mana stones for this, biggest denomination, and get a scribe sent in here immediately!"

The man bowed and rushed out of the room, already talking through his sound transmission device.

The scribe rushed in just a few minutes later.

"Lai Yi, good! Just record down what we're saying," Old Hei said, seeing the scribe.

She nodded and sat in a chair with writing materials, readying herself. "Do you wish for a recording crystal?"

"Yes. Have a few of them to make sure nothing is lost," Old Hei said.

Erik was a little confused but he waited.

"Okay, so density—please tell me more about it, and heat changing it!"

"Okay. Do you have ice?" Erik asked.

Hei had some brought in and Erik put the ice in the cup.

"As density changes with the temperature change, the colder ice is actually less dense than the oil and floats in it but the room temperature water is more dense. Increasing or decreasing the temperature of certain substances might allow them to combine together, or separate out from one another. The centrifuge spins items at high speed, pulling the denser items to the bottom of the vial due to the gravitational force applied..."

Erik continued talking, with the scribe looking on with shocked eyes as Old Hei asked question after question. Feng Fen arrived but stood off to the side, listening to Erik.

***

Feng Fen had heard about Erik before, the man who had helped Old Hei create a Master-level pill. Seeing he was only a Journeyman-level alchemist, Feng Fen felt there must be a hidden history between them but that Erik probably wasn't that talented.

Hearing Erik explaining concepts in great detail that he, as the secretary to one of the three pill heads, had not even heard about before shocked him to his core.

Phenomena that had been half assessed and recognized were clearly and succinctly described—even demonstrated—by Erik.

Alchemy focused on the ingredients and the formula, fighting to control the ingredients to conform to the formula to create a concoction. Erik was talking about the underlying knowledge of why substances and items of the world acted the way that they did.

Hearing his words, Feng Fen's mind and heart couldn't help but tremble. Erik had exposed that their seemingly firm foundation was only standing on shifting sand.

***

Old Hei forced himself to stop sometime later.

Erik checked his timepiece, seeing that three hours had passed while he had given his impromptu lecture.

"Thank you, Lai Yi. Could you make some copies and pass me one? Also, would you be able to copy the recordings on the crystals?" Old Hei asked.

"Certainly, Pill Head." Lai Yi stood and cupped her hands as she bowed deeply.

"Thank you. I will review your notes later and add in my own thoughts and deductions behind the questions," Old Hei said.

Sensing her dismissal, she quickly cleared up her items and left through the side door she had entered. Before she left, her eyes drifted to Erik, who sat there calmly, drinking some tea that Old Hei had personally brewed.

"Feng Fen, with this information, will you help me apply for a teaching reward from the Alchemist Association?" Old Hei asked.

"Certainly." Feng Fen cupped his hands and bowed his head. He was a high Journeyman-level alchemist but the words that Erik had shared left him shaken. Pill Head Hei could give out a reward himself but he didn't believe that it would be worthy of the information that Erik had shared. Also, with his personal connection, he wanted to make sure that others didn't call his actions into question. Another, hidden, reason was the interest it would spark in Erik's information and in Erik, himself. It could allow Erik to reach new heights he couldn't touch before and allow the information to propagate through the Alchemist Association at an accelerated rate.

"I have also retrieved them payment," Feng Fen said.

Old Hei waved him forward.

Feng Fen pulled out a number of boxes.

"Seventy Earth-grade Mana stones, eight Mortal Mana cornerstones, fifty-six Mortal Mana stones, nine hundred thirty-three gold, seventeen silvers, and fifty coppers."

"Thank you." Erik put the payment into his storage ring and accepted the token back from Feng Fen.

Feng Fen bowed to them both and left. He didn't think that it was at all inappropriate for him to bow to Erik; after all, he had learned a great amount from what Erik had said. Today, he had been Erik's student.

"It was hard for many of the alchemists to complete the age rejuvenation potions and only a few were able to complete the pill. I know that a number of Expert-classed alchemists have started to work on this pill too, as it is one of the most challenging for one's Alchemy skills. Though it is cheap in resources, making it a great tool for those of the higher skill levels. I suspect in the future, as people learn more and are able to make this pill and potion, that they will do so repeatedly. Decreasing its price by some but increasing the overall amount created," Old Hei said.

Erik was a bit stunned by the amount of money given to him. After the money that Matt had made with the restaurant, even though Erik hadn't seen an Earth-grade Mana stone yet, he had eighty-six of them in his possession.

Feng Fen closed the door behind him as Erik leaned forward.

"I had something else to ask about while I am here," Erik said.

"Go on." Old Hei leaned forward as well.

"I am aiming to head to the Fourth Realm and I wanted to get as much information on it as I can beforehand. Maps, different groups and their alliances, dangerous areas, safe areas. Alchemist Association and Blue Lotus locations."

Old Hei took a deep breath, letting it out as he stood and stretched his legs. "The Fourth Realm is not a simple place. The regions and the groups fighting in it change all the time. There are many people in the higher realms who have their eyes on the Fourth Realm. You've heard about dungeons, right?"

"A bit here and there." Erik nodded.

The corner of Old Hei's mouth lifted slightly but his expression disappeared as soon as it appeared. But Erik was sure that Old Hei knew more than he was letting on as he turned serious once more.

"The Third Realm is still within the Mortal realm, while the Fourth is in the Earth realm. Having traveled through the lower realms, you know that as one increases in realm, the density of Mana only increases. But the Fourth Realm is an anomaly. There was apparently a massive war some time ago, and as a result, the Mana in the Fourth Realm became chaotic and saturated as people from other realms were dragged into it and the power of the Fourth Realm underwent a change. Dungeons occur in areas of high Mana concentration. They consume the ambient Mana in the area, cleaning and purifying it, and creating a multitude of things. A dungeon could be called a Mana holy land. The walls of a dungeon can give rise to rare resources, and perfect growing areas. It is believed that the dungeons are a way for the Ten Realms to attempt to regain balance. They calm down the Mana in the realm.

"But the war that was started so long ago over the dungeons in the Fourth Realm continues. People fight for dungeons and for the regions they occupy. There are constantly more dungeons appearing and being fought over. It is one of the richest realms, which means that the competition is even higher. A dungeon could hold Earth, Sky, or even Celestial grade materials, and unlike mines that are found naturally in the realms, the materials will come back with time. Imagine a cave that re-grew every day, holding Earth-grade iron, or Sky-grade iron, with jewels and other materials.

"Also, as one goes from Mortal to Earth, the Mana increase is a major step up so people are more likely to experience breakthroughs. Children born in these higher realms will have many more Mana gates open from birth and have a higher chance of awakening a hidden constitution, making it possible for them to increase their level faster. In the Third Realm, the Alchemist Association is the overlord because of our strength but in the Fourth Realm there are no set leaders. Even someone who dominated a continent for decades could be toppled in a week. As such, the city structure is different. Each of the cities not only has a strong fighting force, they also have crafters of all kinds supporting them. It is a dangerous land but it is the first land where most of the population at least have a passing knowledge of the different crafts.

"In the Mortal realms, a sect that controls a city or even a region will usually study just one thing in the area that they control.

"In the Fourth Realm, these sects gather together in alliances, solidifying their bonds. So, say there is one that is good with making weapons, another with Alchemy and formations, others with using shields or swords. They get together to make up for one another's weaknesses. Specialization sects are amalgamated into multi-tiered sects. In the Fifth Realm, these sects are no longer loose alliances but become one complete sect, many different disciplines working together as one entity. It is the only way that the sects of the lower realms can compete with the sects in the Seventh and higher realms. In the Fifth and Sixth Realms, Journeyman-skilled crafters and fighters are seen as chaff and Experts gather increased attention and support. Once the sects reach the Seventh Realm, numbers don't matter. Groups and sects of the Seventh Realm are rated almost solely by the Experts that they have been able to raise. Beyond that, I do not know. The reason I say this is because while I can give you maps and locations for different places in the Fourth Realm, the lines of war are constantly changing—territorial lines are shifting, nations falling and rising on a monthly or yearly basis. I will have the maps collected but they are useful for the geographical information more than anything.

"In the Fourth Realm, there are also trading cities. These are cities that are controlled by one of the larger powers in the Ten Realms, like the Formation Emporium, Alchemist Association, Blue Lotus, and Celestial healing houses, they fight among one another like siblings but unite when facing outside threats.

"Then there are the Crafter's and Fighter's Associations. The Fighter's Association contract mercenaries and they can be found wandering the Fourth Realm. They have a code of conduct but they are mainly mercenaries trying to increase their fighting strength. The Crafter's Association was made for the crafters who do not have a patron god, to support one another and avoid being trampled by the other powers. In the trading cities, anyone is allowed to come, to sell their items, attempt to join the powers or buy new items. The powers are always bickering with one another but fighting is strictly prohibited by the charters of each of the powers. As the gods of the Ten Realms, although they might have arguments, they still work together.

"That is not to say that everyone keeps to these rules. In the higher realms, the powers work together, remaining neutral in conflicts and looking to increase their people's strength. The trading cities are neutral and if there are dungeons in their vicinity, they fall under the control of the different powers. An agreement is made up where the Fighter's Association will protect or clear the dungeons while the other powers will come to an agreement to split apart the products of the dungeon. Trading cities are attacked from time to time but the powers working together are hell to fight, so attacks are rare. They also act as a mediator when requested but they stay out of wars and the rest. If someone wants to enter a trading city, they will need to pay a fee and be accepted as a citizen or get a pass that will only allow them to stay in the city for a limited time. People up to the Sixth Realm will sometimes choose to enter the Fourth Realm. As a result, fighting is not simple. Armies are a factor but in the Fourth Realm and higher, tempering and unlocking one's Mana gates is more common. Body and Mana cultivation is more widespread, a person that can go to the fifth or the sixth realm but stay in the fourth realm are usually only there for one reason, to kill the people that are the same level as them to gain experience. These are people that have increased their strength by killing those stronger or on the same level as themselves. Do not take them lightly. They test out the people from the lower realms in the fourth realm, keeping them there until they can reach the seventh realm or they are capable enough in their skill to warrant sending them to an academy in the fifth or sixth realms. The Fourth realm is a complicated economy as the materials from the Fourth Realm are used by the higher ups within the realm or channeled to the higher realms to improve the progress of talented sect members."

"How will forces fight?" Erik asked.

"Cities are usually built on top of dungeons, with the entrances controlled strictly by the different powers. I have heard of an imperial city that stood on top of three different dungeons. Even under siege, they were able to last until they trained up a new batch of fighters who turned the tide of battle and destroyed their enemy. Warfare in the Fourth is focused on killing off the controlling power and asserting control of their dungeons, or defending one's cities and dungeons against exterior attacks.

"Once a battle begins, that city's totem is rendered inactive by the ten realms. Teleportation formations still work but there are few people who have the knowledge and power to create teleportation formations and their power consumption, although less than the totems, is still high.

"To assault a position, thousands of soldiers will be needed to assault the defenses, along with powerful tools like siege weaponry, spell scrolls, combined spells, and magical items. All will be used to open up the defender's walls and break their Mana barriers. The normal troops are fourth realm fodder used to control the population and gain access, allowing the Elite armies who are made up of members between level forty to fifty to assault the Elite defending army. The real battle will happen between the Masters. Masters are people who have not only stepped on the path of cultivating but they have made some progress reaching the second or third stages of progress and they will be between level fifty and sixty. Those Masters in the city will fight against those from the attackers. Masters are at the peak of the Fourth Realm. Think of them like tactical weapons, once they enter the battlefield, whoever has the most remaining at the end is the victor. They fight those of the same strength to increase their level, power and gain wealth from the defeated. Once they have killed their opponent, they will move on to the next enemy Master. Then they will help their Elites in destroying the other Elites, reducing the strength of the attacker's nation. Finally, they'll clear out the regular soldiers. Raising an Elite, or a Master, is a costly exercise. In the Fourth Realm, tens of thousands of people die every day and all of those resources and money are gone, never to be recovered. Killing Elites and Masters is a heavy blow to the group that raised them."

"So if you were to kill the Masters of a group, basically they'll run and try to recover?"

"Essentially."

"What if you were to kill the regular soldiers?" Erik asked.

"Others can be brought down from the higher realms that haven't performed well or raised up from the lower realms within a few weeks, the Elites take months, and the Masters take years or decades. Regular soldiers are more like slaves, conscripted and then ordered forward to soak up the damage so the Elite forces don't need to." Old Hei looked at Erik sadly.

***

Old Hei knew that Erik was not like others. Even though he was interested in Alchemy, there was a darkness to him. He was not a man to avoid violence. It was part of the reason that Old Hei didn't want Erik to go to the Fourth Realm.

He knew Erik had a good head for when to act and not but the threat in the Fourth Realm was extreme.

"So human wave tactics—beat them with numbers, much like the Medieval ages. With some new tricks in the way of magic, on the open field it might be possible to use tactics, or over time if the dungeon doesn't supply food, cut off their supply and starve a group out, or try to cause issues in their back lines. Get the people to fight against them. Morale is going to be a big issue in a place like that where wars are so common and people know what happens at the end of a siege."

Erik was talking to himself but Old Hei understood what he was talking about. When he was young and stupid, he had gone to the Fourth Realm, looking for glory, only to come racing back to the lower realms to escape the Fourth Realm.

He was a peaceful man but there, he had seen so much death and waste of life—and all for little more than a dungeon. *The rulers tell their people what to do and spill the people's blood for their goals.* Old Hei listened to Erik, who was breaking down the fighting tactics that Old Hei had talked about.

"Okay, so in the wilderness, other than moving militaries, what is out there?" Erik asked.

"Powerful beasts roam. The Mana in the Fourth Realm gives birth to many treasures other than the dungeons. Beasts can find these and can increase their strength greatly. Bandits are common, often cast-off soldiers from various militaries. There are also cursed lands, places filled with creatures that are hard to deal with, or have leftover formations that create strange anomalies or natural phenomena that have led many to their deaths," Old Hei said.

"What about the food situation?"

"Foraging is limited. Many of the armies, when retreating, will destroy any crops they encounter to deny their enemy. There are few farmers outside of the different cities. Stamina potions are used more often than actual meals in the Fourth Realm. After all, people there earn more income than those in the lower realms. It is a jump by a force of magnitude, with gold there being what copper is in the lower realms, a Mana stone is a silver and a Mana cornerstone is a gold. Many people have spells, so farms use these to increase their yields. It is rare to find a place that doesn't have a food shortage in some way. If you have the money or the Strength, you are well fed. Otherwise, you starve. This is part of why people join the various militaries."

"Water sources?"

"Dependent upon region." Old Hei sent a message to Feng Fen to gather the different maps. "Is there nothing that I can do to stop you from going into the Fourth Realm?"

"I don't want to but I need to." *If they do nothing but train then are they really soldiers? I need to increase their strength so if something happens to Rugrat and I then they'll be able to look after themselves.*

Old Hei felt that Erik wasn't telling the whole truth. Seeing that he did not want to talk on it, Old Hei simply nodded. "All right. I will get Feng Fen to get all of our current information on the Fourth Realm as well as the included maps."

"Thank you, Old Hei." Erik bowed slightly at the awkward atmosphere between the two of them.

Chapter: Through the Realms

"Good to do business with you." A man in swarthy clothes and a tanned complexion stood and reached out his hand.

Blaze took it with a wide smile on his face. "The Adventurer's Guild will look forward to completing the missions you put forward." Blaze laughed.

"Though I must ask, just where might one be able to find your Triple S class party?"

"They're off completing a mission in the Third Realm. They should be coming back to the Second Realm sometime soon," Blaze assured the man.

"You talk of realms so easily—it is rare to find!" the man said with a big smile.

Blaze simply nodded. After saying their goodbyes, the trader and his people left the room, leaving just Blaze in the office.

He looked out the back, where he could see Taeman city. If he looked down, he could see the training grounds where men and women from Alva were training and testing the new recruits from Taeman. Their style was not like other mercenary bands. They tested those who came through their doors and those who passed were then trained by the other adventurers. It was possible for a person to walk off the street and become a trained adventurer in just a month.

They would then need to sign a contract with the Adventurer's Guild, agreeing that they would be loyal to the guild, could not reveal its secrets, and that they and the Guild would both honor their agreements.

Even if something about Alva slipped out around someone who wasn't invited to the dungeon, they wouldn't be able to repeat it to anyone else outside of the association.

Once they completed their oath, they would then have to pick a party to go with. It would have at least two or three experienced adventurers and they would go out on a few missions to get their confidence and levels up.

Then came testing to see what kind of quality they were, after which they could go out on their own and pick out missions that were rated for their skill level.

It had been nearly six months since Blaze had left the First Realm. He had placed Jasper in charge of managing the Adventurer's Guilds that were in the First Realm and taking his place on the council.

If Blaze was ever needed, he could be reached by someone crossing into the Second Realm and reaching an Adventurer's Guild. All of them were in cities that had a totem, so one could teleport to them. Blaze and Jasper passed messages back and forth once a month.

The Adventurer's Guild had exploded in the First Realm, as they could give training and offer to sell equipment that was hard to find in the First Realm. Upon seeing their strength and ability, the traders, the different nobles, and people with coin learned that they were not just another mercenary company. They had oaths, a code of honor and they were *good*. They didn't know how to just swing a sword; they had real training behind them. With the added rating system and the Adventurer's Guild business approach to the whole matter, many people were swayed in their favor.

Learning that the association spread up into the Second Realm as well and that many of the core members were above level twenty-five, making them powerful people in the Second Realm, their prestige only increased, and applicants and job offers rushed in from the First Realm.

The core of the Adventurer's Guild trained these applicants, testing their character, energy and willingness to improve. They would gather them close, train them and then they would then watch them. Over time, selected people would be exposed to Alva, and were given a chance to increase their Strength by challenging the battlefield dungeon, training with the teachers from Alva, or taking up a craft. They could also join the Alvan army and even the special teams with time and effort.

Though, it was early for that for most applicants.

Blaze had been spending his time growing the Guild's strength in Taeman city, emulating what had worked in the First Realm. It was harder but the hard work was starting to show fruit.

Over one thousand people had applied and they had made contracts with three large trading groups and multiple smaller ones. Crafters looking for rare resources in hard-to-reach places had also put forward orders.

The Adventurer's Guild proved their ability through completing mission after mission. Each day, the number of applicants increased and their ranks swelled.

Blaze had sent out three different parties to other cities, using the funds at his disposal to increase the reach of the Adventurer's Guild. The location in Taeman city would remain their headquarters in the Second Realm, unless they found a better location someplace else.

Slowly but surely, Blaze wanted to increase the reach of the Adventurer's Guild. Jasper and Rose had already had talks about turning the guild into a financial backbone for Alva's interests. One could pay a fee at one location and at another location, the money they transferred could be dispensed to the recipient. Rose was looking at sending people from the treasury to the different locations. They would not only transfer money but also lend and create savings accounts after the successful model in Alva Dungeon. She was currently working out the security measures.

She had picked Rugrat and Erik's minds; then, through discussions with her own treasury department, they were building a strong Alva Bank.

The Alva traders still used the Adventurer's Guild religiously, appearing in the Second Realm with the goods they had saved up over time from Alva Dungeon. They were making massive profits.

Everything is growing.

Blaze shook his head, looking away from the training grounds. Nearly two years ago, he had been leading his village to defend themselves against a beast horde.

Now, having nearly quadrupled his original level, he would live for four hundred years if he didn't run into problems. He was a member of a dungeon. He was running an association that had some two thousand members, and was growing by the day. Blaze just shook his head at how life has changed him.

There was a knock at Blaze's door, and he looked up, having just sat down.

Before he could say anything, the door opened and a dust-covered person entered his office.

A scarf and goggles came off, revealing her sand-stained face.

Blaze's melancholic look turned into a wide smile.

"Had to go through a damn dust storm to get here on time. You totally owe me dinner," Elise complained. Blaze turned in his seat; she jumped on his lap, wrapping her arms around his neck and landing a gritty kiss on his lips.

Blaze held her close, sandy ass grit or no sandy ass grit, life is good!

She leaned back and smiled, looking at Blaze before she buried her head in his shoulder, moving until she got comfortable and letting out a satisfied sigh.

"Good trip?" Blaze asked.

"Long," Elise complained.

Blaze had to tilt his head at an awkward angle to see the cute pout on her lips. He moved his arm, bugging her for more information.

Elise made a noise of displeasure. "Trade went well. We ran into some bandits but your people took care of it easily. We also met up with some other trading caravans, did some easy trades, and got to the Quanbei Quarry. We obtained raw resources, metal, jewels, enhancers for healing concoctions, Stamina concoctions, high-quality mining equipment and food. Made a decent profit. The trade caravan is already selling it to the crafters from Alva in the city. The rare goods were sold to one of the Alva trade caravans, and the other items will be sold to the traders inside the city in exchange for food and other items. We'll be establishing an exclusive route to Quanbei Quarry, maybe even a trading outpost, as there are several quarries in the area with high-quality ores. They're pulling out Mortal-grade iron in decent quantities, as well as other jewels.

"With refining in Alva, most of it could turn into Earth iron. We might create a cooperative refinery, where others bring in their raw resources, we refine it and then sell it. The refineries there charge a large amount to buy from. With the refinery that Taran and Tan Xue made, Erik and Rugrat's knowledge, and Matt to do up the plans—we could reduce the costs and increase the productivity," Elise said.

"We went to Hermal city. They do make formations there as Erik said but they're low grade. It might be a place that we can get information from but I would not suggest any of our people going there. It is run by a sect and anyone who shows ability, the sect will take and teach, making them one of the sect's people. Though, if that metal we got from the quarry is turned into formation plates here, then we would double or triple our income. They go through hundreds of formation plates and then most of them are thrown out after just a few uses. We can purchase those, use a Butcher spell to tear them down, and reforge them."

"The bandits?"

"They were hiding between Quanbei and Hermal, as there are plenty of rich people going in between." Elise shrugged.

"Gear?"

"Simple, tattered stuff. They didn't even get close to the caravan. Your people saw them before they even launched their attack. We let some of them escape. Seemed that they spread the word as there were no more problems on the trip," Elise said.

"So, good trip overall," Blaze said.

"Yes but the next one will take me toward the imperial city of Idel—plenty of opportunity but also plenty of greedy people." Elise sighed.

"We don't always get to do what we want to," Blaze said.

Elise nipped at his ear before letting go. "Dinner!"

"Fine, fine! I'll get absolutely nothing done today," Blaze said.

"Good! You can tell me all about the nothing that you've done!" Elise hopped up and stretched.

Blaze smiled, not hiding the fire in his eyes.

"Time enough for that later. I need a bath," Elise said, a demure smile on her face as she stretched more.

"Everything can be arranged." Blaze put his hand around her back as she continued to stretch. He kissed her deeply before pulling away. "I missed you."

Elise simply smiled, biting her lip as she stopped stretching and turned, putting her arm through Blaze's. "Food!"

Blaze laughed as they walked out of his office, talking about everything they had been doing in greater detail. Blaze passed her the messages that had come from the First Realm while she had been gone.

They walked through the front of the Adventurer's Guild. It was like a restaurant, with people eating and drinking all around. Off to one side, there was the administrative booths and the mission wall. One could take the poster from the mission wall and apply for it at the administrative booths. They could also sign up, receive their pay, as well as buy goods from within the Adventurer's Guild armory, potions, pills, equipment, armor and weapons—all of it could be found in the Adventurer's Guild armories.

All of these goods were sold to the guild with an agreement with the academy. To buy items from the armory, one needed to be a person of the guild. This was another thing that made it appealing to join the Adventurer's Guild.

"It's grown," Elise said, as they made it through the tables to a private booth. The two of them greeted people they knew and were stared at by the new people from the Adventurer's Guild. Blaze was usually in meetings or having his meals in his room.

He went out to train and to fight but it was rare. There were few things that could challenge him in the Second Realm. He wanted to reach the Third Realm soon but didn't want to rush the development of the Second Realm Adventurer's Guild.

"New people every day." Blaze looked over the front of the guild.

***

Erik and Old Hei's meeting came to an end. The two agreed to meet later that day at the Sky Reaching Restaurant for a meal.

Erik headed to his second meeting. With his token, he was easily able to make it to Ebeneezer's office in the Blue Lotus.

After a quick greeting, Ebeneezer, seeing Erik was in a hurry, passed over the money from the Age Rejuvenation concoctions.

"I am sure that production will increase in time and we would be more than willing to pay top price for the processed Lidel leaves." Ebeneezer pulled out a number of boxes.

"I will keep that in mind but I might not be able to in a short period of time." Erik smiled. *I could get Delilah to get a number of the alchemists to refine the leaves and then I can courier them to the Blue Lotus and sell them, another way to earn money for Alva.*

Ebeneezer smiled and presented the different boxes. "In total, there are eight Earth-grade Mana stones, six Mortal Mana cornerstones, forty-two Mortal Mana stones, six hundred twenty-six gold, and forty-eight silvers."

Erik accepted the boxes into his storage ring. They said their goodbyes and Erik headed over to the Sky Reaching Restaurant, where he was assigned a room. He looked out at the city and sat on the balcony, then he closed his eyes and circulated the Mana within his body.

He checked on the thirteenth Mana gate in his body. It had been continually weakened over time. Still, it was only open about halfway.

Seems that some things cannot be rushed.

Erik wanted to advance his Body Cultivation and open his remaining Mana gate but he had learned from Rugrat that rushing forward would lead to more issues, instead of gaining anything.

"Either I will need to increase my Mana pool, or I will need more tools to open up my remaining Mana gate." Erik tapped his storage ring in thought. He couldn't deny he was tempted to use the Mana stones that were contained within to break through his bottleneck.

"When I return to Alva, I'll give Rugrat his half and then I'll use the Mana gathering formation under the dungeon core. Even if I waste the Mana contained within the Mana stones, the formation will gather it and pour it into the dungeon core, allowing it to grow more."

He wanted to use every resource to the limit, not wasting any of it.

Chapter: Battlefield Trials and Specializations

Rugrat woke up feeling like a bag of ass. He grabbed a stamina and healing potion, drinking from both as they set to work, righting his brain. He had been in the smithing room and on the focusing pills for so long that it had drained his Stamina. He'd kept on going with sheer willpower but paid for it by sleeping for nearly an entire day and waking up with a splitting headache.

George, who had been lying at the end of the bed, let out an annoyed growl. He was bored from being cooped up and not having Rugrat play with him.

"Sorry, boy." Rugrat pulled out a fresh steak.

George's annoyed looked turned excited as his tongue hung out of his mouth.

Rugrat laughed and tossed the steak. George snapped it out of the air and tore into it.

As the potions started to clear his head, Rugrat held out his hand. A simple rifle appeared in it. It had a wood grain stock and enhanced Mortal iron that had been covered in an alchemical oil.

"Nothing like gun oil in the morning." Rugrat pressed a lever under the rifle, releasing the high-capacity curved magazine. The rifle looked like a combination of an SKS body with a removable magazine and the bolt action from a Lee-Enfield. On the body of the weapon on either side, there were formation sockets.

Rugrat removed the magazine as he closed his eyes and opened the bolt action, feeling the action. He opened and closed it a few times, not feeling any grittiness, catching or scraping.

It was *smooth*. Rugrat nodded, an excited expression on his face as he pulled the bolt to the rear, checking over the weapon.

He closed the bolt, aimed, and fired off the action. He then put the unloaded magazine in and pulled the action back. He tried to push it forward but the unloaded magazine stopped him from ramming it forward. Rugrat pulled out the magazine, pushed the bolt forward and fired.

"Time to do some testing," Rugrat muttered to himself as he started to get up.

There was an archery range that ran the length of the barracks and a little beyond, running a kilometer in length.

George rose up, wanting to follow.

"You can come but I'll just be shooting guns," Rugrat said.

Through their connection, Rugrat could tell that George could understand. He didn't know human speech but. He could pick up certain things but not complex ideas. It was like when two friends looked at one another across the room and communicated with a series of looks and gestures, they couldn't communicate anything complex but simple things like 'grab me a beer jackass' was pretty easy to understand.

George pouted at Rugruat, his wolf-like muzzle somehow managing to frown.

"You can go to the beast stables as long as you don't bug anyone," Rugrat said.

George flapped his wings in interest.

"All right." Rugrat scratched George's side and the back of his neck.

Rugrat left his room. George walked off toward the stables before he stretched out his wings and took off.

Rugrat shook his head, passing people going to different courses. Rugrat pulled out a piece of paper that had his courses listed on it.

His first course was on in-field repairs and gear maintenance. He would be doing courses on all weapon systems, showing them how to take them apart, use them and then repair them. This was a mandatory course for everyone. His next course was the marksman course. Trials were being held by range officers, checking how accurate people were with the crossbows and bows that they had.

These scores would then be submitted to Rugrat with everyone's files. Rugrat wanted to create a marksman program at first, and with time he wanted to add in a further course that would turn marksmen into snipers.

Rugrat had made extended magazines and smaller ten-round magazines. He loaded up rounds that were specially made, based on his previous testing and put together with the loaders he and Erik had brought from Earth.

He found a firing lane and set himself up. He placed down vises, clamped the gun into them, cycled the action and loaded a round. He then stepped behind protective barriers he had put up and pulled a string attached to the trigger.

The rifle fired and Rugrat waited a few seconds before going around the other side. Rugrat gave a relieved smile as his newly designed rifle did not actually blow up.

He cycled the action and returned behind the barrier. He took out all of the rifles, triggering them one after another, firing off all ten rounds and using his Simple Inorganic Scan. All of the rifles operated straightaway, although a few of them needed changes as there was a half millimeter too much metal here, or a sliver too little there.

Rugrat used his Mana blade, modifying the different weapons to bring them to full unctionality. Other rifles would take more work, or he replaced the parts with spares he had and tested them again.

Everyone who was there to do their marksman test waited, watching Rugrat carry out his quality checks. The loud noise was enough to throw off their aim and mess up their tests.

Rugrat finished off his tests and cleaned up his equipment. With a pleased smile, he stored the rifles away. The barrels, the bolts and trigger assembly were nearly all made by Alva. The extractor and the bolt head needed Rugrat's hand and although he had given them plans, they didn't know how to put the weapons together. For Rugrat, putting the weapons together was too simple, muscle memory of a lifetime's work was a great thing.

"Okay, time for class." Rugrat wiped off his hands and walked away from the archery range as the range officer took over and began the next round of testing.

***

Everyone sat upright as Rugrat entered the room.

"At ease." Rugrat looked to the front of the room that had a repeater bow, ballista, grenades and a sword and shield.

Rugrat pulled out a rifle and put it next to the weapons.

"Okay! So today, we're going to be visiting the basic weapons of the Alva army and how to keep them operational! Everyone here has used a crossbow. The repeating crossbow is just an upgraded version, with a formation that doesn't directly enhance the weapon's attack power but increases its effectiveness." Rugrat grabbed the repeater, pulling off the magazine, checking it was clear and seeing that there was no bolts loaded.

"Okay! All of these weapons are at least semi-automatic. They are not like magic wands that will just have power in them. You will need to load a round or bolt into them to fire them. So, every time you pick one up, you *must* remove the magazine! Then, you remove the ammunition that is loaded into the barrel of the weapon, then you visually inspect that the ammunition has been cleared and then, just to make sure, you fire off the action." Rugrat aimed into a corner and pulled the trigger. The bow arms snapped forward. "If a weapon is loaded, and you decide in your infinite wisdom that it is a good idea to hand off that weapon to someone else, let that person you are handing it to know that it is a live weapon. . This repeater bow is unloaded." Rugrat passed it to someone at the front desk, along with the magazine.

"Does anyone not know how to look after a crossbow? Know the signs that you need to replace your bow arms, bow string, or other components?"

Rugrat looked around and no one put up their hands.

"Fan-freaking-tastic. Seems that I taught you well! Everything is the same here—the only difference is the formation." Rugrat pulled out a blue gem. "This is your power source! When you inspect a weapon, you know what its durability and charge is. When this weapon's charge reaches zero, the formation will not work anymore, so you will need to use a Mana stone or one of these to charge it back up!"

Rugrat grabbed the repeater, blind firing it, and draining the power some.

He then held the gem against the weapon.

=========

Compatible power source and formation.
Do you wish to charge this formation?
YES/NO

==========

"Yes," Rugrat said. Energy was transferred from the blue gem to the formation. "Now, that's how you charge it. Trust me, you want to have your weapon charged at all times. Now, since it creates light, what are you going to do at night?" Rugrat fired out, looking at the class.

"Simmons!" Rugrat pointed at someone who hadn't raised their hand.

"Put it under something so people don't see the light!" Simmons replied.

"Good. Now, next time, put up your fucking hand if you have an answer!" Rugrat threw the gem at the man.

Simmons flinched as it hit him in the shoulder and flew off.

"Go get my gem and sit back down." Rugrat put the repeater on the table.

"Everyone in the Alvan army will be issued one repeater crossbow as well as a minimum supply of twenty magazines, which hold sixty bolts each. Two repeating ballistas will be issued to every section. They have a stronger formation, string and bow arms, as well as a bipod."

Rugrat grabbed the much larger ballista. It was heavier, made of more metal and had stronger wood components. Rugrat made sure that it was unloaded.

"Instead of sitting on top of the weapon, you are behind and in line with it. This reduces your profile so you are harder to hit. The bipod will now also assist in allowing you to aim. Unlike your old crossbows, these both have aiming devices called sights." The sights were a simple reinforced ladder sight that went up and down but even this could help increase their accuracy greatly. "Now, you might notice that the magazine is a bit off to the side so that you can use the sights. You will need to look through this circle here and line it up with the post up here." Rugrat held up the weapon, pointing out the sights.

"Pass these around," Rugrat pushed the repeater crossbow forward and it started to circulate. "This is just a scaled-up version of the repeater crossbow but much stronger. It also comes with a bipod so that you can rest it on the ground and move it around. Also, it has a capacity of one hundred and twenty bolts so you can lay a lot more power into the enemy.

"Grenades—I'm not sure why these are up here. Keep them in your storage ring and use them as you need to. Remember: once the pin is pulled, Mister Grenade is no longer your friend.

"Your shield and sword, like any metal, scour off the rust and apply the proper oil to the weapon to keep it clean. Don't put a sword covered in shit back in your scabbard. It'll be a bitch to clean and you might just have to get a new scabbard. Same with your spears, maces, and whatever.

"Mages! Charge your fucking staffs! You don't want to be standing there, trying to use your staff and nothing happens. We call that a deadman's click. You've got nothing to do but try to pull out another weapon, charge it up again, or get fucked by the person trying to kill you!"

Rugrat grabbed the rifle and displayed it. "Now this—this is something special." Rugrat removed the mag and opened the bolt.

"This is a bolt action magazine-fed rifle. It uses rounds like this." Rugrat pulled out a round. "They contain gunpowder here in the cartridge and this bullet is fired out of the barrel and will hit your enemy with enough force to send them on an early trip to meet their maker! The metal used in this weapon has been enhanced for increased durability, increased heat loss, and to channel formation power.

"These circles here one the sides are formation circuits. You all know about Journeyman weapons and enchantments. Well, these slots can change enchanctment formation plates. Also, you can get enchanted rounds. Want an Explosive Shot? Just get a bullet enchanted with it. Douse a round in poison—now you're firing out a grenade that will kill a few and poison even more. Add in the enchantment capabilities on the weapons and you can shoot further, penetrate armor or even add fire damage if you want!? Explosive Fire Shot with a poison cloud afterward—imagine that penetrating your enemies armor. Good-bye! All right, everyone gather around and pay attention. I'm going to go over the parts of this rifle, then explain how to take this apart, to clean it and add more parts, then explain on how to put it back together. Then you will be repeating this process after me so pay attention, dipsticks!"

***

Niemm nodded to the sergeant in charge of the half section. For this exercise, he would be under Niemm's command. Yao Meng and Yuli stood to the rear acting as the other two members of Niemm's training cadre. The section commander would lead and they would evaluate and assist as needed.

Niemm started off their delve with, "All right, the battlefield dungeon is not some vacation! This is a test and assessment of your skills. Done right, you'll get to put your training to work. You'll adapt everything that you've learned over the last couple of months into action. Listen to commands and do what you have been trained to do."

The formation ahead of them flashed as a new section departed for the battlefield dungeon.

"All right, let's get moving!" Niemm shouted and then led them forward to the teleportation pad.

He signaled to the person in charge of the teleportation pad. A flash of light consumed the squad and they found themselves in the battlefield dungeon lobby.

"Okay, arrowhead formation. Zhong Da and Ye Tai, once inside, cast detection spells to see if the beast is hiding," Niemm ordered.

They moved into formation and Niemm touched the door. Yao Meng covered him with his repeater crossbow.

The door opened and beyond it was a barren and flat world, with cutting wind slicing over the ground as tornadoes and funnels appeared randomly.

"Detection spells!"

***

Lucinda waited as everyone got into line in front of her. On either side, there were a number of beast tamers, both those who worked exclusively at the beast stables and those who were part of the military.

"Alright, today you will be issued with a mount and a special storage item that you can keep said mount in when you're not riding them," Lucinda said as she saw a red streak headed toward the beast stables, chasing Night Terror.

Night Terror let out a shriek in alarm as the streak pursued him.

"George!" Lucinda's voice cut through the skies. The red streak stopped moving, revealing George flapping his wings. The look on his face seemed to ask whether she was looking for him, as though he had done nothing wrong.

Night Terror landed on Lucinda's shoulder, squawking, annoyed and angry as Lucinda patted the pissed-off Grand Eagle who's wingspan was as large as a human's.

"Down, George," Lucinda commanded.

George came down, moping.

"Night Terror is not for you to play around with!" Lucinda said as she scowled.

George's tail curled down as he looked at the ground, not meeting her eyes.

"You will be helping us today," Lucinda said.

George lifted his head and then turned it to the side in question.

"You'll make sure that the panthers are all obedient and don't cause problems for their new riders."

George let out a mewl of displeasure. Seeing Lucinda's expression, he lowered his head again, not pleased but agreeing.

"Night Terror, do as you want," Lucinda said.

Night Terror looked sideways at George once again, before flapping her wings and letting out another squawk. She jumped off Lucinda's shoulder and flew away again.

"You need to care of your mount but also make sure that they know who is in charge. As beasts increase in level, their intelligence and Strength will increase as well. How soon they develop the ability to think independently will depend on the strength of their bloodline and their species. Night Terror has not reached that stage yet but George can already understand simple sentences.

"Your mounts will be placed in your charge but they are property of the Alvan military, so they can be removed from your care if you mistreat them. They might also be moved around if they are needed for other missions," Lucinda said. "We will teach you how to ride your mounts, how to ride different kinds of creatures, as well as a bit of their anatomy and their habits. We will also teach you how to care for them including their anatomy so you can assess medical problems in the field and so if you are up against similar beasts, then it may help you to find their weaknesses.

"We'll then cover how to ride other mounts, as you might need to use a horse, a flying beast or something else in an emergency. We will show you how to care for them as well so that they don't starve in the field and are kept in good health. We will mainly be working with panthers. These are the main mounts of

Alva. With breeding initiatives, using high-leveled beast meat, monster cores and Alchemy concoctions, these panthers have greatly increased Agility, Strength, and Stamina. They can run for days at a decent speed. They have had armor crafted for them and have gained a resistance to the elements and severe temperatures." With the end of Lucinda's words, some of the beast tamers from the beast stables brought out some of the panthers.

George stood to his full height and preened at the panthers, showing his dominance.

Each of the panthers were at least level twenty-five. They were a meter and a half to two meters tall, reaching four to six meters in length. They were nearly twice the size of jaguars back on Earth. Their shoulders were level with the riders' heads.

Each of them had a glossy black coat with thick corded muscles underneath. They were fast creatures but they were now also built for long distance.

Wearing armor, they looked terrifying. Lucinda watched all of the troops around her; she could see their excitement, anxiety and respect looking at the powerful mounts.

Although the panthers were powerful beasts, none of them were aggressive while in the presence of George. George was already a creature close to level thirty-five, ten levels higher than them. He came from a purer bloodline and was capable of not only physical attacks but magical ones as well.

"Head Tamer Kolick, would you take over please?" Lucinda asked.

Kolick nodded and stepped forward. He was a simple man, wearing tough hide clothes with scratches on them from the different creatures that he worked with.

"Okay, so when meeting your mount, you will need to gain their trust. You might go through a great number of different mounts but the trust you gain between an animal and a person is powerful. A beast will not forget you or your scent and when fighting together, your strength will triple or quadruple if your coordination is good enough," Kolick explained.

Chapter: Haul

Old Hei watched as Erik disappeared through the totem. He didn't know where he was going and he didn't ask.

"Truly, the young will outgrow the old," Old Hei said with complicated emotions.

"Do you want us to send someone to protect him?" Khasar asked.

"I think that it will only be more of a hindrance to him and they would be in greater danger than him. You felt it, too, didn't you?" Old Hei asked as they headed for his carriage.

"Felt what?" Khasar asked.

"His progress to Body Like Iron. He has already entered that realm. Knowing him, once he has a path, he will push forward to reach the pinnacle," Old Hei said.

"For him to make it this far in Body Cultivation—only relying on himself—it is rare. Though reaching higher will require a lot of willpower and greater resources," Khasar said.

"I think he has the resources and the willpower secured. What he needs now are the levels and the access to those different items that will allow him to temper his body further. When it comes to the Fourth Realm, I can only support him. Holding him back is impossible. He is a grown man but it's hard to not worry about him. He is a rare and true friend."

They reached Old Hei's carriage. He stepped up into it and Khasar was left with a hard expression.

**

Erik returned to the First Realm with a number of the people who had gone to the Third Realm originally to build the restaurant. He had checked out the dungeon that was below the restaurant as well. It was about one hundred meters wide and five hundred meters long, with a small stream that entered from the dungeon and pooled at the far side.

Dirt had been shipped in and covered the ground as growing arrays were placed and farmers worked to replicate the fields that could be found in Alva Dungeon. If possible, all of the basic foodstuffs needed by the restaurant would be supplied by this garden. The hidden growing grounds would make sure that the restaurant never ran out of cheap but high-grade ingredients.

Erik felt that since he had attempted to temper his body, he had only been dealing with the business side of Alva. Even the weight of his new valuables were burdening him.

He moved with the people from the Third Realm. Some of them decided to go their own way, others came with him to the teleportation array, reaching Alva Dungeon quickly.

"Egbert, I have some things for you," Erik said as he walked away from the teleport pad.

It wasn't long until the flying bones appeared before Erik, with an excited expression somehow showing through simple bone.

"Could you place these please," Erik took out a box of twenty-five Mortal Mana cornerstones and tossed it to Egbert.

Egbert scrambled to catch them and make sure it didn't fall. "Calm down, will you!" Egbert said in a panic as he opened the box. He quickly closed it and looked at Erik. "Which trader did you rob?!"

"Why did you think that I would go and rob a trader?" Erik asked.

"Well, how else did you do it?"

"Hard work," Erik said resolutely.

"Gambling?" Egbert tapped his chin in thought.

"Please just go and place them," Erik muttered.

"Alva Dungeon is a righteous place. Stealing from others is a bad thing," Egbert said, starting to lecture Erik.

Erik pulled out a book and tossed it to Egbert.

"*Cocky Mistress*," Egbert read the book title aloud and then looked around. The book disappeared into his bones. "Understood, boss!" Egbert snapped off a salute and shot into the sky.

"Why did I have to get the broken skeleton?" Erik shook his head as he continued to walk toward the dungeon headquarters. On the way, he sent a message to Delilah and Rugrat, letting them know he was back.

Erik went to the large block building opposite the restaurant. The homes there had been bought and rebuilt into the administration office that Erik now entered.

"Where is the treasury office?" Erik asked the man at the reception.

"Upstairs at the back right." The man stood, looking flustered.

"Thank you. Signs or posted directions might be useful in the future, like in the healing house," Erik said. They had used colored lines on the ground like back on Earth, to allow people to quickly navigate to the different areas of the hospital. The idea had expanded to the academy as time passed.

Erik walked through the different halls of the administration office and found a room with a sign on it.

Erik knocked on the door and opened it.

There were three people at desks, that had been pushed together and two more in side office.

Looks like there will be cubicles and offices in any world. Erik thought as the people in the office looked over to the door.

"Mister West!" A man stood up from where he was working.

"I'm looking to make a deposit into the treasury," Erik said.

"Please, I'm sure the treasurer would be glad to see you." The man quickly moved to one of the offices. A woman inside that office looked up from what she was working on, and seeing Erik, she jumped up as the man opened the door for Erik.

They looked at odds, Erik wearing his armor covered with his duster and her wearing comfortable business clothes.

"Hello, I am the treasurer, Rose. Can I get you something to drink?" Rose asked rapidly.

Erik could easily tell that she was overwhelmed meeting with him as she wrung her hands, not sure what to do or say. Erik smiled, putting her at ease as the other man closed the door behind him.

"I wanted to make a deposit into the treasury." Erik indicated to the seats.

"Please! Please take a seat," Rose replied.

Erik did so and pulled out a heavy wooden box with silver metal inlaid into it.

Even with the box sealed, the Mana in the room seemed to swell. Pressure increased on them both as if they had just plunged underwater. Instead of being a powerful, crushing force, it was relieving as their Mana systems relaxed.

Erik pulled out three more pouches that made noise, then opened the box. A glow filled the room as twenty aquamarine Mana stones were revealed, lined up nicely inside.

"Twenty Earth-grade Mana stones, one thousand ninety-three gold, six silver, and twenty-five coppers."

Rose looked at it all. It was more money than she had ever seen in her life. "I was just talking about tens of Mortal Mana stones with Delilah and there are Earth grade ones in front of me, a thousand Mortal Mana stones each," Rose said absent-mindedly, not realizing she was talking out loud.

She took some time to collect herself. Erik cleared his throat, bringing her back to reality.

She blushed and coughed before she looked to Erik. "I can accept these on behalf of the treasury. Do you want them to be used for anything specifically?"

"Just help to develop Alva. Add them to the budget or increase the academy buildings all to tier three. How much will it cost to increase the buildings to tier four?" Erik asked.

Rose coughed again, so stunned that she half choked herself. It took her some time and a glass of water to recover. She still had tears in her eyes when she recovered.

"One tier-four building will cost ten thousand Mortal-grade Mana stones, or ten Earth-grade Mana stones," she said with a weak smile.

"Okay, use this all to grow our abilities. Use this for the loans and for incentives and support. Then, when we have two Experts in different skills, look into upgrading the academy facilities to tier four." Erik stood.

Rose stood as well.

"Good work. Keep it up." Erik might not have met her before but he had paid attention to her reports. It seemed that she had been listening to what Elise had relayed about banks and the banking system, as well as the role of the treasury. Erik and Rugrat never thought their joy about not having loans, a mortgage or to worry about their savings, would have had such an impact.

Rose saw him out and he headed for the dungeon core.

He looked up at the ceiling. Different people were talking to one another, looking at Egbert, who was up on the roof of the dungeon, affixing the twenty-five new Mana cornerstones into the Mana gathering array.

They acted like batteries, which grew like salt crystals across open surfaces—so *weird* batteries—but they could only accept a certain amount of power from their surroundings before they were full. The dungeon core had been storing a lot of power in the original cornerstone. It sped up the rate that it created Mana stones but there was too much power from the dungeon core and so some of it was lost. But with the Mana gathering formations, it was merely funneled back into the dungeon core and pushed back into the Mana cornerstone. Now, with twenty-five more of them, the power was spread out and all of it was being greedily absorbed by the different cornerstones. The first cornerstone dimmed as the others started to glow. The thick stream of Mana was split into smaller threads, creating a spiderweb with Mana cornerstones located where the Mana threads intersected one another.

Erik entered the dungeon headquarters and reached the room that the dungeon core was held in. It opened up automatically for him. A wave of pure Mana rushed over Erik as he quickly recovered from a stumble.

"Damn," Erik said. It was like entering a sauna. His body relaxed, the wave of Mana penetrating deep into his body.

He sat down on the ground and started to circulate his Mana. The Mana he let out was pulled toward the dungeon core as it hungrily devoured the impurities contained within. Erik drew in the pure Mana from within the dungeon core. The fresh and pure Mana seemed to scrub his Mana channels, clearing out impurities he hadn't even known about.

Is this why the people in the higher realms have an easier time increasing their ability with their Mana systems? If there are fewer impurities in the Mana and it is denser, then it would be easier to cast a spell. It would also allow them to be born and grow up with fewer impurities entering their body, giving them a stronger starting point and making it easier for them to open Mana gates and have more of them open from birth.

Erik continued to clear out all of the impurities in his body that he could. The pure Mana circulated through his channels, each time carrying fewer and fewer impurities until there was nothing more that could be cleared from Erik's body.

Erik felt the power that filled him. His Mana pool had increased with the higher purity and density. Now, with fewer impurities taking up space in his Mana system, removing more was a slow process. Still, with enough time and pure Mana, he felt he could draw out even more impurities from within his Mana channels.

Erik's Mana flowed easier, like water that had passed through a filter, removing mud and detritus.

His attention turned to his thirteenth Mana gate. It had reduced in size slightly, the opening becoming wider but it had still not yet opened fully.

Erik pulled up the dungeon interface with just a thought. It appeared in front of him as he turned off the Mana storing formation. The power around the dungeon core was no longer being beamed into the cornerstones above and started to gather in the room that the dungeon core was located in. The Mana gathering formation underneath the dungeon core stopped the Mana from leaking out into the surrounding area.

Erik felt the pressure on him only increase. It was as if he had been next to a waterfall before, getting splashed by mist. Now it was like he was inside a valley and the waterfall was still smashing down only now it was filling the entire valley with water.

He hadn't realized how much power was being channeled into the dungeon core. Ambient Mana from around the Beast Mountain Range: from the people casting spells, circulating their Mana, using ingredients and items, from the battlefield dungeon, from the fields, the academy, everyone was like a small Mana gathering formation. As they cast spells or it was released by the world it became tainted with impurities. The mana gathering formations concentrated it and the Alva dungeon purified it all, providing nutrition to the mana cornerstones to create mana stones.

The Mana density within Alva had increased since they had settled the dungeon. The mana gathering formations only drew mana in, it did not allow any out. Alva Dungeon was still a large space. It took a lot of Mana to increase the overall density. It wasn't until Erik was drowning in the new Mana that he realized just how much the Mana in Alva Dungeon had grown.

Erik turned off the mana storing array on the roof. The mana gathering array that was under his feet contained the mana that was pouring into the dungeon core room and entering the dungeon core. With all that power being contained and not being channeled everywhere else in the dungeon notifications started to appear in Erik's eyes. He watched them increase, slowing down with the speed that they appeared as the mana density struggled to increase again.

Erik pulled up the last notification.

==========

You have entered an area with a high Mana content.

While in this area, your Mana Regeneration will increase by +6.

==========

Erik could feel the power at his fingertips. With his Mana King title, the room fell under his domain. The rush, the *feel* of that much power under his complete control—it was like a drug.

It took some time for Erik to concentrate. As he circulated his Mana, the Mana within the dungeon core room moved. It entered through the Mana gathering formations, was pulled up into the dungeon core and then captured by Erik, pulled in and expelled through his Mana gates with his Mana circulation path, pulsing in sync with his breathing.

Erik could feel his Mana gate growing weaker, and thinning out.

His progress started to slow.

Erik took out a handful of Mortal Mana stones. They dissolved with a thought. The power within the room increased again, the Mana turning chaotic. Erik didn't pay it any attention as he continued to force more Mana through his Mana gate, widening it even further.

He took out more Mana stones. They turned to dust, adding to the Mana within the dungeon core. Erik felt a cracking sensation.

His entire body relaxed as Mana rushed through him. His tension relaxed as a notification appeared in his vision.

Erik quickly sent commands to the dungeon, the Mana gathering array starting up again.

The stream of power heading to the Mana cornerstones was as thick as a man's leg and a wave of Mana was released over Alva.

He looked up at the dungeon core and then the Mana gathering formation above. "Well, this is a strange life."

Erik laughed to himself before he stood. He pulled up his notifications.

==========

You have opened another Mana gate!

==========

+1 to Mana Regeneration

==========

==========

Quest Updated: Opening the Fourteen Gates

==========

Congratulations! You have opened your thirteenth Mana gate.

==========

Requirements: Clear all of your fourteen gates (13/14)

==========

Rewards: +1 to Mana Regeneration base stat

Undergo Mana Body Rebirth

1,400,000 EXP

==========

==========

Title: Mana Emperor

==========

Your Mana control has increased greatly.

==========

The strength of your spells has increased by 30%. Your Mana Regeneration has increased by 30%.

(Replaces Mana King)

==========

==========

Name: Erik West

==========

Level: 32

==========

Race: Human

==========

Titles:

From the Grave II

Mana Emperor

Dungeon Master II

Reverse Alchemist

Poison Body

==========

Strength: (Base 27) +39

==========

660

==========

Agility: (Base 20) +41

==========

335

==========

Stamina: (Base 30) +9

==========

585

==========

Mana: (Base 6) +35

==========

410

==========

Mana Regeneration (Base 10) +40

26. 00/s

==========

Stamina Regeneration: (Base 28) +33

13. 20/s

==========

Erik looked at his different notifications that had piled up while he was working with the Alvan army. While he had been training them, he had been rediscovering his old skill set, taking the time to improve his own abilities as he trained others. It had been a good review for him.

==========

Skill: Stealth

==========

Level: 48 (Apprentice)

==========

When in stealth, your senses are sharpened by 5%
==========

==========
Skill: Marksman
==========
Level: 61 (Journeyman)
==========
Long-range weapons are familiar in your hands. When aiming, you can zoom in x2. 0. 15% increased chance for critical hit.
==========
==========
Skill: Throwables
==========
Level: 43 (Apprentice)
==========
Your throws gain 5% power.
==========
==========
Skill: Blade
==========
Level: 17 (Novice)
==========
No bonuses at this time. You must prove your skills first.
==========
==========
Skill: Shield
==========
Level: 15 (Novice)
==========
No bonuses at this time. You must prove your skills first.

```
==========
==========
```
Skill: Spear
```
==========
```
Level: 22 (Novice)
```
==========
```
No bonuses at this time. You must prove your skills first.
```
==========
==========
```
1,212,986/1,215,000 EXP till you reach Level 33
```
==========
```

Erik's eye twitched seeing the Experience he had earned. He had killed a few beasts but they had only added up to less than a hundred Experience. Nearly all of his Experience had come from increasing his different skills.

He'd got a stealth potion of the Journeyman level, which he stored away, and a Mortal sword for raising his blade skill to Apprentice. It was lower than his other combat skills. Learning how to use a sword other than for simple things wasn't easy. The spear was much easier as it was made as a simple infantry weapon. Erik had read about the spear in his past life and there were plenty of spear teachers to listen to. Though, he had cheated: using his throwing and marksman skills with his spear technique, he'd been able to land accurate and deadly hits on animals, hurling it through the air.

He'd even gotten his best haul with the spear, the Wind Spear technique book. It increased one's striking speed and attempted to confuse the enemy's eyes.

Erik had read it over and added it to the library. His last prize was another potion, an increased Strength potion that he had earned for becoming a shield Apprentice.

"Just a few Experience potions and I'll be able to level up," Erik muttered to himself.

Erik waved the notifications to the side and looked at Egbert, who stood outside the doorway.

"Ahh, you were opening up your Mana gates!" Egbert exclaimed. "Thought you broke a formation in there."

"You could have a little bit more faith," Erik replied.

"Could I?" Egbert asked, skeptical of Erik's words.

Erik rolled his eyes as he headed out of the headquarters. Egbert followed him.

"The council leaders, please allow them access to the dungeon core to clear out their Mana channels, increase their Mana density and purity and to help open their Mana gates. Is it possible to create areas to cultivate Mana so others can do the same?" Erik asked.

"If I modified one of the Mana gathering formations slightly, say in a private courtyard within one of the parks, then people could use that," Egbert offered.

"Okay. Also, release the controls on the Mana gathering formations. We're sucking it all up into the formation above but increasing the Mana density in the dungeon will increase the chances of someone making a breakthrough in their Mana Gathering Cultivation. It could also increase the chances of a powerful item being made and increase the growing speed of plants."

"With some changes, I could isolate the dense Mana to the buildings, living areas, then the stables and barracks," Egbert said.

"Talk to the council first. Make sure that they and others know what is going on. Are we able to store all of the energy that the dungeon core is producing now?" Erik asked.

"We are able to store all that is produced. With the increased production, improvements to the Mana gathering formations, and their propagation outward, we are pulling in more Mana than ever before. However, the dungeon core is unable to refine it all and remove the impurities," Egbert apologized. "We need to increase the dungeon's core grade so that it can refine and purify more mana."

"We've stored up a considerable amount of Mana. Instead of hoarding it all, lets increase Alva's mana density," Erik said.

"Why?" Egbert followed Erik as he continued walking, headed for the barracks.

"Mana not only increases one's mana circulation. It can also increase the production of different ingredients in the farms, reduce mana loss in materials that are being crafted. When someone is working or living in a Mana rich environment, they are able to focus faster and for longer periods of time. Which will help Alva grow in strength." Erik glanced at the skeleton.

"No I mean, why do all of this?" Egbert asked.

"It's the right thing to do?"

"But giving your money away, helping other people to get stronger?"

"We only get stronger together. What use is money if I can't use it? I still have a bunch but that's because I simply don't know what we might find in the Fourth Realm and we might need it. The rest—if the merchants turn a profit, then the bank turns a profit. Then Alva can grow faster than before. We can hoard all of this Mana but we can't even use it all. If the people grow in Strength, then they will create more Mana for the dungeon core to grow and they'll increase their Strength further. In Alva, we work together for the future. Since I can help them out, why wouldn't I?"

**

Rugrat was completing his third lecture on different weapon systems and how to maintain them.

"What's this?" He pointed to a part on the table.

"Firing pin, First Sergeant!"

"This?" Rugrat asked.

"Rear iron sight, First Sergeant!"

Rugrat nodded and continued on, asking a few people a few questions.

"Reassemble!" Rugrat said.

Each person in charge of a rifle, bow or ballista put them back together, with Rugrat and the other staff watching over them. With just a glance, they could tell who was messing up their reassembly.

There was no yelling or screaming. All of them had made it into Alva's army. As such, they were treated like adults.

For everyone in the army, the lessons were about sharing ideas and increasing their knowledge. When they were going through tests, to see what they remembered and to make sure that they were paying attention, that was when the yelling would start.

Everyone knew that this information would be vital, so they paid attention and talked to one another, asking questions where prudent.

Rugrat nodded in approval. It wasn't long until they had their different items assembled.

"Alright, your next lesson will be going over shooting and incorporating these weapons into your tactics. Then we will have a follow-up lesson to make sure you weren't sleeping in my classes! Get to your next course. Dismissed!"

The students filed out of the room as Rugrat took back the rifles. After collecting them all he headed out after them and to the range.

"You finished the guns?" Erik asked as he saw Rugrat walking.

"Yeah. How was the Third Realm?" Rugrat pulled out a rifle, clearing it with quick, fluid motions before tossing it to Erik.

"It was busy." Erik tossed Rugrat a bag.

Rugrat opened it and looked inside at the pouches of coins, as well as a box. Rugrat looked up at Erik who was looking over the rifle.

"Our split from the restaurant at the Division Headquarters. Three Earth-grade Mana stones. I gave the Mortal Mana cornerstones to Egbert, so I exchanged them for Mortal Mana stones, nine hundred twenty-eight of them. Well, I don't have them exactly, so I can give you another Earth-grade Mana stone or get you more from the treasury but it will take time to get the Earth Grade stones exchanged down to Mortal. Or you can leave them in there and they'll get interest." Erik shrugged. "Then four hundred sixty-six gold, fifty-eight silvers, and seventy-five coppers."

Rugrat looked at Erik with wide eyes. "Shit. Well, looks like I'll have plenty of material. The rest I'll dump in the treasury for loans."

Erik laughed as he pushed the action forward on the rifle and dry fired it into the ground. "Well, you want to shoot some guns?"

"Got to do safety and handling checks with them first." Rugrat sighed as he continued walking toward the range. Erik walked with him. They were both on the courses staff.

"Should be a pretty fast gun." Erik pointed the weapon at the ground and worked the bolt handle. The bolt came back but not to the point where he had to move his head, meaning he remained on target.

"I'm hoping so. Give them a ten-round mag to start off and for long-range shots so they're not resting the magazine on the ground. Then a thirty-round magazine for patrolling and general purposes." Rugrat took out the curved magazines and passed them to Erik.

"Smart." Erik played with the gun, finding the simple safety catch that stopped the trigger from moving.

"If there is one thing I know, it's guns and messing around with them," Rugrat said.

"Don't remind me," Erik said. "How is ammunition?"

"With the assembly line, we combined the powder and primers from the alchemists the cartridges and bullets from the smiths, well. Tan Xue and Taran used my plans and had another line making the bullets and the cartridges. They've been running this entire time, day and night with a few managers. Got about four hundred thousand rounds, with about forty thousand of them enchanted one way or another. With more being made every hour," Rugrat said. "The powder is from those test samples you made. It burns at a lower temperature but it has about two to three times the power of the mixed powder I used back home, which was shooting hot anyway. The bullets we've got are enhanced iron that will expand under the pressure but not damage the Mortal iron-enhanced barrel. With time, I want to upgrade to Earth-iron barrels. That way, we can shoot Mortal-iron bullets with stronger enchantments."

"Nice. Never enough ammunition." Erik tapped on the sockets. "What are these for?"

"Ah, so I had a mini breakthrough, I guess. I didn't think that it was that big of a deal but it's a formation socket." Rugrat scratched the back of his head and explained what formation sockets were and the possibilities that came with them.

Erik wasn't as shocked as the people of Alva, simply nodding and turning it over to look at the two sockets. "Two enchantments—so is this an Expert-level weapon?"

"No, the metal is enhanced to make it stronger and the weapon has the innate ability to dissipate heat. I wasn't able to pull out two innate effects. Also, it is not capable of being bound to someone and the enchantment formations that can be used can only be of the Apprentice grade. A higher level might cause problems with the gun," Rugrat said. "Still, I'm not a high-Journeyman-level smith. Tan Xue has been locked up in her smithing room for a couple of days now. She eats and sleeps in there between working on something."

"Do you think that she will be able to reach the Expert level in her smithing skill?"

"Who knows?" Rugrat shrugged.

They had made it to the range, where thirty people waited for them. Their ranks ranged from sergeants to privates. Their talking ended as they saw Erik and Rugrat entering the range.

"All right, so all of you have passed the preliminary tests. You are the best shots that we have in the army, supposedly! You all know how to use crossbows or bows but this is something else entirely." Rugrat looked them over. They had all been in his weapon handling and maintenance classes.

"First, let's see how you are with the repeater crossbow and ballistas!" Rugrat wanted to build them up and seeing as no one had fired the new weapons, it would be best to start there and then move to the rifles.

All of them listened to Erik and Rugrat with rapt attention. There was no side chatter in their classes.

They set up targets as Rugrat lectured them on the effects of wind when firing at range. Different things that they had picked up while using their own weapons were put down into cold hard facts.

The class was not a short one. They shot, reshot and worked to improve their skills. It was organized but it wasn't regimented.

There was a lot to learn and it took time and practice to go from knowing the information to hitting the right place on a target with a bolt.

"All right, gather around." Rugrat pulled out his rifles and passed one of them to each of the people there. They took their weapons and checked that they were unloaded first thing. Yep, someone had been listening.

"Looks like not all of my lessons were wasted." Rugrat took out his new rifle. It was a similar copy to their rifles but it was made to shoot the much larger fifty caliber round. His modified Big Momma was a good weapon but it had a lot of parts and it was easier to break. So Rugrat made a new rifle, with fewer moving parts, adding in the formation sockets and the same big, easily enhanced round. His striking power had increased to a crazy degree.

They had gone through iron sights with the new repeater weapons, then he went through the parts of the rifle in greater detail. Then he got them on the firing range and got them firing. They were shocked by the noises but they kept on going. They went over their targets, then Rugrat and Erik checked and changed them. They repaired the targets and went again. Rugrat and Erik asked them questions as they were firing, getting them to shoot from different positions. They asked them how they would aim if there was a cross wind. They had them shoot from standing, shoot from kneeling and a prone position. They could fire their repeaters from the same positions but their magazines were much larger, their range shorter. Their stopping power was lower but as a tradeoff they were much quieter than the rifles.

"All right, so now you've shot a bit. That's nice but being scouts, if you're shooting, something has gone terribly wrong or you have found an enemy that only you can eliminate and which prevents the rest of us out from a lot of dangerous work. As scouts of the army, you will sneak off, find an enemy position and report back. So, we will be going over maps. We will be going over scouting. Then we will be going over camouflage and cover. It will be in more detail than what you've had before but there will still be more to learn to eventually become snipers. Rest now. Report back here tomorrow. This will be a test of endurance and of your mental abilities," Rugrat promised.

They dispersed as Rugrat and Erik watched them.

"Not bad. Also, most of them were hunters or had fought with their bows before, so it should go smoothly," Rugrat said.

"When are you thinking of starting the sniper program or making more rifles?" Erik asked.

"I made the first few and I gave an example to the smiths. They're working to make more. They make them part by part and I've ordered plenty of spares just in case. Though it takes a Journeyman-level smith to make the parts, anyone with knowledge can assemble it. Right now, maybe a rifle a week."

"I thought there might be a reason that you had thirty in the class," Erik said.

"Even if they're using repeaters, if they can hit the damn target, it's better than them just wasting their bolts," Rugrat said.

"You ready?" Erik asked.

"For the Fourth Realm? Hell no. Is anyone actually ready?"

Erik shook his head. "No but it's about time you tried opening that fourteenth Mana gate."

Rugrat's hand shook as a shiver ran down his spine. Fears that he thought he had forgotten appeared in the back of his mind.

"Yeah." Rugrat could feel his anxiousness, the light-headed feeling. His stomach turned into an acidic soup and his wet palms wouldn't dry as he put a smile on his face.

Erik nodded.

When you had to do something you were scared of, you did it mainly because of the ribbing your peers would give you. Rappelling? Didn't matter whether heights scared the piss out of you; you did it because you were a damn soldier and you would do what you were told. They would laugh and joke at one another to push them over the edge and then force themselves right after them.

More than a fear of dying, fear of letting down others pushed you past what your brain thought were your limits. It pushed you to a state of 'fuck it' When you got to the edge of that plane's jump point, when it was your turn to do live fire along-side the worst shot in the company, when you needed to run through incoming fire to get to your friend who was lying wounded on the ground.

You gritted your teeth, embraced your death and just damn well did it.

Erik smacked Rugrat on the back and they headed toward the dungeon headquarters.

Chapter: Cultivation

Rugrat and Erik arrived at the dungeon core. Erik talked about the increased Mana Regeneration, trying to allay Rugrat's fears. He had also asked Egbert to join them. If something went wrong, then Egbert could get help or assist them as needed.

Rugrat was thankful that more people weren't going to be around to see him trembling as he sat down in the dungeon core room.

His Mana pool and his Mana Regeneration were already high based on his increased stats and thirteen open Mana gates. The Mana Channel Revitalization pill had changed his channels' innate composition. Although he had an idea of what might happen in the future, for now it made it easier for him to control and refine his Mana.

Erik turned off the Mana storing formation. The pure Mana, with nowhere to go, was gathered back in by the Mana gathering formation. The density in the dungeon core room climbed once again.

Rugrat closed his eyes and focused on his Mana system, on the three combined Mana drops and the last remaining separate Mana drop.

He started to circulate his Mana, increasing its density. As he exercised his control over the Mana in his body, the Mana around him rippled with his actions. As he moved, the Mana followed just a second behind, like a puppy realizing its mother was gone and trying to trail after her.

Rugrat increased the pressure in his body, bit by bit. He paused regularly. After he had recovered from his injury, he hadn't pushed his Mana system to the limit, afraid that he might cause more damage.

As the pressure increased without any issues, Rugrat continued, bringing in more and more Mana. His Mana gates turned into small vortexes as Mana glowed within his expanded Mana channels.

Rugrat felt the explosive power held within his body. He circulated the Mana, removing the impurities as Erik had talked about. That took him less than a fifth of the time it had when he was combining his second and third Mana drops, his focus and control over his Mana system had improved substantially thanks to the Master level pill.

Rugrat then started to push his Mana toward his last remaining Mana drop.

Instead of forcing them together, Rugrat formed the Mana inside into a whirlpool. On one side, there was the combined Mana drops; on the other side, there was the remaining single Mana drop.

Rugrat was much more powerful than he had been last time. With his high Mana Regeneration increase, even further improved by the dungeon, Rugrat pulled the two separate clumps of drops into the whirlpool of Mana. They fought against him, shaking to free themselves but Rugrat only increased the rotation, fighting against them. Sweat started to appear on his forehead.

Rugrat let out a low growl, opening his eyes, angry at himself. He was playing it too carefully, he hadn't even begun to push himself.

Power surged through Rugrat like a tidal wave, and the whirlpool picked up speed. The vortexes at Rugrat's Mana gates increased in size, from just a few centimeters to a half meter.

The single drop came into contact with the already combined drops.

A light appeared between Rugrat's belly button and his solar plexus. The light filled his Mana system as the Mana in the room seemed to pause.

Then, like sound coming back after an explosion, Mana shot into all fourteen of Rugrat's Mana gates. Rugrat's Mana channels started to glow brighter, then began to grow. Instead of just being a series of channels, threads started to appear.

Rugrat might only have a basic knowledge of the human body but he could see that his Mana channels were shifting, becoming aligned with his circulatory system. Those threads of mana channels arranged themselves around his veins, arteries, and capillaries.

Rugrat let out a yell as Mana was drawn in through his Mana gates, concentrated within the compressed Mana core and then pushed out into his body. The Mana density in his body had increased once he compressed his core, without him needing to do anything else. The Mana in his veins was no longer a mist. Half-condensed drops appeared here and there instead of the mist, pooling where Mana gathered naturally.

Rugrat's Mana veins spread, connecting to his muscles, nerves, organs, tendons and bones. He no longer had just blood flowing in his veins and supporting his different organs and systems. Mana now supplied its own kind of energy, deeply changing his body, recreating it on a cellular level and bringing it closer to the Ten Realms. Closer to the Mana that was all around him. Mana was no longer a separate system that lived around and within him;, it became a part of his entire being.

Rugrat opened his hand and a Mana blade appeared. His expression was blank, assessing and taking it all in. His eyes shined blue as power spread throughout his entire body.

I thought that I knew magic, that I was a true blue mage? I was merely an idiot playing with nuclear bombs and saying I knew nuclear physics.

Between Rugrat's eyebrows, a fifteenth Mana gate opened.

Everything seemed to snap into place as Rugrat was lifted up by the Mana all around him. Rugrat closed his eyes, tired. If he damaged his Mana veins now, then they could be repaired with a healing potion as they were now a physical part of him.

Rugrat lost consciousness. So he didn't feel the Mana being gathered inside his body and the impurities being expelled. Within his body, there was no longer any elemental Mana.

Out of his fifteen Mana gates, the impurities of the five Affinities were released. The dungeon core absorbed them hungrily. Rugrat's body continued to draw in Mana and expel the impurities, the dungeon core absorbing them and growing slightly.

Egbert and Erik watched on as Rugrat changed. Erik felt the Mana within his Mana channels shake, being actually drawn towards Rugrat slightly as Rugrat's mana gates tried to consume all of the mana around him.

The power dimmed down within Rugrat's body as he returned to normal. He returned to the ground, completely spent and unmoving.

Erik lifted him up and put him over his shoulder, then activated the Mana gathering formation again.

Mana surged upward. It was too much for the formation and the Mana spread out in a wave. The wave from Erik had been barely noticeable but this highly concentrated Mana hit people like a shockwave. Their Mana systems trembled. The beasts in the beast stable roared in excitement as the plants and magical items of Alva were recharged or grew faster.

People stared at Erik as he carried Rugrat over his shoulder.

Erik stopped, as if a burglar caught in the act. *He mentally waved his hand and thought, "These are not the people you are looking for."*

"Nothing to worry about, folks!" Erik announced as he turned and quickly headed for the barracks, with Egbert following behind.

"I think that will put them all at ease!" Egbert hissed.

"Don't you have to go back to the library?" Erik responded.

"With everyone staring at us like that? I'm more likely to be asked questions and bugged there. I'll just hide at the barracks for some time."

"Scared of people bugging you?"

"Hey, I was all alone here for a while. Now it's nothing but noise and 'Egbert, do you have any information on formation reactions? Egbert, do you know the best stitching pattern for shoulders? The water-to-flour ratio in pancakes?'!"

"Need a new job?"

"My job is actually rather rewarding. It's just the ones wanting to get you to do the work for them who are annoying." Egbert's eyes thinned.

Erik didn't say anything and just nodded.

It was only now that Erik realized he hadn't asked Egbert his opinion about the changes that were happening to Alva and what he wanted.

"Egbert..." Erik started. Egbert looked over with a curious gaze. "What do you want to do?"

"Do?" Egbert asked, confused by the question.

"You might be bound to serve Rugrat and me but we don't want you doing things that you don't enjoy. I realized that we've kind of taken you for granted. Things like not asking what you think about what is happening to Alva, about what you want to do."

Egbert looked confused, looking to Erik before he slowly started to catch on. "Oh," Egbert said, at a loss for words. It took him some time to think on it.

Erik shifted Rugrat around on his shoulders when Egbert started talking.

"I do want to go out into the Ten Realms. I am linked to the dungeon, so the more the dungeon increases in power, the higher I can go in the realms, the more strength I wield and the longer I can last without needing to get charged up by the dungeon core. Yet with you heading to the Fourth Realm, someone needs to watch over Alva. There are a lot of changes and I'm excited to deal with them and work things out."

Erik nodded. "Very well but do know that I consider your position to be similar to the academy head. If you find someone to take over your role, you can do as you want."

Egbert nodded, his words coming out in a quiet voice. "Thank you."

They continued walking. Something bugged Erik. "How powerful are you?" he finally asked.

"How am I supposed to know?" Egbert shrugged, waving his arms around.

"Well, you keep saying things like 'Oh, I'm super powerful but also dark and mysterious.'"

"You been reading my books?"

"No!" Erik exclaimed. People that they were passing looked over at Erik arguing with Egbert and carrying Rugrat over his shoulder.

"I'm keeping it all mysterious because I don't know," Egbert argued back.

"Like, put it on a scale of that flashy spell in the metal floor?"

"Flashy spell? You mean Cleansing Light? A large area spell that kills enemies and supports allies?"

"Yeah."

"I'm sorry that such a spell is just some flashy light! You would think that such a spell would earn a moniker better than some night light!"

"Well, how powerful?"

"Pushy, pushy!" Egbert warned as he waved his hand, looking through a list that only he could see."I could cast one of those every minute. While the dungeon's power stores wouldn't increase, they wouldn't decrease either. I could also create one of those artillery spells that use four mages to cast about every ten seconds without drawing from our power stores. I can cast any spell that was learned by my old master or by you and Rugrat. Though you have to come into contact with the dungeon core for that information to be transferred.

If you are in the dungeon, you can also have the dungeon cast them but it's not like you learn how to cast the spell the way you would using spell books," Egbert finished.

"So how much firepower if you were to go all out?" Erik said.

"I don't know. It depends on who I have to fight. To kill me, someone needs to take control over the dungeon core and then destroy me. I might be linked to the dungeon core but I gave Rugrat and you my oath and the Ten Realms oath supersedes anything else. If I was looking to do damage, then I could destroy the mountain, the dungeon and anything in a radius of five kilometers, maybe? Instead of doing that though, I would raise more dungeon monsters and send those into the enemy, then support them with spells—create doppelgangers."

"Doppelgangers?"

"Yes. I can recreate myself into multiple versions. It takes a lot of effort but I can make up to one thousand copies. If they are destroyed, I start losing information and my abilities become limited. In this form, if I am destroyed, I come back with all of my information and I am able to channel all of the power of the dungeon. I also do not lose my personality."

Erik had been thinking about leaving people from the army behind in Alva but with Egbert's words and his confident smile, Erik felt sorry for anyone who tried to cause a problem for the dungeon.

"Who gave you the name Egbert?" Erik asked.

Egbert looked up at something on the roof of the dungeon, "Some asshole."

Erik looked up, not sure what Egbert was staring at, and nodded.

***

Rugrat woke up to a flurry of notifications and an influx of information from his senses, which had been altered to see and feel the fluctuations of Mana around him. It was a lot to take in but he fought through it, excited that he had passed the barrier that had scared him ever since he had destroyed his Mana system.

Rugrat had earned 2,800,000 Experience opening his fourteenth Mana gate and forming his Mana core. His Mana core also increased his base Mana capacity by ten points. Opening his fourteenth Mana gate opened his fifteenth Mana gate as well, between his eyebrows, increasing his base regeneration by two. Though the biggest change came from his Mana Body rebirth.

He closed his eyes, feeling the mana moving through his body, it was peaceful as he studied his mana gates. There were one in each foot, in his upper leg, at the base of his spine, located in his dantain in his stomach, between his shoulder blades where his back rounded, at the base of his neck along his spine, where his spine connected to his skull and at the back of his head. One in each of his upper arms and then the last two located in his palms for a total of fourteen mana gates.

He drew in mana, feeling his body come alive, all of his cells vibrating with energy as his wider channels started to glow as he circulated the mana, drawing it through his mana gates, causing the air to stir around him, turning into light blue streams that entered his mana gates, being drawn into his dantain where his core floated above his last mana gate, the mana became thicker, viscous as it was compressed and refined, he held on, drawing in more, testing his new limits.

The mana density increased but Rugrat wasn't able to form a mana drop to fill his core.

He let out a breath his eyes glowing in excitement.

"Well, end of one journey, start of another." He pulled up his notifications.

His title of Mana Emperor had been replaced.

==========

Title: Blessed by Mana

==========

You have become closer to Mana, exerting a greater control over it.

==========

The strength of your spells has increased by 60%. Your Mana Regeneration has increased by 60%.

Can create a Mana domain.

(Replaces Mana Emperor)

==========

"Mana domain?" Rugrat wondered to himself. Rugrat tested his power and felt all of the Mana in the area come under his command. In a five-meter radius, the Mana was cut off from the rest of the realm, no longer under its control but under Rugrat's instead.

"If I was able to get someone into this domain, then wouldn't I be able to cut them off from Mana so that they couldn't regenerate it? I could also call down spell after spell on them." Rugrat moved his fingers. A Mana blade appeared in his hand; he moved it around. "I could use my new Mana control in smithing, allowing me greater control over the entire process. I could compress the Mana around the item to a greater degree and make sure that there's no external interference."

With just a thought, Rugrat was able to call up spells. He could see through the Mana, see it flowing all around him, flowing into his body through his Mana gates. Then, with his greater control, he could manipulate it and force it into a new form.

Rugrat looked at these different stages and sank into thought. He looked at the Mana gathering in his body and wondered whether he could optimize it a bit. The Mana blade, from a normal person's view, looked like a beautiful piece of compressed blue Mana. To Rugrat, he could see the chaos that was barely controlled within the blade, the parts of the spell that worked but were wasting energy or stunting the flow of Mana. Seeing that natural Mana flow in the Ten Realms, Rugrat wanted to see whether he could emulate that flow into his spells. He worked for a few minutes without results.

He put his new theory to the side as he checked his character sheet. With the massive amount of experience, Rugrat had been able to increase two levels.

Seeing it was still dark outside, Rugrat checked his timepiece.

He took out a sleeping potion. It looked like with the changes in his body and the sheer exhaustion they brought, he had bypassed the screen where he could input his stats. It was like the time Erik drained all of his Stamina and passed out and couldn't input his attribute points.

Rugrat drank the potion and laid back. When sleep took him, he increased his stats and slept until the morning.

He woke up with Alva's sun. He stood slowly and stretched, feeling the massive changes that had happened in his body. With a thought, he could look through the Mana makeup of the Ten Realms. He didn't even need a spell. This was an innate ability like the Mana domain.

Rugrat looked at his Mana system. His core sat at the center of his being. It gathered a tremendous amount of Mana within it, spreading Mana out to Rugrat's body through his Mana veins. His system had changed. He was faintly emitting Mana through his pores, his Mana circulating without conscious thought, being released through his Mana veins and then gathered back in by his Mana gates.

Rugrat's body was at ease. He closed his eyes, feeling connected, part of the Ten Realms. Rugrat stretched out his arms and tensed up. His body vibrated with power as the Mana surrounding him shook. With that feeling of explosive power hidden within his muscles and his body, he felt like he could do anything.

"Maybe I'll try flying later. I've got courses to run." Rugrat laughed as he checked the time and headed for the showers. He had a course to teach in just a few hours.

***

Erik was in the cafeteria, talking to Glosil about the Fourth Realm and the importance of logistics and supplies. They had also been looking over the information that Erik had brought back from Old Hei.

Glosil had changed. When he worked as the captain of the guards in Alva, he had done it knowing that he wouldn't go anywhere in the military. It wasn't because he didn't try but because he lacked patrons to help him increase his Strength.

Knowing that he couldn't advance any further in the military, when his senior, Blaze, had offered him the position of Alva's guard captain, Glosil had debated over it. Thinking about what the small camp might become and Blaze's kindness, the young man accepted his offer.

He trained people to be guards but he hadn't lost his edge as he hunted all the time to drive off beasts and protect the people under him.

Still, there were few ways for him to increase his Strength. There were no trainers, no crafters, no one other than Blaze with true fighting experience. So Glosil trained and fought, helping Alva Village to grow but his own personal power hadn't advanced much.

When Erik and Rugrat arrived, he had become used to his routine. They broke him out of it, showing him so much more that he could do and that he could learn. In the defense of Alva against the beasts, he had lost people but he still saw the strength of the people of Alva. Coming to the dungeon, he had done all he could to pass on his knowledge and grow his own techniques, ability and knowledge.

When Alva's army was formed, Glosil was placed in charge of it all. He pushed its members with all he had. He worked side by side with Erik and Rugrat. Both of them had led men and women across different theatres, fighting across countries. They'd been in a trained military, then mercenaries in foreign lands. For them, fighting was in their very bones.

Their thought processes and their actions had all been optimized to convey information and carry out their mission with precision and brutality as needed.

Glosil was no longer a guard captain. As leader of the army, he took time to listen to everyone but when he gave an order, the others snapped to respond. He worked harder than anyone, was always asking questions and was always there for the hardest training. He'd gained the respect of his soldiers, instead of just being appointed to his position. There was a large difference between the two.

"So, we will be entering the Fourth Realm together without the use of a guide," Erik said. "We will head from the First Realm in different groups through different totems, rally in Taeman city and then head to the Fourth Realm.

We're going in blind, so we'll need to adapt on the ground. Once we exit the totem, we need to assess the city we're in as fast as possible. Then either gather ourselves there or head for the nearest neutral city as fast as possible. We'll look for dungeons along the way and then once at the neutral city, we'll create a base of operations and then advance on possible dungeon locations, intending to occupy or destroy them. It seems like even the dungeons controlled by the different sects are not owned by them as Dungeon Lords, from what I was able to get from Old Hei and these," Erik tilted his chin toward the papers.

Erik looked over his shoulder, his eye catching something. He beckoned with his hand.

Glosil looked over, seeing Rugrat with a plate loaded with food. The air seemed to move with him as he approached the table.

"How you feeling?" Erik asked.

"Like a million bucks. Just made it to level thirty-three," Rugrat grinned.

"This fucking guy," Erik pointed at Rugrat and complained to Glosil.

Rugrat shrugged his big shoulders and set to the task of eating.

"So, Mana rebirth?" Erik asked.

"Basically, merged my Mana systems into the rest of my body," Rugrat said between mouthfuls. "Greater control and power."

Seeing they would only get half sentences and a bare minimum understanding of what happened from Rugrat, Erik just continued talking about the Fourth Realm to Glosil.

"Once we've all increased our levels and reached level forty, we'll return to Alva, recuperate, fix up our gear and challenge the metal floor," Erik said.

"You think we'll be ready?" Glosil asked.

"Beasts are powerful, much more powerful than their levels say but humans are sneaky fuckers. They draw out all the power that they can possibly summon. If we're fighting in the dungeons of the Fourth Realm or against veteran forces, it will be a true test of everyone's abilities. In training, we give people the basic tools but it is only when you're in the fight do you decide how to use those tools. The highest level we sensed in the metal floor was level thirty-eight. There might be stronger creatures, too. If we play it smart, if we work the formations, re-establish control over the floor piece by piece, I don't see why we couldn't slowly but surely take over the floor," Erik postulated.

"Going to the Fourth Realm with the army kills five birds with one stone. It bonds the army together, bloodies them, exposes them to the higher realms, gives us the strength to deal with the lower floors here, and adds strength to the dungeon as we capture other dungeons and dungeon cores," Glosil said.

Erik simply smiled.

"The metal floor will have lots of resources," Rugrat interrupted between mouthfuls. "Maybe replace the iron mine that's thinning out.

Got maybe another year of production left in it."As time went on, the methods of mining had improved. The miners' abilities had all increased and they'd had new technology created to make mining safer, faster and much more profitable. It meant that they were cutting through the iron vein that they had found quickly but they had opened up two more mines on areas where surveyors had sensed metal. They'd left a number of spots untouched, not wanting to draw attention with a massive mining operation above ground, focusing instead on hidden operations in the mountains.

"The Fourth Realm isn't going to be easy. So for the next two months everyone gets weekends off to see their families. During the week, we'll press every damn course that might help them down their throats," Erik said.

"Yeah," Glosil said, hidden emotions in his voice. He had been in the military and he'd seen iron meet flesh and bone.

Erik could read his mind because he had the same thoughts. *Will it be enough to keep them alive?*

As well as another thought that neither of them wanted to acknowledge. *Who won't make it back?*

***

Specialization courses continued. People learned the new weapons. Their armor was reissued with formation sockets; adding them in wasn't too hard, just required a smith or a formation master to add in the socket and the effect lines so that the entire armor would be affected.

Formation coins were being produced at an impressive rate.

Rugrat had gone to the formation workshop to work on a few ideas and found another use for his new Mana sense. He was able to see the flaws in the different formations that they had been working on. He didn't know how to fix most of them but knowing that there were issues allowed the formation apprentices to think of ways to work on solutions.

His formations were also stronger and used less power as they were directly aligned with the formation plate and ambient Mana. Rugrat also created a lecture on formations, which was attended by formation apprentices, architects, smiths and anyone else who was interested.

He made this comparison with formations and the environment they were in. If one was to make a formation that was aligned with the area it was set, then its strength would increase. This would help formations reach the Use External Mana stage. At this point they didn't rely on their stored power to create an effect. They also used the mana in the surrounding area to increase their effectiveness.

Formations that were just mass-produced still worked but a formation made for a specific weapon would have a greater effect in increasing the weapon's lethality.

All of Alva was working to prepare for the expedition of its army. The cooks created meals and supplies for the Alvan army. Smiths created and altered armor and weapons for the army and fitted armor to their mounts. The woodworking shop was making more repeater bows, replacement parts and massive quantities of bolts for the repeaters and the ballistas combined with enchanted heads from the smithy and formation workshop. The military workshop located in the barracks gathered and assembled gunpowder and explosives from the alchemists; bullets, cartridges, and the fragmentation shell for the grenades from the smithy. Lines had been set up to create ammunition for all weapon systems in massive quantities.

Raw ingredients and metal would go in, being refined into different shells, cartridges, rounds, powders and explosives.

Rugrat's testing proved to be invaluable with Erik's notes on explosives, through testing in the last few months the different formulas for gunpowder, primer charges, explosive charges, propellant charges had been refined. The process for making rounds had improved as well.

People had thought Erik and Rugrat were crazy with how much ammunition they wanted to be made, that was before the army had gone out on exercises. With a section of mortars with their rate of fire at one every five to seven seconds of sustained fire, they burned through two hundred, to three hundred mortar rounds per minute. Rifles were even worse in an exercise people could go through hundreds of rounds, with the repeaters thousands wasn't ridiculous if they were in large firefights.

Erik and Rugrat were using these exercises to understand just what their consumption of supplies would be and stocking up so that they would always have ammunition.

They had not stopped production in five months. They had stockpiled enough items to fill up several warehouses, luckily the kick ass storage devices solved that potential problem.

High Mortal-grade storage rings were purchased in large bulk orders. Inside each, equipment and supplies were laid out for combat medics, ballista repeater gunners, repeater gunners, mages, marksmen, leadership and so on.

As the weekend came, the troops in the barracks were released to do what they wanted with their two days of free time.

Erik and Rugrat headed toward the teleportation array.

They passed a group heading back from the dungeon. They looked tired but pleased with their spoils as they went to the trader tables that had been set up to purchase items from the returning soldiers.

Erik pulled out one of Rugrat's modified rifles—the MK1 bolt action rifle, though most just called it the Mark One. Erik put the magazine in, chambered a round and pulled off the magazine, putting another round on top.

Rugrat had his larger rifle, simply named Big Poppa. Fondly named after the retired Former Big Momma. It was a fine rifle but the rounds he was firing were too hot and the materials that Big Momma was made from were too weak to handle the new power.

Rugrat's eyes had a faint blue glow to them when he used his magic. If it was large scale or he wasn't trying to hide it, his Mana veins appeared, his eyes glowed brightly and his Mana gates appeared across his body.

He looked different but he was still the same old idiot.

"One fiery hot crotch of a level coming up!" Rugrat shouted.

George landed on the teleportation array, looking excited.

Erik activated the teleportation pad with his dungeon master controls. They reappeared, looking at a familiar door.

"Two years, huh?" Rugrat asked.

"If I knew about the prize hall, I would have thought about staying in the First Realm for longer," Erik answered.

Rugrat pointed his rifle up with a smile on his face. "Well, let's just see how many points we can get." Rugrat had an excited look on his face.

"You just want to show off your new skills," Erik muttered.

"I heard that. And don't you just need a few thousand to level up?"

"Yeah," Erik said, still annoyed with just how close he was to leveling up, as he pushed on the door.

It opened to an icy tundra.

"Fuck, I hate the cold." Rugrat cast his Detect Life spell.

He looked up and grabbed his rifle. He moved it around, following something. He changed out the formation socket and cast Direct Shot on his rifle. He and Erik had added a number of spells to their different internal spell books.

The formations increased penetrating power and decreased the effect of wind on the round. Direct Shot sped up the projectile.

Rugrat fired the loud round shot into the sky. Erik continued scanning with his rifle, not seeing anything. The round was enhanced to explode on impact. Erik saw an explosion in the air, hearing it a few moments later as he tracked a bird the size of a man dropping to the ground.

"Fetch," Rugrat commanded.

George's tongue hung out as he rushed out over the snow, flapping his wings.

"You have passed the first level of the battlefield dungeon," Egbert's voice intoned through the dungeon room.

"Hey, at least this time he's not annoyed we're sleeping in the entrance." Rugrat laughed and kneeled to touch the ground. Using his Simple Inorganic Scan, he was able to see through the ground to scan for items below its surface.

Combined with his new Mana sense, even if he wasn't sure about something, seeing the density of Mana that was collected inside it allowed Rugrat to pick out the useful items hidden in the ground.

Rugrat pulled out a pick and stored his rifle. He marked some items on his map and shared them with Erik, who pulled out his own pick.

"It's off to work I go!" Erik yelled.

Rugrat laughed as they headed to the marker positions, clearing the snow and ice, cracking the ground and extracting resources from the floor.

It wasn't long before they returned to the door. The bird was messed up, so after Erik examined it and Rugrat took the good bits, the rest was left to George to consume, including its monster core.

It had only been a level twenty-five beast but still could have been dangerous had it swooped down from above with its razor-like talons when they weren't looking.

They exited the battlefield and were teleported to a new one.

The door opened and they found themselves facing a flat field. A large den sat in the middle of the plains.

Rugrat looked to Erik, holding a grenade in his hand.

"Worth a shot," Erik said as he shrugged.

Rugrat pulled the friction rope and tossed the grenade into the den.

"Nice toss," Erik complimented.

The den and the ground around it exploded. Dirt, rocks and wood quickly came back to the ground.

Erik looked around but there was no notification.

"Looks like we're not done," Rugrat said. The three of them scanned the area.

The ground started to shake and holes appeared in the ground.

Small horns appeared first, followed by the rest of the creatures.

"What kind of crazy bastard makes a unicorn rabbit?" Erik complained as he fired on the rabbits with his rifle. Using Explosive Shot, he could take out a group of them if they were close enough together. The single-horned rabbits turned their beady eyes on Erik, Rugrat, and George and charged toward them.

"Get in the air!" Erik shouted as they rushed closer.

They were taking out handfuls of them with each shot but the bunny tide was still coming in.

Rugrat jumped on George, who then jumped into the sky. Exhaling a powerful fire breath on the rabbits, George killed tens of them in a line and set the plains on fire.

Erik cast Hallowed Ground and quickly increased the range. As the rabbit wave got within ten meters, Erik put his rifle away and began gathering Mana in his fists. He clapped his hands together and lowered himself into a fighting stance.

The rabbits charged forward, valiant one-horned furry missiles.

Erik spread his fingers out and fired Mana bullets from every finger. It wasn't accurate at all but there were so many of them packed together that it was hard to miss. He jumped to the side; a rabbit sailed past, struggling in the air to try to make contact with its horn.

Erik jumped to the side, right into the path of another that hit him from the side, leaving a cut on his left butt cheek as he felt a breeze through his torn pants.

"God dammit!" Erik yelled.

Rugrat was in the air. The rabbits couldn't get that high, so George was just circling and using his fire breath, leaving burning tracks of ground as the bun-pocalypse continued.

Rugrat switched out his formations and cast Explosive Shot. Each round was like a mortar, destroying anything within a few meters of where it landed.

Erik jumped around, the Hallowed Ground hurting the rabbits, as they charged toward the person who dared to blow up their home.

They hit Erik's armor, one spearing his shoulder right on. Its horn pierced the armor and stuck in his arm.

"Ow! Little fucker!" Erik loudly complained.

The rabbit kept trying to chew or scratch him but couldn't, as it hung off Erik's arm by its horn.

Erik punched the rabbit and it exploded, leaving the horn imbedded and covering Erik in rabbit bits.

"Shit!" Erik shouted as he jumped through a line of George's flames. Some of the rabbits jumped over but others went around. Those that had been blocked off on the other side attacked as Erik used Mana Detonation, clearing a path for him to keep moving. With punches or kicks, he could kill them easily. Yet with their numbers, it wouldn't be enough, he had to go for large area attacks.

Erik tossed out grenades, opening up pockets and paths for him to advance through the mass of rabbits as they charged him, primarily hitting his armor and bruising him. A few more even pierced his armor with their sharp horns.

Erik laid down more Hallowed Grounds, and started to move through them, weakening the charging horned rabbits and healing himself.

Once he had a system set up and a route to run, with George and Rugrat running interference and supporting from above, it wasn't long until the last rabbit was killed.

The ground shook. A horn appeared from the ground as a massive rabbit, easily five meters tall, dug its way out of the ground.

"I think that's their mom!" Rugrat yelled.

"Shoot it!" Erik yipped as he pulled out his rifle.

Rugrat fired a round. It pierced the rabbit's eye and blew up. The horn was launched, cutting through the ground before it came to a stop.

"You have passed the second level of the battlefield dungeon," Egbert announced.

Most of the rabbits were left to George, who crunched through them happily. A few were salvageable and their horns all remained.

Erik took a look at his notifications that had updated with the fight.

```
==========
```
You have reached Level 33
```
==========
```
When you sleep next, you will be able to increase your attributes by: 5 points.
```
==========
```
```
==========
```
14,266/1,300,000 EXP till you reach Level 34
```
==========
```
"About time," Erik muttered.

"You level up?" Rugrat asked.

"Yeah but I'll input the stats later. Still need to make it to a Fire-based battlefield," Erik said.

Rugrat looked at the still burning plains. "I made this for YOU," Rugrat said in some horrible, messed-up accent.

"Just go and get the resources," Erik replied.

Rugrat grinned and went off.

**

With their rifles and Rugrat's ability to see through Mana, they quickly passed through three more battlefields before they finally reached a Fire battlefield floor.

The temperature soared as they looked out over the barren wasteland of rocks and lava. Lakes of lava weaved between the broken landscape, bubbles of sulfur would pop as they scanned the area.

A tiger with black paws that turned into reds and yellows, making it look like a moving volcano let out a roar, stirring up lava and blasts of fire to shoot out at Erik, Rugrat, and George.

George seemed offended more than alarmed by the attack and let out his own roar and charged forward as Erik and Rugrat jumped into cover.

"That's it, show them who's the fire attribute boss around these parts!" Rugrat yelled.

The Tiger dodged George's charge and sent a few dozen fireballs at Rugrat and Erik, destroying their cover.

Erik jumped up as the blasts passed and fired his rifle at the tiger. It was focusing on George, who let out a challenging howl. The Fire Mana that had been under the control of the tiger was now under George's command. As he opened his mouth, fire breath shot out, slamming into the tiger and sending it flying.

The tiger's fire resistance was high, saving it from dying outright. It fought to get up but Erik and Rugrat hit it with rounds. George swooped down from the sky and raked the tiger's side with his hind claws. The tiger let out a pained yell and lashed out, hitting George's wing and damaging it, bringing George to the ground.

George's teeth flashed forward as he sunk his teeth into the tiger's neck and shook his head.

The tiger fought back frantically but its strength waned as it bled out before collapsing. A tombstone appeared above it.

George backed off from it.

"You have passed the sixth level of the battlefield dungeon," Egbert reported.

Erik and Rugrat stood and lowered their rifles.

"Will this area work?" Rugrat asked.

"It should," Erik replied as he looked at the lava and felt the hot Fire-attribute Mana in the air.

He took a quick look at his Experience.

==========

162,918/1,300,000 EXP till you reach Level 34

==========

Erik scoffed. As he increased in level, it was harder to increase his Experience with just killing creatures.

Though now that I've reached level thirty-three, my Experience gain is based on that level even though I haven't accepted the changes. Erik thought that this was the case based on his previous experiences but he'd had little time to think on it when being chased, attacked, and/or mauled by a variety of creatures.

Rugrat looked around, seeing something that Erik couldn't.

"That has the most concentrated Fire-attribute Mana, unless you get into the lava." Rugrat pointed to a small island that rose above the lava, curving to create a bowl-like shape in the lava. Erik moved closer but he wouldn't make it even if he jumped. He didn't really want to fall into lava.

George flapped his wings, coming over. He grabbed Erik with his paws and set him down on the island.

"Good boy. Thanks, George." Erik patted the proud fire-wolf."Go eat." Erik pointed to the fire tiger.

George let out an excited noise and rushed over, his tail wagging in the air as he dug in.

"Wait! Let me skin it first!" Rugrat yelled, rushing over as George's tail dropped. "You big puppy!"

Erik shook his head and pulled out a Mana gathering formation. He took off his armor, wearing just his clothes.

The Fire Mana gathered, creating embers that floated on the breeze, concentrating and forming an ember tornado.

Erik circulated his Mana, pouring out the dense, refined Mana in his body. The Fire-attribute Mana rushed in, warming Erik's body and making his skin turn red as a faint haze appeared around Erik's body.

The Fire-attribute Mana was refined through Erik's circulation, becoming more pure as it was expelled. A part of the Fire mana was left behind, too much for Erik's Mana system to fully remove.

The Fire-attribute Mana continued to increase with every circulation. The faint haze turned into a heat halo, warping the air much like the heat waves one would see on asphalt roads in summer.

It took time but the build up of Fire-attribute Mana overcame even Erik's fire resistance from taking the Internal Burning pill. Erik's body was being refined from the inside out, the Fire Mana burning away weakness.

Those weaknesses were part of Erik and he grit his teeth in pain as he was being burned from the inside out. He continued to circulate his Mana, drawing in more Fire.

***

Rugrat watched the dance of Mana as it was pulled in by the formation, entered Erik's body, was refined and then pushed out. His breaths were like the bellows on a furnace. With each inhale, he would drag the embers into his body; with each exhale, the Mana would burst into new power within his body and shoot out from his Mana gates.

Erik sunk deeper into meditation, pushing the pain to the side, trying to just focus on the circulation.

Rugrat finished cleaning the tiger and got George to carry him over to Erik. He took out an IV stand and inserted needles into Erik's veins, giving him a low dose of a Stamina and Healing cocktail.

He took out a painkiller and added it to the drip.

Erik's breathing became easier as the painkiller took effect, removing him from what was happening to his body.

Rugrat sat against the curved sides of the island, watching Erik and pulled out a book on formations and a formation plate that had been cut to the book's specifics.

Rugrat studied the power flow and checked information in other books. "This will be so much easier when I can get to the Journeyman stage," Rugrat complained.

The Mana in the battlefield was surging but it all seemed to avoid Rugrat.

George was stuck in his meal. The fire tiger was of the same attribute, so eating it increased his Strength much more than eating other attribute animals.

The embers above Erik started to strike one another, their intensity increasing as they turned to flames.

Erik let out a grunt as the flames entered his body. He was covered in sweat, his body burning. He suddenly moved, grabbing the burning crescent dagger, and stabbed it into his leg. The furnace inside him turned into an inferno as the blade was enhanced by the environment and the Mana inside Erik's body.

Erik's blood boiled, becoming thicker as his bones were also hardened. His organs were burned away and then rebuilt even stronger.

His skin browned and then flaked off, repeating the process again and again. His skin looked clear underneath, pure almost but its strength only increased. Erik had taken many kinds of concoctions; he had thought that he'd cleared all these impurities from his system but he was proved wrong. A pungent steam rose from his head as the last hidden vestiges were seemingly removed from his body.

Rugrat watched silently, examining Erik. The Mana ran through his Mana system but the attacks from the dagger went through his body. It was a two-pronged assault. Rugrat stood and opened up the Stamina and Healing bags.

Time passed. George napped after his meal, Rugrat worked and Erik tempered his body.

The faint flames had turned into a fire tornado. At its peak, there were yellow flames and embers, then red flames, and finally, concentrated blue flames.

An explosive noise came from within Erik's body. He tilted his head back and let out a wordless yell.

"Fuck!" Rugrat jumped from his spot, about to throw the formation in his hand at Erik but held back. As the Mana in the area was blown backward, power from the Ten Realms rushed in toward Erik while Rugrat watched. He had passed out during his mana rebirth so he wasn't entirely sure what had happened to him.

Now Rugrat had a chance to watch and saw a majestic tsunami of golden energy rushing toward Erik, it was truly majestic. Erik stood, his body releasing steam as the Mana within his body came under his control.

Erik's body made popping noises as it passed through a bottleneck, progressing from Body Like Stone, to Body Like Iron. His shed skin fell from him. His muscles were more defined. His movements contained a deadly heat to them as he stepped forward. Rugrat jumped up and grabbed the IV as Erik took another step; he was working on instinct instead of conscious thought.

Erik stumbled. The blade was still in his leg as he hobbled forward to the edge of the island.

Uhh... Rugrat wasn't sure what to say or do as Erik straddled the edge of the island and hung his foot over the side.

Erik didn't hesitate, plunging his foot into the lava.

Rugrat's eyes went wide as Erik let out a howl but didn't remove his foot.

"Fucking bat shit," Rugrat muttered to himself as he took out another bag of Healing and Stamina potion and hooked it up, ready to switch to it when the first set was depleted.

He put his hands on Erik, using his Simple Organic Scan to see the damage as he healed Erik.

Erik was breathing through his gritted teeth as he adjusted to the lava. The fire tornado over the Mana gathering formation shot toward him. Rugrat stared at it, the raging energies finally calmed down, weaving around Erik like a snake before it slammed through his open Mana gates.

Rugrat increased the dosage of painkillers. He could see Erik's body continued to increase in Strength. He had entered Body Like Iron but it was only the start of the transformation. His power was further consolidated and increased.

One foot became two feet in the lava, and then he sunk in up to his knees.

Rugrat didn't need to heal anymore as Erik's body was able to deal with the trauma itself.

Then Erik jumped forward, dropping completely into the lava.

The IV stand followed Erik into the lava and started to melt.

"Erik!" Rugrat yelled out in a panic. He looked to see Erik just floating in the lava with the blade still in his leg.

Rugrat was about to dive in when he saw Erik move. He rose out of the lava until he stood on top of it.

Rugrat could see the Fire-attribute Mana had attacked his body but the tempering caused it to infiltrate his body instead, making it a part of Erik.

Erik stood on top of the lava as if it were solid ground. The waves of heat no longer affected him as he turned to face Rugrat.

"Put some fucking clothes on, you nudist!" Rugrat complained.

Erik came out of his meditative state and said, "Says the guy who wears American short shorts in the damn smithy! You know how many complaints I get a day?! The best thing about those smithing rooms is that they keep your hairy ass out of sight! When you went to the formation workshop, did you realize what you were wearing?!" Erik yelled as he walked across the lava.

Rugrat looked up, remembering the day. He had been so laser-focused he hadn't realized he was wearing his cowboy boots, short shorts, apron, and cowboy hat.

"It was hot in there," Rugrat complained.

Erik's lips moved but no words came out. He stepped on the island, letting out a tired sigh as he pulled clothes on.

"So, did you do it?" Rugrat asked.

Erik snorted, with a smile on his face. "Of course." Erik gave a tired laugh as he stretched to the ground and laid down. "I'm taking a nap."

"I'll take watch."

***

Erik opened the notifications from his ordeal.

==========

Quest Completed: Body Cultivation 2

==========

The path cultivating one's body is not easy. To stand at the top, one must forge their own path forward.

==========

Requirements:

Reach Body Like Iron Level

==========

Rewards:

+6 to Strength

+6 to Agility

+6 to Stamina

+10 to Stamina Regeneration

+1,000,000 EXP

==========

==========

Your personal efforts have increased your base stats!

==========

Stamina +3

Strength +3

Agility +3

Stamina Regeneration +3

Mana Pool +2

==========

==========

Title: Fire Body

==========

You have tempered your body with Fire. Fire has become a part of you, making your body take on some of its characteristics. You have gained:

==========

Legendary Fire resistance.

Increased control over Fire Mana.

Physical attacks contain Fire attribute.

Can completely purify the Fire attribute in Mana.

==========

==========

Quest: Body Cultivation 3

==========

The path cultivating one's body is not easy. To stand at the top, one must forge their own path forward.

==========

Requirements:

Reach Body Like Earth Iron Level

==========

Rewards:
+12 to Strength
+12 to Agility
+12 to Stamina
+20 to Stamina Regeneration
+10,000,000 EXP
==========
==========
1,162,918/1,300,000 EXP till you reach Level 34
==========

"Fucker. Just one hundred and forty thousand to go," Erik complained in his dream state.

Erik was unaffected by heat anymore and the Fire-attribute Mana that had spread through his body had been cleansed thanks to his new ability.

Erik opened another notification and a familiar screen appeared.

==========
You have 5 attribute points to use.
==========

Erik placed two into Strength and Agility, with the last point for his Mana pool. He was confident that in time he would open his fourteenth Mana gate and follow Rugrat. Still, his Mana pool wasn't large enough to give him the power he needed in order to combine his five Mana drops and compress them into his Mana core.

Erik looked at the changes on his character sheet. Even as he was half-asleep, a grin appeared on his face.

I wonder just how far we can make it in the battlefield dungeon now.

==========
Name: Erik West

==========

Level: 33

==========

Race: Human

==========

Titles:

From the Grave II

Mana Emperor

Dungeon Master II

Reverse Alchemist

Poison Body

Fire Body

==========

Strength: (Base 36) +41

==========

770

==========

Agility: (Base 29) +43

==========

396

==========

Stamina: (Base 39) +9

==========

720

==========

Mana: (Base 8) +36

==========

440

==========

Mana Regeneration (Base 10) +40

26. 00/s

==========

Stamina Regeneration: (Base 41) +33
15. 80/s

==========

Chapter: Trial of Strength

Erik's fist was covered in flames as he punched the Loch Ness monster-looking creature in the snout as it powered up another water breath attack. His fist cracked the ice armor over its body.

Rugrat rode George, compensating for the rough movements as George moved to miss water spears that the creature had launched earlier. Rugrat trusted in George completely; so he focused on the creature as the shattered ice revealed its football-sized eye that was so blue it was almost black.

Its eye was already a mess, with signs of previous attacks.

The creature was unable to move its head; Erik's attack had landed perfectly.

Rugrat fired. The round shot through the sky, hitting the creature in the eye. He had used a round with a blunt damage enhancing formation while the formation coins on the rifle increased the speed of the round and its ability to puncture. It broke through the creature's eye and all of the bullets kinetic energy was let out in a wide blast. The pressure wave scrambled the creature's brain and a tombstone appeared above it. Its spells fell apart and it dropped forward, slamming into the water and raising waves across the icebergs, which shook from the force.

The large body floated there as Erik rested his hands on his knees and forced his breathing under control. "Fuck, that was a hard one," Erik stated as he pulled up his notifications.

"What's that, number twenty five?" Rugrat asked as George came down to rest on the ground.

"I think so," Erik said.

It had been a tough fight, with Erik and Rugrat having to use different ploys. Their battle had gone on for nearly four hours. Several times, they had thought about quitting.

"You have passed the thirteenth level of the battlefield dungeon," Egbert said in a surprised voice.

"Thanks for the vote of confidence," Rugrat said as his eyes rolled.

George turned his head back at Rugrat with puppy eyes.

Rugrat got off his back and patted George's side. "Let Erik and me clean it up."

Erik, Rugrat and George hauled the creature onto the shore and stripped it. Erik and Rugrat took anything that looked valuable, leaving the rest for George to dine on.

Erik and Rugrat had taken the time to adapt to their new abilities with their changes in cultivation and to get to know their new weaponry.

Rugrat was still ahead of Erik in levels, close to breaking into level forty.

George had the biggest increase in levels, reaching level forty-three. After all, he gained Strength by eating other creatures' flesh and their Mana cores, as well as eating treasures and being in high Mana areas.

Rugrat gave George the Loch Ness like creature's Mortal-grade monster core. The core broke easily in George's teeth. They concluded it must be a beast thing as neither of them could bite the monster cores and only Rugrat's Mana blade could cut them. Or they could be consumed in crafting.

As George was eating, Erik sat down and looked through his notifications.

==========

Skill: Hand-to-Hand

==========

Level: 59 (Journeyman)

==========

Attacks cost 20% less Stamina. Agility is increased by 10%.

==========

"Only one level increase—it's a lot harder to increase at the higher levels," Erik said to himself. He felt like he was much stronger with hand to hand than he had ever been on Earth, but the techniques on Earth were only half developed compared to the fighting styles in the ten realms. *I'll need to find a teacher or someone to help me.* Erik thought before looking at the next notification.

==========

You have reached Level 37

==========

When you sleep next, you will be able to increase your attributes by: 20 points.

==========

==========

543,188/1,660,000 EXP till you reach Level 38

==========

Erik looked at his timepiece. They had arrived on Friday night but it was already closing in on Monday morning.

Once George was done with his meal, they broke their medallion and appeared in the prize hall.

=========

Erik West

Dungeon Points: 83,379

=========

Erik scrolled through the different items that he could buy from the prize hall. He had enough to get just one mid-level Expert item or he could get sixteen high-class Journeyman items.

"I could get high-Journeyman-level armor and then maybe a mid-Expert-ranked piece of gear," Erik muttered to himself. "Or I could get maybe three pieces of low-Expert grade armor and some other items. Are there any armor sets?"

Erik looked through the information. His Ass Kicker set was mid-Journeyman level. He had relied on Rugrat to make his armor up to this point but Rugrat was dealing with multiple different projects: the formation sockets, his own armor and weapons, the rifles, as well as learning formations.

If he could get armor and save Rugrat from having to work on it, then it would be for the best.

Erik looked through the armor and then stopped.

Rugrat might not be able to but Taran and Tan Xue are also Journeyman-level smiths and looking to reach the Expert level. If I just replaced the plates in my carrier, that would be fine.

Instead of making traditional armor, Alva's army used plate carriers and vests like those used in the modern militaries back on Earth. If the armor was broken, instead of needing a whole new set, one could take out the plate and replace it easily.

With this in mind, Erik went to the Expert-level smithing materials. Realizing that he had little idea what to look for, Erik sent Rugrat a message.

"I might not be able to turn those materials into a weapon but I can turn them into an armor plate," Rugrat responded a few moments later. "Why not get something for hand-to-hand or Alchemy or cultivation?"

"There is no guarantee that whatever I get will increase my Strength right away. I want to check the tempering of my body before I get some unknown pill. I've already got some fighting techniques, getting more will only complicate things. Having armor to help me against powerful enemies—it's one of the easiest things to get to improve my overall combat strength."

"That makes sense. All right, send the points on over and I'll see what I can get."

Erik cut the channel and looked up into the air. "I, Erik West, swear on the Ten Realms to give Jimmy Rodriguez seventy-five thousand of my points to be used in the dungeon prize hall."

A golden glow fell over Erik and the numbers on the notification plate changed.

=========
Erik West
Dungeon Points: 8,379
=========

Erik opened up the Alchemy and healing tabs, looking at the books that were there to see whether they had any books that could further his learning or could answer Alchemy questions he had been asked since he returned to Alva. Compared to the armor it was a secondary concern. The armor would increase his Strength in the shortest time possible and increase his survivability.

***

Tan Xue finally woke up. She didn't know how long she had slept for or how long she had worked for. She moved to get up, feeling more energetic than she had in days, weeks—or maybe it was months?

As she moved, she found that she was grasping something. She focused on it instinctively. It felt as if it were perfectly balanced for her.

Her mind went back to the lost time, to what she had been working on—the Expert-level weapon she wanted to create. Then the idea had emerged. She knew weapons and farming equipment down to her bones but her smithing hammer was the other part of her soul.

With this delirious thought, she had set to smithing a new hammer. A hammer that would act as her tool to change all that stood in front of her. It was covered in runes and lines, with a formation socket on both sides.

It had brown veins running through it and as she reached out toward it, her Mana embraced the hammer, the two merging like a hand and glove. The hammer shone with power and faint smoke started to rise from it.

She didn't need to look at her notifications.

"*This* is an Expert-level item," she said with approval, feeling the strength of the hammer. Not only was its strength incredible but that strength enhanced her own abilities.

"Formed of enhanced Earth-grade iron, with innate attributes to increase Mana flow from me to the item I am smithing and an Earth attribute to increase and decrease the weight of the hammer as needed. The hammer is linked to my soul, bound to me with the possibility of two enchantments."

She turned it in her hands, studying it, confused and excited by it. She had made it but believing that she had made it this far was hard.

She stood with a smile. "First, to get some formations and then I'll need to find something worthy to smith!" Her hammer glowed, seemingly agreeing with her and eager to land its first blow.

She smacked its side and let out a hearty laugh, her excitement bubbling forth as she checked her skill sheet.

Expert level smith, I finally made it.

Chapter: March on the Fourth

All of the specialization courses had been completed. If they had been rough ore before, their training outside Alva refined them into finely worked metal. With their specializations, they had been forged.

Training was tested in the battlefield dungeon, with the sections using what they had learned to overcome their opponents.

It was eye opening as they could directly see the changes in their combat strength when they had only increased a few levels but their tactics and methods had changed completely.

Tan Xue had broken through into the realm of Expert smith. Instead of taking a break, she gathered the materials given to her and created new armor plates to be inserted into the soldiers' carriers.

The soldiers, in turn, pooled their point earnings together and bought rare metals that Tan Xue indicated from the prize hall that would be best for her work.

With the armor's simple interlocking plates design, she worked with the Journeyman smiths to enhance the Expert-level metals and added alloys to the Earth-grade metal. They stretched out the new metal as best as they could. They only had enough materials to create the breastplates. Their helmets, arms, backplates, and leg armor remained of the Journeyman grade.

The army, standing row upon row with their armor just visible under their cloaks, had a solemn air. No one dared to move or make a sound as they looked out at these assembled soldiers.

Beside each of them was a powerful black panther wearing its own armor. They had trained in it so much that they had become comfortable in its use. Each of them was level thirty-one or higher.

The lowest ranked soldier was thirty-one, while the strongest was Glosil at thirty-six. When they had started training the lowest soldier had been level sixteen.

Erik remained at level thirty-seven, while Rugrat was level thirty-nine with George beating them all at level forty-six.

Erik's own mount was a black panther with purple eyes. Her name was Lola. She was level forty-one and the pack leader. Many alphas had tried to rise up, only to be thrown down by her. She had awakened her bloodline, a rare and lucky achievement.

Winter had ended and spring was coming, the fresh air entering Alva.

"We will meet again in the Second Realm and then move on to the Fourth Realm. Remember your training and follow your superiors' orders. Alva will no longer passively defend but instead will begin to make its own quiet mark on the Ten Realms." Erik looked out at those men and women, seeing the same emotions he had felt when walking up to a plane that would lead him to a warzone in a foreign land.

He had those same feelings now: the trepidation, the smiles and jokes to cover the crippling fear inside. The cold sweats and sleepless nights of waiting when he just wanted to get there and start.

He knew that once he got there, that his reality would change. He would still love be the same person but there would be a wall between him and what happened back home. The craving to spend time with his brothers and sisters. The complaints they had, and the way that everyone could be relaxed but change in a moment, reacting to any potential threat.

The way grabbing a rifle and your armor to run to the watchtower was just what you *did*—the lack of conscious thought, the need to just react, to just do.

They had a duty and they would carry it out even if it lead to their death.

Erik held their eyes.

"Let's go," he said, just as if they were going out for any other training exercise. Erik stepped forward and Rugrat followed him.

The soldiers moved into action. The sergeants grabbed their people as the special teams talked to one another. The gates opened and the families outside of the barracks saw them exiting.

They cried and hugged the soldiers as they flowed past, many heading to the teleportation pad, others heading out of the Alva Dungeon entrance.

Erik and Rugrat mounted up and rode out of the entrance.

They looked at each other and then looked away silently. They were riding to war again. They both knew what would come.

To avoid making a commotion, the soldiers dispersed to different cities through the teleportation pad, moving in groups of no more than four. Over the last couple of months, Erik and Rugrat had been taking people to the city Kaeju in the Second Realm so that they all had the location logged.

As they rode, Erik took time to look at his character sheet and his new gear, just to take his mind off where they were going and what would happen.

"Still no increase in Alchemy," Erik sighed to himself. He had spent time lecturing for the alchemists of Alva while the Alchemy Lab was being raised up to tier three.

He had worked with the Iron Castle but didn't make anything of a high enough level to increase his skill level.

He had gone and seen Old Hei, to ask questions on the Fourth Realm and to ask about Alchemy.

"Don't chase the skill level—chase the knowledge," Old Hei had said, like an old sage.

Although his words sounded strange, they made something click for Erik. He took his time to examine his weaknesses in Alchemy and thought about how to fix them, not much else to do on a march.

He wouldn't see immediate results and it wouldn't increase his skill level directly but it would make him a better alchemist and that would eventually lead to further advancement.

Erik had integrated his latest twenty attribute points into his character sheet already. When fighting he hadn't needed to rely on his strength, agility and mana was more useful, agility to move and react faster,. Bringing his weapon onto target and the mana to heal people.

So he split it, ten points into mana pool to make up for his weakest stat, five into mana regeneration and five into agility.

```
==========
Name: Erik West
==========
Level: 37
==========
Race: Human
==========
Titles:
From the Grave II
Mana Emperor
Dungeon Master II
Reverse Alchemist
Poison Body
Fire Body
==========
Strength: (Base 36) +41
```

==========

770

==========

Agility: (Base 29) +48

==========

423

==========

Stamina: (Base 39) +9

==========

720

==========

Mana: (Base 8) +46

==========

540

==========

Mana Regeneration (Base 10) +45
28. 50/s

==========

Stamina Regeneration: (Base 41) +33
15. 80/s

==========

==========

1,031,924/1,660,000 EXP till you reach Level 38

==========

Erik's eyes moved to his armor.

==========

Commander Boots

==========

Defense:
180
Weight:
3. 7 kg

Charge:

1,000/1,000

Durability:

100/100

Slot:

Takes up foot slot

Innate Effect:

Stamina cost is reduced by 6%

Socket One:

Flow of the Healer—heal 8-15% faster

This is a set item. When two or more set items are combined, the abilities of the set items will increase.

Requirements:

Agility 34

Strength 23

==========

==========

Commander greaves

==========

Defense:

207

Weight:

9. 7 kg

Charge:

1,000/1,000

Durability:

100/100

Slot:

Takes up leg slot

Innate Effect:

Defense increased by 9%

Socket One:

Flowing Water—Increase speed by 12%

This is a set item. When two or more set items are combined, the abilities of the set items will increase.

Requirements:

Agility 41

Strength 35

==========

==========

Commander carrier

==========

Defense:

279

Weight:

35. 3 kg

Charge:

4,082/10,000

Durability:

100/100

Slot: Takes up chest slot

Innate Effect:

Strength of the user increases by 8%

Mana can be stored within carrier, increasing Mana pool by 10,000

Socket One:

Stone Wall—Defense increases by 15%

Socket Two:

Overclock—Increase users stats by 150% for 5 minutes. Can be used (2) times.

This is a set item. When two or more set items are combined, the abilities of the set items will increase.

Requirements:

Mana Regeneration 15

Agility 23
Strength 35
==========

The commander carrier was made from Expert-level materials, with Erik commissioning custom formations and Tan Xue able to pull two innate effects from the metal for Erik. He had only got the upgraded breastplate; the rear was still of the Journeyman level, so it could only be called a half-step Expert-level piece of equipment. Instead of increasing the effects of the armor, the innate abilities increased Erik's stats and Strength. This was what made an Expert-level piece of gear so powerful.

His overclocking socket took two thousand Mana to activate but it was a massive increase and a last resort. Tan Xue, Taran, and Qin had added in the innate effect of storing Mana in the breastplate. Even now, as he drew in Mana from the surrounding area, he was pushing it into the armor, which lined up with his upper body's Mana gates, increasing its charge without needing to use Mana stones.

It allowed him to use overclock, power his increased defense, and draw upon extra Mana when he needed it in a fight. If he wanted to, he could also use his armor to power others' armor. Erik kept checking his gear.

==========
Commander Helmet
==========
Defense:
212
Weight:
3. 7 kg
Charge:
1,000/1,000
Durability:

100/100
Slot:
Takes up helmet slot
Innate Effect:
Increase defense by 5%
Socket One:
Stone Wall—Defense increases by 15%
Requirements:
Agility 14
Strength 21

==========

==========

You have equipped the Commander set.
For having 4 pieces:
Your defense increases by a further 10%
Stamina consumption reduces by 6%
Natural healing is 4% faster

==========

Gloves and eyewear weren't part of the set. Erik examined the gloves that Rugrat had made when making his breakthrough about formation sockets.

==========

Tropic Thunder

==========

Defense:
157
Weight:
1. 8 kg
Charge:
0/0
Durability:
100/100

Slot:
Takes up glove slot
Innate Effect:
Stores blood energy
Socket One:
Blood drinker—Consume blood from opponents to increase attacking power.
Socket Two:
Transference—Energy stored within can be shared to the user or their items.
Requirements:
Agility 41
Strength 51

==========

"Why Tropic Thunder?" Erik asked, knowing he would regret the question.

"Cradle the balls, stroke the shaft? Don't you remember?" Rugrat asked.

Erik's fear was right, he did regret asking. He let out an annoyed groan as he half remembered the long-forgotten scene.

"I hate you so much." Erik gave Rugrat the middle finger.

Rugrat snorted and shrugged. "Still, that innate effect and the sockets make it one hell of a weapon. If you land five hits with the gloves, then the blood energy increases. The more you hit, the greater the increase in stored blood energy. If you kill someone or get someone powerful's blood on the gloves, then the blood energy will increase in strength. You can use the blood to increase your physical abilities, including your recovery.

"If you had enough power, then you could basically reverse damage done to you and come back at your peak," Rugrat said.

"How much power do I get for every hit and every person?" Erik asked.

"Depends on their Strength. The stronger they are, the more power in the blood, the more power that you can drain." Rugrat explained.

"If you said something like that back on Earth, they'd think you were crazy."

Rugrat looked at Erik. "Dude, we *are* crazy." Rugrat grinned and turned to face the direction they were heading.

Erik checked out his weapons.

==========

MK1 Crossbow Repeater (Repeater)

==========

Damage:

Unknown

Weight:

5. 8 kg

Charge:

1,000/1,000

Durability:

100/100

Innate Effect:

Increase formation power by 7%

Socket One:

Rotating formation allowing automatic fire.

Range: Medium range

Requires: Crossbow Ammunition

Requirements:

Agility 51

Strength 55

==========

==========

MK1 Heavy Ballista Repeater (Ballista)

==========

Damage:
Unknown
Weight:
15. 2 kg
Charge:
1,000/1,000
Durability:
100/100
Innate Effect:
Increase formation power by 7%
Socket One:
Rotating formation allowing automatic fire.
Range: Long range
Requires: Ballista Ammunition
Requirements:
Agility 47
Strength 57
==========
==========
MK1 Bolt Action Marksman Rifle (Marksman Rifle)
==========
Damage:
Unknown
Weight:
4. 0 kg
Charge:
1,000/1,000
Durability:
100/100
Innate Effect:
Increase formation power by 7%
Socket One:

Punch Through—Penetration increased by 8%
Socket Two:
Supercharged—Increase bullet's velocity by 7%
Range: Long range
Requires: 7. 62 rounds
Requirements:
Agility 53
Strength 41

==========

Erik looked ahead and moved Mana through his body, storing it in his carrier plates as a familiar city appeared in their vision.

***

Lola prowled at Erik's feet as George lazed on Rugrat's shoulders, both of them wearing collars to reduce their size.

They made their way through Chonglu, checking their timepieces.

"Three minutes," Rugrat said as they walked through the streets. It was around midday.

The city that had once seemed large now looked quaint in their eyes. People knew one another. Traders and farmers came in to sell their wares. Things were simple.

Looking at it, Erik felt a closeness to this place that he had reached when first entering the Ten Realms.

The time continued to run down as they approached the totem. People looked at them.

"More hooded strangers. Been a number of them over the last couple of years. Hear that they might be from the higher level sects that go to the Beast Mountain Range," one person said.

"I heard that they're rejects from the higher realms," another said.

"My cousin's brother-in-law is a guard and he said that the guards don't intervene because they're so strong. And they don't talk when questioned," someone else said.

"On my mark." Rugrat held his timepiece, his hood hiding his face.

Erik held up his hand and a screen appeared.

==========

You have reached Level 30, meeting the requirements to ascend to the Fourth Realm.

==========

Do you wish to ascend?

==========

YES/NO

==========

Erik tapped on the NO and went through the menu, finding Kaeju city located in the Second Realm.

Chapter: Battlefield Realm

Bayar accepted the entrance fee and allowed the trading caravan past. Kaeju was as busy as ever, with traders moving through all the time and the different powerful groups working together or against one another to gain power. Some things never change.

He was thankful that his guard post was at the totem. He didn't have to deal with the politics and alliances that happened in the places of power.

He looked over as a group of five people appeared in front of the totem. He didn't know what interested him about the people initially but more appeared in a flash. Suddenly there were over one hundred people around the totem. They all wore the same cloaks that hid their features and Bayar could see armor and weapons underneath their cloaks.

He started to stand up. Some were looking out, covering one another as all of the guards went on alert.

Bayar felt a tremendous pressure weighing down on him. *Level suppression.* He felt the weight that came from the people that had appeared. It was not merely a few levels but an entire realm's difference.

"Is everyone here?" a man called.

"Yes, sir," another replied.

"Good." The first man turned back to the totem. In a flash of light, they all disappeared. The pressure was removed and the traders who had been frozen in fear looked around.

The guards stared at the totem.

Was that real? A mirage?

***

Alva's army disappeared from their rally point at Kaeju and Erik made sure everyone was linked as he used the totem again. This time they were all teleported to the Fourth Realm.

They appeared in a random city that looked like it was made from rough rock. The buildings all looked like bunkers with thick walls that rose around the totem, like a castle all on its own.

There were signs of fighting and bodies around the totem.

"Spread out! One Platoon, hold. Second Platoon, special teams—clear the defenses!" Erik called out. Repeaters were revealed as people rushed forward, their cloaks flapping as they moved.

They barged through doors facing the totem. They were tough but the Alva soldiers were stronger and broke through easily.

"Where are we?" Erik turned to Rugrat.

"On it." Rugrat pulled out his map and checked their location while the sergeants moved the sections of First Platoon, nicknamed Dragon Platoon. Second Platoon was called Tiger Platoon.

"Defenses secured. Captain, you'll want to see this!" Sergeant Niemm called.

Erik leapt up, grabbing onto an arrow slit and throwing himself up as if he weren't holding nearly a hundred kilos of gear. He dropped over the parapet, looking at the city beyond.

They were in the midst of a mountain range.

He had declined Old Hei's offer of a guide. He trusted Old Hei but he didn't know whether he could trust everyone else in the Alchemist Association.

So they had rolled the dice and it looked like they'd landed right in the middle of a fight.

The city beyond was gray and simple, built to be a fortress.

"What do you see?" He asked Lucinda.

"There is an army out there, people are preparing defenses, it looks like they're getting ready to fight."

We were able to get in so this must be a sneak attack and they haven't declared war, closing off the totem. We can run back to the second realm. Or we try and escape the city.

Erik looked in the opposite direction.

"Even the houses are built like bunkers," Erik said.

"We've got guards coming from the southeast!" Lucinda yelled.

"Time till they get here?" Erik asked.

==========

Event

==========

The city of Aberdeen is under attack! Pick a side!

Defend Aberdeen

Attack Aberdeen

==========

"Lucinda?" Erik asked again, getting her to focus on her job instead of the pop-up.

"Fifteen minutes maybe?" Lucinda shot back.

Rugrat jumped over the wall. "We're in the city Aberdeen, which is in the northern area of continent seven. It's a mountainous region and we're right in a crucial pass. Aberdeen is controlled by the Sanem family, who control twenty-five dungeons, seventeen cities, and forty-three towns. That's based off of what Old Hei gave us. What's new is the attackers are the Marceola Sect. They occupy territory in the south. It looks like they've taken nearly ten dungeons, four cities, and six towns from the Sanem family to get this far. The Sanem family uses what is called the iron fortress formation: they have heavy infantry, great at defending but attack slowly. The Marceola focus on long-range weapons, using them to starve out a city over the space of months. The siege must have just started for us to be able to make it in. The warfront is facing south but there are exits to the north, back toward Sanem family territory."

"To the west is the Halberd Sect; to the east is the Chaotic Lands. There are tens of dungeons and even more groups fighting in them so we can't get a good read on the Chaotic Lands. The closest neutral cities are Pasinidi to the east, Shashi to the southeast and then Tareng to the south," Rugrat reported, checking the map that Old Hei had given them and they had copied.

"Options?"

"War has just started—things will start to get clamped down. We move to the north, get the hell out of here, head to the east," Rugrat offered.

Erik and Rugrat looked at one another.

"We try and head back do it again or go for it. With the event being started I'm betting that the totem is locked down. We rolled some one's on this." Rugrat said.

Erik made a decision in that moment. *We're here, there is no telling where we'll be next time.*

"Niemm, Roska, Glosil." Erik used his sound transmission device.

"Glosil, gather our people. Ready them to head to the north. Niemm, Roska, go around the city. Niemm, go east and then move to the south. Roska, do the same in the west and go north. Find out if there is anyone heading northeast or west. East is preferred," Erik ordered.

"Understood," the three replied, leaving to carry out their tasks.

The special teams moved out immediately. If they could find traders leaving, then they could get out of the city more easily and learn more about the area, including safe routes away from Aberdeen.

Beast masters released their flying creatures into the sky as the Alva company broke down into their sections, moving for the north wall.

Erik got reports from the special teams and the reconnaissance beasts, allowing the Alvan soldiers to avoid patrols.

Erik took time to assess the Fourth Realm. The skies were gray and looked as if they would start raining at any moment. He watched people moving through the streets. Looking into their eyes, he could tell this was not the first siege that they had been involved in.

There were injured and crippled people moving around, dealing with the feebleness of their bodies, broken by wars and battles past.

The Mana concentration was much thicker. The difference in the Mana density from the Third Realm to the Fourth was equivalent to the jump Erik experienced going from the First to the Third Realm.

Even though it was more concentrated, it was stirred up with all kinds of impurities. Casting would be stronger here but it would be harder to compress and purify the Mana that entered their bodies.

Erik could see the effects of the heavily attributed Mana. The quite young seemed in poor health but the older kids were much stronger. Growing up in harsh conditions, only those whose bodies adapted would thrive, increasing their Body and Mana Gathering Cultivation.

Erik's eyes hardened. This was not an easy place to live. Even the children had to fight to survive.

The Alvan soldiers moved past the people moving to and fro, who cleared a path for them, offering questioning looks but otherwise leaving them alone.

***

Hadard looked over at the ranged attacks being traded back and forth between the Aberdeen protection force and the Marceola army.

"Shit, weren't they supposed to attack in a week? We just got here," one of the traders complained.

"Less to pack!" Hadard exclaimed.

"Bad news," A trader announced as he ran up to Hadard. He had been sent to bring the mercenaries back. "All of these mercenaries are from the north, so they've been called to the wall."

"Shit, we need more mercenaries." He had hired them because they were from the north and could ease their passage. The north had recently turned into a war zone after it leaked that there was an item defense dungeon. A party would protect an object in a dungeon; with every wave that they defeated, more power was injected into an artifact. At any time, they could carry the object and run away. Dungeon defense was the easiest as one could set up defenses and defeat many creatures, gaining powerful tools that could increase an entire cities, maybe a ruling bodies, overall strength. Even Expert and Master weapons weren't out of reach.

The Marceola Sect had allied themselves with the Halberd Sect. The Marceola attacked from long range while the Halberd protected them. It might become a merger of the two forces if they were able to come to an agreement, defeat the Sanem family and take their land. Hadard didn't care. All he cared about was making his coin so that his family could live well in the neutral trading cities.

A woman holding a spear appeared. She looked over the armored beasts, the heavy carriages that covered their drivers and had arrow slits one could fire from.

"Are you leaving Aberdeen?" she asked.

The traders looked at her. Their own guards held their weapons, ready to fight if they needed to.

"Yes. Why?" Hadard said. Even if she raised the alarm, they could be gone quickly.

"We are looking to leave as well," she said.

"Deserters? Won't you be killed by your oath?"

"We're not from Marceola or the Sanem family," she said.

She doesn't know about Marceola allying themselves with Halberd? Could she have just been swept up in this?

"We are looking for fighters but you won't be enough on your own," a trader said.

"There are more of us but we need to leave quickly. It looks like the protection force are rounding up people to work for them," she said.

"How many of you are there?"

"Over a hundred."

"Okay, we need to leave now, so we can't wait around."

"They can meet us on the way to the gate. We have our own mounts—you just lead the way."

"Can you speak on their behalf?"

"I can't but I can say that as long as you don't attack us, we won't attack you." Her eyes were clear.

Hadard's hand glowed behind his back, secretly using a spell to see the truth in her eyes. He didn't like it but he didn't have any other choice.

"Fine. Have them meet us on the way. My name is Hadard and I run this convoy." Hadard looked to the others, "Mount up!"

They all got into the iron box-like carriages. The four tusked beasts that pulled them shifted in their armor and harnesses, ready to move.

The woman waved her hand and a panther appeared.

The convoy moved out of the house they had been staying in and picked up speed as they got into the streets.

The rear gates were open, allowing nobles and other privileged individuals, and those that were too weak to be useful in the upcoming battle, to leave for the other cities.

Out of the surrounding roads, others wearing armor and cloaks like the woman appeared, surrounding the traders.

Hadard looked at them, impressed in their numbers and their ability to ride as the woman guided her mount over to them. Hadard watched them but they moved off to the perimeter and rode behind the convoy.

When they got to the gate, Hadard had a quiet conversation with a guard, passing over a few glowing stones. The guard nodded and then moved to the group following Hadard. A man paid a bribe and they were allowed through as well.

They swept out of the gates and picked up speed.

"Looks like we made it out," the man sitting beside Hadard said as Hadard scanned the gate behind them with a spyglass.

"Looks—shit." Hadard saw a group of riders leave the city and head toward them.

"You think that they caught on?" the man asked.

Hadard looked at him and then back at those running out of the city.

Hadard wasn't just a trader of goods; he had sold the information to the attacking sects weeks ago. He'd made enough to retire and aimed to leave the Sanem-controlled lands before they ever attacked. Yet it looked as though that was no longer possible.

Hadard pulled out a map. They were in a mountain range. To the south, there were plains; to the east, there were swamplands that gave way to forests and then the Chaotic Lands.

To the west were the mountain ranges, more of the Sanem-controlled lands and the Halberd Sect lands after that.

The Chaotic Lands were hell but there was a chance of living. If he continued through the Sanem land, the trading caravan would be hunted every step.

Hadard looked back at the goats that his guards were riding. They were good at both running along open areas and climbing mountains.

"Turn for the Chaotic Lands." Hadard checked his map, looking at the plotted routes. There was an old route, one that most had forgotten. He'd never heard of anyone who had been able to cross it.

He looked at the riders who had joined them.

"Tell them that the riders from the city are looking to take our goods for the defense. Say that we have a route," Hadard said to one of the people in the caravan. That man nodded, waved his hand and a beast appeared.

"Tell them that I'll make an oath once we leave the guards behind," Hadard added.

"Understood, boss." He jumped onto his beast with practiced ease and dropped back to the panther riders.

If it's a cursed land, then we have a few who we can sacrifice to ensure our escape.

***

Erik was wondering what the traders might do. He'd already had everyone prepare to rush away if the traders turned on them after discovering they were getting chased by the guards.

Looks like they really don't like people showing up unannounced at their totem.

A trader released a beast from a storage item and jumped on it, dropping back to the Alvans.

The group stopped next to Tully, who relayed everything to Erik with her sound transmission device so the traders couldn't pick up anything.

"It looks like they want our goods but my boss has a path out of here," the trader said.

Seems that he thinks that they're following after him. Erik wondered just who they were actually chasing.

"We'll follow. Once we shake the guards, my boss wants to make an oath with you," the trader said.

"Understood," Erik said to Tully who was acting as his mouthpiece so the traders were none the wiser as to who was the leader of the soldiers.

He didn't know whether there was more to why the trader wanted to flee but as long as they got away from the guards, they could split up and work on their own.

"I sensed a dungeon," Rugrat transmitted.

Erik checked his map, looking at the shared way point. "The first one but I think we'll have to check it out later."

Rugrat made a noise of agreement.

Their path changed sometime later, moving from the well-maintained highway to an older road. It was made with worn stones that had withstood the passage of time and led toward a large forest that appeared in the distance.

They rode for the rest of the day, entering the forest as darkness descended.

The guards charging after them kept on coming as they continued on the road that seemed to cut through the forest. Debris fell on the road but nothing grew through its stones. The large beasts of the caravan smashed through the trees or tossed them aside with their tusks. Nothing slowed their advance, these things were truly massive beasts.

"Feral beasts are coming," one of the outriders said.

They had pushed scouts out into the forest. The panthers moved as easily in the forest as they did on the road. They changed out from time to time so that they didn't get too tired and to share the duty.

There was a roar off in the distance as a forest beast found people trespassing in its territory.

"Roska," Erik said.

She nodded, rising up in her stirrups and Special Team Two rushed out to meet the noise. Special Team One became more alert.

More beasts called out as they rushed forward to attack.

The special teams led. They had all trained to shoot and ride at the same time. It wasn't as accurate as when they were standing but Rugrat and Erik's standards weren't low so everyone was still proficient.

The trading convoy continued, keeping up their pace, only pausing to clear the road and rushing on.

The trader who had talked to them before appeared again. "My boss wonders if you are up for traveling through the night? With that, he is sure that those chasing us will be far behind by tomorrow night."

Tully looked around but didn't make clear eye contact with Erik, giving him time to think.

They all had strong constitutions. It would be rough but they could stay awake for up for two weeks.

"That is fine by us," Erik sent to Tully.

The night didn't become quieter. The types of beasts just changed to more predatory species.

Erik moved with the group, watching as a mage turned the ground to quicksand, the beast she targeted unable to do anything as repeater bolts penetrated its sides. The soldiers landed five shots before the beast died from the potent poison on their bolts. They recovered its monster core and headed back toward the rest of the convoy.

The beast would attract predators that wanted a simple meal instead of chasing after the convoy. Its body was already poisoned and would kill or greatly harm any creatures who ate it. It was better to leave it instead of filling their storage rings with useless meat. They already had high level meats stockpiled for the trip.

The night was a long one but they made good time through the forest.

***

Hadard had heard the noises from the beasts being killed but he hadn't seen the fighting so he didn't put it in his mind.

"Maybe I was overthinking this all," Hadard said to himself as he relaxed a bit. He had been scared of the path but it looked as though its dangers were exaggerated.

The sun rose but a fog had covered the road and the trees, making it hard to see through. The mist was annoying but in the valleys and mountain ranges around this area, mist and fog was a normal occurrence.

"It'll be good to return to the south and the sun, boss. I can feel the sun on my skin already," a new driver said with a laugh.

Hadard smiled. He and the rest of the caravan had been able to sleep and change watch. The mercenaries were all still riding on their beasts and charging off to kill creatures that got too close.

They must be tired. We could rest but then I would need to make an oath and I don't know who they are. If we're better rested than them, we can escape if we do run into danger.

Hadard moved his heavy furs around, looking at the mercenaries, who didn't seem to be affected by the wind. They had masks hooked to their helmets that covered their faces and protected their eyes.

Watching them, he finally took in their identical appearance. Their gear was clearly functional, with any superfluous extras removed. They looked strong.

Chapter: War Immortal

They continued traveling for three more days with the fog only getting worse by the day.

Erik had Tully ask to see the trader boss but she was denied.

"Think that there is something strange going on?" Rugrat asked with his sound transmission.

"Well you obviously think something strange is going on or else you wouldn't contact me," Erik replied.

"Saying I can't give you a social call now? That's cold dude," Rugrat complained.

"You got a point there?"

"They're keeping the leader hidden, we're doing the same. We don't really know one another, think we should remind our people that these aren't our traders," Rugrat said his voice a few degrees colder.

"Agreed. We'll make camp soon, everyone is tired and we've only stopped once this entire trip. We'll check on them, make sure that they're good to go. We arrived and were just dropped in the shit, they might have their nerves up. Get them adjusted to it all and keep them focused," Erik enthused.

"They've done good though."

"Yeah, they aren't bad coming right out of training," Erik looked at them. They were hidden under their clothing but their eyes were sharp and they rode as if they had been born in the saddle.

Without needing to say anything, the section leaders were getting them to cycle out watching and just riding. A human couldn't be alert all the time and it showed how the leadership understood their soldiers enough to care for their needs so that they could carry out the tasks they needed to, when they had to.

"You want to send out the scouts from Tiger Platoon and follow them?" Erik asked.

"Sounds like a plan. Be good to make sure that they didn't lose all of their training just because it's the real thing now. I can organize that."

"Alright I'll wait back here."

Erik shifted in his saddle and patted Lola.

She shook herself, getting comfortable as they continued moving.

"Tully, tell the traders that we're sending out people to look for a place to rest up. We'll camp tonight and move out in the morning," Erik said through his sound transmission as Rugrat and the scouts headed out ahead.

"Yes boss," Tully responded as she sidled up to the traders, talking to them quickly before she moved off and used her sound transmission device to contact Erik again.

"They want to push forward, said that they don't need sleep."

"What did you say?"

"Said that they might not but we do, up to them if they want to go ahead. They agreed that we need to rest," Tully said dryly.

"Good work," Erik said, the corners of his mouth lifting up.

"No worries boss."

Erik cut the sound transmission as he looked around. He moved his body around, tensing and untensing his muscles to get the blood flowing while regaining feeling back in his limbs. It was only barely working as he rubbed his gloves together, using his legs to keep him on Lola as he moved with her motions.

Why is it you can rub your hands together for hours but they never get frigging warm?

He let out an annoyed grunt and put one hand under his ass and grabbed the reins with the other.

Could I use my fire body?

Erik circulated his mana into his bones and muscles, his fire attribute body started to warm up rather nicely.

He hid a smile on his face, not wanting to tell anyone his newfound ability.

The road was well made and wide, big enough for four carriages to go side by side. There were even regular rest areas that had been carved out of the side of the road that reminded Erik of truck stops back on Earth.

Though these had been long overrun with trees and shrubs, making them hard to find and a good challenge for the scouts.

Where the hell does it lead though? There is no way a road that would be this expensive in time, labor, and resources to build, would be just left here if someone had a choice.

Erik looked at the massive trees that closed them in on either side, seeming to loom overhead. Their size and the fog made it impossible to see more than a hundred meters to either side of the road, even with their magically enhanced vision.

Down the road they could see around three hundred meters, a clear corridor in the darkness. Erik had a greater sensitivity to mana and this place just felt *dead.*

Erik used his sound transmission device again.

"Commander?" Yuli asked as he contacted her.

"Have you got any new theories for why the mana in here is so still?" Erik asked.

"Well, I have three theories. One, there is a kind of anomaly in the area that stops the mana from moving. Two, there is some anomaly that is drawing in the mana and the mana is more attracted in that direction. Out here the pull of the rest of the realm and the pull of that object are equal so it doesn't move. Three, there isn't enough things to move the mana in a large area so it has become stagnant."

"That last one sounds kind of awkward."

"So I think of mana like water in a lot of ways. It lies over everything equally but there are forces acting on it all the time to move it, whether it be the wind, tides, the moons, maybe temperature. If you removed those factors, then it would remain relatively still. Wherever we go, we stir up the mana, though it's dense and hard to circulate as we move into it. Looking at the map, we're in a large valley to either side which makes this area protected. We haven't run into that many strong beasts, so the tide or temperature of the mana isn't stirred up like when there are cities where the mana density is higher from people creating items, using resources and spreading out mana, circulating it." Erik was impressed with her reasoning. She had incorporated a lot of information that Erik and Rugrat had shared with the people of Alva, allowing her to make an informed decision and not just accept the facts as they were as she tried to understand the situation.

"What else?" Erik asked.

"People haven't come down here much, otherwise the mana wouldn't be this way. They haven't come down here for a long time and there is a city right next to this road. I'm not sure what happened here but it is enough to stop a sect with thousands of soldiers from pushing this way." Yuli shivered as she finished postulating.

Erik fell silent, checking his timepiece and using his dungeon sense. *If there's an anomaly, there is usually a dungeon close by or something really damn powerful.*

"Captain?" Yuli asked.

"It makes sense," Erik said.

"You don't think I'm overreacting?" Yuli sounded like she wanted to be proven wrong.

"I don't think so," Erik said, with his higher sensitivity of mana that came with his title increase to Mana Emperor. He wasn't that well versed in the intricacies of mana but now he heard Yuli's hypothesis he didn't think it was far from the truth.

Rugrat sent Erik a sound transmission. Erik took the message immediately as it was to all of the command staff.

"We were scouting ahead for somewhere to rest, we came to the end of the forest. There is a clear cut area that the road goes into, it's hard to see through the fog," Rugrat paused. "It looks like a battlefield. There are ancient siege weapons, broken weapons, armors and bodies. It must've been a long time ago as the bodies are nothing more than bones. I pulled the scouts back and we're now just observing."

"Is there any movement?" Erik asked.

"Nothing so far, don't feel good about this. There is limited vision and there are signs of a fresh battle."

"We can't turn back, we'll be heading right into a siege. Check the map we have, can we skirt the battlefield?"

"This place looks like France after World War One. There are craters all over the place, it's rough and hilly. Moving the carriages around is going to be a pain. We can do it but we'll lose a few of them and the faster we go, the more we'll lose."

"I'll get Tully to talk to the traders, see if they have any information and then tell them."

"Rog." Erik sent Tully her orders as she went up to the carriages again. A map was brought out and she touched her map to it, adding the information to her map as she went back into the Alvan Army formation, passing the map around and it was shared across all of their maps.

"They said that there is an abandoned city ahead. We can skirt around it, go north and then hit the eastern road and take that," Tully suggested to those on the leadership channel.

Erik was shared the map and then shared it on to others, trying not to bring attention on himself as he looked at the map.

The map was rough, with the city lying to the south along the mountain walls of the valley. They were going down a road that cut from the east to west down the length of the valley and diverted into the southern city.

"We'll go straight down the east to west road. We'll move fast but quiet, try and do it stealthily. We'll have scouts up front. If we encounter an enemy force, the scouts will hold position and suppress the enemy forces, covering us as we move through. We'll push out Special Team One to replace the scouts, then Special Team Two, then scouts from Dragon Platoon and back to the scouts from Tiger Platoon, rotating through to create a rolling barrage of fire and cover for our movements. At the same time, the convoy will speed up, going as fast as we can without our formations falling apart. Thoughts, questions?" Erik questioned.

"What about the traders?" Glosil asked.

"If anything breaks or is too slow, they have to get on their secondary mounts and keep up," Erik replied. "If it comes down to it, we protect our own first."

"Understood," Glosil said. "I'll pass it on to the company."

The Alvan army all started to move around, becoming more alert as they shifted around the convoy.

The traders passed messages to one another as they prepared for what was ahead. They kept going until the trees started to fall away.

The scouts suddenly appeared out of the fog some twenty meters away. They were spread across the road looking out at the battlefield before them.

The fog thinned a bit, allowing them to see forty meters away, the air: the smell of decay, rot, and of blood and iron.

They looked to either side of the road and saw the fields had been turned into a battlefield. There were skeletons holding rusted and broken weapons along the ground. The ground was strewn with fragments from siege weapons that had been destroyed. The battlefield was old, layered with signs of fierce fighting over decades. There were bodies from people across different generations, their flesh in different stages of decay.

"These skeletons..." Glosil said looking at a few of the older bones among the dead.

"Not human," Erik said.

The traders were all looking around. Seeing the bodies, they all started to fidget and move around.

"Stay in close with the traders, make sure that they can't cause a problem. Push the scouts out ahead," Erik ordered.

The army moved like a fine tuned machine. There wasn't even a slight pause in their actions. They were awake and alive, their eyes now sharp, the last few days of monotonous riding had dulled their reactions but now, thanks to their training, they were switched on once again.

As they rode forward, the destruction around the damaged fields increased. They had to navigate the roads that were damaged and broken in places.

No one dared to breathe too loudly.

"I hate this shit," Erik muttered himself, calming himself down with his own words. It was like a million eyes were watching him, toying with and keeping him on tenterhooks. *Fight me or piss off, he thought to himself.*

They pushed on as nothing happened.

"The intersection is just ahead," Rugrat reported from the scouts.

"Stay alert, we're halfway there," Erik told all of the Alvan Army, using his words to try to calm and reassure them.

There was a terrible battle cry off to the north that couldn't have come from a human, closely followed by the clashing of weapons. Mana was stirred up as a fight broke out.

The traders and their mounts were all startled by the ruckus.

"Calm it, calm it!" A trader called out as the traders looked around with large eyes, eyeing the road ahead.

A wave of air cut through the fog, clearing it off to one side.

"Incoming, three o'clock!" a scout called out.

"Move it, follow the plan!" Erik barked over the sound transmission.

"Move, come on!" Tully yelled to the traders as they picked up the pace. Erik rode Lola, his face cold as his body was no longer tired or cold.

He was just reacting to circumstances as his training kicked in.

"Pushing ahead, there are undead fighting one another, hopefully they continue to do so!" Rugrat announced.

The mana was stirred up. he fog was being rapidly thrown clear so Erik could see further. A large spell went off as the fog finally cleared The lighting was still dull with the fog above, blocking out the sun but now he could see the group of a hundred or so undead fighting one another. Their powerful attacks had caused the fog to lift.

The Alvans had all seen Egbert, so undead weren't all that unfamiliar to them. The traders had never seen them before and started to panic.

"Calm the fuck down, the're only undead," Tully said, trying to manage the traders.

Trees were tossed to the side by a skeleton knight's attack. They were just under one hundred meters away but a wave of air cut at Davos, who turned, using his shield. The force of the attack pushing him and his mount sideways. Being a member of the special teams his mount and gear was the highest quality.

"Strong fucker," Davos said, getting seated again, grabbing his reapeater.

The scouts pushed out to the sides of the road as another group of undead that were further down the road started to attack them.

Repeaters fired into the fog aimed at the glowing eyes of the undead or using their spells as points of aim.

"Covering!" Rugrat barked.

"Special Team One!" Erik yelled.

Niemm led Special Team One out from the pack and moved ahead as they all sped up. The traders whipped their beasts in the hopes of increasing their speed as they all increased their pace.

"Covering!" Niemm yelled as they started to fire on new groups of undead.

"Shit," Erik said to himself. They didn't have clear sightlines, the battles were clearing some of the fog but they didn't know what was further ahead of them. His stomach turned over with anxiety as he started to question his own orders.

"Push on!" Erik yelled. The trader beasts were already startled, trying to turn them around would take forever and was a quick way to kill them all.

They couldn't do anything else, they just had to fight through as he pulled out a repeater. He held his reins in his left hand and put his repeater in the crook of his arm to balance it as he fired on the undead that were emerging out of the fog on either side of the road.

"Rugrat get up high. Glosil have our aerial scouts in the sky. I want to know what's happening around us," Erik commanded.

George let out a roar and jumped into the sky as the beast masters and mages started shooting off spells and releasing their aerial beasts to see what was around and ahead of them.

***

Hadard looked at the undead that were coming out of the fog in droves. They were rushing forward and were getting ever closer.

The undead are focusing their attacks on the groups that are firing at them. He thought as he looked out of the caravan. *We don't need to be the strongest, just the fastest.*

Each of them was emitting an aura that was on par with some of the Masters he had seen. He looked around and saw other carriages that had been destroyed with newer items littered about.

Hadard used his sound transmission device.

"Flavus, Otho and Wido! Get your slowing spell scrolls ready!"

He unraveled his own spell scroll as they were nearing the intersection that led to the south and continued on to the east.

Hadard shivered as he saw undead turning to face them.

He opened the door to the trading carriage.

"Get ready to go left around the main road," Hadard said.

"Yes boss," The driver was pale, his hands tight around the reins as his eyes were as wide as saucers, his whole body shaking.

Hadard looked to the south where a city emerged out of the fog like a titan rearing its head, watching them coldly.

That's bigger than any city I've seen. It must be an imperial capital.

Part of a massive spire reached into the sky but it had been struck by something and collapsed on the buildings below.

Other spires reached into the sky. They were all in various states of disrepair, except for the one that wasn't a spire at all but a totem of the Ten Realms.

The walls of the city showed multiple breaches. Skeletons, armor, and weapons lay across this battlefield. The siege weapons had fallen apart and rotted. Now there was nothing left alive, only the undead waging a forgotten war.

The sight of the skeletons struck Hadard with fear to his core. Never had he witnessed this anywhere in the realm.

Hadard turned and focused on the road ahead. He had lived in the Fourth Realm all of his life, it was not a place filled with merciful people to say the least. He had only survived this far by doing what needed to be done, sometimes wielding the blade himself, other times using others to do it.

Hadard saw the mercenaries start to pull out their spell scrolls. *You think you can slow us?!*

"Flavus, Otho, Wido, use your slowing spell scrolls!"

He started to use his speed increase spell as he kicked the door.

"Go left as soon as the spell hits!"

***

"Covering!" Roska shouted.

"Dragon Platoon, ready spell scrolls to open a path!" Erik ordered as he saw the undead on the road facing them. He fired on them. It might have done some damage but the undead just took the attacks, firing back powerful attacks that had already injured more than one person.

Once we get in close it's going to get bad.

"We've been slowed!" Glosil called out as a spell landed on the army.

==========

You have fallen under the spell Slowed Reactions
Ends in 9:59

==========

Another spell landed on the caravan. Instead of slowing, they sped up as they cut north, breaking from the Alvan formation as they did so.

A few of the Alvan Army that were closest fired on them, one would have to be blind to not figure out what the traders were doing.

Erik gritted his teeth and looked at his options."Who isn't debuffed?" he asked.

"Dragon Platoon's scouts are good to go!" Domonos reported.

"I'm good," Rugrat said.

Erik was studying the road around him and figuring out his options.

We can follow the caravan but anything they stir up and pass is going to be right in our path. We can charge down the road, though we're going so slow we're going to take heavy casualties. Head south towards the city? We'll have better visibility but we have no idea what is in there. It will be close quarters fighting but then we're not caught out in the open and we can use our numbers to overpower their strength. The larger skeleton knights were the stronger ones, some reaching up to ten feet tall. Only a few of them would be able to fight at once in the city. *The number of undead, the dead mana, it must be linked to the city somehow.*

"We're going to go south across the battlefield. Rugrat, take Dragon's scouts and scout ahead. The rest of us will follow behind and find a defensible position to hold up in. Switch formation sockets on panther's armor in fire teams to speed enhancing," Erik ordered.

The grouping of soldiers started to move under Glosil's orders as the Alvan Army cut to the south.

Rugrat dropped to the ground on George in the middle of Dragon Platoon's scouts who were in two lines of five. They'd inserted speed enhancing formations into their mount's armor sockets as they took off ahead of the majority of the army.

"Captain, there is a dungeon core in the city!" Storbon shouted.

"You sure?" Erik responded.

"Used Dungeon sense!"

"Rugrat, find that dungeon core."

"Spread out to ten meter spacing! Heavy repeaters and rifles!"

Glosil yelled as they raced across the battlefield, the panther's throwing up dirt and mud. Erik put his repeater away and pulled out his rifle. He fired on a group of twenty mounted undead knights that were rushing towards them.

Rifles and repeaters peppered the knights and their mounts, hitting the ground around them and throwing up dust devils. A few mages waved their staffs, sending a holy light attack and dozens of needle sized rocks.

The knights came through the cloud of destruction with only three of them being knocked out of the fight running on an angle to the road, trying to catch their rear.

The remaining undead had slight damage but had only been slowed slightly.

"Aim you fuckers!" Yui yelled as everyone tightened up their shots as they pushed forwards.

I hope to hell that dungeon core is the center of this shit storm. Erik prayed to himself

"Glosil, I need to know what we're going into," Erik said as he fired and worked the action, hitting one of the knight's mounts. The round exploded, making them miss their footing. Their speed, the terrain and the weight of the knight riding them caused them to slam into the ground as they rolled over, tossing the knight free.

"Aerial scouts move out towards the city, populate the map!" Glosil ordered as the magical constructs and beasts above moved forwards as fast as possible. The army had linked all of their maps already.

Erik pulled out his map and stuck it on Lola's back in clips as he looked at their destination.

Fuck it's massive.

He glanced up and then back down. He threw out waypoints for entrances into the city. Rugrat and his scouts had just made it into the city as Erik and the rest of the army were fighting their way into it. Repeaters, rifles and spells were being unleashed as the undead charged at them with melee range weaponry.

Their arrows must have been used up or destroyed long ago. I hope they don't have fucking mages.

"Yui, have your mages fuck up the ground in front of the undead charging at us. Use grenades if they get in close enough!" Glosil shouted. Yui and Domonos worked well under the pressure, moving their people around even on the move. They were halfway to the city, heading for the broken walls. Without the carriages they could now move across the battlefield as well as they could move on the road but the speed debuff was still kicking their asses.

An undead that had been under a number of corpses stood up and they stabbed out with their spear, hitting a soldier in the chest and throwing them off of their panther.

Erik stood up in his stirrup, firing and working his action. He was using blunt force formations on his weapon and explosive rounds with a powerful acid poison. The undead was pushed back with the force of the round. , The bullet exploded inside their ribs as the acid ate their bones away.

Others fired on the lumbering undead as the section behind altered their path. One of them reaching down and grabbing the rider that had been tossed from his panther, tossing them up on their own mount as they checked them over.

They pushed past the recently fallen undead. They didn't have time to waste on it to make sure it was dead.

Come on Rugrat, get the fucking core.

Chapter: Imperial Capital Vuzgal

Rugrat rushed into the city with the rest of the scout section right behind him. The buildings' glory days had been shattered with the fighting that had happened in the city.

Bodies lay in the alleys and the streets. All of them were worn away with the passage of time so that only bones remained.

==========

Event

==========

You have found the undead imperial capital Vuzgal, which lies cursed by its last emperor. Forces wage war, even in death, until their bodies are broken and destroyed, neither side ever able to secure victory.

Investigate Vuzgal and stop the curse. Release the soldiers from their fighting and reclaim this lost land.

==========

"Yeah, you can fuck off with your events and all," Rugrat hissed. He checked on his people as they rode through Vuzgal's streets.

Fighting was still going on inside the city as well as the outside. They could hear the clash of weapons in the distance as the undead continued their never-ending war with each other.

A dragon bear lay in a collapsed building, its rider nowhere to be seen. A wall of stone had been melted with a powerful destruction spell.

Rugrat used his Mana Sight.

"Turn left down the next street," he called out. "Use your mana sight if you can, the undead are made from mana so look for where the mana is concentrated. We'll avoid those areas, we don't have the time or the numbers to get stuck in a fight."

Rugrat used his dungeon sense, which had recovered from their three day rush, getting a precise location of the dungeon core which he waypointed and shared with the others.

"Our goal is this dungeon core. If there is one of us alive you will get that damn dungeon core. Understood?"

"Understood," they called back.

"Go straight for two streets and then right," Rugrat ordered.

The scouts had their own beasts and spells to reveal the area and terrain, building out a map of Vuzgal for them all to use.

They kept advancing, avoiding the roving packs of undead and those that were locked in battle.

Rugrat checked his map and looked up at the broken spire in the middle of the capital. *Of course it's right in the middle of all this.*

"Rugrat, are you there yet?" Erik asked over array.

"Nearly, this place is fucking huge!" Rugrat heard wings flap as George alerted him to incoming enemies.

"Shit! Contact left!" one of the scouts shouted. They fired their rifle at the incoming mob, winging one with an explosive shot.

Rugrat and the rest of the soldiers turned and fired on them as the approaching, winged pack of undead got in range. The winged creatures couldn't deal with the explosions, which blew away bones and disrupted the magic that they used to keep their bodies together and afloat, forcing them to the ground.

Sergeant Dong Ju pulled out a spell scroll. It was an Earth scroll, so as it activated the local dirt and stones shot out, pelting the undead. The onslaught forced them backwards as they tried to defend against the ground underneath their feet.

"Let's go! There are others coming!" Rugrat yelled. He saw the skeletons that had been patrolling now looking over in their direction.

There were just too many inside the city to avoid them all.

Rugrat could feel their strength with his heightened Mana sense. He knew that, although the rest of the company was coming, they could get bogged down in the fighting and torn apart.

The dungeon core was a Hail Mary but if they could take control of it, then even if this wasn't a dungeon, they could turn it into one and make it their land. They had the Mana stones; they could power it and change the landscape into a defensive camp, giving them a terrain advantage. Fighting these creatures out in the open was not an option.

They raced forward on their panthers and George, moving through the broken buildings and the rubble, raising dust as they skirted through the tight roads.

They fired their rifles at anything that moved. Rugrat stood up on George with the other marksmen, moving with their mounts that had been trained to ignore the rifle fire.

Rugrat aimed for the eye sockets and mouths of the skeletons, hoping to penetrate inside the skulls with the explosion from the round to tear their skulls apart. Even with his super-human aim, he wasn't able to hit his target every time. They might be powerful creatures but without their heads, they collapsed into piles of bones. The other scouts were trying their best to mimic Rugrat's shots.

They were making progress but there were more undead closing in, attracted by the noise.

"*Fuck.*" Rugrat cursed to himself. He could see that there was a group of undead that were attracted by the noise that were coming down a side street that was directly ahead of them and to the right. If they kept charging forward, then the scouts would run right into them.

"*Come on boy!*" Rugrat mentally shouted to George.

George understood his thoughts as he accelerated, weaving around the other panthers as he jumped up into the air. His wings unfurled as he started to gather mana in his body. His red fur looked like flames as motes of red, almost blue, flames appeared around him.

Rugrat grabbed onto George's armor as he slung his rifle and grabbed a half dozen stick grenades from his storage ring.

They cleared the buildings, looking down the street at the undead ahead of the scouts.

George breathed deeply and then washed them out with flames, coating the entire street and the undead in cackling fire. Rugrat grabbed the pull tabs at the bottom of the grenades, tugging on them to pull the tabs before throwing them. He tried to get them to blow up all over the street.

Their momentum carried them over to the other side of the street as George glided to the ground, digging his claws in. He left scrapes on the ground and tossed up debris as they turned back to the street.

Rugrat unslung his rifle as he yelled out commands.

"Patrik, Sabina, hold your position on your end. The rest of you, move across as fast as possible. Strosic! Once you're across with me, we'll cover Patrik and Sabina."

Rugrat got to the corner of the street and started firing his rifle at the moving skeletons covered in flames.

George blasted out fireballs, their momentum causing even the large undead to be thrown backwards.

"Covering!" Patrik and Sabina yelled as they had taken positions in a broken building, shooting at the undead down the road.

The rest of the group raced across the street, not taking the time to shoot.

"Dong Ju, keep going!" Rugrat shouted.

Sergeant Dong Ju kept them moving down the street as Strosic wheeled out, his panther finding grip on the road as he moved up to beside Rugrat.

"Move it!" Rugrat yelled at Patrik and Sabina.

Patrik and Sabina's panthers moved as fast as they could, rushing across the street. A sword came flying down the street passed them and an undead mage shot out a string of curses that hit the ground or other buildings around the two, cutting holes wherever they landed.

George turned, leading Strosic's mount as Patrik and Sabina passed. They all raced after Dong Ju.

"Cleared, regrouping with you," Rugrat said as he reloaded his rifle.

"We've got incoming from the sides and ahead!" Dong Ju yelled.

Rugrat looked at the road with his mana sight, looking through the buildings.

"Shit, okay, what if we go up? Broken building to the left!"

Dong Ju's panther led the way up the building, the others following.

They climbed and clambered up the debris pile that was left of the house, parts of it collapsing as the riders relied on their panther's reactions as they jumped and clawed their way onto the buildings next to it.

George opened his wings, flapping them and using a few touches on the old destroyed building to reach the roof. The other three scouts with Rugrat charged ahead, looking to catch up with the rest of the section. Rugrat looked over the capital from his new high vantage point.

The streets are turning into a mess. We need to go across the rooftops but they stop before the interior walls. I could make the leap to the walls with George but the others couldn't.

Rugrat's eyes fell on the top section of the spire that had dropped onto the city.

Sections of one of the roofs collapsed under one panther. The panther reacted, jumping up and clearing the hole as the others moved around the new hole or jumped over it.

"Spread out, twenty meter spacing!" Rugrat yelled.

The scouts rushed across the roofs, getting closer to the inner wall. Running from roof to roof across the city, the panthers pushed their limits for their riders.

"Contact left!" someone called out, firing their repeater on a skeleton that had climbed up to a roof.

The new threat was hit with three rounds. They'd changed their formation sockets and their rounds, penetrating the skeleton and exploding. The poison laced on the round was acid based, melting the skeleton. The skeleton dropped back to the ground with its skull smashed.

There was sounds of fighting in the city from every direction.

"The undead are fighting one another in droves over there," Tullia said as they pointed off into the distance.

"Better them than us!" Rugrat announced.

They continued on as Rugrat pulled out a speed scroll and cast it.

==========

Speed increased by 23% for 10 minutes

==========

Their speed increased dramatically, as they bounced ahead of the fighting and the high concentrations of undead, now lumbering behind them.

They must have been fighting with one another for centuries. With all of that killing, their Strength must be enormous.

The group of panthers and riders passed areas where undead were fighting one another, as they had for lifetimes. With this cycle of constant war, the strongest beings had continued to rise while the weak were left as bones, leading to these powerful monsters.

Dong Ju led them to a breach in the wall, where the broken sections of wall had created a lower bridge from the outer to the inner city.

They rode their panthers down the rubble of the wall. ,Once on the ground again they bounded into the inner area of the city.

They passed through the into the area where the more affluent members must have lived. It had larger buildings, that were better built and had wide streets with higher quality crafting workshops arranged in a wagon wheel shape. The roads led to the broken main spire that reached into the heavens and the circular castle that lay underneath it.

"Move towards the broken spire. Those walls look sturdy and the spire is lying right on top of it," Rugrat said.

The lead panther changed their direction as Dong Ju checked their groups limited map, trying to plot a route.

"Contact!" Sabina yelled out as her rifle cracked.

"Shit," Rugrat moaned. He looked at the undead that were fighting one another ahead of them. Just being hit with the shockwaves of their fight would kill them.

"Roofs!" Rugrat shouted.

The scout squad ducked down a side street as the lead scout led them towards a broken series of buildings that led up to rooftops.

Undead appeared from within the rubble around them.

"Shoot em and keep going!" Rugrat ordered He could see that there were undead closing in from all around them. His mana sight was limited by the buildings; these inner city buildings had much thicker construction and thus were harder to see through.

The squad fired on the undead as their panthers used all of their speed to sprint ahead. They felt like the devil himself was chasing them as they bunched together.

Rugrat fired on the skeletons, not looking to kill, just to push them back.

They finally got onto the roofs, cutting a straight line towards the spire. Strosic, who was the last man in the section, threw a grenade down to welcome the skeletons in the rubble pile.

A small dust cloud exploded behind as they continued to move over the roofs, trying to avoid the roiling mass of death that roamed the streets below them. There were a few times when tiles slipped or people lost their balance but with the taller homes, few undead made it up to reach them in time.

Rugrat saw the horde of undead that now lay below them, blocking the streets leading to the dungeon core.

"I'm getting a look from above!" Rugrat shouted as he patted George. They jumped into the sky. They were getting close to the spire. There was undead all over the streets around them, patrolling, running to battles or just standing there.

Thankfully none of them had climbed on top of the broken spire that was Fifty meters wide and taller than most of the buildings in the inner city.

He looked back at the scout section.

They had barely slept for three days and rode nearly the entire time but there were no complaints, no words that needed to be said as they followed him.

Death was all around them but there was little that they could do. Throwing grenades here would be a waste, hurting a few of the skeletons at best.

The squad continued to cut through what looked to be higher class areas. The panthers jumped from the buildings to the large spire, scrambling up it and then rushing for the central castle.

Rugrat nudged George and they drifted down, rejoining the scout section on the ground once again.

"It's pretty much a straight shot from here to the castle, where the dungeon core should be!" Rugrat explained before he got close to Dong Ju. "How they doing?"

"Minor scrapes and bruises, all loaded up and ready to go First Sergeant," Dong Ju said.

"Good shit," Rugrat nodded and then raised his voice. "The rest of the company is relying on us! Keep your heads on a swivel and call out anything that looks like a threat!"

From the inner wall to the castle district it must have been close to two kilometers, a distance that they were crossing quickly.

They passed over the barracks and training grounds for the capital's military. Now, there was no more life, and bodies were everywhere—both the non-human people with tails and humans. There were mounts and beast skeletons across the whole area. The large-scale destruction here all looked to be done with people's own physical abilities and magic instead of with siege weapons and war machines.

This must have been a battleground of their Elites.

A part of his mind couldn't help but wonder just what kind of war machines and loot that they might be able to find here.

Rugrat looked at the damage as they kept on going. The castle was broken in areas, with openings here and there but Rugrat could see into the castle. Only the main entrances were made of a size for beasts.

There was a cry in the sky. Several flying beasts that had been resting at the top of the jagged spire that jutted out of the castle jumped off, diving as they gathered speed directly towards the scout squad.

"Check your spacing and zig-zag! Change to repeaters, explosive distance shots!" Rugrat ordered.

The squad continued moving forwards but moving randomly side to side, making it harder to aim on them. they put their rifles away and grabbed their repeaters, changing their bolt magazines and their formation sockets.

"Just three hundred meters more!" Rugrat exclaimed.

The flying undead came out of their dive, snapping up and shooting down by the base of the spire.

The undead flying beasts opened their bony faces and let out cries. The skeletons on their backs with black swirling eyes let out their own yells, eager to spill blood from those who had dared to enter their city.

Rugrat had changed one repeater around and had put it back in his storage ring. He was working on the second as George raised his head and started pumping out fire balls that exploded in the sky, making it hard for the skeleton fliers to pass through.

The undead flying beasts altered their paths to avoid the fireballs with angry noises as their riders were jostled around.

The squad started firing on the airborne threat. Their repeater bolts reached up into the sky, most of them missing but still exploding in the air, filling it with acidic gas that the airborne undead had to fly through or dodge.

Rugrat finished with his second repeater and pulled out the first as he laid back on George, shooting them up into the sky.

Shooting with two different hands was highly inaccurate—if you were just a human, without marksman skills and an innate knowledge of the movement of the world of Mana around you.

Bolt after bolt flew from Rugrat's crossbows. The undead creatures dove and rolled as the squad were lying on their backs, their expressions stony as they filled the sky with explosive bolts.

Rugrat could feel the Mana gathering as the riders of the winged creatures readied themselves to create a spell.

Rugrat felt the Mana within him moving to his will and the Mana around him was clamped down. A suppressive atmosphere followed him as the bolts in his repeaters started to glow red. Rugrat's body started to light up with the glow of contained Mana. The Mana around him was turned to chaos. A grin appeared on his face as the hairs on the back of his head raised up at the power under his command. The others in the group felt a deep-seated, almost evolutionary fear and excitement from Rugrat as he fired his bolts.

If Rugrat's bolts from before were like rounds, they were now like artillery shells.

The undead birds might not be afraid of death but they couldn't disobey the laws of physics and air resistance. The explosions knocked them to the sides, causing them to try to fight to stay on their trajectories.

"Disrupt their flight path! We just need to get past them!" Rugrat yelled. Even with his custom rounds, he couldn't defeat them in a few shots. He was only try to gain space and create openings.

The others in the group obeyed, trying to disrupt the casters and their mounts as much as possible. The undead mages riding on the creatures seemed to realize that they wouldn't be given the time to call down large spells.

Mana bolts shot out from a mage's hands instead, peppering the broken spire and sending out shards of stone, making the scouts flinch at the near misses.

Lightning attacks played across the spire from the undead mages. Water turned into arrows and shot down at the scouts below.

"Fuck!" Someone yelled out as they were hit with water arrows.

Rugrat glanced over, seeing them holding their chest but still firing.

The first scouts had reached the base of the spire and were climbing down the broken wall, rushing towards the castle.

A mana bolt hit the spire above, right in front of Sabina.

Her panther was killed as they were tossed off of the spire into a free fall.

She slammed into the ground and rolled, no longer moving.

.

"Sabina!" Patrik yelled out. He was the closest to her and moved to her as the aerial undead were starting to circle around to follow up with a second attack.

"Keep moving!" Rugrat yelled as he saw the squad start slowing down as Patrik stopped next to Sabina. He jumped off of his mount and put his hand to her neck and started to resuscitate her.

"Patrik?" asked Dong Ju.

"I-I can't get a reading on her pulse, nothing," Patrik said, his voice turning professional and analytical.

"Get her into your storage ring, move it!" Rugrat yelled. "Get your fucking heads in the game and keep going!" Rugrat yelled to them all as George kicked up the ground. Patrik stored Sabina in his storage ring as they rushed for the castle.

Rugrat checked his map.

We just need to get through the castle!

Strosic let out a scream-grunt as he was hit with a lighting blast. e entered the castle last, smoke coming off of his armor.

He and his panther slumped as they flopped forwards. Their momentum still carried them as if they were puppets with their strings cut. hey slowly smoked on the ground.

"Move! Get to the dungeon core, I've got him!" Rugrat turned back, knowing George was the strongest and the fastest.

Rugrat jumped off of George as they got close to Strosic. Rugrat grunted has he dove on the ground, using his legs to get over to Strosic.

He used simple organic scan on him and his panther.

Gritting his teeth, Rugrat put them in his storage ring and then jumped back onto George.

They're just so strong here that even a slight graze could kill us. Mother fuckers.

He pushed the rest of his emotions down as he raced to catch up with the rest of the squad.

What he had thought was the actual castle was merely the outer wall protecting the compound inside. There were training grounds, open gardens, crafting buildings and housing. It wasn't a castle but rather a castle district.

They had passed the barracks and now ran across a large open area with broken fountains and a massive garden, whose glory had been lost long ago.

Rugrat heard the aerial beasts with their mages that were now behind them.

"Move it!" Rugrat yelled as they sped across the inner area. The actual castle and cover from the aerial mages, lay ahead of them.

"Nothing is more important than getting that dungeon core!" Rugrat yelled. He hoped that they would all make it out of the blast zone of the spell but hedged his bets.

"Yes, First Sergeant!" they yelled back.

Rugrat nodded as they rushed on. Seeing their friends hurt and possibly killed, they had already changed.

Clouds converged above them as lightning rained down.

"Spread out! Move through cover!" Rugrat yelled. The lightning struck the ground, creating new craters in the dirt and destroying the bones and debris that lay there.

A fountain was struck, turning it into flying rubble that struck one scout. They were able to remain on their mount but their left arm dangled uselessly by their side.

The rain transformed and turned white, its speed increasing as ice arrows shot down from the sky.

Mana lances also shot towards the soldiers. Spells were cast on the ground and plants were revived and slithered through the skeletons, weaving through their bones and turning them into humanoid plant creatures.

Rugrat and the others fired at them blindly as they focused on moving erratically because their lives did depend on it.

Using fire superiority to force the enemy back failed as, unlike live opponents, the undead continued to charge into their attacks with no regards for their well being.

Quagmires appeared, one panther was unable to dodge the newly created obstacle. Its paws entered and its rider was tossed, landing on the ground a meter away as multiple fireballs rained down from above.

The ground was torn up by the spell rain as the scouts all shifted around, making it harder to hit them.

Rugrat was hit in the shoulder and then the back with rocks from a near miss spell hitting the ground.

The first scout made it through a broken castle wall, their panther's legs turning quickly as they tried to find purchase on the floors that were covered with bodies and rubble.

The rest of the squad pushed forwards into the corridors, clearing space for those following behind.

They all piled in through the breaches in the true castle.

The mages stopped firing on Rugrat's group as they banked away with angry cries and yells.

"Store your mounts!" Rugrat ordered. Inside they would be more of a hindrance than an aid.

George shrunk in size, now about the size of a dog as the others were returned to their creature storage rings.

"Reloading!" one called out.

"West, this is Rugrat. We have entered the castle. We have a location on the dungeon core. Two KIA at this time. There are multiple undead in the streets, as well as aerial undead," Rugrat reported into his communication device as they moved.

"Understood. We're trying to disengage with a group of undead at the moment. We shook off the enemy outside the walls and are heading for one of the spires in the outer areas to use as a defensive position," Erik relayed back.

"Understood." It sounded as though Erik was having a tough fight as well with the company still under the slowing reactions spell for another two minutes.

"Rugrat, remember—focus on the dungeon core. It might be the thing controlling all of this or it might be our only hope to make a defensible position."

"Understood. Rugrat out."

It's on us. They can send everyone in but there is no guarantee that they'll be able to get this far.

Others in the remainder of the scout squad checked their ammunition. Rugrat pulled out his modified bolt action and moved forward.

"Back in!" Rugrat ordered. Those who needed to reload said so as they followed Rugrat, who was moving and visually clearing as he went. The rest of the squad fell in behind him. All of them had training on how to fight in enclosed spaces and were putting it to use as they turned corners and moved toward the spire that the castle was attached to as fast as they could

There were signs of heavy fighting in the halls. It looked as if the attackers had died in great numbers here, seemingly unable to use those numbers effectively against the defenders in the small corridors. Not only when they were alive but when they were fighting as the dead as well. Whole sections of walls had been torn apart and the roof was collapsed in places.

The medic of the squad Shi Song was going between people, administering concoctions and applying a few healing spells as he could. By his expression, things did not look good.

Rugrat didn't have time to worry. *First, win the firefight, then look to the wounded.*

That was a law Erik always told him that bound all combat medics, and it was one of the hardest.

Even as they were fighting, they were thinking of the wounded and wanting to care for them, knowing that vital seconds were passing. They were soldiers first and medics second. If they didn't secure the area then when they were working on the wounded they would be the next casualty.

They kept on advancing, the woman with the busted arm applying self aid to fix herself. She could at least cradle her rifle in the crook of her arm and work the action with her right hand.

They entered a large room that looked as if it had once been a majestic hall. It rose up over two floors with sweeping stairs on the right and the left with what once were hanging chandeliers adorning the ceiling.

Now the chandeliers were broken glass and crystals on the ground. The ceiling showed holes to the sky beyond. Parts of the ceiling had collapsed onto the floor below. Some corpses were crushed under the rubble, while others had died in combat on top of it.

The room was marked with the scars of different spells. Blades had torn through support pillars and heavy weapons had smashed into the ground, leaving craters. Broken arrows littered the floor and archer corpses perched on the second floor of the room, spears pinning some of them to the wall behind them.

There was a doorway that had been blasted open at the end of the hall, behind what looked like it once had been a formation enhanced barricade.

It's just through there and then below. We're right underneath the spire.

Rugrat could see a light shining down behind the door as light filtered in through the top of the broken spire in places.

The squad advanced into the room, their weapons raised. They searched for threats as they moved over the bodies and rubble that covered the room.

As if triggered by their actions, undead stirred and started to rise from the ground. Three large skeletons started to shift. The dust moved from their bodies as they grabbed their swords and other weapons.

"We protect," one of the skeleton knights moaned somehow as it rose up from the ground.

The remaining members of the squad fired on the rising skeletons. The squad had white faces as the skeletons took damage but didn't seem affected by it at all, even as their bones melted and the explosions pushed them back to the ground.

"First Sergeant, keep moving on. We'll hold them here!" Dong Ju yelled.

Rugrat and Dong Ju shared a look. Rugrat gritted his teeth. They both knew that they were working on a hunch, that the dungeon core might help them overcome the undead here or it might be useless. They both knew that their squad could be sacrificed so that the rest of the company lived. Rugrat could tell the others knew it too but they didn't stop fighting.

He knew that it was the right action to take but it tore at him something fierce. George increased in size and Rugrat jumped on him.

George rushed forward, dodging between the recently animated skeletons that lashed out, trying to catch them with their blades. George used a fire spell behind him, creating an explosion that tossed them forward through the doorway. They dragged bodies and armor out with them as George shrunk in size. They tumbled through a doorway and rolled right off the platform on the other side. The inside of the spire was hollow with stairs in it.

Rugrat was now falling down the stairs, seeing the several floors below him and a group of bodies all around a single ritual formation in the middle of the bottom of the spire.

George grabbed on to Rugrat with his claws and expanded as large as he could, stretching out his wings to stop them from falling. George saved Rugrat from crippling injuries but they weren't able to stop all of their momentum as they hit the bottom floor and rolled.

The armors, weapons and bodies that they had hit and carried with them flew through the doorway behind them and fell several floors before raining down on the ground around George and Rugrat.

More skeletons were rising up in this bottom room. Rugrat and George were now underneath the center of the spire.

"George, fire," Rugrat said. His voice was rough from the jumping and constant shouting. He grabbed his rifle and fired at the closest skeleton that was getting up.

Their head snapped to the side but they kept on rising. *Stronger than the ones outside.*

George breathed flames in an attempt to coat the room but the skeletons only seemed more pissed off. One attacked with a spear, the attack drilling a hole in the wall that sounded like an explosion.

Rugrat grit his teeth again. There was no way he could win this in a stand-up fight. The majority of the skeletons were piled around a fancy skeleton wearing a crown, with his hand on the dungeon core. The core was fitted into a pedestal in the middle of a formation that connected to the spire.

The man with the crown, who must have been the emperor, slowly started to move and looked up at Rugrat, his undead eyes a mixture of browns and black. He opened his mouth and let out a scream that reached into Rugrat's very bones. The shout caused the skeletons around him to move faster.

Rugrat didn't have any more time to wait as skeletons were still chasing him from the higher levels. One of them fell from above and smashed into the floor, breaking into individual bones that quickly started to reassemble.

Rugrat cast his most powerful explosive shot on the round within his gun, pouring his power into it before firing on the emperor.

The resulting close range explosion made Rugrat immediately go deaf as he felt the heat bleed off the explosion while the Emperor flew backward, slamming through lines of rising skeletons and into a wall. He started to get back up, looking more pissed off than wounded, the only damage mark being his crown was now askew. He stared at Rugrat who was already rushing forward.

A blade appeared to Rugrat's side, swinging for his hips.

Rugrat leapt, his heart in his mouth as he landed near the dungeon core.

He felt his legs being cut off as he let out a cry in the air. A Mana blade appeared in his hand as he fell towards the core. He dug the Mana blade into the stone pillar and reached out with his other hand to touch the dungeon core.

==========

You have come into contact with a dungeon core. With your title: Dungeon Master, new options are revealed.

==========

Do you wish to:

Take command of the Dungeon

Remodel Dungeon

Destroy the Dungeon

==========

The emperor let out a yell and launched a metal spear.

"Command!" Rugrat yelled.

Everything seemed to freeze as the undead stopped their movements with sudden jerks.

Rugrat looked around a few times, the tension in his body not getting any weaker as he looked at them all

"George, legs!" Rugrat said, feeling all of the pain of his missing legs.

George grabbed Rugrat's dismembered legs in his mouth. Gingerly he took them and put them next to Rugrat.

Rugrat pulled out a repeater, holding it ready as he used one hand to force his stump together with his severed leg. He let out a scream between his teeth before he poured healing potion liquid over the two different stubs and held them together the best he could. The two halves merged back together and started repairing themselves as he looked around at the skeletons, making sure that they hadn't moved.

He grabbed his other leg and then repeated the process.

There were tears running down his face as he noticed that there was a call on his sound transmission device.

"Rugrat, did you get it? The skeletons just stopped fighting here," Erik asked.

"I think I did," Rugrat responded, still looking at the skeletons that had been attacking and trying to kill him moments ago. He was not really sure whether he had control of them.

==========

Event Cleared!

==========

Vuzgal has come under your command, staking your claim on this once lost land, returning stability to the region.

==========

Rewards:

2,000,000 per participant for clearing the city

==========

==========

You have taken over control of a Capital.

==========

Do you wish to:

Take command of the City?

Take City as a vassal for another?

==========

==========

Quest: City Lord

==========

You have the land but not the people. To become a true city lord, one must have both.

==========

Requirements:

Have a population of at least 100

==========

Rewards:

Gain Access to City Interface

+10,000 EXP

==========

"Did you just get a bunch of notifications?" Rugrat asked.

"Got the event cleared one. Why?"

==========

Population verified

==========

==========

Title: City Lord

==========

You have taken over the Capital Vuzgal and filled it with a population greater than 100 people.

==========

Rewards:

You gain access to the Capital Interface

==========

"Yeah. Yeah, I think I got it," Rugrat said, breathing heavily in both relief and agony.

"You good?" Erik asked.

Rugrat looked at his legs and then leaned back against the pillar, looking up at the top of the broken spire. His breathing was restricted by his body armor and he was also covered in grime and sweat.

His mind started to wander, flashing back to those broken bodies of Sabine and Strosic. He swallowed and looked to the undead, focusing his mind somewhere else.

"Yeah. Yeah I'm fine." Rugrat said as he used simple organic scan on his legs. They were quickly being repaired. He'd need to take some time to fully recover before he could even move.

"What's your situation?" Rugrat asked Erik.

"Some wounded, some pretty bad. Currently checking on them. See what you can learn about the city and the dungeon core. I'm going to check on our forces here and then move to meet up with you and your section at the spire."

"Understood."

"West out."

Rugrat called up the city interface. "Well, this is crap. I can only build things, impose taxes and appoint leaders. There isn't even a map function like the dungeon. I can't alter the area either. I guess it makes sense as it's a city, not a construct built with a dungeon core at its center," Rugrat started to talk his thoughts aloud. Rugrat tried to cover over his pain and refocus his mind.

George looked around, guarding his master incase anything else tried to attack him.

"Looks like I took control over the city, not just the dungeon core," Rugrat continued.

Rugrat then checked the dungeon core interface. With his knowledge of formations and dungeon cores, he was able to piece together just what it was doing.

"Dong Ju, sitrep," Rugrat said into his communication device.

"This is Corporal Valvo. The sergeant..." Valvo took a shaky breath, recovering and putting on his soldier voice, attempting to push his emotions to the side. "He didn't make it, First Sergeant."

Rugrat cleared his throat and nodded to himself, taking in a sharp breath. "Understood. Tend to the wounded. I'll be there in a minute."

"Yes, First Sergeant," Valvo said, just as he would've in training, separating himself from the loss of his sergeant to take command and help the rest of his squad.

"Rugrat out."

George was looking over at him with a worried expression, trying to support him with his presence.

Rugrat tested out his recently stitched together legs. They were mostly healed, and the bones were fully fused together, allowing him to stand up on his own.

Rugrat pulled out formation plates—first, Mana gathering formation plates. They were simple but the Mana in the air was so dense that the Mana that gathered was a visible mist already, with a few drops condensing and dropping onto the Mana gathering formation plate. Rugrat put down defensive formations that could use the power in the gathering plate around the dungeon core.

Rugrat looked around, his eyes falling on the emperor's storage ring. He grabbed it and looked at the other storage rings on the dead.

He just waved his hand, sucking up the undead corpses into a ring and then slumped over George who had made himself smaller in size so Rugrat didn't need to jump up on to him.

George made sure to be careful, climbing up the stairs that lined the sides of the spire back towards where they have left the rest of the squad.

Rugrat braced himself for what he might see as they entered the hallway into the main chamber.

They passed the still smoking doorway they had just burst through to see the four members of the squad that were still standing. One was watching for threats, the other three using healing spells and concoctions on their brothers and sisters.

There were two bodies off to the side, covered in a blanket.

Rugrat looked at the bloody mark on the floor and then a wall, with a thick trail leading to the blankets.

Rugrat got off of George. "Come help!" Rugrat said. George took the watcher's position.

They had IVs of Stamina and Health potions already lined in the different members of the squad.

The medic had sewn them together in places where bits had been blown off. There were two people who were unconscious but recovering; the others were in a battle between healing and Stamina loss.

They had to tread a fine line to heal them enough to stay alive and repair damage but not to over-exhaust the patient's body or else they might die, despite the healing.

One more person was stabilized and left to the side to recover. Rugrat and the medic worked on the last person. The others made sure to check that the other three were stable, answering Rugrat's questions and checking their Stamina IVs.

Rugrat and the medic stabilized the last patient as they checked on the other three'.

George let out a low yowl in warning.

The remaining squad members looked up to see the rest of the company filing in. They looked like the scouts felt. Everyone was covered in grime, their eyes looking for threats. There were no smiles of greeting as they fanned out and started to build fighting positions as Glosil organized them.

Erik and the company medics moved up, Rugrat and the squad medic relaying to them what had happened.

The company medics took over as Rugrat went over to the two corpses that had been put to the side. Rugrat took out a stretcher and laid down Sabina from his ring and put a blanket over her as well. He stood up, making eye contact with First Sergeant Han for Dragon Platoon and then to the scout squad.

Han had a grim look on his face as he nodded, looking over at the three bodies to the side. Rugrat saw his eyes shake as he came up.

Han cleared his throat, getting the attention of the scouts. "You did good, let's get you cleaned up." The medic made to talk but Han held up a hand.

"The company medics have them now. You did good," he said.

The medic lowered his head as Four Section were moved off to the side, away from the injured and the dead.

Glosil shifted the platoons and companies around, checking the new defenses so they were ready for anything.

Erik talked to the medics some more before turning to Rugrat and indicating a place off to the side. Roska and Niemm joined them as well. They sat down on some rubble and a broken pillar.

Rugrat gave them the blow-by-blow of what had happened since they left the rest of the company outside of Vuzgal.

***

"It looks like the dungeon core wasn't being used as a dungeon core but rather the central command node for a massive formation. It looks like the Mana barriers of the capital failed, then the emperor used a dungeon core at the center of the barrier's formation, allowing him to take the core over easily. He might have used the dungeon core's ability to manipulate the area under its control. He turned it all into a massive spell formation. Things must have been going badly. He didn't actually cast a spell; he just gave the dungeon core an order and it carried it out. Problem was, he gave the wrong damn command. He ordered the dungeon core to turn the people into undead and fight on. So it turned *everyone* undead, including him, and had them fight. No matter the side, humans and the other creatures fought one another. They were powered by the dungeon core so they couldn't leave its area of effect and became monsters of the dungeon. If anything was to leave its domain then they'd collapse. He probably meant to raise the dead and turn the battle on the attackers but..." Rugrat left the rest unsaid.

"Okay, so what are we working with here?" Erik asked.

"All of the undead are minions of the dungeon. The entire city and some of the land beyond it, all of it is under the effect of the dungeon. The heavy mist around this place is like captured Mana. Usually the heavy attribute mana is cleaned by the dungeon cores, like a purification system. With this the dungeon core has a domain over the entire area, which draws in mana right. Now, it was part of a spell formation instead of just being allowed to do its own thing. So think of all the mana around here like water in a lake and the dungeon core is a dam. It's an impassable dam that will never let the water break the banks or go anywhere, just stay there. A pocket of unmoving mana. If we break the spell then the dungeon core will go to work, drag all of that mana in and purify it. It's a big dungeon core," Rugrat looked at the ceiling. "Got to be like maybe three times the size of the dungeon core in Alva."

"Okay, so what is happening right now?"

"I guess I've just kind of stopped everything. The core doesn't have orders from me to do anything, so the undead are just dormant. If I use it as a dungeon core instead of part of a formation I think all of the undead would collapse. If we destroy the dungeon then we might get the plans to make undead and then we can use those plans with the bodies to get back the undead."

"Let's hold off on that for the minute, we need to secure our position and make sure that our people are good. Then we can come up with a plan."

"Are we staying here?" Roska asked.

Erik and Rugrat looked at one another.

"There is a shit ton of loot here. If we can neutralize the threat of the undead, just the resources alone that we could get from here and ship down to Alva would be worth it," Rugrat said.

"We did see a totem here, maybe we can get that working," Niemm said.

Glosil came over and joined them now that his people were settled or would be soon.

"How confident are you, if we're to hold this position?" Erik asked.

"If those undead start moving again, we're fucked," Glosil said point blank.

Erik and Rugrat looked at one another.

"We'll take a look at the dungeon core and see if we can neutralize the undead threat. Be ready to move in the meantime," Erik said.

The others nodded.

"You want to take some people with you?" Glosil asked.

"We'll be fine. If something happens, get our people out of here," Erik said.

Rugrat nodded, he didn't want them to get stuck trying to fight for him and die with them. With that, their meeting came to a close.

Erik and Rugrat checked their gear and their weapons before they passed the dead and wounded, passing through the blown open doorway into the spire.

George padded over to them. Rugrat opened his mouth to argue and then thought better of it as he moved to catch up to Erik, George following behind.

Erik looked up at the broken section and then down at the glowing formation.

"You good?" Erik looked at Rugrat.

Rugrat looked at him but didn't say anything. Erik nodded and then started walking down the stairs, kicking off random armor and weapons through the broken railing, causing the pieces to slam into the undead below.

"What are you thinking with the dungeon core?" Erik asked.

"We see what we get for destroying the dungeon, destroy it if we can and then remake it. Otherwise, remain in command and figure out just what the hell is happening with this formation and mess around with it," Rugrat said.

"Let's hope the first option works," Erik said as they lapsed into silence

Rugrat's legs were stiff and a bit painful but he ignored them, taking it like some kind of punishment.

"I'll cover," Erik said as they moved closer.

"Got it," Rugrat said.

They moved over the undead, there were some that were in states of standing up and a few with their weapons at the ready. It was like they were walking through a park filled with statues.

Erik and George looked outwards, watching Rugrat's back.

Rugrat used the dungeon interface and went through the options.

==========

Destroy Dungeon: Corrupted Vuzgal

==========

You will receive:

1x Common Earth-Grade Dungeon Core

Undead knight blueprint

Undead mage blueprint

Undead aerial beast blueprint

Undead beast blueprint

Undead skirmisher blueprint

==========

Do you wish to destroy this Dungeon?
YES/NO

==========

"That kind of makes sense," Rugrat muttered to himself.

"Speak up," Erik said, scanning the area.

"The city must have been made before the dungeon core was added. The core only controlled the formation, so we'll only get the blueprints for the undead," Rugrat said.

"Okay, so if we destroy the dungeon that should just destroy the spell formation. Then we can use it to create a new dungeon. We could then use the bones and skeletons here to fill in the blueprints," Erik said.

"That's the idea," Rugrat responded and looked at Erik.

"Do it," Erik commanded, raising his rifle so he would be ready to snap it at anything and shoot in a moment.

Rugrat tapped on the destroy button.

He stopped the flow of power to some of the undead. The undead inside the city walls collapsed into piles of bones as Rugrat took the dungeon core. Power was drawn in by the dungeon core in waves. It was much stronger than the one in Alva, creating a vortex of Mana as the released attribute Mana rushed to the dungeon core. It came in, feeling almost like sewage to Rugrat's senses, before the dungeon core consumed it.

Gold Ten Realms energy drifted from the undead that had collapsed, it was thick like a river as the whole city lit up. The Experience travelling through the walls and streets of Vuzgal as the Alvan Army members were slammed with Experience.

The core started to shake in Rugrat's hand, drawing in that highly impure and stagnant mana.

It was being drawn in from across the former capital, the pure mana spreading around the dungeon core quickly, only being restrained by the mana gathering formation plate that he had set up earlier, which was helping contain it but also bringing in more mana from the surrounding area.

"Crap!" Rugrat yelped as he quickly started selecting options on the dungeon core, establishing a dungeon once again with the spire as the focal point. Designating it to spreading over the former capital and the battlefields beyond.

The dungeon core was drawing in a truly massive amount of mana as it floated in front of Rugrat as he raced through menus.

The mana gathering formation couldn't contain all of the mana. The pure mana started to leak out. The Mana rose up through the spire and spread out over the city. It kick started the cycle of mana in a very visible way.

The clouds above started to clear and the ground around the spire started to show life; the sun looked down on them from above.

The broken city was revealed to the heavens again but now there was spots of color in the broken fields and open areas as plants started to recover and peek out of the ground.

The power being released was incredible. The dungeon core had been supporting the thousands of undead for centuries, turning this into an inhospitable land, devoid of life. Now, that power that had been held within the skeletons and lying stagnant over the capital and surrounding area was pouring out of them and being drawn into the dungeon core.

I need a place to put this power. These kind of mana fluctuations are going to be picked up by someone else otherwise. I need a mana gathering formation and cornerstones, though I've only got the undead. I'll start reviving as many of them as possible so that they consume the pure mana.

"What's going on?!" Erik yelled.

"There was so much impurities in the mana, it's like primetime dining for the dungeon core. It's sucking it all up and then the pure mana is shooting out of the spire like a beacon to any damn mana capable person or beast in miles. Blueprints, undead, there you are!" Rugrat shouted back as his fingers and eyes flickered through menus.

The undead started to move again as power flowed back into them.

"Glosil, this is Rugrat. The undead are under my control. I'll have them move to the barracks," Rugrat said, mentally kicking himself. He'd wanted to do something and he'd rushed ahead and shot himself in the foot.

Using the blueprints and the power that was coming through the dungeon core, Rugrat was able to redirect the energy coming in to revive some of the strongest undead. Instead of being powered with Metal, Water and Earth attributed Mana, they were now powered with pure Mana, increasing their Strength. Their brittle and old bones regrew to look like polished ivory; instead of the crazed black and brown eyes, their eyes were clear and blue as Rugrat sent them out to wait in the open areas of the city. He had to work quickly to spend the Mana. To try to contain it, the sheer density of the Mana—if it was released into the realm, it would draw beasts from a large area around and alert other nations.

"West, get a formation specialist, I need them to put together a mana gathering formation. We need to see if anyone has mana cornerstones. If not, look for them inside the city. We're leaking pure Mana all over the place and it's going to start drawing people's attention. I'm using the pure Mana to improve the undead, trying to find as many ways to burn the power as possible. Take out the Mana gathering formations, all of them, and place them around the city. Charge up everything we have off the formations. Gather all of the impure Mana we can," as he spoke, Rugrat raised more of the knights. Those in the spire were reassembled, emotionless as they were reborn. The undead moved to their new task of clearing up the city. Rugrat finally contained the power that had been leaking out and stopped himself from reclaiming more power back from the skeletons.

"What just happened?" Erik asked.

"Just released a bit too much Mana—wanted to contain it. We're going to need Mana cornerstones and a Mana storing formation if we want to stay here and not alert people about us being here," Rugrat explained. "And, well, I guess we killed the undead so we got the Experience for that. They were animated by the dungeon core but it was part of a ritual, not a dungeon core. So now they're dungeon monsters, they were just regular monsters before."

Rugrat peeked at his notifications, taking in a cold breath.

"Damn."

"We can go to the sixth Realm!"

"Focus," Erik said while Rugrat could hear people above yelling out. "Do you have a map on that thing?" Erik asked.

"Yeah," Rugrat replied as he moved to the side and Erik transferred the map from the dungeon onto his own map, filling in the previous blank areas.

Rugrat tested a few things out.

"It looks like I can see much further with the dungeon core being above the ground but I can only remodel the same amount of area that it would be able to affect if it was underground," Rugrat explained.

"Huh?" queried Erik.

"Larger map can only alter things with the dungeon in a smaller area."

"Okay, you good down here? I'm going to have the special teams move out to look for Mana stones. Have the undead drop off their storage rings in front of the castle and we can start going through those to look for what we need to make the Mana storing formations."

"Okay," Rugrat waved Erik off. "I'll manage things here and see if I can learn more and divert more power here. I'll start getting the undead to gather the dead together, see if I can make some more undead or get more storage rings."

"Do it," Erik said as he was already walking sideways, having to raise his voice as he broke into a jog, taking off like a bullet for the main floor.

***

"Special Teams One and Two on me. Glosil, there will be undead dropping off storage items in front of the castle. I need formation specialists that know how to make a Mana storing formation to go down into the spire and help Rugrat. Collect any Mana cornerstones from among the troops that you can," Erik said, slowing from a run to a jog as he entered the main hall.

The Special Teams that had been sitting to the side grabbed their weapons and followed Erik.

"Cap?" Niemm asked as they ran through the castle. Erik checked his map as he looked for the places that would likely hold cornerstones.

"We need cornerstones. The dungeon core is purifying a massive amount of mana which could create a storm of Mana that will most definitely alert people to us being here. Unless we can find a way to store it," Erik explained.

"Why would it just start purifying the mana if it hadn't for this long?" Roska asked.

"That's what dungeon cores are supposed to do." Erik slowed his pace and then altered his advance, pointing towards where they were supposed to go, Storbon and Yao Meng taking the lead.

"They take in impure Mana, clean it all up and push it out. The gnomes of Alva Dungeon were geniuses. Instead of letting that pure Mana escape, they set up formations to use it for their own means. Sometimes, dungeon cores can't consume all of the impure Mana, so they turn that excess impure Mana into creatures that are naturally more aligned with the various impurities. A dungeon located in an area with high Metal is going to have Metal attribute creatures. Water and Earth area will mean creatures from each type or creatures that are aligned with both. These monsters are created to hold those impurities. However, when used in spells then the Mana gains an attribute and impurities. Dungeons are a mana filtering and impure mana burning center; think of them like the evaporation stage of the water cycle but for mana. The creatures are like Mana stones for the impure energy. Killing them releases that energy to be purified and will allow more impure mana to be dragged in to spawn a new dungeon monster. When the creatures are killed, that Mana is released and the dungeon core consumes it, purifies it and it is returned to nature, where it is once again consumed by everything and anything. Like the cycle of water, there is a cycle of Mana. So, when the formation was interrupted, the power that had been stored up in the undead came rushing toward the dungeon core and it carried out what it was meant to do: purify Mana and return it to the Ten Realms," Erik added.

"So you put the pure mana into the creatures, turning them into pure Mana stones, so there wasn't pure Mana shooting off," Roska said, connecting the dots.

Erik nodded as he added four different waypoints for potential locations. "Bingo. Niemm head to waypoint alpha, then bravo, Roska, head to charlie and onto delta. Give me two people. We'll check through the rooms between you to look for anything useful and support if needed."

***

Several of the soldiers that had an understanding of formations were sent down to Rugrat as well as three smiths.

"Welcome to the party," Rugrat said. He had the undead groups clearing the floor, putting skeletons together from different bodies, piling up weapons, armor and storage rings in a pile, allowing Rugrat to animate them and put more Mana power to effective use.

The formation specialists got to work, taking out a blueprint.

They activated the blueprint and it turned to motes of light that spread around the dungeon core, overlaying the dead formation. They pulled out their carving tools and got to work at the different edges, tracing out the formation.

"One second," Rugrat called as he used the dungeon interface, simply consuming the floor, clearing it of the old formation. The pillar that had been holding the dungeon core disappeared, revealing a Capital Interface underneath the pillar that Rugrat couldn't destroy with the dungeon core. He ignored it and followed the blueprint with the dungeon core controls, cutting out the ground perfectly.

"Alright, now it just needs to be filled in," Rugrat explained.

Rugrat left the dungeon core as he and the other smiths pulled out mobile forges, firing them up and powering them with ambient mana. They melted metals and combined them with the right enhancers, passing them to the formation specialists to pour them into the formation's grooves.

They worked quickly, following the formation blueprint. It was much simpler and smaller than the Mana storing formation that was located in Alva, making it easier and faster for them to build as the first mana cornerstones were retrieved and passed back to them.

Rugrat returned to the dungeon core from time to time, looking up at the air that was clearing above the capital. In his mana sight he could see the pure Mana drifting above like a smoke signal trying to draw attention. The Mana pulse was much smaller than before but the amount of mana being drawn in was still like a raging waterfall.

Rugrat reached down and touched the Capital Interface as he was waiting for metal to heat.

```
==========
```
City interface.
```
==========
```
Lord: Jimmy Rodriguez
Population: 104
Grade: Imperial City
Build
```
==========
```
Rugrat clicked on Lord and added Erik as well before he dismissed it and continued working.

***

Glosil squatted down next to Domonos, who was checking his map.

"Problem?" Glosil asked.

"The castle has three floors. I'm comfortable about holding just the room we're in, but this place is massive," Domonos said.

"We just do our best. Rugrat has control over the dungeon so we'll know if any threats are heading our way. Get two lines of defense set up and dug in, then rotate shifts, get your people to drink and eat."

"Got it," Domonos said as there was movement from the doorway to the dungeon core.

Rugrat and George were walking out with the rest of the formation specialists and smiths. They had been in there for three hours working on the design.

Rugrat was guiding undead as well, sending them out beyond the defensive lines and into the city.

Glosil patted Domonos on the shoulder and went over to Rugrat.

"The formation is done. We still need more cornerstones. The formation is throttling the power leakage and the Mana should disperse over a large enough area that it shouldn't bring too much attention to us. We'll need to update the cornerstones from Mortal grade to Earth grade and increase the power that the formation can store. I have the undead out there cleaning up the streets and the area around the totem in case we need to run for it. I'm also having them collect storage items and drop them at the front of the castle," Rugrat said.

"I sent out Lieutenant Yui to recover the items," Glosil responded.

There was some noise at the front lines as Yui returned along with two sections carrying boxes of storage items.

Yui had them stack the boxes over by the wall. There were already twenty or so boxes against the wall, with three people looking through storage items and then tossing them to the side. This was where the cornerstones they had already set up had come from.

"There are a lot of storage items. The undead are walking in from across the city, collecting them as they go and dropping off theirs," Rugrat said.

"Damn," Glosil said. *Just how many undead are there in the city. How many people did there used to be in this city?*

"Get some people to start going through the storage items, looking for corner stones. We still need another thirteen to fill in the formation. It's strained right now but stable for at least a week in its current state," Rugrat said.

Glosil nodded.

"We'll have a leadership meeting in thirty," Rugrat said, looking out at the sun that was hanging lower in the sky.

"Understood," Glosil said.

Rugrat contacted Erik and had him pull the special teams back.

***

Rugrat had found a corner of the main room, the blood had been cleaned up and the room, while still showing signs of battle, had been cleaned up as well. The pillars were repaired slightly. The dead on their stretchers were resting inside of Glosil's storage item.

Erik, Glosil, Niemm, Roska and Rugrat were sitting on chairs with a field table between them.

"How are we looking?" Erik asked.

"We've got a perimeter of this hall. The castle is too big to do much more than that. We're building some defenses now," Glosil reported.

"Well, we should start thinking about our next moves." Erik sat forward."I propose we secure our position, check on the totem, loot this place and then check out the nearest trading city. We need to know more information about what's around us."

"We should definitely get in contact with a neutral trading city," Rugrat said.

"We need to secure our position here. I'll go with Roska to the nearest trading city. Keep the skeletons active—use them to ward off people and keep the changes to Vuzgal a secret," Erik ordered.

"Safest when they don't even know we're there," Rugrat said as he nodded in agreement.

"We'll do a sweep of the city. Have the undead clean up the dead and gather up the rest of their storage items. Have our people search through the city too. I want to know where every sewer goes and the inside layout of every square foot of this place." Erik looked at Niemm, Rugrat, and Glosil.

"Can do," Rugrat said. "What do you want to do with the city?"

"I'm not sure," Erik said. "We'll talk about it later. I'm going to check in on Dragon's Scouts—give them some light duties and time to take this in. We'll have a funeral ceremony in three days. We'll take their bodies back to Alva and bury them there."

With that, the meeting broke up. Erik and Rugrat headed to the spire through the corridor and then down to the dungeon core.

"So, what are you thinking?" Erik asked Rugrat.

"I'm thinking we have a massive city under our control and an undead army, including our own small one. I want to say that this would be a good place to put down some roots but the Fourth Realm is a constant warzone. If we take over this city, then others *will* try to take it from us. They might not find out that we're here instead of the cursed lands for some time but somehow, it'll get out," Rugrat said.

"Hasn't yet with Alva," Erik offered.

"Alva is underground and only we know about it. People know about this capital and it's right out in the open. We can't keep the dungeon core from expelling Mana all over the place. Already, the city has changed from my lapse of judgement."

"This is quite a large city. There should be a dungeon around here—maybe more than one," Erik said.

"Well, this might help," Rugrat offered as he pulled out a book.

"What is that?"

"It was inside the Emperor's storage ring. Looks like a journal of some kind. I'll read through this, see if we can get any clues. I think the biggest thing we can get from Vuzgal is loot and the totem. If we can take that stuff down to the First Realm—well, no one ascends to the First Realm, so we can use it as a way to go to the other realms and other totems without having to use the other Totems in the Ten Realms. Saves on power usage with the teleportation arrays," Rugrat said. "Maybe with the city lord title we can make an extra totem here and send it down. Otherwise, we just dismantle the one here and take it with us."

"Okay, so we get the undead to make the totem, if we can, or break down the other one. Then, we have the special teams scout outside of the city and find out what's around us, terrain, cities and so on. Have the Company start organizing the loot inside of the city. Start sending materials down to the first realm if we can, once we've got control over Vuzgal, then we go and check out the neutral trading cities in the area and hopefully get updated maps too. Build up our strength here as much as possible so that when someone does find out about Vuzgal, they can't take it from us."

"I was thinking about something," Rugrat frowned. "Grenade launchers and mortars. Grenade launchers can add a lot of combat power, without being all that complicated, same as mortars can. Now that we're in a city, mortars can be a powerful defensive weapon," Rugrat said.

"You spearhead their creation," Erik said.

The two of them sat there for a few guarded seconds.

"You good?" Erik's tone changed as he looked at Rugrat, holding a different meaning.

"Never good when you lose someone but I'll deal with it." Rugrat breathed out of his nose as he moved in his chair. Feeling as though he was missing a part of his body, numb once more.

He'd trained and worked with them for nearly a full year now. He had known some of them for nearly two years, laughed and ate with them, their families, talked about dreams and aspirations. Now it was gone and they were but corpses lying underneath blankets, where not even the concoctions and healers of the Ten Realms could bring them back to life.

"They did good but shit happens," Erik said, patting Rugrat's knee.

Rugrat let out a grunt but didn't say anything else.

"Try and get some food and sleep. I'll move with Niemm and Special Team One to scout the totem," Erik said.

"Alright," Rugrat nodded.

They stood up and headed their own ways.

Rugrat moved to the defensive lines, walking them to understand where the different members of the company were and making sure he remembered how it was laid out.

He didn't miss the quiet conversations, the dark atmosphere that lay over them all. He found a position and pulled out his repeaters, reloading them, followed by his rifle.

Scanning the area, he pulled out the book he had seen in the emperor's ring. Rugrat opened the book and started to read. The afternoon was turning into night as Special Team One and Erik headed out on their mounts.

Rugrat's body was tired but his mind couldn't rest, so he read the book and monitored the dungeon with his dungeon interface.

Chapter: Vuzgal's Strength

They rode on their mounts through the streets, they passed undead that were moving orderly down the street. They were clearing a path from the totem to the castle and collecting storage items. Small piles were appearing along the streets some undead collected these storage items dropping them off at the castle.

"Fucking weird, with them all walking around, feels like they might turn on us at any second," Yawen said.

"Just keep your finger off the trigger," Storbon warned as they kept moving.

Erik heard them but didn't pay any attention as they got close to the totem. Around it there was a miniature castle with gates to allow people in and out, to be checked on their way.

The walls were in disrepair like those around the city.

They padded across the open ground.

"Spread out, cover the entrances and exits," Niemm said. Special Team One fanned out, their mounts prowling around.

Erik dismounted and went up to the totem.

==========

Ten Realms Totem

==========

This totem allows one to move between cities and realms.
Status: **Disabled**/Enabled
Functional
Charge: 1,000/1,000,000
Controlled by: Vuzgal City

==========

"So I guess you can disable a totem. You can turn it on and off, then in a fight the Ten Realms shuts it down to limit movement. If we enable it now then it should be good to go. It looks like the fighting wasn't centered around here."

216

Erik patted the totem and then walked over to Lola, getting on her back.

"Okay let's head back," Erik said.

They rode back to the castle district, passing the section of Dragon Platoon that was gathering up storage items in boxes from the pile that the undead had created.

"Get some rest, you'll be out scouting in the morning," Erik said.

Special Team One complained and grumbled as Erik headed back to the spire.

The dungeon core was only added after the capital was built and it had no power over the current standing architecture. If they wanted the materials or the items in the capital, they would have to take them themselves.

Erik didn't see Rugrat in the corner where they'd had the meeting or down where the Mana storing formation was. Erik looked at the stairs that went upwards.

He shrugged and started to walk up them as night started to settle in. It took some time before he reached the top.

From there, he could look over the capital, the large road that ran from east to west.

Erik turned around, his eyes narrowing. To the south, the former capital butted up against a valley. The original castle and inner walls closing the valley off as the newer outer wall grew out of the valley's side.

The mountains circled the entire valley, closing it off from East to the South and back West, creating a pinched U that opened up towards Vuzgal, reaching higher than the spire Erik was on. Along the mountains, spires and walls could be seen watching over the surroundings. The tallest spire on those mountain ranges would have been shorter than the main spire that Erik stood upon before it was destroyed. "The capital is massive as hell, holy shit." Erik shook his head. The city must have been filled with millions of people when it was at its height.

The mist previously covering the area had been pushed back but it hadn't been completely removed. Erik looked at the valley that was left untouched by the death and destruction of the constant war in Vuzgal.

Erik pulled out his personal rifle and sat down. He used his marksman ability and the scope to zoom in on the valley. The ground was lush with various growths. Groves of trees lay here and there. A small road exited a sturdily-built gate, heading deeper into the valley, hidden by the low-lying mist.

Creatures were moving about, eating the vegetation or hunting, moving from one location to another. They seemed separate from the rest of the world, untouched other than for the road cutting through the valley.

Erik checked his map. The map of the capital was highly detailed, including all of the damage but the valley must lay beyond the influence of the dungeon core and the capital.

***

Erik went back down to the castle interior. It was getting darker. Night stones had been put up so people could work in the darkness.

Smiths had set up shop next to the dungeon core, repairing gear and setting down mana cornerstones as they were found.

The wounded were all back on their feet except for one, who needed some monitoring overnight.

People were eating and sitting around, talking. Some laughing nervously about how close to death they'd come; others talked about things that they'd learned or seen. Others were off to the side, dealing with their grief. Everyone dealt with loss differently; no one way was right or wrong.

Erik checked on the defensive lines and talked to a few people here and there before he found Rugrat tucked away in a room. He was sitting on a foldable chair, with his rifle across his lap as he read a book.

"Good read?" Erik asked.

Rugrat looked up. His hand touched his rifle for a moment before returning to the journal. "It's the emperor's diary." Rugrat answered as he grabbed the map on his leg. "And this is a map of the dungeon that Vuzgal controlled. They called it The Armory. It is a dungeon that gives set armor for completing every level of the dungeon. If one clears the levels with fewer people, then they can get higher level gear—they pulled out an Expert-level blade from there once.

"They used the dungeon to supply their military, free weapons and armor. It was a Water and Earth attribute dungeon. Seems that they were farming the hell out of the dungeon to arm their people. The quality of the weapons and armor allowed them to fight harder and for longer while they grew their empire. They covered the north and controlled the Scarlet Rivers as they once called it or the Chaotic Lands as they're called now. To the west of this continent, some thirteen dungeons were controlled by them as well.

"Then they advanced further on the Chaotic Lands. Back then, there was a race of lizard people living there. Nasty bit of fighting to clear the land, blood feud kind of stuff. Then we get what we've got here. Has to be a long time ago that this old war happened. Lizardmen attacked the empire directly. Seeing that the empire was weakening, other bordering groups attacked from the west and pincered the empire.

"Cut off from the rest of the empire, the capital could only rely on itself.

"The lizards attacked and battle raged on for months. The lizards broke the main spire, paid for it in blood though. It seems that the base of the spire is where Mana stones were stored to power the shields. The formation was actually located at the peak of the spire and linked to the other spires to cover the entire capital.

"They were getting closer to the center and the emperor, seeing death coming—" Rugrat turned back a couple of pages. "Well, I inferred that—he basically stopped after reporting that they had slaughtered a large portion of the lizard's army but the remaining lizards still weren't stopping. Though he makes a reference to the dungeon core and about its abilities, the royal family primarily used it as a training aid to increase their cultivation. They called it the Purification Stone. Raised a pretty powerful family, it seems. I guess he took a long shot, using the formations at the base of the spire, to try to connect to the rest of the city. Then, he cursed the whole city and the people in it to wage war eternally. I'm thinking that the rest of the lizards in the area didn't make it back—all of them were stuck here. Then the lands to the east turned into the Chaotic Lands and people kept on fighting for control over the other cities.

"Others probably came here, only to be killed by the two fighting forces and turned into more undead."

Erik shook his head, thinking of those who wouldn't make it back to Alva alive, wondering whether his actions were the right ones. He forced words out to clear his head. "The dungeon—is it to the south in a valley?"

"Yeah," Rugrat said.

"I went up to the top of the broken spire and looked out. I could see it."

"Ten Realms Totem?" Rugrat asked.

"Looks like it's functional but purposefully disabled. Looks like we can activate it when we want," Erik said.

"As soon as we activate it, then someone could ascend accidentally into it or randomly get sent to us," Rugrat put his hands up. "I know, low chance but there is still a chance. No knowing if they'll be on our side or not. I saw a building option on the city Capital Interface—it's underneath the dungeon core. Might have forgotten to tell you anyway we can possibly build a totem, well we get the undead to build it. Then we break it down into parts and ship it down to Alva. Set up a totem there and start shipping materials back and forth," Rugrat said.

"I'll go look about building a second totem and start it if I can. Then we'll scout Vuzgal out tomorrow, scout the surrounding area too. We should push out observation posts and alarm formations so we know if we're going to have any guests. Day after the ceremony, we'll check the dungeon out with the special teams?"

"Sounds like a plan to me," Rugrat nodded.

"Alright, I'll go check on the city interface." Erik said. "Let me know if you learn anything else."

"I will." Rugrat nodded.

Erik left and Rugrat continued to read through the journal. Erik found a corner and checked his notifications.

==========
You have reached Level 50
==========

When you sleep next, you will be able to increase your attributes by: 75 points.
==========

==========
15,921,992/16,500,000 EXP till you reach Level 51
==========

==========

Skill: Healer

==========

Level: 63 (Journeyman)

==========

You have become familiar with the body and the arts of re-pairing it. Healing spells now cost 5% less Mana and Stamina.

==========

==========

Skill: Riding

==========

Level: 35 (Apprentice)

==========

Melee attacks while riding are 10% stronger

==========

==========

Skill: Marksman

==========

Level: 62 (Apprentice)

==========

Long-range weapons are familiar in your hands. When aiming, you can zoom in x2. 0. 15% increased chance for critical hit.

==========

==========

Skill: Throwables

==========

Level: 45 (Apprentice)

==========

Your throws gain 5% power.

==========

I need to increase my level to be ready for whatever comes. Erik sent a message to Glosil telling him that he was going to take a short nap.

Erik then used a concoction to send himself to sleep.

==========

You have 75 attribute points to use.

==========

He couldn't feel excited it was the largest increase he had ever gone through but the cost was too high, taking three of his people's lives.

"Okay, so I need to be as combat effective as possible. So far I have been increasing my physical attributes over my magical. As a commander I'll be at the rear with the gear instead of on the front. So I need to increase how alert I am. Agility is still useful, if I get into a fight, it's more likely that I'll be using a rifle instead of my fists. If not, then mana blasts and bullets. Strength isn't as important. Ten into stamina should keep me easily recharged after sleep, twenty into stamina regeneration would decrease the amount I need to eat and sleep. Forty five points. Fifteen into Agility. Speed up reactions. Then twenty into mana pool and ten into mana generation, my mana pool is still really small."

Erik looked at his stat sheet, feeling anxious, knowing once he added these stats he couldn't undo it. He accepted it before he could think on it too much and looked at the results.

==========

Name: Erik West

==========

Level: 50

==========

Race: Human

==========

Titles:

From the Grave II
Mana Emperor
Dungeon Master II
Reverse Alchemist
Poison Body
Fire Body
==========
Strength: (Base 36) +41
==========
770
==========
Agility: (Base 29) +63
==========
506
==========
Stamina: (Base 39) +19
==========
870
==========
Mana: (Base 8) +26
==========
740
=========
Mana Regeneration (Base 10) +55
33. 50/s
==========
Stamina Regeneration: (Base 41) +53
19. 80/s
==========

***

Rugrat read the journal through the night, learning about different hidden treasures and armories, checking it against the dungeon map, he was able to find them easily.

The imperial city must not have been touched in centuries, Rugrat was eager to see just what kind of loot it held. Some would be affected by the fighting and time but any that were held within storage items might have been preserved. If so, the capital was a place of untold wealth and riches.

Rugrat rubbed his tired face as dawn was fast approaching, checking his notes against the markers on his map.

As the sun came up, Erik appeared at his door.

"Briefing is about to start." Erik stated.

"Did you start building the totem?" Rugrat asked.

"Yeah, it is going to need special parts, though they're all pretty simple. It shouldn't take long to organize them but it'll take three months for the totem to be built. Guess the Ten Realms has to do something with it," Erik said, passing Rugrat a coffee as he got up.

"Thanks," Rugrat took it and followed Erik, a side room had been cleared out for their meeting. The rubble had been pushed along the walls and used in parts with magic to repair the walls and supporting pillars and arches.

"Morning," Erik said as he greeted the group of Yui, Glosil, Storbon, Roska and Han. Niemm and Domonos were out on watch, leaving Han and Storbon to watch over the briefing.

Rugrat stopped Glosil as he went into the room.

"I've marked down a number of locations that should have items useful to us. Just watch out—it looks like there are a number of them still with traps set up." Rugrat passed Glosil his notes on the different areas and their possible traps and then transferred the information on his altered map to him as well.

"I'll see to it," Glosil said.

Erik pulled out a large map and put it on the table so everyone could see it.

"Welcome to Vuzgal, the once Imperial Capital of this area. It used to house millions, now it only hosts us and the undead. We have turned the undead into dungeon monsters. Minor change but means greater control and follow our commands. They are out clearing roads, building a totem, collecting storage items and dropping them off at the castle. A totem that will take three months to complete! Now, what we need to do is get to know Vuzgal. We have this map here and within a kilometer around the dungeon core, we know everything above and below ground. Beyond that, we're going to need to scout it out. Domonos, your platoon will hold here and continue to sort through storage devices and repair the castle. Yui, your platoon will head out in teams to scout out the city. Roska, your team will head to the east to scout the forests and set up alarm formations along the road. Special Team One will do the same in the west," Erik looked to Storbon.

"How far out do you want to have the alarm formations?" Roska asked.

"At least five kilometers," Erik said.

"For the next three days we will scout the roads and the city, then we will move onto the second phase," Erik looked to Rugrat.

"There is a dungeon in the valley to our south. The special teams will assist Erik and I in entering and checking this dungeon out. At the same time," Rugrat tapped his map to the large map as markers appeared. "The Company will be looking to loot these areas. These markers are locations that I found with the dungeon core map or based on the Emperor's personal notes that look to be of interest. There will probably be traps and it could be dangerous, so we need to take every care in entering these areas," Rugrat said.

"Once we have an understanding of the dungeon, we will start to allow the rest of the company into the dungeon to increase their skills. We will have rotating times to give people some time off to decompress as needed." Rugrat looked to Erik who moved forward again.

"We'll have a ceremony for the fallen in two days, figure out who will be on watch. Make sure everyone's kit is good to go and look after your people. Questions or issues?"

There were none, bringing the briefing to a close.

***

Glosil checked on the monster cores that they had gathered while killing the different beasts in the forest. They'd been on the run, so they'd just collected the cores and kept moving.

Now, he saw they were different from the monster cores that had been in the First Realm.

"Toth, you have an appraisal ability, right?" he asked one of the nearby soldiers.

"Yes, sir." She nodded.

"Can you have a look at these?"

She took the monster core from his hand, looking at it and then pulling out some notes. "I can't say for sure but I think that this is an Earth-grade monster core." She handed it back.

Glosil made an impressed noise. A grand mortal grade monster core could go for one hundred and twenty gold, though to the people in the Alvan army, that wasn't important. The looting might have been removed from the army but they all lived comfortably and many of them had made a lot of money off the different things that they brought back from the battlefield dungeon. The battlefield dungeon was a proving ground for them to hone their abilities, earn rewards and learn to work as a unit.

They had become close with one another in their section but now their role was to defend Alva and its interests, not to keep on fighting in the battlefield dungeon.

Also, with a stable income and the responsibility that they were given, they weren't like a regular military that looked at looting as a bonus. They looked at it as a job to be completed, organizing resources and sending them back to Alva as was their job.

"Thanks, Toth," Glosil said. *A Lesser Earth grade monster core is worth 24 mortal mana stones. Not that much in a realm that can produce Earth mana stones.*

She headed back to continue working on her repeater while Glosil checked the other monster cores. All of them felt similar, so if Toth was right about the first one, then all of them were Earth-grade monster cores.

We are in an Earth grade realm now.

Glosil looked up as he heard people approaching, he looked up seeing Lieutenant Yui and First Sergeant Frost, commanders of the Dragon Platoon, appear by him.

"You ready to step off?" Glosil asked, standing up.

"All set," Yui said. "You got your route?"

"Right here," Frost, said holding out his map. Glosil transferred the information to them and included time spots when they should be in different locations.

Glosil nodded at it all. "Make sure that you don't miss a building. We don't know how long we'll be here or when we might need to bug out. Anything that we can take back to Alva can increase our strength."

"Understood," Yui said.

"Be back before dark," Glosil said.

"Yes, sir." Yui and Frost nodded, holding back from saluting. No one saluted on the battlefield just in case there was an archer out there. It was something that Rugrat and Erik had drilled into their heads.

They headed off, rounding up their platoon. They checked their gear one more time.

They moved out of the main castle and got onto their mounts in one of the gardens that was starting to recover, shoots of color peeking through the ground. They left, leaving the camp in relative silence. The special teams had already ridden out on their mounts shortly after the briefing.

The Dragon Platoon took the time to increase the strength of their defenses, sort through the storage items, check on their mounts and work on their gear.

Glosil moved through the castle and paused in a large room with a broken window looking out at the capital. It was the first time that he had a minute to breathe.

Glosil opened his creature storage item. His panther appeared and stretched. The panthers loved activity and being stuck in the creature storage items didn't give them much freedom. Glosil moved her armor around, releasing some catches so she could move more easily, and scratched her fur underneath.

The panther purred at the relaxing feeling from Glosil's scratches.

A weak smile appeared on his face as he looked out at the capital, his thoughts on the men and women he'd already lost.

He took in a breath through his nose and let it out. He forced his emotions down, his eyes growing wet. He turned away from it and gritted his teeth, removing the man from the rank. All he could do was his duty to the best of his ability and try to keep the rest of his people alive.

Chapter: Looting

Erik and Rugrat were inspecting where the Totem would be built while a half section from Dragon Platoon watched the area.

"Smart idea," Rugrat said.

"Got it from you making the mana storing formation," Erik said. "With the houses and buildings in the area, we can easily destroy them with the dungeon's interface. If we just cut lines in the walls, then the buildings will collapse, we don't get all the mana impurities from the material and then the skeletons can clear the big sections quickly, clearing the area and making sure we don't miss storage items or anything useful. We might need the materials to repair the city or build up the totem. It needs a lot of stone."

Rugrat looked at the big circle that was formed in the slums of Vuzgal. Most of the buildings had been in bad condition with the fighting so there was little left to destroy.

"They've cleared, what, seventy percent of it?"

"Should be ready to start building the totem this afternoon. I gave a list of materials to the people looking through storage rings." Erik passed Rugrat a piece of paper.

"What is this?"

"Everything that's needed."

==========

40,000 stone bricks

10 Earth Mana stones or equivalent power source.

5,000 iron ingots

Will require: 90 days to complete

==========

"That doesn't seem that bad, isn't there a way to make it quicker though?" Rugrat asked.

"We'll have to see but we need a ton of stone, and iron ingots. Thankfully there is a crafting area in the city," Erik said. He patted Lola who turned away from the construction site.

"Group up, we're heading to the crafter's district." Erik yelled.

They used their maps, crossing the city as they reached the crafting district, there were all kinds of workshops here.

They dismounted and began checking on the stores, in different states of disrepair, or in some cases, just piles of rubble. They searched through the buildings, collecting iron and other materials that were easy to collect.

Rugrat sent two mana bolts into the hinge of a door, kicking it back and sending it flying as dust was thrown up.

Rugrat stepped into the room. There were three furnaces along the wall and ten or so workbenches and anvils.

There were still words written on the board to the side of the room for orders that the customers had placed.

Rugrat moved through the room systematically, checking storage items he found and tossing the anvils or other solid iron items into an empty storage ring. He moved through to the front of the store and saw a staircase going downstairs.

He saw a formation on the door leading down but it had long since run out of power. Rugrat used his sound transmission device, "Erik I found a door going down in the place I'm at."

"Coming over to you, this place it empty," Erik said.

Rugrat took out a knife and cut through the locks.

"Must be Earth Grade Iron to take that long to cut through," Rugrat muttered as he pushed on the door. With the Wood and attribute mana the door hadn't degraded at all but the hinges were squeaky, making Rugrat wince.

"You trying to open some damn doorway into hell in there?" Erik asked, entering the store.

"You know it," Rugrat said. He pulled out his rifle as he cast night vision on his eyes and then he stepped onto the stone staircase, heading below.

Erik already had his rifle out as he followed Rugrat down.

They scanned the room, there was nothing but crates along one wall and another locked door.

Rugrat and Erik looked at one another.

"Check the crates first?," Erik asked.

Rugrat checked the boxes. "Minor storage devices, cheap and easy to make but have a greater capacity. I've got Mortal Mana stones here," Rugrat said. "Must be used to power the forges."

Erik stepped back from the boxes. "Take a look," said with a grin hanging from his face.

Rugrat looked inside the boxes. There was Mortal iron ingots and other metal ingots as well as enhancers.

"Jackpot." Rugrat grinned as he kept looking through the boxes.

Erik pulled out his sound transmission device. "Going to need some help at my position, we've got a bunch of iron ingots here needing to be transported," Erik waited for the reply. "Oh, good work, see if you can find more, that would make things easier for us," Erik said and cut the channel.

"What was that?" Rugrat asked.

"They found some carts in storage devices, can hook them up to a mount, transport more storage items."

"Now, the real question," Erik turned and gestured with his rifle "What's behind that?"

Rugrat created a blade in his hand.

"Want to find out?"

"Might as well, that means hell yea!" Rugrat moved to the door, using his mana sight to make sure that the formations around it weren't powered and then used his inorganic touch on the door. Then he used his mana blade on the lock.

"Earth Metal again," He said as he cut through it. Erik's rifle was at the ready.

"Open!" Rugrat shouted, moving to the side as he readied his rifle. Erik pushed into the room, scanning it.

Rugrat flowed in behind him going left where Erik went right.

"Clear!"

"Clear!"

They lowered their rifles. There was a locked weapons rack along the wall and there were a few large iron storage items off to the side. Rugrat went to the storage boxes as Erik went to the weapon rack.

"Looks like they were in a hurry, they're unlocked," Erik said, holding up the lock and pulling out the chain that held the doors closed.

Rugrat looked in the storage items.

"Shit yea, Earth grade ingots, high journeyman level enhancers, Expert grade tools," Rugrat said looking through it all.

"Journeyman level weapons and armor, most mid level a few high journeyman pieces," Erik said.

They cleared out the smithy and kept going, they still needed a metric assload of iron ingots.

They spent most of the morning and afternoon clearing out the crafter's district, they still hadn't gone through it all but they had the metal they needed for the totem so they headed back.

Erik took out the Totem blueprint and placed it down. It projected itself over the cleared area.

Rugrat altered the orders of the undead as they started to gather the materials that the half section as dumping out and that the skeletons had put to the side, starting to build the totem formation. The undead knights would cut the materials to size and shape with their weapons, others would move the materials and place them down, undead mages would use their spells to fuse the building materials together.

"I think that's about it," Erik said as they were watching the undead building the totem in record speed.

"'Bout time we headed back," Rugrat said looking at the sky as it was darkening.

"Bring the cart with us, let's head back," Erik said to the half section of soldiers with them.

***

Erik, Rugrat, and Glosil were at one of the fire pits they'd made, eating their dinner as Yui appeared, he pulled off his helmet and sat down in a chair.

"Tiger Platoon's all back, safe and sound," Yui reported as he pulled out a map, the others put their food down and grabbed their own maps.

"How did it go?" Erik asked.

"This place is massive. I had my people spread out in an extended line and we moved through the buildings. Skipped those that didn't look structurally sound and marked them down. We collected storage items and left them in the piles that the undead made. We should be able to cover the inner city in three days, get to the outer city a bit later."

"Concentrate on scouting the area, grabbing easy loot and storage items. Mark down locations with traps. Once we have a complete map of the place, return to the places with a lot of loot but wasn't easy to get in the first pass, then the places with traps. Don't rush it, take time and get it all," Rugrat said.

Yui nodded as they had all tapped their maps on his to get his information, then he put it away.

"Still, our people are a little jumpy around the undead but it should get better with time." Yui reported.

"We can hope," Glosil nodded.

Chapter: Roll Call

Three days ago, they had arrived in Vuzgal, the totem had been erected but there were mana fluctuations happening throughout it as it changed internally and externally. Alarm formations were added to the roads up to ten kilometers out. The inner city had been scouted except for the buildings that looked unsafe and were leveled by the skeletons. Half of the outer city had been scouted as well.

The morning sun lit up the city but within the castle it was gloomy, no one was out on patrol and there were only a few people watching the defenses.

Those that were free filed into a room with rubble that had been put into rows. At the front, there stood three crossbows pointing down, each holding dog tags of the fallen.

The company fell in, all but a few keeping guard.

Rugrat stood up to the side as everyone filed in. He started roll call.

Men and women stood at attention as they were called.

"Private Strosic." Rugrat's voice rolled through the otherwise perfectly silent capital. That loneliness and loss was brought back to the surface as some people shook; others looked higher, trying to force the tears in their eyes back to where they came from. "Private Jan Strosic."

Still there was no answer, and they knew that he would never answer roll call again.

That pain and emptiness of loss settled in the stomach of everyone there.

Roll call continued before another name was left unanswered.

"Sergeant Dong, Sergeant Dong Ju."

"Corporal Sabina, Corporal Helena Sabina."

Roll call fell silent.

People started to move up. They saluted the three crossbows; tears might be running down their cheeks but they saluted. They took a knee in front of them, a personal item or something of the deceased at the bottom of the crossbow. They only had a few seconds before they stood back up and saluted again before turning away.

As they left the room, some just couldn't hold it back again, crying openly but still they didn't make a sound. This was not their day, it was their friends' day, and they wouldn't make a noise to take away from their day.

Finally, it was Erik and Rugrat's turn. They walked up and saluted the three crossbows, taking off their shades, revealing their red eyes.

Dong Ju was a solid sergeant; he looked after his people and made sure to pay attention to everything and anything. He was firm with his people but always there as a fatherly presence. Rugrat had found out that he was thinking about proposing to his long-term girlfriend. Corporal Watson had been a quiet type, a hunter and a tracker who had become a sharpshooter and come into his own. Corporal Qin Da loved to ride with her trained beast. Now both of them would rest together.

They were only in their early twenties, people with a future—none of them would have a chance to have children, to see more of life.

Thinking of the people that they were, the lives that they didn't get to live, weighed on Erik and Rugrat. They had trained them, led them, and given them the mission. That weight was not easy to bear.

It wasn't the first time that they had lost people but it never got easier. Neither of them hoped that it ever would.

***

People headed out to search the Capital again and to see to their tasks as Rugrat, Erik and Glosil met up in the ad-hoc command center.

"Were you able to find any cornerstones?" Erik asked.

"I believe that there were several. We added in Earth grade cornerstones and switched out the Mortal Grade cornerstones," Glosil responded as he took out a sheet, checking its contents before passing it to Erik. "This is the basic inventory of all the items recovered."

"Good. Then we can set up that Mana gathering system to reduce the outflow." Erik passed it to Rugrat.

Glosil nodded and Rugrat passed back the inventory.

"Tomorrow, Rugrat and I will head out with the special teams to open up the dungeon. Once we understand the floors we'll open them up to the Alvan Army sections to increase their levels as well. The battlefield dungeon is useful but there is only one beast to fight at a time and the terrain, while varied, is still limited." Erik announced.

Glosil was reminded that although Erik and Rugrat had been into other dungeons, the members of the army had only been into Alva Dungeon and the battlefield dungeon. This would offer them more practical practice and with more beasts to kill, they could level up faster. They would be forced to use new tactics and it would make for good training.

"Understood," Glosil said.

The capital was massive, it had housed nearly one million people when it fell. Their leftover wealth and items were now Alva's loot.

Chapter: Into the Dungeon's Maw

The sun was just rising as the Special Teams moved through the city, with Erik and Rugrat leading them past the working skeletons and the streets they were clearing of debris.

Thousands of undead had been destroyed since they were revived, but there were still thousands left. They were all high-powered creatures, allowing them to use large-scale spells or throw sections of buildings and walls that were as big as a cart with ease.

The assembly phase of the totem was complete, the materials had been placed down as the power of the ten realms slowly altered them. Changing it from a pile of precious materials into a true ten realms totem.

The skeletons were clearing out the debris and tearing down buildings that the Dragon and Tiger Platoons didn't feel were structurally sound. With the skeleton's abilities it took a matter of seconds and then they started to sift through the building's remains, organizing the different materials and valuables.

Nothing was wasted or left out, broken rocks could be fused together to create bricks, twisted metal could be melted back into ingots. The Alvans didn't want to waste anything.

For the first time in centuries, the lizard men and human skeletons worked beside one another instead of fighting. They put the capital back together as they mended the damage they had done in the wars. Mage skeletons used spells to put the walls back together as war beasts carried stone and debris.

The people of Alva passed the skeletons with their weapons ready but unneeded as they moved toward the large gate that stood to the south. There were four gates in a row and the section of wall here was built to defend against the valley beyond their walls.

The gates had been sealed shut some time ago. They sent up beasts over the walls with lines, secured them to the wall, and started climbing.

Erik looked out over the wall into the valley. It was much clearer than it had been yesterday. Even with the Mana stored in the different creatures, the dungeon core in the capital was starting to cleanse the mist around the valley.

There was a dead area of the valley, close to the former capital's walls but it was recovering quickly. The rest of the valley beyond the battlefield was untouched. Just seeing the green grasses and the trees made the Alvan soldiers relax a bit after leaving the broken city, swarming with undead that had so recently tried to kill them.

They rappelled down the wall into the valley.

Roska used her Dungeon Sense but wasn't able to locate the dungeon.

They pushed on into the valley. Mounted on their panthers, they made good speed.

Most creatures they encountered were startled by them and ran off, while others moved in closer. The scouts took them out if they seemed aggressive and stored their bodies as they kept on moving.

They rotated using their Dungeon Sense as they went.

"I've got something!" Storbon said after they had been traveling for an hour. He marked the point and shared it with everyone.

They continued through the valley, fording small rivers that ran toward them from the direction of Storbon's marker. creating a natural irrigation system through the valley that ran into the Vuzgal water system.

They came over a rise and slowed to a halt.

"Well, I think we've found it," Rugrat stated.

There was a massive tree that looked like a weeping willow. It stood at the end of the valley, with two streams dropping down in waterfalls from the mountains around it.

The water trickled down to meet at the base of the massive weeping willow before diverting once again and spreading out into the rest of the valley like roots, forming pools or disappearing into the undergrowth to create creeks.

"Must be fifty meters tall," Tully said.

"Well, let's go and see what's underneath," Erik said.

They moved forward once again.

The water covered a large area but was no deeper than a puddle. The tree rested on a sandbar forming an island.

They parted the branches that drooped down, sweeping against the ground and water. It was darker inside but not impossible to see as light still came in from above.

They looked around as Rugrat pointed at the roots."I think I see an entrance at the base of the tree."

They all moved closer, checking the area but focusing on the roots.

The tree had roots like a mangrove, rising out of the ground and supporting the massive tree above. They looked all jumbled together when viewed from the side. The roots parted in the middle, making an entrance that led down underneath the tree.

"Let's have a look," Erik said.

As they moved to the entrance they saw a set of stairs that led down, like a large open mouth. It wasn't completely dark as they could see a doorway all the way at the bottom of the stairs.

"Dungeon, if I've ever seen one." Rugrat picked up a stone and tossed it at the opening.

A formation activated as a barrier of water flashed into existence, shredding the stone before the barrier disappeared.

Rugrat took out the blue, rune-covered rock he had found in the Emperor's ring and tossed it.

The water wall appeared again but it surrounded the pebble, holding it momentarily before the water wall dropped down and a formation carved into the ground was revealed.

Rugrat tossed another rock at the entrance and this time it wasn't shredded. "Well, magical marbles—looks like we're in," Rugrat said. "Duck!"

Rugrat dropped to the ground, as did everyone else.

The tree that had looked as if it was on its last legs was rapidly revitalized, growing taller and stronger. Its leaves covered in fresh blossoms, filling the air with sweet smells. A wave of Mana emanated from the dungeon entrance, spreading out over the valley before dissipating. The Mana that had been bottled up in the dungeon calmed down after having been released.

The Mana was highly purified, causing plants to turn into high-level alchemical ingredients and beasts to undergo breakthroughs simply from the Mana's passage. The beasts of the Alvan army were the closest; some of them directly increased their levels and abilities. Others surged to the next bottleneck to increase their level.

"Well, I think that just sent out one big Mana signal," Niemm sighed.

"Crap." Rugrat got up and ran to the entrance as he tossed down some Mana gathering formation plates.

"Place Mana gathering formations around the tree!" Rugrat yelled.

"Team One assist, Team Two watch the perimeter!" Erik yelled.

Everyone worked quickly as the Mana was contained.

Rugrat then went around, moving the Mana gathering formations so that they drew in the most pure Mana to the cornerstones that had been placed in the middle of the formations.

"Not as good as the Mana storing formations in Vuzgal, but if we can get to the dungeon core we can put one around here directly," Rugrat said.

"Why is there so much Mana and why is it so pure?" Niemm asked.

"The capital has Mana gathering formations to increase the Mana artificially, though they don't work perfectly so Mana continues to pile up and be released at different times. This dungeon was sealed off and there are no Mana gathering formations around. So the dungeon core never stopped refining the Mana in it. Similar to what happened in the capital, different ways," Rugrat explained.

"How do you know that?" Niemm asked.

"A mix of going to different dungeons, a sprinkling of magical knowledge and my own senses. This mana feels almost stale, it's so pure because it has been purified again and again of any type of attribute. So probably got trapped in there for a long time to get to its current state."

"Team Two up front, followed by Rugrat, Team One and myself, will clear room by room. After each room consolidate before moving ahead! Anyone not clear?" Erik asked, looking around. There were no questions as everyone turned serious.

"Gong Jin up front," Roska said as she got her people organized into two five man teams.

They sorted themselves out with Gong Jin going first down the stairs, her rifle up and searching for targets.

***

Roska had her repeater ready, following right behind Gong Jin. Her spells were more powerful but the repeater only required the strength of her finger to fire.

Casting a spell, on the other hand, would take from her Mana reserves.

==========

You have entered the dungeon: Bala Dungeon

==========

==========

Quest: Re-open Bala Dungeon

==========

Remove the barrier around Bala Dungeon (Completed)

Clear Bala Dungeon at least once

==========

Rewards:

55,000,000 EXP

Bonus

==========

Roska cleared her vision with a thought as they continued down the stairs. There was light but it was dim, making it hard to see.

"Use night vision," She whispered.

Roska used a night vision spell, allowing her to see as if it were daytime. The others all cast their own night vision spells as well.

The stairs were made of compacted dirt and had water traveling down either side, trickling into the dungeon.

She reached the end of the stairs. Seeing a wall to her right, she turned left into the room. "Wall right, turn left!"

Creatures let out noises at her sudden arrival.

Roska pushed into the room, firing at anything that moved. She was hit with a web that tangled up her repeater.

"Stoppage!" she yelled. Spiders hung from the ceiling and there were large rat-like creatures on the ground.

Roska dismissed her repeater and took out her staff. A magical circle appeared and floated in front of her, shooting out icicles. Other soldiers flowed in behind her, their weapons firing and cutting down the spiders above and rats below.

Tully was hit in the face with webbing but was pulled back by Davos, who took her position and fired freely on the creatures.

Gong Jin let out a yell. His body glowed white with a self-buff as he drew the attention of the creatures, reducing the pressure on the rest of the special team.

The creatures were easily defeated, merely tens of bolts having been fired but noises came from an archway across and to the right from where they stood.

"Jin, Simms, Davos—cover that right entrance. Shoot anything that comes through. Xi, Imani, Han—with me." Roska ordered as she advanced as the rest of the group entered the room behind her. Yang Zan helped Tully to remove the webbing, which had left her panting from the lack of air.

Roska advanced toward the archway. A bipedal creature that looked like a mini T-Rex, without arms or a head, appeared.

The group opened up on it as it released a cloud of acid from small holes in its body. Xi was hit with a concentrated dose in the leg and went down screaming.

Han Wu fired his self-made blunderbuss at the acid spewing creature. The shrapnel peppered the creature and it backed up, clearly in pain as its skin and body burned from the poisoned metal.

It flopped down on its side silently as another two appeared.

Bolts pierced through them, filling them with wood and fletching. They tried to spit out a concentrated form of acid but their range fell short, hitting the ground instead of the humans.

An explosion went off from the other side of the dungeon as Yao Meng, who had joined the other group, used a Fire grenade and burned whatever was in that other room.

Roska and the rest moved into the room of the acid T-Rex creatures.

There was a half-covered mural that had been carved into one wall and a pit of dirt with different ingredients growing in it. The ingredients glowed with vibrant colors, poisonous and powerful.

Reinforcements moved up from behind as they stacked up against the wooden door. They smashed it down, moving into a connected corridor that went to the right.

They followed the corridor, finding a burned-out room and linking up with the other group, moving to one of the two remaining doors in the room.

Storbon was in the lead and stacked up on one door with others flowing behind as Davos covered the other door, ready to fire his repeater if anything came through it.

Storbon used his foot to bash in locked door and move to the side.

"Dead end!" Yao Meng yelled out as the two groups with Roska moved to the other door, it was locked as well. Yuli, who was with Roska, used a flame spell to melt the hinges and kicked the locked door.

A roar came from the room beyond as Han Wu, the first person in the breach line tossed in grenades. The grenades went off and the floor shook with the movements of the creature on the other side. Yao Meng pushed into the room, firing as he entered with Tully and Roska flowing in behind. Roska was third.

She saw two dead beings that could only be trolls and a third falling to the ground. All three were covered in wounds from the grenades and bolts. Even dead, it took the troll bodies a few moments to realize they were already dead before their wounds stopped trying to close. Their natural healing ability was incredible, despite only having levels in the low thirties but the grenades had confused and wounded them badly, the powerful and poisoned bolts were the end of the line for them as their bodies couldn't deal with the cumulative damage.

As the teams advanced through the hallways of the dungeon, a labyrinth of tiles appeared. They attempted to skirt around it and ran into two traps. Either a section of ground would open up to reveal spikes or toxic spores would be released into the air.

Tian Cui fell victim to a spike trap, but her teammates were able to care for her wounds and get her back into the fight without needing Erik's assistance.

They weaved through tunnels after clearing the traps, updating their maps as they ran into various dead ends. They passed through a row of water traps that shot water at pressures high enough to cut through their armor. Fortunately an inorganic scan had predicted the water traps and were avoided. They just had to crawl under where the jets shot out.

They eventually broke into a room filled with more rats, spiders and with trolls thrown in for good measure. They threw in grenades and backed up, tossing in magical curses afterwards until everything was dead.

Then they entered a large corridor that was filled with plants and a few roaming creatures. They killed the creatures and found deadly plants hidden alongside their more benign brethren in the idyllic corridor.

On Erik's order, they used Fire spells to burn everything down in the corridor as they advanced through.

Even as the plants burned away, they started to reform. The dungeon was bringing them back to life.

Erik hauled up a portcullis that lie at the end of the corridor, letting everyone through into a smaller hallway as they advanced on a large room. It was much darker than the other rooms they had been in thus far.

They all cast night vision, allowing them to see in the darkness.

They had just exited the small hallway into the large room when three creatures that looked like raptors without eyes appeared. The soldiers fired their already readied crossbows on the creatures, who then opened their mouths and unleashed destructive screams that destroyed the bolts and threw back the three closest Alvan's, Xi, Setsuko and Davos.

Bullets from marksman rifles, that had been quickly swapped out after the bolts disintegrated, were fired. The bullets were able to make it through the shockwaves. The rounds exploded and disrupted the sonic attacks as the raptors. With a higher pitched screech the raptors closed to make use of their sharp forelegs in melee range. Roska couldn't hear anything thanks to the previous attack bursting her ear drums but she could feel the pressure and pain on her brain as blood dripped from her ears.

Rugrat got a clear shot on a raptor's head and it disappeared in a fountain of blood, reducing the sound pressure on the Alvans.

Those in the front row recovered and stayed prone on the ground, where they had dropped at first contact, as they fired so that those behind them could safely fire over them.

It wasn't long until the creatures were killed off in very short order. Each raptor was broken into tiny and tinier pieces. Brutal overkill is a damn fine thing.

The healing effects of the standard-issue armor worked to supplement the healing spells people used on themselves. The medics saw to the worst affected people, who had been up front, their brains rattled to the point that they had become unconscious.

They cleared the rest of the room once everyone was back up and their heads at least screwed on right enough to move.

There was a dais in the middle of the room, its sides were made from roots that gathered up to support an altar of water above it. A set of boots rested on top of the water fountain.

The boots were their prize for clearing the first floor.

Roska used a healing potion by dripping it slowly into her ears. That allowed her to hear a rustling noise from the freshly opened doorway that led to the second level of the dungeon.

A creature moved through the new doorway, its large body too wide and too big to walk forward normally. It looked as if it were made entirely from soil but it had mouths and eyes covering it, moaning and letting out hissing noises at the same time.

It was like it had run into a firing line as everyone aimed and fired their repeaters.

The beast was too big to dodge. The bolts pierced through the beast or exploded next to it, tearing chunks out of it until it stopped moving and a tombstone appeared.

"Big but dumb as hell," Han Wu said as they all looked at the dirt creature.

"Organize a watch. The rest of you check your weapons and drink some water. Tend to the wounded," Erik ordered. The sergeants moved to him as Rugrat took over the lance corporals, organizing the wounded and the defense of the room.

Roska took out her repeater and started to clear the webbing off of it to get it functional again.

"The beasts up here are difficult to deal with but manageable. We'll recover here and then head to the second level," Erik said.

Roska and Niemm nodded.

"Any issues?" Erik asked.

"Good to go," Niemm said.

"Same here," Roska agreed.

Erik was about to say something else when Rugrat came over.

"Don't you think that these are a bit harder to deal with than just regular level thirty-twos?" Rugrat asked.

It took them a moment of thinking before Roska nodded.

"Yeah, it felt like they were almost as strong as us," Roska added.

"Check your Experience gain," Rugrat ordered.

They all did, looking at one another with surprise.

"These guys haven't died in a long time and have just been pumped with more Mana. When they die, do you feel like the Earth and Water Affinity Mana increases exponentially in the area?" Rugrat asked.

Roska had felt a slimy feeling like mud covering her but she had been in the midst of fighting and didn't pay much attention to it.

"The dungeon seems to be about three times the size now of what it was listed as being in the journal. So, the dungeon must have been putting that power into expanding as well as pumping it's creatures up. If I was a betting man, I'd think that the creatures on the lower levels are going to be stronger as well. If they're level fifty-four, then next level after that they might be level fifty-six." Rugrat's words hit them like a bucket of cold water. "I can already start to feel the purified Mana from the dungeon core rising up, while the impure Mana we released by killing these creatures is being drawn down. Whatever dungeon core is controlling this place, it's much stronger than the dungeon core in Vuzgal."

"Get everyone sorted out. We move out in ten. We'll head back to the surface to make sure our exit route is clear. Then, we'll come back down tomorrow and clear the second level. Slow and steady wins it," Erik commanded.

Roska checked on her people. Yang Zan already had everyone back on their feet, if a little worse for wear.

They all checked their gear. Erik grabbed the boots and then they headed for a large door framed by roots behind the water altar.

They found a corridor beyond. To the left, it led down a level; to the right, there was an elevator-like pad.

Rugrat inspected the pad for traps before everyone got on.

They shot upward, a section of ground opened, revealing the dazzling sky above and making them flinch from the light as water dropped down around them.

The elevator stopped suddenly. Looking around, they were about fifty meters away from standing in one of the streams that flowed out from the dungeon tree.

They stepped off the pad and the ground moved back together, covering it and preventing re-entry.

Morning had turned to midday. They had been down in the dungeon for a few hours.

"We'll head back to the Vuzgal castle today. Sergeants, collect the loot," Erik said.

Now that they confirmed that they could exit the first floor, tomorrow they would clear the first floor faster and move to explore the second floor.

They made it back to the castle with no problems. Erik and Rugrat traveled back to their room. Erik pulled off his body armor.

"We're making progress," he said as he made his armor stand up on the floor to air it out.

"Bit by bit. I'm going to check on the Vuzgal dungeon core and the Mana storing formation," Rugrat said as he dropped his gear on his bed.

"Alright. I'll check with Glosil and see how things are going," Erik said, using a clean spell on his armor and then himself.

He looked up seeing Rugrat with a towel, wearing his American flag short shorts and boots.

"Dude, you've been wearing that all day?" Erik asked.

"Yeah, pretty funky," Rugrat said, pushing back the sheet that covered a hole in the wall that led out to the hall where they'd set up sleeping quarters and a shower at the end of it.

"You can make him an officer, even a first sergeant, still can't get rid of the marine," Erik muttered as he pulled out some food and started eating. He pulled out his map and checked it, looking over the tree dungeon and adding new markers to it.

Chapter: Clearing the Second Floor

The special teams moved ahead into the second floor with a group of twenty from the Tiger Platoon waiting until the monsters on the first floor respawned. They had all increased their levels quickly. With the dungeon they could adapt to their new-found strength faster so that they were ready for battle at any time.

The second floor was filled with camouflaged creatures that blended into their surroundings. They didn't have a great fighting strength in a prolonged battle but their sneak attacks could easily be fatal if one wasn't careful.

It took them a full day just to reach the boss room of the second floor. They'd gone around every single pathway in the entire floor before they found the right way to get to the boss.

It was similar to the last room on the first floor. There was an altar at the back of the room and behind it there was a door. A small stream fell from the altar, where a pair of shining greaves lay on top. The walls were covered in tree roots, weaving over one another.

Erik and the others advanced into the large room, looking everywhere for danger.

Erik swept the room with his rifle. Rugrat moved out to the other side, sweeping the other side of the room as the rest of the teams moved in doing the same.

"Do you smell that?" Erik asked as he sniffed the air.

There was a faint dust in the room.

Someone started coughing as Erik's eyes narrowed.

"Spores! Everyone hit the deck! George, use your fire breath!" Erik shouted.

Everyone dropped to the ground as George expanded in size. His chest blew out and glowed brighter. He took in a powerful breath and he released it in a large flow of bright-red flames.

The whole room exploded. The pressure wave wreaked havoc on everyone's ears and sucked the air out of their lungs as it shot through the rest of the floor.

"Up!" Erik yelled but with the ringing in his ears, he couldn't even hear himself. He looked around in assessment. The spores had all been burned up, with some of the roots on fire.

A large creature rose from the floor, shaking itself as the flames attacked its body. It looked like an octopus but instead of flesh, it had limbs that looked like tree roots.

Erik fired his rifle at it, working the action as fast as possible. The rounds hit the creature, spraying green blood around the room behind it.

The creature ignored its wounds as its long, tentacle-like limbs shot into the ground. They burst back up from the ground under the Alvans, hitting people who were still recovering from the fire burst. Yawen was hit in the leg; while Deni took a hit to the chest and was sent flying.

Erik dodged a root tentacle before he punched it, using his Mana Detonation and covering his fist in poison. The limb was blown apart. The poison mist entered the creature's body through the remains of the tentacle, making it shiver, shake and slowed its reactions to a degree.

Erik glanced over to see Rugrat use a large Mana blade to cut the limbs around him. They all raised their rifles and fired. The creature was resilient, using its limbs to create a shield around it and sending others through the ground to attack or lash out.

Those who could still fight fired on the Tree-topus. It was in bad shape in short order. Modern weapons are devastating. Its body glowed green; its limbs and body became smaller but it healed itself and it became faster as it shrunk. It rushed Rugrat, who was doing the most damage.

Erik rushed forward to block whileRugrat moved to the side. The creature's thorn-covered limbs missed him by inches as he moved forward through the offending limbs. His rifle touched the creature's main body and he pulled the trigger.

The round forced the creature back before it exploded. Parts of it rained against the Mana barrier that appeared in front of Rugrat.

Erik looked over to Rugrat, who cycled the action on his rifle, chambering another round.

The door behind the altar opened, meaning that they had cleared this floor's boss room.

Erik and Rugrat used healing spells on themselves and started to organize the wounded and security details to watch for other dungeon creatures that might be brought up by the noise.

A few people were reloading their crossbows, a few were still holding their ears. Some who had been hit by the creature's attacks were rolling around on the ground and crying out or silently trying to deal with their pain as they frantically tried to heal themselves.

The medics set to work, organizing people by their wound severity and stabilizing those who were in the worst condition, getting IVs into their veins or needles into their bone marrow as quickly as possible. They stabilized each person and moved on, figuring out each person's separate issues.

Some people just got a few healing potions. Four had amputated limbs by the creature, its limbs had cut through their unarmored portions of their legs or arms. The tiny and numerous thorns along the roots had acted like a saw, tearing people apart.

Using potions and healing spells, the medics were able to put the worst of the wounded back together. Erik couldn't help but just wonder how many lives he would have been able to save back on Earth if he had the same abilities then as he did now.

Erik had some people do self-aid and assigned others to assist the medics.

Cut arteries and amputations needed concentrated healing potions or powerful healing spells. The person with the opened artery could get back into the fight rapidly and the person with the amputation would have to have their open wound sealed over and slowly stitched together with the missing limb.

Yao Meng had had his leg cut up badly, with an open artery in it and a busted shoulder. He had done some self-aid with a potion. Yang Zan was working to seal up the artery but Yao Meng would be good, just unable to move for now.

Han Wu, crying out through gritted teeth, had also been hit badly. He had done some self-aid as well and had a tourniquet around his leg, applying a second above the first tourniquet as it was still bleeding. Han Wu cried out again as he tightened it more, stopping the bleeding.

Erik stored his weapon and pulled on medical gloves as he moved over to the last patient who needed immediate care.

Setsuko had taken a nasty hit that had torn her glasses off and shredded her face. She had been panicking from the pain and not being able to breathe, hear or see.

Erik poured healing potion in her ears and used a hand to keep her down on the ground. "Setsuko! Get a hold of yourself!" Erik yelled. "Setsuko! Setsuko, can you hear me!"

She calmed down a bit as she could hear Erik, who poured the rest of the healing potion on her tattered face and used Focused Heal with his left hand, focusing on her neck and mouth.

Setsuko made a noise and then a wet coughing noise.

"Recovery position," Erik said. Deni, who was assisting Erik, put Setsuko on her side as she was coughing into the dirt, unable to breathe.

Erik pulled out a tube and a breathing bag.

"We've got you, Setsuko; don't worry about it." Erik slapped on Iodine Touch. It was modified Wraith's Touch, numbing and cleaning the area it was applied to, turning it yellow. He took out a clean scalpel and held her with Deni's help, quickly opening a hole in her neck and inserting the tubing.

Setsuko flailed, not knowing what was going on.

"Storbon!" Erik yelled, seeing that he was close. "Hold her down!" He applied his fingers to Setsuko's neck, checking her vitals.

"I've got diagnostics—Deni, you get an IV in her." Erik pulled off Setsuko's armor vest and tossed it to the side.

He used Simple Organic Scan to check her for any other hidden wounds. Deni got the IV in and fed Setsuko Health and Stamina potions.

"Low blood pressure, high heart rate," Erik observed. Deni was pouring a healing potion on Setsuko's face directly.

From her eyes down, she was a wreck. Erik didn't want to think what would have happened if she wasn't wearing her helmet. Its straps had been sawn apart, the helmet falling off some distance away.

Erik took out the painkiller potion he called Ket and injected it into the IV tubing before storing it away.

Setsuko stopped freaking out as Erik sat back. Deni was using healing spells and healing potions on Setsuko's face, rebuilding it.

"It's okay, Setsuko. It's okay. You're going to be fine." Storbon kept her pinned to the ground so she couldn't interfere with Erik or Deni's actions.

Erik kept checking on her condition but she was good now; she had plenty of Stamina and the healing potions were working well. He focused on repairing her skull surrounding her brain and healing her brain, which was showing signs of swelling. Deni focused on healing her upper airways and neck.

Erik dosed her up on more painkillers. There wasn't enough space for them to numb the connecting nerves with Wraith's Touch, so they could only speed up the healing process so that she didn't have to suffer quite as long.

Erik poured in his own healing spell as her healing accelerated.

Setsuko was bucking but with the tracheotomy she wasn't able to make a noise other than raspy breathing, since the air wasn't passing her vocal cords.

Erik didn't want to force her into unconsciousness; they didn't know what condition her brain might be in and she had lost a lot of blood.

Erik scanned constantly to see what the condition of her brain was.

"Setsuko, we're moving to somewhere more secure." Erik looked into her eyes. He pulled out a stretcher and put it beside Setsuko.

"Roll her on her side," Erik ordered. They did so and he slid the stretcher under. "Roll back."

She was on top of the stretcher as Erik used a carabiner to attach the IV potion bags to his chest.

"Storbon, you take the front; I'll take the rear. Rugrat, we're good to go!" Erik shouted after Deni had secured Setsuko to the litter.

Rugrat had organized everyone else in the meantime. "Medics and patients in the middle; security front and rear!" Rugrat hollered. People moved to their positions, creating a battle ready formation.

"Three, two, one!" Erik and Storbon lifted Setsuko. Deni had applied some Wraith's Touch to Setsuko's face. Enough of it had been rebuilt enough for her to use the numbing agent.

Erik used his thumb to touch Setsuko's shoulder, to keep scanning her vitals to see if anything changed while in transit.

Setsuko kept on breathing through the tube hanging out of her neck.

"Move out!" Rugrat ordered, leading them. The boss creature's body and the greaves had been stored away.

They headed out of the room and went straight for the platform that led to the surface. They all rose up together on the platform, finding the sun giving off fading rays of light. Rugrat sent a message to Glosil on their current situation as Erik worked on the various wounded.

By the time they reached the gate to Vuzgal, Yao Meng, who'd had his leg cut up and his shoulder smashed from hitting a wall, was able to walk on his own power. Deni had been controlling and checking on Setsuko the entire trip. The next thing they had to repair was the damage from her eyes to her jaw; it was all superficial damage, thankfully. Deni packed the wounds with bandages to stop the bleeding.

They got back to the castle carrying Han Wu, who had regrown a stub of a leg but was exhausted, and Setsuko, who still required heavy healing, into the medical wing that they had created.

Erik checked her once more. Her breathing was good. The brain swelling he worried about hadn't appeared and her blood pressure and heart rate were normalizing. He took out a syringe, adding a potion to the IV that was still attached.

The tension in Setsuko's body faded as she passed out.

"Okay, we're going to focus on repairing any remaining damage." Erik said as he looked to the other medics with him. He assigned them different areas to focus on and they started, rebuilding Setsuko's face.

Erik removed the tube from the tracheotomy and healed up the damage to her neck and once again used his Simple Organic Scan to make sure that there were no other issues that he had missed.

He checked on Han Wu afterwards.

"Will she be okay?" Han Wu asked.

"Setsuko will be fine." Erik responded. He wasn't sure what kind of mental state she would be in after all of this, though. The Ten Realms were amazing but Erik hadn't figured out how to magically heal psychological wounds yet.

Han Wu gave a short nod, as if understanding Erik's unsaid words.

Erik and the other medics then reviewed everyone who had come back from the second floor. The spores had gotten into most of their systems. With their Body Cultivations, it hadn't affected them yet but if the spores mutated it could go bad quickly.

The spore infections was all solved with some quick heals and they were sent on their way. The spores used hosts as food and a large enough infection would have eaten them from the inside out.

"Fucking Ten Realms," Erik cursed as he wiped his face, tired as hell. He checked the rest of the medical wing before he headed out to the debriefing.

Rugrat, Glosil, Yui, Choi, Roska and Niemm were there already.

"Setsuko's wounds are healed—keep a watch on her. Han Wu's tourniquets were released and his limb is regrowing. We'll keep him till he's all good but shouldn't be long with how ad-

vanced his Body Cultivation and levels are. The dungeon team
has been cleared of spores. We will be doing spot checks on those
who came in contact with the dungeon team over the next couple of days to see if any spores became airborne and infected
others," Erik summarized as he entered the room. The tension
seemed to snap and everyone took a breath.

"All right, the first floor is cleared. What squad will be going
in next?" Erik asked.

"Yes." Glosil sat upright. "Tiger Platoon's first section."

"Good. We'll start a rotation, the day after tomorrow. Get
them used to their new strenght, how did the loot recovery go?"

"Well, we have put more Mana cornerstones to the side. The
Mana cornerstones that are located at the Mana gathering formation plates are already showing signs of growth. We were only
able to open a few vaults and other secured storage areas in the
capital today—it had too many traps. I'd rather do it slow than
get people hurt." Glosil took out an inventory of items.

Rugrat took it and passed it to Erik.

"Good call. Tomorrow, Special Teams One and Two will
clear the second floor. We've thankfully got a map on most of
the floor now, so it should be much faster. Then, we will head to
the third floor and scout it—if possible, push into it a little," Erik
said.

Niemm moved in his seat.

"Issue, Sergeant?" Erik asked.

"Sir, we took bad casualties," Niemm offered.

"We took casualties but we were lucky—no one was left with
permanent damage. Everyone has their own way to deal with
that kind of trauma. We lost people taking this capital. We don't
know how long we'll have peace. We need to be ready to fight.
We can't just go home because it is getting a little hard," Erik explained.

"I was wrong, sir," Niemm said as he saluted, still slightly uneasy.

Erik nodded, letting it go and looking to the rest of the room. "Tomorrow night, we'll have the memorial service for our fallen." His said as his voice softened.

The others in the room refrained from making eye contact, each of them seeing and remembering something that only they knew.

Erik left the meeting and checked on his notifications.

==========

Skill: Healer

==========

Level: 64 (Journeyman)

==========

You have become familiar with the body and the arts of repairing it. Healing spells now cost 5% less Mana and Stamina.

==========

==========

16,026,992/16,500,000 EXP till you reach Level 51

==========

It had been months since he had seen an increase in his healing skill. He had a bitter feeling looking at it. For his healing skill to increase, someone needed to be injured.

Chapter: Talking Monster

Setsuko looked up at the unfamiliar ceiling. Thoughts and memories rushed back as she grabbed at her neck, finding nothing but healed skin. She rubbed her face, which felt fine. She pulled out a mirror from her storage ring and she looked back at herself. There were no signs of any damage. She turned to the side, seeing where fresh skin met tanned skin.

She touched the faint line around her face with shaking hands.

"You're awake." One of the medics came over. "Are you in pain anywhere?" he asked gently.

Setsuko took a few seconds, trying to talk, and coughing instead. She pulled out some water and drank, her mouth and throat were dry and rough. "I feel fine," she warbled, not really believing her own words.

"Tough damn bastard," Han Wu said from where he was lying down. He had been napping but hearing Setsuko, he had woken up. His leg was still regrowing and he had an IV in his arm to accelerate the process.

Setsuko looked at his leg but he waved it away, sitting upright.

"What happened?" Setsuko stuttered, her voice still rough.

"You were hit in the boss room. Erik and Deni stabilized you and brought you back here. Then they knocked you out and healed the remaining damage," Han Wu said.

His words were flippant but Setsuko knew that the process must have been anything but.

"Where is everyone?" Setsuko asked.

"They're back at the dungeon, clearing out the second floor and then heading to the third floor. The rest are still clearing the city," Han Wu said.

Setsuko nodded.

"How are you?" Han Wu asked after a few minutes, his voice concerned instead of being filled with his normal joking tone.

Setsuko paused, trying to assess herself. She remembered one of the last lessons that they had gone through in their training. It hadn't been official and had more of a relaxed air. Erik and Rugrat sat with them, telling them that they would change through war. They told of how their mental processes might change—they might get angrier or depressed. Those who had served in the military, that had been in battle, or lost people to conflicts before, understood their words. Setsuko had understood it in theory before but now, they'd taken casualties and the reality hit home for her. The pain, the feeling of helplessness; it was vivid—images, emotions, and feelings that she wouldn't be able to leave behind.

She knew that these feelings would be a part of her now until the day she died. She didn't brush Han Wu off but sat there, thinking. The medic left them, his job done.

"I don't think that I will be the same but I won't quit or leave the military," Setsuko said firmly. She had gotten hurt but her brothers and sisters had banded together to help her, to save her life. She couldn't dwell on it for too long. She had nearly died, yes, but only nearly. She wasn't dead yet and she had people relying on her.

She looked into Han Wu's eyes.

"You're one tough mother." Han Wu laughed.

Setsuko laughed as well, touched by the care that Han Wu showed. The Alvan army wasn't just a job for her anymore; it was a calling. Knowing that she was a soldier of the Alvan army was a powerful feeling; it gripped her guts. It made her see everyone in a different light: There were those who were her people, who could understand what she had been through and relate, and then those who would never be able to truly understand.

***

Erik and Rugrat were having a little meeting before the second floor boss room. They had gone through the first floor, taking the most direct route, and then headed to the second floor. They searched the rest of the floor, only running into a few new beasts as they uncovered the entire floor.

"Alright, Roska, your team is up first. Use Detect Life. Find the fucker and we'll move in," Erik said.

Roska nodded as she moved to the doorway leading into the boss room. She used a Detect Life spell and headed into the room.

The rest of the group flowed into the room behind her.

Roska opened fire with a crossbow as soon as she found the Tree-topus. Her Fire-enchanted and poisoned bolts struck the creature, making it cry out and its limbs collapse. The powerful paralytic on the bolts slowed it. A half dozen other bolts hit it as it started to crawl away, trying to use its tentacles. Immobilized by the poison and burning from the enchantment, it wasn't long before a tombstone appeared above its head.

Everyone felt a little more relaxed as the door to the third floor opened.

Erik and Rugrat looked at each other.

They needed that win. Without it some of their people might have started having doubts. It was like when someone was in a car crash; they needed to get behind the wheel again or else risk developing a phobia.

For combat, that meant that they needed to get the person back into battle or else they could change in a negative way that put their life or the life of their fellow soldiers in danger.

"Check your gear. Check on one another and take a cure poison potion so the spores don't affect you. We'll be heading to the third floor next!" Rugrat yelled.

Everyone reloaded their weapons and checked one another, reloading their magazines.

"Sergeants, on me," Erik said.

Roska and Niemm jogged over.

"We're heading into the third floor, have the marksmen up front. Their bullet rounds can hit harder and we might be up against creatures that could be up to sixty. We need to play it safe here. We'll advance slowly but surely, clearing each room completely, recovering and then moving to the next if we can. In the first couple of rooms, I want to set a casualty collection point and defenses. If we run into something we can't deal with right away, we need to back up to the defensive point. We can retreat to the surface from there or we can focus our firepower and use the defenses to stall whatever creatures we run into," Erik said.

"If we run into powerful creatures on entry, Erik, George and I will look to block. If that happens, everyone moves to supporting and buffing spells on us and curses and poison on the creatures, with everyone backing up into the last cleared room," Rugrat said.

This was where military operations from Earth met the realities of the Ten Realms. On Earth, everyone was essentially equal. They might have better protection gear and weapons but their basic strength and speed was at least similar. With levels in the Ten Realms, that changed. If your enemy had a greater strength or speed than you, they might be able to dodge weapons fire. Or in a close quarters fight, one punch might enough to kill their opponent. It was this kind of overwhelming power that necessitated changed tactics.

They had gone over these tactics before but they wanted to make sure that they were ready. They hadn't needed to use the more drastic tactics on the first two floors.

Briefing done, they went back to their tasks. The greaves from the altar went into Rugrat's storage ring. The items so far were all of the Apprentice level because they were clearing the dungeon with so many people. Erik was interested to see what kind of items the group that came behind them might get with just their ten-person team.

Erik took the lead as they headed down to the third floor.

He got to the bottom of the stairs. There were two doorways ahead of him that led into dark corridors.

A roar sounded out, followed by two others. The first was from right in front of Erik. He moved forward and fired his rifle at a massive minotaur as it charged from the doorway on the right with twin axes in its hands.

"George, Rugrat!" Erik called out. It looked as though they would need to use their trump card already. Erik could feel that the minotaur in front was level fifty-eight.

Erik rushed forward to give more room to the people behind him. The minotaur was slowing as poisoned rounds and bolts affected it.

Erik fired at its feet. The minotaur lost his footing and slammed into the ground.

George jumped from the stairs and glided in the air across the room, breathing fire on the corridor through the doorway to the right, catching the two other minotaurs and setting their fur on fire.

Rugrat was moving and shooting. His rifle punched holes in the minotaurs but they were tough bastards. Their bodies regenerated even with the attacks still plucking into their flesh.

One minotaur slammed its axe into the ground. A green magical circle appeared around the axe and wooden spears shot out of the ground, aimed at George.

George burned them with an indignant roar of fire and lunged to tackle his attacker. His front claws tore bloody stripes into the minotaur as Rugrat targeted the other one, hitting it as it tried to slash George.

The round tossed the minotaur back and slammed it into the wall. Rugrat put two more rounds into its chest and one into its head. It stopped moving after it slumped to the floor.

Erik treated his target like a punching bag. With his new increases in speed, strength and Stamina, and with his stamina cost decreased by his armor, he'd turned into a boxing monster. Each punch was like a sledgehammer raining down on the minotaur.

Erik used One Finger Beats Fist when a fist flew unimpeded at his opponents head, piercing through the creature's skull and into its brain. A red mist appeared around Erik's gloves as they drank greedily and a tombstone rose over the minotaur.

"Defenses!" Erik called out. He pulled out his rifle, pulling the magazine to check his ammunition and slammed it back into place.

George had destroyed his opponent and was covered in blood, not caring for his appearance. With both of his ears raised he looked down the corridor that the minotaurs had come from now that the minotaurs were dead.

Special Team One covered Special Team Two, who pulled out large barriers from their storage rings and placed them on the ground and used fuse spells to create a barricade.

A scratching noise came from the corridor opposite the one the minotaurs had come through.

George took a deep breath and sent fireballs down the corridor, illuminating the rats as big as motorcycles and spiders as big as horses.

"Fuck me," Rugrat muttered as he pulled out a formation plate and tossed it down at the left entrance.

Erik pulled out gas grenades and tossed them into the left corridor. They were packed with poison powder and an air-type formation to disperse the poison all over the place.

"Formation plates!" Niemm called out. Special Team One pulled out their plates and put them on the ground.

"Roska?!" Erik yelled.

"All good to go here!" Roska yelped back.

"All right, everyone behind the defenses!" Erik ordered.

Everyone moved behind the simple but tough barricades, and looked through the slits at the approaching chittering horde.

As the horde moved forward, heavy repeaters and rifles opened up on the corridor, landing Fire shots and Explosive Shots in the left passageway, turning it into a bloodbath. Everyone felt the flow of Ten Realms' Experience flowing into their bodies.

Four heavy repeaters continued covering the corridor. As one paused to reload, another would start firing, reducing the creatures' numbers. The rats ran into the poison cloud and even the spiders that were resistant to poisons were affected as they rappeled down to the floor to get to the doorway. The forward formations came to life. Rugrat had placed down the lightning formation near the doorway, which zapped the rats and spiders, reducing them to nothing but smoking husks.

After just a few minutes none were left alive.

"Cease fire!" Rugrat called out.

Erik and Rugrat looked at each other.

"Advance or try to pull them to us?" Erik asked.

"Bring them to us. We've got some summoning scrolls and Yawen learned some summoning from Matt," Rugrat said.

"Yawen!" Erik called out.

A few minutes later, an ostrich-like creature shot off through the corridors. It went where the spiders and rats had come from. That corridor led to a dead end, with nothing else in it.

The ostrich ran back and then went down the other corridor. It was linked to Yawen, so his map increased in detail, revealing the dungeon beyond.

The summon reached a new room filled with creatures and ran back. These creatures were forest golems. They were large creatures made of trees and dirt.

Erik felt them coming before he saw them. Their large bodies caused the entire dungeon floor to shake. The three golems had to run in a line as they barely fit through the corridors.

Yawen dismissed his summon as it came into range.

"Light them up!" Rugrat shouted and shot, hitting the first forest golem's head. The dirt and tree parts were blasted apart but it quickly started to reform from its remaining mass. A golem was based around a monster core; one needed to disconnect the monster core or exhaust the Mana of the golem in order to stop it.

The heavy repeaters and sharpshooters struck the creature following Rugrat's shot. With that much firepower, it wasn't long until they saw its monster core crack.

The golem fell to the ground, collapsing in a wave of rotting tree parts and dirt as the next one stepped on its fallen sibling and continued charging forward. The special teams adjusted their aim and kept firing.

The second fell and the third struck the lightning formation, dropping to the ground as it smoked.

Rounds poured down on it until a tombstone appeared.

"Cease fire!" Niemm called out.

Everyone paused as they looked at the three dead juggernauts.

A formation flashed as a part of the ceiling disappeared. A worm-like creature fell through the ceiling. The formation lashed out more, breaking the dirt ceiling and dropping the stunned worms.

Erik fired his weapon as they fell. "Fire!" Erik yelled.

The defensive formations lit up as twenty or so worms appeared from the roof, about half the size of a human adult and with powerful serrated teeth. They were nasty-looking creatures but their defenses were weak.

The shooting died down as more tombstones appeared.

There was a sound of rushing water. Erik turned his head to the right corridor. It sounded as if it were getting closer.

"Yawen, send out your summon. What is that noise?" Erik asked.

Yawen's summon ran out but was cut down suddenly.

Blue light appeared in the corridor followed by calming sounds. They sounded like the sounds of the sea. It was a pleasant sound that relieved everyone's tension made them feel better. The soldiers felt that it would be a fine place to take a nap; it was rather warm, like a good summer day, perfect for sleeping outside.

Suddenly, a powerful force swept through their minds, making their bodies tremble and tighten their relaxed grips on their weapons.

"You think that you can win with illusion spells?" Rugrat let out a laugh. The area around him had fallen into his domain, reducing the effectiveness of the spell. He aimed and fired at the approaching blue lights.

A horrible noise came from the hall as the new enemy revealed themselves. They looked like a form of water fae. They floated through the air with water waves appearing underneath them. Their eyes were like a fish's and their teeth like sharks. They had humanoid appearances and fins across their bodies with white, grey and blue scales that shone in the minimal light. They raised their tridents with a war cry.

Everyone opened fire without having to be told a single thing.

The creatures wove their hands, walls of water appearing and neutralizing the Explosive Shots and Fire rounds.

They sent out water spears that shot through the corridor, colliding with the defensive formations that visibly dimmed under the powerful impacts. The fae rushed to get closer. There had to be a half dozen of them in the hallway.

"Change to lightning rounds!" Rugrat shouted as he popped out his magazine and pulled out another with a lightning bolt painted on its side.

He fired a lightning enhanced round as the first fae ran into the lightning formation. The formation sent a jolt of lightning through its body. As the fae shook, screaming through its locked-up muscles, the lightning round hit its defenseless body. The blast of additional electricity caused it to fall from the sky. Steam rose from it as a tombstone appeared. The other face continued attacking, destroying the first formation in their way. Some of the other Alvan's started firing their recently equipped lightning rounds. The main heavy repeaters were taking longer to switch.

Mages fired spells and George let out a howl of fire breath. The fae covered themselves in defensive water spheres and shot out water spears in retaliation by waving their tridents that glowed blue with power.

Storbon tossed grenades under the creatures and they detonated, creating a lightning storm around the creatures.

The water fae fought through three formations before they were destroyed.

Everyone looked around and reloaded as the corridor lit up with blue light once again.

⁎⁎⁎

There were two more waves of creatures: another group of the water spirits and four minotaurs. By the end, the soldiers' formations were all used up and it came to close-quarters combat, with Erik and George each holding back a minotaur. With Erik's blood stacks on his gloves, he was able to fight one on one with the minotaur without needing his overclock ability on his breastplate.

It was a slow battle. He released poison into the minotaur's wounds and slowed it to the point that he could land the final blow.

The Alvan dungeoneers regrouped, recharged their formations and repaired or replaced their barricades.

Yawen's summon was sent out once again to scout. It passed through a number of rooms before it finally reached the boss room.

A large toad-like creature, looked around the room the scout was currently viewing. "Meat, not tasty," the mouth said as it eyed the summoned creature.

"So, a talking creature," Rugrat said as they held a meeting to discuss the floor boss.

"Let's go and check it out. We'll have booby traps if we need to retreat to slow it down. We can fight back here or go back to the surface if we can't handle it," Erik said.

They were all tired but they had come so far. As long as they took their time and were careful, they could possibly deal with the floor boss.

So they headed through the dungeon, preparing formations and mines, marking them with small flags. They put down defenses and obstacles that would be easy for them to pass but would stall anything following them.

The preparations took them a few hours before Erik, Rugrat and George stood in front of the boss room. Being the strongest, they could gauge how strong the boss was and call in reinforcements or retreat as necessary. If they needed to run, having more people with them could lead to chaos.

Erik moved up to the door that the summon had previously broken through.

Rugrat squeezed his arm when he was ready.

Erik moved in through the doorway and saw the toad sitting in a muddy pool of water, the room was shaped like a hexagon, with them coming through two intersecting lines, an altar and a door behind the toad creature.

"Mmmm, tasty metal! Ugh, not tasty meat underneath!" The toad harrumphed as his eyes opened and it licked its lips, studying Erik and Rugrat.

"Can you understand me?!" Erik yelled.

"Yes! Oh, other people to talk to! But they have metal. Do I talk or do I eat?" The toad muttered as its head tilted back and forth.

"Rugrat, ingot," Erik said.

Rugrat shot him a look but didn't say anything, taking out an iron ingot and tossing it towards the toad.

The beast jumped on the ingot, putting it into its mouth to chew on it.

"Good adventurers, treat Old Xern to nice meal. Ah, it has been so long since I've had metal! Blood still has the foul taste of meat on it!" Old Xern crooned in delight.

"I'm Erik. This is Rugrat and that's George. We don't want to fight if we don't have to," Erik said.

"Don't want to fight—are they trying to get past? Well, if they have more tasty metal, would it be easier to get than have to touch nasty meat?" The creature mumbled to itself.

"Two tasty metals each!" it declared proudly.

Erik looked to Rugrat. He sighed and pulled out five more iron ingots. It was only the most basic iron, so it barely cost Rugrat anything.

The toad called Old Xern hurriedly took the metal and scurried back to a corner, as if they might try to take back his 'snacks'.

"Take the dirty armor as well. It looks tasty but only hurts Old Xern," Old Xern complained.

He looked to the door that wasn't opening.

"Open door! They pass floor dungeon!" He commanded. The door started to open, slowly, as if complaining. "Other Xern will be beyond. They not nice like Old Xern. They tricky tricksters who don't mind meat in their metal. Beasts! Monsters! Uncultured!"

"Could you tell us more about the next floor?" Erik asked and shot a look to Rugrat, who pulled out an iron ingot, reluctantly.

"Yes, yes! Old Xern can for three clean precious snacks!"

Rugrat coughed up the iron ingots. Old Xern stored them away with a pleased expression.

"Much tastier than armor with all the weird things in them and without crunch. Old Xern did well in trade. Should accept more snacks for allowing people through!"

"The next floor?" Erik asked, motioning a hand towards the open door.

"Ah, it is a floor of Xern like me. All of them are not as strong as me but they sneaky tricksters. They have mind of the young. They burrow through ground, distract with one and attack with many." Old Xern nodded his head repeatedly.

Erik and Rugrat became wary of their surroundings. George was alert sniffing the air before he settled down again and continued staring at Old Xern.

"That floor is smaller than this one and doesn't have metal. This one has more metal and the other creatures bring me my tribute. There is a pretty miss down there but she is lonely and one of the higher creatures. She thinks but can't talk like Old Xern—terrible, terrible. She also metal eater. We talk but she like talking to lower creatures." Old Xern looked a bit sad before he rebounded.

"If you can pass the young Xern, then you can reach Metal Devourer Miss! She doesn't like meat but also not like visitors. I will give you introduction!"

The Xern slammed his foot against the floor, sending water everywhere as he smacked out a few times. There was nothing for some time as Old Xern chewed on his new metal.

A roar came through the open doorway that shook the room.

Old Xern put down his metal. "Moody miss!" He smacked his foot against the ground. Roars of the hidden boss of the fourth floor and Old Xern went back and forth.

"She not had metal in long time. Young Xern stole from her. She grumpy I have some. Make sure to give her a snack or else she might not mind the taste of meat." Old Xern went back to chewing metal.

"We might have to kill other Xern," Erik warned.

"Things die and they are bad young ones," Old Xern said.

"We will come back tomorrow with more metal snacks and to meet with Metal Devourer Miss." .

"Good, good!" Old Xern said, his mouth filled with metal burrs as he crunched on another metal ingot.

Erik and Rugrat backed up and were about to leave Old Xern.

"Take armor too!" the Xern shouted.

Erik and Rugrat shared a look. Erik went to the altar and grabbed the breastplate and then headed back. They left the room Old Xern was in, as he was humming happily to himself. They collected their people and previously placed traps, heading back to the second floor exit and leaving the dungeon.

"The beasts of the third floor should be strong enough to increase our level with. Once everyone is level forty-six, then we can head to the fourth floor." Erik said to Rugrat.

They fell silent as they walked back toward Vuzgal with the rest of the special teams, looking around them and scanning the valley for danger.

"Tonight is the remembrance ceremony," Erik said.

"Yeah," Rugrat said in a flat voice, holding the weight of a lifetime as a marine.

Neither of them said anything, organizing their emotions and bracing for what lay in front of them.

***

They learned of Setsuko's recovery on their return and went to go and see her. Erik and Rugrat went to the command center where Glosil was working on schedules and maps.

"Eyo," Erik said.

"Cap," Glosil nodded as he put another marker on the large wall map that showed Vuzgal.

"Looking good," Erik said walking up to the map.

"There anyone over at the crafting workshops?" Rugrat asked.

"Yeah," Glosil grabbed a clipboard that was hanging from string. "Staff Sergeant Han is over there."

"I'm going to head over. Gonna work on those mortars and grenade launcher designs," Rugrat said.

"Have fun," Erik said as Rugrat walked out of the room.

"How are things?" Erik asked as he put his helmet on the table and sat down, pushing his thumbs under his vest, pushing it out.

"We cleared this section here, got undead breaking houses and fixing up the castle walls. I was wondering if you could use the dungeon core to open up holes underneath the castle for waste water. The sewage system here is messed up, we could dig holes but if we get a decent water system going that would help. Especially if we want to stay here," Glosil looked at Erik.

"Yeah we can do that. We'll need to make pipes, see if you can get some of the crafters to help the undead make pipes that won't break. Make them big so they can take a lot of volume. See if we got anyone who does blueprint work. The crafting facilities are busted up but they still work, we can upgrade them later. We should focus on leveling up, gathering all the loot and finishing the totem."

Glosil looked at the map with his eyes moving back and forth. "I think it'll take us another week, maybe nine days, to get all of the easy loot. Then picking locks, breaking traps and such, not sure how long that will take but all of the nobles, big trading houses and crafters have some kind of locked or trapped storage."

"We've got plenty to keep us busy. Once we've secured the dungeon then I'm hoping to increase the range of the scouted area to the west. We know that there are the Chaotic Lands out there, we don't need any uninvited guests," Erik got up with a sigh and grabbed his helmet, feeling all the aches of his body. He used a healing spell on himself, making it a bit easier to bear but most of it was just pure fatigue.

"I'm going to get some sleep, send a runner if you need me," Erik said.

"Will do," Glosil said.

Erik headed out of the command center and to his room, dumping his armor and boots.

He looked over his notifications as he lay down to get some shut-eye.

==========

You have reached Level 51

==========

When you sleep next, you will be able to increase your attributes by: 5 points.

==========

==========

164,581/20,200,000 EXP till you reach Level 52

==========

Erik's eyes closed as another screen appeared.

==========

You have 5 attribute points to use.

==========

He couldn't feel excited and mechanically placed his attribute points: two into his Mana pool, one into Stamina regeneration, two into Agility.

His character sheet appeared.

==========

Name: Erik West

==========

Level: 51

==========

Race: Human

==========

Titles:

From the Grave II

Mana Emperor

Dungeon Master II

Reverse Alchemist

Poison Body

Fire Body

==========

Strength: (Base 36) +41

==========

770

==========

Agility: (Base 29) +65

==========

517

==========

Stamina: (Base 39) +19

==========

870

==========

Mana: (Base 8) +68

==========

760

==========

Mana Regeneration (Base 10) +55

==========

33. 50/s

==========

Stamina Regeneration: (Base 41) +54

20. 00/s

==========

I have reached Body Like Iron but I still have Body Like Earth iron to reach. The soul grounded. He repeated the mantra that he had first heard about Body Cultivation from Egbert. Now he finally knew what it meant.

I need to find a place that is heavy in Earth-concentrated Mana. A place of a natural phenomenon or variant Mana stones that are filled with Earth-attribute Mana. I need to suffer under the crushing gravitational pressure that comes with high Earth areas, letting it crush my body. I'll need to hold myself together, to heal myself and be crushed until I can deal with high gravity or rapid gravity changes. The Fourth Realm is a place of phenomena and Mana chaos that go against the laws of nature. If I can find a place that can help me in tempering my body, then I can increase my Strength again.

Chapter: Dungeon Grind

The next day was filled with bleak skies. The mist that had been thinning the last couple of days seemed to return, as if to fit the current mood of the army. Just a quarter of the capital had been searched.

Han Wu and Setsuko returned to the special teams; a new section of the army was pulled from their recovery operations so they could go into the dungeon as well.

The special teams moved through to the third floor, using the monsters there to increase their levels. They would leave after clearing it. The newly spawned creatures' levels had dropped back to normal and they weren't as strong. Once the teams cleared the floor, they passed Old Xern some metals and headed out to the surface. They started the dungeon again, once again reaching the third floor and grinding out more kills against the beasts on the floor.

They cycled the third floor three times, with nearly everyone increasing their base levels by one.

After talking with Old Xern, they learned he truly didn't mind other creatures of his race dying. He was a beast, after all, and death was normal cycle of nature.

What was shocking was Old Xern's level. George reported that he was level sixty-three, which made them exceedingly wary of the Xerns of the next level, even as Old Xern maintained that they were nothing but weak young ones.

They took their time to create a plan to clear out the fourth floor using Old Xern's intel.

"So the Xerns' weakness is their love of metal. They've been deprived of it for centuries. Old Xern hates the taste of meat so now we meet him while wearing leathers instead of metal.

Though these other Xern might not have the same hang-ups he does.

"So, we use some metal to lure the Xern and we do what we did on the third floor; we set up defenses and lay into them. Their vulnerability is to fire. We lace the area with poison, formations, and just bring them right into the trap," Erik schemed.

"What if they don't go for the metal?" Rugrat asked.

"Then we will retreat out of the dungeon. I think that they will go for the metal but we need to watch out. They're smart and sneaky creatures. Old Xern has talked about how they will talk and entice someone close, with one Xern talking as bait, and then the other Xern will appear from the ground and ambush the person the first Xern is talking to," Erik said.

"There are notes from the emperor talking about the Xern. Seems that he wasn't the biggest fan of them," Rugrat added.

They went over how they would place the barriers in the room beyond. They'd looked into it but they hadn't seen anything inside the first room of the fourth floor. With the Xern being able to move through the ground as if it were water, they didn't trust the emptiness.

***

Rugrat passed Old Xern his snacks as the two teams moved through the room.

Old Xern couldn't hide his excitement, getting two iron ingots for every single person who passed him.

The soldiers reached the stairs down to the next floor.

"There are creatures hiding underneath the ground," Roska reported, having used a Detect Life scroll.

"Plan three," Erik confirmed.

The others all nodded. They had rehearsed it all night and this morning to make sure that they could carry out any plan they chose rapidly.

Rugrat held an iron ingot in his hand. He threw it hard to the other side of the room.

The ground exploded as Xern, similar to but smaller than Old Xern, jumped out of the ground to try and get the iron ingot.

"Oi!"

"It's mine!"

"Metal!"

"Tasty treats!"

They went wild. Six Xern scrambled over one another, biting, scratching or sending Water and Earth attacks at one another.

"Floor clear!" Roska reported. Her only job—along with Simms, Xi, and Imani—was to sense into the floor to make sure that they weren't ambushed from underground.

The front rows dropped to the floor and threw down barricades. Storbon, Deni, Yuli, and Setsuko put up defenses as Erik, Rugrat, Niemm, Han Wu, and Gong Jin threw grenades forwards at the Xern's scrum. The others all opened fire with their weapons.

The Xern were packed in close together. Seeing the grenades were made of metal, they stuffed them into their various faces.

Explosions went off inside stomachs. Three died from the explosives, another two were badly wounded, and the last had taken a bite of the first metal ingot thrown by Rugrat.

"Ah, I hate reincarnating," he complained as rounds and arrows focused on him, killing him in seconds.

People watched the distance as more watched the earth beneath them. The defenses were up and heavy repeaters and bolt action rifles were prepared for threats.

Rugrat threw out formation plates, circling the half-chewed iron ingot.

The ground started to shake as a Xern jumped up to get the ingot, only to be stunned by the formations and attacked by the defenders.

They kept on complaining as they were shocked, shot and blown apart, merely annoyed by the prospect of death.

It was hectic, with dozens of them appearing. A few tried to sneak around and attack them from the rear but Roska and her squad dealt with them before they could threaten the group.

It was systematic and cold slaughter. There were moments of panic but they were the special teams, the best of Alva's fighting forces. They quickly recovered and adapted.

It took some time before the soldiers ceased fire. The room was a mess. Formation plates were broken. Bolts and bullet holes could be seen all over the place. Smoke rose and Xern corpses with tombstones covered the ground.

An annoyed but resigned deep and feminine roar came from further within the dungeon. Erik and Rugrat knew this roar. It was from the Metal Devourer Miss that Old Xern had talked about.

"Yawen, send out your summon," Erik said.

Yawen's summoned beast went out, scouting the entirety of the dungeon, and found nothing left. It entered the floor boss room, seeing a deep pool of water with an altar in the middle of it. A head rose out of the water. The skin of the beast was composed of brown scales with blue lines carved into them that formed symbols that traced down the sides of her head. Her head was large, nearly a meter in size with beady and deep blue eyes that were difficult to make out in the darkness of the cavernous boss room.

It looked at the summoned creature before letting out a snort and lowering itself back into the water.

"Well, shall we go and pay a visit?" Erik asked Rugrat.

"Sure," Rugrat said. "All right, same as we did with the third floor!"

Even with Old Xern's words, they made sure to add in a number of traps behind them.

Erik, Rugrat, and George went to the fourth floor boss room.

A brown, white and blue scaled dragon head rose lazily from the waters. She looked at Erik, Rugrat, and then George. Her eyes thinned as she hissed at George.

George grew to his full size as he growled back. Her head was a size and a half larger than George's when he was at his full size

She let out a series of hisses.

George looked confused with his head to the side and then let out a few yaps back.

The two of them looked at each other, the atmosphere tense as they seemed to be communicating with each other.

"What is going on, Rugrat?" Erik asked under his breath.

"She can't speak human tongues but she can speak the beast language, same as George. Seems he's arguing about us and she's making fun of him being contracted to me," Rugrat replied as he realized what she had said about George's tiny human.

"Oi! It's harder to level up for a human! Plus he gets all the monster cores and meat from the bits that aren't good!"

George looked annoyed by Rugrat's words as the dragon-like head laughed at Rugrat.

The two beasts got into an argument. It looked as if they were trying to outdo one another.

"What is she, some kind of water serpent?" Erik asked.

"Not like one back on Earth. Look at those scales—they connect to one another like armor, like an exoskeleton. If I was a guessing man, I'd say the scales are pretty strong, too. Close to as strong as iron armor and as thick," Rugrat said. " She kind of looks like a dragon mixed with a naga."

During the argument, Metal Devourer Miss had lifted the majority of her body outside of her pool as she slithered about, somehow making it look like she was imitating Rugrat. She had two powerful back legs, two smaller forelegs and with her natural serpent like shape it would be easy for her to move through water. Though her forearms were stunted, on land she would probably use her back legs to run, kind of like a T-Rex. She was certainly as big as one. She was two times the height of George, who was already the size of a small truck.

Erik and Rugrat stood there as George and the floor boss spoke to each other.

George flashed his wings at one point and Miss let out a shriek, nipping at him. George yelled back and they seemed to get in an argument about something before George ruffled his wings but kept them down.

It was some time before George's conversation with the dragon slowed down and George looked to Rugrat.

"What's he saying?" Erik asked.

"Not really *saying* anything, it's kind of like frigging mental Scrabble," Rugrat said.

"Putting letters in the right place?"

"No, the one with dancing around, and pictures and other people guess." Rugrat snapped his fingers, trying to remember.

"Like you trying to communicate to other humans?" Erik deadpanned.

Rugrat just looked at Erik with a 'what the hell, man' look on his face. He shook his head from side to side, shrugging a few times, unable to form words.

"So, what is he saying?" Erik asked again.

"She's the floor master, been stuck here a long time and doesn't like it. He said that we can control the dungeon and set her free. She's all like, no, you can't—you're too weak and stuff, back and forth. But then she said if we can do it, then. . . Holy shit, she said she is willing to become your sworn beast!" Rugrat said.

Erik looked at the dragon looking at him with big eyes. He felt excited but also apprehensive, considering that such a large beast that might become his sworn companion.

The power of the Ten Realms descended as the creature seemed to have made an oath.

==========

Gilga has sworn on the Ten Realms that if you take control over the dungeon and free her from its constraints, that she will become your sworn beast. If either break this oath or harm the other, then it will result in their death.

==========

Do you accept this oath?
YES/NO

==========

Erik thought for a second before he nodded. "Yes."

Gilga turned her head, examining him more closely.

The door behind her opened, revealing another stairway down.

Gilga swam back in her pool so she was closer to the doorway and roared into it.

"Gilly! It has been some time! What are you talking about? More people? Why are you telling me? You swore to be their companion!?" The man's voice, which was calm in the beginning, turned to rage with the last sentence.

"I'll tear them apart! I'll destroy them!" The man's voice turned more bestial and deeper.

Gilga turned around and rolled her eyes, making *muah muah muah* noises before she roared back through the doorway.

"Fine. I'll meet with them." The man still sounded angry but not bestially so now. "Okay, okay! I swear I won't kill them, or allow someone else to kill them if they come down to this level of the dungeon unless they intend me or the others harm."

Gilga roared again.

"On the Ten Realms," the man said with gritted teeth as another oath was made.

Gilga waved her head toward the open doorway.

Erik pulled out a Mortal-iron metal ingot. Gilga's eyes went wide as she cruised across the water and looked at the iron in his hand. Her tongue hanging out. She looked exceedingly cute, like a puppy eager for a treat.

Erik tossed it up and she caught it in her mouth, chewing on it with loud noises.

"Metal-eating beasts, great, just great," Rugrat sighed.

"Don't think I forgot when George got loose in the Alchemy garden," Erik reminded as he walked ahead, his rifle up and ready.

Rugrat let out a dry laugh and then shot a look at George, who let out an indignant yowl. Gilga made some *hukhukhuk* noises as she laughed at him.

George let out a bark; a tongue of flame appeared from his mouth.

Gilga only seemed more amused. She continued munching on her metal, watching as they headed forward.

"Glosil, this is Rugrat. We have met with the boss on the fourth floor. They were amenable and we are heading to the fifth floor to meet with a new entity. We are safe for now. Be ready to support or pull back if needed. Do not open fire on the boss on the fourth floor. We have made an oath with her," Rugrat reported through his communication device.

"Understood. We'll wait it here." Glosil responded.

"Rugrat out."

The three went down the stairs. As they did so, Rugrat used his Dungeon Sense, locating the dungeon core and then shared it with Erik and Glosil via the sound transmission device.

It was brighter in this room, the first of the fifth floor. The light emitted heat, as if the sun beat down on them. A calm stream trickled through the room; in the center of the room there was a large humanoid creature. He had deep-brown eyes, a full mane of thick, bushy hair, and a full beard. His mustache was rolled up like tusks. He was squat but had a powerful body.

"Humans," he spat, as if the word brought up a sour taste in his mouth as he looked at them.

The floor's Mana was dense and moved quickly. The air around the man shook as a vein appeared on his forehead.

George let out a low and confused yowl.

"Wolf?" The man looked at George before Gilga said something from behind them.

"Hello, I'm Erik and this is Rugrat," Erik said.

"I'm Dromm, the first beast of the fifth floor. Well, don't you want to kill me and take my Experience?" Dromm's body started to grow bigger and power started to roll off his body. He was much stronger than even Gilga and had passed level sixty-five.

Erik and Rugrat locked up for a second. A feeling of doom filled them, a feeling that any action they took could lead to their deaths, ran through them.

That crippling fear wasn't unfamiliar to a soldier, it was something they mastered long ago.

Erik and Rugrat took deep breaths, coming out of the black and not focusing on their fear. They looked around, focusing on something else.

Fear was the mind killer; giving in to it would make them irrational. Using it as motivation, though, that could allow a man to do things they didn't think possible. Using it they could run through a field under fire to reach their friend who had been wounded or run toward the enemy to kill them so that their friends could survive.

"If we don't have to kill, we won't," Erik stated.

"Strange humans. Wouldn't make good beasts," Dromm huffed.

A tree appeared beside Dromm, growing from the floor in seconds. A face looked at them both from the tree bark.

"Elder," Dromm intoned as he dropped to a knee, greeting this tree that studied Erik and Rugrat. They both bowed their heads slightly but didn't lower them fully, checking the area for threats still.

"Humans, why are you here?" the tree asked.

"To take control of the dungeon," Erik replied.

"Take control of it?" The tree questioned, sounding skeptical.

"We're Dungeon Masters. Once we get to a dungeon core, then we can control it," Erik said. "I want to ask, just what is going on here?"

Gilga, Old Xern, Dromm—Erik felt that something had gone wrong. In the earlier levels, the beasts were just beasts. By the way he looked and the way he talked about humans, Dromm wasn't one. He was powerful but he must still be a creature of the dungeon.

"An accidental evolution. My name is Elder Fred. Please take a seat." Roots appeared from the ground, weaving together to create seats. "I swear with my life on the Ten Realms that no one in the fifth floor of the dungeon will attack you or your comrades unless provoked."

Erik and Rugrat lowered their weapons as the oath settled over them.

"Fred, huh? Never thought I would...what are you?" Rugrat asked.

"That is a bit complicated. Anyway, I want to ask what your plans are?" Fred asked.

Dromm moved to the side, eyeing them all. George stood next to Rugrat, who was petting him absentmindedly.

"We want to take control over the dungeon. Then, we can assure its safety and use it in the future," Erik said.

"Would you be able to free us from this place?" Fred asked. Dromm perked up and looked over.

Erik thought on it for a bit before answering. Egbert was a creation of the dungeon but he could technically leave it. He was a creature that relied on magical power, so he needed Mana stones to sustain himself and cast his spells apart from the dungeon.

On the other hand, Fred and Dromm were beasts. They consumed Mana to stay alive, yes, but they could also eat other items, like Old Xern with his metal. They could just consume other monster cores or Mana stones to increase their Strength. Either way, it should be possible.

"I believe so." Erik nodded.

"Would you?" Fred asked, his eyes holding a greater weight to them.

"I would." Erik confirmed. He didn't know how long they had been down here but it seemed that they had gained the ability to reason. To be stuck in this dungeon for centuries—he couldn't imagine it.

"So what are you—tree, beast, human?" Rugrat asked.

Dromm huffed at the last word.

"I was once the tree that this dungeon is built under but with the power of the dungeon core, I was able to create an avatar. That avatar is currently in the main boss room. This is just one of my apparitions. With the laws of the dungeon, the bosses can't leave their rooms and the creatures can't leave their floor. Dromm is a water-tusked boar but has turned into a demi-human. The majority of the creatures on this floor have as well. With the power on this floor, the creatures here have increased their level, attaining sentience and the ability to have a humanoid form and speak the human tongue. I was the first to gain sentience at level sixty. Then, I taught the others. They have reached level seventy or so. Most beasts only attain a humanoid form when they're level eighty. Some might get it earlier or later—it depends on the beast's bloodline, how they are taught, and the resources that they consume."

Erik looked at the tree that was talking calmly. Level sixty—he could enter the Seventh Realm!

From the two entrances behind Dromm and Fred, four more people appeared.

There was a woman with gray skin and blue eyes. Her brown hair fell down her back, her body flexible and dextrous as she moved toward them, a playfulness in her eyes.

There was a thin man with a brown robe and long hair that fell over half of his face, revealing brown eyes so dark they looked black.

Next to him was a pale man floating above the ground with a trident in one hand. He looked like the god of the seas. His blue hair danced in the wind as he stroked the back of a tanned woman with long brown hair, her arm around the man's shoulders. Her body was highly toned her muscles were like corded wood.

He aura seemed solid and powerful as her deep brown eyes looked at them with the same timeless quality as the man. As if she was seeing through them.

Being in their presence was like being in the presence of a god and goddess.

Who also didn't seem to care about what others thought of their PDA, and treated it as if it was completely normal.

"Racquel, Reaper, William, and Elizabeth. Snake, treeling, Water spirit, and Earth spirit," Fred said with a proud but also caring voice, like a grandparent talking about their grandchildren.

They all looked at Erik and Rugrat.

Erik was stunned, looking at them. They looked at Erik and Rugrat casually but he wasn't able to gauge their levels. Their strength was beyond his guess.

"Strong." Rugrat's eyes glowed with his Mana sight as he looked at them.

"We can make an agreement that you allow us access to the dungeon core to take over this dungeon and we will free you from the dungeon. I was wondering if you might want a job?" Erik asked.

"A job? What does this mean?" Fred asked.

"Prison!" Dromm rose from his seat.

"Dromm." Fred's tone didn't change but Dromm quickly sat back down. "Sorry about that. Please explain."

"We have control over another dungeon. We have built a city on the first floor but there are another five floors underneath it: Fire floor, Earth floor, Metal, Water, and Wood. The thing is, we're not strong enough to clear these floors. With your help, we might be able to. You would be paid for your help and any materials you recover you can sell to us. You would have a place to live and do as you wanted, as long as you lived by the rules of all the people in Alva," Erik said.

The creatures of the fifth floor looked to Fred.

"We would want to see this place before we were to make a decision," Fred said apologetically.

"Understood. It is not an easy decision to make." Erik paused before continuing. "As you know, you all look different from regular humans. That isn't a big deal to Rugrat and me but in the Ten Realms, unless you're with other demi-humans, then you might be at risk of prejudice. Even if you decide to not come with us, I would warn you to alter your appearances or come up with a reason for your looks to explain to other humans." Rugrat nodded in confirmation.

"A fighter but one who also cares—you are interesting men." Fred looked at them both.

George let out a proud bark.

The other creatures showed amusement at George's actions but didn't say anything.

"Once we are freed, will we be able to procreate?" Elizabeth asked. William looked down at her with a smile.

"If there is a restriction, I can remove it and you would be released from the dungeon's control. Beyond that, I don't know." Erik shrugged. He hadn't dealt with Water or Earth spirits procreating before.

Elizabeth looked up at William. He smiled and squeezed her tighter. She had a pleased expression on her face as she wrapped her arms around him and squeezed him tighter, rubbing her face against his chest.

"I, Erik West, swear on the Ten Realms with my life that if you give me access to the dungeon core, then I will release you from this dungeon so long as you don't attack anyone from Alva, unless they attack you," Erik said.

"Well, guess I should do the same." Rugrat repeated Erik's oath.

"Bring them to my room." Fred announced as his tree form seemed to reverse the growing process and disappear into the ground.

"Come," Dromm told them as he led them along with the rest of the creatures through the dungeon.

They deactivated traps and opened doors on the way. After that, it felt like they were being guided through someone's home rather than a dungeon.

They reached a large room, one much larger than the previous rooms they had been in. There were three doors out of this room.

Sunlight warmed the room, streaming down through holes in the ceiling. Water created a pool in the back right of the room, its turquoise waters looked refreshing and inviting.

The room looked like the inside of a massive wooden hall and had roots growing throughout. They moved across the ground to roots that had created a throne. On it, sat an elf.

He looked like a heavenly figure. His eyes were blue and seemed to dance with amusement. He had a strong body and as he stood up, there was a grace to his movements, as if he would never place a foot wrong even if he tried.

Around his head, there was a wreath of golden tree branches. A green cloth grew from behind his shoulders, creating a cloak behind him.

"It is good to meet you in person," Fred said, his current voice easier to hear than the rough voice of the tree he had used before.

"I didn't think that elves were real," Rugrat said in a slightly awed voice.

"Elf?" Fred asked.

"Or maybe they're not," Erik chuckled.

"I remember something about elves and trees." Rugrat shrugged and left it alone. "I think the dungeon core is under the throne."

"May I?" Erik asked.

"Please," Fred insisted. Although Fred looked calm, his emotions were easy to read as everyone in the room looked at Erik.

He stepped forward towards the throne.

The roots of the tree parted, coming to life once again as a bright blue glow was revealed from behind them. The Mana in the room was stirred up, collected into the dungeon core and refined, while pure Mana escaped the dungeon to change the rest of the world.

Erik was a bit shocked by the Mana density around the dungeon core. He saw that there was a chip in the dungeon core as well. With time, it had been smoothed over. *That must have been where the dungeon core in Vuzgal was hacked off.*

The dungeon core rested in mid-air. A mist of concentrated Mana appeared around it.

Erik reached out and touched it.

==========

Do you wish to:

Take command of the Dungeon

Remodel Dungeon

Destroy the Dungeon

==========

==========

Quest Completed: Re-open Bala Dungeon

==========

Remove the barrier around Bala Dungeon (Completed)

Clear Bala Dungeon at least once (Completed)

==========

Rewards:

55,000,000 EXP

Bonus: 18,250,000 EXP

==========

==========

You have reached Level 53

==========

When you sleep next, you will be able to increase your attributes by: 10 points.

==========

==========

18,657,376/30,600,000EXP till you reach Level 54

==========

"Take command," Erik said.

Erik saw his dungeon controls update as his dungeon interface activated.

He could see throughout the dungeon now, all of it his domain and under his complete control. "Creatures?" Erik moved to the Creatures Tab and went through the options there.

Power started to seep from the dungeon to the sentient Beasts they had just met, increasing in speed as they absorbed it all.

Erik felt the connection between them and the dungeon decreasing as more power entered their bodies. Finally, they separated from the dungeon, no longer listed on the Creatures Tab.

Erik looked at them as the power in the room settled down. There didn't seem to be anything different about them.

"So?" Rugrat asked.

"I don't feel the floor restrictions anymore," Fred marveled as he looked to the others.

"I don't feel the presence of the dungeon anymore, telling me where to go," Racquel said with a hint of triumph in her voice.

"Glosil, this is Erik. The dungeon is now under our control. Clear out the traps and meet us on the surface," Erik relayed. All of the tension in Erik's body fell away. He raised his rifle, pointing it to the ceiling. "Want to see outside world?"

The demi-humans talked among themselves. Even the cold Reaper looked excited as they went to the platform at the back of Fred's throne.

The ceiling opened above them and they shot upward. The roots moved away as they accelerated faster.

Light poured in, burning their eyes and forcing them to look away.

Erik and Rugrat cancelled their night vision spells and blinked, rapidly adjusting to the sunlight.

It took the demi-humans a bit longer to adjust to the light.

They all looked out over the valley once they could see again.

Dromm was the first to take a step forward, leaving the pad and stepping on the grass. He started to cry as he dropped to his knees.

The others laughed or cried as they looked out over a world that they'd never seen before.

Racquel grabbed Rugrat and kissed him. He barely kept his rifle up, stunned by her speed, strength, and technique. She pulled away and smiled, her tongue flickering before it disappeared.

Fred looked at the tree standing over the dungeon. That tree was his old body and the structure of the dungeon. "Thank you, Erik."

Erik simply nodded as Rugrat laughed and clapped him on the back.

"We've got to clean up a few more things in the dungeon, like Old Xern and Gilly," Rugrat said.

"There is a city named Vuzgal to the north. We control it right now. There is a man called Glosil controlling it; I'll send him word. There are undead in the city but they're under our control. Don't break them, please," Erik said.

"We will take some time to adjust. We might stay in the valley for some time, if that is alright," Fred said as he marveled at the world around him for the very first time.

Chapter: Dungeon Trials

Now that Erik and Rugrat controlled the dungeon completely, they didn't have to worry about the remaining beasts and could directly use the different pads at the end of each level.

First they went down to Old Xern, releasing him from the dungeon and sending him up to the valley above. He started sniffing around the valley, having agreed to not eat the metal from the city.

Then they went to see Gilly.

She looked at them both before she bowed her head to Erik.

==========

Gilga has voluntarily created a bond with you, making you her master.

==========

Erik immediately felt closer to her; he could understand her thoughts and translate her actions into words. He patted her head, scratching at her armored scales. He used Simple Organic Scan on her body, finding only minor issues.

"Come on, let's get out of here," Erik said. The special teams had already packed up their gear and were headed to the surface.

They headed to the travel pad as Gilga stepped out of the pool. She stood at ten meters long from head to tail.

George, who was on his shoulders, scratched at his cheek.

"Ow!" Rugrat yelped.

"Now everyone else is a higher level," Erik pouted to himself. He was one of the strongest in Alva but he was now weaker than his own beast, Rugrat, and George.

They found the special teams ready and waiting at the surface. The meandering creatures of the valley were studying them. Dromm was eating some beast he had hunted, raw. Racquel was with him, enjoying in the feast as well. Fred, Reaper, Elizabeth, and William were nowhere to be seen. There were holes in the valley floor were Old Xern had burrowed his way into the ground to find metals below.

A Fred tree appeared from the ground. "If you need us, at any time, just call my name. I am able to sense anything within Vuzgal and the valley beyond," Fred said.

"If you want to, come and visit us in the capital," Erik said.

"We might do that with time. It has been a long while since we have talked to others and it might take us some time to get used to it," Fred said. His tree reversed its growth.

"All right, let's head to Vuzgal," Erik said. The special teams set off as Erik and Rugrat talked with Roska, Gong Jin, Niemm, and Storbon, letting them know what had happened and telling them to pass word to the rest.

Erik and Rugrat went to the debriefing with the rest of the leadership before they grabbed some food in a remote corner of their new base.

Gilly was off somewhere, hunting creatures with George. Both of them were strong and smart, so there wasn't much risk of them getting into trouble that they couldn't handle.

Erik had been able to sense the powerful bloodline within Gilly during his scan and he hoped that with his help, she'd be able to awaken her bloodline faster.

"Well, that was one hell of a day," Rugrat stated as he got comfortable on his cot, taking his rifle apart to clean it.

"Thought it might take us months to clear the dungeon," Erik commented.

"Don't always need to kill our way through. Plus, you finally got a companion, too," Rugrat said.

"Now, we can focus on putting people through the dungeon to increase their Strength and build a sixth hidden floor underneath the valley for the people of Alva to use. I only just realized that we should get a few more store interfaces set up in our various dungeons. I wonder if they work in the other realms. If we can put one in the Sky Reaching Restaurant, our traders could trade all across the Third Realm—same with our Adventurer League locations in the Second Realm's Kaeju. Need to know if trading on the store interfaces could lead back to us. But if it doesn't, we've got a new fat revenue stream."

"Look at you, thinking like an empire builder." Rugrat laughed.

Erik threw a dirty rag at Rugrat as he pulled apart his own rifle as well to clean it.

Rugrat kept laughing and working.

"CLP?" He asked, offering a bottle of liquid.

"You do know it's not CLP right?" Erik said.

"Ten Realms gun lube sir yes sir? You want some CLP or not?"

"Yeah, I'll take some," Erik put some on the rag he was working with and stuffed it into the magazine well with his pinky finger.

"Though I have been thinking about making something new," Erik said as he worked.

"Oh?" Rugrat asked while putting down one freshly cleaned part and moving to the next.

"Crafter trial dungeons," Erik said.

"Which are?" Rugrat wondered as he glanced up from what he was working on.

"So, dungeon cores work to pull in impure mana and then pump out pure mana. They can also exert control over impure mana, turning it into things like items, dungeons and dungeon monsters. They kind of contain all that impure mana so it doesn't mess up the area more. Also it acts as a way for the Ten Realms to increase people's power and reward them while doing it. Though sometimes a dungeon core doesn't make monsters. Sometimes, dungeons can create resources. Or sometimes if there isn't enough impure mana around, they're just kind of there, slowly growing and purifying whatever it can get around them."

"I've got you so far," Rugrat said, still focusing more on the rifle more than Erik.

"Well, sometimes the dungeons can have trials in them right? Like the beast mountain trial. Most of the time, the trials are just killing things but what if we could get the dungeon to make a trial for crafting things? In a way, crafting things is refining the base materials into something more. It is also a way to increase the power of people. When we're crafting, we're spending mana all over the place. There is no such thing as a spell that uses all of it's power. That wasted attribute Mana power can be consumed by the dungeon core."

"So, you're basically banking on the Ten Realms wanting to make people stronger with the dungeons?" Rugrat asked, using a length of wood to push small rag he was using through the barrel of his rifle.

"Yeah and then adding in one of those dungeon point reward systems so that if we clear out the battlefield dungeon in Alva, then we still have a way to use those points," Erik said.

"Worth a shot to try your idea. Be a win win for both sides. The dungeon gets to clear the impure Mana in the area, it creates a trial for people that the Ten Realms seem to love, it increases people's skills and power like other dungeons and then maybe it gives some rewards at the same time. Seems like standard dungeon procedure from the Ten Realms to me. It should work. People might freak out about it though, non violent dungeon rewards and all," Rugrat said.

"Yeah, it might make waves."

"The dungeon core in the valley is pretty powerful so it will be faster to set up. Could maybe even have Expert level testing facilities. It's just a tester dungeon, if it works here, then we can get it to work in Alva as well as other places."

"Break the damn system—alright." Rugrat shrugged. "I'm going to make grenade launchers."

"Redneck."

Later that day as Erik was going to sleep he was greeted with a new screen.

==========

You have 5 attribute points to use.

==========

One into agility, two into mana pool and two into stamina. Agility and Mana pool so my hands are more dexterous when crafting and then the larger mana pool to increase my cultivation and work for longer. Stamina to work longer as well. Time to focus on building instead of fighting.

==========

Name: Erik West

==========

Level: 53

==========

Race: Human

==========

Titles:
From the Grave II
Mana Emperor
Dungeon Master III
Reverse Alchemist
Poison Body
Fire Body
City Lord

```
==========
```
Strength: (Base 36) +41
```
==========
```
770
```
==========
```
Agility: (Base 29) +68
```
==========
```
533
```
==========
```
Stamina: (Base 39) +21
```
==========
```
900
```
==========
```
Mana: (Base 8) +71
```
==========
```
790
```
==========
```
Mana Regeneration (Base 10) +55
33. 50/s
```
==========
```
Stamina Regeneration: (Base 41) +56
20. 40/s
```
==========
```

***

The next day, the special teams joined the searchers in the capital. They had been fighting for nearly a week straight and a break would do them some good. There were two army sections heading into the dungeon to increase their levels

Rugrat looked over administrative efforts while Erik headed back to the dungeon. Gilly and George had hunted all night and day. The hunt had gone well and their Strength had increased as a result. Gilly showed gains already by increasing in size. Up to this point, she had been largely sustained by the Mana of the dungeon instead of meat and monster cores. By eating these, her Strength was developing even faster. She might be a beast of Earth and Water but she had dragon's blood in her.

Erik entered directly through the fifth floor's exit. He created a chair from the roots on the floor with a thought and looked at the dungeon core that floated between the tree roots that were bent down towards it in reverence.

"I think that it might be bigger than the dungeon core in Alva at this point." Erik observed as he looked at the soccer-ball sized dungeon core. "No time like the present." Erik reached out and touched the dungeon core.

"I, Dungeon Master Erik West, wish to create a dungeon agreement with the Ten Realms. To create a trial to be administered by the dungeon. Crafters will be allowed to access areas based upon their ability, turning materials and ingredients in the Ten Realms into finished products."

A golden light came down and surrounded the dungeon core.

==========

Blueprint required

==========

Erik took out the rough plan he had had one of the blueprint soldiers whip up. They had basically stitched together the plans of different crafting workshops from Alva and then stacked them on top of one another to make Apprentice, Journeyman and Expert level floors of all kinds of crafts. The trial construction would take a truly monumental amount of resources to build but thankfully they had a cities worth of items to use.

At the entrance of the trial there was a prize hall where one could use their earned dungeon points at. When someone was done with their trial, they would be returned there.

==========

Blueprint accepted

==========

==========

Terms?

==========

A shiver ran down Erik's spine. He didn't know what he was talking to, really—what the Ten Realms actually was. But he knew that the changes in his body were due to the Ten Realms. Now he was talking to it directly.

He didn't know whether it was like a computer program, or whether it was sentient. He didn't really think that this was the time to figure it out.

The golden glow stayed around the dungeon core, waiting for his response.

Well, it didn't reject me right away.

"Power to the Alva Dungeon," Erik said.

==========

Unable to comply. Dungeon located across realms.

==========

"Prize hall points for every person that completes the trial."

==========

Plan understood, Blueprint added, terms agreed.

==========

The golden glow around the dungeon core disappeared.

He thought that this might happen. Egbert had told him that the dungeon master had to propose the dungeon to the Ten Realms, then actually make it. After that, the Ten Realms might accept the dungeon and take control of it.

Erik accessed the dungeon core and used the dungeon map to place the new floor and added in emergency access tunnels that would be hidden in the valley and the surrounding mountain ranges. The strength of the dungeon core was such that the entire valley was under its domain.

The plans disappeared and the power that had been leaking out from the dungeon core was focused instead on the changes.

Earth started to move and firm up. Roots extended through the structure, weaving through the earth to create strong walls as the crafter's trial was built beside the original Halls of Bala dungeon. Underneath it all, a new sixth floor was being created.

The sixth floor was laid out similar to Alva Dungeon, with the dungeon headquarters in the middle housing the dungeon core. Around it, there would be buildings made of roots and wood. Erik felt a little more relaxed. Now if something happened, they would have another place that they could move to and hide in.

It was being built but it would take time before it was completed.

"Going to need resources, I can get the monsters in the dungeon to help out, might need to transfer a few undead over to help with the building." Erik said to himself.

Erik input the crafting trial dungeon project to the dungeon core. The blueprint turned into a wire diagram in his eyes.

He altered the stairs from the tree above and made a new path, one that entered the original dungeon filled with five floors of beasts to be killed and armor to be claimed.

Erik queued up the building process, so that the trial rooms would go after the sixth floor with the dungeon core. The expansions would take time and it would take a lot of resource contributions to finish but if it worked here, then they could destroy it and recreate it in Alva.

They could also use it as a way to recruit new talents as they watched what was happening in the dungeon, finding candidate fighters and crafters who were good matches for Alva.

It would also create changes in the dungeon itself. Instead of being just an Earth and Water attribute dungeon, it would turn into a dungeon with all of the Affinities. Thus allowing it to draw in and cleanse more impure Mana—improving its function in the Ten Realms and also serving to help Erik and Alva.

Chapter: Changing Future

Erik woke up and pushed his sleeping bag to one side. He turned, sat on his cot and rubbed his face. A lot of things had happened yesterday. They'd taken over the Halls of Bala dungeon; he had come to an agreement with the Ten Realms and there was no knowing whether that would work out.

They'd freed the sentient creatures on the fifth level that had never seen the sun or known anything other than their one tiny floor in the dungeon. Beyond the the demi-humans powerful levels, they were like children and also wise elders at the same time. Erik couldn't even begin to think of how old they were, or how they had lived in the dungeon.

After working on the dungeons new plans and setting it to work, Erik had toured the dungeon some more.

The rooms had been turned into houses for Fred and the others, each fitting them perfectly, complete with beds and chairs. They also had treasures and items that they played with; ingredients that grew from the walls of the dungeon, nurtured by the pure mana of the dungeon were nothing but food ingredients to them. There was a Mortal-grade cornerstone that created a massive mine of mana stones. The demi-humans ate the Mortal stones to increase their level but they also carved designs into them, creating glasses, sculptures, games or furniture.

To anyone else, such acts would be extravagant and wasteful with all of the Mortal stone chippings; to them it was normal.

Erik checked his Experience bar.

==========

18,657,376/30,600,000EXP till you reach Level 54

==========

He was 54 but he didn't feel all that secure in that knowledge, knowing that there were people from the fifth and sixth realm who were just soldiers here.

He really wanted to rope the demi-humans in to help out Alva but at the same time, he vowed to not push it. They might be old souls but everything was new to them. He hoped that they weren't discriminated against by humans but he knew it was a faint hope that was bound to be crushed.

He let out a tired sigh. He had seen people from across Earth and across the first four realms. He lived in a dungeon once built by the genius gnomes but destroyed by a human's greed. He'd seen the best and worst of people: those willing to give their lives to save their friends and those rushing into battle for the sheer chaos and destruction of it.

All I can do is be who I am and hope it's enough to help a few people.

That belief was why he wouldn't push a job onto the demi-humans but let them make their own decisions. They might have hard lessons ahead but they were not his choices to make.

He got up and headed to the showers. "Hot showers in the field—come a long way." Erik laughed to himself, trying to clear his mind of worries.

***

A broken man's head lolled forward. He was strapped to a chair, unable to do anything. Blood and spittle covered his face. His teeth were broken and there were cuts across his body. He couldn't open his eyes anymore.

The man who had punched him stepped back and bowed to a woman working at a desk, calmly checking over reports and passing them back to another officer, who didn't even blink at the casual torture happening off to the side.

The woman, even when working on reports, wore her armor and her sword was close by.

They were in a tent that was large enough to be a normal person's home.

"So, he came from the west," she said with a snort. "Is it so hard to tell us the condition within Tareng? You have the token of someone from the neutral cities."

The man talked through cracked teeth and lips.

She shot a look at the interrogator, who flushed in embarrassment and stepped toward the man, listening to his words.

"He said that he came from Aberdeen, fled through the woods to the west. When he got to Tareng, they wouldn't allow him in, General Ulalas."

Ulalas put down her report. "How did he make it through the west?"

The interrogator listened to the man in the chair.

"They were moving with a mercenary group. They went past some place, a city filled with undead. The mercenaries bought them time. They lost two thirds of their people escaping."

Ulalas smiled and picked up her report. "Take him out of my sight." She looked at one of the interrogators behind the man. She nodded to him; he pulled out a blade and stabbed it through the back of the chair into the man's heart. He let out a hiss of pain before slumping forward as the poison from the blade entered his bloodstream.

They picked up the chair and carried the dead caravan leader out of the tent and past carriages that were being searched. They tossed him into a pit of other bodies, a mage expressionlessly using flames to destroy those in the pit.

Back in the tent, Ulalas finished her report.

"He might have come from the west—put some scouts out in that direction. We can't let the people of Tareng get away. It will take another two weeks before the madness overtakes them. We can't let anything go wrong," General Ulalas said.

"Understood, General." The officer standing next to her moved out of the tent to send out her orders.

***

The Alvan army's leadership was gathered around the briefing table for an early morning meeting. All of them had breakfast in front of them as Erik took a sip of coffee.

"Starting today, Special Team One and Two will clear the dungeon completely. I want to have a gauge of just how difficult it is. We will have one section from the army entering the dungeon in the morning and clearing the first two floors, then a second section heading in the afternoon. One half-section will be compiling all of the items recovered from the city for half a day, alternating with the other half section to get some free time. We will have two sections on standby at all times, ready to react if we come under attack. The remainder will continue to recover items from the capital.

"Once the special teams have assessed the dungeon, they will alternate clearing the dungeon and assisting in recovering items from the harder traps we've found in the capital."

"How are we looking inside the capital?" Erik looked to Glosil, who stood, while Erik took his seat.

"We have cleared most of the unstable buildings and are in the process of clearing the land, having the undead turning the stone into bricks and organized in open areas. The castle's outer wall has been repaired and our area of the castle has been repaired while the undead are focusing on the inner wall. We have piled up most of the storage items and valuables that were easy to gather. I'll direct you to the trap map," Glosil pointed to a map with different markers on it, from blue, green to yellow and red.

"Blue, lock pick or can probably bust it open with some tools. Green, formation detected, yellow, powerful formation. Red, looks pretty damn bad, I have picked out teams for the red and yellow locations, the others we'll sweep through.

"We have most of the valuables out of the houses, most of them are piled up on the street and need to be organized. The undead are working on collecting and dropping them off at the castle district to be sorted. We've found more carts and have prepared them near the totem. The sorted items are organized into storage rings and added to the carts, so if we need to bug out we can have our mounts hook into the carts and take most of our loot with us."

With that Glosil sat back down.

Rugrat raised his hand and everyone looked over.

"I will be working on making weapon systems, one called a mortar that will shoot explosive projectiles over very large distances and a grenade launcher that shoots an explosive over pretty far distances. Rifles are good with dealing with one or two targets but if we can get an explosive into a group of tightly packed combatants, it'll be pretty damn effective. Also, I'd suggest we have the scout sections and the special teams scouting the area around us to the east and particularly to the west. We have alarm formations but we don't know the terrain or what we could find down there," Rugrat said and looked at Erik.

"Good point, I forgot about that. They can set up observation posts as they go so they can go on longer patrols and out further. Do you want to coordinate?" Erik said.

"Lieutenant Yui took the scout training as well, why don't we leave it to him?"

"Yui?" Erik looked at him.

"I'm up for it," Yui nodded.

"Anything else that we're forgetting?" Erik asked.

Domonos put up his hand.

Erik pointed at him.

"The troops are asking how long till we're done." Domonos asked, almost sheepishly.

"Well, the totem will take just over two months, something like sixty two days, once it's done and we've got it all packed up we'll use the other totem to send people back and figure that all out," Erik said.

Domonos nodded and added it to the notes that he had been taking.

"Okay, lets get settled in for the long haul and see if we can repair up the castle a bit more, so we have some firm defenses. Rugrat I added in a Mana storing formation to the Bala Dungeon but could you take some formation specialists down there to make sure it's working and add the mana cornerstones?"

"Can do," Rugrat said as he added the note.

"At the end of a week, we'll have a barbecue. We made it to another realm and took over a city, two beers per person and a healing potion after if they're going on watch," Erik said, tapping his notebook against the table as he stood up. Chairs squeaked and creaked as the others all stood up as the meeting came to an end.

"Also, I know we talked about it last night but make sure everyone knows to treat the demi-humans in the valley with respect. Treat them just like people from Alva. I'll deal with anyone who causes trouble personally." Erik stabbed his finger into the table.

All of them had dark expressions on their faces. They had all been trained by Erik and Rugrat. Although they respected them, they also understood just how they could make a person's life hell.

"Alva is a place that accepts all. Wherever we go, we will demonstrate those same values."

Glosil raised his hand.

"Why don't we send supplies down to Alva?" Glosil said. "We can send them to the third or the second realm, have the adventurers, the traders hold them. If it is in their hands and not up here then no one can take it from us. We can place orders for formations ammunition and other supplies from Alva? Also it'll raise morale getting messages from their family member back home."

Erik looked at Rugrat.

"What is your plan?" Rugrat asked.

"We send people down with the carts, have them contact our people, let them know the situation up here. We set up times that we open the totem up, our people teleport back between those times and then we close it down again. Saves us having to sort through the loot, have Alva council look after that issue. We just have to ship it down, get the carts back and then repeat," Glosil said.

"Chances are slim that someone will randomly make it into the city. I think getting supplies up here and ship them back down to the lower realms instead."

"It's a fair point, we can get their help and aid," Rugrat said and looked at Erik.

"Alright, I still hate leaving the back door open like that."

They swallowed and nodded as they felt that deadly calm that Erik and Rugrat showed before they turned into demons.

"Good. We've all got work to do. Let's get to it." Erik concluded.

***

Fred was lying on the ground, taking in the sun. He chewed on a piece of grass, looking like a teenager just wasting away the day in the sun.

Fred's smile turned into a frown as loud snoring disrupted his rest. He cracked an eye and looked over to Old Xern. He had spent the last few days searching for metal in the surrounding mountains around the valley, only stopping when he was tired and passing out wherever he was comfortable.

He was on his back in a pond close to Fred. The beasts of the area had all left them alone, not having the strength or willpower to try to get close to the high-leveled creatures of the dungeon.

Old Xern's mottled brown and blue skin had changed, taking on a more metallic finish, and the blue lines and runes on his body seemed to be brighter than before.

Reaper was off looking at the different water and dirt deposits in the valley. To the former tree spirit, good dirt and water were like metal to Old Xern.

Racquel spent most of her time sleeping in the sun, enjoying its rays like Fred. Then, at times, she would go off hunting, capturing strong animals, fish, and beasts on the land. None of the local creatures were her match and she consumed them whole. Roots pushed Fred upright and created a chair underneath him. He pulled out a book. The chair moved across the valley as he headed for one of its sides.

He had borrowed the book from one of the people in the Alvan army. It was a book on Alchemy. Fred was fascinated—it was a practice of combining plants together to create a stronger product that could change one's body.

Alchemic study had then led him into healing studies and then to the makeup of human bodies.

Fred might look like an elf but his body wasn't like a human's on the inside. Humans had a Mana system; he did, too but it was like a tree within his body that was centered around his monster core. His Mana system had grown with time but his monster core was more effective at drawing energy from what he consumed: other monster cores, the nutrients from the soil, from other beasts. This was much more effective at progressing one's Strength. Which returned him to Alchemy. What might be poisonous for humans wasn't necessarily the same for beastials who had much stronger bodies and consumed items, not just for survival, but to increase their Strength.

"I wonder if the person who created Alchemy got the inspiration from watching beasts consuming each other?" Fred held his chin, thinking on it as he reached the top of the valley.

His thoughts turned blank as he looked over the landscape: the rolling hills of black, gray, and white mixed with shoots of green. The low-lying mist and the clouds created a ceiling above, with rays of light breaking through the natural cover.

Fred stood. The wind whipped at his body as he looked around at it all. Indescribable emotions and thoughts made him smile. Silent tears fell from his cheeks. He was stunned as he touched his cheek, looking at the water on it.

He laughed and blinked, trying to clear his blurry vision to take it all in. *There is so much to discover, so much beauty to be found.*

Fred closed his eyes and raised his arms to the side, stretching them out, feeling the wind on his body, smelling it—cold, wet, and earthy.

Slowly, he opened his eyes again.

"There is always a valley beyond this one." Fred grinned as he ran forward. Vines started to grow out from his body, expanding, changing his form as he jumped off the peak.

He waved his arms and they turned into wings. The wind fought and tried to pull him down as he fought against it, growing larger and turning into a massive wooden hawk.

On that day, a tree that had been rooted in the ground and buried, spread its wings and soared in the skies.

Chapter: Boom Tubes

Rugrat and a group of smiths reached a large building. Half of the building had been destroyed, revealing the forges inside.

"All right, it's time that we got to work!" Rugrat exclaimed. After talking to Erik, he had called an emergency meeting. Shifts changed as people were expected to work for two days before resting. Most of them had only been sleeping for a few hours a night anyway. Their Stamina and Stamina Regeneration had all undergone a change with their increased levels and their Body Cultivation. Sleep just wasn't as necessary for them anymore.

Now all of their free time disappeared as searches continued through the night and four army sections headed to the dungeon every day now. The panthers moved on patrol and went to hunt beasts with the roving patrols, increasing their Strength and their understanding of the area.

Rugrat had studied the road toward the west, comparing it with the information Erik had sent over. He worked on a plan of action, noting down locations where they could make an advancing armies life hell, if they did come.

They had been bloodied with the fighting at Vermire, their missions in the different realms and the battlefield dungeon. Their minds and actions refined with the training provided. Given time and materials they were able to come up with plans to make the enemy's lives a living hell. The more time that they could prepare the harder it would be for someone to try and dig them out of Vuzgal.

The smithy, under Rugrat's control, produced ammunition and casings, repaired armor and heavy repeaters.

When riding on their mounts, Rugrat couldn't help but think of heavy weapons that could be mounted on vehicles. He had been thinking about trucks and how he missed having one. That errant thought gave him an idea.

"So I thought, why not add weapons to our mounts? Attach them to their armor, mounted between their shoulders and above their heads. As we charge the enemy, we fire the mounted weapon. Our tactics are not to attack an enemy formation straight on. We go around them, we hit them from the rear, from the sides, from the air. Stay mobile, stay deadly stay hidden," Rugrat said.

"What weapon system would you want to mount?" Gong Jin asked.

"I'd like two heavy repeaters. If we shorten the limbs of the repeaters but increase their strength with new reinforced bracers, then they will hit with the same power. While the shorter size will allow us to mount them side by side. With the ammunition being top-fed, it's not hard to reload them. And we add in a charging handle so that one can yank back, clearing the old bolt and pulling the string into position," Rugrat said. "Thankfully, we made a few extra, so we can use those as a test bed."

"How many extra do we have?" Gong Jin asked.

"Well, after a month, Alva produced three heavy repeaters and five regular repeaters every week, so around seventy or so? Thankfully, I brought them, the extra mortars, and all of the ammunition," Rugrat said.

All of the smithing teams looked at him. Their expressions seemed to bounce between praise and just sheer inability to understand his reasoning.

"Never know when you need more firepower," Rugrat muttered, not acknowledging his weapon hoarding.

Han Wu had been released from the medics' care and was in a private house in a corner of the city. He had made a number of bombs while they were training back in Alva and a firearms assembly line had been created at the limits of the Alva Dungeon. He was recreating that facility, to produce more bombs and explosives.

Glosil went over refresher courses with the people who had learned how to handle the new mortars, checking their ranges and observing the area around the city, creating firing zones so they would only need a few adjustments to turn onto target.

"Also, I want to see if we can get this to work. I've been thinking about it for some time but the rifles came first." Rugrat showed them a blueprint—it was a monster, Rugrat's latest brainchild was a thing of beauty, destruction, brilliance and simplicity.

Rugrat headed out to the wall and pulled out a grenade launcher.

Once he had finished creating the rifles, he turned to his other passion, explosives—specifically, explosives delivered through someone's window at range.

It took Rugrat a day to complete the first prototype. His ability with smithing was such that he might be faster than machines back on Earth.

Now, in his hands, a bastardized version of the M32 appeared in the Ten Realms. It had been an obsession of his and if there was a grenade launcher to be found, he would find it.

It looked like an oversized six shot revolver mated a potatoe gun and then had a fling with a flare gun. The gun industry was an interesting one. It had the cylinder of a revolver, but held forty milimeter grenades, six beautiful, and *highly* destructive grenades, then a stumpy barrel with a foregrip to try and tame the beast, a butt stock to beat your shoulder into submission or to clamp in your sweaty pit.

The one main difference between this grenade launcher and the one someone would find on Earth, this one didn't have a sight on it.

As a Master level trainer of the M32 it was childsplay for him to recreate it. Making the grenade rounds had been the hardest part.

They weren't chemical explosives. Instead, they were metal packed around a poison vial. When the round hit the ground, the enchantment on the round would activate, causing it to explode. Rugrat was excited to see what kind of destruction the power pouring into the formation carved into Mortal metal could create.

Rugrat went to the wall and split the weapon system. He pulled out a filled six shot and clicked it into the weapon. He had made a second release on the front of the weapon so that one could replace the entire magazine or they could choose to reload it while it was still in the weapon system.

Rugrat twisted the magazine, charging the spring inside. He shut it and aimed out from the wall and pulled the trigger.

Doumpfh. The grenade arced and landed on the ground a few hundred meters away. Rugrat was easily able to see and rate the explosion. Dirt was tossed out and smoke appeared before he heard it.

"Shit!" Rugrat only smiled wider as he fired the launcher again, working to improve his accuracy.

"Who needs sights anyway, made some of my best shots just guesstimating ranges. The sight just gets in the way of explosions," Rugrat snorted to himself a wild smile on his face as an vein on his head thumped with excitement.

He dumped the entire magazine and then reloaded the weapon. He cast Sure Shot on the rounds and fired. They reached out nearly twice the distance, nearly a kilometer away with only a few seconds delay.

Rugrat laughed and he patted the weapon with affection. The casings were all there, too; he just needed to clean them out and reload them.

"All right, so need to make three per section, so twelve for a Platoon, and twenty four for the Company. Then twenty for the Special teams, one a piece, give them options. Need to get an assembly line up and running to make the rounds, we'll manufacture at least one hundred and twenty rounds for all of the grenade launchers before making more. I want to have everyone armed with a grenade launched if we can." He let out another laugh and tapped the weapon system. "Now that is some impressive fire!"

He looked around and loaded up another six shots and fired into the now-pitted target area a southern sized grin on his face as explosions bloomed over the battlefield.

The grenade launcher was simple and to rush the build, Rugrat had only added one formation socket to it, the weapon system not able to handle a second. Still, with the first one, he had upgraded the blunt damage of the round so when it hit something, it would destroy it and then the enchantment on the round was activated, causing an explosion. The blunt damage would still be active, tearing apart everything in the area.

"Instead of acting like the forty-millimeter grenades they were modeled after, they hit with the strength of a mortar," Rugrat muttered. He wanted to get more grenades to play with. "Awesome," he said in a breathless voice.

These test rounds didn't have the poison within them but were still hollow. If he were to make solid enchanted rounds, then the area of effect would increase and the poison-filled rounds would spread death over a large area, affecting people outside of the blast zone, or those who ran through the area afterwards.

Rugrat's excited expression focused as he heard a mortar firing behind him.

The area in front of him was torn up with mortar rounds landing.

They had brought ten mortars. They were simple to make but so were the rounds they used. There was: the shaped metal charge filled with shrapnel, a concoction that would make smoke when it was exposed to oxygen, filled with poison gas, or the close-range Mortal-grade iron mortars with an explosive enchantment. Rugrat stood there, watching the mortars land. They did the different rounds one by one, checking their effects. They had tested dummy rounds in the Beast Mountain Range but they didn't want to draw attention so the testing had been limited.

Now they might need them and they were away from anything that might care; they had the perfect range to play with.

"The smoke was effective and the shrapnel rounds' blast zone was around fifty meters, about what to expect with an artillery piece," Rugrat said to himself.

"We're going to be testing the heavy round now," Glosil said.

"Okay, let it rip," Rugrat said.

There was a deeper noise as the round disappeared into the skies. The ground exploded where it landed.

Rugrat ducked slightly from it. "Hot damn! been some time since I've been around shit blowing up." Rugrat laughed at his own actions as he looked at the damage.

He took out a rifle, using his optics to observe the blast zone. "I'd say that's a seventy-five-meter blast zone. Damn. Max range of about two klicks? If we were to use Sure Shot on the round, might hit three or four klicks. The stress on the firing tubes isn't much as the rounds are the lethal part of the system. Shit yeah."

Rugrat lowered his weapon and put it across his chest, resting his arms on it. He looked at the blast zone.

What will Alva's military become in the future? It's not inconceivable that we could have artillery batteries, mounted cavalry, scouts, infantry, broken into mages, medics, hand-to-hand and the like. Would it be one role-one unit, or do we continue down this path where any unit can use any weapon system?

The first would turn the military into a machine; the second would turn them into groups that worked as part of an organic whole. It would take more time and resources to develop the second group but Rugrat felt that it was the right path to take.

"All right, now we need some more boom tubes." Rugrat put away his weapons and headed back to the smithy, whistling the whole way. There was plenty to be done still.

***

Roska looked over the convoy, there were five carts packed with storage items filled with items from Vuzgal.

There were two panthers for each of the carts, they were annoyed at being made to take the carts.

"Good to go?" Erik asked from behind Roska and Davos.

"Ready," Roska said.

"I hear that Hersht is great this time of year," Erik said.

Rosja let out a whistle and the convy moved through the gates of the totem. She pulled up her hood as power surged through the totem as it went active.

The rest of Special Team two followed her.

She reached the totem teleportation area as Erik used the totem's interface, light appeared around her as they chill of the mountains was replaced with the heat of the desert.

"Welcome to Hersht," Erik said.

"Get to work on my tan," Davos said, grinning under his hood as he led the panther's forward.

"See you later, stay safe" Erik used the totem again and disappeared in a flash of light. He had only been there for a few seconds so there were only a few people with confused looks on their faces, the wind carried off the earth mana stone dust behind Roska and Davos.

People looked over at the carts with their towering goods and their war beasts pulling them. The four other carts followed behind as they went to the guard watching the trading entrance.

"Three silvers each," The man said.

Roska checked through her bag.

Damn I only have mana stones and gold.

Davos pulled out fifteen silvers and passed it to Roska, she nodded in gratitude and passed it to the man.

He took the funds and waved them through.

They entered the dusty city, Roska checked the map that Erik and Rugrat had worked up. It didn't take them long to reach the Adventurers guild branch there.

Roska jumped off as the others all stood around the carts, standing guard as people looked on. Roska had to blink a few times, to clear the light from her eyes as she went up to the front desk and presented a medallion and put it on the table.

"Please come with me," The person at the desk said. They guided Roska back to a room hidden in the back of the building, they knocked on the door as a man who looked like he got too little sleep and smelled like he hadn't showered recenetly opened the door. He peered out at the secretary who presented a medallion nervously.

"Thank you," The man said , becoming alert and straightening. The woman bobbed her head and quickly left.

The man waved her inside and looked around. He shut the door and activated a sound cancelling formation.

Roska took down her hood as the man's eyes went wide.

She pulled out several letters.

"These need to be sent out, I have goods that I need to leave here. We will be departing tomorrow, I need five new carts and twenty beasts to pull them as well as a location to drop them off in Hersht. In return I need ammunition and supplies from Alva. Rugrat has given me designs for new reloading equipment to increase the speed for creating mortar, grenade and rifle rounds."

The man took the letters and nodded.

"I can send these out within the hour and we should have an answer by tomorrow," The man said, he still looked like hell but he was alert and focused.

"Do you have a place we can store the carts?"

"Bring them around the back of the guild building, we have a courtyard there, we can hold the carts there."

"Make sure you keep an eye on the goods, they're valuable. Nothing should be lost in transit to the dungeon."

"I will look into it personally," The man drew himself up.

"Good, I'll get the carts moved around to the back. I will need quarters for my team."

"I can get you a place to stay in the guild, wear these," He opened up a drawer and pulled out Adventurer's guild emblems and passed them to Roska.

"Thank you," Roska said.

"It's my job," The man smiled.

Chapter: Agreement

Rugrat tossed some water on his face, cleaning up his appearance. He had been working in the smithy and then heading into the dungeon to increase his level by fighting the higher level creatures with Special Team Two and the leadership from the Alvan army.

He had reviewed the teachings about the Mana Heart, which was the next step on the Mana Gathering Cultivation path.

He needed to condense the Mana Mist in his Mana channels into drops and then introduce them into his Mana core. His core had turned into a sort of container. The drops were pure Mana. As he filled up his Mana core with more drops, he felt greater strength in his hands. With his fourteenth and fifteenth Mana gate opening, he had already condensed five drops and was increasing more with time. The power contained within each drop was close to the power of half of his normal Mana. They offered another trump card, allowing him to draw on an incredible amount of energy in an instant. Though if he released just a few of them, he would temporarily be in the same situation as when he had ruptured his Mana channels.

Now, that his Mana channels were no longer separate from his body, healing potions would repair his Mana channels and his control over Mana had reached an incredibly high degree. Another benefit was it increased his endurance and the amount of power he could deal with.

There was another cost to using the drops. When he had all of the drops in his core, then it would transform into a Mana Heart. Spending one drop was destroying several hours' worth of work spent compressing the damn thing.

Rugrat was able to fight creatures that were level 50 but humans who were level fifty there was no knowing what advantages they might have, in cultivation, trump cards, fighting styles or tactics.

It didn't matter just how strong he was but how he was able to use that strength.

Rugrat left his room to find George there in the hallway.

"All right, let's go see Fred and his people." Rugrat got on George's back as he took a run out of a second-story opening where the wall was still broken and flapped his wings.

Rugrat looked at the city as he soared over it. The two inner walls had been repaired but the main wall was taking time due to its sheer size.

Rugrat had had them focus on the barrier systems instead. On the walls and in open areas, one could see trees that had been grown to create catapults.

Rugrat had used the power of the dungeon to create trees in the form of catapults or ballistas. They were simply designed and they could keep on attacking without needing any of the Alvan army.

The undead workers shone in the light, wearing armor that they had recovered from the city. There were still thousands of them, each of them a powerful entity in their own right. Rugrat was still shocked that they had survived their mad dash to the dungeon core when they had first entered the city. If they didn't have their dungeon master abilities, they wouldn't have made it. Some of them still didn't.

They crossed over the wall. A section of the army headed back from the dungeon and another got ready to enter. They waved to Rugrat, who waved back as he went off toward an idyllic pond further into the valley where there were five grown homes. Grown because their owners had grown trees, weaving them together to make their homes.

Racquel was outside, wearing a pair of short shirts made from some kind of hemp like material as she wore a string bikini made of a similar material to cover her chest as she lay out near the lake. She looked up, a smile on her face as if she had seen Rugrat staring at her.

Rugrat grinned as George laughed.

She stretched in her lounger, showing off her curves.

Rugrat shook his head before he dismounted George and remembered that kiss from when she had been freed from the dungeon. *I should talk to her.*

"Racquel, stop distracting our guest." Fred's voice came from his house as his door opened.

Racquel pouted and turned to face Rugrat, showing off her cleavage. "But he's handsome and interesting. Look at the images in his skin."

"They're called tattoos," Rugrat smiled in response.

"Ohhh, and I would be interested to see where they go," she said with a coy smile.

Rugrat laughed as Fred sighed from inside his house, the entire house sighing with him. "I'd be happy to take you out for a meal and show you. Do you drink beer?" Rugrat asked.

"Beer? I haven't heard of it before but it sounds interesting." She put her finger to her lips in thought before she bloomed with a smile.

Rugrat could see her snake eye like pupils and he knew on some level that she was a powerful snake. *But she is also a babe. She'd totally be a tattooed-up badass babe back on Earth. Ugh, I am too weak!*

"Could you at least do it away from here? I can hear Elizabeth and William all night already and they're two doors down," Reaper said from inside his house, sounding like a surly teenager.

"All wood but no fun. Trees." Racquel sighed.

"Talk later? Just need to have a word with Fred," Rugrat said.

"Make sure you don't take too long,"

"I'll do my best." Rugrat winked at her and headed into Fred's house. The door closed behind Rugrat. He found Fred sitting at the back of the house, reading a book. He didn't look up as Rugrat came in.

"Being Demi Humans we get some of the desires that humans feel, being a tree and an old one at that. I thankfully don't have any of those issues but what brings you here?" Fred asked. He didn't care for societal norms; he wasn't used to them.

Does that make him and Ent or something?

Rugrat quickly shook his distracting thoughts away as he focused.

"There might be a fight eventually coming our way. Knowing our luck, there probably will be a fight. I don't know what might happen. We have always trained to expect the worst. That being said, we might stop them before they get to the city walls; they might fight us on the walls or they might take Vuzgal. If they take the capital, we will be pulling back to the dungeon or escaping through hidden tunnels. I wanted to pass this on to you so that you are able to make your own preparations," Rugrat said.

"I feel like there is more." Fred turned the book's page.

"You're all strong, much stronger than we are. I would like to ask for your help, only in a support role. You might be strong but I don't know how you fight and it might cause chaos on our front lines. But, supporting the special teams, you could help out a lot," Rugrat said, not hiding anything.

Fred's hand paused before he turned the page in his hand. "Don't you want to use us?"

"Well, it would be nice to work with you, might help out in the coming battle but we wouldn't force you into it. Like everyone in the army, they do their jobs not just because it is their duty but because they wanted to."

"You are interesting humans. The others will follow me and we will help you."

"Okay, so what are your capabilities? Your strengths, your Mana, your healing and Stamina?" Rugrat asked.

"Why such complicated questions?" Fred asked.

"To know how to use your strengths to the greatest result, I need to know what those strengths are," Rugrat said.

"Racquel is good in close combat. Reaper as well but only in short spurts. William and Elizabeth have powerful spells but that will drain them and they are also good fighters in close range. I believe William would be a terror if he was fighting in the rain.

"Dromm is good at charging when in his beast form. I am best with support. I can heal, and unlike you humans, I am able to split my concentration, allowing me to support people across a large area. I do have other attacks and I can create or call upon different creatures.

"Old Xern is much like Dromm—the two of them are actually good friends. Dromm can clear a path and Xern will tear apart anything in front of him. He was limited in the dungeon by how far he could jump. Now that he is outside, he is jumping all over the place," Fred said.

"We've noticed, tell him to stop trying to eat weapons out of people's hands. I know we said all metal not inside the walls, but that includes people's armored boots," Rugrat pleaded.

"I will talk to him. Also, these books you have are rather interesting. Are there more on this Alchemy?"

Fred's door opened as he continued reading.

"Erik has the most but there are other alchemists in the group; you can ask them at the meeting tomorrow," Rugrat said.

"Very well. Also, treat Racquel well." Fred looked up for the first time since the meeting.

The house shifted. Rugrat felt the power that was hidden within the placid-looking elf.

"Just talking." Rugrat held up his hands as he forced a smile. Cold sweat ran down his back.

Worse than Lucy-lue's father when he was cleaning his shotgun in the front room while staring at me. I was in the tenth grade! What could I have. . . Well, I could have done—well, we did but...

Rugrat coughed as he scratched the back of his head.

Then there was Sarah from two towns over. Only had my boots and my hat when I got into the truck and booked it out of there. I don't have the best luck with fathers.

Fred lowered his gaze as Rugrat left the house.

He let out a breath. George was on his back, waving his paws in the air, his tongue hanging out of his mouth, looking like nothing but an oversized puppy.

Rugrat stopped in his steps, looking at the big dolt.

He heard Racquel laughing as George jumped up and then rushed Rugrat, jumping on him. It seemed that he had been bored while Rugrat was working.

Rugrat pulled out a big stick that looked more like a tree. George jumped up and down, backing up as Rugrat turned and threw the small tree.

George ran after it. The tree splashed into the water. George pranced in the water before jumping into it fully and swimming over to the tree, and started bringing it back.

"Still nothing but a puppy," Rugrat said.

George wrestled with the tree and turned around, coming back to shore as Rugrat went over to Racquel.

"So, when do I get this beer?" Racquel asked with a playful smile.

"Thankfully, I've got some extras." Rugrat took out two cold beers, pulled the wax covered cork out of one and passing it to Racquel. He pulled out a foldable chair and put his beer in it as George came back.

Rugrat grabbed the branch and hurled it again. George ran off again.

Racquel sipped the beer, then held it at arm's reach, examining it before she took another sip.

"What do you think?" Rugrat pulled off his armor vest and tunic, leaving on his t-shirt underneath as he sat back in the chair.

"About the beer or you?" Her eyes fell on the tattoos on his arms and her finger traced some of them out.

"Both?" Rugrat smiled and took a drag of his beer. Drinking was allowed in the Alvan army. With a healing concoction, they could clear a hangover or sober up in just a few seconds. They were only allowed to have one mixed drink or two beers per day, following along with the rum rations that the British navy had.

"You intrigue me, you're a blacksmith, a fighter but also a mage. You are used to fighting in the front even if your body is weaker. Mages usually hide at the back, doing a lot of damage but aren't useful if they're attacked head on. Many people look at smithing as a rough craft but it takes patience. The items that you make—I've had a look at them and they're not only well made, they're complicated, works of art, many pieces all working together in harmony. A rough man with a soft heart." She smiled, withdrawing her hand and drinking her beer.

Damn, is my body that weak, I should talk to Erik about body cultivation again? Even the Special teams are starting to surpass me.

George came up with his tree and barked at Rugrat.

"Sounds like you've been looking into me." Rugrat grabbed the tree and hurled it.

George ran after it, jumping up and using his wings as he raced after it.

"Well, a man in body armor and tattoos—guess you're my type." She drank from her beer.

Rugrat let out a laugh, a heated feeling in his stomach. "So, what do you want to do?"

"Now?" Her eyes ran down Rugrat's body and then back to his eyes. "Or *later*?"

"While I would like to know both of those, I meant more like do you want to stay here, do you want to explore the realms, does Alva interest you?" Rugrat said, trying to not look back and see if Fred was watching them.

"I want to explore. I want to see the other realms, see this Al-va. I want to experience life and take risks." Racquel's eyes glowed as if picturing that future as she took a big drink from the beer.

George splashed through the water and dropped off his tree and shook himself dry, covering Rugrat and Racquel in water.

"Oh, George! Stop it!" Rugrat complained as Racquel laughed at George's puppy dog look of innocence as he looked up at Rugrat and pawed the three meter branch, his tongue hanging out of his mouth.

"You silly pup." Rugrat rubbed George's head. Racquel stood up and passed Rugrat the beer back.

"Thanks for the beer but I should go and clean up, you should come around my place tonight if you're free," She said, somehow getting close to him and pressing her full chest against his stomach.

"Yes," Rugrat said in a rush not realizing how desperate it sounded. "I uhh."

"I look forward to it," She kissed him, her tongue flickering over his before she released and walked towards her house.

"I'm never going to sleep!" Reaper complained from his house.

"Shut it, tree house!" Racquel yelled back.

Chapter: News from the Fourth

Delilah wiped her brow as her sound transmission device started beeping at her.

She had just finished working on her latest concoction. She let out a sigh and took the message. She knew that unless it was of vital importance she wouldn't be interrupted when she was working on her skills.

Delilah took a shaky breath. She wasn't someone originally from Alva, but now, as the council leader, she had come to know the people in Alva. She frequently met those proud parents talking about their son or daughter who had worn the armors of Alva to fight for their home. The boyfriends, girlfriends, wives, and husbands of those who were looking forward to their return—the hidden darkness in their eyes as they were worried about their loved ones.

Delilah lisened through the message she had recieved.

She quickly sent a message about ammunition production to Taran, with her authority to hire more people and use more resources to increase the ammunition production. She sent the letter about the loot to the treasury department and Jia Feng, the two of them would supervise one another and break down what items were useful to Alva and what could be sold.

Another letter was passed to Jia Feng with all of the different items that the Alva Army needed help with, making formations, different tools, replacing broken weapons and armor. Another batch of letters went to her secretary to be sent out to the family members of the Alva Army serving in the Fourth realm.

She felt numb as she wrote down names, the successive hits making her feel weak. With each name, it was as if she were putting them to death herself. It was like admitting that they were dead. Writing the names made it so permanent, seemingly unable to take it back. She felt a wave of nausea as she gritted her teeth.

She was the council leader for Alva, but she was still just a young woman. Dealing with this kind of loss was hard for her to bear, but she also knew it was her duty.

She stood and read the first name on the list.

"What are the names for?" Fehim asked.

Delilah's hands trembled as a soft smile appeared on her face and her vision blurred. "They're Alva's heroes." She sniffed; then she cracked, letting out a few tears, quickly trying to hold back the flood.

Fehim was shaken by her words. His eyes widened and a pain could be seen in his eyes. He reached out and pulled her into a hug, patting her on the back as she took a few moments to pull herself together.

She backed up and wiped her eyes, setting her face and pushing the emotions away. *Now I have to be there for the families; it is their loss.* She ground her teeth and tamped down her emotions.

"What are you going to do with the list?" Fehim asked.

"Rugrat and Teacher taught me how to tell people about their loss. I'll go and tell the families."

"I'll come with you," Fehim said.

She was about to deny him, but instead nodded. She needed someone there to help her.

She read the first name again and then they headed out of the Alchemy lab. It wasn't long until they reached the farms. They asked around before they found a man working in the fields, using a spell to increase the speed that they grew at.

He saw Delilah and Fehim approaching. He smiled and nodded and tilted his hat to them in greeting. His expression turned strange as he saw that they were headed for him. He took off his hat, a confused smile on his face.

"Mister Ershman." Delilah stopped in front of him.

"Miss Council Leader Delilah, what brings you to my corner of the farming fields?" he asked with a hearty and kind smile.

"I wish I brought better news today, but I have been informed that your daughter, Lily Ershman, fell in battle in the Fourth Realm." Her words were more brutal than any bullet.

Ershman's kind features dissolved. His face turned as white as a sheet. He dropped his hat, forgetting it as he gripped his shirt, brought to his knees. He shook his head, trying to deny it, but tears appeared in his eyes.

"She will be returning as a hero in two days." Delilah moved to try to comfort him.

Others in the fields heard what she had said and moved to come over, helping Ershman.

"Lily—no, baby girl. Not my Lily." Ershman's words tore the breath out of Delilah's lungs and turned her throat into sandpaper.

That day, Delilah met with people and watched as their worlds were shattered.

A somber air filled Alva as Jia Feng found Delilah and Fehim in Delilah's office with pale faces and tear streaks on their faces. Jia Feng took them back to her homestead, feeding them and helping them. The two of them emotionally spent.

Chapter: Changes in the East

General Ulalas stood on top of a sand dune, looking in the direction of Tareng. She couldn't see it through the tall sand dunes but she knew it was there; prey just waiting for the jaws of her army to bite into.

"Targeting Tareng was a move of brilliance. Once we kill the people in the city, we can blame the actions on the Hang-Nim Alliance. Allowing us to take the riches of the city, and destroy the alliance through the Crafter's association and Blue Lotus' retribution. Returning strength to the Blood Demon sect," one of her top commanders, Minor General Damel, said.

"Now is not the time to get complacent, how are the communication disrupting formations?"

"They're still trying to send out messages regularly to see if there is any weakness but none of the messages have been able to get through. Even though they weaken with the transformation concoction in their veins, they're sending out their people to try and sneak through our lines so they can get far enough to send a message or reach another city."

"I agreed with your suggestion to extend our forces out to make sure that there was no space between the camps," Ulalas said.

"Thank you General," Damel beamed and saluted.

"What about direct visual observation?"

Damel grimaced. "If we have anything that can see them, they have spells that they can drop on us. Still can't get within that envelope without them knowing."

"We have time on our side, they reported the plague two weeks ago. We have another six weeks before their headquarters will even send someone out to check on Tareng. We want the transformation concoction to drive them to madness and then we have our spies open the gates and we kill them all," Ulalas said, her voice calm and composed.

"Ready the army. In one week, we will move." Ulalas turned from the sand dune.

Damel bowed as she left. As soon as she had, he started to send the orders as the camp readied for the coming battle.

A total of fifty thousand soldiers in several camps sharpened their blades and checked their armor. They were dealing with the people of the Blue Lotus and the Crafter's Association, so they had brought an overwhelming amount of fighting power, including those from the higher realms. The Blue Lotus and Crafter's Association guards were strong, the kind that could be a general within any army that they went to, best not to take chances.

***

Qiu Jun waited as the patrol was passing him. He had been waiting three days for them to come back again just for this moment.

He activated his movement technique, flitting across the top of the sand dune, passing behind the patrol without any of them noticing as they walked across the peak of the sand dune. He threw himself forward, landing further down the sand dune, allowing himself to tumble down without making a noise.

He slammed into a rock ledge, he held in his cries of pain, his arm and leg broken as he flew off the edge, landing some thirty meters down on the sand again, the pain almost making him black out as he continued to roll.

He opened his eyes at the bottom of the sand dune. He could feel the madness coming closer, the new wounds on his body and his exhausted state was nearly too much.

Using a detection spell he searched for new observers and alarm traps.

He didn't detect any as he pulled out his mount. The reptilian creature looked around with red rimmed eyes, looking dangerous and fast.

Qiu Jun got onto the mount and took off towards the forest.

I'll cut to the west and see if I can send a message to the Crafter's association, or head north to Aasoir city. If I can just stop this concoction from taking over my body in time.

He clenched his teeth, rushing off into the night as he kept on using his detection spell. It truly looked like he had left the scouts behind as the desert started to turn into forest with some fog hanging over it ominously.

***

Storbon was with Yao Meng, using Earth moving spells to clear out a square area inset into a hill underneath a large boulder. Yuli was transforming the dirt and materials, making them stronger to support the boulder and the hidden structure underneath.

Lucinda was standing nearby using her beasts to scout the area in greater detail.

They were hidden from the road but there was a break in the canopy below the hill, allowing them a perfect overwatch of the main road that ran all the way to Vuzgal.

Yawen had his rifle ready as he scanned the area.

"Looks like we have a visitor," Lucinda said.

"Who is it?" Storbon said, still working.

"Unknown, coming from the East. Quick mount, looks banged up."

"Not ours?"

"Not ours."

Storbon sent a sound transmission to alert headquarters. "Niemm this is Storbon, we've got a contact."

"A man and a fast mount, possibly wounded," Lucinda supplied. Storbon repeated it to Niemm.

"Understood and reporting higher. Forward me waypoint with real-time updates," Niemm said.

Lucinda added a waypoint, moving it as the man moved on the map.

Everyone gathered their gear and called their mounts back who had been patrolling the area, investigating their zone and catching other animals that were worth their effort.

***

Qiu Jun was suddenly awake.

He didn't know when he had closed his eyes, it felt like it was just a moment ago but from the position of the sun it had to be a few hours ago. He was feeling delirious, the madness was fighting for control over his body. He had escaped into the forest and his injuries were healing with his high body cultivation but his body was now weaker from the extended abuse, allowing the concoction to take over and change him faster.

His bones were itching as they were changing. He opened his eyes forcefully, looking up into the sky as he saw a beast circling above.

"Shit," He cursed as he pushed his mount to move faster, dodging through the trees.

He checked his sound transmission device and activated it, gritting his teeth as he saw the sound transmission formation consuming the scroll.

The message was sent with Qiu Jun looking at the device, making sure that it was operating properly. A wave of relief rushed over him as a pressure lifted from his shoulders. He took out another sound transmission scroll and used it with the device, sending the pre-recorded message three more times.

His mount moved to the side, his grip had relaxed and he barely held on as his mount changed directions again, tossing him free.

He slammed into a tree and dropped to the ground.

He lay there, the fight draining from him as he felt relaxed, his duty was done. His mount came back for him but he was too tired to get back on. He took out a Stamina potion and drank it down, waking him up some.

There were noises in the bushes around him as people appeared on panthers.

"State your name and your purpose," A man asked, wearing a helmet as he aimed a strange device at Qiu Jun.

Qiu Jun had been preparing to detonate his mana core and kill as many as he could when he saw the weapon.

"Are you Sha?" He asked, they were the only people with similarly strange weapons.

"It doesn't matter, who are you?" The man asked.

"You Blood Demon Sect dogs can all die! Know that the Crafter's association will come for you!" He threw open his cloak and showed off his crafter's association guard badge proudly.

"Never heard of the Blood Demon Sect. What is a Crafter's association guard doing out here?" The man asked, moving his weapon so it wasn't pointed at Qiu Jun but it would only take him a moment to change that.

"Lies!" Qiu Jun shouted.

"I, Storbon, swear on the Ten Realms that I am not of the Blood Demons Sect, nor are any of my people. We do not wish you harm but if you attack us we will kill you. If you answer our questions truthfully, we will answer yours. I so swear on the Ten Realms and on my life," Storbon said.

Qiu Jun blinked, taking a moment to recognize the oath wasn't fake as he saw a screen in front of him, giving him the terms for accepting Storbon's oath.

"I am Qiu Jun, guard of the Tareng Crafter's association, who are you?"

"Specialist Storbon. What are you doing here?"

"Sending a message to the headquarters," Qiu Jun coughed.

"Why?"

"Blood Demon Sect poisoned our city, made it look like a plague. hen they blocked us from communicating or fleeing. We're too weak to fight them. Need help," Qiu Jun said.

"Which city?"

"Tareng," Qiu Jun said as his sound transmission device flashed.

He quickly accessed it and listened to the message.

"You will have to wait until someone can be sent from the Blue Lotus or the Crafter's association. We are sending your message higher but there are protocols to be followed. If this report is inaccurate, it will be reflected on your personal file. You will get a response within a week," a secretary at the crafter's association said.

"You mother fuckers!" Qiu Jun wanted to slam his sound transmission device against the ground. *They're still following the protocols in case we really have a plague. They get one message from us weeks ago saying that we're locking down the city and then another saying that we're under attack but not from the main sound transmission arrays in the city but from me.*

"Why are you here?" Qiu Jun asked, his eyes latching onto Storbon and the others.

"Working," Storbon said.

"On what?"

"Can't answer that."

"Can you take me to the nearest city?" Qiu Jun gritted his teeth. He didn't care about his own life now but he needed to get help for Tareng.

Storbon talked into his sound transmission device.

Qiu Jun could tell that there were more people in the forest watching them. Qiu Jun started to look at them closer, they didn't mean him harm it looked like.

Qiu Jun was level forty eight, sensing their auras he could tell that none of them were lower than level forty seven.

Why are they hiding in the forest? To have this many late level forties in the fifth realm, who are they?

Qiu Jun didn't know what to do.

Storbon relaxed on his mount.

"My boss wants to know everything before we do anything."

Qiu Jun looked back to Storbon, "Everything?"

"Everything that happened to Tareng. He is a member of the Alchemist Association and has an agreement with the Blue Lotus."

Qiu Jun felt himself relax some more.

Chapter: Sending Aid

"Grenade launcher," Tan Xue said, looking at the bastardized blueprints.

Matt couldn't help but laugh, shaking his head as if he was in on the joke.

"Something you care to share?" Fehim asked.

"Rugrat loves his explosions, never knew how this thing worked, he must've takena few of them apart."

"So, what are we looking at?" Taran asked.

"Firepower," Matt said and then cleared his throat with the looks from the different academy department heads.

"Okay so basically there are three parts to the weapon system, the barrel, the rotating chamber and then the buttstock and trigger assembly. Rugrat has said that it can all be made out of metal, we're not trying to reduce weight, with everyone's strength in the Army, they should be able to use these without strain. If we can make a plastic chamber and shrouding then it will reduce the weight and save people from burning their hands," Matt looked at Fehim.

"We have been able to extract tree sap and other ingredients to create plastics to support the Alva healers and the military medics. This would not be a flexible plastic, we will need more time to figure out the formula and then a way to set it," Fehim said.

"Taran can proabably help you with injection molding," Matt said.

"Huh?" Taran asked.

"Cast weapons and armor," Matt said.

"Oh," Taran went quiet. "I didn't think of that but yeah I guess anything that can be poured as a liquid and then solidifies could be cast, right?"

"Right, for this we can cast most of the parts, the ammunition will be cast as well. Breaking it down, Qin and Julilah, it will be up to you to create and streamline the process to make ammunition for the weapon system, then either have a rotating formation for the chamber, or we will have to use a spring mechanism that wue will need to create and will take longer."

"Should be able to make the formation but it depends on the materials. If we make the chamber with gears inside it will be easier to control. How does it work?" Qin asked.

"Well he sent an example," Matt grinned as he pulled out a complete version. He'd spent the night playing. . err. . Studying it.

"Okay so, if you press this release here, the chamber comed to the right, you can handload the rounds in here, but then Rugrat wants to make a speed loader which will take the plastics from the alchemy department and the smiths,": He looked at Fehim and then Tan Xue.

"You load the rounds in here, then you close it up."

He followed his words with actions and pressed the buttstock with his shoulder, "then you take it off of safety, which Rugrat went simple with, it's a level with a metal block that stops the firing pin from hitting the base of the round. The trigger system is simple but effective, you have to let the trigger go all the way forward, then when you pull on it the sear will engage the geared firing pin assembly."

Matt pulled on the trigger lightly, taking it under tension, "Then when the sear disengages"

Click

"Okay so then when it fires then the cylinder rotates, through spring or through formation you just pull the trigger again and it fires?" Julilah asked.

"Correct," Matt said.

"Okay seems like a mainly geared system," Tan Xue said. "Need high tolerances on the interior workings so that they stand up to wear and tear, probably best to have the formation trained smiths work on sheet metal."

She saw the looks of others.

"We can cast the barrel as well as the buttstock. Our ability to make reliable springs has improved though for small parts it is better to make a sheet of enhanced meta and then use mana blades and cutting tools to keep them uniform. The parts will all have similar tolerances and they can easily be replaced if necessary," She looked at Taran.

"Rugrat and Erik told me that the biggest thing with weapon systems is the ability to repair them and the fact that the parts from one should be interchangeable completely with another. We don't need to make specific parts for each weapon system. That way they can replace the parts in their weapons and keep them functional without needing a crafter on hand," Taran said.

"Rugrat wants to have one of these weapon systems for each of the Special Team members and then two per section to start, he really wants to make this a standard issue firearm."

"Understandable, it should be very versatile," Qin said. "New ammunition can greatly change the effects. If we add a formation to rotate the cylinder, it won't take much but it will mean that we can only add in one formation socket to the system if we want to mass produce them. If we took our time, different materials and different techniques we could increase that."

"Plastics will take time to build up, it might be better to go to the woodworking department, they have plenty of different types of trees that might be able to create coverings that will save people's hands and something to soften the blow with the buttstock," Fehim said.

"If we use casting for the rounds then we can create dozens of rounds at the same time, then check the formations, make sure they're properly inlaid," Julilah said.

"Then repeat the assembly line for rifle rounds, we'll need more powder from the alchemists department though," Taran looked at Fehim.

"We have made a system to create the rifle gunpowder, it has increased the production speed by thirty to forty percent. We will need to check the formula that Rugrat has identified and set up another gunpowder mill but it should take us less time to make more rounds. As long as we have the funding we can shift all academy related projects to creating more gunpowder and accelerants as well as explosives," Fehim said, looking to Delilah who was sitting in the corner listening.

Everyone looked over at the council leader of Alva.

"From now until the end of the conflict in the fourth realm, all production will be shifted to support the Alva military, funds have been released to this effect. Departments with personnel issue will call upon students in other departments to increase their numbers," Delilah's stood up as everyone watched her.

Matt looked at them all, most of them were older than Delilah, some nearly twice as old, but all of them respected her orders.

"Yes Council leader," Taran said, the others nodding their heads.

"Taran you have been liasing with the military and the smiths, now you will be in charge of military supply, you will coordinate the creation of any and all supplies that the military require. It will be your job to increase production while decreasing the resources and time required to create these supplies. I have sent a message to the Adventurer's and Trade sectors, they will be at your beck and call to gather required resources," Delilah's gaze fell on Taran as he bowed deeply with a grave expression.

Matt felt something in his core, something he didn't realize. He felt a part of Alva, he didn't care if he was worked to the bone if he could help. It was part of being and Alvan, pitching in and putting yourself to the side to help the whole.

It felt *right* and it felt powerful to be part of not just a group, but a community.

Seeing them all, thinking of how they had worked together to break down and build up the grenade launcher, Matt remembered that they had been dealing with swords and shields just months ago.

***

Erik started the briefing as Rugrat entered the room, his clothes in disarray and he smelled different.

Took him twenty minutes to get here and he came from the south. I should start sending my messages to Racquel if I want to get him after hours.

"From what the messenger is saying," Erik began, "Tareng was affected by what looked like a plague. As per their Standard operating procedure, they messaged the headquarters and locked down the city, no one in or out, containing the spread. Sound transmissions are being stopped by the attacking sect. They found out afterwards that the plague wasn't a plague at all but it was a concoction that had been introduced into the water systems.

"To others, this would be a failure of a transformation pill but it is also an incredibly effective poison because it doesn't act like a poison. Healing spells accelerate the poison instead of counteracting it. Many citizens of Tareng have already died, mainly the old and the very young. Apparently, the people with Body Cultivation aren't affected as quickly.

"The pill has been added to the water but in amounts that are hard to detect. Though a person needs what—three to five liters of water a day, more in the desert? Add that up over weeks, the potency increases, like poison building up in the body. This is a city, not the road, so people drink water from here instead of what's in their storage rings. If you went looking for poison, you wouldn't find anything. The body reacts positively to the failed pill after all, so healing spells actually accelerate the process. The change takes a lot of Stamina, so the people who have died were due to Stamina exhaustion. The chemical release of the body from the vast changes probably affects the chemical balance of the brain—turns them insane. Looks like it's pretty violent too.

"This is not a plague but a ploy. It seems that someone knew that Tareng would be cut off from the rest of the neutral cities if a plague started there. With this imposed isolation, when Tareng tried to report the poisoning, they found that they were under an isolation barrier. Moments later a war was declared on the city, locking up the totem so they couldn't leave.

"So to the various headquarters, nothing is wrong and it allows this Blood Demon Sect to do as they want," Erik concluded.

Everyone was quiet. It was a smart plan that took cunning to carry out but it removed the advantages of the Blue Lotus.

"Can they hold out?" Rugrat asked.

"The Blood Demon Sect is watching the city As the concoction progresses people will enter a stage of madness, where they will attack others wildly and randomly. After causing the people within Tareng to attack one another, then the Blood Demon Sect will walk in and clear up what's left," Erik said.

"Ways to cure it?" Domonos asked.

"None so far, just use Stamina potions to keep the body active, no healing potions, same reason for no healing spells," Erik said.

"So, what options do we have?" Yui asked.

"Leave them to suffer and get destroyed by the Blood Demon Sect and keep Vuzgal a secret, or help them escape to here and expose Vuzgal," Glosil said.

Erik turned to the map on the wall, it was a copy of the rough map Old Hei had given him.

"Tareng used to trade with Vuzgal back in the day. They're the closest city to the road that acted like a major trading center between Vuzgal and the Chaotic Lands before the fighting. We can take them supplies, Stamina concoctions and clean water so they can recover from the concoction over time but Tareng's got a weakened army of ten thousand. The Blood Demon Sect has a fifty thousand strong army. The Blood Demon Sect came to destroy Tareng one way or another. We will only be able to do one supply run in. The scouts aren't watching the forest as much as the desert and the messenger knows a weakness in the detection formations. While we can probably get in and out once, I wouldn't risk it a second time. They'll know someone came from the west. They might head this way and attack us at Vuzgal afterwards and we'll have to run. The other plan is," Erik paused "A little insane. We pull everyone out of Tareng. We get people from the higher ups on the fastest beasts we have, get them through our totem and to their headquarters."

"We need more information, have Lucinda do what she can to find out about the Blood Demons Sect numbers and their position. See what people in the lower realms know about Tareng, their fighting force numbers," Rugrat said.

"We should still send out forces to prepare for fighting, reainforce the observation points, clear out positions for the mortars," Glosil said.

"They will die without us," Rugrat said not trying to play to either side.

"They might die sooner because of us," Erik rebutted.

Rugrat seemed to have a response ready before he deflated and shrugged non-committally.

"Can we use the undead?" Glosil asked.

Erik looked at Rugrat.

"Only within the dungeon's area of influence. The undead rely on the dungeon core's power to keep them active, they can go beyond the dungeon's reach but they consume the power that is within their bodies quickly, while fighting it goes even faster. They'd be effective fighters in Vuzgal but outside of it, they're effective bombs if we just get them to detonate their mana core."

Glosil nodded.

"What are your orders?" Roska asked, looking between the three of them.

Rugrat looked to Erik who crossed his arms.

"I don't like how many unknowns we have and frankly the plan is more of an idea than a plan," Glosil said. "That said there was a time when Alva needed help. You helped us against the odds. I would suggest that we focus on building up our defenses here and making ammunition, using the undead to aid in both of these processes. We dig in like tics. If the battle is going bad on the road we risk it and send what we have to Alva and pull out as many people as we can."

"We should cut down the totem before we leave, Special Team One will volunteer to take it and flee to the North, we'll find another city with a totem and then bring it back to Alva, it's use and value cannot be denied," Niemm said.

"If we want to delay an army of fifty thousand, we're going to need a lot of shells. We'll need to clear those firing positions as well. What if they have aerial creatures or go through the forests?" Yui asked.

"The forests will be hard for them unless they have jungle mounts, there are a lot of monsters in there that will get stirred up. If they move into the forests it means that they won't be able to use large area defenses and we can tear them apart with artillery. If they have aerial creatures, we'll need to use explosive grenade shells to create flak," Erik looked to Rugrat.

"Otherwise we have spell scrolls, say we call in a lightning storm, tornadoes, high heat or low cold will make it hard for anything to fly in the skies," Rugrat offered.

"My current plan is that Domonos and Glosil will remain here with Rugrat to build up our defenses and complete looting the place," Domonos and Glosil nodded as Erik looked to Yui and Roska."I will move to meet up with Special Team One and this messenger to head to Tareng. Special Team Two and Tiger Platoon will come with me. Tiger Platoon have trained extensively with the Mortars. Special Team Two will start plotting out ambush points along our projected retreat path. Tiger Platoon will start clearing and readying positions where they can fire their mortars from. We'll adapt as things change on the ground. Special Team One and I will head in with supplies for Tareng. If they just take the supplies, that is all we can do. If they only send a few people out with us that's all we can do. We'll plan for all of Tareng coming with us and the sect trying to chase us down."

"Thankfully Han Wu has been studying how to make explosives for a long time so shouldn't be much of an issue getting him to adapt to the mines and IEDs," Rugrat said.

Roska's eye twitched but she nodded in agreement.

Erik looked at the others in the room. It was clear that they had their doubts.

"It won't be easy, but it's worth a shot," Glosil said getting nods of approval from the others.

***

"Well this is one big fucking mess," Rugrat said as Erik was packing up his gear in their shared room.

"Yeah," Erik said, stuffing items into his bag.

They could hear the rest of Tiger Platoon gathering their gear as well, people checking weapons or on their mounts. Vuzgal was in motion once again.

"Didn't think that we would be putting the mortars into use so soon," Rugrat said.

"They're good to go, right?"

"Yeah, though it will be the first time using them in combat and they weren't trained all that long ago."

"You sound like their mother. Mortars are much simpler than artillery."

"The two are pretty similar actually." Erik checked the room with a glance, it felt as if he had never been there. He pulled out his rifle, checked it and put it away as he grabbed his helmet and pulled it on.

"Keep the lights on," Erik said.

"Kick some fucking ass," Rugrat commented. They fist bumped as Erik walked out of the room and into the chaos of people getting their gear together and moving to the muster point, jumping up on their mounts.

***

Supplies were still going back and forth between Vuzgal and Alva, they were using multiple routes to bring up supplies while a small trickle was making it Alva. Most of the supplies held in different locations across the realms, waiting to go down so that it didn't raise people's suspicions seeing so many trading convoys heading into the Beast Mountain range. Loot travelled down and ammunition travelled back up.

"So you got all of this to play with?" Han Wu asked, his eyes shining as he looked at the crates that filled the abandoned warehouse.

"We've got shell casings, over there, bullets there, then we have the powders for them in those crates. Then we've got the solid explosives there," Rugrat pointed to different areas of the warehouse.

"Alva are making mortar and grenade rounds, they have casts down there that make it faster for them to cast the rounds, formation masters clean them up and fill in the formations. Alchemists add the charges to the mortar rounds, they can make five thousand rounds per day reliably. Now that will increase with needing to cover the people from Tareng.

"Which brings up this part of the warehouse, explosives."

"I'm guessing that they haven't been broken down into charges?" Han Wu asked.

"Bingo, Erik made this stuff when we were finding out the right mixture of stuff for gunpowder," Rugrat explained.

"And the world has never been the same," Han Wu grinned.

"Yeah explosives are pretty sweet," Rugrat and Han Wu shared a look of appreciation between pyrotechnics.

Rugrat cleared his throat.

"This is C4, the name doesn't relate to what it is, I just like it."

"C4 this stuff is pretty stable though. Can throw it around and it'll do nothing, you compress it or set it on fire, going to be an issue. Great for making mines without building the casings," Han Wu said.

"Seems you've learned a bit about it?"

"Well, I do deal in explosives and make my own mixes, get talking to alchemists and you had this in production and my clearance is high," Han Wu coughed under Rugrat's gaze/

"I've done stupider shit. This is your main go to IED making mix. I have the alchemists in Alva working overtime to make more, it's up to you to figure out how to use it. Here are a few ideas," Rugrat passed Han Wu a few pieces of paper detailing ways to set up different charges and what they would do.

Chapter: Tareng

Special Team One raced ahead with Erik to meet up with Special Team Two who were looking after the messenger who was sending messages to the Crafters and the Blue Lotus continuously, trying to get them to break their plague protocols.

The Tiger Platoon followed behind, making sure to not tire their mounts that were at a lower level than Gilly and the special team mounts.

Gilly, finally free from the dungeon pulled ahead, stretching her legs happily as she raced down the road.

Erik was surprised with her speed being level sixty-five it started to make sense.

The ride was short. A few creatures tried to challenge them but with ten battle-tested panthers and Gilly, they didn't stand much of a chance, not even including the humans riding them.

It took Erik four days with only a small break to rest before he arrived in the camp that Special eam One had created.

"He's this way," Niemm said, Erik was covered in dust from the road as he dismounted the blue scaled beauty known as Gilly.

Gilly shook her body, even she was tired after the hard riding that they had done over the past few days.

Erik used a healing spell on himself, his legs were chafing and burning something fierce.

Erik entered a tent where the messenger was staying He looked like hell as he drank another Stamina concoction.

"I'm Erik, the leader of this group," Erik pulled out two medallions and handed them to the messenger, he looked at them, the medallion that showed him to be friend of the Blue Lotus and the other that made him a Journeyman of the Alchemist association.

The man's eyes relaxed a bit.

"My name is Qiu Jun. I'm told that you have a plan to help the people of Tareng."

"Yeah, we're going to get past these Blood Demon Sect scouts, and meet up with the leaders of Tareng then convince them to flee Tareng with us," Erik said. "Are you good to move? We need to get our plan in action as soon as possible."

"I'm okay to move but I don't think that they'll agree," Qiu Jun said

"I can only give them options," Erik looked at Niemm. "Get the supplies cross loaded, we'll head out in two hours."

"Sir," Niemm said.

Erik left the tent and looked at a notification that appeared.

==========

Event

==========

You have found that the Blood Demon Sect has poisoned the people of Tareng.

Save the people of Tareng or leave them to die.

Rewards will be based upon your end result.

==========

***

Qiu Jun's body had healed up some more, with the clean water and stamina potions his body had been able to recover enough to allow him to walk and calmed down the changes happening in his body. He looked down from the sand dune, his enchanted clothing blending in with the sand naturally.

"Looks like there are a few scouts in the area. They are looking away from the west, toward Tareng," Lucinda said, her eyes murky as she was looking through Night Terror's eagle eyes.

"We'll move at night and use spells to remove our tracks so they don't spot us," Erik said. "Are you sure that this pass will work Qiu Jun?"

"They're looking to detect people exiting Tareng, not those going in. The formation will detect those going into the valley but along the pass I saw it won't detect people coming out. I wanted to pass through there but instead had to pass when a patrol was going through so that I looked like part of the patrol," Qiu Jun answered.

Night came and they moved forward between two sand dunes that created a valley. There was a rock face at the end of it that they scaled down with ropes.

They got to the edge of the detection formation and dug, the sand collapsed back on them and left a gap under the detection formation.

They crawled through the new gap, using spells to mask their progress, stirring up the sand and returning it to how it used to be and passive anti-detection and stealth spells that made it harder for formations to see them and would trick the human mind.

They used hand signals and looks to communicate as they moved on, Qiu Jun leading them past random detection formations he had laid out on a map during his exit.

After clearing the last detection formation, he got back on his mount, the rest of them following on their own mounts as they quickly crossed the desert.

The sands gave way to a landscape that was dotted with massive naturally formed stone pillars that reached into the sky.

The sun was coming down on them as a city appeared between the red stone pillars.

The city had the same red sand-colored walls as the pillars around it. The buildings inside were shaped like pyramids, stretching above the city walls. There were four entrances to the city, each of them large enough for four carriages to ride side by side.

Currently these roads were empty and the gates were closed.

"Not a good sign," Storbon said.

"Nope. Keep a lookout," Niemm said. The two of them looked at each other, shifting their worn cloaks so it would be easier to fight.

Qiu Jun used a spell, sending up a signal flare.

Nothing happened as they adjusted in their saddles, becoming more alert.

"What was that?" Erik asked Qiu Jun.

"A signal to let them know who I am," Qiu Jun said.

Erik gritted his teeth but didn't say anything, he wiped the sand from his combat glasses and watched the area as they rode up to the massive city.

It was a large city, about a third the size of Vuzgal. The powerful, formation-inscribed walls had patrolling guards and weapon emplacements showing that the city wasn't empty.

They kept on riding toward the walls but the gates remained closed.

They arrived in front of the gate as it opened.

There were soldiers waiting behind the gate wearing the armor of the Crafter's association and the Blue Lotus.

"Hands up!" A voice came from above as archers appeared on the walls.

Qiu Jun and the others did as they were told.

"Don't fight," Erik said.

They were quickly pulled from their mounts and had chains put on their arms as they were dragged into the city, their mounts growling angrily as they were captured, even the high leveled beast masters had a hard time calming the beasts and pulling them inside.

Erik didn't miss their surprised looks, the beasts had been fed plenty of monster cores, with the supplies of Vuzgal they had reached the same level as their riders. Mid level forty mounts were expensive and harder to find in the fourth realm.

*   *   *

Head of the Tareng Blue Lotus Xue Lin let out a sigh as she heard everything that the messenger Qiu Jun had to say.

"Thank you for your efforts," Daniels, the Head of the Crafter's association in Tareng said.

Qiu Jun bowed deeply before leaving the room.

The doors closed and the room remained in silence, feeling desolate. *Our own headquarters won't listen to us and the only people that our messenger met are this mysterious group that have an alchemist who is also a friend of the Blue Lotus.*

"What do you think Xue Lin?" Daniels asked. They had worked together for years before this and with the latest issues they had become friends.

"I think we don't have many options right now, it sounds that at least this Erik has a plan," she shrugged.

Daniels nodded and then looked to a guard."Bring him in."

It was a few minutes before a bound Erik appeared before them.

"What is your full name Erik?" Daniels asked.

"Journeyman Alchemist Erik West, direct disciple of Expert Alchemist Hiao Zen, pill head of the Third Realm," Erik said.

There was some talk among the leadership as Erik continued.

"If you need confirmation you can look at my emblem, the information is all there. Now I'm not here for small talk, so there are two things I offer. A shot at escaping this trap, and supplies to help you," Erik said.

Close to reaching level forty but he has confidence and he's smart. Telling us his qualifications and linking him to the associations and offering options, allowing him to take control of the discussion so we are the ones that have to ask him questions as if he knows everything about our situation already.

"What is your plan?" Xue Lin asked

"Leave Tareng," Erik's two words were like a bomb.

"How can we leave the city? There are wolves at the gate and you want us to rush into them! Do you want us to fall on our swords for them too?!"

"At least we have walls here, in the desert we'll be caught without any defenses!"

"There are ten armies all around us, that can react to cut off our line of advance!"

"I thought you would have more brains than this!"

Daniels cleared his throat, silencing the other voices in the hall.

"The army will intercept us before we get to any of the surrounding cities," Xue Lin said calmly.

"We won't be going to any of them. We will be heading east," Erik said.

"East? There is only the cursed lands there and the remains of the Edar Empire."

"It used to be. We need to move and fast. We have a lot of people to move."

"How long will it take for us to reach the forest and them?"

"It will take them three days to gather their units and then reach the forest road. It could take us," Xue Lin frowned, thinking. "Around two days if we go all out."

She looked to Daniels who nodded in agreement.

"They'll be right behind us, on the road they will move faster than us and catch up."

"I have people on the road that are getting ready to greet the Blood Demon Sect. I have a few plans to attacka nd ambush their army along the road and slow them to give us space and time between the two groups," Erik said.

"You have been able to clear the Edar Empire's capital Vuzgal?" Daniel's asked suddenly.

This sent ripples through the room as the different men and women talked to one another.

"Something like that. It's not important but if we get to the capital, we'll have defenses and a totem to use. Also, we will have the forests which will naturally funnel the Blood Demon Sect armies. With the right tactics, we can slow the speed of their advance. If we don't slow them, then we will die. If we go in any other direction, we will die. If you stay here, they'll wait till you're at your most vulnerable and everyone will die."

"We will need to take time to think on this," Xue Lin responded.

"Don't take too long. There are supplies of Stamina concoctions and water within some of our storage devices that could help the people of Tareng. The longer you wait, the worse it will be. I hope that based on our associations goodwill that you will release myself and my guards within two days so that we can escape the Blood Demon Sect encirclement," Erik said.

Xue Lin and Daniels shared a look.

"We will release you in two days," Daniels confirmed.

Erik was led out of the council room again as everyone started talking to one another.

"We will take a break," Daniels said as he and Xue Lin left the room, stepping into a meeting room.

Daniels took a seat in one of the chairs as he let out a sigh.

"What do you think?" he asked.

"I didn't detect that he was lying, he was confident in what he was saying. What do you think of his plan?" Queried Xue Lin.

"I think that it will be hard to tell others about it. To leave Tareng? The walls are the only thing that people have confidence in anymore."

"A fish can be flushed out and a crab's shell broken," Xue Lin said. "We are running out of time and supplies. His emblems can't be faked, they're as authentic as they come. If they really control Vuzgal then they're not pushovers. There have been generations that have gone there to try and claim the treasures of the capital but none have been able to. If we stay here we will die, if we flee through the desert it might be the only chance that we have," Xue Lin sighed, feeling the full weight of her position.

"You're willing to place that much trust in him? It could be a trap," Daniels said.

"If we get him to make an oath on the Ten Realms would that satisfy you?" Xue Lin asked.

Daniels seemed to be stumped for words.

"I guess it's not really having an oath or not, more the fact that it feels like we're just running scared," Daniels sighed.

"We run today, so that we can fight tomorrow," Xue Lin consoled him.

Daniels was quiet, thinking if there was any other option. Finally he stood up, "Alright, shall we get back in there?"

They walked back to their seats as Daniels motioned for Xue Lin to speak.

"The Blue Lotus agrees to Erik's plan, we will order our people to pack up their goods as well as the people of the city to follow us out towards Vuzgal," Xue Lin announced. This had mixed reactions among the people there. Those from the Blue Lotus kept their mouths shut, there was a strict hierarchy among them so what their head said, they would follow through with.

Daniels cleared his throat and looked at Xue Lin.

"Our two groups have worked together for an unknown number of years. We will stand with the Blue Lotus at this time and listen to your counsel. We are crafters, not people of war. Though I want to raise a few questions. If it is indeed true, what will we do? Our fighting forces are badly affected by the concoction and from what you have said, it will only get worse before it gets better. If the enemy attacks, we will be unable to defend. We have sealed the totem; the seal will remain for another month. Our options are limited. I have wracked my brains and not found answers. I don't like this plan but out of what we've got, it's the best one."

He'd brought up other's fears and showed that he was not deaf or blind to them and was also sympathetic to them.

He might not have fought in any battles but he knew the way of things in the Fourth Realm.

"For this, I hope Head Xue Lin will take command."

"I thank you for your trust Head Daniels," She stood and bowed her head slightly to Daniels and looked to the rest of the people in the room. "Gather your people, we leave in two days."

***

"Sorry about that, I am to escort you all to the Blue Lotus," A guard said as he undid the chains of Special Team One and Erik, their mounts were there waiting for them.

"Please follow me," The guard mounted up on a lizard.

They all got on their mounts and made to follow him. The guard waved to someone that opened the gate into the compound. They passed through and walked into the actual city.

Tareng was an oasis in the desert. There was nothing but rocks and sand outside the gates, with the trading road cutting through it all. Inside the walls there were desert plants reaching up to the skies, parks with ponds, streams of water that curved underneath bridges and through the city.

Tareng was made up of tall but thin buildings, like the towering rocks outside of the city. Pyramids rested on pillars, the interior filled with gardens and water features, the pyramid keeping the sand and wind out, while the gardens naturally cooled the interior.

There were markets that filled the interior of the pyramids with color, but remained silent with the plague keeping many at home.

Some of the pyramids were connected by walkways. Between the Pyramids there were streets lined with palm trees, stores, and living quarters. A second city that hid in the pyramid's shadows.

Erik pulled back his hood and took his sunglasses off, the newly revealed clean skin striking a contrast as the rest of him was covered in dirt.

All of the squad looked hard traveled.

Although the city was a paradise, the people in the streets moved around with fear on their faces, looking around as if skittish.

There were massive trading areas dotted around the city. Entire pyramids were dedicated to different crafts but the forges were cold and the tailors' needles were still.

The city seemed to have ground to a halt.

They reached the middle of the city. A Blue Lotus building rested in the center of the city. It was massive—about the size of the Colosseum in Rome. Instead of being a pyramid, it was shaped like a blooming Blue Lotus flower, reaching into the sky.

The normally busy doors of the Blue Lotus were open and barren. The wind rolled through the main square, pulling along non-existent tumbleweeds.

The guards standing at the gates of the Blue Lotus building were each level fifty. Their cold eyes watched the group as they dismounted. Someone collected their beasts and they walked passed the guards who stood there like statues.

"Has to suck standing for that long," Erik thought to himself as they continued into the Blue Lotus. Remembering the parades and the all too long speeches he had needed to suffer through.

A man cupped his hands and bowed to them as they entered. "I am Lee Jung. I will take you to see Head Xue Lin."

The guide guard cupped his hands and bowed deeper to Lee Jung, backing off, his job done.

Erik cupped his hands. "Thank you."

The man looked at Erik's clothes covered in dust and his dirty face.

"I can only allow two of your guards with you," His smile became a bit more forced as he led them through the Blue Lotus.

"Yao Meng, Tian Cui, keep up. Niemm make sure that those supplies get passed out," Erik said as he walked up the stairs.

"On it," Niemm replied.

Tian Cui and Yao Meng followed Erik up the stairs.

"This place is loaded," Yao Meng said to Tian Cui. She nodded as they passed different cabinets with items on offer and entered a private area with expensive paintings and sculptures.

They passed roaming guards but there was no one trying to auction any items. It was eerily silent as they reached the head's door.

The guards didn't seem to have a presence; if Erik didn't see them breathing, he would think that they were statues.

They moved to open the door as Lee Jung stepped to the side.

"Wait here. Don't break anything," Erik said to them before focusing on Yao Meng, who looked hurt.

Tian Cui snorted. "I'll try my best to keep him out of trouble, boss."

"Thanks." Erik headed in.

Xue Lin stood from where she was sitting. She looked delicate and classy wearing a finely made blue dress.

She nodded to Erik, who cupped his hands to her and gave a slight bow.

"Head Xue."

"Journeyman West, if you are able to get us out of here, then you'll gain recognition from the Crafters Association and Blue Lotus that few have," she said.

"I only have one term I need you and Daniels to agree on," Erik said.

"What is that?"

"That the Blue Lotus and the Crafter's Association will call Vuzgal a trading city. That I will be able to remain in control over it. I will offer preferential treatment to both associations, the same terms that I would give to my own alchemist association," Erik said.

"You have big aspirations," Xue Lin said. "Though I won't lie, it is good to know your terms and that you're not just doing this out of the goodness of your heart. People that do that in the Fourth Realm have another angle they're working, or they'll end up dead soon enough."

"I wouldn't know, I'm pretty new around these parts," Erik said and sat forward.

Xue Lin sent a message with her sound transmission device and then pulled out a contract, writing it out in front of Erik and then signing it with her blood and passing it to Erik.

Erik checked the contract and put it away.

A light appeared on her sound transmission device.

"Daniels will have the contract sent over shortly," She said.

A screen appeared in front of Erik.

==========

Event

==========

You have found that the Blood Demon Sect has poisoned the people of Tareng.

You have chosen to save the people of Tareng.

Rewards will be based upon your end result.

==========

"Can you tell me more about what is going on?"

"We have been trying to pass messages out to the Blue Lotus and the Crafter's Association Headquarters. Yet it looks like from what you've said that we need to send one of our more prestigious people there to tell them in person. They won't trust outsiders. We have an army of ten thousand here, all of which have been affected by the concoction. We estimate that they have an army of fifty thousand circling us in ten different camps, with a heavy concentration of Elites and Masters. We are swiftly running out of clean water to drink. We won't get aid for six more weeks but we will likely not last that long. I have a responsibility to my association and to the people here. I haven't heard of you Erik or your group but you came to help us, are a member of an allied association and a friend of my Blue Lotus.

"Your identity checks out and well. There are no other options left to us, so, you're it."

"No pressure at all," Erik said.

Xue Lin didn't offer any consolation as she shook a bell.

A woman appeared through a side door. Looking at her, Erik couldn't see through her level and he could tell that while her Mana systems weren't as developed as his in terms of Mana gates, it was a step further in overall cultivation. The same went for her body cultivation.

"This is Olivia, she is the commander of the Blues Lotus forces here, and now all of the guards. She is currently getting everyone ready to leave the city."

"Good to meet you Olivia," Erik said

Chapter: Movements

"The staff of the Alva Healing House in Vermire have arrived and the previous group are returning. Jen from the Healing department has already sent people off to the higher realms to assist the adventurers to gain more practical information when dealing with different injuries and increase in overall experience for solving complications that come with mana and body cultivation," Jia Feng said. "It is possible for us to increase our skills in the first realm without the need of rare resources, we just need more information and practical application."

Healing was one of the few skills that didn't need better materials, only worse or different injuries to increase in skill level. As long as someone continued to learn about the human body their level could increase dramatically.

It was how Jen had been able to reach the mid-level Journeyman level in healing and there are a dozen others who had reached low-Journeyman level skill in healing.

"Tan Xue is now an Expert smith, Taran is a high-Journeyman-level smith, and there are seven other smiths at the mid-Journeyman level. Fehim has reached the low Journeyman level in Alchemy and there are a dozen high-Apprentice-level alchemists.

"Zhou Heng has increased the ability of the clothing workshop. His trained tailors have reached the mid-Journeyman level; he has reached the high-Journeyman level. Shu Wanshu of the woodworking department has also reached high Journeyman, with his people at mid-Journeyman level.

"Qin Silaz has just reached the mid-Journeyman level in formations but most of her people are at the high-Apprentice level, with only three others as low-Journeyman level. It is a heavily theory-based course, and although Qin is forging a path, there are still plenty of questions they don't yet have answers to.

"We have collected a great amount of material but as we can see, having a person of higher skill levels will pull up the others in the department by helping them learn better techniques faster," Jia Feng said.

"How has the search for Experts gone?" Delilah asked.

"We have been able to find a few people but trying to convince them to come to Alva and confirming that they are of good good character is the hard part. Many of them are used to having powerful forces fawning over them." Jia Feng sounded dejected.

"We do not need to take the ones who everyone else wants. We want the outliers, people who don't have a position of strength, the ones who have made a name for themselves on their own hard work and the people who don't care about games but want to increase their abilities. We have Expert-level workshops and resources that are almost impossible to find in other realms. That is why they should come to us. If we're just bringing people interested in wealth, as soon as they have made enough money from us, they will move on to the next person to offer them more money," Delilah said.

Jia Feng winced at her words and cupped her fist. "Council leader's words are correct. I am sorry. I was blinded by their prestige."

"Honestly, if there are strong people of the Apprentice level or Journeyman level, they are a gem to us. It will mean that we do not need to train them on the basics and with what we have here, they might be able to increase their Strength faster. And if they are younger, they will feel a greater attachment to the place that took them in and taught them." Delilah's words were basic truth but Jia Feng's eyes widened; a faint flush appeared on her face as she made to speak once again.

"We have all been busy. This change will not be easy to go through," Delilah said, saving Jia Feng from having to say more words of apology and embarrass herself. "We are all doing jobs we didn't think that we would be doing. We need to help one another and we will do so, as a team."

Although they were members of the council, they all had their own areas of expertise before they were council leaders.

"Egbert, what is the current population of Alva?"

"Our population has rapidly increased with the Adventurer's Guild and the traders heading to the higher realms. There are currently five hundred cases under review, with our population in Alva reaching six hundred and another three hundred outside of Alva, not including the army in the Fourth Realm," Egbert said.

"Very good. It seems that for now we have been able to stabilize Alva. Upgrading to the fourth tier of workshops and departments will take time and a lot of wealth to do so. So, in the meantime, we will have to work with what we have, look to recruit more people to Alva, and gain more opportunities for our people to grow. Is there anything else that we need to talk about?" She looked at the council members.

Jasper raised his hand. "The Adventurer's Guild has increased to three thousand current members and we have even more applicants. Right now, most of the people are working in the other realms to earn more money, meaning that we will need to make special requests for people to come back to Alva if some of our students want to go to the higher realms and need security. We still have adventurers training with the dungeon battlefield and others who are teaching their fighting art or learning at the academy as well. I think that organizing trips after the different semesters might be for the best—take groups of people to different places in the realms without having to pay exorbitant fees."

Delilah looked to Jia Feng.

"We can talk afterward," Jia Feng said.

Jasper nodded as Delilah looked around the room, seeing that there was no one else with points. "Very well," Delilah said.

Delilah got up and stretched. "Well, I think that should be all for our meeting, thank you all for your continued efforts."

The others stood, stretching and working out the kinks from having to sit for so long. Outside of the dungeon core meeting room, one could see the academy, which had undergone another set of revisions. All of the different buildings were now tier three. A large two-story building stood over the growing fields, the first growing house. They only had a limited amount of land that they could grow on and they had covered the free land in farms and doubled the size of the Alchemy garden.

The rest of Alva was filled with crops in different stages. Once they had covered the ground, the blueprint office and the farmers got together, wondering whether they could build upward instead of out, creating a second floor to increase their farming land. It added a new challenge as the plants on the first level would be getting less light, the farmers were excited to work with creating strains of plants to work in low-light areas while the formation department was working to create formations that could recreate natural sunlight.

In the fields, different monsters moved around. These were from the Earth's Divinity Temple. As they moved through the fields, they released Earth and Wood Mana, increasing the nutrients in the soil and in the plants, increasing the speed that they grew. It meant that even with the increase in land, the time to harvest decreased and the farmers could focus on their projects. A field of trees had been started. There were regular fruit trees and then synthetic trees that the farmers were experimenting with.

Alva was no longer a place that was grasping at anything and everything to try to grow. Now, they had the ability to take their time and plan. They had matured and grown steadily. Now there were more people who weren't originally from Alva than there were people who had been from the small village in the wilderness.

Still, everyone had heard the stories of Erik and Rugrat, how they had brought people to the dungeon and put everything they had into increasing the strength of others and Alva as a whole.

One only needed to look at the academy, a kind of institution that was unheard of in other places and something that people definitely couldn't just pay a fee to enter. In the rest of the Ten Realms, they would need to dedicate their life to the people who taught them, being a sect's pawn under restrictive oaths for the rest of their life.

In Alva one could learn to advance themselves but no one demanded any oath other than to keep Alva a secret.

The council members talked to one another and started moving out of the room. Delilah found Jasper as they were leaving.

"Have you been in contact with Elise?" Delilah asked.

"Periodically. She set up a new trade route in the Second Realm and she headed to the Third Realm. She should be in the Sky Reaching Restaurant. It seems that she had thoughts of expanding our influence there. She took out a sizable loan from the Alva treasury," Jasper said.

"Happy not to be dealing with all of it?" Delilah smiled.

"You have no idea." Jasper grinned. "Much happier managing things and letting Blaze deal with all of the meetings and the like."

"You've both increased the size of the Adventurer's Guild rapidly, that is nicely done."

"Yes but we've got plenty of applicants. We have to limit how many we bring in to keep up the standard that we've created."

Delilah nodded. The guild and the traders were the biggest borrowers of money. They also purchased the most goods from Alva and had the greatest profits. Alva now had the financial capital to go up against a powerful sect in the Second Realm in terms of wealth. In terms of population, they would be able to compete with some of the weaker sects in the Third Realm. This showed just how strong they had become.

Jia Feng approached as Delilah said good-bye to Jasper, leaving them to talk as she headed for the academy to read the latest books that had been purchased from the Third Realm. She smiled and waved to people as she moved through Alva.

If one tried to commit a crime, then the oath that bound them would incapacitate them, needless to say, there was no crime in Alva. Other places didn't use oaths as it was seen as a big hassle and if the stronger power players killed a few of their subjects there wasn't a backlash. Without an oath, it created a double-edged sword; with it, the people at the top had to do what they thought was best for the people under them and the people under them would follow the laws that they passed.

The policing force was a few people who didn't want to be soldiers or adventurers. They were older in their years but they were still powerful. There were only ten of them but their Strength increased rapidly. They were allowed various resources to increase their Strength so that they would be able to deal with any issues within the population, should any issue arise.

They were also a neutral force that only listened to Egbert. He acted as their judge and commander as well as teacher.

Many people wished to get the positions but very few were accepted, needing to be older to have experience and an education and Strength.

They also served as a regulatory body for the government to make sure that everyone was doing their job. Even with oaths, there might be something that wasn't covered and people were able to steal some funds.

Delilah pulled out a pad of paper and checked to see whether there was anything else she needed to do and then checked her planner. She was free for a few days. A smile crept up on her face as she put it away and looked at the library ahead of her.

Her smiled turned somber. *I hope that Teacher and Rugrat are safe.* They were the strongest people she had met but with everything she heard from the Fourth Realm, it was hard not to worry.

***

"I hope that we are able to come to many more agreements in the future!" The man laughed and his eyes danced in joy at the deal they had made as he bowed to Elise.

"Pleasure doing business with you." Elise bowed to a man wearing flowing robes and a medallion on his chest to show what trading company he belonged to as she saw him out at the entrance to the Sky Reaching Restaurant.

He took his leave, chatting happily to his cohort about his successful deal.

Elise turned, looking at her aides. Matt came out from a doorway he had been behind.

"Another deal made. I really do have a lot to learn from a trader of your caliber." Matt laughed, cupping his fists.

"Jackass." She rolled her eyes at his jokes as he laughed and followed her through the restaurant. "I heard that you're going to be leaving the Division Headquarters?"

"Yeah, I've been stuck up in here making plans for people for a long time. My designs are getting stagnant. I'm going to travel to a few other cities I have heard about and check out their designs and architecture. I'm also interested in studying item design and blueprints. A building is a lot of work but it's a lot of repeating yourself. I've had more people from Alva requesting me to make blueprints and technical drawings for weapons, clothes and armor. I want to see what other crafters do to make these drawings or blueprints and see if I can adjust my style. Why try to recreate the wheel when I can use what others are doing?"

"Are you sure that the Sky Reaching Restaurant can survive without you?"

"I'm pretty sure. Manager Yi is rather capable and she has already brought the men of the Division Headquarters into her hand. I was wondering if I could talk to you about another matter though." Matt's voice turned serious as they reached the back gardens of the restaurant, the private area where the people of Alva stayed.

Elise looked at him with interest.

"While you are traveling the Third Realm, would you be able to find other locations where we can put more Sky Reaching Restaurants? They can act as stops for the traders and adventurers, as well as information gathering centers and generate an income. We have a large income here but we are limited by our size. If we were to make more, we would also be able to act as the banks for the people of Alva," Matt said.

"You sure that you don't want to be a trader?" she asked.

"I have plenty of money and I want to grow stronger." Matt's playful smile fell away. "You might not have seen it—the risks that Erik and Rugrat take all the time, the way that they're able to smile after it all, as if it were nothing and hide all that they've done from everyone else. They hold the weight of Alva on their shoulders and I want to do everything I can to help them. With blueprints, it can help those of a lower level to increase their skill and ability or at least should help some.

"I want to make Alva strong, stronger for them. Also, I want to find more information on my summoning class and gain more creatures that I can summon."

Elise nodded. She had seen Erik and Rugrat when they had defended Alva the village. She had heard of their fighting from the people on the special teams, from Delilah and now even from Matt. While she had been sitting back and growing her trade network, even now they were fighting. If it wasn't for them, they wouldn't have gotten to this stage.

"We were lucky to find them," Elise said.

"I also want to see if I can find any more people from Earth. There's no knowing where they are but it is worth looking to find them if we can."

**

Olivia got a message from one of the scouts that she had sent out of the city. She had only sent the strongest, the reserve force of the Blue Lotus. They were kept hidden and moved between Blue Lotus locations frequently, a hidden trump card that moved before they were discovered so people wouldn't know the abilities of the new group.

They were also the trainers of the guards of the Blue Lotus locations, making sure to keep their skills in top form and increasing their skill constantly.

She was confident in their abilities, which were only slightly less impressive than her own.

Her expression darkened. "Roi!" she barked. She pulled out the black armor with faint blue sections and a lotus embossed on its front. She started putting on her leg guards as the door opened.

A tall man with crystal-clear green eyes opened the door.

"Commander." His deep voice was powerful, even when speaking quietly. He knelt and saluted Olivia.

"The enemy has started to move." Her voice was chillingly cold as she put her boots on and tightened them with quick movements. She was still feeling the effects of the concoction but with her powerful Body Cultivation and Mana gathering ability, its impact had been weakened.

Roi's hand clenched as killing intent leaked out from his body. Someone weaker than Olivia might have been sent into a state of shock and covered in cold sweat.

Instead, she simply pulled on her breastplate and pulled the ties, sealing it up. "Alert the others and ready the guards."

"Yes, Commander," Roi said. The killing intent from before had disappeared, which was even worse than letting it leak out. It showed his control over his emotions. A person blinded with emotion would be a liability. One who could use them, who could make the enemy think that they were soft, could lead the enemy into making a fatal mistake.

He stood as Olivia pulled on her gauntlets.

"We might have to run now but the Blue Lotus doesn't forget," Olivia said.

"Yes, Commander," Roi said. His green eyes were cold now. A switch had flipped, turning him from man to guard.

Olivia pulled on her helmet as he turned and left the room, sending out messages.

She looked out of her window out at Tareng city and the desert beyond that was shrouded in darkness.

Chapter: Run

The door to the compound that Erik and Special Team One were resting in opened as Xue Lin entered.

Erik and Storbon were lounging next to the fire, both of them grabbing their rifles as her guard's hands touched their weapons.

They lowered their weapons, Xue Lin paying no attention "The enemy has started to move," she said.

She wasn't wearing her flowing clothes anymore; instead, she wore armor of the Blue Lotus. Erik could tell that it was a peak-Journeyman-level armor with a few pieces that had reached the Expert stage based on referencing other armor he had seen and conversations with Rugrat about armor and weapons.

Erik looked at Storbon. He took off at a run, his speed impressive. Erik put away the report. "Communications?"

"They're blocking us and we're blocking them."

"Hopefully that can give us some more time."

"The caravans are ready, we move within the hour."

"Understood," Erik nodded he pulled his armor on and grabbed his helmet.

"Once we break through the scouts, Daniels and his people will move with their guards and your people towards Vuzgal at their best speed to go through the totem. They can go to visit their higher-ups and pass the word to their people and to the people of the Blue Lotus in person. We know they won't accept what you say without proof, so Daniels' group will be our proof."

"Understood. I'll hang back and command my people at the road to hold and slow the Blood Demon Sect," Erik said.

"Olivia will command the Tareng forces."

"Got it," Erik finished with his gear as the rest of the special team were jogging out of their rooms and checking their gear.

She also noticed that there was no fluctuation in his emotions, as if he were detached from it all. It was as though he were more machine than man. It was something she had seen in men and women who had been in the Fourth Realm for a long time and had seen too many of the horrors of war.

***

The city started to move. The streets were filled with caravans; storage chests and items were stuffed to the brim as extra carriages that had been made just for this were hooked up to beasts.

Some people didn't want to leave; they weren't forced to. Xue Lin didn't waste her time with them but sent some of her people to investigate them in case they were spies.

A few spies had been found and they were questioned. Some of them gave information, enough for them to determine the identity of their enemy.

The Blood Demon Sect.

The sect had been facing trouble recently, with two powerful forces creating an alliance for the purpose of tearing up their lands.

By mid-afternoon, the convoys were ready to move. They moved out of every gate in the city and headed east. There was no attempt to hide their movements. Winged beasts took off into the sky as forces moved ahead of the caravan, taking the locations of the scouting outposts from the Blood Demon Sect. It would be their role to sneak up on the scouts and kill them.

In a coordinated strike they cut down the scouts in the observation posts. Clearing a path through the Blood Demon Sect's lines.

Olivia and the others knew it wouldn't be long until the Blood Demon Sect learned of the hole.

Olivia didn't allow anything to stop them as the stream of people left the capital, nearly Eighty thousand people. All of them were powerful. The members of the neutral cities were strong in their own right, be it in skills or in connections and wealth.

The Blue Lotus and the Crafter's Association were the overlords of the city, so no one dared to get in their way.

Erik and his special team were in the middle of it all, the nerve center of everything. They were calm, sending out their orders. Olivia didn't like being under command of someone who wasn't from the Blue Lotus and had picked the guard detail around Erik. No matter what, if something went wrong and Erik betrayed them, they would lay down their lives to make sure that he didn't survive.

She had done the same with the group that was with the Crafter's Association and had placed some of the hidden eyes and ears of the Blue Lotus with the guards. It would be valuable if they were able to observe where they were going and pass information back to the higher members of the Blue Lotus.

They rushed across the desert, heading to the East.

An advanced force had gone ahead with half of Erik's group, Qiu Jun and the Master level Tareng fighters.

Olivia rode up to Xue Lin's carriage, the wind whipping at her armor.

"The scouts and the Master level forces that we sent out killed the Blood Demon Sect people in the outposts, they're not sure if they triggered alarm formations or not."

"Make sure no one falls behind. If a carriage is broken, leave it," Xue Lin ordered.

"Yes Head Xue!"

They had punched a hole in the Blood Demon Sect's ring of outposts and rode through it in a race to live.

The sect would learn sooner or later of the hole in their screen but it would give the people of Tareng more time; the convoy looked like a black snake moving across the desert in the middle of the night, a large cloud of sand rising up behind them as they ran.

***

As they were fleeing, an older, kind-looking woman stepped out of Tareng as if to see them off. She had tears in her eyes as she looked away at the desert and kneeled in the sand, touching it.

Her sleeves touched the ground; a worm-like creature dropped to the desert ground. It burrowed into the sand and disappeared. With a wave of her sleeve, there was no sign of the disappearing worm on the sand's surface.

"Are you okay?" One of the people who had decided to stay in the city and had seen off the convoy moved to help the older woman.

"I'm fine, thank you." She gave them a warm smile as they helped her up.

The younger man smiled as he nodded to her. "Do you need more help?"

"No, I will be fine. Was just having a moment to take it in."

He nodded, none the wiser as he turned and headed back into Tareng.

Different spies—those who were with the convoy or in the city—sent messages...or tried to. A number of people were killed in the convoy as they were sending their messages, the agents of the Crafter's Association and the Blue Lotus finding them.

Bodies were left behind and the sand covered them as is the deserts ancient right.

***

Night arrived as Ulalas sat on her lizard mount, wearing her full armor. They were resting for the night but they only had a few fires built.

One of her aides rushed over to her with a bloody note in his hand.

"Tareng knew about the concoction. They're still weakened and they're fleeing because they're not strong enough to repel us and they have no way to get support in time. They are heading to the east." The aide lowered their head and offered the message with their hand.

Ulalas opened the note and quickly scanned it. "Break camp. We will be heading to the east. Damel!"

The minor general rode up.

"You take your army and clear out Tareng city," she said.

"Yes, General." He rode off to gather his army and ride for Tareng through the night.

"It looks like that merchant wasn't lying after all. The group that went to Tareng, they must have been the survivors he left behind. Though they're heading to the east—is it a feint?" She spoke aloud, thinking. "It doesn't matter. Contact our scouts to the east. We need to know how far the people of Tareng are."

Messages were sent before an aide, with a grave voice, reported, "We have lost contact with a number of our scouts to the east of Tareng. It looks like the people of Tareng have passed their positions."

"Get up some flyers. They know about us already. I want to know where they are!" she yelled.

Flying creatures and their riders took off from the massive moving caravans that were moving with the army. Each of the various carriages was the size of a manor, hauled by dozens of large beasts. They were moving command posts, storing siege weapons, ammunition, and supplies. They also held beasts and acted as mobile launching platforms for flying creatures; large posts reached up into the skies on each of four points.

***

Rugrat was working on shells for the M32s when he got a message.

"Rugrat, we're on the move toward Vuzgal. How are the preparations?" Erik asked.

"Han Wu and I will move out with Special Team Two immediately to start planting the charges and prepare our first present for the enemy. I will have Dragon Platoon move out immediately to start to prepare following locations," Rugrat said.

"Understood. I want you to remain in the capital."

"Why do you want me to stay back?"

"You can directly control the dungeon cores and the people of the Blue Lotus have a bit of information on you. They'll respect you more. Also, you are one of our best smiths. With you making weapons and explosives, I'll feel better," Erik said.

"Got it." Rugrat was annoyed. He wanted to be there on the ground. He felt he was the best person for the job but he knew that Erik had thought it through.

"Sorry, brother. Don't worry—I'll be with them," Erik said.

"Got it. They're smart people but this will be their first time using the new weapons or seeing what they can do. I wanted at least one of us with them. The first time we hit the army will be when we can inflict the most casualties and once they have an idea of what to do, they can adapt from there with everything we've taught them."

"I was thinking the same. It's going to be a tense few days, though," Erik said.

"Yeah," Rugrat said. There was an army of what might be fifty thousand. On Earth, an army of that size would have been incredibly hard to support requiring massive amounts of food and water.

In the ten realms mages could call down rain to make water, and a stamina potion could replace a day's worth of meals. It was why the third realm's greatest profits didn't come from healing potions or transformative pills. It can from simple stamina recovery potions and powders.

Chapter: Discovery

The people from Tareng continued to travel through the night. As midday approached, they were in sight of the forest.

Instead of rejoicing, people could only look with fear at the fast and evasive flying creatures above them that kept their distance. They were the scouts from the Blood Demon Sect. It was clear that they had been discovered. All they could do was race toward the forest.

The enemy knew where they were but they didn't know where the enemy was. They continued their pace. People started to panic but the leadership clamped down on it.

They had already sent out their fastest creatures toward Vuzgal. It would take them three days to reach the capital. By that time, the people of Tareng would be in the forest, and either Erik and his people had slowed the Blood Demon Sect, or the Blood Demon sect had caught up with the people of Tareng.

Erik told Xue Lin his plan of staying behind with a number of his people and creating a line to slow the Blood Demon sect army.

"I will send a group of our strongest Blue Lotus guards and Crafter's Association guards with you," she said.

"Okay but it would be best if they are skilled in stealth or if they have long-range abilities, and can hit a target from a kilometer away or so," Erik said.

Xue Lin looked over to Olivia, who was by her side.

"I will gather those who are capable and I will stay to assist," Olivia said.

Erik felt that she didn't trust him but he didn't care as long as she listened to what he said. He could care less about what she thought about him when this was all over.

Erik nodded. With their help, his plan would be more effective. The first attack they landed would give away a lot of their tactics, so they needed to make it as effective as possible.

"It would be best if we have people who were capable of dealing damage to the strongest people in the Blood Demon Sect's army. We can distract and hurt them. When the time comes, it will be up to your people to kill them. You've got powerful mages and ranged attackers which we can use to wear down their numbers if we concentrate that firepower in one location," Erik said.

Olivia looked at him in question *Firepower, ranged? Doesn't he know our main strength comes from attacking the enemy directly?* She was frustrated being treated like some little girl who didn't know how to fight. He should have been looking to *her* for advice. *Is he looking down on me because this happened on my watch?*

It was a fear that had grown ever since they knew that the Blood Demon Sect was outside the city.

I need to prove to him and to everyone else that I didn't mess up.

***

The tension in the people from Tareng increased as time went by, understandably so.

Special Team Two were waiting for them as they entered the forest.

Seeing them, the people of Tareng felt a little better. But they had no idea how just ten people would be useful in a battle against thousands.

"Sir," Roska said in greeting as Erik rode up on Gilly.

Gilly nipped at Roska, who smiled and patted the big creature.

"How are we looking?" Erik asked.

Olivia was beside him, studying them all. She had a group of Blue Lotus guards behind her.

"We have Tiger Platoon with twenty mortars pre-placed and ranged in on the main road. We've already pre picked some ambush locations and laid down mines. We used some formation traps on the first couple, just to see if they can sense them. If they do then we can try and catch them off guard with the mines, we'll have to adjust that as we go. Also, Rugrat wanted me to show you this." She pulled out a M32 grenade launcher.

Erik took it and opened it up as if he were familiar with the weapon system. "Of course, a grenade launcher. I'm guessing this was the surprise that he was keeping from me. How many do we have?"

"We have ten in total," she said.

"Okay, show me the locations that you've picked out," Erik said.

Roska pulled out a map that traced the road from the beginning of the forest all the way to Vuzgal. She had picked a switchback with two turns that would force whoever was going through it to slow down.

There were also areas where the road was higher or lower than the rest of the forest; areas that had swamps or other challenging terrain on either side.

Erik looked at them and picked out several locations. The first would be the switchback, which went up a hill.

"Where is Han Wu?" Erik asked.

"Working on more explosives," Roska said.

"Okay, let him continue working. I want the mortars zeroed in on this area here. Stagger them out at different locations. This location here, does it have good sight lines to the bottom of the switchback?" Erik pointed from the bottom of the switchback to an area off to the side.

"One would need to get up in a tree," Gong Jin said.

Olivia listened to them and wondered what they were talking about. Explosives, grenades, mortars—she didn't know what language they were even speaking in.

Erik looked to Olivia. "What kind of range do your mages have?"

"A kilometer," she said.

"Okay, we'll have them targeting the bottom of the switchback. We'll have the mortars hitting the rear of the army lines. They want to go forward—they go through a minefield; backward—they're into mortar fire," Erik said.

Olivia saw the grim looks on the people Erik was talking to. She didn't know what these items were but it seemed that they were powerful.

"Okay, we'll start digging into the road. I want IEDs underneath the road. I want sniper pairs here, here, and here." Erik pointed to different locations. "We get them in the switchback, packed together and slow, blow the IEDs, let rip with ranged Blue Lotus and crafters, then with the mortars. Snipers hit the leadership and powerful-looking people, spell scrolls and call in a few batteries of mortars, only using rifles when necessary. Spotters on this location will guide mortars onto high-density targets."

The members of the special teams nodded but Olivia only understood a portion of it.

"What are IEDs, mortars, and snipers?" she asked.

"IEDs, improvised explosive devices, are like mechanical spell scrolls. Mortars are like long-range destructive spells, and snipers are people like rangers who use extreme range to create havoc in the enemy's camp by hitting their leadership and valuable targets attempting to cause chaos and confusion," Erik said.

She nodded. With that, she could understand it a bit more.

"All right, let's get people in position and get ready. The second location will be here." Erik picked a flat area at the bottom of the valley. "We'll use mortars, IEDs, and mines. Niemm and Roska, you will be in charge of this area. Gong Jin, take three from your team and a section from Dragon Platoon to prep the next location."

Gong Jin headed off on his mount to gather his people as Yui, the leader of the platoon, Erik, Roska, and Niemm addressed any remaining questions.

Olivia listened to their final plan. She hadn't heard of these types of tactics before. They were cowardly and although they might be effective against the chaff forces, they weren't made to kill the powerful forces of the enemy.

What does it matter if we kill a lot of them? If we don't kill the powerful Masters in their ranks, then this will all be for nothing.

Chapter: Stage Is Set

Taran looked up from the forges. The forges had been going twenty-four seven there was an area being run by Tan Xue with the Journeyman level smiths and formation masters that were working on the grenade launchers. The rest of the smithy was turned over to making ammunition, mortars, bullets and mortar rounds were cast here, then handed over to the formation master workshop, their edges smoothed, the formations cleaned up and inlaid, then it was off to the ammunition mill where the rounds and cartridges were mated together with the accelerants from the alchemist association where they would be packaged and readied to ship to the fourth realm.

There was a similar assembly line for repeater bolts that was being carried out by the woodworking division. The spell scroll students were all working to make support spell scrolls, they cooking department were making meals for the soldiers. The medics were preparing supplies for the wounded as well as pills and resources to increase body and mana cultivation. Beast masters prepared meals and regiments for the beasts up there to increase their levels and care as they increased in level.

The people of Alva bore the three names of those that had already fallen in their hearts. They turned into a machine, the different limbs of Alva dungeon were active, moving resources to and from Alva and Vuzgal, across all the realms they were gathering resources that would be of use to support the troops.

He saw Delilah walking through the smithy, she waved for people to get back to work as she went up to Taran.

"How are we looking?" She asked.

"We've got about ten of the grenade launchers completed. We should have another ten completed in the next three days, production is ramping up quickly. Our main focus is on ammunition, we can go through thousands of rounds in just a few minutes of sustained fire. Rifle round production has increased through new techniques we've added to the production lines. Grenade launcher ammunition is becoming faster, though like the mortar rounds it takes more time with the larger formations. Looking to perfect the casting situation," Taran said in a deep voice.

"I heard that there was an issue with the castings not being as clean as you hoped."

"That's correct, the power of the rounds would be lower and it takes more time for the formation folks to work on. Want to get to the stage where we can use a machine to clean the rounds, engrave and inlay the formation. Got the Blueprint group working on it."

"Do you need anything?"

"More hands, but that'll be hard. We're automating as much as possible, or at least reducing the amount of labor required. Even the Novice and Journeyman level applicants are being utilized," Taran said.

"I would say don't push yourself too hard, but I know that wouldn't be possible," Delilah said with a smile.

"I heard that there was a certain Council leader that has taken to brewing gunpowder in her office and helping with the gunpowder mill every spare minute she has," Taran said in a sarcastic tone.

"They need us, they're fighting for others as they fought for Alva they went up there for us," Delilah said.

"They're our people," Taran finished for her.

"Yes," Delilah nodded.

Taran looked around, he *really* looked at Alva, seeing the tired men and women around him, their movements like machines, even if they were tired, their minds were focused with iron-like will.

He couldn't put what he felt into words, he felt that they couldn't convey what he was feeling.

"We'll get them the ammunition and weapons," Taran said. It was a promise he made not based on production speeds or material needs. It was based on the fact he knew that they would all sacrifice their time, their blood and tears. What was a few hours of overtime when it could save one of their friends of family members lives?

***

Xue Lin sighed as another person left her carriage. The strongest forces of the Blue Lotus as well as Erik's people had left the convoy and disappeared into the forest, no idea where they were or what their plan was.

If they had told us, it is possible that the spies in our ranks would find out what they were planning and warn the Blood Demon Sect, she assured herself. "Still, just sitting here and working to calm people's nerves is not what I thought my job would be."

She felt a sense of defeat as she thought about the events of the last few weeks.

She looked out of the window at the forest. The farther they went, the gloomier it became. They had people farther up the road, clearing it and then hurling debris behind them so it would make it harder for the Blood Demon Sect to follow.

"Edar Empire, one of the four main empires of this northern continent when it was at the height of power. Just how were they able to get control over it?" Tareng was a large city and it had been around for a long time indeed. It had even been there when the Edar Empire had existed. In her free time, she had been interested in the nearby location's history.

The Edar Empire was a massive trader, with Vuzgal their capital, being the center of that strength. In the forest, there were plenty of natural resources for them to harvest. They had rich ore veins in their mountains and it had two secondary cities that blocked off the road that entered the passageway between two mountains to Vuzgal. The area inside was all controlled by them. They were one of the few places in the Fourth Realm where crops were actually grown. Though the capital only had access to one dungeon, that dungeon would be exceptional even in the upper realms.

"A set dungeon, capable of giving one a set of legendary armor or a weapon based upon one's fighting abilities." No one had been able to get access to the capital as there was a powerful spell that was cast on the capital that revived the undead and made them keep fighting. They killed anything that entered their range, beasts and people as well as other undead, thus ever increasing their Strength. *Just how did they enter it?* Xue Lin thought back to her original question.

"In the end, it doesn't really matter. What does matter is if they can really slow down the Blood Demon Sect 's army."

***

There were mages moving dirt and people using shovels as they dug underneath the road around the switchback. It looked like a construction zone as Han Wu, Erik, and the others who had spent time with explosives went around, checking the holes and then placing premade charges. They had made a few IEDs back in Alva, and Han Wu had been making them ever since Erik found out about the concoction they were made with.

He checked the command wires that were gathered together.

Olivia was looking around at all of the work, not understanding it but doing what Erik had told her to do.

Not for the first time, he felt that there was a tension between them. It might be because she was under him; it might be because he was an unknown to her. He could understand that and left her to deal with her own thoughts as he focused on the fight ahead.

Niemm rode up to Erik on his mount and jumped off it, landing next to Erik.

"How are the assigned observation posts?" Erik asked.

"We checked all of them and had spotters on the road and using a few spells. We're looking good," Niemm said.

"Good work." Erik nodded. "What about the trip wires?"

"The trip wire formations that we placed show the Blood Demon Sect's army to be about five hours away."

Erik looked up at the sun and gauged its position. "All these different realms and suns are doing my head in," He muttered and looked at his timepiece, thankfully it adjusted to the different day lengths of the other realms. The fourth realm's days were three hours longer than the first realms. He took a few minutes to check his math.

"So they will either march through here as night is coming, or they'll camp up somewhere and come through in the morning."

"They haven't stopped one night yet," Niemm said.

"Neither have we. Fuckers are a goddamn pain in my ass. If they try to come through here at night, it'll be better for us, though."

"Pitch black, hard to see who they're next to. Probably using night vision, throw in explosions, mess their sight up, create confusion, people wounded or dying with no sign of where the attack is coming from. Sounds like hell from a command and control perspective," Niemm added.

"Right. Can you check with Yui and make sure that his mortar teams have illumination rounds? If it is at night, we'll need to see where the hell they are," Erik said.

"Sir, I've been thinking. Why don't we keep our beasts stored and then when we need to bug out, we pull them out? That way, their night vision won't be messed up and we can rely on their eyes instead of ours?" Niemm asked.

"That is a good fucking idea. See to it and pass the commands to Olivia as well as update her on the situation."

"Yes, sir," Niemm said, happy to be able to help.

He left and Erik watched him go.

The special teams had meshed well once combined together in training and had become a well-oiled machine in combat.

Erik looked over as a mage came closer.

"We have buried most of the devices and your man said to say that 'we're burying the command wire now.'" The man made an odd expression as he said the foreign words.

"Thank you," Erik said. The mage headed back to work as Erik looked over the switchback.

***

Yui checked over the mortars once again, moving between positions and checking that they were dialed in. Storage rings allowed them to prepare hundreds of rounds of ammunition ahead of time then just let it out of their storage ring, right down the tube.

One person worked communications, another was the gunner, and a third was the ammunition prepper and weapon loader.

They had trained with the mortars and fired them off at Vuzgal but this would be their first combat fire run, so they were ready to adjust on the fly.

They had worked out the ranges and the angles but now it was the real deal.

"How we looking?" Yui asked Strode, his second-in-command.

"Looking good. We've got crews manning all twenty mortars. Got five different firing sites, so even if we get marked we'll be able to keep firing from the other positions. We have at least one secondary site for every team to move to if we're getting targeted. We're ready," Platoon First Sergeant Strode said.

***

Roi walked up to Olivia, who was looking at the switchback. The holes had been covered over and the wire was just being laid down now. People were headed to their different posts around the road to get some food and hunker down for the Blood Demon army to appear.

"Commander?" Roi asked.

"Take the Wind Unit. You will separate from the ranged forces and move close to the road and lay in wait. When the first attack begins, you will lead the Wind Unit into the enemy forces to attack the Masters," Olivia said.

Roi's face was grim. It would be a vicious move, a deadly blow on the strongest people in the Blood Demon army. It was well known that Masters decided a battle. It could take tens of regular troops to kill just one Master.

The Blue Lotus and Crafter's Association didn't have the numbers to bleed and to kill some Masters. With a single strike they would impress on the Blood Demon Army the strength of the Blue Lotus and the Crafter's association. Strike fear into their hearts as they remembered who they were attacking.

"I will carry out your orders," Roi said.

Olivia turned to him and pulled out a dozen green and red potions. "You honor the Blue Lotus." She handed them to him.

He took a deep breath and accepted the potions. "Please, look after my family."

"They will forever be members of the Blue Lotus," she promised. She didn't want to send them out but, in her judgement, she needed to. Xue Lin had ordered her to follow Erik West. She was going against that order.

She didn't know the man and she wanted to stack the odds in their favor as best as she knew how to.

***

The sun started to disappear. The asteroid belt around the Fourth Realm lit up the night—there were no noticeable moons around the Fourth Realm planet.

Darkness came, revealing the stars in the night sky.

Erik lay on his back, looking up at the sky, the asteroid belt, and the stars beyond. It was a sight that couldn't be seen on Earth.

He heard noise in the distance, a low rumbling.

Erik looked away from the sky and he used his binoculars to look down the road. The asteroid belt's faint light reflected off the Blood Demon Sect army's armor, as their vanguard appeared on the road.

"This is Captain West. Enemy spotted on the road. Hold positions and wait for my orders." Erik's stomach tightened as they waited, filled with adrenaline. He moved his fingers, rubbing them against one another. He breathed and cleared away distractions, looking at the army, checking the markers that they had placed along the road.

He looked over at the formation plate and the wires that lay beside it.

Everything was in place; now all that was left was to wait. Waiting for an ambush made minutes seem like hours.

Chapter: Thunder Without Lightning

General Ulalas ordered her people forward. They had sighted the people from Tareng. A day ago, a group had disappeared—riding on ahead, according to her spies.

She had no idea of where they were but she needed to wipe out the people from Tareng. She had no idea what messages that they had sent already but she knew that she needed to stop them from talking. Nearly three days had gone since they had left Tareng. Now, her army was just a half day behind the fleeing caravan.

She ordered the army to eat on the move to keep up their pace. It would tire them out but she had numbers on her side. Tareng's people didn't have any defenses to hide behind while on the move, leaving them open for slaughter.

They passed through switchbacks and crossed over hills.

Another switchback appeared as they continued to march on.

***

Erik watched as the Blood Demon Sect's army appeared. It was massive, unlike anything he had seen before. Seeing the dark snake that was moving down the road, each man and woman a warrior heading to battle, was an incredible sight.

They entered the switchback, climbing to the top of the hill. Erik got the first good look at the army. The basic soldiers had simple black and red armor. The leaders had more red in their armor, it wasn't something that was easy to pick out but thankfully the crafter's association had a few people that had worked on their armor in the past. There were massive carriages, with a large team of beasts pulling them up the incline. On top of them, there were posts where flying creatures could fly from or land on.

The first group of soldiers passed through the switchback, then a group of carriages moved through.

Erik got a communication from Olivia.

"What are you doing? Hit the carriages," Olivia said.

Erik frowned before replying, "The carriages will force them to stay on the road. If we take out the carriages, then it will make it easier for them to move through the forests. On the road, they need protection, which makes it harder for the army to spread out."

Erik scanned for signs of leadership. He saw a number of flags around a heavily armored and mounted group. Around them, there was a large unit of mounted soldiers. Erik had now found his target as the army continued to push onward.

"They contain siege weaponry and supplies for the entire army!" Olivia hissed.

"Obey your orders, soldier. I do not have time to hold your hand. If you call me again to try to get me to change my orders, I will relieve you of command," Erik curtly responded into his communication device. He didn't have time to deal with her second-guessing his orders.

"Understood." Her voice was cold.

Erik gritted his teeth. He could tell that she would be a problem. He didn't have time to deal with it now but if he had to, he would send her back to Xue Lin. *I'll deal with it later.*

He watched his targets entering the switchback, riding on their lizard creatures.

"Mortar teams, ready. Ready trigger devices," Erik said, using sound talismans to send out his orders.

He grabbed the formation and took the wires, removing their caps and putting them into the formation. He tightened the two screws, securing the wires in place.

"Mortar teams confirmed ready," Yui replied.

"Trigger device one ready," Han Wu said

"Trigger device two ready," Niemm said.

"Trigger device three ready," Erik said.

Erik pulled out his timepiece. He had cast Night Vision so the darkness of the battlefield had no effect. .

He looked at the road once again. "Mortars, you are free to fire." Erik clicked on his timepiece as it counted down.

"Mortars understands. Firing!" Yui shouted.

There was some faint noises in the distance. Erik didn't know whether they were the mortars or the noises of the forest.

"Trigger devices, on my mark." Erik checked his timepiece as it ticked down. "Three, two, one—MARK!"

Erik pressed the formation device three times to blow three different mines. A spark appeared and three flashes of light went off just seconds apart from one another in the switchback.

***

General Ulalas looked out of the command carriage she was riding in.

Then as she watched the switchback disappeared; smoke, dust and debris flew up into the sky. Explosions rippled through the army.

General Ulalas wanted to yell out but the noise from the explosions and the wave of pressure blasted across the army, making it impossible to send messages or orders.

A piercing whistling could be heard from above. People looked up but didn't see anything.

More whistles could be heard. A shiver went down even the veterans' spines.

The first whistle ended in an explosion, killing everything within fifty meters and pushing back everything within eighty.

Explosions continued to go off among the army. Chaos took over as hundreds of packed-in soldiers were killed in each blast.

Conscripts ran for their lives but their oaths forced them back to their positions, unable to run or find cover they couldn't retreat, only charge forward into the destruction ahead or stand still hoping they weren't hit.

Commanders tried to get control over their soldiers but there were no spell formations in the skies or signs of where the attack had come from.

"Defensive formations!" she yelled out to all of her commanders as explosions continued to go off.

The explosions were getting more accurate, finding pockets of densely packed soldiers.

With the carnage and flashes of light, her soldiers were in chaos.

"Form up and move forward!" she yelled. She needed to get them moving. She was used to losing people; it was sudden and the effects were devastating but if they fell into despair then they wouldn't be able to pull back together.

Even as they ran to cover on either side of the road, the ground exploded, killing and maiming dozens who cried out in panic and pain.

There was no direction that they could move in, they were boxed in with undetected traps around the road and the whistling thunder rain that cut them down from above.

"General Divaz, move into the forest and find out where the attacks are coming from. General Hummel, find out where those mages are hiding and attack them! General Kalim, form Mana barriers to cover our people!"

***

Olivia saw the attack. The switchback had simply disappeared in the explosion. There was nothing there anymore. The army was in chaos, trying to find their attacker, thrown out of rhythm but they were people from the Fourth Realm and used to seeing death. They were starting to reorganize themselves but the mortars continued to come down. It only took one round to clear out a hole in the road, leaving behind a crater and killing anyone who had been there.

The mortars dropped on the command groups that the different spotters had identified.

The shooting went on for five minutes. Olivia was shocked by the repeated explosions that overlapped one another, making it seem like the end of days had come to the Blood Demon Army. The fire was accurate anyone caught outside of a mana barrier could only last for a few seconds.

Olivia started to feel more confident but the Blood Demon Army started to recover as officers regained control over their panicked troops.

"Pull back. Mortars—five rounds and move to position two," Erik said.

The observation posts started to dissolve and pull back.

We have the advantage—we need to push it! Olivia punched the ground. "Roi, do it!"

***

The Wind Unit was the strongest group within the Tareng Blue Lotus, entirely comprised of people who came from the higher realms.

They were people who were completely loyal to the Blue Lotus.

Roi got the order and nodded to the others. They were surprised by the destruction but they had their orders.

They drank the red and green potions.

Roi felt a new surge of strength through his body. His power skyrocketed while he felt a strange tug on his body.

He was one of the strongest from the Tareng Blue Lotus. Seeing the Blood Demon army coming after them, he felt a kind of rage that he hadn't felt in a long time.

The Blue Lotus had found him in the Second Realm, nurtured him to this point and given him opportunities he'd never thought possible. They had cared for him and his family. Without the Blue Lotus, he would have died in the Second Realm.

The squad had twenty people in it. They rushed out of their cover, running through the tree line.

Spells shot out. The defending soldiers who were looking outward were Elites but they were unable to stop the sudden attack. They had only just gotten into a defensive formation. A few Masters from the Blood Demon army fired at where the spells had come from, lighting up the forest.

The Blood Demon army that hadn't had a target before, now found it.

Every bow that could be aimed or spell that could be targeted on the area fired almost at once. The Blood Demon sect army wanted to hit something.

The Wind Unit appeared out of the tree line and slammed into the Elites. Destruction fell behind them. They were wounded by the incoming spells and attacks but they didn't fall; their armor was all half-step Journeyman level or above.

They smashed through the lines of Elites, turning it into a bloodbath as they charged toward the Masters who appeared for battle.

They were like demons, stepping through the ranks of Elites, leaving only the dead lying behind them. The road turned into a bloody battlefield with the Blue Lotus guards showing the Blood Demon Sect what real demons looked like. The Elites could only hope to slow them.

Roi let out a laugh. It was a grim and powerful thing. His body overflowed with power. He didn't feel the arrow that cut the side of his leg, or the fireball that hit him in the side, sending him flying. He rolled on his shield and came up; his sword flowed through the gaps in the Elite's attacks.

Blood fell around him and madness filled his eyes. He cast buffs on himself, turning into a blur.

A sword cut through the air, aimed at his back; he turned to face the attacker, a smile on his face. He had found a Master, his target!

The two swords clashed. The power was enough to throw back the level thirty-seven Elites in a five-meter radius. The trees on the sides of the road bent back.

Their weapons repulsed apart. The two rushed together again. They were no longer humans but monsters.

Their speed accelerated, making it hard to follow them as their sword and shields met one another. Attacks rained down again and again.

Others couldn't get near due to their speed and the force of their attacks.

Roi sensed something and used a movement technique, rushing away. An arrow hit where he had been, leaving a crater and burying itself into the ground. A sonic boom was heard afterward.

"Rat! You think you can get away!" The Master fighting Roi laughed as he rushed forward, aiming to pin him down.

Roi's weapon glowed red as a red mist appeared around his body. The potion he had taken increased his power dramatically. He let out a laugh; the master had a cold look on his face as he rushed in. They clashed once again but the Blood Demon Master was thrown back with the attacks, struggling to contain Roi.

Roi ducked; his shield deflected an arrow. He used his sword to push back the Master.

Roi pulled out several darts from his storage ring on his shield arm. He threw them forward. The Master, even having just been pushed back, was able to stop two of them but three hit him—two in the armor and one in the neck.

He grabbed his neck. His complexion changed as the poison overtook him.

Roi activated the formation in the darts. Wind blades shot out of them, shredding anything in front of them. The Master fell down dead as Roi tossed darts at the archer in the forest and detonated the formations, clear-cutting trees in the forest. The archer was thrown off guard and a body fell from the trees, a tombstone overhead.

Roi let out a laugh, seeing the other members of Wind Unit slaughtering their way through Elites and cutting down Masters.

He ran into the Elites again.

He could feel the powerful fluctuations in the air. The strength that came from Masters was easy for him to identify.

His darts flew and cut down dozens. He collided with a woman with a spear. As he went, his strength only grew and the madness in his eye increased. He was willing to take wounds to kill; he knew that this was his last mission.

"Lotus!" he yelled, taking a hit to the side of his body. He had reached Body Like Earth Iron, yet the weapon still cut through his armor and damaged him.

They used a defensive scroll, stopping Roi's attack and tossing him back.

Roi was disorientated as the spear user and other Masters attacked him.

"Lotus!" members of Wind Unit yelled back. Their voices filled with laughter as they rushed past Roi, killing the woman. A Wind Unit mage was exchanging magical fire and supporting the others.

Roi got up and rushed forward, stepping over the dead spear-wielding Master.

"Lotus!" The war cry of the Blue Lotus could be heard as Wind Unit left destruction in their wake. The Elites couldn't match them, so the Masters were sent in. Although the Blue Lotus Wind Unit was strong, they weren't invincible. Their powerful Body Cultivation could only help them recover from so much. Dealing with the powerful attacks of the other Masters, even with their powerful strength, they were wounded like common mortals would be.

With each attack that could kill an army of people from the First Realm, the Masters clashed with one another.

It was a terrifying display of strength that destroyed the land around them.

For every Wind Unit member's death, the Blood Demon Sect had to pay with countless Elites and over ten Masters. The Wind Unit had taken berserk potions to increase their current Strength, at the cost of their long-term cultivation and power.

The magical users, knowing that they would die, detonated the Mana within their bodies, clearing an area one hundred meters wide. Not even Masters could survive their final attacks.

Roi was no longer a human but a beast in human skin, taking on anything that was within reach. He fought with all the power left in his body, which was covered in wounds. Even his Expert-level armor was unable to take it, breaking under the strain, and the damage was beyond his ability to heal himself anymore.

He lost his sword arm; using his shield arm instead, he deployed spell scroll after spell scroll. More of the Wind Unit fell from devastating wounds.

Roi lost track of where he was, who he was fighting.

He was hit by a spell, sending him flying. He waved his shield, throwing back those in its path. The Elites were blown away with the power; their armor mangled by his strength.

Attacks continued. He lost his other arm, and someone sealed his cultivation. His body was trying to repair itself as someone took his legs.

He was unable to fight back anymore as he coughed up blood.

There were ten Masters watching him. Around them was a land of death. He was the last Blue Lotus Master left.

He'd taken down nearly thirty Masters on his own.

A woman approached, wearing armor that didn't lose out to his own. "What is the plan of the Tareng people?"

"To destroy the Blood Demon Sect." Roi laughed as he was stabbed. He cracked a tooth in his mouth, consuming the poison inside.

"The Blue Lotus army comes for you." Roi laughed, not seeing them anymore, instead remembering the days that he had trained within the combat groups of the Blue Lotus, how he had fought across the realms, and adventured across hostile lands. The massive training facility for Blue Lotus guards, the ranks and ranks of Blue Lotus warriors being trained.

His path might end but his brothers and sisters from the Blue Lotus would wipe out the Blood Demon Sect and it would fall. He knew it with certainty.

He saw that the Masters were shaken by his words, his understanding of who they were, and saying that the army was coming.

"The Blue Lotus army is nothing but an urban myth."

"You'll see soon." With that, the potent poison caused Roi to take his last breath.

One of the Masters saw a colored liquid in Roi's mouth.

"Poison!" she yelled, calling down a spell on Roi. They burned his body, to make sure that all of the poison was destroyed.

***

General Ulalas snorted at the man's last words and looked around at the battlefield. She had lost nearly three hundred Masters. Thankfully, few of them had been high-tier Masters between level fifty and sixty.

Her eyes turned to the switchback. Craters covered the switchback and her army was split in two. It would take time for them to advance through the broken ground and transport the carriages. Still, they hadn't been able to find out what spell created the whistling destruction.

In just a few minutes, they had lost hundreds of her soldiers, with only this squad of twenty people attacking directly.

This is not a low level fighting force. Instead of taking us head on to grind us down, they hit and ran, then launched a sneak attack. I have never heard of the Blue Lotus using this type of attack before. The Blue Lotus usually just hides in their walls, using their overwhelming weaponry to destroy any force that dares appear and then deploying forces from other cities to attack through the totem.

For the first time in this campaign, General Ulalas frowned. She didn't know where they were heading but she didn't want to break up her army. There were only a few thousand ahead of the switchback. Sending them to attack the Tareng convoy would only lead to their deaths.

"Get me a path through this rubble," she said. It might take a few hours but with the Earth mages, they could slowly repair the road and continue on.

Chapter: Making an Enemy

The people from the Blue Lotus were quiet, with stiff expressions. They had lost twenty good people. Olivia was moving through them, reassuring them, as Erik's killing intent locked onto her. She sneered, looking at him in disdain.

"A word in private?" Erik said, his face stiff and his blue eyes frigid. Olivia could feel his power fluctuating, affecting his aura and pressuring those around him.

Being a higher level and with more advanced body and mana cultivation it was no more than a mild irritation.

She gave a stiff nod and walked off with Erik.

They walked into the forest some more. Erik stopped, trying to control his breathing and emotions.

He turned around, his composed expression twisted.

"What in the fuck was that!" He demanded.

"Are you or are you not under my command?" His voice barked as Olivia bit back her words, tightening her fists in indignation. *Do you know who I am and what I've done! You are only a member of the Alchemist Association with a trade agreement with the Blue Lotus!*

"I am trying to run a damn stalling action here, to give the people of Tareng time to pull back and my people time to prepare Vuzgal to face the Blood Demon Sect. I need people that can follow orders, *not* people that are going to do their own thing and sacrifice people's lives for," Erik opened and closed his fist unable to find the words.

"What *was* your goal in sending out those people?"

"To send a message, to remind them just who they're facing. To show that we're withdrawing because we decided to, not because they forced us. Your weapons and attacks are effective in

418

killing and stunning the enemy, but they need to know that they're fighting an enemy!"

Erik took a deep breath and let it out of your nose.

"Here are two scenarios for you, you are chasing the enemy, you know that they're there, just, *just* beyond reach, you *know* that you can defeat them if you get close enough. You can taste the blood, see the fear in their eyes.

"This is an enemy that has looked down on you all your life, but now you're the one with the power. Got it?"

Olivia nodded, feeling frustrated and stifled.

"So the first scenario, you're chasing the enemy but then you keep on getting ambushed by them, they keep popping out of the road, you lose people, but you kill those ambushers, see their corpses, show off that you've defeated the enemy. Even if you lost two, three, even ten to one. That enemy that looked down on you all that time. You got them!"

Erik paused.

"How do you feel? Honestly."

Olivia shifted on her feet, not liking what her brain was coming up with.

"I feel like I'm losing people," She said, but her voice sounded weak.

"How do you feel," Erik's voice snapped.

"I feel vindicated, we can defeat the enemy," She snapped back.

"Now, what if you are advancing, night and day, there is whistling and explosions, there are explosions going under your feet, the sides of the road are a death trap, the forest a sure way to die. What are you thinking now?"

"I'm protected under the shields!"

"Oh, but are you?" Erik's voice was conversational but it sent a shock through Olivia's system as she started to play scenarios through her mind, sinking into thought.

"If, after being attacked by an enemy you can't see, the enemy now attacks you. Would you be scared stiff, or would that fear, change to anger and you go all out to kill those bastards that made you feel scared?" Erik crossed his arms.

"When they engage us in battle later then they'll go all out anyway," Olivia said.

"Probably, though how much will they have slept, how alert will they be? Will they think that they are stronger than us? Will they think that we're sheep? Oh they can think that we're cowards all they want. Does it matter what they think, or does it matter if we win?"

"We need to show our strength!" Olivia said.

"We need to win, I don't need a commander trying to prove herself. I need a commander that listens to my orders. Work with your people, make sure that they're combat ready for Vuzgal. We won't be able to stop the Blood Demon Army on this road, we can reduce their numbers and bleed them. Most importantly, we need to break their spirit."

He seemed older as Olivia looked at him she felt something had changed.

Nothing changed but there's a side of him that I didn't see before. Did I keep thinking of him as a young upstart because of my own failings?

Olivia had taken a sever blow to her confidence.

"Go and speed up the people of Tareng, Olivia. Our job is to slow them, to break them before they reach Vuzgal. Don't get in our way." Erik took Gilly out of her storage area.

The powerful aura covered Olivia.

Gilly stood there proudly as Erik got on her back.

"Do your job."

Erik's words burned something fierce as she wanted to lash out, to prove to others this wasn't her fault. She had been stuck in this situation and had to work with what she had been dealt with.

A golden light appeared around her.

==========

You have broken the oath between the Blue Lotus and Erik West. Losing his trust and going against an agreement between your two parties.

==========

"Wait, what? How did the entire Blue Lotus make an oath with you?" Olivia yelled.

Erik didn't look back as he rode his mount over to the rest of his group and headed off into the forest.

Olivia felt that she had more questions about Erik than ever before.

**

Elder Lu Ru was walking through the halls of the Blue Lotus headquarters in the Fourth Realm. This Blue Lotus controlled all of the Blue Lotus locations in the realm. Elder Lu Ru was from the Seventh Realm. Given the nature of the Fourth Realm, it was necessary to have someone of his Strength managing this realm.

He got a message as he was walking to his meeting with Emperor McMahon, who controlled nearly one hundred and fifty cities.

"What is it?" he asked in a grave tone. Being late for his meeting was no small matter.

"A contract has been broken by a friend of the Blue Lotus," the man said on the other side.

Elder Lu knew that it wouldn't be insignificant if they were calling him now. "Do you know which?"

"No, the information is only saying one thing: Alchemist West."

Lines appeared on Elder Lu's forehead and his stomach turned.

Few knew what that meant, but he did. His wife had a bad constitution, it took her more resources to increase her cultivation and she aged rapidly. While he was still in his prime from a cultivation standpoint his wife was quickly aging. Anti-aging concoctions had helped her, but they couldn't be used repeatedly. Her life was coming to an end. But then the Age Rejuvenation potion had appeared. The weakest one was able to give her two to five more years; the strongest could give her another fifteen. It would give him more time to look for other solutions.

He had the position to look into who had invented the potion; information that was hidden away from most.

A man called Erik West had created the concoction, then given the recipe to the Blue Lotus and the Alchemist Association. He was a mysterious man—a healer and an alchemist. Direct disciple to one of the Three Pill Heads of the Third Realm. A man who continued to travel through the realms even with his position.

He was a fighter but his abilities hadn't been recorded since he had appeared in the First Realm just a few years ago. They didn't know how strong he was now or the abilities he had developed.

Erik had helped out the Blue Lotus and shown that he was a good man. He controlled a restaurant in the Third Realm that the heads of the Alchemist Association often frequented.

He had even healed a Blue Lotus head's son of an affliction no others had been capable of, for free.

"Alright Cui Chin, what the hell is going on why did Erik West break the contract with us?" Elder Lu asked.

"He broke it because he lost trust in the Blue Lotus," Cui Chin reported.

Elder Lu flicked his sleeves. His face turned thunderous. "Have you reviewed the entire situation?!"

"We have not. I thought that it would be best to inform you."

"Did he break faith with him, or he break faith with us?" Elder Lu didn't think that he would do something so stupid but he needed to check.

"We're not sure," Cui Chin said awkwardly.

Elder Lu's expression turned from calmly listening then to one of anger. "So, we don't know how it happened but after all of that, someone broke his trust as they're fleeing from this Blood Demon army?"

Elder Lu was a calm man but now rage twisted his expression, causing him to pace. A terrible pressure appeared around him; his guards, standing by his sides, shook with the weight of his anger.

"As it stands, yes," Cui Chin reported not flinching at the anger in his voice.

"Why was this information about Tareng not brought to me sooner?"

"There was already protocol for a city potentially affected by a plague," Cui Chin responded in a displeased tone.

"Come to my office. Bring everything that you have found out. Contact the head of the Crafter's Association. Get someone to look up the rules we must follow." Elder Lu flicked his sleeves cancelling the sound deafening formation and cancelling his communication and turned around.

"Tell the emperor that I am deeply sorry. I will agree to his request minus seven percent. I will give him three extra percent because of my rudeness," Elder Lu said to a woman in his entourage.

"Yes, Elder Lu." She answered as she hastily walked toward where the emperor was waiting.

Elder Lu looked to his personal guard's commander. "Wake up the army."

The man opened his mouth before closing it, a stony expression on his face. "Yes, Elder Lu."

"Get me the contact information of Head Xue Lin, now." He looked at another aide. The aide started talking into his communication device rapidly as Elder Lu stormed through the halls of the headquarters. Everyone moved away from him as if pushed by an invisible force.

***

Erik had no idea what had happened. All he knew was that twenty people died who didn't need to. This was only their opening engagement; he wanted to know how the enemy reacted, what their actions would be. From there, he could adapt his tactics to work against them.

"Han Wu," Erik called out as they rushed through the forest.

"Sir?" Han Wu said, closing in on Erik.

"I'll take care of position Bravo. I want you to move to Charlie and start preparing it. Take the crew that was with you at the observation post and gather an army section from the reserve," Erik said.

"Sir." Han Wu dropped back and then moved off with Gong Jin, Imani, Xi, and Tully. They altered their direction to make best speed for position Charlie, their third planned ambush point.

A section from the mortars would meet and assist them.

Erik and the rest of the group reached position Bravo in just an hour; with their map and their mounts, they had made good speed.

Erik and the rest looked at the creek and started to get creative now that they had seen the effects of the IED's and compared it to what they had learned back at Alva.

"Mortars, this is Outpost Four. Fire mission, point Alpha—fire point codename Crater City," Roska said.

"Outpost Four, Mortars. Fire mission, target point Alpha, marker Crater City confirm," Yui replied.

"Mortars, fire for effect. Will adjust as needed," Roska said.

Erik was linked into their channel. He looked to the new position of the mortars but still he didn't see anything in the night as they fired for the second time.

***

"Target point Alpha, Crater City! Confirm!" Yui barked to his mortar pits.

"Target point Alpha, Crater City! Pit one confirms!"

"Target point Alpha, Crater City! Pit two confirms!"

"Target point Alpha, Crater City! Pit three confirms!"

"Target point Alpha, Crater City! Pit four confirms!"

"Fire when ready. Shift fire east to west, down the road! Pit one, you will fire one illumination round for every three high explosive rounds!"

"Pit one will fire one illumination rounds for every three HE rounds!"

"Fire!" Yui yelled out.

The gunner confirmed that they were on target. The assistant gunner pulled a round out of their storage ring, dropping it into the mortar tube.

The mortar tubes fired, the assistant gunner dropping round after round. On Earth, it took at least two to four seconds for each round. The mortar teams cut that time in half, firing a round every second or two.

The gunner adjusted their sights and changed the trajectories of the mortars. Even a small half turn on the traversing gear or elevating gear could change where they landed by tens of meters at these ranges.

***

Roska and her team watched the Blood Demon army from their observation post. They had moved to a secondary observation post just in case.

The switchback had been repaired by the mages. The healers and alchemists dealt with the wounded; the dead were held in storage rings.

It was hard to see what had happened to them exactly under the cover of night. They knew that the Blue Lotus fighters had killed a lot, but the damage from the switchback and mortars was hard to assess.

They estimated that they had critically injured or killed two to five hundred with the mines, two or three times that number with the mortars and the Blue Lotus suicide squad had killed maybe three hunred.

With the healers and the alchemists among them, they'll be able to save a lot of them, still in our opening attack we hurt three percenrt of their force in one go. That has to hurt.

Roska clenched her hand, feeling the power within her body. Everyone in the Alvan Army had increased their levels rapidly, now they were all the levels of Masters themselves.

They were wary of the people from the various associations but now they could at least hold their own ground in terms of sheer power. In techniques and abilities the association's guards would still win out.

Seeing the effectiveness of the different tactics up close and personal was a first time for Roska. She knew that they would be effective in theory, but without even showing their faces, they had taken out up to fifteen hundred people and ruined the road, slowing them down and showing that they could hit the enemy at any time and inflict mass casualties.

People were moving up the new switchback when that whistling from just a few hours ago could be heard again. Rolling explosions covered the switchback as the fire moved down the road.

Roska and her team watched as an illumination round appeared in the sky. Suspended from a parachute, it lit up the entire road.

The mortars came down without pause. The overwhelming firepower caused people to jump off the road and into the tree line. Mana shields appeared, the mortars landing on them from above.

"Let's get moving." Roska and her people moved out of their observation post and got on their mounts, moving to meet up with the rest of the forces at position Bravo.

"Mortars, this is Outpost Four. Fire mission complete—bug out," Roska said.

"Understood. Moving."

In two minutes, Roska and her people disappeared from their position, while the mortar section had packed up their tubes and were on their mounts, headed to another mortar position that they'd sent an advance team to scout out.

In just those three minutes from ten mortars they had dropped nine hundred mortar rounds on the Blood Demon Sect. Everyday there were more rounds coming up from Alva producing ten thousand mortar rounds per day. They would stagger their attacks spacing out mortar fire, using more or less mortars, so they did dig into their reserve ammunition but kept continuous pressure on the enemy. Even a handful of mortar rounds such as smoke could disorientate and make it hard for the Blood Demon Army to move forward, or illumination rounds could keep them awake during the night.

***

Rugrat spent nearly all of his time making weapons and ammunition. He had only went to the dungeon once because he got an alert that the dungeon was complete.

He had offered the Ten Realms the same agreement as Erik had with some minor alterations.

"I, Dungeon Master Rugrat, wish to create a dungeon agreement with the Ten Realms. The Ten Realms will administer over this crafter trial dungeon with additional terms," Rugrat said.

==========

Agreed. Additional terms?

==========

"People can get tokens if they prove their skill. If they make a Journeyman-level item, they get a token that will allow them to reach the Journeyman-level crafting area. They can only enter the trial once a month and with the token once every two weeks if there is space."

==========

Agreed. Additional terms?

==========

"Sixty percent of the power in the dungeon will be used to expand the crafting dungeons and the main combat dungeon. The remaining forty percent will be held in the Mana storing formation and used to build out the sixth hidden dungeon floor."

==========

Agreed. Additional terms?

==========

"That's it," Rugrat said.

==========

Agreement reached. Breaking this agreement will result in a permanent loss of ten percent to each attribute.

==========

Do you accept this agreement?

==========

Rugrat let out a deep breath at the severe penalty, but nodded. The Ten Realms would manage the dungeon; trying to reclaim it was practically impossible.

"I agree." The golden light of the Ten Realms descended on Rugrat and covered him. It had a stifling pressure as it seeped into Rugrat's body before disappearing.

Rugrat felt that his control over the dungeon lessened. He was able to create, but no longer destroy. A big grin appeared on Rugrat's face as he ordered the undead in the dungeon to get moving.

"Okay, so looks like we'll have to do this the old-fashioned way!"

Rugrat made five tunnels branching off from where the smithing dungeon trial intersected with the stairs heading down to the original set armor dungeon.

These different tunnels would each house a different craft testing area.

Rugrat went forward into the smithing area. In a few minutes, he was able to pass the Novice test and use the Novice smithy to create a Journeyman-level weapon.

With it, he was rewarded with a token that allowed him to skip through the other areas. He entered the next floor, finding himself in a low-lit cave.

He pulled out his blade and started cutting the metal away from the deposits. He went through the Apprentice and then into the Journeyman mine and finally into the Journeyman-level smithy.

Rugrat felt his mind calming down as he changed into his smithing gear. He moved around in his short shorts, checking his range of motion and put on his apron, affixing his cowboy hat on his head.

"It's time to pound some metal," he said. Thankfully, since he was in the crafting dungeon rather than Vuzgal's smithy, everyone was spared the terrifying image of him standing in front of the furnace burned into their memory.

He tossed some ingots into the flames, adjusted his American flag booty shorts and worked the bellows.

Chapter: Snake in the Grass

Elder Lu listened to the information that had been gathered at his orders. The more he heard, the darker his expression turned.

"I want those people isolated and checked as soon as they arrive. Call the Alchemist Association and the healing houses. In the meantime, bring up all available information on the Blood Demon Sect: their allies, their enemies—I want to know it all." He was calm but the vein that was popping out of his neck showed that it was only on the surface. "Do we have anyone in the Fourth Realm who has ever come into contact with West?"

A woman reading over papers raised her hand, reading at the same time.

"Yes?" Elder Lu asked as he nodded at her.

She looked up to check he was talking to her. "Hiao Xen. He had descended the realms for a place for his son to recover from his injuries. He was given leave to do so. His son was healed by Erik West and he has climbed the realms rapidly since. He is currently a deputy head in the Fourth Realm."

"Have him come here immediately. I wish to talk to him." Elder Lu had read the files but he didn't know Erik personally. It was only the break in the contract that had alerted him. He needed to know just what kind of person everything was resting on.

"Also, see if the head of the Crafter's Association is free for a meeting. At this point, we will not make any moves. We must find fact from fiction before we act. All of our actions are watched and we do not have much time to decide what action to take."

Everyone had stopped making noise, looking to Elder Lu.

"*If* the Blood Demon Sect has perpetrated this crime, we will contact the enemies of the Blood Demon Sect. We will come to

431

an agreement with them, and push our armies forth to destroy the Blood Demon Sect. We might trade in goods, but we are not some weak group to be stepped over. We are fighting for the Blue Lotus' honor and our standing—do not forget that." He looked at them all, seeing the weight of his words settle on them.

"We have plenty of work to do." He tapped the table and stood. The others stood up as well.

***

Hiao Xen, once getting his order to report to the Fourth Realm's headquarters, was taken by a guide through the totem to the headquarters of the Blue Lotus. *What do they want me for, and why so urgently?*

He hadn't been to the headquarters in the Fourth Realm before, but he could see from the expressions of the people in the halls that it looked as though something important was happening.

He was led to a large office with powerful guards standing outside of it. Both of them wore armor that identified them as personal guards for the Fourth Realm Head. They were people from the Seventh Realm.

There was no aura around them, as if they were the abyss. Their movements were smooth but Hiao Xen didn't feel any power in it.

He saw their skin. It looked as smooth as polished marble. *Body Like Sky Metal?*

Hiao Xen examined the Mana around them, but there was no sense of Mana entering or leaving their body. It was as if they existed in perfect harmony. *Is this peak Mana Heart or Five Aperture Mana Heart?*

The door opened to show a man talking with another man and woman, who looked at maps and reports on the table in front of them.

"Deputy Head Hiao Xen," one of the guards said respectfully.

"Come in." The man leading the conversation looked over and stood.

Hiao Xen moved into the room and bowed deeply. "Elder Lu."

"Good." Elder Lu nodded as he looked at the deputy head and then up at the doors to make sure they were sealed.

"This is head of the Fourth Realm guards, Lei Huo." He gestured to the woman.

Hiao Xen bowed once again and sincerely.

"This is head of intelligence gathering, Cui Chin." He looked more like a guard than an intelligence officer. He was a swarthy man with focused eyes and large muscles. He had an easy smile on his face but Hiao Xen felt as if he was stripped naked in front of this man.

Hiao Xen's body trembled and he bowed again. There was a hidden side to the Blue Lotus, one that gathered information throughout the Ten Realms. All of the main associations had members like these, to keep track of what the other associations were doing and to gain information on the people they had to deal with. What someone said and who they were could be very different things. If one didn't know their allies better than they knew themselves, it was possible to be taken advantage of.

"Erik West, do you know him?" Elder Lu asked.

"I have a benefactor by that name who was a healer I met in the Second Realm," Hiao Xen said. The pressure from the other people decreased as Hiao Xen's eyes thinned.

"What do you think of the man?" Elder Lu probed.

"I think he is brash, bold, strong, in all the meanings of the word strong. He's the kind of person who has seen the best and the worst of life and knows the thin line we walk upon. He's not a simple man. He is a healer but he must have a history of fighting as well—the way he worked and reacted, the way he wore armor most of the time. He also looked into using Alchemy for fighting purposes—also, he had cultivated his body to a small degree."

"Would you trust him?" Cui Chin asked.

"With my life. He treated my son of a disease I could not find a cure for without asking for rewards or compensation. He is a good man."

Elder Lu nodded and his expression relaxed. He waved to Cui Chin.

"Nearly a week ago, Erik West came into contact with our Blue Lotus location at Tareng, on the Yaleir continent in the Fourth Realm. The city had been affected by what we thought was a plague..." Cui Chin got Hiao Xen up to speed on everything that had happened.

"Before you ask, I have looked into it—there are policies in place for this kind of thing. We do not have a guide for this totem that they have found at some cursed capital city that no one has seen in hundreds of years. There are people from Tareng rushing to it to teleport over to us here. We will need to examine them with healers and alchemists to confirm that they are not plagued and are, in fact, under the effect of a concoction. These are the rules of the Blue Lotus and we are bending them slightly due to the circumstance. You will be there to liaise, put Erik at ease and pull our combined forces together. Coordination on the battlefield can be the key to winning or losing.

"I have to wait until we get evidence of the Blood Demon Sect's involvement from their higher ups. We can't destroy a sect based on their actions of just one army. If we start attacking people because of one issue then our image will drop." Elder Lu explained.

Hiao Xen nodded, *looking at it from Elder Lu's perspective, we have thousands of locations across the Fourth Realm. Losing one is bad, yes, but having our image tarnished can spread through all the realms and affect all of the Blue Lotus locations.*

"Once they are cleared of the plague diagnosis, then we can start sending out our forces. We will destroy whoever organized this attack, but we must be completely sure." Elder Lu continued.

"While on the surface it looks like the Blood Demon sect is at fault, there are certain facts that don't add up. The attack looks to be well thought out but there are too many flaws. At any time, our people at Tareng could send out a message through a number of ways saying that the Blood Demon Sect was attacking. Something is wrong," Cui Chin conferred. .

"Anything that I can do to help, I will," Hiao Xen said. The Blue Lotus had given him his current life. They had looked after him and his family. They had allowed him to go to the Second Realm so that he could look after his son and see that he had a good life despite his shortcomings.

They had accepted him and allowed him to ascend once again after his son recovered. He was just one of four deputy heads at a lower Blue Lotus branch, three or four positions below what he had been before, but it was more than he expected.

"Do you know about Age Rejuvenation potions?" Elder Lu asked as he took in a deep breath.

"I do know that he made a number of them and sold them to the Blue Lotus. I made sure that he knew that we would take any he made. I saw that there was an update on his file some time ago and that he was made a friend of the Blue Lotus," Hiao Xen admitted.

"He signed a contract with us for two formulas an Apprentice and Journeyman-level Age Rejuvenation potion, that had the effects of Journeyman or Expert-level concoctions. We do not know what happened, but the contract and oath between the Blue Lotus and him has been broken."

"I don't think that he would go back on an oath." Hiao Xen frowned.

"He didn't. Someone on our side did, by breaking his trust."

Hiao Xen's fists tightened. *If someone in the Blue Lotus has attacked Erik...* Hiao Xen's emotions were mixed as he looked at the ground, thinking on it. His eyes moved back and forth.

"It was a blessing in disguise, as it brought the issue to my attention. There are rules and regulations to everything in the Blue Lotus, but they can get in the way at times."

"How long until we can get people there to help them?" Hiao Xen asked.

"It is best that we have the element of surprise. As such, we cannot send more people to support them until we are ready to act," Lei Huo spoke up for the first time.

"Seven days," Elder Lu answered with a stiff expression. "Thank you for coming on such short notice. Someone will get you a residence to stay in. We may have more questions."

"Elders." Hiao Xen bowed deeply again and headed out, knowing that they had much more important matters to do than answer his questions.

He left the room and found an attendant ten levels stronger than he was waiting for him.

This headquarters is filled with monsters. All of them come from the Seventh Realm, completely separate from the regular promotion chain.

***

Rugrat heard the yells as the flying creatures could be seen. People moved to positions as they loaded their dual heavy repeaters and aimed them at the sky.

"Vuzgal, this is Storbon. We are coming in to land. Where would be best?" Storbon asked.

"Stand down!" Rugrat shouted to the men and women of Tiger Platoon, and got the undead to continue their work.

"Take them right to the totem," Rugrat ordered.

"Understood, First Sergeant," Storbon replied. The flying beasts cut across the large capital, riding through the thinning mists. They could see the full city; its buildings might still be in disrepair but the walls stood strong in the sunlight. There were undead moving everywhere, carrying out different tasks: making arrows, hauling rubble up to the walls, walling off the gates, creating a labyrinth inside the city, opening up holes in the ground for IEDs and mines, or plain pits for people to fall into.

Rugrat knew what they saw; he had seen it while flying with George. The main pillar of the city still lay on its side, but with the undead and powerful spells, they had been able to get it off the walls and push it into the middle of the city.

There was a large open area inside the city as well.

Rugrat patted the string holding ten rings numbered one to ten. With Mana blades and the undead's help, they had been able to tear down the freshly built totem. They had only built it and not activated it, not fusing the building together. This allowed them to take it apart piece by piece and those with some art or blueprint ability had recorded the plans down. It was a reach to see whether it would work after being reassembled in Alva, but if it did, it would solve one of their biggest security concerns.

***

"Come on, George," Rugrat said as he put his hammer down.

George got up, moving his wings as Rugrat got on his back. George ran down the street and flapped his wings, causing them to rise into the sky. George used a heating spell underneath him, causing them to shoot up into the sky, a little trick that Rugrat taught him about hot air rising.

They rose above the houses and banked toward the Vuzgal totem.

Rugrat rode on George, looking over to the group with Storbon. There were members of the Blue Lotus and the Crafter's Association; all of them had tired but determined looks on their faces from riding constantly for four days.

They landed in front of the totem, looking at George, who landed with them. Rugrat got off, his face covered in soot. He and the rest of the armies smiths had been working in the smithy all this time to make more ammunition for the mortars and the M32's.

"Warrant," Storbon nodded to Rugrat.

"Good to see you back. I've got work for you to be doing," Rugrat said.

"I didn't think it was true that you had been able to take over Vuzgal. I have heard stories about this place," one of the crafters said, looking around.

An undead moved through the city nearby, jogging with crates that had been strapped to their bones so they wouldn't fall off. One of the people from the Blue Lotus used a powerful sound talisman that disappeared.

"So, what now?" Rugrat asked.

"Now we wait. They will need to ready everything on the other side. After we travel through, we go through testing; we tell them what is going on and then we bring back reinforcements to destroy the Blood Demon Sect," one of the people from the Blue Lotus said.

"Very well. Let me know if you need anything," Rugrat said as a sound transmission arrived in front of the person who had used the powerful sound talisman previoiusly.

"They are waiting for us," the man said.

The Alvan army backed up as the people from the Crafter's Association and Blue Lotus pulled out Mana stones for their passage.

The Mana stones turned into energy and the totem activated.

Light covered their bodies and they were all gone.

"Well, that wasn't quick at all." Rugrat looked to the members of the special team. "Get some hot food into you—we've got plenty to do!"

Rugrat's sound transmission device lit up with a message.

"Warrant, I think that we've found an armory, but the traps are difficult. I wouldn't be asking if I didn't think it was important,"said Glosil.

They had continued the recovery efforts to see what supplies and resources they could draw on if they needed to flee.

Rugrat's eyes flickered to a building near the totem. Inside it, several carriages with crates were filled with valuables ready to be moved. There were three such buildings around the totem. With these carriages, resources would no longer be a problem to Alva in the foreseeable future.

Their next shipment was ready to go, thankfully there were some traders that were a high enough level to make it to Vuzgal that were helping the Dragon Platoon to take the carts down to the lower realms to the different branches of Alva.

The carts filled with ammunition had been already stripped bare and divded up. The mortar rounds were shipped out on the fastest mounts. They had trained beasts with storage items around their legs flying to the mortar teams. Other teams were moving to the ammunition caches that had been set up along the road. The mortar teams had to watch their ammunition consumption closely so they wouldn't run out as Han Wu and his people had to get creative with IED's to make the explosive that they had go as far as possible and create the most damage.

"All right, I'm on my way to you." Rugrat was interested to see what was in the armory. They might be able to outfit their people and the skeletons in better gear. They had put the best armor on the Alvan army with the strongest of what was left being placed on the undead.

"Come with me. I've got presents," Rugrat said.

Storbon and the others followed, getting back on the winged lizard mounts that had been leant to them by the Blue Lotus and Crafter's association, following Rugrat over to the castle.

Three or four days until the people from Tareng finally get here. We still have a lot to do by then. Rugrat looked to the valley, thinking of the dungeon beyond.

There was a movement off to the side. He saw Elizabeth raising her hands; dirt rose up and compressed, becoming stronger than stone and creating a new wall in the city.

Reaper was with her, creating traps formed from small trees. They looked like nothing but weeds—a perfect disguise.

"The worst thing you can give a defender is time," Rugrat said to himself as he looked at the city.

***

General Ulalas was resting her eyes when she heard the whistling again.

A half dozen explosions went off before peace returned.

I've never heard of the Blue Lotus or the Crafter's association fighting like this before.

She sighed and rubbed her face, pinching the bridge of her nose as she rose slowly, she was still wearing her armor.

The world seemed to be made of noise as Ulalas' eyes went wide, she reached out and grabbed the wall as the carriage came to a sudden halt.

She stood up, her sleep forgotten

Ulalas grabbed her helmet and ran outside, looking at the Mana shields that were erected, waiting for the whistling attacks from the sky.

There was nothing but screams that could be heard as a seventy-meter section of road had been torn apart—another unit destroyed.

"Have the scouts spotted anything?" she asked Minor General Damel, who had been in command as she was sleeping.

"They haven't," he said.

"Sneaky fuckers," Ulalas muttered, looking out at the forest all around them, she *knew* that they were watching them. They had tried using life detect spell scrolls and other means to find out where these attacks were comign from. They hadn't found any trace of the enemy that had to be attacking them from well beyond eyesight range.

They'd pushed out the cavalry to move through the forests to look for spotters. They knew that someone had to be guiding the long-range abilities on top of them.

"Get the road repaired and get us moving again," Ulalas said. She lost hundreds of soldiers with every attack but so far they had only killed some twenty Masters from the Blue Lotus. She looked over the army. She could see their nervousness, their anger; they wanted to attack the enemy but were unable to fight or even see ghosts.

If we could send up scouts to clear the road ahead, it would be for the best. But we just don't know what kind of strength this hid-

den force has. Maybe, this is for the best. The longer this drags out, the greater chance of the Blue Lotus reporting that the Blood Demon Sect is attacking them.

The wounded were cleared away as Minor General Damel went off to get the army moving again.

Ulalas wasn't blind to the sentiment of the soldiers. When they had started after the Blue Lotus and Crafter's association, their morale had been sky high. They were chasing two of the assocations!

They had even killed some of their masters! Their bodies were paraded around as proof of their strength.

That was yesterday and this is toady. The incoming attacks placed a constant pressure on them, kept them from sleeping, from having a meal in peace. The ground they walked on could turn into a trap.

Already some of the people from armies not normally led by Ulalas were starting to show morale issues with their generals trying to reassure them while looking for help from Ulalas.

It took two hours before they were moving

They were a half day or more behind the Tareng people now.

Just who are the people in this forest? They aren't from the Blue Lotus. I've never heard of anyone using these tactics or attacks before.

A report was passed to her. Four hundred had died today. A percent of their fighting force.

We've only killed what, thirty of their people, out of an army of ten thousand.

Ulalas gripped the hilt of her sword. *This will become a fight of morale instead of numbers. I need to make sure that I bind everyone properly with oaths so they can't turn back and escape.*

"Lets make sure that people reaffirm their oaths," Ulalas said, looking to General Damel.

They shared a deep look before he nodded slowly.

"I'll make sure I pass the order on."

A dark cloud hung over the Blood Demon army as oath keepers went through the ranks to reaffirm people's oaths to the Blood Demon Sect.

Forty minutes later the whistling started again.

"Take cover!" people yelled out and ran to the sides of the road as explosions went off.

Why does it look like the ground is exploding instead of the sky?

***

"We hit them with mortars as they put down the Mana barriers. A bunch of them ran into the forest and found our mines there. They've deployed a large number of flying beasts and are scouring the area," Niemm reported.

"Okay, that will make it harder to use the mortars," Erik said after he listened to the report. It had been two days since they started their attacks.

"They've got their scouts out around three hundred meters on either side of the road," Niemm reported.

"Maybe we can turn that into a trap?" Roska asked.

"How?" Erik asked.

"Well, we've got these spells scrolls we haven't used, turn the sky into a mess with tornadoes or something?"

"Could use spell scrolls to mess with the ground around the road. Raise golems, make it hard to travel across the ground. Won't stop them, but it would be annoying to deal with," Niemm suggested.

"Their mana barriers get disrupted by the trees, looks like it doesn't go through solid objects. If we can get a few mortars in there?" Gong Jin asked.

"We're running low on mortar rounds. Well, really it's not that we don't have the rounds. We just don't have the ability to get them from Vuzgal to our positions fast enough. We'll need ton conserve our rounds until we get to the prepared caches along the road," Yui sounded frustrated.

"Suggestions?" Erik asked

"We're not going to crack through their shields anytime soon with our mortars, they'll have a greater effect on their morale, I can send some of the mortar team back to the caches or meet up with the supply beasts. Then they meet up with us and transfer ammunition."

"Okay, we'll coordinate weapons fire, keep it low unless we see an opening, hamper them but not waste rounds. Test with Gong Jin and see what we can do against those scouts in the trees."

"Sir," Gong Jin and Yui acknoweldged their orders.

"Then those not manning the mortars can stay on watch and use spell scrolls on any aerial assets," Yui added in a questioning tone.

"You run it how you want, you know the situation with your people better than I do," Erik said.

"Understood," Yui said.

"Questions?" Erik asked, stretching in his armor, the middle of his back aching as he tried to loosen up.

No one responded.

"Good stuff. Gong Jin, report to me when the enemy is in our target zone."

"Will do." he confirmed.

Erik closed the channel. He sat against a rock, looking like unsleeping hell. He was covered in dirt and grime, his left leg raised up, with his helmet resting on his knee.

He took a deep breath, rubbed his face and pulled out some luke warm coffee he had been nursing focusing on the map in his other hand.

He checked his updated map and the different ambush points that were still marked out and the mortar positions and observation points that they had already checked out. There was a section from Yui's Dragon Platoon and Han Wu with a group of people from the special team that had been withdrawing ahead of them, locating and preparing observation and firing positions as well as picking out ambush locations along the road.

The two groups had quickly become experts at their new roles.

Erik put the map away and opened up his notifications.

None of them had slept in two days, meaning that they had been unable to accept their new increase in levels. Erik knew that most of his men wouldn't actually sleep until Vuzgal. All of the company were linked up as one massive group; most armies didn't do this as the Experience would be so spread out that few people would increase their Strength. The Masters and more powerful people would revolt; the strong fought the strong and so it went.

The Alvan army was only one hundred and twenty or so people strong. When the fighting started, the average level in the company had been late thirties early forties; the special teams, had all been around level forty-five. The average soldiers in the Blood Demon army were level thirty-three as well. Their Elites, thirty-seven; their Masters, forty-three. The Blood Demon Army's levels hadn't increased, but the Alva Army's had. As they counted as a group, even the members of the army that were working in Vuzgal increased their level.

With the deaths coming via tools instead of direct combat using their own Strength, the Experience was decreased by half.

Still, the amount of Experience that they had earned was daunting.

The Experience that was required to advance past level fifty was even more so.

==========

You have reached Level 54

==========

When you sleep next, you will be able to increase your attributes by: 5 points.

==========

==========

7,189,530/30,600,000EXP till you reach Level 55

==========

It was an incredible amount of Experience and had raised everyone within the army to the level of low-level Masters in the Blood Demon Sect's army. Instead of celebrating, they continued on. The fight wasn't over.

Erik was proud of them. Combat could be trained for, but until they were in it, he didn't know how they'd react. They had performed well, but still they had a long way to go. It would be another day or two until the people of Tareng reached Vuzgal.

"Wake me up in an hour," He said to Gilly who was scratching her back against a tree. She let out a warble, before returning to her look of bliss as she scratched her back.

Erik had a light smile as he took a sleeping aid.

==========

You have 5 attribute points to use.

==========

Erik saw his character sheet and studied it.

Looking at it, his Stamina Regeneration was at 20 per second while his Mana recovered at 33. 5 per second. With stalling the Blood Demon Sect, he really felt the effects of his Stamina Regeneration. It allowed him to need only a minimal amount of food and sleep to remain in functional condition. He put two more points into stamina regeneration, two into mana pool, he was still keeping an eye on advancing his mana cultivation. He took the last point and put it into Agility. Agility would give him a greater reaction time and make him deadly with fists, a rifle or a M32.

He was strong and his armor only increased that with the innate Strength buff. He had also been able to fill up his carrier with Mana, increasing the pool he could pull from to increase his defense and overclock his body. With pills and his Body Cultivation, he could deal with the resulting damage from him overclocking his body.

It was very rough, but for now it would work.

He accepted the changes and looked at his new character sheet.

```
==========
Name: Erik West
==========
Level: 54
==========
Race: Human
==========
Titles:
From the Grave II
Mana Emperor
Dungeon Master III
Reverse Alchemist
Poison Body
Fire Body
City Lord
==========
```

Strength: (Base 36) +41

==========

770

==========

Agility: (Base 29) +69

==========

539

==========

Stamina: (Base 39) +23

==========

930

==========

Mana: (Base 8) +73

==========

810

==========

Mana Regeneration (Base 10) +55

33. 50/s

==========

Stamina Regeneration: (Base 41) +56

20. 40/s

==========

Erik woke up with Gilly using her snout to push him. He nearly jumped up as he was instantly awake, he grabbed his helmet and saw that everyone was relaxed, eating drinking and taking care of their gear as the other group were working.

Roska came over and gave him a warm drink that one of the soldiers had made.

"Thanks," Erik said.

"No problem," Roska replied as she took out her own cup and drank her coffee beside him. "So what's our next move?"

"We need to stall the Blood Demon army for another night. Then, the only way they could they catch up with the people from Tareng is if they made a run for it. What I'm thinking is we start having the people of Tareng and those in Vuzgal to dig out places for us to put down IEDs.

"For tonight and tomorrow, we spend all of our remaining ammunition and make the Blood Demon army's lives hell: mines in the forest, mortars through the night, random one shots and barrages, IEDs all over the place. Use up our spell scrolls too. This will be our time to inflict as much damage as possible on them before they reach Vuzgal. They take a position; we back up. We can give ground here, we just have to be slow about it. They have to fight for every inch, we don't," Erik said.

"They've started scanning the ground for the explosives. They caught one of them this morning," Roska reminded him.

"Yes but we still activated it—didn't get as many though. We need to bury them deeper, or instead of in the road, we put them into hills around the army's sides—this point here." Erik pointed to a slight depression in front of them that the road went through. The sides of the road sloped down, only slightly, but the depressed area was nearly two kilometers long.

"Pack explosives and shrapnel into the sides. Hit them with mortars when they're right in the middle; target the carriages there. It will be hard for them to move around and clear them. Get them to throw up their Mana barriers as the mortars are coming down. They'll umbrella over the sides of the road. As they're trying to find cover or relying on the shields, we blow the IEDs along the road that are still inside the shields," Erik said.

"That is three ambush points ahead of where we are," Roska commented.

"I'll send Niemm and two sections of Dragon Platoon to prepare it," Erik said. "They'll focus on just that all night while the rest of us will be hitting the Blood Demon army."

"It looks like our attacks are having an effect, with the reduced mortar attacks there are more lulls. When I was watching I saw a few people escaping into the forest. Looks like some people have figured out how to get around their oaths," Roska murmured.

"The more that run, the less we have to fight," Erik stretched as Gilly's head appeared behind him and nudged his back.

"Hey girl," Erik said with a bitter smile as he patted her head.

Roska smiled and released her panther mount. He stretched out and looked at Gilly, lowering his head in greeting before he went to rest beside Roska.

"Something calming about animals," Roska said.

"Other than when we're fighting them?" Erik snorted.

"Other than when we're fighting them," Roska agreed.

"Why do you think that the Blood Demon Sect are trying to wipe out the people of Tareng?"

"Riches? Some kind of blood feud? I don't really know," Erik shrugged.

They fell silent, just taking some moments away from command.

"How are you Roska?" Erik asked.

"Hmm?" Roska asked.

"It feels like yesterday I healed you, but also a lifetime ago. Then you joined the defense force at Alva, then the special teams and have led people across the realms, growing in strength, becoming a powerful leader respected by those that she leads and by the Alva Army. We have always been training or working on something but, how are you?"

"I'm good," Roska shrugged.

"You enjoy being in the Army," Erik asked. Roska looked at him making him smile. "Asking as a friend, not the guy running this. Trust me it is weird as hell to say that sentence."

The corner of Roska's mouth lifted as she sat back against her panther who opened his eye and then closed it, comfortable lying there.

Gilly turned her head to the side and made a noise then looked at Erik. He looked at her, feeling that she wanted to go hunting.

"Alright, just don't alert anyone or anything."

She let out a pleased noise, nudged his face with her snout and ran off.

Erik sat there, waiting for Roska's answer she seemed to be pondering.

"I like my job, to some that might seem crazy, but I have a purpose here. When something needs to get done then it is done. There are challenges, times are hard but I like the challenges. The hard times bring people together and remove the weak from the strong. I've learned that being physically strong will only get you so far and the mental strength will push you further. I couldn't let down the people around me here."

Erik listened as she fell quiet.

"I've never had a family really, the one I did have left me as soon as I became a burden. The people in the Army, the people in Alva, they're more of my family now than my family ever was," Her eyes fell and looked at Erik, captivating him.

"If not for you then I would have never had this life, never been able to stand properly. I will follow you and Rugrat into the depths of hell if you ask me to. You gave me a second life."

Erik was a bit stunned by the emotion behind her words.

Erik looked away, at the stars above.

"There is a saying, not really sure how it goes, but the gist is, live your life the best you can, that is the way to repay me for saving it," Erik said and looked to Roska with a smile on his face. He felt that gritty tiredness that gave clarity but allowed one to see through emotions to the heart of the matter.

Roska looked at the ground, thinking on his words.

Erik saw her looking at the ground, one of his strongest commanders as she dealt with her own thoughts and emotions. She was only in her early twenties but she had the responsibility of ten lives on her back as well as Alva dungeon. Erik felt proud of her, he wanted to express just how astounded he was at her ability.

The silence stretched before Roska cleared her throat.

"So why do you think that the Blood Demons are doing this?"

"Who knows what motivates them. I was sure that we would break their morale but we've only seen a few people breaking away. Those Oaths are stronger than I thought," Erik sighed, tired. "All we can do is try to thin them out as much as possible. The hill ambush will be our last big attack. The IEDs are forunately still effective at killing them, though."

"What about the formation traps?" Roska said.

"They're prepared for the formation traps, be useless for them," Erik countered.

"Exactly," A sly smile formed on Roska's face. Erik tilted his head as she continued.

"They know how to detect trap formations, if we throw them down here and there, they'll have to slow to deactivate it and then continue, maybe they'll miss it a time or two. We only have a certain number of IEDs but if they have to slow or stop to clear the formations, we have plenty of mortar rounds, when they're stopped we hit them with mortars. Get them used to fighting the formations and then throw in an IED to break their morale and take down as many of them as possible."

"We do have plenty of trap formations, the more we can slow them down then the better. We could deploy them in the forest actuall," Erik rubbed his face.

"You said that expect the unexpected, well if they're expecting IED's and we throw in formations it could throw them off balance," Roska said.

"Sounds like a good plan to me, talk to the teams working on pre-placing the ambushes."

"Yes sir," Roska smiled and headed off with her new orders.

Erik grunted as he moved around in his armor, his back was tight and he'd long become numb to his own smell.

He took solace in his warm drink, looking at his people that were resting, but not really seeing them. He was plotting to kill thousands of people, but it was the only way that he could save the innocents from Tareng.

If the Blood Demon's , he wouldn't chase them. But they kept on moving toward his city and had planned to kill defenseless people to take their goods. He wasn't going go let them continue without an even greater fight.

***

Glosil greeted the special team as they headed down a corridor. It was wide enough to fit five people across. They passed a few smithies that were long cold, armories that had been emptied and were in a state of disrepair. There were undead hauling out crates of weapons and armors. There weren't many sets of gear left; most of them had been used to arm the people of the city as the last battle had arrived.

Glosil led them past the armories and then through a barracks area where people could don their armor and weapons.

Then they went through an armored door. Inside was different. There was still plenty of room to move but there were private rooms for people to get armored up in.

Weapons and armor that had been left here looked as if it needed some care but it wasn't falling apart like the gear in the other rooms.

They got to another, larger, armored door, where a number of Tiger Platoon examined the floors and walls.

Rugrat stepped forward and used his Simple Inorganic Scan and opened up his Mana sense.

"Back up, everyone!" Rugrat ordered loudly. Everyone moved away as Rugrat raised his hand. A large amount of Mana gathered in his hand, forming a Mana bolt. Instead of just wild Mana raging around, it was compressed. Barely any of it leaked out.

It shot forward from Rugrat's hand and hit the door.

The door exploded. The noise made everyone grab their ears; a few started yelling, unable to hear anything.

The hall filled with dust. Rugrat fired out a Mana bullet; the speed of the Mana bullet cleared the dust, blowing it out of the hall. A few people coughed on it all as Rugrat stepped forward. Glosil gritted his teeth, using a healing spell on his ears. He followed Rugrat, looking into a room with several chests. Even covered in dust, they were clearly higher quality storage chests.

There was a rack of swords at the rear of the room that Rugrat moved toward, his eyes shining. He took out a Mana blade and jammed it into the wall. A formation flashed into existence and then faded as Rugrat overloaded it with Mana, destroying the formation.

He reached out and grabbed a sword. Rugrat's aura changed, making one feel a cold cutting wind by being around him.

"Damn! So that's what an Expert-level weapon feels like," Rugrat said with a touch of awe.

A shiver ran through Glosil's body as he heard Rugrat's words.

Rugrat crossed the sword in front of him lazily. The blade hummed, as if excited to be used.

Glosil moved to one of the crates and checked inside. There were only a few items inside. "Three Expert-level bows." He reported as he moved to the next. Three spears were inside that crate; then armors—one full set, another only a partial.

"Take an inventory of everything here. Write up commendations for who should get what. This should give them an increase in Strength in the coming battle," Rugrat said.

"I'll see to it, First Sergeant," Glosil said before coughing from the dust.

Rugrat touched the wall in the armory and smiled. *There you are.*

He put his hand in a hole that Glosil hadn't seen and pressed something. There was a clicking noise. Glosil's hand dropped to his weapon as a section of the wall turned to reveal another area beyond. It was in chaos, with pieces of paper flying everywhere.

The paper resonated with the Mana in the room.

"Spell scrolls?" Glosil asked.

"Seems that they used a bunch of them but not all of them." Rugrat collected the ones off the floor and passed them to Glosil. He checked them over as Rugrat pressed his hand to the wall and opened another cubby hole.

"This is where the dungeon core was hiding," Rugrat said as they looked at the open space. There were spell scrolls, formation designs, and other information pieces that the royal family must have kept hidden.

"These should make it easier to get into the different caches." Rugrat observed as he looked at the formations. They were defensive or offensive in nature. He opened up one of the books; he put it on a crate and pointed to the map inside.

"Looks like there are plenty of hidden places in the castle," Rugrat said.

"Well, they would need to have some kind of record for what changes happened to the building," Glosil said.

"If that out there is their armored division, then this is their nuclear missile silo," Rugrat said, checking in the different crates. He grabbed two of the crates and moved items from the remaining to the two he was holding. "I'll be taking these."

Glosil nodded, not sure he wanted to know what items he was keeping, if he was willing to have Glosil look after Expert-level equipment.

Glosil followed Rugrat out.

"Good work on finding this place. I'll be checking over everything personally. Head to the next location of interest," Rugrat said.

The others took another look around the room and headed off to their other tasks. Glosil took a look around the room and pulled out a notepad. He started to list down the different weapons and their stats. He picked up the sword that Rugrat had been holding.

==========
Chilling Breeze
==========
Attack:
361
Weight:
4. 2 kg
Charge:

2,234/5,000
Durability:
84/100
Innate Effect:
Strength of the user increases by 14%
Agility increases by 20%
Enchantment One:
Call down Storm of Swords. 10X10m radius. Speed of user increases by 50% for 3 minutes.
Costs 500 charge
3 hour cooldown
Enchantment Two:
Chilling Strike
Imbue sword with the effects of frost. Increase attack power by 100%. Frost attack reduces opponent's speed by 5%; lasts for 5 minutes.
5 hour cooldown
Costs 750 charge
Requirements:
Agility 51
Strength 47
Stamina Regeneration 25

==========

Glosil let out a whistle. The Expert blade served to enhance one's Strength by a large margin. Also, it's enchantments didn't just increase the weapon's ability, they were killing moves that could be used tactically, like Erik's overclock enchantment on his armor.

The line between Journeyman and Expert-level weapons appeared thin, but from the stats, one could see it was much wider.

One needed to have three stats that reached the requirements in order to wield it. The enchantments that Journeyman level or half-step Expert-level armor and weapons had were usually based toward a percentage increase instead of a hidden technique that one could execute with their weapon.

Glosil looked at the three other weapons that were hanging up on the wall and then the storage crates.

Rugrat appeared again, dragging his boxes behind him. "Well, so, uh, I might have not actually realized this." Rugrat pulled out a few undead bodies—the emperor and his personal guard that Rugrat had found around the dungeon core."Yeaaah, they've probably got some good gear too." Rugrat let out an awkward laugh.

"You forgot?" Glosil's eyebrow twitched.

"Well, yeah. I know that there is supposed to be Expert-level gear here and it is a big place, but I didn't look at their gear. Honestly, I just thought that it might be useless and smell nasty," Rugrat said.

"Aren't you a smith?" Glosil's voice rose.

"No need to point that out." Rugrat looked around. "Anyway, they can be your helpers."

Mana seeped through the ground and into the bodies of the fifty or so dead that were on the ground.

They started to rise up, turning into undead as Rugrat used the power of the dungeon. Though the problem was they'd been thrown haphazardly and quickly into Rugrat's storage ring. There were a few cases of someone's foot stuck between someone's arm bones or a foot in another's chest as the undead started to get up, dragging one another undead upside down because their foot was stuck in the other's ribs, so their head was on the floor.

"Good luck!" Rugrat left, quickly dragging his two high-quality storage crates with him. "All elbows and knees with that lot. Maybe should have just had them walk over."

Glosil was sure that the undead looked confused and scared as he looked at their pitiful state. *Is this how it is for Egbert?*

Glosil looked at the skeletons, looking at their actions with pity and shook his head as they tried to get themselves out from one another and stand up without being connected to each other. "Go outside the room and get yourselves upright!"Glosil commanded.

They stumbled out of the room, even the undead emperor, who had one arm in one guard's neck and a foot stuck in another's arm as he flailed around with one free arm and one of his legs.

"Poor bastards." Glosil looked at his notes and started with his work.

***

Rugrat headed to the city's dungeon core. Using a spell stone, he was able to pass through the security barriers and formations.

They had collected three dozen Mortal Mana cornerstones and nearly ten Earth-grade cornerstones.

With the power of the area and the dungeon core, the crystals had grown at an alarming speed. They were growing at a rate visible to the eye as they spread across the interior of the pillar, only a small road leading from the stairs to the dungeon core.

Rugrat could sense that the polluted Mana around the capital was becoming cleaner with time. Right now, every three or four days, the people of the army needed to circulate their Mana while being around the dungeon core so that the polluted Mana didn't remain in their system.

A few had been able to get a day or two off in order to use this opportunity to increase their Mana Gathering Cultivation. More people were forming Mana drops. Roska had formed three drops already. With her natural talent and focusing on Mana Gathering Cultivation from the beginning, she was one of the strongest, though she was currently out fighting with the rest of Dragon Platoon and the special teams.

Rugrat put down the boxes and opened them. They were filled with a number of spell scrolls.

Spell scrolls were rated, much like regular spells, by the force that they could exert. The difference between spells and spell scrolls was where the power came from. A ninth-tier spell needed a tier-nine caster to cast it. A tier-nine spell scroll had a similar effect, but it didn't need the mage in the equation.

Rugrat looked through the scrolls. Many of them were buff-like scrolls, mass scrolls that could increase the power of a fighting force in times of need. There were mass healing scrolls as well as spells and formations that would weaken the enemy as they were attacking.

Most of the defensive and attacking scrolls had been used, but there were still a few fifth-tier spell scrolls he could use.

The defensive scrolls could enhance the walls making them sturdier all around. There were also some earth and stone scrolls that could increase the level of the materials in the walls for a period of time.

There were dozens of tier-three and tier-four artillery spell scrolls or damage-enhancing scrolls.

It was a treasure trove, if used right.

The amount of gold coins that they were worth—well, it could probably only be calculated in Earth-grade Mana stones.

Rugrat checked on the dungeon. Everyone was working in the capital right now, but construction had not stopped at the Bala dungeon. A rudimentary sixth floor was completed and the basic layout of the first floor of the Crafter's trial dungeon was under construction. It took a lot of Mana and materials that Rugrat had had the undead drop off.

Rugrat hoped their scheme worked but it wasn't his primary concern right now.

He felt more Experience entering his body. Rugrat paused and looked over to the east. He couldn't see Erik and the others fighting but he knew that they must be with the new Experience flooding into him and the rest of the defense force.

Even without fighting, their levels were increasing. It would give them a better chance when they had to face the Blood Demonarmy.

***

"What happened?" Xue Lin asked as Olivia entered her carriage.

Olivia relayed everything that had happened and handed Xue Lin the medallion.

"We can't trust them anymore, now that they have broken their oath. He was just looking for a reason to do so," Olivia said.

"Looking for a reason to do so..." Xue Lin clenched her teeth.

Olivia had an ominous feeling in her stomach as she looked up at Xue Lin.

"I have been in contact with Elder Lu."

Olivia's eyes went wide. "Elder Lu, the one in charge of the Fourth Realm?"

Xue Lin nodded. Something of this caliber had to be sent to him.

"Hiao Xen is a deputy head in the Fourth Realm. His son was healed by Erik West in the Second Realm just over a year ago. At that time, he was close to reaching level twenty and was under the tutorship of Third Realm Pill Head Hei Zen. I got a message from Elder Lu, asking why *we* broke trust with Erik West. His oath jade is kept in the headquarters of all the Earth realms." Xue Lin let that sink in.

Olivia gnashed her teeth, thinking of the arrogant fool West and unable to compare it against this other man she heard explained to her.

"So, I ask again, *what happened*?" Xue Lin asked with narrowed eyes.

Olivia gave a full recounting of everything that had happened since she and Erik had left the rest of the convoy.

"So we don't know if Erik's people at the capital will be hostile or friendly to us."

"We are the Blue Lotus—we can destroy them," Olivia said.

"And that is the flaw." Xue Lin nodded, as if putting it together. "Because of our position, do you think that others should blindly obey? That the realms can bend to our rules and orders? We might be one of the pillars of the Ten Realms but that is only due to our backing. There are many who would like to see us fall. We are strong but we cannot take on the Ten Realms. We were attacked, yes. We were forced to flee, yes." Xue Lin's words made Olivia wince, bringing up her failures again and again. "We had to rely on another group to save us. We look to make connections and friends like Erik West so that we have people to assist us in times of need. It is not when we should be pushing them away!" Xue Lin's voice rose into a yell as she shifted her armor and adjusted her hands to calm herself.

"He wanted to use these mortars and IEDs, too scared to attack the enemy head on," Olivia complained.

"Maybe, but I gave overall command to him, not to you. He was in charge and you went against *my* wishes and *my* orders," Xue Lin said.

"I didn't..."

"It doesn't matter what you meant to do—it's what you *did*. Even now there are strangers fighting for us to escape and our fighting forces were sent away because the people saving us couldn't trust them! Do you know what kind of stain this is on our reputation?!" Xue Lin's anger was fully revealed, finding it quite hard to keep under control.

"You are dismissed of command and you will report to Commander Femi. You will carry out his orders as a person of the Blue Lotus. Am I understood?" Xue Lin's eyes burned into Olivia's.

Olivia felt a pressure on her very soul; she wanted nothing more than to drop out of the bottom of the carriage. "Yes," she said in a small voice, unable to look Xue Lin in the eye.

Chapter: Elan Silaz Surfaces

Elan Silaz looked rougher than when he had left Chonglu just a few months ago as he stepped down from his carriage.

A woman came up to him with a smile. "Head Silaz." She bowed to him.

"Come, little niece Lidia, is that any way to greet your uncle?" Elan smiled. He had grown a beard while he had been traveling around the different outposts around the Beast Mountain Range.

Lidia giggled as she and Elan hugged.

"It is good to see you, Uncle!" she said with a pleased smile.

Elan laughed happily and released her. "I have heard that you have turned into the trading devil of Vermire." He grinned.

She played with her hair, pressing her foot into the ground.

Elan let out a laugh. "I knew that you came from my side of the family!"

Lidia blushed but couldn't help smiling.

"Come, it has been a long road and your uncle smells!"

"I was wondering what that smell was," she teased and waved for him to follow her.

They went through the back entrance into the Silaz trading house. It was one of the biggest traders of monster cores in the city. They also dealt in certain high-quality weapons and armor that couldn't be found in other stores.

"The meeting with Lord Aditya?"

"It has been confirmed but it has taken a lot of work to do so. He has become a powerful man since the Zatan Confederation was turned on its head. Did you see the construction?"

"Looks like they are expanding the city walls?"

"The outpost has more people visiting it than any in the region. Getting a place to trade or stay within the outpost has turned out to be incredibly expensive now. There is also the healing house. People are even willing to come from cities far away to go to our healing house due to their agreeable rates that don't fluctuate with a person's medical issue." Lidia's tone dropped.

"So it has turned into a gold mine. Thankfully we had a position here already," Elan said, a hidden smile in his eyes.

"I heard that you brought a number of skilled people who are looking for employment with you, as well as Mana stones and wealth?"

"Why do you think that I had so many guards?" Elan laughed.

"A number of them are lamed as well." Lidia's eyes narrowed as she looked at Elan. "What are you aiming to do, Uncle?"

Elan simply smiled, not revealing anything.

Lidia let out a flustered snort. "Of course, always keeping your little tricks to yourself!"

"When will I be meeting Lord Aditya?" Elan asked.

"Tonight. It was the only time that he was free. In four hours," Lidia said.

"Very well," Elan said. "Before I go, I want to take a look at this healing house."

***

Elan looked a bit cleaner, his beard trimmed up and the dirt of the road cleaned away before he walked toward the Alva Healing House.

There was a line down the street with people wearing a uniform of green clothes and white masks moving along the line, checking people over, giving them each a colored emblem for them to pin to their jackets.

A man screaming was rushed to the hospital by a group of fighters. Someone wearing a uniform rushed over, halting the group. They used a healing spell and then had them continue inside.

Elan walked around the building. There was a garden to the back of the healing house. It was gated off, with some people outside, being monitored as they began to walk, or doing tasks for people inside the fenced area who were wearing the same uniform.

Elan saw a few people with stands next to them with bags of liquid that dripped into their arms.

A mysterious smile appeared on Elan's face.

He had been able to get information on what Erik and Rugrat had done for Lord Chonglu's children; it wasn't a big secret. The way that they healed people was different than healers who used spells and alchemists that used concoctions: they used a mixture of tools, concoctions, and spells.

Elan had heard about the bags before. Seeing them attached to the patients within the healing house, he felt closer to Yui, Domonos, and Qin than he had in a long time.

He turned away from the healing house and looked toward the lord's manor. His guards followed him as he headed off to his meeting.

***

Jen checked Lord Aditya's leg. It had healed well, fully recovering, and now he was looking to restore his Strength. "You'll be making a full recovery soon," Jen said as she released his leg.

"I can't thank you enough," Lord Aditya said.

"Just doing my job," Jen said.

Lord Aditya laughed. Things had changed from that night when in this very room he had been visited by that mysterious woman and her companions.

The new Vermire couldn't be compared to the one of old.

They had items for sale that would be hard to find in some capitals of the First Realm. There were dealings from multiple countries and nations that happened in the back taverns of Vermire. Supplies moved hands here on the scale that could supply a country.

There were more mercenary groups than ever in the outpost and they were even making strides toward becoming a true city in their own right.

The healing house, the items that they sold, the spell scroll trump cards, weapons and armor: all of it came from Aditya's benefactor. Even the construction plans for the new wall and the layout of the city that would go between the new wall and the old wall was written up, designed and then passed to Aditya.

He had accepted it fully. He didn't know when it happened, but at one point, he had become simply a vassal for this power. He added his suggestions and he was listened to. He didn't know where this path would lead but he was excited and content for the first time in a very long time.

It was as if he were hunkering down before, just living a blind existence. But now he had been able to step forward; the realm was his oyster and there were endless possibilities at his feet.

"Head of the Silaz trading house has arrived," an aide said.

"No rest for the wicked," Jen said. "You should be good in a week. Try not to lose any more limbs. Oh…" Jen pulled out a letter and passed it to Aditya.

He opened the letter and read it. Then he took it to the fireplace, burning it. He looked to Jen and raised his hand as if making to talk.

"Will you just tell me what is on your mind?" she asked.

"I have been picking up chatter. The Beast Mountain Range's beasts have been decreasing. People are able to get farther than ever before and they aren't able to meet their quotas. It looks like the beasts have been thinned out to a large degree and a few of the stronger beasts that have been around for decades have disappeared. It will take time for their numbers to come back. People are going to start to ask more questions," Aditya said.

"Your suggestion?" Jen asked.

"If you don't want people looking into this deeper, less beasts should be killed. If not, people will start to look at the source of the issue," Lord Aditya said.

"I will have a talk with my people."

"Thank you." Aditya cupped his hands.

"Well, I will leave you to your next meeting. With Head Silaz, is that right?"

"That is correct, Elan Silaz," Aditya said.

Jen seemed to be lost in thought for a second. "Interesting. Well, until I see you again." She turned and headed out. The guards, seeing the head of the Alva Healing House, bowed their heads to her. All of them had been healed by her or her staff.

"Have you been doing those exercises you were told to?" she asked one of the guards in a severe tone as the door she went through closed, making Lord Aditya smile.

Another door opened and a large man entered the room.

"Head Silaz!" Aditya said in greeting.

"Lord Aditya, thank you for making time to allow me to visit." Elan smiled and held out his hand. The two of them shook hands before Aditya waved toward two couches.

"I heard that you have an important matter to discuss?" Aditya asked.

"I have recently been looking to advance my trades and make more acquaintances and trading partners. I heard of what Lord Aditya accomplished and I couldn't help but be shocked."

Aditya waved the comments away with a proud smile. "It was a simple matter."

"Simple matter? Then I do not know what would be a big matter!" Silaz laughed.

Aditya smiled as well, but his eyes remained on Silaz, wondering what his angle was. "Your words are too kind, though I'm interested in what I might be able to help you with?"

"It is I who is looking to help you, Lord Aditya. With increasing the reach of my trading, I have been able to create a number of contacts that deal in the buying and selling of gold and Mana stones," Silaz said casually.

Aditya's attention tightened. *Buying and selling Mana stones is not like a stroll in the garden. There is an incredible demand for them, but the supply is simply too low.*

"I must applaud you, Head Silaz. Mana stones' rarity is only too high in the First Realm," Aditya said.

"They are but there is a number of monster cores that are going through this outpost and there are powerful people visiting all the time. I have an offer to put forth to you." Silaz adjusted his jacket.

"Please." Aditya's senses told him that this deal's ramifications could be big.

"Vermire is a powerful entity right now, a place of true neutrality—a rare thing to find in these turbulent times. I am proposing that the Silaz trading house, with your approval, set up an auction house within the city. A regional auction house, with items collected from all over to be sold here. There are a number of rare items that can only be found in the Beast Mountain Range, even weapons and armor from Experts who have tested themselves in the Beast Mountain Range and failed. Vermire is expanding and it would be good to make use of this. The Silaz trading house has secured a number of Mana stones. Our supply is not that vast, but it would increase interest of other parties to come," Silaz said.

Aditya gave Silaz a deep look, his mind putting the pieces together. *The Silaz trading houses—Mana stones would get people to come here and trade with them. At the same time, they have an auction that would sell high-quality items from across the realm and the Beast Mountain Range. This would be a good cover for me to sell items from my benefactors. Also, I can change money into Mana stones and increase my Strength and Mana Gathering Cultivation.* Lord Aditya had a massive wealth now. The walls and the expansion were being paid for by him, but once that cost was removed, he would have a large amount of wealth coming in every day.

He might have become the lord of Vermire, but it didn't mean he had given up on his goal of trying to advance his Strength.

"If I was to do this, what would you offer?"

"I have heard that Lord Aditya is looking for people who are willing to work but are unable to, or have been injured and dismissed from their previous work," Silaz said.

Aditya made sure to hide his reaction as Silaz continued.

"I have a great number of contacts in many cities. I know that Lord Aditya's reach is much greater than my own but I can help in these recruitment efforts. I have brought two hundred people with me who are at least Apprentice skill level in one craft, most of them in two or three. Though they have been disowned, cast out, or wounded and unable to complete their tasks. I would also pay for the construction of the auction house and I would charge a ten percent handling fee, taking five percent myself and paying the other five percent to you."

"Seven percent would be better," Aditya said.

"Or would you be interested to get the first opportunity to buy a Mana stone outright, at one thousand two hundred gold, with the price set at that amount?" Silaz asked.

"How many per month?"

Silaz let out a breath, looking at the ceiling. "I would say one Mana stone a month. More as time goes on."

"For recruiting people?" Aditya asked.

"Three gold each for transportation here, or to any other location," Silaz said.

Aditya looked at Silaz for a few tense moments, the two of them getting a grasp of the other.

"Very well. I will have a contract written up to that effect." Aditya stood.

"A pleasure doing business with you," Silaz said with a big smile and reached out his hand to Aditya.

They grasped hands, still trying to understand one another.

Aditya saw Elan out personally.

As he left in his carriage, Aditya returned to his office and took out his sound transmission device.

"Jen, we might have an issue," he said.

***

Delilah called an emergency meeting with Jasper and Qin.

Jasper and Delilah were talking when Qin knocked on the door.

"Please come in," Delilah said.

Qin opened the door.

"Council Leader Delilah, Deputy Head Jasper." Qin bowed her head. She was only a few years younger than Delilah, but they were the council leader and head of the formations department. The people of Alva grew up quick and age wasn't a big difference in power, there were people in the same class who might be ten years old or thirty.

"Please, come and sit," Delilah said.

Qin moved to the seat.

"What is your father's first name?" Delilah asked.

"Elan," Qin said.

Delilah and Jasper shared a look.

Jasper let out a short laugh. "Well, your dad gave Lord Aditya quite the scare. It seems that he appeared in the city, and talked about recruiting people and he had an offer to sell him Mana stones and set up an auction hall."

"I didn't tell him about Alva, nor did my brothers. We did, however, suggest that he find more Mana stones to trade," Qin admitted.

"I believe you." Delilah fell back into her seat, not looking like the council leader of anything. "Jasper, you're about as neutral as they come. Would you be willing to go and check on Vermire? At the same time, look into Elan Silaz. Just need a neutral outlook at him. I know he's your father," Delilah said, seeing Qin getting riled up. "But we've got an entire city of people to look after. I have to look at all of the angles. If he is clean, then we can bring him in on some secrets. If not, we will have to keep him at arm's reach."

Qin deflated in her seat. "I understand."

Delilah smiled. It had been easier for her to bring her parents in on the secret that was Alva. They had come from another realm, given an oath, and they weren't powerful or prominent people.

With the Silaz family, their brother and father were both large traders with a large amount of money at their disposal. It could be a blessing having him on their side, or a curse if they had to deal with the issues he created.

"I'll head out right away. There isn't much for me to do here except meetings and watch over the training programs anyway," Jasper said.

"Thank you, Jasper," Delilah said. "I should also tell you as you're here that the mercenaries and the people who hunt in the

Beast Mountains are starting to talk about how few beasts there are to hunt this year. I am going to talk to all of the council and the department heads about what we can do for this problem. The less beasts and the weaker they are, the more chances that people find us."

"Be easier if we could just rear them like the mounts in the stables," Qin thought aloud.

Delilah and Jasper looked at her then each other.

Jasper shrugged. "There's not much that can defeat us in the First Realm now. We don't want to kill them all off, only the ones that we need for materials and those materials are usually things that we can purchase or get from other places."

Delilah made some notes. "Well, looks like I will be having a talk with the beast training department. I don't know if it would be wrong for us to help the beasts here increase in numbers. They do kill people, after all."

"They know the risks coming here. And the stronger or the rarer the beast, the more people will come to the area. Though if we just focus on helping the animal population, that should be enough to recreate the balance of the Beast Mountain Range ,since we were the ones that caused the imbalance to start with," Jasper said.

***

"Morale is low with the hidden attacks. We still do not know where the enemy is hitting us from or how. We know that they bury items in the road and the roadside. When we find one of the explosives, even if we try to remove them, the enemy makes them explode and kills our powerful mages looking for them. They change the placement often, alter their depth so that it is harder for us to find them next time. The whistling explosives—we don't know where they come from. But a plan has been raised to get the flying forces up in the air at night. Then there might be something that they can see in the surrounding area to pinpoint where the whistling devices are coming from. Once we discover them, we will attack them with everything that we have to destroy them and stop them from hitting us," General Ulalas's aide said.

There was agreement from everyone in the meeting. The generals all looked tired, many of them unable to sleep with the constant mortar's attacks day and night. Ulalas could see that this fight was weighing on them. Dealing with an enemy they could see was one thing; an enemy that they couldn't even find a shadow of, losing hundreds of soldiers without gaining any confirmation that they had hit one person—it eroded their morale and initial confidence.

Every night people disappeared, some said that they were killed by the people from Tareng.

What assassination groups packs up all of their belongings? They had lost two to three thousand people to desertion.

Oaths weren't perfect, someone could find a way around them if they desired.

"We will continue to use the Mana barriers to cover us from the falling explosive formation devices and have rotating scouts moving off to the sides of our formation and looking for the buried devices. Better to lose a few instead of a thousand. We need to keep on moving. Say that we will give an Earth Mana stone to whoever kills thirty people from Tareng. Incentivize them to fight and remind them what the Blue Lotus will do if they try to escape. Make them affirm their oaths." Ulalas stabbed her finger into the table with each of her points.

"Should we report our progress to the rest of the Blood Demon Sect?" Damel asked.

"I have been in contact with them this entire time. My silence order is still in effect. This matter is too big for us to have people randomly sending messages," Ulalas said.

"Yes, General." Damel cupped his hands and bowed, not wanting to offend the commander.

Ulalas looked at the other general's out of the corner of her eye, the sour looks on their faces. They knew Damel was her right hand man and that she was doing this as a warning.

"Monitor all messages. Anyone who attempts to send messages will be seen as spies for the Blue Lotus or the Crafter's Association and will be killed on the spot. Even a small slip-up will cost us this battle," Ulalas said.

The Generals kept their emotions hidden, but she could feel the cold looks. They were losing the trust and strength of their armies grinding their way forward to hopefully catch the people from Tareng who they hadn't seen since stepping on this road.

She dismissed the generals, sending them back to their armies with their orders and to reaffirm the army's oaths to make it harder from them to deny orders.

She retired to the back of her carriage. Checking that there was no one around, she took out a formation that would block any noise from escaping her room then took out a sound talisman.

"The Blood Demon Sect's army knows nothing. Communications are cut off. The enemy continues to flee down the road into unknown territory. Everything is going according to plan. The enemy has probably already sent a message to their leadership at this time."

The sound talisman was consumed as her message was transmitted.

If one looks hard enough there is always a way to escape your oath. The ones that deserted are the smartest.

Chapter: Danger in the Night, Hell in the Day

Erik was in the observation post as he watched the army move forward. Their pace was a bit slower but one could hear the generals and commanders yelling at them to be faster.

Erik was using binoculars to look at the target zone. With the scouts that the army was putting out, it was hard to get within a kilometer of the main army. Still, at night, it was easy to see them moving up the road.

With their enhanced senses and the magnification on Erik and Rugrat's weapon sights and binoculars, the forward observers were able to see the targets. They were trying to make copies of the sights and magnification but it was stuck with the people of the academy trying to make better glass and rebuilding the knowledge of optics from Erik and Rugrat's faint recollections. Rugrat was much better, having dealt with a number of scopes, but the manufacturing processes to make a weapon sight he wasn't too familiar with and was still under development.

Erik looked at the sweeping party moving through the blast zone and continuing on their way.

The army kept on moving, looking around them for ghosts they couldn't see.

Erik moved his binoculars and looked at the planned road of death. It was still under construction, with everyone who was free working on it.

Then there was a noise in the sky.

Erik moved his binoculars. He could see a number of creatures in the air, silhouetted against the asteroid belt hanging in the sky.

"All forces, watch out for aerial attacks. Mortars, be ready for these guys to rush you," Erik said.

"Understood. Countermeasures are deployed," Yui reported.

"Very well." Erik watched the army as it continued to move.

An IED went off, tearing the carriage above it to pieces. Three other charges exploded in the midst of the army around the same carriage.

The exploding carriage was the one that the generals had met in earlier that day. Erik meant it as a message to make them nervous, to show that they could hit them at any time. He had wanted to hit the carriage as it was moving but with those Mana barriers, mortars couldn't get through and they didn't have any IEDs near where it passed over.

It was also meant to show that even with their mages looking through the ground, they couldn't pick up the IEDs. It required a ton of mana and causing many to suffer the effects of mana exhaustion causing them to be rotated out all the time.

They had buried them so deep that Erik was using shaped charges to punch through the ground and still be effective. Instead of targeting the troops they targeted the wagons. They were a bigger target and the shaped targets were better against a single target instead of trying to cause massive casualties.

"OP Charlie bugging out," Gong Jin reported as a new flood of Experience filled the members of Alva's army.

"OP Alpha has visual. Ready for action," Erik said into his sound transmission device.

"Mortars are online and dialed in," Yui reported.

***

Ulalas ducked as she heard the whistling. Her heart stopped for a second before she looked around, becoming embarrassed and then angry as the Mana barriers were already activating to stop the explosives from hitting them.

A message came from her airborne forces.

"We think that we can see where the attacks are coming from. There are a series of bright flashes in the distance, about four kilometers away."

"I don't want you to tell me where they are! I want you to destroy them! Go and tear their fucking throats out!" Ulalas roared, ending the channel. She wanted to throw her sound transmission device in frustration. She took a few breaths, calming herself. She looked up at the flying beasts in the air above, flapping their wings. They shot toward the direction that they saw the light flashes from.

***

"Mortars, be advised, you've got fast-moving airborne coming in. Scramble to your next position and trap your first location," Erik said. He had Yuli calling in the artillery while he kept an eye on the skies and Yao Meng watched the ground for the scouting forces.

"Mortars are mining and bugging out," Yui reported.

"Scouts are moving out. We'll have to get a move on in five," Yao Meng said.

"Let's get going," Erik said. They couldn't fire any mortars with them on the move back anyway.

***

Ulalas looked at the sky. Not long after the aerial forces started to charge forward, the whistling explosives stopped going off.

Found you.

The aerial forces cut across the skies and rushed toward where the mortars had come from.

They fired down spells, lighting up the ground as they arrived, showing holes in the ground and an area that had been cleared by humans.

Spell formations appeared all around the aerial forces. They were so excited to close with the enemy that they hadn't even seen, that they hadn't been thinking about watching for an ambush.

A freezing white spell formation appeared in the sky. A blast of cold air shot out and covered a square kilometer. The ice covered the mounts, making it hard for them to move and affecting them with an armor debuff.

More of the spell formations appeared in the sky. Some people directly dropped out of the sky, their mounts unable to handle the stress of the cold.

Seeking frost arrow formations appeared. Thousands of frost arrows shot out from these formations into their victims. The mounts and their riders had nowhere to hide as other spell scrolls activated in every direction. Simple Mana detonations peppered the fliers, artillery spell scrolls combined with wind attacks—these attacks pulled them in from across the sky, pinning them down into kill areas. The sheer amount of wealth needed to create the spell scrolls was impressive. The Blood Demon Sect were played with to their deaths, the aerial forces slaughtered. Bodies dropped from the sky across the forest.

The magical assault lasted for ten minutes before the skies settled down. Of the five hundred aerial forces, less than a hundred were able to fly back to the army.

***

The morale of the army, which had skyrocketed when seeing the flying forces charging away and hearing them attacking the enemy positions, now plummeted, lower than ever as they saw the broken aerial forces limping back to the army.

Ulalas ground her teeth but didn't say anything. IEDs and more mortars went off through the night. The remaining and freshly healed aerial forces found the positions and sent out scouts. The scouts found mortars landing on them as they moved through the forest. The trees turned into shrapnel, tearing them apart.

Her expression darkened when, ten minutes later, the air once again filled with whistling.

She had sent out groups of scouts into the forest, with the display of spell scrolls they were charging towards where they had been cast.

"Brace barriers," Ulalas' voice sounded monotonous.

Ulalas heard the whistling again but they didn't land on the army that was trying to advance. Instead, they landed in the forest, in the direction of the scouting forces.

Her knuckles popped as they turned white.

The army was at their lowest point, trudging forward knowing that only death lay ahead. If they could win this fight, they might get wealth beyond their dreams. If they died, they wouldn't get anything.

It was a fine balance: life on one side, falling into the abyss on the other.

The night was a bloodbath. The minutes turned into hours and the night turned into day. The enemy couldn't be spotted in the daylight either. They trudged on, resigned to their fate. If they made it to the actual battle or not, it all depended on one's luck now. The Blood Demon army had lost all of their initiative.

In the night, one of the army leaders had directly left, the general took with him all his family members. The army gritted their teeth, cursing the cowardly general in the open and wishing that they had escaped with them in their hearts.

***

"Determined bastards," Niemm said.

Erik grunted as he rubbed his face and drank coffee. His face felt as though it were covered in grit as he sat on a log, looking at what they were fondly referring to as the road of death.

Everything was torn apart—the banks, the road itself. Nothing resembled the old landscape from before.

In the dirt, one could see explosives and wires that disappeared into the distance. Teams laid the wires to the different firing points that they had already sighted, having good overwatch over the position.

Han Wu checked the explosives. He was covered in dirt and grime, but his hands were clean. He rested the back of his hand against the ground to make sure he wasn't carrying a charge.

"Thirty mississipi," Han Wu said before he started working with the explosives, checking every connection point, every meter of wire.

"What is mississipi? And why is that a measure of time?" Han Wu muttered to himself, using words to keep himself awake.

Erik left him to it.

"Keep an eye out. Once this is all set down, we're going to have to make it blend in." Erik waved his cup at the road.

"You make it sound so easy, sir." Niemm drank his own coffee.

"Hey, that's why we get paid the big bucks." Erik drank his coffee and grimaced. "Guess that I'm paying you the big bucks now. How much did this all cost?"

Niemm let out a short laugh and just drank his coffee.

"That much, huh? Should do some audits—accountants and taxes!" Erik scratched his beard. "All right, time to stop dicking around." Erik headed over to a group of explosives.

He took another big drink of coffee, eternally grateful the drink existed in the Ten Realms, putting it down and wiping his hands clean. He moved over to a bomb, then placed his hand against the ground to make sure he got rid of any residual shock.

Just a little bit of static energy and soon, arming explosives is no longer my problem. Erik laughed at his own dark humor and clicked his tongue as he counted down twenty seconds before he took out his tools. They were specially made by Rugrat so that they could be used to work on explosives.

Once he was working, he zoned out the rest of the world.

He laughed as he remembered when he had been a young man setting up explosives on the range. Putting down a claymore, makiong sure he didn't have a static charge, checking it over, running the wire, then attaching it to the claymore, terrified that it might go off, but more scared of the sergeant who was watching him. Talking him through it as if he were an idiot, his entire being focused on the claymore he was working on.

Then he had backed up into a trench, attached the firing line to the clacker and clicked it three times.

He didn't even know whether he did it three times, but he knew he was clicking it after the explosion went off and rocked his world. The feeling of the pressure wave in his chest, the thrill of being alive, and adrenaline flooded his system.

How he'd realized at that point, he'd just used a claymore.

"Pretty badass." Erik laughed as he thought of the times he had used grenade launchers, rockets, automatic grenade launchers, TOWs, and every damn thing that went off with a big bang.

"It's a strange life, but we do as we can," Erik finally muttered to himself as he stood and backed away from the charge that he was working on.

He cracked his back and went to find his coffee. It was a good ten explosive charges away, and cold.

"Ugh, I should have put it into my storage. I should have some more." Erik took out another cup and put the first away. He grinned to himself. "Storage rings are the fucking shit." Erik laughed; others looked over and then shrugged and chuckled, getting back to work.

Erik continued his work. Behind him, people were tossing dirt back over the explosives by just pouring it back out of their storage rings. They had Yuli, Simms, Roska, Niemm, Deni, and Yang Zan all using spells to make the grass and other plants grow over the ground, making it blend back together.

The road took more time but it was going along quickly. The sections that had been pulled out were put back down and fused together.

As they worked, Gong Jin's team, which had been split into two, called in mortars and blew up IEDs, slowing the enemy even more.

By mid-morning, they had finished on the road. They took precious time to to make it look like how it had when they started: blending more plant life across the sides of the road, leveling it out a bit more here and there. They checked the trenches that they had dug and buried the wires in, making sure that they couldn't be seen from the road. This would be their last big operation before the Blood Demon Sect reached Vuzgal.

Erik drank a Stamina potion, regaining his lost energy, but he knew that the eventual crash would be even worse and the Stamina fatigue afterward wouldn't be fun to deal with.

"Okay, let's get ready," he said as everything was checked for the third time.

They disappeared, leaving the road alone.

Two hours later, one could hear an explosion down the road. Then they could hear the marching noises of boots and the whistling noises of the mortars.

The army continued onward, only stopping to rebuild the freshly destroyed road and then forging ahead.

Erik was lying on a hill nearly two kilometers away as he looked at their death road.

The army finally appeared, marching forward.

Minesweepers were out front, looking to see whether they could find the bombs. Erik continued to watch them. If they made the explosives, then all of their plans would be put to waste and they would have to blow everything, hoping to kill even a few and destroy the road.

They passed the first blast marker and continued on.

Everyone watching the march forgot to breathe as they continued on. The road shook with their footsteps. They didn't sound as in-time as they had when they had first stepped onto the road. They were powerful people, but the mental strain had sapped their Stamina, leaving them as robotic automatons.

"Come on, keep on coming," Erik said as the sweepers passed the midway point and kept moving.

"That's it. Just a few more meters. You can do it. Yeah, yeah, just keep on walking...nothing under your feet," Erik coaxed the sweepers and their accompanying army forward, his entire body tense, ready to act at a given moment.

The front of the army passed the forward marker without pausing as Erik continued to entice them forward.

They willingly moved along the road, getting into the road of death. The army was pinned in with the rises on either side of the road.

"Wait till they're in a bit more...just a bit more," Erik said through his sound transmission device.

They had set up all the mortars for this one attack. Erik had been holding back on the high-power rounds and were using the regular rounds that were explosives on the outside with a poison core.

The high explosive rounds Rugrat had made were resource-intensive and took time to build; their range was nearly half of the regular rounds. Erik had kept them in reserve, wanting to use them from behind the walls of Vuzgal. Here, with the distance away from the enemy, they had time to move the mortars and run if they needed.

"Ready there, mortars?" Erik asked.

"Smoke loaded, OP Alpha," Yui replied.

"Very good, very good," Erik said, his voice calm and distracted as he looked at the approaching enemy.

"Ready." Erik pulled out his formation and the wires, attaching the two.

"Ready," Niemm reported.

"Ready," Roska said.

"On my mark." Erik looked at the army, picking out a group of Masters. "Mortars, fire for effect."

The mortars, nearly four kilometers away, fired. Erik and the others heard the whistling. The entire army cowered with the noise and the Mana barriers snapped into existence.

As they got closer to Vuzgal their supply lines had less distance to travel reaching them faster. They had stockpiled ammunition of all kinds while Alva's production only increased.

"Three, two..."

The mortars landed on top of the barriers. Clouds of smoke covered the barriers, enveloping the army.

"One, mark!"

The entire road shot into the sky. The white smoke was filled with gray debris and dust.

"Smoke out!" Yui reported.

"OPs, take individual mortar teams. Adjust onto fire zones!" Erik barked.

They had split up the road into arcs for the different observation posts to observe and to guide mortar fire onto. This allowed them to make sure that they didn't overlap fire. Each of them had three or four mortars under their command.

Erik watched his blast zone as the mortars were dialed in on their new target. He checked where the rounds were landing. "Elevation increase by one turn. Confirm?"

"Elevation increase, one mark confirmed!" the mortar team commander called back.

"Fire!"

Erik knew where the mortars were firing from and how they were orientated. He didn't need to call in directional cues to adjust their targeting, but could directly tell them the changes to the weapon system. It wouldn't fly in the military on Earth, but he just so happened to own this ragtag group.

"Seven minute mark!" Yui called out.

"Switch to poison rounds. OPs, bug out!" Erik ordered. They had shelled as much as possible, each mortar putting down nearly two hundred rounds into their blast zone.

The four thousand rounds destroyed the road, the trees, everything within fifty meters was shredded around the Blood Demon Sect.

The posts collected their gear and got on their mounts, rushing away from the army that was covered in a haze of smoke, debris, and poison gas.

Their Experience climbed crazily, but they had no time to check on the changes as they rushed away. Every noise seemed to be the enemy coming after them. They rallied together and went to ground, facing outward and holding out their rifles and repeaters, ready to engage anything that chased after them.

Everything was quiet.

Nothing moved as Erik got them collected together and they moved on. Gong Jin was already in position at the next ambush point. He was also able to see the road of death.

"Fuck," Gong Jin said simply over the open channel.

"What do you see?" Erik asked.

"They got cut down, sir. Not much left. They're all over the road, trying to pull together. The Mana barriers must have been destroyed in the blast. They had no idea what was happening with all of the dust and smoke. The poison is affecting the people behind the barriers. They're a mess—going to take them time to reorganize. Request permission to hit them with mortars?" Gong Jin said.

"Give them five minutes. Let them try to establish order, then hit them again," Erik said.

"Understood, sir," Gong Jin said.

Chapter: Enemy on the Horizon

"City ahead!" a scout called out as they rushed toward Xue Lin's carriage.

She opened the door and asked him. "How far?"

"Must be a few hours' ride," the man said with a wide smile.

They had been on the move for nearly a week now. Seeing their destination, those in earshot started talking excitedly.

"Get my mount and have a security detail readied. We will ride on ahead. Send messages to the Crafter's Association to see if they want to join us," Xue Lin said to two messengers nearby. They raised their sound transmission devices as another waved their hand; a large lizard beast appeared.

It looked around before cooing at Xue Lin.

Xue Lin rubbed her mount's head and gave a slight smile, her mind working as she looked over to where the scout had come from. *Just what is waiting for us there?*

"The Crafter's Association agrees to send a few crafting leaders with you," one of the messengers said.

"We will move out in ten minutes," Xue Lin said.

***

A skeleton let out a roar, making Rugrat jump up, crossbows in either hand. As he was about to fire, he saw that his alerts were beeping. He passed his Experience gains and looked at the alert coming from the Vuzgal dungeon. He had ordered it to alert him when someone was in range of the undead scouts.

Rugrat sent orders to the flying undead and pulled on his armor as he opened his door. "Stand to!" Rugrat yelled through the castle and his sound transmission device.

The sleeping men and women leapt to their feet, pulling on their boots, armor, and helmets. They had all slept in their underclothes.

Rugrat was running, George hot on his heels, expanding in size.

He ran ahead of Rugrat and expanded to his full size as they reached a broken balcony. Rugrat jumped up and landed on George's back. They shot up into the sky like a rocket. Mounted undead rose up around the city. Several flights circled the city as streams of undead stopped their tasks and moved to the walls.

They were no longer equipped with just bones. They had been armed with weapons and armor from the armories within the city. All of them wore mid-Journeyman weapons at the least. There were roughly ten thousand undead within the city, but none of them were below level forty.

Rugrat looked over at the five demi-humans who walked through the sky towards him.

Racquel, Fred, William, Reaper, and Elizabeth had found out that with their control over Mana, they were able to just walk through the sky, crossing vast distances quickly.

Hearing about it, Rugrat had tried it out. He was able to do it for a few minutes, but not much longer. That was before he had increased in level as he had slept.

Rugrat opened his special stuff storage ring and threw a robe and crown to Fred. Fred caused the Mana around them to float them to him. It was the mage's robe from the emperor and his crown.

Rugrat threw Racquel two swords, Elizabeth a ring and gloves, William a necklace and trident. Reaper gained a new robe as well as a staff.

All of these items were of the low-Expert level at least.

They looked at the items and then Rugrat.

"It's the best that I can do. Take this as well." Rugrat tossed out armor that he thought would be best for them as well.

They put on the items and fastened the armor over their clothes.

Rugrat felt an immense pressure coming from them with their newfound strength, but it subsided quickly. Rugrat focused ahead. He pulled out his rifle and scanned where the dungeon had sensed people.

Rugrat saw a group of a hundred or so people charging down the road from the east. "I want to find out just who they are. If they're hostile, we'll fight. You ready for that?" he asked Fred and the others.

"We are," Fred said.

Rugrat gave him a look of thanks and focused on the oncoming forces.

George and the mounted undead tilted downward, diving toward the oncoming forces.

The Mana in the air was stirred up as the undead mages on the flying mounts gathered their spells, ready to cast them at a moments notice.

Rugrat pulled out two M32s and checked that they were loaded and prepped, holding them ready by his sides.

***

"Aerial beasts!" someone called out.

Xue Lin and the others looked up into the skies. Coming from the sun, they could barely see a group shooting toward the ground.

"There are people walking through the sky!" another called out.

"Be ready to fight but don't attack first!" Olivia called.

"On my order." Xue Lin looked to the people from the Crafter's Association.

"On your word," they said.

The oncoming flying beasts and people walking through the skies dropped in altitude sharply, racing toward Xue Lin and her group.

Xue Lin saw a wolf approaching. It had wings that looked as if they were on fire as it cut through the sky. Its wings let out powerful beats as the other flying beasts banked around Xue Lin and her group, who had to slow down.

"Are those undead?" One of the crafter's voice shook, looking at the mounted beasts and their riders. They looked like people from a distance, but when they got close they noticed their powerful auras and the lack of any life in them. They were undead, hundreds of them wearing Jourenyman level armor and using Journeyman level weapons. were nothing but bones; they circled the group, spells readied in their hands.

A man sat on the flying wolf that had a red and orange mist around it as it naturally drew in the Fire-attribute Mana in the area.

The five people who had been walking in the sky were behind the man on the beast, on either side of him.

The man held two odd-looking devices in his hands, pointing them up at the sky. Behind them was the former capital city. Its walls reached up into the skies. Movement could be seen on the walls even from this far away.

They really did take over the capital.

Xue Lin made a gesture to calm the guards, who were all ready to fight.

"I am. Xue Lin." Xue Lin nudged her mount forward a bit. "Mister West told me to say pickles," Xue Lin said, confused by the foreign word.

Rugrat put his weapons away and patted George, calming him. The mounted undead stopped gathering Mana and turned back toward the capital.

Rugrat moved towards Xue Lin.

He got off of his mount and cupped his fists awkwardly, it wasn't natural for him.

"Head Xue Lin, my name is Rugrat, City Lord here. I am glad that you have made it. May I know where Head Daniel's is so that I might pay my respects?"

If he wanted then he could be arrogant, instead he has lowered himself, showing himself to be subordinate to us. Xue Lin felt a bitter taste in the back of her mouth, thinking about how the guards of Tareng had been forced to stay with the people of Tareng.

They were bitter about having to stand guard when a group that they had only met days ago was defending their rear.

They has used this indignation to remove the poison in their bodies as quickly as possible, the concoction turned into a tonic as the healers and alchemists believed and their strength had increased.

Unable to find fault with their protectors and wanting to take action, they were eager to fight, to prove their abilities alongside those from Vuzgal.

"He is here," Daniels said, walking over with his personal guards. He clasped his hands in greeting and lowered his head slightly, a sign of subordination, "I am sorry for the trouble that we have brought you."

The people of Tareng heard his words and dropped their heads in shame.

Xue Lin read Rugrat's approval as he relaxed slightly.

"We have only helped a token amount, I hope that our people can stand together on the walls of Vuzgal and make the

Blood Demon Sect Army pay for their actions," Rugrat said as he seemed to realize something.

"I am sorry for being so rude, welcome to Vuzgal. It's a work in progress but we've made a lot of headway. Your people left through the totem three days ago—haven't got any word from them or movement from the totem."

"Only when they are cleared by the people of the Blue Lotus will they return with reinforcements," Xue Lin said.

"Well, let's hope that testing doesn't take very long! We can talk and ride on our way into the city." Rugrat turned to the others behind him. "You can return now if you want."

"Trying to get rid of me?" One of the women stepped forward and pouted.

Xue Lin looked at her, alarmed by the woman's eyes. They were captivating. She had vertical slatted eyes, like a snake. *A conscious body alteration, special constitution—or is she a demi-human?*

"You can come if you want," Rugrat offered.

The woman with animal eyes flew through the air and landed on the fire wolf, wrapping her arms around Rugrat, who coughed awkwardly. She had a pleased look on her face.

"Take this as an advanced payment for taking so long to ask me out on a date."

Rugrat turned bright red at her words.

"Manners, Racquel," a man wearing a crown and robes said. He was easy to overlook as there were no Mana fluctuations from him. It was as if he blended in with the Mana makeup of the Ten Realms perfectly.

Xue Lin became wary as she looked at him and the others with him.

He was incredibly handsome, enough to make even Xue Lin's heart beat faster. There was another person hidden in a magical cloak, and a man and woman, blue and brown coloration to their skin.

Just who are these people?

"Elizabeth and William do it all the time," Racquel pouted.

"Behind closed doors, because of complaints," Elizabeth replied.

Rugrat gave Fred a pleading look. Fred didn't seem to see the look

As he stepped into the sky.

"Come on."

The others followed, crossing tens of meters with each step.

They were wearing a selection of Expert-level items. But to be able to walk in the sky—it means that they have formed their Mana Heart at the least.

Instead of getting more answers, she found that Rugrat and Erik were only creating more questions.

They continued their journey toward the city, Xue Lin and the others with Rugrat.

"We have cleared out a section of the inner city for your people to rest in and barracks for your guard forces to assist our forces on the walls."

"Do you intend to use necromantic magic on the fallen too?" someone asked from the Crafter's Association.

"Didn't plan on it," Rugrat said, confused by the hostility in the man's words.

"We cannot work with someone from the dark guilds," another said.

"Dark guilds?" Rugrat said. "I think you have something wrong, when we took over the city, we took over the undead that have been fighting in the capital for centuries. There ain't no necromancer. But, they're under my control. If you can't stand that, you can wait outside because I'm not getting rid of them inside the city. We've offered to help you. I really didn't want to let you know about this city, which is why everyone who enters this city will need to make an oath: to confirm that they will not attack anyone and that they will recognize Erik and my commands as the city leaders."

The crafters were riled up as their expressions turned indignant. They were the ones who gave others orders. This rough-looking man who looked as if he hadn't showered in days was nothing but a fighter.

"Who do you think you are?! We are from the Crafter's Association!" one of the Crafter's Association called out in a cold voice.

"I'm the guy with the city, the walls, and the fighting force," Rugrat said simply.

"And we are the leaders of Tareng's Crafter's Association," the leader of the clothier's workshop said.

Daniel's coughed, the normally quiet man's power leaked out as everyone felt a pressure wash over them.

The man who had been speaking shut his mouth and bowed deeply, claspiong his hands towards Head Daniels.

"I am sorry for their outburst, tensions have been high," Daniel's said.

"Understandable," Rugrat said, smiling, Xue Lin noticed that he hadn't even flinched with the power that Daniels had applied.

How is his level so high? Erik's level was only around level fifty, but Rugrat feels as though he is closer to level sixty. And he's clearly enhanced his Mana system.

"I still need to make some preparations, but please come to the castle tonight, we can discuss our plan to defeat the Blood Demon Sect over some tea. I am sorry that our accomodations are not in the best repair," Rugrat said awkardly.

"Having a roof over our heads will be a welcome change and I will come with Tareng's military advisors tonight."

"I look forward to it," Rugrat gave a quick smile as Racquel wrapped her arms around his stomach. His mount stretched out his wings and flapped them, taking ot the skies and going ahead.

Xue Lin could only sigh and start to pass back word back to the rest of the convoy.

"He has only taken over an empty former capital and has de-mi-humans with him," one said, spitting to the side.

"We are from the Crafter's Association and Blue Lotus. What right does he have to look down on us?" another said.

Xue Lin understood their line of thinking only too well.

They were the leaders of the Crafter's Association; in Tareng, no one could question their authority. This kind of power had made them arrogant, looking down on everyone who was not part of their group or others like it.

They had been forced to flee, already a stain on their records and their hearts. Now, as they looked to exert that control again, someone appeared. Instead of being honored and bowing to them, being servile, he dictated to them a set of rules causing the feelings of rage to be stoked once again.

"Anyone who goes against what he has said will become an enemy of my Blue Lotus," Xue Lin said in a tired but firm voice.

Everyone looked at her in alarm.

"We would not be alive right now if not for Mister West, Rugrat and their people. We will follow their wishes.

"We will establish communication with the higher realms and we will do as Mister West and Rugrat tell us. If I see one person trying to make a play for power, or to undermine their orders, I will cut you down. This is not the time for politics; this is the time we band together to face an enemy that will not stop until they slaughter us, our families, and the people of Tareng who are under our protection."

She looked at them, Daniels standing behind her. No one dared to cross her, she wielded the full power of Tareng.

Olivia's actions, although they were against her orders, were understandable. They wielded such great power; few dared to act arrogant in front of them. Power equaled the ability to dictate the way that the Ten Realms moved.

Rugrat and Erik offered safety but the people of Tareng needed to lower their heads a bit.

The oath is reasonable but it will make sure that if there are any spies in our ranks that we will be able to find them, or they will be unable to help the Blood Demon Sect Army. On the surface it looks like they will gain the ire of Tareng, but the Blue Lotus and Crafter's association have made their own agreements so really it makes the people of Tareng want to prove their loyalty and their strength, to work closer with the Blue Lotus and the Crafter's association. In the end their loss will be very minimal but it raises everyone's fightin spirit and protects our rear.

Xue Lin's eyes lit up, since Olivia's actions, the Tareng leadership had been bitter, herded around like children.

***

Elder Lu got messages relayed from Head Xue Lin. He had a contract drawn up, assuring the command of the capital stayed with Erik and Rugrat, but that the Blue Lotus and the Crafter's Association would be allowed to stay and conduct business there.

It would add security to all sides involved, and turn the capital into a neutral trading city. It was a rare case, but it wasn't the only time that it had happened.

Elder Lu looked at the maps of the area that had been sent over to him. They had records of Vuzgal, so they used a set of older map records and updated them with information coming in from Xue Lin.

"Is something the matter?" Lei Huo asked.

"Doesn't this attack seem a little...stupid?" Elder Lu pondered.

Lei Huo frowned, motioning for Elder Lu to continue.

"The Blood Demon Sect is facing the Hang-Nim Alliance, which, in the ancient dialects of their two sects, means friendly alliance, made up of the Nezzar and Red Sword sects. Both of them are newer sects in the Fourth Realm but they are anything but friendly. They are sneaky, underhanded sects. The Blood Demon Sect is an older, well established sect. They have a great amount of wealth, which assures their position, but it also makes them a big target. We know that the Blood Demon Sect has added transformation concoctions to the water of cities that they have had to abandon before in the past. Turning the city behind them into a city of demons that will kill anything on sight and feel no pain until they die. We originally thought that this was a plague, but when the dust settled, how was the Blood Demon Sect thinking that they could keep an army of half a million people quiet? How would they hide the evidence of the concoction in the water?"

"Maybe in their desperation, they didn't think of it," Lei Huo replied.

"Why would they attack Tareng? What would they gain?"

"Wealth? Maybe blame it on the alliance?"

"Although they are greedy, they already have fifty dungeons under their control. Just for wealth would be a waste. Again, they're an old sect. They have a lot of wealth and they are playing the long game, not the short-term gain. Cui Chin, are we getting any kind of chatter from the Blood Demon Sect?"

"I am not getting anything about this attack. They might possibly have been able to keep this information to only a select few people," Cui Chin said.

"Who would have the most to gain if the Blood Demon Sect were found to be attacking the Blue Lotus?" Elder Lu asked.

"The Hang-Nim Alliance," Lei Huo answered.

"Look into the alliance more closely. I want to know what they're saying behind closed doors and tell me the actions of the greater militaries on either side," Elder Lu said.

"Yes, Elder," Cui Chin and Lei Huo said.

"Someone bring Deputy Head Hiao Xen to me," Elder Lu said after a minute.

An aide left the room and Hiao Xen appeared a few minutes later.

He bowed deeply to Elder Lu.

"Deputy Head Hiao Xen, I have a request to make of you, but it will place you into great, possibly grave danger," Elder Lu said.

"Hiao Xen awaits his orders," Hiao Xen said, without hesitation.

Elder Lu pulled out a medallion. "With this, you wield the authority of this headquarters. You will be able to command the Blue Lotus forces of any city within the Fourth Realm." Elder Lu watched Hiao Xen closely. He saw Hiao Xen's face pale and him hiding his shaking hands. He could tell it was out of fear and anxiety, instead of excitement. He was young by the Blue Lotus standards, but it showed that his judgement was good. Anyone who was excited to wield this item usually didn't deserve to. The power that one gained was great, but the responsibility was greater.

"You will go to the city Vuzgal, with a contract for Mister Rugrat and Mister West. You will take over the forces from Tareng's Blue Lotus and work with these two men to speed things up and give them the full support of the Blue Lotus. Do you understand what I am telling you?"

"I do," Hiao Xen said, his voice solemn.

"You might be exposed to the poison or concoction that the people of Tareng are affected by. You will not be allowed to leave the capital until you are confirmed to be clear of any plague."

"I understand. I am still willing to go," Hiao Xen said.

Elder Lu knew it was a lot of power, but Hiao Xen had wielded a lot of power in the past. He was also known to Erik and Rugrat. With the issues that had appeared and the friction between the people of Tareng and the two men, he needed to do something to smooth things over.

Hiao Xen was his best way to demonstrate his willingness to work together and get the people of the Blue Lotus in line.

"Very well. Don't let down the Blue Lotus," Elder Lu said.

Hiao Xen bowed and left the room.

"Send a message to the Alchemist Association with the information regarding Erik West, about his direct disciple status. Use them to apply pressure to the Crafter's Association to fall in line. Also mention that we believe Rugrat is an Expert-level smith. Now is not the time for them to be fighting one another, but to be working together," Elder Lu said.

People got to work as Cui Chin moved next to Elder Lu, activating a discreet sound-cancelling formation.

"You are betting on Erik and Rugrat?" he asked.

"Yes. It is a risky bet, but our other option is to try to take over the city. Do either men seem like the kind who wouldn't have a backup plan?" Elder Lu asked.

"Latest intelligence from our people say that the undead are all around the mid-level forties, wearing Journeyman-level equipment. There is a group of possible demi-humans who may be stronger and who are equipped with Expert-level items. There are also human members all around level fifty and with a mixture of peak Journeyman and Expert-level items."

"With a fighting force like that and the fighting forces of Tareng, they should be able to hold out for a long time," Elder Lu said.

"Yes, but Vuzgal is massive. The Blood Demon Sect have numbers on their side: thirty thousand regular troops, fifteen thousand Elites, and five thousand Masters, not including their mounts. While they are ten different armies, they're all from the same military. While the forces of Tareng have trained together, they're in new territory fighting beside a new mostly unknown force."

"What about the plague testing on the people who used the totem to cross over?"

"We have pretty much confirmed what we knew already, but the higher-ups want us to wait the week to make sure that there is nothing hidden. It could be a ploy to have us send the army out and then have them affected by the plague."

"Find out who sends the orders to the attacking army. We can send the army into cities that aren't affected by the plague just fine," Elder Lu said. "If we take out the person giving the orders, then the rats in the Blood Demon Sect will lose their backing. Either they will fight harder or run. I am willing to bet they'll try to run."

"I will have answers within two days," Cui Chin promised.

"See that you do. I don't like waiting."

***

"The totem is activating." Rugrat stood, using his connection to the city and the dungeon to know what was happening with the totem.

Just two people appeared before the totem stopped working.

Undead surrounded them, as did the Alvan army section that was watching the totem.

Glosil had his hand on his sword, ready to act.

His sound transmission device activated.

"One of the people we sent to the Blue Lotus returned and he brought a man called Hiao Xen, who wants to meet with you. He says that he is from the Second Realm."

"And he's all the way up here?" Rugrat muttered to himself.

"They're good. Have the man who returned give an oath and allow Hiao Xen to come to the castle. Ask him—what formation did he give Erik?" Rugrat asked after a moment.

Glosil relayed the message and got a reply.

"He said that he didn't give him a formation but theFlames of the Rezi cauldron. He asked how Tan Xue is doing."

"Looks like he is our guy," Rugrat confirmed with a grimy smile.

It didn't take long for Hiao Xen and his guides to reach the castle.

"It is good to see you, Head Hiao." Rugrat cupped his fist.

"I wish it was under better circumstances." Hiao cupped his fist in reply. He looked tired. "What can I do to help? I have been sent to make things a bit easier with you and the people of Tareng, and I have a medallion from headquarters. They want me to speed up how fast people can enter the capital and they want to know just how effective Erik has been with delaying the Blood Demon army."

"We can raise it to thirty thousand per group, but you will be responsible. I will have people watching over and undead acting as backup. Everyone will need to make the oath, even the kids and the elderly," Rugrat said.

"I can get that done," Hiao Xen assured him.

Rugrat pulled out a map and put it on the table. Markers showed the advancing Blood Demon army and other markers showed the people from Tareng and Vuzgal.

"Erik and his group have slowed the army by about a day, maybe a day and a half. I have new forces moving out to relieve them and pull them back to the city. The pressure on the approaching army will decrease and their speed will increase. For casualties, we estimate that the death toll on the Blood Demon Sect has reached between eight thousand to twelve thousand."

"Are you sure?" Hiao Xen looked from the map to Rugrat.

"That's our best estimate. We haven't been able to calculate accurately, but based upon the Experience we've earned, I would guess about that many."

"I was able to bring the Weight Reduction spell scrolls with me. What will you be using them for?" Hiao Xen put a box on the table.

"We will be using them on the pillar in the middle city. The formation inside it is still pretty good. If we put it back on top of what is left of the pillar, we can activate Vuzgal's Mana barrier. It will take all of our people and time if we have to do it; if you can get the crafters to help out, then we can get it done in a few days. If you can get them to work in the smithies, we can make more ammunition so we can keep raining hell down on the army. I need to have the mages organized so that they can use long-range destructive spells. I need the armies organized so that they can be used to defend the walls. Others to run ammunition, to carry the wounded. I can fight by myself, but I won't if I don't have to," Rugrat admitted.

"I'll get you your help," Hiao Xen said.

***

Storbon and two sections of Tiger Platoon had been riding since the day before. They got to the meet-up point with Dragon Platoon and the special teams.

"'Bout time you showed up." Yao Meng harrumphed as he rested his rifle on his leg and as he sat on his mount.

"Fashionably late," Storbon laughed in response, studying Yao Meng. He looked tired, covered in grime, but that he had long ago stopped caring about it.

His weapon had dirt on it but it was well maintained, unlike his own face and hands that were covered in dirt.

"Follow me." Yao Meng and Imani led them to where Erik and the rest were waiting.

"Sir," Storbon said as the group dispersed, moving to talk to their friends they hadn't seen in a week. It felt like a lifetime ago.

"Storbon, good to see you. All right, I'll be leaving Gong Jin and his half section with you as well as a few commanders from Dragon Platoon. Get you all sighted in and good to go. Your people been using the mortars in Vuzgal?" Erik asked.

"Yes, sir."

"Good. They're going to be using them all the time. I hope you like digging. The enemy is using their Mana barriers nearly all the time and they're pushing through our IEDs as fast as they can. IEDs are our best killers. The mortars are more to put the fear of long-range artillery into them. We've been adding in batches of poison rounds that can get through the Mana barriers. They have to be running low on antidotes by now and they lose a number to the poison gas. But they're building up a natural resistance, I swear.

"We checked the land a bit and these look like good places to hit the enemy. These are the locations that we've used. They're wary about anything that makes them slow down or get packed in together, so we're starting to hit them in wide open areas—do the unexpected. Your aim will be to inflict casualties, wear down their supplies and their morale. They're already three to four days behind the people in Tareng. Thankfully, with Hiao Xen now in the city, things should speed up a little bit.

"Now, you need to watch out for their strong roving patrols. Damn well got close to finding our observation posts a few times, and they're pushing out far to the sides and in the forest. It's hard to track them."

Storbon and the rest who came with him were sponges, absorbing all the information that they could in just a few hours.

Explosions could be heard in the background as Niemm called in mortars on the enemy and blew an IED. Storbon and the others jumped but those who had been there for a while already didn't even flinch, smiling at their reactions.

"You get used to it," Erik said as he shifted in the dirt. "The things I would do for a shower."

He continued briefing them on everything that was useful, Storbon copying it down into notes. Then Erik's group got onto their beasts and left, leaving Storbon with just a few people left from the first group.

"We have three positions set up right now. We should mix our teams so that we have old and new working together," Gong Jin said.

"Agreed." Storbon turned back from their departing friends and focused on his mission.

***

The Blood Demon army pushed on, slugging it through the repeated explosions. They were barely staying together, a fifth of their force dead along the road and more affected by poison as they were running low on antidote concoctions.

Erik rode toward Vuzgal, cutting through the forest to make the best possible speed. They exited onto the road, seeing the people of Tareng entering the capital.

Though all eyes were on the pillar that for the first time in centuries was moving.

"All right, let's not fuck this up!" Rugrat yelled from inside the city as he had the undead soldiers, the flying mounts, and mages from Alva working together. Underneath the pillar, vines grew out and gripped the pillar as well.

It had all been checked over and the damage repaired and fused together.

"Ready!" Glosil reported.

"Use the Weight Reduction scrolls!" The scrolls were activated, falling onto the pillar; it stopped weighing thousands of tons, now only hundreds of tons.

"Lift!" Rugrat commanded as he grabbed the pillar himself. They worked together, lifting it up.

"Pass to the central city!" Rugrat ordered.

The repaired wall had an opening in it again as the pillar was moved, the end pointing toward the center of the city.

"We're lined up!" Rugrat said. Everyone stopped their movement.

"Forward!" Rugrat yelled.

They marched forward. Their Strength allowed them to deal with the pillar as if it were nothing but a big plank that they had to move around a worksite.

They entered the main city. Vines covered the castle and the other pillar, and rose up under the pillar that they were moving, taking some of the weight. Vines that sprouted from the top of the broken pillar were pulled out to the top of the upper half of the pillar.

They reached the castle in short order.

"Earth lifter!" Rugrat called out.

Mages used a Raise Stone spell. Stone columns rose out of the ground, bracing the top of the pillar and pushing it free of those holding it.

The mounts that were flying above pulled; the vines grew larger and contracted. The pillar moved upright as vines from the castle and the bottom half of the pillar hugged the top section and pulled it closer. It rose up over the castle, then reached the broken pillar and started to climb. The flying mounts used all their strength to pull upward. The vines, like tentacles, moved together like caterpillar feet to push the pillar up meter by meter.

The pillar rose up into the sky, being seen for miles around.

The top pillar was on top of the bottom half once again. The wind at that height made it sway slightly. It was turned to line up with the magical formation that was inscribed inside the pillar.

Mages poured out rubble from the pillars and stuffed it in the gaps and fused the pillar. Quickly, the pillars stopped being two separate parts and were one complete whole.

"We're looking good from inside," Domonos reported five minutes later.

The pillar no longer swayed, but stood above the capital once again.

"All right, now let's go and put that wall back together!" Rugrat clapped his hands. The crafters went to work on the formations inside. Rugrat had created a false floor so that they wouldn't be able to see or find the dungeon core or their Mana stones.

The people of Tareng looked at the pillar as it rose into the sky.

Rugrat activated the Mana gathering formations across the city in each of the pillars.

They covered the entire capital and the lands beyond, drawing in and concentrating mana as it entered the main defensive wall, it became thicker and more concetrated, compressing further as it passed the inner wall before focusing on the main pillar. Unseen by those watching the mana was directed down through formations into the hidden underground dungeon control room.

The excess mana passed through a mana storing formation that was rooted in the walls of the pillar.

Earth and Mortal Mana cornerstones started to create mana stones that slowly started spreading across the interior of the pillar. While the concentrared and purified mana was directed into a mana storing formation in the hidden room away from prying eyes.

The mist around the city started to clear at a rapid rate, no longer trying to hide their existence. As the sun was revealed, the pillars glowed with a blue light from the sheer density of Mana, lighting up the city.

***

Early the next morning, as it was still dark, Erik arrived in the city.

Rugrat and Erik gave each other knuckles.

"Good to see you," Rugrat said.

"You've gotten a lot done," Erik admired.

"We've got hot food, showers and beds. Get some rest. We won't have much of that in the coming days. You did good," Rugrat said.

"Thanks." Erik went passed the others and released Gilly to the stables with a hug and an ear scratching.

He used his Clean spell. His greasy hair and his dirt-stained face and hands looked fresh as the dirt and grime on his clothes were removed.

He took off his gear. Even as tired as he was, he made sure that it was stored away, easy to reach.

He took a shower. Even with the Clean spell, it wasn't the same as a shower, which allowed him time to decompress, to allow his muscles to relax.

"Notifications," Erik said. A list of information appeared.

==========

14,379,060/30,600,000EXP till you reach Level 55

==========

Erik dismissed the information. He trudged over to his cot and flopped down on it, pulling his sleeping bag out of his storage ring and dragging it over himself.

Even though we killed thousands of them, killing people that are a lower level than you comes with severe experience penalties. Each level higher I am than my opponent, I get half of the experience. So others that were a lower level quickly leveled up as they were part of killing much higher leveled people. For Rugrat and me, being a higher level meant that we didn't get many gains, only barely increasing by a whole level.

It's no wonder that higher level people don't waste their time fighting those from the lower realms, the experience that they'd gain would be pitiful.

***

Workers at the top of the pillar took in the sight of Vuzgal and the asteroid belt above. They saw flashes of light in the distance that must be the Blood Demon army being hit with weapons.

The army kept on coming despite the flashes of destruction, just on the horizon.

Chapter: Hidden Machinations

Jasper left the teleportation pad. They had placed one of them close to Vermire in case of emergencies. He stepped forward and headed off into the forest before he circled around to one of Vermire's gates.

He paid the fee and entered the city gates, looking around at the construction that was happening everywhere. It was progressing quickly, with the walls already up in a few sections, others in different states of completion.

Jasper kept walking and headed toward the city lord's manor.

"I'm sorry. The city lord is not seeing anyone," the guard at the front door said.

"Tell him it is Jasper." Jasper smiled and said in response.

The guard sent the message, flinching from the messages he was getting back. "I am sorry, sir, about my disrespect." The guard bowed to him.

"You didn't know." Jasper walked past the guard. "I know the way."

"Yes, sir." The guard said, still bowing as Jasper continued walking as if he owned the place.

He found a flustered-looking Lord Aditya in his office, the same office that Aditya had pressured Jasper in on their first meeting so long ago.

"Mister Jasper." Lord Aditya bowed directly from the hip, cupping his hands.

"You make it seem like I'm some monarch. It seems that you have been doing well these past few years." Jasper walked to the windows, looking out over the city.

"For my actions, I cannot try to make up for them," Lord Aditya said.

"Oh, I don't know about that. We gained a good subject at that time and you have kept faith with us. As such, you should be rewarded." Jasper took out a box and passed it to Aditya. "This pill will allow you to temper your bones."

Aditya looked at the box, his hands shaking in excitement.

"Seems that you have not been able to temper your body as yet—we should look to changing that. Though I have not just come with rewards. I have come for other issues. Have you heard of the Beast Mountain Trials?" Jasper moved to one of the couches and sat down.

"I have heard something about it—a dungeon that is located in the Beast Mountain Range, but one needs tokens in order to access it. The sects come from higher realms to make use of it," Aditya said.

"I have ten tokens that I can give to you. You will hold a contest among your fighting forces and the top three fighters will get one token each. The others you can use to barter with mercenary leaders, nation leaders, and do as you desire. If you find someone of good standing and a capable fighter, you should also pass them a token. You can use two of the tokens to barter; the others would be for these independent fighters. They could return with powerful items, indebted to you, or they might disappear," Jasper said.

Aditya nodded, finding the hidden meaning in Jasper's words. "Understood."

"Now, I also must ask about Elan Silaz. I have heard that he has made some hints about our operations," Jasper said.

Aditya told Jasper everything that Elan Silaz had said and he picked up the contract that he had written up.

Jasper listened and reviewed the contract. Silence fell in the office until there was a knock at the door. Aditya's expression turned sour.

"It's fine—deal with it," Jasper said.

Aditya went to the door, talking to the person on the other side before returning to the couch. "Elan Silaz has offered me a Mana stone for twelve hundred gold," Aditya reported.

"Seems he is working quickly. But where did he get a collection of Mana stones from? I will have to look into this further." Jasper stood and started to walk to the door. "Oh!" Jasper pulled out a scroll and ten tokens, passing them to Aditya. "Listed here are items that we will make available for purchase for you. The gold required is listed as well."

Aditya saw Jasper out and then looked at the scroll: there were Alchemy concoctions—true Alchemy concoctions, not items from an apothecary—formations, weapons, armor, and spell scrolls.

"These would be trump cards for older nations, but these are things that I can get with enough money. The prices are high, but I have time and my income will only increase with the city expansion. It's about time I expanded the guards again, yes indeed."

***

Jasper read through the information that Aditya's doves had collected on Elan as well as the information from the traders from Alva and their associates across the First Realm.

He had started the Silaz Trading House by himself. He had been an adventurer of a large mercenary group but when he found his wife, he wanted to put that behind him. So he left, turned in his weapons and started trading in monster cores. He knew the ropes from being a mercenary.

Knowing the different fighting groups, he traded weapons and armor for monster cores at a better rate. Then he sold the monster cores to higher powers at a profit.

He expanded his operations to even more outposts around the Beast Mountain Range to acquire monster cores, then he had set up a headquarters in Chonglu. It was one of the largest hubs around the Beast Mountain Range, with the Blue Lotus bringing in a high number of nobles and powerful figures.

There wasn't any other city that was close to the Beast Mountain Range and had a Blue Lotus location, making it ideal.

He was smart and although the Silaz Trading House mainly dealt in monster cores, they also sold weapons and armor as well as maintenance services.

Many others had tried to replicate his business model and they had done well, but not on the level Silaz had achieved.

"There are several hidden companies that he controls, such as those dealing in furs and meats. He also has several trading caravan services—hires out the mercenaries who are tired of the Beast Mountain Range life, gives them some training, a contract and a job. It's highly lucrative due to their levels. Several mercenary groups have him as a silent partner, giving him a constant flow of monster cores and beast parts. He has also groomed a group called the Twelve Mediators. If someone crosses him, attacks his caravans or his different businesses, then these people will appear, dealing with the issues and disappear once again. He must have a training facility hidden from people's eyes...or maybe it is part of the mercenary groups that he controls?" Jasper reached over to his tea and took a drink, looking over the cup and the paper in front of him at the building opposite as Elan Silaz left the trading house's Vermire location and greeted an architect.

"Now he wants to move into regional auctions," Jasper muttered to himself. Silaz's background was not shallow and it had hidden depths.

I can make conjectures at every turn, but I need to know what he's actually thinking. For that, I need an oath or a contract that allows me to ask him questions freely. Jasper leaned on the arm of his chair, holding his chin. *He has been requesting to meet with the head of the healing house. That would give me an opening.*

Jasper sent a message to Jen.

A few minutes later, she called him back. "Do you know how busy I am?" Jen complained.

"I only need you to bring him in for a meeting. I don't need you to be there for it," Jasper said, drinking his tea.

Jen let out a sigh. "Okay, I'll get it set up, but you owe me one of Jia Feng's own meals!"

Jasper nearly choked on his tea.

"Something wrong?" Jen said in a sweet voice.

"Can't it be someone else's food—like Diana's? She's a mid-Journeyman—and that tender roasted meat she makes is amazing!"

"Three meals from anyone else and tell her I want my special!" Jen said. It was as if she had regained all of her lost energy.

"Okay, okay, I'll see to it," Jasper acquiesced, thinking about all the work Jen had been piled under.

She was the Healing Department Head, managing things back in Alva and also managing everything at the Alva Healing House. She only had a few more months before she had to head back to Alva. One of the rules that the department heads and councilors had to obey was returning to Alva every six months at the least and remain there for a month to deal with any issues that had appeared.

Jen was already over that number but Erik and Rugrat had allowed it.

"Deal!" Jen closed the channel before Jasper could say anything. "I should've asked if he can move any of the items we've had shipped to us from the Fourth realm." Jen grunted in complaint. Vermire had become a powerful trader so it was easy to move supplies into the city, which were now stockpiled underneath the healing house and the Lord's manor, being transported undercover to teleportation formations hidden in the forest with ammunition and supplies needed by the army coming out and being sent to the totems and to Hersht where members of the army would transport supplies through the realms.

"Everything is complicated now. I wonder what they want with Elan Silaz?"

***

Elan Silaz felt something was up when he got a message from the head of the Alva Healing House. He had requested the meeting but it was only a day after he had talked to Aditya. *He probably pulled some strings to show his ability off and then he can change the contract to his benefit.*

Elan got out of his carriage and looked at the healing house.

He entered the door, seeing people coming in, being assessed, and healed in just a few moments before they had to go to collections. Two large and powerful guards stood there. They wore the emblem of the Alva Healing House as their only adornments. They looked simple but Silaz's senses told him that even his Mediators wouldn't be able to take them down.

He couldn't even read their level.

The speed that people were processed through the healing house was much faster than any other healing house he had seen.

Other healing houses deal in one or two powerful and rich members with a high retainer. Here they work on numbers, getting people through quickly. The profits wouldn't be any smaller, but it means more work. It also means that they get all kinds of cases from different people.

Their public sentiment would be much higher of course. I would think that the people would blame them for the attack by the Zatan Confederation, but there isn't any animosity. They have become a pillar of Vermire, with a strength that is only less—no, maybe on par—with Lord Aditya's.

"Mister Silaz, please come this way." A man wearing healing robes and a mask led Silaz to the top floor of the healing house. "Only you." He looked at Silaz's guards.

Silaz smiled and waved for his guards to wait outside. *Time to make a leap of faith. Maybe I've really found out a connection to Domonos, Yui, and Qin.*

The man opened the door for Silaz.

"Elan Silaz for you, Department Head," the man said.

"Thanks, Kyle." A tired woman's voice came from inside.

Silaz entered a double office. On one side, there was a woman standing up and looking at a number of books on her shelf.

The door closed behind Silaz as a formation activated.

Silaz grabbed his communication device in alarm, turning for the door. His fist was gripped and wrenched around his back; his other hand grabbed too. He was unable to fight back as two chains were applied.

"Don't be too rough with him. I am a healer, Jasper," the woman said, still looking up information.

"I just want to have a private conversation with him—don't want any guards in the way," the man behind Silaz said as he pulled up on the cuffs and forced Silaz into the room.

"Guards!" he yelled out and struggled. "Guards!"

"They can't hear you, sound formation or something." The woman looked up at him and then the man behind him.

"I don't want to hurt you, Mister Silaz. I just need to ask you some questions, privately. Qin sends her regards," Jasper said.

Silaz relaxed as he looked at the woman, who was jotting down notes, and back at Jasper, turning his head. "Qin'er?"

"Yup. But I have to do my job, so…" Jasper dropped him into a chair and attached him to a chain in the floor. "Let's start negotiations!" Jasper moved around in front of Silaz and sat down.

Silaz tried to access his Mana, but he wasn't able to. He felt as if his Strength was being sapped as well. It was no wonder it was easy for Jasper to wrestle him into a chair.

"First, I will need an oath from you on the Ten Realms that you will tell the truth, according to my wishes." Jasper pulled out a contract and held it in front of Silaz.

He stared daggers at Jasper before he checked the contract. Everything seemed to be in order. If he didn't say the truth, then he would be electrocuted, the Mana in his system acting against him so Jasper would be able to visually see that he had lied.

"I agree to the contract," Silaz said. The Ten Realms confirmed the contract, covering it in golden energy and then covered Silaz. He felt chains, stronger than the ones around his wrists, tighten on his very soul.

"Your name is Elan Silaz, correct?" Jasper asked.

"Yes," Silaz said.

"You have three sons and one daughter?"

"Yes."

"What are your intentions with coming to Vermire?"

"I wanted to find out more about my children. I have seen them, but I don't know where they have gone. I'm guessing that you're the power that they are learning under?"

"I guess, kind of?" Jasper shrugged. "Why did you offer people to Aditya?"

So they control this city. He wouldn't tell anyone that lightly.

"Qin hinted to me that the people she was learning from needed people and Mana stones, so I looked to find people and

Mana stones," Silaz said. "I just want to be able to see my children more often. I am a trader. I can trade in things that Aditya can't."

"Are you looking to attack the people teaching your children?"

"Not unless they are hurting my children."

"So you came here looking for information on your children, rattle the tree and, well, essentially have this meeting. Do you want to become part of the power teaching your children?"

"Pretty much. I am looking to see just what kind of people are teaching my children. If they are people I can work with, then I will. If they aren't and my children are fine, I will go separate ways. If you are treating my children badly then I will do everything in my power to bring you down."

Jasper was unaffected by his words.

"Sounds like Elise is going to have some competition," Jen said from her desk and stretched.

"If he goes to the other realms. Okay, Mister Silaz, I will give my recommendation that you be given more information. This conversation didn't happen. Domonos and Yui aren't in this realm but Qin is. I'll have her meet you and bring you over to our headquarters. I will need an oath that this conversation will not be repeated to anyone else," Jasper said.

"I swear on the Ten Realms with my life that I will not repeat the contents of this conversation unless you allow me to," Silaz said. A golden glow appeared around him for the second time.

Jasper released Silaz, deactivated the formation, and used his sound transmission device.

Elan rubbed his wrists.

"Are you done yet?" Jen asked from her desk.

"Mister Silaz, are you free tonight? Qin can meet you tonight. You will need to make one more oath at that time."

"Yes, I am," Silaz said.

"No guards. Meet me here," Jasper said.

***

Qin exited the teleportation array, finding her father and Jasper standing there.

"Dad!" She hugged her father. It had already been a number of months and seeing him, she realized just how much she had missed him.

"Little Qin'er." His tone softened.

"You better not have beaten him up!" She pouted, looking at Jasper.

"I wouldn't think of it. Your brothers could kick my ass all over the dungeon!" Jasper laughed.

Qin smiled as she grabbed her father's hand and pulled him toward the array.

"He needs to make an oath to Alva," Jasper said.

"Ah," Qin said, embarrassed as she let go of her father's hand.

"Repeat after me: I, Elan Silaz, of my own volition, swear upon the Ten Realms that I will not pass on information about Alva Dungeon to any outsiders. I swear to protect Alva Dungeon, no matter how far I might venture from the dungeon. I swear to uphold the rule of law within Alva Dungeon and to follow the orders of the Dungeon Masters Erik and Rugrat as long as their orders are reasonable."

Silaz repeated the oath word for word.

"Well, that's that sorted out," Jasper said.

Qin led the way to the teleportation array.

Elan had never seen anything like it before. A light consumed him, much like the light he had seen around people heading to higher realms.

The light fell away. They were still in a darker place but lights revealed a much larger rune-covered ground. There were a few people with weapons around the pad. They talked to Jasper as Elan looked around.

"This is Alva Dungeon. Erik and Rugrat made it—well, kind of took it over and then built up everything inside it," Qin said.

"I thought that they might come from some powerful group—I never thought that they would have made one," Elan said.

"Take him on the tour. I'll be in my office. I still have more I need to talk to him about," Jasper said.

With his oath, Elan wasn't a danger to Alva anymore.

Qin happily took Elan around the dungeon. They passed through the fields, where plants were growing quickly. They passed the Alchemy garden that looked mysterious, scary, and peaceful depending on the different ingredients one was looking at.

She took him to the academy, showing off her workplace and then took him to the library.

"Egbert," she said.

A skeleton wearing robes and with blue fires in his eyes turned around as he was reading a book. "No shouting in the library," Egbert admonished as the book disappeared from his hands.

Even without cheeks and lips, Elan could sense Egbert's smile as he reached out his hand.

"You must be Elan Silaz. You've got three very talented children. Haven't met the other, but he sounds like a troublemaker," Egbert said.

Elan coughed and looked at Qin.

"Egbert taught all of us and I spend most of my time in here trying to get information on formations." Qin offered.

"Wren was a bit of a trouble maker, but he's doing better. Thank you for helping Qin," Elan reached out and shook Egbert's hand.

Egbert's hand fell apart.

"NoOoOoo!" Egbert said.

Elan jumped back, smacking the bones off his hand. A shiver ran down his spine as he tried to forcefully erase the feeling from his hand.

"Egbert," Qin admonished.

Egbert cackled as the bones showed runes on them and started to reassemble, recreating his hand.

"Did you see his face! Oh, priceless!" Egbert continued to cackle.

Qin couldn't help but laugh.

Elan pulled on his jacket feeling another shiver up his spine with the sensation coming back.

"Oh, if I only had tear ducts. Ah, that's got to be the best one yet!" Egbert rubbed a finger underneath his eye as if clearing tears.

"I've got to take him to meet Jasper again. Try to not prank so many people!"

"Oh, I could never promise that." Egbert chuckled.

Qin led Elan out of the library. He looked at the trading area near the academy, the different buildings and surrounding grounds.

"So you said that you work on formations and spell scrolls," Elan said, recovering as they walked through the dungeon, reaching a park.

"Well, I do formations mostly. Julilah is better at the spell scrolls. Formations need to be carved into a metal medium and then have reactants added. Spell scrolls need a cloth-like medium; then, instead of carving anything in, they have a mixture of reactants combined into an ink and then applied to the scroll. We tried to print them in bulk as Erik and Rugrat said, but one needs to inject Mana with the reactants or else the spell scrolls won't work. With formations, we can have the formation plates pressed or carved by machines and the reactants filled into the carvings. It is good to mass-produce them but their strength is less than if a person did them. And they are bigger, but we are looking at making them smaller. The machine-made formation's failure rate is lower. Though different materials need a person working on them instead of a machine. It's complicated." Qin sighed. "Thankfully, we have been able to get a number of books so that we have a complete heritage from Novice to Apprentice. The simple things are easy, but it is so information-based that passing through the Journeyman level is complicated and a long process, like Alchemy and other disciplines that have a lot of theory behind them."

Elan understood most of what she was saying but there were terms and thoughts he didn't understand. "You've been working hard," he said in a soft voice.

"There is still a lot to learn," Qin said, deflecting his words, embarrassed by the praise.

He pulled her close, hugging her from the side and kissing her head. "So, any boys I need to warn off?"

She pushed him away and fixed her hair. "No!" She pouted. "None of them want to talk to me. Think that I spend too much time working. What do they know? Not mature enough." Her words trailed off as she played with the cuff of her jacket.

He wanted to know what she was thinking, but he didn't at the same time. Elan coughed. He had meant to embarrass her as any father ought to and know which boys he needed to watch out for.

"So, your brothers—do they have girls they're interested in?"

"They've been training so much that they haven't had time to see girls. But there are a few who have tried to get me to introduce them. Few of them are able to build up the courage—guess it is because I am a department head." Qin sighed.

She has had to grow up fast with her problems from before, but now, seeing her here, it looks like she's finally found things to interest her. His pride in her ability and her temperament were something he couldn't express in words. He only wanted to cry out how lucky he was and hug her tight.

"This is our house," Qin said as they reached a simple house looking over the park and on the edge of town, near the barracks and a short walk from the academy.

"It looks great," Elan said.

Qin smiled and opened the door, leading him inside. Elan felt that the house was smaller than what they deserved but he knew that it had been a big move for them and he didn't want to belittle their achievements.

They stepped inside and he found that the house was warmer than outside. The layout was different, with large open spaces, making it feel airy and bright.

Qin pressed on formations as lights turned on.

"We had to make all of the formations in the house—for the ones to heat and cool the house, heat the water and to pump the water into the showers. We also made stovetops that have regulated heat, and cooling boxes that Erik and Rugrat call refrigerators. The water is clean to drink from the tap." Qin quickly showed Elan around, showing off the different rooms.

Although it looked simple on the outside, it had more amenities than their manor in Chonglu. He took back his original thoughts; the home might be smaller but functionality and form were combined together here.

"What about the large home near the center of the city?"

"That is the manor owned by Erik and Rugrat. It was left by the gnomes. It was where the master of the dungeon lived. Egbert looks after it now. Delilah lives there as the council leader of Alva. The large three-story building near the dungeon core is the government building. The adventurer's building is next to the trading and warehouse district, with a number of bars there, too. I will take you to Jasper in the morning. He will need to talk to Delilah tonight and tomorrow they'll have more information for you I'm sure," Qin said.

Silaz nodded. He knew that there would be limitations with him finding his children. Not knowing what those limitations would be was the hardest thing.

***

"Well, what do we have to eat?" Elan asked his daughter.

"I was able to get some food from the cafeteria. It's soo good." Qin moved to the kitchen and pulled out already prepared meals.

"What about all of those cooking classes you went to?"

"I can make some food, but not as good as the actual cooks. I don't have time for that!"

Elan sighed. She might be an adult, but she would always be his daughter.

***

Elder Magnus tapped his fingers on the chair before he couldn't take it any longer. He smacked the armrest and stood up, pacing.

Elder Jalli looked up at him as he started pacing and then went back to reading the scroll in her hands.

"Why has there been no word? Shouldn't the Blue Lotus or the Crafter's Association have attacked the Blood Demon Sect by now? They couldn't still think that this is a plague. Even though our original plan didn't work, the people of Tareng have had plenty of time to communicate with their higher-ups that they were under attack by the Blood Demons!" Elder Magnus threw his arms up into the air.

"Patience, Elder Magnus. Once our plan is finished, then the Hang-Nim Alliance will be able to control the Blood Demon lands without issue. The Blue Lotus and the Crafter's Association couldn't let such a thing go easily. They are slow to act on anything." Elder Jalli's expression was passive as she continued to read the scroll in her hands.

"Do you think that General Ulalas has turned?" Elder Magnus looked right at Jalli.

Jalli looked at Magnus with an annoyed expression. "We wouldn't have allowed this mission to go ahead if we didn't have complete faith in Ulalas. She was meant to marry one of the sect's higher echelon, but just as it was supposed to happen, they were married to another person from a different sect to increase the Blood Demon Sect's ties.

"Since then, she understood that the Blood Demon Sect has only been using her. She would not betray us, happily hurting the Blood Demon Sect. Even if she dies, she would only fight to hurt the Blood Demon Sect more." Elder Jalli looked back to her scrolls as she murmured, "Beware a scorned woman's wrath."

"You are right." Magnus put his hands on the back of his chair and rested there, looking at the table.

"We surround most of the Blood Demon Sect, but they might not even use us. The Blue Lotus army hasn't even been heard of in generations. They're something of a myth. Might need time to pull people together from other cities, group the guards together. That is probably it. We don't know if the Blue

Lotus army is a real thing." Magnus laughed to himself and smacked the chair.

"Would you be quieter? Some of us have other work we need to do."

Magnus rolled his eyes. He was an elder of the Red Sword sect. They were fighters who lived their lives on the edge of a blade. Their fighting art combined with Fire elemental magic to turn them into powerful magical swordsmen.

They were more direct and forward, while the Nezzar sect were mainly mages and technical fighters. Their main attribute was their ability to work together to create powerful multi-mage spells quickly. Their teamwork and intelligence were high and robust.

They were a powerful force; they were smart about luring their enemy into a trap instead of being drawn in themselves, giving them an aloof temperament.

The two groups—who didn't agree with one another—agreed that the Blood Demon Sect, the old monster in their backyard, was a greater threat and they had worked together, combining their forces to make up for the other's weaknesses. There were some talking about making the alliance permanent with the victories that they had been able to pull off and the stability they had created. Being able to hold their ground in front of much older sects and groups in the Fourth Realm was a powerful thing.

"I hate waiting," Magnus said.

"Go and swing your sword. The Blue Lotus and the Crafter's Association will move when they want to. You talk of the Blue Lotus army, but you haven't talked about the Crafter's Association's assassins. They're a much bigger problem, so make sure that you keep your mouth shut. There is no knowing where they might be or who is listening," Jalli warned.

"I've got it." Magnus waved his hand and left the hall.

***

Elan woke early. Qin was still asleep. Even now, when she left home, it seemed her habit of sleeping in still hadn't changed.

He left the house and walked around. The 'sun' was appearing above the dungeon's residents. People started to stir; many hadn't gone to sleep, their Stamina at the point that they didn't need to sleep for several days. There were children heading off to mandatory lessons at the elementary school in the residential area. Classes were starting in the academy; the workshops had people going in to work on their production. Stores opened their doors and those who had been working through the night or drinking until the early hours went back home to sleep it off or to the alchemists or healers to sober up.

Elan took a closer look at the stores near the academy. They sold items for the residents of Alva and then items for the academy and food. There were stalls all over the place, selling food of different kinds. It was the closest stall to the back of the cooking workshop.

Elan looked at the items for sale at the stalls, surprised by the large selection. There were simple items, to rare ores and materials that would be hard to find in the Second Realm. There were things that he had never seen before on display.

There were some items that cost hundreds or even thousands of gold. Instead of being outraged at the prices, people came from the academy and bartered with them, using Mana stones or gold bars worth hundreds of gold to buy the displayed items.

Elan got directions to the warehouse district from a vendor.

He passed the Adventurer's Guild. There were rough-looking people outside and inside, talking to one another, meeting up or heading out. A group of them met up with a trading caravan, greeting them and then heading out of Alva.

Elan went to the trading district. He saw people writing on a large board. Trades were being completed in the thousands of gold. The area around a simple-looking building with the sign Trading House above it was the center of everyone's attention. People ran in and out of the building. It had a roof, but there was only a formation in the middle with people on either side that would monitor one at a time on the formation before they had to leave and line back up again.

There were a number of bars, restaurants, and tea houses around the area. A few that were open were filled with people waking up and those who were meeting up and completing their first deal of that morning.

Elan stepped up to the line for the formation. He got to the front of the line. The two people looked at him, stopping him.

"Name?"

"Elan Silaz." He realized that he might not be allowed access, or that he might not be registered. A dozen bad scenarios passed through his mind. *Maybe I should have woken Qin'er up before I left.*

"Sounds familiar," one said.

"My sons are Domonos Silaz and Yui Silaz, and I have a daughter, Qin Silaz."

"You've got some powerful kids." The other laughed and smiled, waving Elan forward.

"Thank you," Elan said.

"You have ten minutes," the man replied.

Elan used the interface and was blown away with the information there.

Is this a city trading interface? I thought only the rulers of a city and their own trading houses could gain access to this—it was how they're able to amass so much wealth! Certainly no normal person would have this amount of materials or wealth to move!

The more Elan looked through the pages, the greater his understanding became of the system and why people were looking to buy items from their fellow traders outside.

Get the items locally for cheap, bundle them together and then sell them through the interface, or vice versa—buy a lot of items cheaply from the interface here and then sell it on to traders here who sell them in small lots across the local area. Or maybe in other realms? I heard someone talking about a shortage of wheat in the Second Realm and demand for water because of a drought moving in?

Elan left the trading station and walked through the traders, getting more information from them by just listening to what they were saying.

He headed out of the trader's square and passed the Adventurer's Guild. He stopped and then walked inside. He had been buying and selling to mercenaries for most of his adult life. The more he knew about the mercenaries of Alva, the more opportunities he would have to replicate his previous practices or adapt them.

Once he entered the building, he saw stores and administration areas to the right. There were potions, weapons and armor available for sale. There were people who were passing out contracts or organizing them to be issued.

A board was filled with jobs categorized from SSS down to F.

People were examining the job board, going to the different tables, or they sat in the area to the left, which looked to be a pub area.

There were also people who were talking about training coming through doors in the far back right.

They're strong. They range from level eight to level thirty, though they're not chaotic like some mercenary groups. They look more organized.

"Elan!" Jasper, who was walking through the Adventurer's Guild, called out.

He turned to find Jasper, who was walking out of a set of doors that led into the administration side of the building.

"Jasper," Elan said.

"Come, let's get a drink. Now that you're a citizen of Alva, I can tell you a few more things," Jasper said.

They sat down in a corner of the pub.

Jasper pulled out a piece of paper and gave it to Elan. "This is an information flyer from the Alva Bank. You can invest and save your money with them to be pulled out at a later date, or you can get loans from them. These are like the supporting payments that a lord will make to a trader, supporting them financially at the start and then getting a payment later on. Unlike with these lords, you can pay back a loan and then not owe anyone anything.

There is a plan for the person with the money to pay back the lender as well as a percentage ontop of the loans total amount it is meant to help companies and people grow. I know that there are a number of merchants who use the loans to start and expand.

"The Adventurer's Guild is located in the higher realms. It acts as a hub for the people from Alva. A place for adventurers and traders to go and be safe. We also have some locations where there are smiths, alchemists, or tailors learning their craft in greater depth and they've taken over bars, inns, or other infrastructure. The people Aditya hires are vetted by us and then, if we think they're a good fit, we offer them a place within Alva. With the academy and our connections to the higher realms, it isn't hard for someone to increase their skill levels and move through the realms with less problems."

"Why in secret? Most sects broadcast that they have places in the higher realms. It brings in more promising recruits," Elan asked.

"What we're looking for is not the people who are playing political poker with where they want to develop their skills. We want to help the people others have turned away. The people of Alva work together. They might compete with each other but with the laws, oaths, and police force, infighting isn't allowed.

"Sects can get more people, but the moral character of those people might range from not being the best to downright shitty. We won't impede anyone trying to go to the higher realms. We'll help them with the basics, but everything past that, they have to work for. Which is also why we select people with a drive to work. People can be educated, but we can't teach them how to work."

"So if you have a Master in some skill, you wouldn't take them if they weren't willing to work and help others?" Elan asked. Such a thing was absurd. They were in the First Realm; knowing a Master in any skill would give even a massive sect a big step up.

"Again, if they want to grow and advance, we're for it. If they want to just milk us for benefits and allow us to say that they live here? We wouldn't want that, that is not what we do here at Alva," Jasper said.

Elan fell into thought.

"Look, we're still growing, but I know that in the future Alva will birth many Masters in different skills. People can grow in multiple skills here. Want to be an armorer, a chef, and a tailor? You can do it! We allow people the freedom to make their own decisions. Such as trade," Jasper said. "For the auction house in

Vermire, take a fifteen percent commission. You can take five percent; Alva will take ten percent. The items that Aditya would
have given you will come directly from us, making sure that you
have high-quality goods to sell and draw others' attention. You
will be getting a five percent commission on all of the items that
way, and a five percent on anything that others bring to the auction. We will pay for your people to find and recruit people for
Alva, with a profit for you as well. We are trading in gold, monster cores, and Mana stones. The Mana stones are rare to find
but they can be bought for one thousand gold. Gold is used the
most in the First and Second Realm, with Mana stones appearing in the Second and the Third Realm. As such, most in the
First Realm use coins instead of stones. Some people just trade in
these and other basics to make a profit."

"What about Mana cornerstones?" Elan asked.

"We do not have any of those for sale right now. We're still
looking to fill up our Mana gathering array above the dungeon
core. Once it is filled, then we will start replacing the Mortal
Mana cornerstones with Earth Mana cornerstones, and then
adding in Sky and so on," Jasper said.

"What about these loans?" Elan asked.

"It would be easy to get five thousand gold in loans. Higher
than that would be difficult," Jasper said.

Elan was floored. A single store of his might only make
around two thousand gold in an entire year.

"There is a bank located next to the government building
outside of the dungeon core building—might be worth taking a
look," Jasper said.

"Thanks for this information. But why tell me instead of letting me discover it for myself?"

"Alva is built on crafters but funded by traders—two sides of
the same coin. Without one, we wouldn't have the other. Aditya

has ears in different powerful countries, listening to the people in power. We have some people in the different trading spheres in the First Realm, but most of our traders head to the higher realms because of the greater profits. If you can increase your profits, increase the money flowing through Alva and the people we recruit, it is a win for us," Jasper said.

Elan fell quiet for a little bit. "I'll have a look into it, but I do have one last question." Elan looked at Jasper.

"Shoot," Jasper said.

"Where are my sons?"

"You're a person of Alva now, so I guess it wouldn't be bad to tell you." Jasper turned serious. He sat forward, lacing his fingers together as he leaned on the table.

"Right now, both Yui and Domonos are in the Fourth Realm, the battlefield realm, with the rest of the Alvan army—with Erik and Rugrat—to find other dungeons to improve Alva's strength and temper the strength of the army. They left for the Fourth Realm almost a month ago."

Elan's stomach dropped, before he controlled himself. "Is there a way to talk to them?"

"You can send them a letter, they're in the middle of a battle between two powerful forces," Jasper's tone was grim.

Elan knew that he couldn't hide everything from his children for their whole lives. It still made his stomach drop, learning that they were off in some foreign land, potentially fighting for their lives.

Chapter: Standing Tall

The Blood Demon army seemed to breathe for the first time in a long time as the attacks for the last week fell away, with no more whistling from above.

The mist that had covered the forest was rapidly clearing as they were walking down the road. The ground rose up and dipped, making it hard to see too far forward.

"General, there is something ahead," one of the scouts said, moving to Ulalas.

"What is it?" she asked.

Everyone tensed up as they thought it would be another one of the devices under the road.

"There is a pillar reaching into the sky," the scout said.

"A pillar reaching into the sky? What is it from?"

"I sent some scouts ahead and they said that it is standing in the middle of a large city. They say that the city is as big as the Capital of the Blood Demon Sect."

"The Captial?" Ulalas asked.

The Capital was the largest of the cities, housing the headquarters of the Blood Demon Sect.

"We will soon see what lies ahead," she said as the army kept on marching.

When they marched on the rises in the land and could look over the trees, they saw the pillar as they got closer, standing in front of them, as if inviting them in.

People started talking to one another as the pillar would disappear when the road dipped.

It was into the afternoon when the road started to open up and it gave way to fields that had been cut down recently.

A ripple went through the army as Ulalas rode up to the front on her mount. The pillar was now visible even above the trees, the mist cleared around it to show the sky once again.

"Wasn't this supposed to be a dead land?" she demanded, looking at the towering walls of the capital city that lay underneath the pillar. It was based at the entrance to a closed valley in the south so only two-thirds of it could be attacked at any time. The ground surrounding it was anything but even: pot holes all over the place, trenches that were meant to break ankles. Crossing that would be a task of its own.

She cast a viewing spell and could see people on the walls, watching the approach of the Blood Demon army. Eight kilometers of dead ground lay between the walls and where the road met the open killing grounds.

"Form up the army. We will rest tonight and attack tomorrow," Ulalas said.

There was a whistling noise as people huddled together underneath their Mana barriers.

Ulalas gritted her teeth and tightened her grip on her reins, seeing her army cowering underneath the Mana barriers. Her eyes were filled with rage as she looked at the capital in front of her. It was as if they were taunting her, telling her that they were the people who had been fighting with her in the shadows all of this time.

"Find out what you can about this city. It wasn't built overnight," Ulalas said to her generals.

***

A large map covered the central table in the command center. There were runners and messengers for the Crafter's Association and the Blue Lotus, as well as leaders from both fighting forces in the command center looking at the table.

Rugrat had already explained to them the terrain of the cap-ital when they had arrived.

"From the scouts, it looks like the enemy is setting up camp and they'll get ready to attack tomorrow. We'll have roving pa-trols and fighting forces go to ground near the walls to get some sleep. We'll have the undead patrolling beneath the walls. They don't need sleep, so they'll react first if there is an attack in the night. We'll drop regular mortar shells tonight, but to half their range. I don't want to hit the Mana barriers, but mess up the landscape, turn it into a muddy mess for them, and make them unable to sleep. Throw up illumination rounds so we can see what they're doing," Erik said.

"If we shoot short, they might think that is the extent of our range, might not do anything. So far they haven't seen how far our mortars are out. The only ones were the aerial forces but that was one time. If they think that they're outside our range, they might do something stupid beyond it, we can take advantage of it and hammer them," Glosil saw to the heart of Erik's plan.

Erik nodded as Rugrat pointed at the board.

"They have been moving with Mana barriers mounted on carriages this entire time. Now the ground is going to be rough. They might set up a train of carriages, but that takes time and a lot of mana stones to make a tunnel from the rear to the front," Rugrat said.

"We have saved up our spell scrolls thus far, if we use those with your mortars it should have a larger effect," Daniels suggest-ed.

"While advancing down the road they might have the time to check for traps, but few can do that when charging across the battlefield," Xue Lin added.

"Is it possible to add them to the outer walls?" Erik asked.

"Of course," Xue Lin nodded.

Erik looked at everything, trying to pull the different elements together.

"Okay, so when they move forward, we won't be able to hit them from above thanks to the barriers, but we've got IEDs all over in the ground. If we can add in some formations Those can disrupt them nicely. Anywhere that loses a Mana barrier, we can call in mortar fire. Otherwise we'll hopefully be trading hits—our Mana barrier against theirs, with siege weaponry and spell scrolls thrown in for good measure. Which is fine. As soon as they get to the walls, we hit them with close-ranged weaponry. We bleed them—make it hell for them to enter the city. Though we don't have that large of a fighting force compared to theirs, they have three nearly three times our numbers in straight soldiers. Once they're making a push and it's confirmed that we can't hold, we pull our people back through the outer city; we collapse the Mana shield inward, make it look like it failed, thus luring the enemy into the city. That is where we will claim lives," Erik said.

"Why don't we stop them at the outer walls?" Daniels asked. Xue Lin seemed to agree.

"It takes something like three times the number of attackers as the defenders in an entrenched position. We'll bleed them crossing the battlefield, but we don't know how much, what if they take their time, what if they have a massive reserve of mana stones? Though that's not the crux of it," Erik tapped the outlined wall.

"The outer wall that they can attack runs for twenty-seven kilometers, that is nearly three meters for each of our soldiers to cover, that's with no back up support, no artillery or mages on the rears or reserves to help our people," Erik said.

"What about the undead?" Daniels asked.

"They're good with simple tasks, put them among the enemy they'll be great, defend a wall next to allies, they don't know how to control their strength that well," Rugrat explained.

"So the inner wall?" Xue Lin interjected.

"The inner wall is just over five and a half kilometers. That means we would have two people for every meter of the wall if we committed them, but more than that, it concentrates our efforts," Everyone focused on Erik more as he cleared his throat.

"Once inside the capital, they can't use their mana barriers, the terrain is like the forest, random walls, different terrain."

"They'll be within range of our mages and spell scrolls," Evelyn Moss, from the Crafter's Association's guard forces, said. "It might be better to put the traps inside the walls instead of out on the battlefield. There is a chance they might activate it on the battlefield, inside the capital their forces will clump up, easier to get more of them with our traps. Retreating in an organized manner will be difficult."

"Retreating under control is nearly impossible to coordinate but we can train for it," Rugrat said.

"How are your forces looking?" Erik asked.

Moss looked to Xue Lin who nodded slightly.

"They're stronger than before, but we've still got about twenty percent of our force out of the fighting because of the pill. Another thirty percent can fight but their fighting ability is affected by about half. Another thirty percent can use all but a third of their power. And then we have a remaining ten to fifteen percent who are essentially unaffected. They are our Masters, for the most part, so it means we've got a strong reserve," Evelyn didn't hide anything.

Erik looked at Rugrat who shrugged.

"We believe that your masters and Elites should fight alongside your regular forces."

The people from Tareng had skeptical looks.

"Are you sure that is a wise move? If we don't hold back our strength, then we won't have a reserve to pull from," Evelyn stated.

"We will still have a quick reaction force to act as a reserve, but mixing the two groups mean that if we're attacked by masters we aren't constantly rushing and reacting to it. We have people hold on and then hammer them with quick reaction force, or ranged alternatives."

"How is the army still together?" Rugrat asked, looking to the association representatives.

"What do you mean?" Evelyn asked, frowning.

"Their morale is low, we've seen people deserting all over the place, they've lost a quarter of their fighting force but they're still preparing to fight a battle against an entrenched position. Most battles if one side loses ten percent of their numbers then they break," Rugrat said.

"Power of oaths among other things," Xue Lin said. "Oaths are powerful if done right, they can bind people together with powerful consequences. There are ways to get out of it, but some, like oaths to a military are hard to break. If someone doesn't carry out orders then they can even die in some of the more severe cases. The most effective way to break an army is to kill the leaders. With the leaders dead, their orders are no longer applicable."

"So oaths, kind of sort of keep people from breaking ranks and running away. They've got to be a bit pissed at that," Rugrat said.

"They certainly won't be a motivated fighting force. They'll still fight," Evelyn shrugged.

"So if we can we go for their leadership and that should break their oaths, or at least allow them to get past the oaths? Bypass them kind of?" Erik asked.

"Pretty much," Evelyn shrugged.

"We just need to hold for a day or two for the people we sent to our headquarters are confirmed to not have a plague," Xue Lin said.

"Easy," Rugrat said, sitting back in his chair, looking as tired as everyone felt.

***

Storbon looked out over the wall. He was using one of Erik and Rugrat's newly developed sights. With his marksman zoom in skill, he could pick out the individual soldiers who were setting up their camp. They moved as if robots, with barely any energy in them.

Yao Meng let out a burp and stretched.

"Nasty bastard, what the fuck did you eat?" Deni said.

"Perfectly natural," Yao Meng defended.

"Yeah, like you're natural in any way." Deni snorted.

"You been talking to my girlfriends again?" Yao Meng wiggled his eyebrows.

Storbon grinned. He could hear the eye roll as Deni let out a sigh.

"Real original."

"How much longer we on watch for? I've got a hot game of poker going," Yao Meng asked.

"Another half hour," Deni said.

Storbon stopped scanning as he saw siege weapons being deployed among the different formations, the carriages finally revealing their stores.

There were trebuchets, ballistas, and magical cannons. Storbon studied them. They had magical runes running down their length to increase their damage and range. Instead of being hollow in the center like with rifles and other firearms, these were made of magical circle-covered cylinders that were locked into one another, making the magical formation not just some formation carved into metal. It allowed them to channel a greater amount of power and intensity.

"Looks like the materials are all of the Earth-grade and covered in formations. They're not going to be easy to deal with." Storbon opened a channel to the command center. "This is Overwatch Sierra One. It looks like the enemy are deploying siege weapons and defensive measures. Wait one moment." Storbon saw a large totem that people had been assembling powering up; a large Mana barrier appeared, covering the area of four mobile Mana barriers.

"The only time that those barriers go down is when they need to recharge." Deni said as she had appeared at the wall, looking at the camp.

"With that large formation over there active, they can charge their mobile Mana barriers. Just how many Mana stones do they have?" Yao Meng asked.

"A metric fuck ton, probably," Deni said.

"Even the medic is swearing," Yao Meng said.

"Command, this is Overwatch Sierra One. Update on enemy forces. Looks like they've got four ballistas, two trebuchet, and one magical cannon for every thousand people," Storbon said.

"Sierra One, this is Command. Understood. Keep us updated on the situation."

"Understood, Command. Sierra One out."

"That's a lot of firepower." Yao Meng's voice lowered as a heavy atmosphere fell over the trio on the wall.

The sun faded away, the clouds above turning gold and red before it sunk below the horizon.

Deep in the capital, thumping noises could be heard.

Light bloomed above the battlefield, pushing back the shadows and allowing those on the wall to see the sieging army clearly.

The army all looked up from their makeshift camp up at the glowing white balls that were slowly coming back down to earth.

The people in the army moved their siege weaponry into position and worked on their defenses. More of the defensive totems appeared along their lines to take over defense from the mobile Mana barriers.

Tents were erected as people tried to get some sleep with the bright lights continuing to flare outside.

"Fire mission, offset by five minutes down the firing line. Let's see if we can't keep them up past their bedtime," Rugrat said over the command channel.

"Mortars, acknowledge," Glosil said.

There were now forty mortars within the capital. Both Tiger and Dragon Platoon had been training with the mortar system, or using it in combat. The veterans of Dragon Platoon mixed with Tiger Platoon seamlessly, bolstering their combat strength and passing on their recently learned lessons.

The first mortar fired, arcing through the Mana barrier that allowed attacks out but not in.

A whistle made the Blood Demon army still. Those who had been sleeping shivered as they were suddenly awake.

The mortar shell landed between the Blood Demon army and Vuzgal. The explosion didn't even hit their newly raised shields, but there was no one asleep in the Blood Demon army.

Five minutes later, the second mortar fired lazily.

Like clockwork, the guns fired up and down the enemies line, the Blood Demon army unable to get even five minutes of rest as the mental fatigue continued to mount.

Within Vuzgal, people were able to sleep in the prepared residences. As they slept, the soldiers' bodies continued to be tempered by the concoctions. Instead of being weaker, they were stronger than ever before, their bodies increasing in Strength and Agility.

This was part of the trade in the Ten Realms; if you could overcome adversity, your Strength would reach a new level.

***

A sleepless night passed for the Blood Demon Sect.

Ulalas listened to the whistle of a mortar before it landed in no-man's land and exploded as first light arrived.

There are two ways to take a city. The first is to attack at long range, take down the defenses of the city and bleed them of resources—Mana stones, water, food—kill as many as possible and then send in forces to clean them up. The second is to get close enough to their walls that their Mana barrier doesn't cover them and blast them from up close, open up holes and then enter the city and fight it out inside the city. We have no idea of how much power this city can draw on. We have no information on it at all other than it was supposedly some cursed ground and then what that trader said about there being around one hundred people he had left here to die. This doesn't look like the work of just a few hundred people.

"General, it has been confirmed. It appears that there are undead within the city. We were able to spot a group of undead mounted on flying beasts moving low over the city," a scout commander reported.

She nodded. The scout commander saluted and left her tent. The other generals all looked at her examining the rough map that the scouts had updated throughout the night with the flying forces able to get some details of the city's inner layout.

"Move the siege weaponry into range. Let's test their Mana barriers and see if we can find weaknesses along their walls. They're defending a large area. If we can find their blind spots, we can try to force them. Now, we'll be the ones making them run around to our attacks." Her orders got noises of agreement from the generals.

By mid-morning, the army of the Blood Demon Sect was lined up.

A horn blew and the army marched forward. Their mobile Mana barriers activated as they marched forward. The Elites and Masters remained in the main camp as the soldiers and cannoneer teams moved forward.

***

On the wall opposite, Erik watched as the cannon teams moved forward.

"If they pass over any of the IEDs, hit them," Erik told Xi. She and Lucinda had been attached to him to be his helpers and to keep him safe on the battlefield.

Rugrat had Racquel and Simms assisting him.

The Blood Demon Sect's army kept advancing, entering the range of the mortars. They had stored their siege weapons in their storage rings. They walked over what was the Alvan army's firing range, passing over the scarred landscape from the battling of the Vuzgal undead and the mortar fire.

The first IED went off suddenly. The other groups halted slightly and then forged ahead. They had become used to the IEDs. The commanders ordered them forward, knowing that there was nothing else that they could do.

More of the IEDs went off, but there were only a few in their path that far out.

"Mortars?" Erik asked.

"Loaded with smoke and poison as you ordered," Lucinda replied.

Erik nodded, not taking his eyes off the advancing army. He leaned on the battlements and linked his hands together, holding his head as he watched the enemies advance.

"Just what is your range?" he asked himself. Xi and Lucinda remained quiet as they scanned the area, Night Terror above so Lucinda could give Erik real-time updates on what was happening on the battlefield.

The armies finally reached the two-kilometer mark and started to make a new temporary camp. The ground was cleared and organized, with magic making perfect firing positions in minutes as the siege weaponry was deployed and put down.

"Looks like they were keeping some trump cards hidden," Erik said. There was nearly three times the amount of weapons that Storbon had reported.

"Shall we have the undead attack?" Rugrat asked through an open channel between the two of them.

"Hold off for now. When they enter the city or use their Elites and Masters, then we'll use Rising Coffin," Erik said.

With Elizabeth and so many undead mages at their control, it would have been criminal negligence if they didn't alter the battlefield according to their advantage. They had dug a series of tunnels underground, using the ingenuity of different guerilla forces across Earth.

They could place IEDs under the enemy, or have the undead climb up through the ground and attack the enemy from underneath.

"Have them place IEDs under the different weapon teams, and along the path that they traveled down toward their current position from their camp," Erik said.

"Understood," Rugrat said.

Siege weapons were revealed among the Blood Demon army as the aerial forces moved higher into the sky. The smoke screen continued to blind the siege weapons, making them unable to see the walls of Vuzgal.

The weapons were already loaded. Seconds after they were deployed, they were ready to fire.

Trebuchet arms were released and ballista arms straightened as the runes across the cannons lit up with power, draining the Mana stone at their rear. A magical formation appeared around the front of the cannon; a blue beam cut through the smoke, followed with hundreds of five-foot arrows, and enchanted pay-loads from the trebuchets.

The different weapons struck the barriers of Vuzgal, but others, with their view obscured, landed in the ground.

==========

Event

==========

The city of Vuzgal is under attack! Pick a side!
Defend Vuzgal
Attack Vuzgal

==========

==========

You have picked to Defend Vuzgal

==========

The barrier stood strong. Within the main tower of the city, a chunk of Mana stones was turned into dust. It was a large chunk, but before the dust had settled, one could see that more Mana stones were starting to form in the open space. The Mana of the Earth realm was naturally higher, combined with the Mana gathering formations in the city and the large dungeon core in a land that had been fought over for centuries. It might have lost some power, but the interior of the hidden dungeon core room was becoming cramped with Mana stones.

The mortars didn't stop falling but their pace was more sedated now. The army looked through the holes in the smoke, but Vuzgal disappeared once again.

Based on our power usage, it would take nearly a week for them to siege us and open up our barriers. If we leave their army alive, then they might just try to do that. Though there has to be a pressure on them to kill us off as soon as possible. It would be hard for them to drag this out.

Erik was trying to figure out just what the opposing general's plan was. If he could figure out what was driving her, then he could make plans to counteract. If she wanted to wear him down, then he could oblige and wait for reinforcements to arrive.

Aerial mounted forces reported back to the Blood Demon army how the attack had gone.

Erik looked up at them as the soldiers under the Blood Demon army reloaded their weapons. "Rugrat, see if you can come up with something to get rid of their eyes in the sky."

A second volley was fired, the Mana barrier around Vuzgal flashing with impacts.

"I've got a plan," Rugrat said. "I'll need the heavy repeaters though."

"You've got them. I'll only need them if the army charges forward into close range of the wall."

"Understood."

"Get the mortars to split fire, half smoke and poison, half high power shells. Let's see if we can't drain some of those shields," Erik said to Xi.

"Understood."

For the first time, the high-powered shells were deployed. They went off like thunder claps, hitting the back of the Mana barriers, while smoke landed in front and poison landed all around. The army was isolated from their Elites and Masters, being hit from every side. As they drank antidotes, they fired a third volley. Their motions picked up in speed; they felt the pressure as their sections Mana stones were drained to power the siege weapons and the mobile Mana barriers. If the barriers failed, they would be left open to the mortars fire.

***

"All heavy repeaters are ready," Hiao Xen said.

"All right, we'll drive them into you." Rugrat looked around the cleared area. There were hundreds of undead creatures with mages on their backs, lined up in rows, unmoving like statues.

There were hundreds of aerial mounted men and women of the Blue Lotus and Crafter's Association as well.

"Mount up!" Rugrat yelled.

They moved to the open area and got onto their flying mounts.

Rugrat used his sound transmission device, talking to them all at once. "We will gain altitude and come down in the north, using the sun behind us so the aerial forces of the Blood Demon Sect don't even see us. We want to launch a surprise attack and make them break toward the walls of Vuzgal. Let's give our people on the ground some target practice," Rugrat said.

"Move in your formations and don't lose your team leader. Take down anyone you can, but don't chase them into our allies' fire. It'll be impossible for them to fire up accurately."

Rugrat swung his leg over and sat down on George, who wore his full battle armor. The weight didn't seem to affect him much. There was an eager look in his eyes.

Rugrat patted his back and looked at the undead. They had a chilling aura around them, as if a newly sharpened blade waiting to be used. Each wore Journeyman-level equipment, increasing their already powerful Strength. Among them, there might even be the mounted mages who had attacked Rugrat when he had been running through Vuzgal. He didn't know and he didn't want to find out. Right now, they were a tool to be used and one of the reasons that they were able to stay in control of the fight.

"Let's go!" Rugrat shouted. The undead moved with him as the Crafter's Association and Blue Lotus guards followed. Their beasts charged across the cleared area and spread their wings out as they gained speed and climbed into the sky, flying low and away from the city opposite the approaching army.

They left the trees behind quickly. The sun made their armor and weapons shine as they spread out, breaking down into their assigned formations. As they climbed, the undead banked away. They couldn't leave the dungeon's area of effect or else they would quickly lose power. Being from the magical class, it was a given they would burn through their Mana faster than any other fighter.

Rugrat looked to his left. He could see Vuzgal's Mana barrier taking impacts, unaffected by the attacks. He saw the dust given off by the mortars and the flash of the outgoing rounds. He scanned the walls, seeing people moving through the capital carrying out their attacks.

Siege crews were working madly to reload their weapons and fire again.

Cannon fire hit the barrier. The blue blasts burned through the smoke, only for the gaps to be hidden again with the next barrage of smoke rounds.

The Elites and Masters were in their makeshift camp, watching the battle raging. The Elites were grouped together, ready to be ordered into the fight if needed.

Rugrat's eyes searched through the skies as they continued to fly. He saw the black spots that were the Blood Demon aerial forces.

The battlefield was displayed beneath him as Simms reported what was happening to Erik and the command staff. The mortars' fire adjusted, becoming more accurate as the repeaters were all readied for action along the walls.

Rugrat started to bank with George. They turned down and to the left, picking up speed. They dropped lower, aiming above and behind the Blood Demon army's regulars.

"Mortars, hold your fire, hold your fire!" The wind pressed Rugrat's glasses into his face, distorting his face and making his cloak flutter wildly, chilling him to the bone.

"Mortars are cleared!" Glosil said.

"All right, as we discussed," Rugrat said to the other mounted aerial forces.

The undead started using spells against the Blood Demon aerial force's left flank, making them move toward the right as they tried to defend and evade. Coming in the direction of the sun meant that the forces above the sieging army didn't see them at first. But someone in the camp below must've because they turned to react.

"Night night, mother fuckers. Use your scrolls!" Rugrat ordered as he took out two magical scrolls and activated them. The scrolls were torn apart as the other aerial forces used their spell scrolls as well.

Buffs from the mages on the wall fell on Rugrat and his people. Their speed and reaction time increased.

Spell formations appeared in the sky. Tornadoes with winds that could shred a mount and person flew out. Arrows—both those from the spell scrolls and the mounted fighters—were released. The lucky aerial forces were able to dodge and were driven forward, the unlucky ones didn't need to worry about the attack or anything else as tombstones fell to the ground. The only place that was clear of attacks was the walls of Vuzgal.

Rugrat reared up in his seat and pulled out his twin M32s. He was expressionless as he cast Sure Shot on the rounds and fired. The rounds caught the aerial beasts directly, shredding them and their rider, sending them plummeting to their ends.

The mages and archers behind him used everything at their disposal, switching from spell scrolls to their weapons because the spell scrolls took too long to use in a battle like this.

Rugrat monitored how everything was going before he put his weapons away.

"Bank right!" Rugrat ordered. Everyone disengaged and rushed to the side. The enemy was flying low and fast toward the walls, breaking away themselves.

Rugrat checked where everyone was. "Repeaters, you are cleared to fire!"

***

"Fire!" Hiao Xen yelled.

They had only used a few of them at a time on a testing range. Now there were hundreds of mages, archers, and long-range weapon users adding in their attacks.

Hiao Xen watched the explosive arrow tracers that were loaded into the dual-mounted repeaters filling the sky with lines of ballista arrows.

The Blood Demon aerial forces that had just escaped the long-range attack of the undead mounts on one side and the sneak attack from the remaining aerial forces on the other now found that instead of fleeing to safety, they had walked into the maw of the beast.

The aerial forces had been severely weakened with the ambush from the mortar team along the road. Now, they were cut down out of the sky in droves. A lucky few were able to flee and run back toward their camp.

"Heavy repeaters and ranged, cease fire. Mortars, smoke screen. Fire when ready," Erik ordered.

"Cease fire!" Hiao Xen yelled. Along the wall line, they recovered and reloaded. The skies changed owners again as the Blood Demon sect aerial forces feld and the Vuzgal defenders replaced them, the mortars continued to fire on the incoming soldiers who responded by firing their siege weapons at Vuzgal's walls. Their attacks crashing into the other's barriers.

"Ranged and formation mages, begin your attacks," Erik ordered.

Mages who had prepared attack formations activated them. They either cast spells, the formations serving to increase their Strength, or activated the formation and the spell within them and acted as a conduit for their power.

Mages cast fireballs with their hands, hurling them out. The fireballs turned from baseballs to the size of a beach balls as they left the formations, a mage turning themselves into a siege weapon as fireballs were launched over the walls of Vuzgal. Spell formations appeared in the skies; beasts started to appear in the skies or on the ground, summoned by the mages.

Magical artillery fire, Mana bolts the size of a grown man, were group-cast by mages working together.

Catapults that had been built across Vuzgal snapped forward as their payloads cleared the wall. The branches fell back to the ground and reset as the undead loaded enchanted rocks.

They waited until the skies were clear so that the enemy wouldn't know where we have our siege weapons hidden or where our mages stand, Hiao Xen realized as he watched the Blood Demon army.

"Mortars, change to high explosive only," Erik commanded. His voice was cool, as if a boy talking about how he might open a particularly annoying box.

Hiao Xen thought the firepower from before had been impressive, but now—now it looked like the gods themselves had grown angry as Mana crackled in the air.

Spell formations appeared in the sky above Vuzgal as titanic forces of Mana were unleashed. The Blood Demon army's retaliation wasn't any weaker than Vuzgal's. The Mana barriers of the city and the Blood Demon army weathered the storm, glowing brilliantly as spells slammed into their surface. Lightning caused the barrier to flicker with blinding light as spells of Water and Fire exploded, causing splashes like raindrops hitting water.

Hiao Xen's stomach tightened as if it were in a vise as he looked up at the destruction being waged above him. All that stood between them and destruction was a Mana barrier.

"Slow your rate of fire, mages. Conserve your energy; tighten up your targeting. Chain spells together to land in the same area." Erik's voice was calm, a maestro of destruction. Fire continued to rain down from the Blood Demon Sect as Vuzgal's fire dropped but their attacks increased in efficiency.

Spells landed on the barriers, one after another. With the pillars drawing in mana the city's mana concentration was much higher, allowing formations and mages to recover faster than normal.

Without the aerial forces and with the attacks being traded back and forth, Hiao Xen doubted that the Blood Demon Sect knew that they were shooting empty sections of the wall.

It took a lot more fire than the mobile barriers but the barrier along the main wall opened up a few times and through the distortions, the wall was damaged or even destroyed in those sections.

People reported in that they were affected by poisons or curses within the attacks. They were sent back to the aid stations that Erik had created, quickly being cleared and then sent back into battle.

The toughest to deal with were the people affected by the concoction. If they were hit with a poison, then they needed to take an antidote. A healing spell or potion could remove it as well, but if they had not completely resolved the transformation concoction within their bodies, it would flare up and weaken their Strength greatly.

The day continued this way with the two forces exchanging fire. The Blood Demon Sect moved their people around, changing positions and fired at different sections of the wall while the Vuzgal forces mana barriers started to fail in places.

The forces on the wall held their fire, with the melee types waiting below the walls.

As the Mana barriers of the Blood Demon army started to fail more often, they started to pull back.

They passed along the same paths they had advanced, thinking that they would be clear.

The mages from the Blood Demon army continued to fire as they retreated, covering the retreat as the mages of Vuzgal changed their aim and targeted the main camp. Their attacks now blocking their sight, making it harder for them to accurately target Vuzgal that was over five kilometers away.

Erik told everyone to check their gear and to rest and eat. The mages worked on rotating shifts to attack the Blood Demon army as IEDs along the retreating siege force went off.

Hiao Xen's face was hard as he looked at the Blood Demon army. There was no glorious battle, no master dueling master.

This was a dirty war, one that worked on the opponents' minds—making them lose their reason, filling them with fear, and sapping their Stamina.

"I have truly underestimated them" Olivia muttered in a low voice. She was still the highest ranking in all of the guards and he needed her to help him in commanding all of them.

Hiao Xen's face hardened. "Explain?"

He was short with her, she had gone against his friend after all.

Olivia paused, collecting her thoughts.

"They could have attacked the army from underground, but it would have removed the sieging army and then the Masters and Elites would have had to charge the walls. Erik and Rugrat eliminated their aerial support; they're blind to what's happening within Vuzgal now. They showed a lot of power, but it wasn't any of their real trump cards.

"I doubt that we know those even now. Using the mages, they can recover from their lost Mana and fight again and our melee fighters are still fresh. War is about keeping the enemy from being able to find their balance and pushing the advantages you have.

"Sometimes you show your hand, other times you play your cards bit by bit," She realized that her remaining doubts while they hadn't disappeared, she felt more sure of Erik and Rugrat's actions. They weren't just two men playing commander.

"This isn't about how you win a fight—it's about how you win a war. Take a disadvantage now, to win in the end."

"If I've learned anything about these two, it's that they don't do the expected." Hiao Xen said.

Hiao Xen left Olivia with those words and moved to check on the rest of the men and women up and down the line who were checking their weapons, reloading those that needed it and talking to one another. Laughing and joking, attempting to assimilate what they had seen with reality.

It felt as if the fighting from just minutes or hours ago wasn't real.

Some let out yells as they saw particularly big hits landing on the Mana barrier of the enemy camp. Or looked up at the ones that were hitting the barrier of Vuzgal.

Teams moved to the areas where the wall had been broken and were being repaired. Masters, who were revered in the other realms, were treated as construction workers as the wall was rebuilt and reinforced as if nothing had happened.

They weren't pleased with the basic work they needed to do, or the fact that they were all sharing Experience between the fighters, but they were under orders and oaths. And they had seen firsthand for the first time the calculated way that Erik and Rugrat, with their 'company,' worked.

Chapter: Come

The barriers for the camp and Vuzgal traded hits. The mages within Vuzgal used formations , buffing spells and potions to increase their attacking power. Masters, Elites, and soldier-level mages rotated in shifts. All of them worked together to attack different areas of the Blood Demon Sect's barriers, costing the enemy power.

Erik didn't know just how many Mana stones they must have burned through by now. The power kept in store with the pillar was extensive, with the Blue Lotus and the Crafter's Association both adding a sizable amount of Mana stones to the pillar.

Erik didn't know whether they knew about the dungeon core or not, so he had buried the dungeon core underneath the pillar. Even if they broke through the fake floor, there would be nothing but a large collection of Mana stones and cornerstones.

Erik walked along the wall, checking in on those on guard. He even sat down and started to read a technical manual after he was done with his inspection. Gilly lay down and took a nap as Storbon and Yao Meng, who were with Erik, kept a lookout but were playing a card game.

The members of the different groups inside the city all ate in cafeterias with one another. This was to encourage them to be closer and show a united front. The people of Alva's army took the time to talk to those in the Blue Lotus and the Crafter's Association. They might be military members, but most of them had learned at least one crafting skill, others more.

When asked for more information about who they were, the people from the Alvan army would turn silent. They only talked about Dragon and Tiger Platoon, part of the company and then the special teams.

Even though they were defending the same city, there seemed to be a cloud of mystery around them, obscuring who they were.

These one hundred experts who seemed to relate more with regular soldiers than the masters or elites of the other fighting forces.

The demi-humans from the dungeon studied the humans from Tareng. The demi-humans often were the objects of ridicule but they didn't let it faze them. They were centuries old; hearing the pettiness of these other creatures, what did it matter to them? Only the Masters could touch them and there were few who would willingly do so.

Beasts, once they reached a certain stage, were closer to elementals than humans in the amount of power they could draw on. AS they had consumed so many items from the Ten Realms, tempering their Mana channels and their bodies over their lifetimes.

Some creatures had a higher affinity toward Mana or increasing their bodies Strength. This was why there was a difference in the final score of one's Stamina, Agility, Strength and so on compared to their base stats and modifier stats.

When a beast was able to take human shape, it showed that not only did they have a great amount of power, they could now cultivate their body and Mana consciously. Even so far as removing the impurities that had built in their body since they had been born, opening their Mana acupoints or gathering Mana drops. Their strength would be much greater than their human counterparts.

"Boss, why do you think the other groups are nasty to Fred and his people?" Storbon asked.

"Because they're different." Erik answered as he flipped the page of his book.

Storbon frowned as Yao Meng put two copper pieces forward as a bet.

"'Cause people are arrogant assholes," Yao Meng added.

Storbon let out a snort but didn't argue.

"Come far since we defended Alva," Yao Meng said with a soft snort.

Erik looked up from his book at the city walls, then at the magical attacks that rang out against the barrier and the attacks landing on the enemy.

No longer was it a dirt and wood wall with a beast wave coming toward them.

Storbon paused as well.

"Yeah." Erik took it all in again. It was not what he thought he would be doing when he woke up without three of his limbs.

The universe was a strange place, now that he thought back on it—the anger and the rage that just built up in him, after Africa. That same rage that he had turned on himself. He had been blind to it; he didn't know what would have happened if he had continued down that path.

He could have chosen to focus on his sorrow, his pain turned anger, to let it drown him and pull him down. It was harder to fight for something than it was to lay down and die. He had fought for his country, fought for the people around him and the patients he had worked on.

Fighting for himself—that was harder.

Erik lowered his head, not wanting to fall down that road of thought as he forced himself to read more of the book.

Storbon and Yao Meng continued their game of cards as they slowly recovered the relaxing air from before.

Since the Blood Demon Sect had arrived outside of Vuzgal and declared war, the totem was locked down. Thankfully they had casts and materials that had been shipped up from Alva so that they could create their own ammunition dumps, creating their own ammunition.

"How are we looking?" Erik asked up.

"Distributed the remaining ammunition, we can't just fire the mortars anywhere, ammo is limited. For the repeaters we're looking good. Same for rifles. Grenades are lower, but still we've built a stockpile over time. There are some of our people working on making mortar rounds. Have casts and materials for it all, just need to assemble." Rugrat pulled out a chair and sat next to Erik, pulling out a waterskin and taking a big drink.

Erik concured with Rugrat's words.

There wasn't anything that he needed to say. The two of them sat there, Erik studying his hands as Rugrat looked around at the half built city. Soldiers moving in formations, others that were relaxing, taking some time before the fighting broke out.

"So what do you think that they're going to do now?" Rugrat asked.

"I'm happy if they decide to keep on sieging. Honestly, that's the best for us. We can't use the totem to leave anymore. So whatever reinforcements we get, they're going to have to come from one of the nearby cities and then rush over here. Might be even best if they get someone to order the Blood Demon Sect to stand down, but I don't know if that will be possible anymore," Erik said.

"Hmm?"

"They had the balls to attack the Blue Lotus and the Crafter's Association—they're going to want to destroy them all." Erik sounded tired and resigned as he looked at Rugrat. "The strong make the rules and there aren't any rules of war here. The Blue Lotus and the crafter's association are some of the strongest. They can't just let this go."

"Shit." Rugrat spit over the battlements, the single word expressing his tired agreement in Erik's words.

It was quiet for a moment as Erik took a breath through his nose.

"They have two choices really, break our defenses over time or try to do it quickly. If they take their time we can just wait here for the Blue Lotus and Crafter's association armies to get here and we pincer the Blood Demon Sect against the walls," Erik took some more time to collect his thoughts.

"Otherwise they've got to go fast, which means that they need to enter the city. How they get into the city? Bring those mana cannons against the wall and pop it open, would take two or three hits and a big hole. Formations of some kind, spells. To do that, they need to get past the mana barrier."

Erik looked at the attacks that were landing on Vuzgal's Mana barrier. The flashes of light ruined anyone's night vision as they traded illumination rounds with the Blood Demon army.

"We need to hold for at least two days," Erik said.

"If we've got them inside the walls..." Rugrat said.

"It will be shitty, but their numbers won't count as much in the tight corridors and you worked on the outer city yourself," Erik said.

Rugrat let out a snort before he gave a grave warning. "Give anyone enough time and they can adapt."

There was an explosion, but it wasn't from the magical attacks.

Erik and Rugrat stood and scanned the battlefield. There was a smoking crater nearby. It was hard to see as attacks lit up the wall.

"Send out some of the aerial undead, have them scout the area around the walls," Erik said.

***

I should have left with Ian and his group. He didn't know where the confidence he had held in the chaotic lands had gone. The thought that they would win over the Blue Lotus and the Crafter's association. That had been dashed in the first few days of the road exploding underneath the army's feet and that whistling thunder.

He had drawn the short straw and been marched to the front of the army to be given an *essential mission.*

A suicide mission. That they made me swear an oath to complete.

Garek looked at Vuzgal. He was covered in mud while taking cover in one of the whistling craters.

Attacks landed on the Mana barrier ahead of him, lighting up the wall.

Garek rushed forward with the cover of the lit-up Mana barrier.

It looked random but the mages were altering their aim, creating cover with their attacks and moving around to make it hard for people within a region to watch the battlefield.

Garek flopped down as there was an explosion off to the side. His clenched heart was filled with adrenaline and his breathing became rough. His eyes went wide, looking at the wall. Searching for signs that they had heard the local explosion go off, killing one of the saboteurs.

Some, with their addled heads from the pressure waves, ran forward; others turned and ran back. Some remained still like Garek.

Archers and others moved on the walls and they started to shoot at the people running forward. There was little cover and once they were discovered, it was hard for them to hide.

Garek knew that running back to the Blood Demon sect army without succeeding was a death sentence in itself.

The entire army was on the brink of losing their sanity and rushing the walls or fleeing into the forest.

Someone from the camp must have seen what was going on as they increased the strength of the ranged attacks on the city.

Garek saw the barrier light up and he ran forward. Others were cut down; another was torn apart in an explosion to his right.

Garek had no path but forward. As he dropped to the ground, the barrage stopped on the barrier. He didn't care about the cut on his knee or the pain from the rock pressing against his armor. His mind was detached from his body as he bounded forward under the cover of the attacks.

He reached the wall, touching the stone, and forced his breathing down. He could hear people above him.

"Did you see any more of them?" a woman demanded.

"There!"

He heard arrows flying as they fired on a body, adding several new arrows to it.

"Already dead. Stay alert!" the woman said.

Garek waited for some close hits on the barrier. He was underneath it now. The barrier covered the walls, but it was shaped like a dome, barely missing the top of the battlements and leaving a narrow trail underneath protected by the barrier inside it.

He took out a sheaf of papers and placed one by his feet, covered it in mud and then moved down the wall, making sure that he wasn't heard or discovered.

He added another one of the papers to the walls.

He did so another thirty times before he looked out at the open ground between him and the camp.

Just thinking about that run, he shivered. Salvation or death: both lay ahead of him. But there was something about running away from the enemy—the fact that if they did attack, you wouldn't see that it was coming.

He waited for cover of the attacks and ran forward as fast as possible and then dropped into a crater. *So far so good.* He got up and ran again as blasts hit the walls.

He heard a shout and instead of dropping down, he kept on running, pumping his legs as he took off.

Pain spread through his body. He made to scream out but found there was no air in his lungs. He dropped back down in the mud; he gulped, trying to claw his way forward when the poison in the arrow gave him a final release. A new tombstone appeared on the battlefield.

***

"Do we know what they were doing?" Erik asked Niemm, who came up to Erik as he scanned beyond the wall.

"We're not sure, but they made it to the wall and then—"

"The army is forming up!" Yao Meng interrupted as more called in and silent reports came from the undead aerial forces.

"Looks like they have something planned. You were saying, Niemm?" Erik asked.

"They seem to have been charging the walls individually. We don't know if there are any hiding underneath the lip down. I have people checking through the drop slits to see if they can find anyone," Niemm said. The drop slits allowed them to drop rocks and wood on those trying to get up. Or pour tar and fire arrows at them and the defenders could use it to look at the bottom of the walls.

"Stand—"

Explosions went off along the wall as the presents that the saboteurs who had made it went off. Sections of the walls exploded, falling apart into rubble with people on them.

"—To! Stand to!" Erik yelled out. His voice became louder as rocks fell down and dust was thrown everywhere.

"Niemm, organize the injured and try to reinforce our defenses. Rugrat, prepare the aerial forces. Storbon, Yao Meng—you're with me. Storbon, send a message to Hiao Xen; tell him that the saboteurs used something to blow up the wall and the army is coming." Erik pulled out a scope and looked across the wall at the approaching army.

The wind whipped around as the attacks on Vuzgal's barrier more than quadrupled.

"Rugrat, let me know if there is anyone left in their camp."

"On it!" Rugrat jumped off the wall, using his ability with Mana to glide down, mimicking how Fred and his people were able to walk in the sky.

Niemm ran off, calling on medics and working his way toward the blast sites to clear the wounded and repair the walls as fast as possible.

Cafeterias were emptied; bunks were left in disarray as people threw on their clothes and armor, rushing through the streets toward the wall.

Erik watched the oncoming army. They were moving quickly, much quicker than they had been the morning before.

"Mortars, this is Command," Erik said.

"Command, this is Mortars. Go ahead," Glosil said back.

"Full coverage illumination rounds. Ready with the first series of poison," Erik said.

"Full coverage illumination. Ready series one poison. Understood."

"Follow with remaining poison rounds and remaining poisons on my command. You copy?" Erik said.

"Follow with remaining poison rounds and remaining poisons on your command, good. Copy."

"Command out."

Erik watched as seconds later illumination rounds lit up the area around the city, turning it into day.

Mages moved to their formations or got into their groups. The rate of fire continued to climb as they fired back at the Blood Demon army.

The Blood Demon army's barrier lit up with impacts as the renewed fire came down, one after another.

"Command, this is Aerial One. Message, over," Rugrat said.

"Aerial One, this is Command. Go ahead," Erik said.

"Command, the camp still seems to have a sizable force within it, but it's odd," Rugrat said.

Erik lowered his scope. "Aerial One, use a Detect Life spell or scroll."

There was a few seconds of silence.

"Used a Detect Life. There's an illusion on the camp and the army. They're all moving forward," Rugrat said.

Erik turned to Yao Meng. "Get the mages to use a remove illusion spell on the Blood Demon army. If nothing changes, then keep using spell scrolls until we can see what they're really doing."

Yao Meng nodded and started to talk into his sound transmission device.

"Aerial One, watch the skies. Split into shifts. Take out their aerial forces if you can. Otherwise, target their barriers from a distance," Erik said.

"Command, understood."

"Command out." Erik cut the channel and sent orders to the undead and then opened a channel to Glosil.

"Mortars, this is Command. As soon as the enemy gets into range, I want you to lay down a poison carpet for them. If they want to advance, they have to go through our poison," Erik said.

"Command, this is Mortars. Understood."

"Command out."

Erik scanned the enemy as wounded were treated at the wall and then hauled to the prepared casualty collection points, where they would be assessed and treated by alchemists and healers.

Bodies were pulled from the rubble and moved to the side. Mages started to fuse the walls back together, section by section. The openings were massive, ranging from ten to thirty feet wide, and there were dozens of them across the walls.

"Storbon, do we have a time estimate on how long it will take for us to repair the breaches?" Erik asked.

"Three to four hours," Storbon said.

"Well, looks like we'll be meeting the Blood Demon Sect face-to-face soon," Erik said. "Have Han Wu and Special Team Two pick out the holes where we can control the flow of the enemy as much as possible. I want to mine the ground to hell. Make sure that the commanders are ready to pull back to the inner wall." Erik gave Storbon side-eye.

"Understood," Storbon said. Erik and Rugrat had taught them for months; he had learned how to fight and he had learned how to make others fight and the ways that their mind would work when fighting. No one liked to retreat, but sometimes the best option was to pull back and fight later. To others retreat might be embarrassing but it would lead to a greater victory later.

The same couldn't be said about the other two fighting forces working with them.

Spells continued to fall on the Blood Demon army.

"The spells haven't worked yet," Yao Meng reported.

Erik checked his storage ring and then flicked through the spell scrolls that he had from Alva and then those that were from Vuzgal.

"Try this." Erik passed Yao Meng one spell scroll; he activated it as Erik pulled out another three spell scrolls, checking through the others.

"Wish they made names that were a bit easier to understand," Erik complained as he pulled out those that might counteract an illusion spell.

The spell scroll in Yao Meng's hands was used up as a spell formation appeared around the Blood Demon army. The advancing army seemed to be covered in shimmering lights before the spell scroll's power was used up.

The army remained the same.

Erik passed Yao Meng another spell scroll, put away the others he had, and then used a spell scroll himself.

More spell formations appeared around the enemy as they entered the true range of the mortars.

The mortars fired. Their shells landed in the path of the Blood Demon army, covering the ground in poison that killed the bugs and the grass underneath.

The mortars continued to fire, walking their fire across the front of the army and ahead of them.

One of the spell scrolls created shimmering dust that fell on the Mana barrier of the Blood Demon army. The illusion was finally lifted; the army appeared in front of their eyes, nearly doubling in size and a full kilometer and a half closer than they thought—just three and a half kilometers away.

The mortars had been hitting behind them. It was no wonder they weren't being affected by the poison that much.

Their illusion broken, the army started to break down into units, lining up with the different breaches.

The mortars changed their aim and their rate of fire climbed. It looked as if they were pissed off at being fooled and wasting their shells.

"Find out which groups contain Masters and Elites. Use the aerial assets if you need to," Erik said to Yao Meng.

"Storbon, inform the other commanders that they will arrive at the wall in ten to twenty minutes," Erik gauged.

"Sir, do you want them to move back their forces to the secondary lines?"

Erik looked at the army, trying to think like their commander.

"Move half of our forces back to the secondary lines. Make sure that all of our ranged assets are to the second line. I want the mages and the mortars to have at least one breach that we can't repair covered. Wounded are to be moved as soon as possible. Make sure that there are enough people to cover the breaches—at least three formations, group of mages or two mortars. Tell me the ones that you have covered; I'll have the undead cover the others." Erik paused. "Anything that Special Team Two can't mine, get the Crafter's Association and the Blue Lotus to lay down traps. Those traps and the ranged fire will cover the second half of our forces pulling back."

***

Ulalas knew that she needed to get this fight over with soon. The longer her people had time to think, the more likely they were to try to get her to allow them to run and bend their oaths to stay back and request reinforcements.

She had lost ten to fifteen percent of her people to desertion already, the others looking for ways to run.

She couldn't let them call reinforcements; if they did, then the Blood Demon Sect would know what was happening.

She had sent forward Elites with breaching spell scrolls. They needed to be placed on a wall and then they could be triggered remotely.

She knew that with time, the enemy would find out about the detonation spell scrolls. So she used illusion spell scrolls to disguise the camp and her army and started to advance as soon as the saboteurs started to die.

The illusion had done well, as the enemy had fired at the area behind them and allowed them to get closer.

"Have the Masters and Elites get ready to push into the breaches at their best speed," Ulalas said.

Her aide passed her message as she looked at the wall in front. The wall was large, but the holes in it were easy to see.

"We have reports of people being affected by the poison clouds. It's more effective than the previous poisons," an aide reported.

"Well, tell them to move faster and not breathe as much!" she yelled back, her nerves already on edge. What did she care about a bunch of useless soldiers who were only meant to distract from the real forces in her army?

She watched the walls and the aerial forces above. Her own aerial forces had been dramatically thinned out, so she only had them moving above the army where the ground forces could support them. Thus limiting how far they could see into the enemy camp.

Illumination rounds started to hit the ground. The light died down as more of them shot up into the sky. The attacks going between the two forces made one's ears ring and leave light spots on their eyes.

Trebuchets made by the dungeon released their payloads.

A cold smile spread across General Ulalas's face. To her, their actions looked like desperation; they were trying to throw out everything that they could to reduce their strength.

More mines went off, killing hundreds.

One of the barrier totems was destroyed by an IED but another totem activated, covering the group.

Ulalas let out a breath through her nose in fury; others chilled and stepped away as it seemed that a true demon of vengeance had overtaken General Ulalas.

Finally, her mind that had been balancing on a thread, teetering for days, let loose.

"Soldiers are to use their cannons at point-blank range to open up breaches. Order the Masters and the Elites through the breaches." Ulalas's words ran through the Blood Demon army.

Silence seemed to fall for a second.

"Destroy them!" Ulalas's words carried across the army and to the city itself.

The groups who had been marching forward orderly now broke ranks and ran forward. Madness filled their eyes. Their anger, their anxiety, the fear that had turned their stomachs and drained them of energy—it was all channeled into their charge. Their desire to destroy their enemy created a powerful and domineering aura that shook the entire force of Vuzgal, making them take a step back.

Suddenly, laughter reached the level of their charges. A single man on the battlements, laughed at them.

It caused the enraged Blood Demon armies blood to chill and their eyes lose some of their red glow and made the blood of the defenders boil. They knew that voice.

Erik looked at the Blood Demon army and smirked, "Come." His voice rolled over the ground, defiant and bloodthirsty.

Chapter: Drawing Them In

Come. That one word sent the Blood Demon army into a greater fury, losing all sense of reason: They had walked through hell and made it this far, they were the proud soldiers of the Blood Demon Sect! Now they were being looked down on by a bunch of guards that were too sick to fight them face toi face, that had run from their own city and hid behind the walls of a broken capital.

Seeing the Blood Demon army coming, the defenders were scared, yes, but they were not filled with fear. Instead of looking at them as terrible beasts, the Blood Demon army looked more like savage dogs.

Dogs that had dared to attack their home, where they and their families lived.

"You dared to attack our Tareng! I will make you pay!"

"Blood Demon sect! Your days are limited!"

"You may kill me, but your sect will be removed from these Ten Realms!"

The voices of the people from Tareng, the Crafter's Association, and the Blue Lotus spoke out together, their fighting spirit surging.

Hadn't they been chased? Hadn't they been poisoned? Weren't they the people of Tareng? They might bend but they would not break! Come! Yes, come! They would meet them with iron, with spells, with their fists if they had nothing else!

The atmosphere was enough to make one feel drunk on power. Erik looked around. His battlecry had been only one word but it had resounded in the hearts and minds of the defenders, regaining their composure.

People worked harder at their tasks as people headed back to the second wall. Thoughts of retreating disappeared.

They looked over to where he stood on the wall, looking at the enemy approaching as if everything was going according to plan.

Erik saw the sudden changes in the Blood Demon army below.

The army had split into three main groups: one headed straight on and the other two flanked.

"Move our Masters to head off the groups coming in to sector twelve," Erik said.

He had broken up Vuzgal's wall into twelve sectors like a clock. At the base was the valley at the six o'clock position. At the ten and two o'clock positions were the roads that came from the east and west. The army had come from the east but then they had moved their camp to the north, orientated on the twelve o'clock position of Vuzgal.

"Mortars, switch to HE and be ready to fire on the breaches. Mages to do the same," Erik said to Storbon without looking away from the fight.

"Rugrat, you will be leading the quick reaction force. Have the aerial forces keep circling. The undead aerial mages are to head to the pillar and attack from there," Erik said.

"On it."

Erik was anxous, nervous. He had led men and women before, yes, but that had never been more than forty or so people. Now there were ten thousand people under his command and nearly four times that number charging at them. It was unlike anything he had seen before and certainly not something that he had trained for before.

He had delegated as much as possible, leaving the Tareng force as the main defenders, he seeded the Alva forces among them. They operated the mortars, the different repeater batteries, they were the stretcher bearers and part of the quick reaction forces. They knew the capital better than anyone else so they acted as guides for the other units.

Erik was coordinating the figthing, but the Tareng members were leading it for the most part. He agreed with this as he had been stuck in the rear while he firmly believed that the commanders should be up front with the troops knowing what is going on.

The illusion spell scrolls had allowed the enemy to get in close, it wouldn't be long for them to reach the breaches.

Erik took out a big box and laid it on the ground. He pulled out spell scrolls that caused the mana around to move in agitation.

"Rebuild," Erik said as he activated the spell scroll.

The spell scroll was one of the few remaining expert level spell scrolls that had been recoverd from the royal family's armory.

A spell circle appeared on the ground, where there were several breaches piled together.

Blaack arms appeared in the broken parts of the houses and the wall that were touched by the spell circle.

These arms were gathering up the rubble that was laying across the ground, the rubble solidified and the buildings started to repair themselves as a visisble rate, there were people in the breaches as the walls came in on them, bringing rock down on them. A pillar that had been damaged recovered and the shield solidified.

The pressure on the area decreased as the mages and ranged had time to switch their aim, cutting into the would be breachers that were now hacking at the wall that was repairing itself faster than it could be destroyed even the ground was repaired, streets recovered and the ground formed into a ditch that had been worn away with time and fighting.

Erik watched the force coming off of the wall as he got a call from Evelyn Moss.

"It looks like they have mixed their normal soldiers with their strongest soldiers."

"Fortunatley we did the same," Erik said. "How are things looking.

"We can hold for some time, a few hours if we're unlucky, a day if we're lucky."

Trap formations went to work, spell scrolls that had been distributed were used like candy, using money to supplement numbers and save their fighter's strength.

Death filled the breaches as they were pushed back, but other areas were opening up.

A group made it to the wall, being hit with rocks and rolling wood, without the protection of barriers as they took out cannons and set them next to the walls.

Erik used the spell scroll fire trench, the ground underneath the wall and the feet of the attackers. The ground opened up as Erik traced out the trench, running along the line, flames from deep within the earth shot out.

There were seven thousand people on the wall it wasn't enough to cover everything as the first few groups failed, others suceeded.

They activated the cannons, which shot through the walls and were hurled backward by the recoil and the force of the explosion.

The Blood Demon army charged through the new breaches.

"Glosil reports that he has handed over control of the mortars to Yui and is moving to meet up with the rest of the company," Yao Meng reported.

With him there he can keep things stabilized with Rugrat handling the quick reaction force

"Status on the pullback?" Erik asked.

"Second line is established," Storbon said.

Erik opened his dungeon interface. "Just a bit farther," Erik muttered to himself.

"Have the first line begin pulling back."

"We have forces that have entered in high numbers in sectors nine, twelve, and three. The most breaches are in sectors nine to twelve," Storbon reported.

Erik turned, looking at the fighting that was happening all around. Masters and Elites had rushed forward in their own groups and were opening up breaches all across the walls with magical cannons.

"Focus on three and nine. We can't have them cut off our forces that are pulling back." Erik's eyes flicked to the dungeon's map, overlaying the city.

A breach was blown open, into the side of a group of defenders. People were hit with the rubble as they turned to fight off the enemy coming from another direction.

Erik pulled out an M32 and aimed; a Blood Demon soldier appeared through the breach.

Erik fired six shots as fast as he could fire, tracing a line through the breach, lighting it up with explosions and killing anyone inside. He opened the M32 as Yao Meng waited until more people filled the breach and fired.

Erik dumped and reloaded his M32 as he saw a group from the Blood Demon army pushing in.

Storbon was faster as he dropped three rounds into the group, decimating them.

Defenders rushed in from behind the wall, supporting the crumbling defensive line and pushing back those in the breach, allowing them room to collect the wounded and start pulling back.

The defenders left the walls and reorganized down on the ground as they retreated through the streets.

Erik, Yao Meng, and Storbon fired their M32s into groups of Blood Demon soldiers as they moved across the rooftops, leaving destruction in their wake and easing the pressure up on the defenders who were moving through preselected streets. It was organized mayhem at its best.

The enemy tried to flank and move through side streets only to find them filled with traps instead.

Rugrat and the Alvan army had nearly two weeks to increase the defenses in Vuzgal, with the power of the dungeon to alter the landscape and the workforce of the tireless undead. They had turned it into a hellscape as attackers poured into the massive former capital.

Even as they chased after the defenders, who were pulling back in an organized manner, they were cut down by IEDs and traps that activated after the defenders passed.

Erik checked his screen again as he reloaded his M32. They jumped from the roof they were on to a watchtower overlooking an intersection. The local roads all crossed in front of this watchtower, becoming one road heading toward the inner walls. All of the roads were like this, meant to slow an enemy if they entered the city and to create choke points.

"Fire!" the crafter guard yelled. Archers and mages in the back of the choke point or within the watchtower fired over the defenders in the mouth of the square.

A Master in the group of attackers raised her hands; a spell formation appeared in front of her.

An arrow tore through the air, breaking the air ahead of it and leaving white streamers in its path as it pierced her neck.

Her spell failed as she dropped to the ground, pulling out a healing potion.

"Focus your fire!" the commander called.

Another woman stepped out. Her sword turned red as she moved, deflecting arrows with her own power and reaction speed.

Erik, Yao Meng, and Storbon fired on her as more Masters charged into the battle.

She tried to stop the rounds but cried out as one exploded and the two others were toofast for her to defend against.

"Reinforcements are coming in!" someone from the defenders yelled out.

Erik looked over to see a wolf covered in flames and wearing black armor charging down the road. Panthers flanked him on either side, dual repeaters attached to the top of their armor.

The Alvan soldiers watched the enemy over their repeaters as they turned down side streets, spreading out.

The Blood Demon army started to react as the Alvan army depressed the triggers on their mounted dual repeaters.

One could only see every fifth explosive arrow; even the Masters could only defend under the wealth of fire.

"Hold your fire!" Erik barked. The commanders repeated the order.

The mounted forces were like a titanic wave of beast, metal, and heavy ballista repeater bolts.

The Masters of the Blood Demon army had not gotten to their position by sitting back. They looked to find cover from the charge or they rushed to meet it.

They were hit in the flank, throwing their formations into disarray as people reloaded their weapons and others withdrew.

Weapons clashed and people were nearly tossed from their panthers from the Masters' power.

A dozen magical circles appeared around one Master mage as he moved his hands around.

A few rotated around him, meeting the incoming attacks; others shot out arrows of water that cut the Alvan army's armor.

He waved his hand. Ice appeared on the ground around him, causing the panthers passing him to skid away. He waved his hand; a staff appeared in his hand and he shot out an arrow, piercing the body of someone from Alva.

He made to attack again when the Mana in the area diverged. His Strength decreased as his spells could no longer call upon the ambient Mana of the area.

Erik had used the dungeon's abilities to draw in power from the area. An axe hit the mage, sending them backward, unable to recover as panthers rushed over and mauled his body.

The Masters' attacks turned buildings into rubble. Erik didn't know who was alive or dead as the Blood Demon army who were closest suffered the most, cut down from the wild attacks from the defending Masters.

The enemy Masters started to gulp down healing potions and demanded heals from their support as the charging mounted forces raced on.

As soon as they were clear Erik didn't let the opportunity go.

"Fire!" The Blood Demon Sect didn't have time to pull themsleves together as spells, arrows, repeaters, rifles and grenades landed among them.

Erik fired his M32 at them again. Pinned in by the buildings of Vuzgal, the Blood Demon Sect were desperately trying to advance.

A mage lashed out; a black formation appeared and hit the watchtower but it only struck the barrier that surrounded the tower.

A group of Crafter's Association Masters appeared in the street and rushed into the battle.

The difference between the two groups of masters was evident.

The Crafter association guards tore through the Blood Demon Sect masters who were a half a second too slow or fought by themselves, too arrogant to ask for help or had been fighting by themselves for so long they forgot how to fight together.

Watching the Masters fight was incredible. With just their hits colliding, they could force their opponents' legs into the ground, causing the road's bricks to break and a crater to form. Their weapons were imbued with Mana; even a stray cut left marks on stones five meters away. They were chaining together techniques and combos, using their powerful bodies, their levels and attributes along with their talent in magic to clash with one another.

The Masters from the Crafter's Association met them blow for blow. The Masters from the Blood Demon army were enraged. They were supposed to dominate the field of battle but for two weeks they had been attacked with no way to fight back.

Now they were being trampled on, as if they were nothing but common soldiers. They forgot about asking for heals and charged forward, to cut down their enemy and calm the anger in their hearts.

Erik cast Ranged Heal with the other healers, empowering the Crafter's Association Masters. He looked at Storbon and Yao Meng.

"Why do I think you have a very bad idea, sir?" Storbon asked.

"Because I have a very bad idea!" Erik cackled as he aimed from the top of the battlements and unloaded his M32 into the Blood Demon army coming up the road. Storbon and Yao Meng fired with him, their rounds leaving destruction behind.

Erik drew out his rifle, storing his grenade launcher. He aimed and fired, working the action as he saw his round pierce a Master's eye and detonate, he switched aim and another lost a kneecap, a crafter's Master cutting their neck.

Another in the arm, in the head, or in their side.

Storbon and Yao Meng pulled out their rifles as well. Their aim was scary accurate.

They supported as they could, but they weren't as proficient as Erik with the rifles by a large margin.

He racked the bolt back and ejected the magazine, which disappeared into his storage ring. He slapped a new magazine in and continued to fire. He wasn't the marksman that Rugrat was, but with his fine control over his body and with his knowledge of firearms, he was the second deadliest person after Rugrat.

Even if he didn't cripple the Blood Demon Experts, he was able to wound them and help out the Crafter forces.

The Elites were severely wounded or killed while the regular soldiers fell like puppets with their strings cut.

The Masters were stronger than he thought. With his mana and body cultivation he could tell that they had tempered their bodies to a high degree. They had fought across the Fourth Realm, being born into a life of war or coming from other realms to fight. Until now they had never engaged one another in a direct flight so he had underestimated their combat strength.

The Blood Demon army and the Vuzgal defenders traded spells and blows. Buildings and streets were torn apart. The people who were caught in the spells were in worse condition.

Looks like I won't be needing to use my pills, concoctions or armor.

He dropped behind the defenses as he reloaded, some had got smart and hurled spells against the barrier that wasn't looking too sturdy anymore.

Erik checked the map, they were being pushed in all areas, but they were retreating.

Erik pulled out three spell scrolls and started to activate them as he contacted Yui.

"Yui! Use those spell scrolls, lay down attacks to cover our retreat, we're getting bogged down here," Erik yelled as he started to activate the spell scroll in his hands.

"Understood!" Yui said.

"Prepare to move!" Erik yelled. As he finished activating the spell formation.

A spell formation was completed in the sky, ice whistled through the skies as the supporting mages behind the second defenses attacked.

Hail shot through the ranks, killing and maiming those attackers who were lower than Elites.

Shields appeared around the Crafters, two of the three spell scrolls active as Erik focused on the last scroll.

The Elites had to huddle together. Many of them were terribly injured as a large spell circle appeared between the Crafter's Association defenders, who were disengaging themselves from the Blood Demon Masters. Their shields saving them from the hail as they pulled back.

The wind was shifted as the mana in the area was becoming thin with the multiple activations. A large head appeared, rising up out of the ground as if the magical circle conmnected to some hell. It looked like clay, with its savage eyes and mouth closed, as if a doll. The Blood Demon Sect soldiers sent attacks at the creature but they were stopped at the edge of the magical circle.

It continued to rise, quickly now. Its body covered in black scars and opened yellow sores.

It had two arms as large as a man was wide with rusted meat cleavers at the ends, with a tail of skulls hanging off the handle. Blood dripped from the meat cleavers.

The cricle under its feet disappeared, bering drawn into the creature creating tattoos over its body. It opened its eyes. There was a maniacal look in its eyes, a mix between childlike joy and psychotic blood thirst.

It took a step and moved forward. Sharp birds formed of white air appeared in the sky and dove toward the creature. It was hit, cutting into its body. But its magical resistance must have been high: it had deep wounds, but none of them were fatal. It only got angrier and yelled out.

"I didn't think the summoning scroll would be this powerful," Erik muttered to himself.

"Continue on to the next fallback line!" The leader of the group ordered.

The Blood Demon army changed their focus to the approaching and big cleaver-wielding creature that ignored the Vuzgal defenders.

Spells took off its flesh and arrows stuck in him, but his strength was enough to send Masters flying and to cut through mid-level Journeyman armor.

Erik wished that he had been free to charge into the fight but he had more to worry about, Storbon and Yao Meng guided him as he was studying his dungeon map, nothing escaped his eyes.

"Rugrat, sector nine is getting hammered, see if you can hit the Demons there, use a few spell scrolls," Erik said.

"Okay I see it," Rugrat cut the channel and started to coordinate the quick reaction force to whittle down the Blood Demon Sect and give the forces retreating the time that they needed.

Vuzgal defenders continued to fall back as the Masters gave them the space that they needed.

***

Domonos rode on his mount, his hands on his heavy repeaters, mounted on top of his panther's shoulder blades.

Rugrat led the charge with George. Using his knowledge of the local terrain labeled as a dungeon, he could pinpoint where the enemy was and line them up in different streets so they would hit them from the side and quickly escape.

Through the side roads, Domonos could see the rest of the mounted quick reaction force. There were Masters moving to bolster the strength of those on the ground and then the mounted forces smashing into the groups fighting to weaken the Blood Demon army.

They turned a corner, seeing a group of Blood Demon soldiers at the intersection.

George shot out a pillar of fire from his mouth as Domonos pressed the trigger on his dual repeaters.

Bolts passed through the flames, hitting the soldiers, piercing some of their armor, breaking bones and splitting flesh. Poison covering the arrows seeped into the wounds as explosive arrows blew their group apart.

They passed over the soldiers, none of them left alive. They stopped shooting and Domonos checked the ammunition he had remaining as they turned through the streets.

Their real target appeared and they increased their speed.

"Charge!" Rugrat yelled as he cast repeated spells on the bolts in his repeating ballista. His arrows punched through even Elites' armor and tossed Masters back like dolls.

With their sudden arrival, the Blood Demons weren't able to get organized by the time the mounted Alvan army met them.

Domonos pulled the pin holding the repeater to his mount and stored the repeater. He drew out his spear in flowing motions. They had practiced repeatedly so that there was no break in his movements. His panther leapt, grabbed an Elite's neck in their mouth, broke it, then tossed them to the side.

Domonos deflected an attack aimed at him and sliced at their face, then stabbed another attacker on the opposite side. He was hit in the leg but his armor protected him as one of the Alvan soldiers behind him cut down the man who had sliced at his leg.

They plowed through, just actions and reactions. Domonos's spear glowed with a gray light; his spear blurred, moving in his hands as if it were nothing but a broom handle but hit like a hammer, displaying its full weight and strength.

It was an Expert-level spear; that, as well as buffing concoctions and spells, allowed him to compete with Masters.

He looked around, checking on his comrades. They were three-quarters through the enemy's lines. His people were holding up well, but they had various wounds covering them as they fought.

He saw an arrow fly, hitting one in the eye, causing them to slump on their mount.

"Younger!" Domonos yelled out but the man was stuck in his saddle, dead.

Domonos looked at where the archer was, spells already raining down around them.

They crossed the last enemy, rushing away from the active battlefield. Those in the rear threw out smoke grenades behind them, covering their path of retreat and blocking the enemy from seeing their backs.

The Alvan army were like reapers as they rode. Appearing like ghosts, slamming into the enemy and then pushing onward, leaving a harvest of death in their wake.

But they weren't truly ghosts. They reached a safe area, slowing their pace, and moved to take care of the wounded. Some could treat themselves; others were missing limbs or were affected by a curse or poison that wouldn't be easily dealt with.

People from Younger's section confirmed his death. Sergeant Edwards collected his storage rings on a length of string and put his body into a different storage ring, storing his mount in his own creature storage device.

He wasn't the first loss. But they all gritted their teeth, pushed the tears down as their grief turned into anger. Their best way to deal with being attacked, with losing one of their own, was to go out there and to claim the lives of the bastards attacking them.

"We're being ordered back to the second line," Rugrat said.

"Yes, sir." Domonos pulled himself back together, just blocking off his emotions. He didn't have the time to deal with them. He had people relying on him; he could deal with his grief later.

Rugrat held his eyes and clapped him on the shoulder.

There was no need for words. They knew that the other understood what they were going through but they were in leadership positions. They couldn't crumble; they couldn't show weakness, especially at a time like this.

"Once the wounded are stabilized, we'll move out," Rugrat said.

***

Erik used healing spells on himself to speed up the recovery time from the Stone Skin and Defender's Might when Glosil found him.

"How are we looking?" Erik had put Glosil with Hiao Xen. Now he took command; Hiao Xen remained back, ready to take over if Erik and Rugrat died.

They were kept in separate spots so if a rogue magical attack hit them, the defenders wouldn't lose all of their command staff in one hit.

"Nearly forty thousand. Those Masters and Elites came in much faster than we were thinking they would be able to," Glosil said, trying to soften the blow.

"Looks like the general on the other side didn't want to follow the regular rule book either," Erik said.

He got a message through his sound transmission device, letting him know that all of the forces in the outer city were pulled back or in one of the secret tunnels, on their way back.

"The Mana barrier is adjusting," Erik said to Yao Meng; he sent the message as Erik used his interface.

The barrier collapsed and then reappeared, reducing in size and covering only the inner city while the mana formations in the outer city continued to work, reducing the ambient mana in the outer city.

Each of the pillars had been filled with traps, making it hard to gain access and destroy the mana gathering formations.

"Now their Mana barriers will only have a limited effect in the broken-up city. When they come for the walls, we can use the repeaters and our ranged attackers and they won't be just shooting into Mana barriers. This is where we will end the Blood Demon army."

"What about any trump cards that they're holding onto?" Glosil asked, as he kept his voice quiet.

"We'll just have to hope that our trump cards are stronger. How are the civilians?"

"They've retreated into the valley, a number of them volunteered to fight and assist they're with the Tareng forces but there are some that are assisting our medics, the mages and the mortars, I checked to make sure that they all took oaths before they began."

"Good, maximize our effectiveness," Erik said he rekaxed a bit and rubbed his face, taking a seat.

"What are our casualties looking like?"

"Three for Alva, two to six hundred for Tareng force, not sure who will make it or not. They paid for it, estimate seven to ten thousand died in the attack," Glosil said.

"Who?" Erik asked.

"Vang, Chang Ju and Su Dara."

"Shit," Erik said, moving his feet on the gravel as it seemed to turn colder. Erik cleared his throat, he couldn't focus on them right now.

"How many rounds do we have for the mortars?"

"Enough to fire at rapiud rate for thirty minutes, can stretch them for continuous fire with them all going, an hour and a half, maybe two?"

"What do you think about our next moves?" Erik asked.

"They still outnumber us but the margin is slight, with their thirty thousand to our nine or so thousand. We still hold the defenses and our defenses are tighter with support from ranged elements, medics and such," Glosil paused. "I'm interested in how many of them will remain after tonight."

Erik looked at Glosil to explain further.

"So they are under oath, yes, but there are ways to get around that oath. The Blood Demon Sect, especially in the last week has been reducing in size with desertions. Their morale is at an all time low. Why not, instead of attacking them head on, we talk to them."

"I think we're past that point," Erik said.

"I don't mean face to face I mean that we get people with volume increasing enchantments on the wall, vowing that the Blue

Lotus and the Crafter's association will hunt them down, that there is no escape anymore. I'm willing to bet that a lot of people will try to run and escape," Glosil said with a serious expression.

"Smart, they're tired hungry and demoralized. Okay, talk to the Tareng people and see if they're up for it. At the same time, Storbon.

I want you to send out the assassination squads and the special teams out once the Blood Demon army has regrouped themselves. I want to know what is happening over there. They're not to kill anyone unless they have to. Now, we just have to hold this wall. If we retreat, then the people in the inner city won't be able to survive," Erik said.

"Should we take the undead as support?" Storbon said.

With their dungeon control ability, they were the second best controllers over the undead forces of Vuzgal. With them commanding the undead then they could maximize their combat strength.

"I don't want to expose them to the undead too much right now. It would be more of an impact if the first time they have a real fight with the undead is when operation rising coffin begins."

"Yes sir," Storbon nodded to Erik and then stepped away to send the sound transmission.

"What about Fred and his people?" Glosil asked.

"They're a trump card like the skeletons, one that I don't want to use until we have to. Once we do then we lose the element of surprise. With Fred growing his trees throughout Vuzgal, the dungeon, and the assassination squads, we should know every move of the enemy. We also have plenty of spell scrolls to use still," Erik said. "No sense in showing our hand if we don't need to."

The wall turned silent as Erik stopped talking. They looked out at the outer city, where the sounds of fighting had finally stopped. There were small fires burning here and there, as well as distant noises from the Blood Demon army moving in the darkness.

Behind them, the wall was filled with activity: people moving supplies, others standing guard, ready to fight at a moment's notice, wounded being carried and rushed to the casualty collection points where they were attended to and different commanders coordinating with one another to make sure that there was no part of the wall that was left undefended.

People were preparing and checking formations. The mortars, which had been moved back, were being cleaned and checked over by Yui and his people. Ammunition and food were being brought up to the front lines, with people watching the walls, their eyes scanning for the slightest movement.

They had been bloodied by the Blood Demon army other than when Olivia had sent the Tareng forces into the middle of the Blood Demon Sect, this was the first time that they had directly engaged the enemy. It was the second time that they had taken casualties as well.

They had been chased for days, but this was the first time that they had fought one another, drawing blood on either side.

The atmosphere had changed, with the forces under Erik's command becoming closer and trusting one another. They saw the effectiveness of his plan and the limited casualties that they had taken relative to the Blood Demon army.

"There are some saying that while they might be the Blood Demon army, you are the true demon general," Glosil said.

"Oh?" Erik queried, looking at him.

"When someone is your enemy, then they step into hell," Glosil said.

Erik let out a snort and shrugged, not acknowledging or denying the nickname. "How are the supplementary mortar gunners?"

"We had them all make oaths, as you said. It's really simple and easy to drop mortars down a tube and it allows one platoon to operate forty of them, giving us a platoon free to fight," Glosil reported.

"Good. I'll need that other platoon to assist the repeater gunners from the other groups, and act as close-in support with their M32s and rifles. Make sure you switch the sections off—get Yui's people to head out as scouts first. They've been on the mortars the entire time and they're probably a bit annoyed they haven't had any direct action," Erik said.

"I will pass word to Lieutenant Yui," Glosil said.

"Has there been any message from the Crafter's Association or the Blue Lotus?" Erik asked.

"If there has, I haven't heard anything from Hiao Xen."

"it's a week since we sent their people back," Erik said. *Just how long will it take for them to confirm that it isn't a plague to send people to help? We have bloodied and hurt the Blood Demon army, but we have only taken out two-fifths of their army.*

***

Elder Lu was looking over a pile of reports when there was a knock at his door. "Come in!" He put the papers away.

Cui Chin entered the room, his face dark as he approached.

"We know who did it," Cui Chin said without preamble. "It was the Hang-Nim Alliance, in collaboration with General Isa Ulalas. The Blood Demon Sect took away the man she loved; he died and she was being forced to marry another man. She went to their enemies and seems that they came up with some plan. We do not know the specifics. Though we know that the Blood

Demon Sect has been having troubles with contacting the army under her command. We know that Ulalas met with some people from the Hang-Nim Alliance. Connecting the dots, there's the fact that we can't get anything from the Blood Demon Sect but the people from the Hang-Nim Alliance are being really friendly with us and have been making vague inquiries to the Crafter's Association."

"That will be enough for me to move the Blue Lotus army." Elder Lu sent a message. It wasn't long until there was another knock on the door.

"Come in!" Elder Lu said. General Lei Huo marched through the door as Elder Lu started talking, stopping her from bowing in greeting.

"The Hang-Nim Alliance seems to be behind this plan. It is my plan to ask for the Hang-Nim Alliance's assistance in this matter. We can use this as a guise to teleport our forces into their cities and then take them from the inside. What about the Blue Lotus forces near Vuzgal?"

"I have organized two armies, each thirty thousand strong, with the fastest mounts. Cui Chin has talked to a city state in the Chaotic Lands, securing their assistance quietly. Once the seven days are cleared and the people are confirmed to not have some kind of plague, then they can use the totem to move over in seconds and head for Vuzgal. It will take them just two days to reach Vuzgal."

Elder Lu thought on the reports he had just read. "Do you think that the people at Vuzgal can hold out that long?"

Lei Huo looked unsure what to say.

"Speak freely."

"I do not know. If it was just our forces and the Crafter's Association, I would say no. The Tareng city is one of the weakest neutral trading cities in the fourth realm as there are no strong cities or sects in the area. Their combat strength is low, with most of them being weakened by the concoction. They have had successive victories, with Erik and Rugrat leading the offensive. Now, they can't delay any longer. They lost their exterior walls, yes; being in the city will make it hard for them to be protected by the Mana barriers. The roads are large; they can still move their army around in a number of ways. We have reports saying that there are still thirty thousand soldiers on the side of the Blood Demon Sect." Lei Huo shrugged. "Will they last? I don't know for sure. If they had the same numbers as the enemy, I would say that they could. They have a defense force of nearly twenty thousand if we include the undead."

Elder Lu pulled out a scroll and put it on the desk. "This is an instantaneous teleportation scroll, which can teleport anything within a one-hundred-meter-square area. I release my personal guards to you, as well as the headquarters guards. Teleport as soon as you can and both of you make sure that the plan is set for the Hang-Nim Alliance. When this is confirmed to not be a plague, I want the alliance and the Blood Demon army destroyed," Elder Lu said.

Cui Chin and Lei Huo hid the shaking in their hands and bodies as they bowed to Elder Lu. Lei Huo had no room to refuse the instantaneous teleportation scroll, an item that was rare even in the Seventh Realm. The two of them quickly left his office.

Elder Lu sent a message to the head of the Crafter's Association, telling her everything that he had found. She shared all that her people had found, her voice shaking in anger. She was a crafter by training; she didn't have the training that Elder Lu did as a merchant to keep her emotions in check.

"This time tomorrow the Hang-Nim Alliance won't exist anymore!" she declared vociferously.

"What are your thoughts toward the Blood Demon Sect?" Elder Lu asked.

"It will be difficult to destroy them completely unless we want to have a drawn-out battle. We don't have that sort of strength readily available and it would make us look like tyrants." She gnashed her teeth. She might be enraged, but she hadn't lost her senses.

"Increase the sales commission on them for buying and selling any services. Push for the others to agree. I think it would be easy to do so," Elder Lu said.

She let out a cold laugh. "Mercy in the short term but death in the long."

Elder Lu smiled as she understood his words and their implications. It was one of the joys of talking with competent people.

With the Blue Lotus and the Crafter's association charging the Blood Demon Sect more, it might not be much in the short term but over time it would pile up. Slowly the Blood Demon Sect would lose strength, few people wanted to join a sect that was an eyesore to two associations that were pillars of the ten realms reaching into the third realm all the way to the ninth. Less people would want to join the sect that had higher costs.

The Fourth Realm was a realm of unending battle. Wars cost an incredible amount of money. With these kinds of changes, the Blood Demon Sect would lose strength gradually, running through money at an ever increasing rate. If they gave up quickly, they could drop to the Third Realm and try to consolidate their power there. Even with the dungeons they controlled, they would have to sell more dungeon time slots to outsiders to get more money.

Indeed, it was a slow, painful death instead of a war at one's gates.

The Blue Lotus didn't forget its friends...or its enemies.

Chapter: Among the Wreckage

Ulalas looked over her remaining numbers. The sun rose over the battlefield. The exterior walls were broken and the Blood Demon army easily fit inside the city walls.

It was a city meant for millions. There were multiple watchtowers and smaller walls that the defenders had used as fallback positions.

The city was littered with traps. Random areas would be covered in poison gas; others would explode from an IED underground. Trap formations would activate seemingly at random. The death toll wasn't large but it showed how long the enemy had been preparing for them. These distractions also made all of the soldiers of the Blood Demon army jumpy and restless, never knowing where death might hide.

Their Mana barrier formations' coverage was slim as well, encountering walls, destroyed buildings, and so on. The uneven terrain greatly reduced their effectiveness.

She had them sit in the city, to recover. For the first time, they were able to relax.

She had made an oath with the Blood Demon Sect, like those under her command, but there was a funny thing with oaths. If you made an oath to look after someone, if you thought the best way to look after them was to kill them, then you could kill them. Now if the oath said, to look after someone, to make sure others and you didn't harm them in any way or kill them, then you truly couldn't kill them.

Simple oaths were a great assurance, like being under oath and telling someone the truth. For more complicated oaths, then there were plenty of loopholes that one could take advantage of.

She had sworn an oath to do what was best for the Blood Demon Sect. As she had been promoted, her oath had become looser with each position as she needed the ability to order others to do things that might not be the best for them but would be best for the sect.

Now she thought it was best for the Blood Demon Sect to be destroyed. It meant that she would die if she didn't do everything in her power to make sure that came to be.

***

Yui listened as the boots above him moved away. He slowly pushed up on the boards and peeked out, looking to see whether there was anyone nearby.

He pushed the boards to the side and got out of the hole, a blade in his hand. He moved toward the doorway that the boots had gone out of. He peeked around the corner, seeing a group of people slumped against a building.

Others came out from the hidden passage, the last replacing the cover.

Yui pulled out his crossbow, tapping it; he looked at three others and put his finger to his lips. He cast a Silence spell on his arrow and then on the other arrows that they had loaded.

He checked to see whether there was anyone else nearby.

Not allowing him time to think, he stood and walked out of the house. He fired his arrow. It caught a man looking in his direction in the neck. The Silence spell activated on him; he fell to the ground without making a noise even as they grabbed at their neck. One stood up and pulled on his sword before he was hit in the neck as well. The poison on the arrows went to work as the last one who was looking away got the arrow through his back and into his heart; he arched in pain and then fell to the ground.

They looked around to see whether they had been discovered as they stole across the ground, moving to the bodies. They grabbed the bodies and pulled them back to the house that they had come from.

Dirt was tossed over the blood stains in the street before they broke up into teams of two, moving to different observation posts that they had established in the city already and that their aerial forces had been able to check for enemy occupants.

Yui got to a temple. He had to jump up what looked like a broken wall. He found a ledge and pulled himself up, dropping a rope for his partner. Imani, from the special teams, quickly scrambled up the rope and pulled it up after her. He kept moving higher, into the peak of the temple. The spire was broken and opened in places, allowing them to see out over the capital.

"Good spot," Imani confirmed.

Yui nodded. He had been talking to Glosil and Domonos to find the best observation points. With his knowledge of mortars, he knew that they were only as effective as the coordinates they were given.

"You take the northeast. I'll take the northwest," Yui said.

"Got it." Imani nodded as they looked for breaks in the walls of the spire for the best vantage point.

***

Back at the command center, the information from the scouting teams and assassins who had re-entered the outer city came back.

Rugrat listened closely. He had a dungeon map of where people were in the capital, but to know which groups had commanders in it, or which were Masters, they needed eyes on the different groups.

He and Erik had wanted to go out, but they were the commanders of the army. They had been able to fight in the moment before but if they went out on purpose, then others would try to keep them back.

"Your orders?" Hiao Xen asked Rugrat.

"Hold," Rugrat said.

The people in the command center looked at Rugrat. They had the Blood Demon army dead to rights.

"Let them get comfortable—let them relax their security. Then we'll hit them. We want them to waste time for as long as possible. The more time, the closer our reinforcements and the less people affected by the Blood Demon concoction."

***

Night settled down over Vuzgal as the Blood Demon army started to move with purpose. Siege weapons were put down in different locations, hidden from the Vuzgal inner wall, but visible to the observation posts across the city.

The asteroid belt that hung in the sky above the Fourth Realm lit up the night as the Blood Demon army started their siege, attacking the barrier and walls of the inner city.

Imani and Yui called out targets and updated them in real time.

The forces inside the inner city retaliated with the dungeon-created catapults, spell scrolls, formation-enhanced mages, and mortars.

Only a few from each were picked out to actually target the available targets that the observation posts had found. It made them look like random hits and hid the fact that there were observers in the city.

Generals and commanders were the biggest targets, then Masters after that, with siege weaponry thrown in after that.

"Observation posts, this is Command. You are cleared to use firearms," Command said.

"About time." Imani pulled out her rifle and cast the Silence spell on it. She aimed at a building she had been watching for some time. A group of officers hid outside. "Yui! I've got three commanders in a circle."

Yui moved over to where Imani was set up and checked where she was aiming, looking at them in the darkness through the sights on his rifle. "You take the left and middle; I'll take the right?"

"Works. On my mark. Let me know when you've got your target."

"Got it," he said.

"Three, two, one—mark!" They only felt recoil as the Silence spells made it impossible to hear the weapons.

The two commanders dropped to the ground. They both worked their bolt and aimed on the new target. Imani hit them just as they turned. They dropped but started crawling as Yui put a second round into them.

They searched for new targets, looking out of the broken spire for commanders and other high value-looking targets, as hell rained down around the invaders.

Most people started to hide in the different houses in the outer city as they seemed safer with the amount of people dying outside.

The night was not a quiet one as the groups exchanged fire. Imani's eyes burned from the smoke, the explosives, debris and dust that had been tossed up over the night.

No one of the allies inside the Vuzgal inner city slept. They were watching as attack after attack rained down on their Mana barrier, standing tall in front of the attacks but seeming so slim that it could collapse at any time.

Although it was a disturbing night for the people in the inner city, it was another terrifying and all-too-similar situation for the Blood Demon army as they once again went through hell. A hell that they thought was over as they saw Vuzgal's walls.

The whistling noises would forever be burned into their minds: a sound that told them that death was near and there was nowhere for them to escape.

Still, they put in all their effort with the attack and worked like slaves through the night.

As morning came, the city, which had been an ancient ruin moderately repaired, now once again showed the signs of fresh battle.

***

"Well, today is the day," Yui said as the sun started to come up.

Imani looked through the holes in the spire, looking over the damaged walls around Vuzgal. "What day?" She scanned for targets.

"The day that the people from the Blue Lotus and the Crafter's Association will either be cleared and they can act, or they will be confirmed to have the plague and we'll be screwed, with no reinforcements," Yui said.

"You're really positive for an officer, you know that?" Imani said.

"Don't worry—I'm gunning for a spot on the special teams as soon as I can." Yui laughed.

She smiled as the dawn turned into Morningside, fire was still exchanged back and forth between the groups. Some smart people hid their magical cannons in different buildings to shoot out of or used their trebuchets in courtyards, making them harder to find until after they attacked. The mages were the worst as many of them didn't need a direct line of sight at their enemy to unleash their spells, so they were hidden all over the place. The Blood Demon army had all been pulled into the city, but teams headed out into the battlefield and collected the dead, dumping them in several large open spaces in the city.

"Command, this is Observation Post Thirteen. Message, over."

"This is Command. State your message," the man in command said.

"I am looking at what looks like Blood Demon army soldiers collecting the dead and then putting them into open areas under Mana barriers. I wanted to know if we have any information on this being a practice of the Blood Demon Sect?" As she heard Yui's boots scrape on the ground, he looked over to her and then back out on the capital.

"It's hard to see but they're doing it on this side as well," he confirmed in a low whisper.

"Observation Post Thirteen, this is Command. We don't think that this is something to worry about over."

"Command, did you check with someone?" Imani asked.

"Yes, I did," Command said back. They must have been from the Crafter's Association or from the Blue Lotus because they stopped caring about how they spoke on the sound transmission device, annoyed at her question.

"Command, this is Observation Post Thirteen. Who did you ask?"

"Just tell me the targets and what they look like," the man said, in a tired voice.

"Chain of command is nice but sometimes it doesn't work." Yui pulled out his sound transmission device and started talking into it.

"Understood, Command. Observation Post Thirteen out." Imani cut the connection to the annoyed man.

"Talked to Glosil. He asked Hiao Xen directly. He is looking into it," Yui said.

"Thanks. Didn't think that it would be so difficult to get information." Imani sighed.

"Well, that's what happens with three organizations smashed together into one military. Well, that is what I was told by Erik, at least. Apparently, it nearly never goes well unless they have a common enemy and the same background at least. Then he talked about an air force, navy, and army." Yui shook his head and went to staring out over the city.

"They have some strange sayings." Imani scoffed.

***

"Bodies collected in open spaces?" Lei Huo sounded confused. "Why would they do that and not just put them in storage rings or toss them into holes?"

"I'm not sure." Cui Chin looked through information he had been sent by different people who were looking for anything related.

A new message came in to Cui Chin.

"It's a ritual!" the researcher said, looking through the archives of the Blood Demon Sect.

"What?" Cui Chin asked.

"It is a ritual that gives them the name Blood Demon Sect. They use the bodies, combine it with Alchemy and a formation—the bodies turn into demons!"

Cui Chin was pulling out a sound talisman.

"How do you defeat it?" he asked the researcher.

There was a pause as they looked up the information.

"Destroy the bodies completely, the formations or the Alchemy concoction. Once it is done, it will be nearly impossible to reverse. At least, there is not a solution in these notes," the researcher said.

Cui Chin cut them off and used his sound transmission device, sending a message to Hiao Xen, repeating everything that he had heard.

***

"All observation posts, this is Command," Hiao Xen said, talking to everyone in the field. "I want the bodies that are being piled together to be reported in and marked. These are supposedly ritual sites. Look for formations or Alchemy concoctions in the area."

Imani and Yui looked at each other as they started to call out the locations of the different open mass graves.

"Well shit, it must be one hell of a ritual!" Imani said.

The defenders didn't play any games anymore, directly targeting the siege weapon locations and the points of interest that the observation points had marked. Their attack, which had been like scattered rain, now hit with deadly precision as attacks rained down on the ritual sites, not allowing anyone into or out of them.

The Blood Demon army suddenly charged forward. The defenders, who had been watching, quickly moved to their positions. The mortars and other siege weapons changed their aim onto the armies massing and running forward.

Formations that were around the dead started to glow with a red light. Between the arranged formations, lines appeared, connecting them all. People inside the barriers smashed down potion bottles that were filled with black and red blood, soaking the bodies inside.

A tremendous amount of power was drawn in from the surrounding area to the open grave sites, the new ritual sites. The bodies that were grouped together made cracking noises; they started to move, as though there were something alive underneath them. They started to writhe and move, melding into one another. The blood potion mixed with the Mana that was drawn in, entering the bodies and something inside them.

The power from the surrounding area dissipated on one of the ritual sites as the corpses moved. They had been fused together—mounted beasts, humans, armor, and weapons creating an abomination covered in blood.

It stood up, looking roughly humanoid, with two stubby legs. It let out a terrible and miserable wail. Even the veterans gripped their weapons tighter as their faces paled at the tremendous bloodthirst and power contained within the creature.

Its right arm peeled back to reveal dead mages. Mana distorted around the mages, as if broken pieces of spells from each of them were forced together, firing out a chaotic blast of Mana that hit Vuzgal's Mana barrier.

Another and then yet another wail came as the blood demons were formed.

A mortar struck the first raised corpse demon, tearing off bodies. It took a step back, before regaining its balance and pushing forward. Its leg power caused the buildings to shake around it as it wailed and shot out another Mana Blast. Spell scrolls were activated, and ranged attackers concentracted their fire.

Attacks hit it, causing it to lose more bodies. It became smaller, but the remaining bodies that it was constructed from melded back together in front of Imani's eyes.

There were seven massive blood demons about the size of a five-story house, while there were around thirty smaller blood demons between two and three stories tall all being raised across Vuzgal.

One of the larger blood demons opened its chest, revealing mage corpses inside. It fired a Mana bolt. The twisted Mana lost a great amount of power as it flew, but as it smacked into the Mana barrier, it was still stronger than fifty magical cannons.

Fire shifted from the army to the blood demons. The defenders were left to directly engage the army attackers as they rushed through the streets and alleyways. The Blood Demons had not been idle and had been working out paths that would allow them access through the city to the inner walls.

Under the attacks of the focused fire, they could only engage two or three at a time, shifting fire away from the Army.

"Well, I fucking hope that they don't have the plague because we need reinforcements now!" Imani picked out a commander and fired on them. The mortars and the large-scale magical attacks were damaging the blood demons but they weren't able to destroy them.

She pulled out a spell scroll and started to activate it and her communication device. "Focus on destroying the ritual sites. Better to take them out before they can become a threat!"

Chapter: Seven Titans

"Well, fuck," Rugrat said as he heard the information coming in. "Erik?"

"I'm open to ideas," Erik said.

"Burn through the spell scrolls, activate every damn trap that we have. Take out as much of the army as possible. Destroy the small blood demons and then we can focus on the big ones?" Rugrat offered.

"Sounds about the best plan we've got. We'll put everything on the line. All of the guards that can wield a weapon will engage; the ones in bad shape will be as a reserve. Masters target the demi-demons. Have Fred and his people help us. Observation posts, go for commanders—full strength mortars. Break out the M32s as well and fire repeaters like the government is paying for the ammunition. We need to hold out for three more days. Just enough time for the higher-ups to confirm there is no plague today, then send people and then for them to travel over to here. Make sure the reinforcements know what the hell we're dealing with right now."

Erik sounded calm and collected but Rugrat could tell he was ruffled. Magical battles and enchanted firearms, that made sense. Using the corpses of the dead to give rise to demons? It was not your regular Tuesday anymore!

"Why does it have to be demons? Couldn't it be like cute goblin healers or something?" Rugrat muttered under his breath.

"Demons are bad, but no one wants to have to deal with Fibbles," Hiao Xen said with a haunted look on his face.

"All right, you're scaring me, Hiao Xen. What did they do to you?"

"They tried to sing," Hiao Xen said.

Dude has some serious issues. Rugrat nodded as if he understood.

"We need to remain strong on the walls. Deploy Masters through the underground tunnels to intercept the demons and titans. Take away the Blood Demon army's new support. We have the Elites and the soldiers hold the line. Ask Fred and his people for their help. They'll need to not only fight the titans and demons, but they'll be in the middle of the enemy, so they'll need to be the strongest people we have," Erik said.

Hiao Xen nodded, looped into the channel as well. He started to talk on his communication device to get the strongest Masters ready and deployed to the battlefield.

"The undead are good fighters but they're simplistic in their actions. They'll back up the defenders on the wall. Have the mortars be replaced by the people we have been training and are oathed in. Rugrat, I want you with the army and a group of undead. You will act as our quick reaction force. The fighters who are affected by the concoction will be our reserve force. Glosil will be our link to Hiao Xen. I will remain on the wall and command from here. Rifles and M32s are free to be used," Erik said.

"Understood," Rugrat said.

They were using nearly all of the trump cards that they had left. It was Go Time.

***

The demons and the titans were large and slow as they moved toward the inner walls of Vuzgal. They would fire off the occasional Mana Blast when they could. Each blast seemed to take a lot of energy out of them as they advanced slowly.

They weren't alone, either as there were Masters grouped with them, protecting them.

Around the approaching demons, the defenders' Masters ran through tunnels, appearing in the outer city.

The Blood Demon soldiers had reached the inner wall, hurling spells and ranged attacks where they could to try to cover their advance.

They didn't rush forwards, taking their time to cover their advance, they were wary, tired and scared, only being pushed forward by their oaths that wouldn't allow them to retreat.

Special Team One and Two had been scrambled, their target one of the smaller blood demons. They were much weaker than the titans, but that didn't mean that they would be any less deadly.

Imani had been tracking the demon and the group of thirty Masters grouped around it with their Mana barriers covering them and the demon. The Demon left a trail of destruction in it's wake, walking through buildings taking a couple of blows to break them, sending it's defenders running for cover from the falling rocks and building.

It entered an open marketplace with remains of wooden stalls, the buildings around the square in a state of disrepair with craters and signs of fighting marring the surroundings. with all of it's defenders grouping together out in the middle of the square, exposed and all alone.

Hitting them from range would only serve to alert the Masters where they were. Niemm and Roska had set up an ambush with their teams. They were hiding in a row of broken buildings along the road that the large demon needed to pass.

"Fire in the hole!" Han Wu said as he powered his activating formation.

Formations buried under the road and an IED went off underneath the Masters. The barrier formation was shattered as the demon stumbled backward, its body covered in shrapnel and cuts across its body from the wind blades called up by one of the formations.

"Fire!" Roska called. All of the special teams were armed with the new M32s from Alva, they fired into the blast zone as one. The Masters were like cockroaches; even with the element of surprise, a number of them had lifesaving items that kept them alive.

"Advance!" Roska yelled. She turned her team toward the demon as Niemm turned his to face the group of Masters who had been walking in front of the demon.

A wind cut through the air, revealing bodies of Masters on the ground, nearly twenty of them lying on the ground.

The special team didn't need orders.

Niemm saw two moving on the ground. Severely wounded but getting back on his feet, he fired his repeater into them at point blank range. They flopped backward from the impacts. The arrows seemed to have their own eyes, piercing through the openings in their armor as they dropped to the ground. Two new tombstones appeared.

Deni shot an arrow into a wounded man; they had the presence of mind to interpose their armor. The enchanted arrow exploded on impact, peppering the man with shrapnel. Rapid-acting poison that had covered the arrow entered the man's body as he staggered, grabbing at his body where the poison had entered, and dropped to the ground.

Setsuko fired her arrows but the soot-covered Master used their staff, deflecting the arrows, and cast a spell to deflect those that it couldn't get with their staff.

A wail came from the demon but they didn't even pause in their attacks.

Lucinda, who was on an open angle to the mage, fired her M32. A barrier appeared and the round exploded. But the mage was unaffected as spell formations appeared around them. Tian Cui had the highest Agility and appeared behind the mage. Their sneer turned into a look of horror as the poisoned blade stabbed into their back, draining them of Strength as their spells disappeared and they dropped to the ground. Tian Cui jumped back, dodging an arrow from a Master and sending a curse at them, slowing their reactions. As the bow user returned to speeds like a normal human from the curse, Storbon appeared at their side. His spear went through their armpit, making them cry out. Yao Meng fired an arrow at a Master who was charging forward, slowing their advance. The shot forced the Master to focus on defending. Yuli buffed Storbon and Yawen, who dodged underneath a spear aimed for his head. They swung down the spear as Yawen jumped to the side and rolled away. They kept coming for him, their spear jabbing at Yawen. He danced more than he fought; he jumped back and fired his rifle. The Master was pushed back, leaving trails of blood on the ground as Yawen jumped to his feet, that spear chasing him once again.

"Yawen, grenades!" Lucinda yelled.

Yawen jumped to the side and pulled Storbon with him. The two of them rolled away as the exposed spear wielder made to charge forward, only to get hit in the front with an M32 round. They were tossed backward as Lucinda kept firing. Storbon and Yawen got to their feet, with their weapons ready.

They had greatly increased their Strength, but the Masters were still powerful, much stronger than them in not only their attributes but their techniques. The special team was able to hold their ground with the advanced weapons that they could employ.

All of their actions flowed together as five more Blood Demon army Masters joined their allies.

As Storbon and Yawen had been fighting, the others had rifles or repeaters in their hands.

The Masters charged forward after them.

Deni's target dodged suddenly, making her miss her attack. As her attacker faced Deni, they did not notice Setsuko aiming for them.

Setsuko's round pierced their leg and exploded; the master went down, screaming in pain. Only their strong body extending their time left in this world.

Niemm shot at a spear-wielding Master running forward. The arrow hit their armor, making them grimace as they launched their spear in the air.

Yao Meng cried out as the spear hit him in the leg.

Tian Cui fired. The Master with shoulder length black hair defended against her attack and launched one against Yawen who was next to her. Tian Cui's body glowed green as her speed and strength increased. Storbon attacked the black haired Master, forcing her to defend. Yawen placed his life in Storbon's hands as he launched forward; his body showed a red glow as he left a trail of blood behind, cutting the black haired Master's stomach open.

The Master turned, her face filled with rage as her power reached a new high. Yawen's face was grim; he had used a lot of Strength in his recent strike.

The bleeding Master pushed Storbon, hitting him in the chest with such strength that a snapping noise could be heard on the battlefield.

Bullets and arrows threaded through the fight around them. Deni's struck a target, forcing them back as she kept on pumping arrows into them. Lucinda's bullet was explosively enchanted and went off, the force of the spell exploding, blowing them to the side, opening up their defenses and killing another badly wounded Master. Deni's arrows found purchase as the Master looked at her with questions in his eyes as he died.

Ghost-like spears appeared from the ground, finishing off the wounded of the Blood Demon Masters and those who were close to dying.

The three remaining Masters dodged the ghost spear attacks, while also watching Special Team One, giving the Masters no time to counterattack.

Tian tried to fire on another Master but her gun jammed. Niemm's target threw up a barrier; his hasty shot missed while Lucinda's new explosion destroyed their barrier and Storbon launched his spear into their chest.

They were tossed back as one Master used a talisman, that both pushed others back and increased their speed dramatically as they fled.

The other two also used their different escape items, running from the battlefield.

Deni rushed over to Yao Meng's side. Blood covered the ground and a tombstone appeared above it.

***

Roska and her team all knew their roles as they had gone over their plan of attack as they were preparing the ambush. Gong Jin, Tully, and Davos would distract the demon. Yang Zan and Roska would provide support: Yang Zan with healing, buffs, and ranged attacks while Roska disrupted magical attacks. Simms and Xi were floaters and would switch with the tanks if they needed to. Otherwise, they would harass from the sides and do as much damage as possible.

Han Wu and Imani were long range, using Han Wu's modified M32 which had two sockets, not the original one and he had worked on the rounds himself. He'd combined his knowledge of formations and explosives creating rounds that could shoo further and do two to three times the amount of damag as a regular

M32. With him supressing an area and Imani's sniping with her new Expert bow.

They had to completely trust that Special Team One would protect their backs as they fought the demon. If they allowed their attention to wander, then it could very well be a lethal mistake.

The demon had been knocked back by the attacks and it let out a wail.

Gong Jin let out a yell of his own as he executed a sword attack. His body glowed with power as Roska used a spell scroll, buffing her party's Strength and Agility.

Yang Zan and Imani were firing arrows at the demon, trying to find an area not covered in the armor of the dead used to create this abomination.

Said abomination's head opened as it fired out a Mana Blast. Its attack hit the ground behind Gong Jin. The buff from the spell scroll had increased his speed and threw off the demon's aim as it couldn't move its head as fast as Gong Jin could run.

Gong Jin circled back and sliced through the demons leg, making it bow outward as it twisted. Imani's bow glowed purple as the power from the bow leached into the arrow as it was released. It crackled through the air and struck the demon's shoulder, piercing through the armor there and then detonating, taking a chunk of flesh with it.

Davos used his shield to deflect the demon's fist. His feet left behind two lines in the ground as he was pushed back; his face paled as a red curse appeared around him.

Yang Zan sent heals to help Davos recover as Tully, who Davos had been covering for, stabbed up through the demon's leg, the same that Gong Jin had attacked, weakening it further.

She pulled out her spear and sliced at the leg again, jumping back as the demons second fist came at her.

"Grenade!" Han Wu barked as he clicked his grenade launcher back together. He peppered the demon with explosive shots. The demon was forced back but it didn't have any greatly visible damage. The last two grenades of the magazine Han Wu cast Piercing Shot on.

They exploded deep inside the demon. The shrapnel tore into the demon's legs, forcing it to drop forward onto it's knees, using its arms to support itself.

Poison, applied generously to all of Team Two's weapons, appeared on the bodies of the demon; purple snakes twisted and writhed in the demon's shoulder, causing its bloody skin to turn black as the corruption advanced.

Tully ran forward, but misplaced her feet and fell forward.

The demon lashed out with a fist, hitting her. She only just got her spear in the way; she cried out as her arm was broken by the impact.

Davos and Gong Jin attacked, but their attacks hit armor as the demon made to smack Tully again. A green shield snapped around her as a green glow covered Roska's hands; she had just been able to cast Attribute Shield as Tully was tossed to the side instead of being smashed into paste.

Tully hit a wall along the side of the street. Dust sprinkled down on her as Yang Zan fired ranged healing spells in her direction with one hand and fired his repeater with the other. Xi and Simms fired into the demon's exposed back, making it arch in pain from the impacts.

Imani was moving through the rubble at the edge of the street. She pulled back on her bow and released her arrow, striking the demon with another purple arrow and taking a chunk out of its arm, making it bow further forward.

Gong Jin charged in, his body glowing with power and his eyes wild. The Mana in the area was stirred up as he seemed to grow in height, his power focused on his sword.

The demon's chest opened like a grotesque flower. The faces inside screamed out as Mana gathered into a Mana Blast.

A spell formation appeared around the demon as the built-up Mana was dismissed. Roska bit her lips, drawing blood that was in contrast to her pale face. Gong Jin, who had just experienced near death, unflinchingly landed his attack from underneath the bowed demon. Mana focused on his blade, doubling its size as he cut into the demon and sliced into those screaming faces. He pushed off with his feet, using the last of his strength as he rolled onto the ground, three meters away from the demon and up into a kneeling position. His armor moved with every breath; he seemed to become smaller, the power around him dissipating.

Simms, Xi, and Yang Zan fired into the opening on it's stomach left by Gong Jin. Their poisoned attacks made the demon's skin turn purple.

The demon was affected by several poisons, slowing its reactions. As it tried to regain its feet, its body opened again and fired out Mana blasts. The poison continued to attack it internally, decreasing the power it could draw on and further slowing its reaction time, allowing Roska and Yang Zan to dodge the huge Mana blasts and sending Simms spinning through the air instead of taking a direct hit.

Davos attacked again, trying to draw its attention as he left a bloody line and retreated.

Han Wu fired another grenade clip at the demon as it started to raise its body from the ground.

Tully let out a yell, holding her side. Her spear glowed with a ghostly light as she slammed it into the ground. White and black twisting clouds in mirror images of her own spear shot out of the ground, driving into the demon's body, striking armor and flesh. Nearly forty spears hit the demon, with twenty of them actually landing on flesh over armor.

The demon shook with the impact of so many spears.

The spears disappeared as the demon crashed to the ground. A tombstone appeared above its head.

Roska drank a Mana recovery potion and looked over to Special Team One that had been fighting the Masters moving with the demon.

Her stomach dropped as she pulled the potion bottle from her lips. Deni was tending to Yao Meng, a spear right through his leg as he was keening on the ground.

He let out a shrill noise as Deni tore it out of his leg.

"Don't worry nothing big, was giving you ice damage any-way, doesn't that feel warmer?" Deni asked as she worked on the pissed off Yao Meng.

Special Team One, who had just finished their fights, looked over as Roska saw them.

Niemm pulled out his communication device, talking into it.

There was a pause as he listened to the other side.

"Understood, Command. Special Team One Alpha out."

Niemm pulled out his map and showed Roska. "Looks like there is a group of Masters attacking a demon here, but it is buried in a large group of the Blood Demon troops. Can't call down spells or mortars for fear of hitting friendlies, so we're go-ing to be their support," Niemm said, his professional veneer pushing away the loss.

Roska checked the location on her own map. "Okay, do we want to come from the east or from the north? The east has more buildings for cover, but we could charge them if we come from the north."

"Our people are engaging from the western flank. I'd like to come in from the north and then loop around to the west to add to their line. If we're east and they're west, good chance that we miss and hit one another," Niemm said.

"All right." Roska nodded, checking the map once again and putting it away.

"Everyone, check your gear. We move out in five! Listen in while you're changing your gear." Niemm started to brief them through his sound transmission device as they checked their ammunition and their supplies.

Chapter: Difference in Power

Since the beginning, Fred had created tree avatars within Vuzgal, giving them eyes and ears into the Blood Demon lines.

Now, these trees came alive. Their branches and their roots attacked the Blood Demon army. Some that had bombs hidden within them detonated when there were big groups of Blood Demon troops around them.

The Blood Demon army was starting to attack and set fire to every tree that they saw.

Racquel, Reaper, Elizabeth, William, Dromm, and Fred stepped into the skies, their target one of the seven titans.

Old Xern dove into the ground, creating traps underneath and attacking soldiers and Elites by himself. With his ability to run away, he could decimate a group and disappear in seconds, or appear underneath a Mana barrier formation, destroy it and leave the group defenseless.

"Looks like there is something going wrong with our target," William said in his deep voice, unmoved by the sights of violence around him as barriers were struck on either side. The wall was coming alive, with ranged weapons being deployed against the charging army. The demons and titans fired Mana blasts occasionally as more spells and spell scrolls were exchanged between the two sides.

Buildings were torn apart. People were no less than ants or as powerful as gods as the divide between soldier, Elite, and Master became clear and apparent to all.

Fred frowned, looking at the titan moving toward the wall but also firing Mana blasts at the ground.

"It appears that it is trying to kill the Masters that were sent to protect it," Racquel said.

"Disgusting abomination," Elizabeth said.

The others didn't say anything but they all agreed.

"They don't care for the people around them, willing to kill their allies to win the battle," Fred said with tired disappointment

They were all demi-humans, they were closer to nature and the Ten Realms, making them feel a natural repulsion toward such a creature.

When they made alliances then they would rarely go back on them, seeing the way that the Blood Demon was willing to turn on one another made them feel sick.

"Seems that in the race for it to be animated, that it didn't have all the resources it needed. So now it is trying to consume more of the living to sustain itself," Fred said as they started to descend toward the titan.

"I'll go first!" Dromm's howled as his body extended and grew bigger. Hair sprouted across his body. He quickly began filling up the oversized armor he was wearing and his tusks grew larger. The power rolling from his body increased as he became closer to his beast side than his human form. He shot through the sky toward a group of Masters.

He slammed into the ground with such speed that only a few of the Masters were able to react to his arrival.

The dust around him distorted as he appeared. The sound of metal hitting metal rang out as he punched a Master. Their armor deformed from the hit and a tombstone appeared above their head. A silver and gray power covered Dromm's body and his fists as he moved in a blur, his small legs reaching incredible speeds.

Masters hit him but his skin had reached Body Like Sky Metal. With their techniques, it would be hard to inflict wounds unless it was inflicted with a high-Journeyman-level or higher weapon made from rare materials.

Roots moved down Fred's sleeve and around his hand, twisting together into a sharp wooden sword that glowed in the light. A formation written in an unknown language appeared on the blade. The pressure it gave off was no lower than the Expert-level crown on his head.

William drew out a hammer that was covered in blue formations, it looked like it belonged in the hands of a giant. His body turned blue and transparent as he turned into a man of water. Elizabeth held a staff up as her tanned skin darkened and turned into a black crystal form.

Racquel rested her hands on the two swords on her waist. Reaper's thin form started to grow in size. Branches could be seen underneath his magical robe as a green and a blue eye could be seen glowing in the darkness of his hood.

The titan seemed to realize that there were other threats nearby. Its head turned to face the four still in the sky. It let out a moan of excitement as its chest opened up, and a Mana Blast spell started to form.

"Disgusting." Reaper's voice was deeper, filled with the power of the world, as if he were an incarnation of the Ten Realms, its eternal justice sent forth.

A spell formation snapped into existence as a spike, ten meters long and one across, appeared next to Reaper and shot forward. There was no pause or build up like with most mages; he was able to instantly cast it. The magical wooden spike pierced right through the opening in the titan and slamming into the ground, pinning the titan to the ground.

It started to struggle as the wooden spike in its chest started to grow branches. Tree limbs pushed into its body.

It struggled against the attacks within its body to no avail.

Masters on the ground shot out attacks at the Demi-humans in the sky. Elizabeth threw up a defensive spell. The attacks smashed against the brown wall of defensive magic as William let out a yell and charged forward. Spell circles appeared around him; rain shot forward through the sky at speeds where buildings were covered in holes as if they had been shot with a bullet. Masters dropped to the ground, filled with bleeding holes.

William's hammer glowed with a spell formation. He struck the ground with the hammer. The spell seemed to make the ground act like water; The attack rippled out, tossing people away and hitting them with an incredible force.

Attacks shot back at him haphazardly but he dodged through them with a liquid grace. He slashed out with his hammer a thin scythe of water shot out along the path of the axe, cutting through armor, buildings and people.

"You should have been paying attention to me," Fred whispered.

Tree roots shot out from under the feet of the remaining Masters. Reaper waved his hand, tossing out seeds that shot toward the ground, exploding into movement. Green sprouts turned into vines, which transformed into bears, tigers, and wolves as they landed on the ground. The roots from underground tripped and attacked the masters, forcing them to care about themselves instead of others.

Dromm and William cut a path through the Blood Demon soldiers with the animated tree beasts by their sides as more members of the Blood Demon army rushed forward to fight them.

Racquel blurred as she disappeared from the line-up in the sky and Elizabeth cast a spell. Magical circles appeared on the ground; the dirt shuffled moved together over the stones of the buildings and the roads, creating dirt and stone golems.

Masters hit the freshly conjured golems, taking chunks out of their bodies or breaking their heads. But the golems ran forward still, taking the damage and pummeling those who got in their way.

Racquel appeared on the ground, behind the Masters who were fighting various tree beasts and others who were trying to regain their balance or fight off the roots.

Her blades flashed. With every wave of her blade, another tombstone appeared. She cut a path towards the titan who was ripping its own body apart as it pulled against the growing spike in its body.

Fred lifted his sword; roots shot out of the ground and wrapped around the titan's arms, pulling them back. Elizabeth cast a spell, causing the titan's feet to sink into the ground.

The titan seemed to lose its mind. It fired Mana blasts out of its body randomly, breaking some restraints, but killing many of the Blood Demon soldiers who were fighting for their lives around it.

The titans arms compressed as the blood was sucked out of the bodies, making them wither away into nothing.

The titan shifted its now smaller arms under the roots. The withered corpses fell away to reveal bone swords on either arm covered in swirling blood curses that looked like tortured souls waiting to be released.

"Racquel, William and I will be enough." Fred said as he descended through the sky, untouched by the battles around him. Attacks diverted around him, as if he were merely an illusion.

William charged across the ground. The water in the air pooled behind him and formed water soldiers that shot forward, clearing his path. He turned into a blue blur as he struck out at the titan as it struggled to step out from it's legs earthy restraints.

It let out an enraged roar as the Mana around it started to fluctuate dangerously.

William struck its leg, causing an explosion from the power gathered on his hammer. His spell shredded the titan's leg, causing it to collapse forward. The Mana dissipated and it was confused by its lack of balance.

The titan lashed out at William with his bone swords. The curses surged, becoming almost real as William dodged the attack which cut through the ground and struck several nearby Blood Demon Masters, tree beasts, and golems, causing them to wither. A thinner stream of blood-like energy returned to the titan as its leg started to regrow as it pitched forward onto the ground.

Racquel appeared on its back. Her arms glowed with deep-green magical circles as she stabbed her blades into the titan's back.

The titan's blood regeneration stopped as poison shot through its body. The wounds gave off a black gas and the titan started to fall apart.

Fred had an impassive look on his face as he looked at the titan. It was an incredibly powerful beast, but with centuries to test their power and only fighting one another to learn ways to increase their own abilities, their fighting ability was much greater than others of their same level. This allowed them to easily dominate the titan and the battlefield around them.

The poison would kill it in a matter of minutes, but there were others who needed their help sooner rather than in a few minutes.

Four magical circles appeared around the titan. Trees appeared and their limbs sunk into the titan's body and heaved, ripping it into four parts.

"Purify," Fred said simply.

The trees glowed and a golden light started to fall over the battlefield.

The titan's strength was incredible, as even in four different poisoned parts, it cried out as the magic that had awakened it was unraveled.

A tombstone appeared above it as Racquel, William, and Fred turned their attention back to the rest of the Blood Demon army, as if looking at an annoying and unrewarding task.

Racquel sent out green snakes, formed from poison, that rushed over the battlefield while William jumped across the street and slammed into groups of Masters.

Dromm waded into the groups of troops, blunting weapons and sending them flying with every fist, kick, and head butt.

Fred moved forward. His sword whistled and blurred as he remained impassive, as if just walking down the street. Masters or Elites used different attacks and techniques but they couldn't penetrate his defense.

Reaper stood in the sky with Elizabeth, harbingers of doom as they controlled the battlefield from afar by proxy with their creations.

Other groups of Masters from the Blue Lotus and the Crafter's Association clashed with the titans. But even with three or four hundred against the defending Masters and the titan, they were just able to wound it and slowly wear it down. While in turn, the titans used curses, bone weapons, and Mana blasts, killing tens of the defenders and getting closer to the walls.

**

Erik got the call about the KIA. They didn't know who had died on the special teams and now wasn't the time to confirm as they were assisting Masters to take out the other demons and titans.

Right now he couldn't focus on that as he was on the walls, watching as spells and mortars landed right outside of the Vuzgal barrier into the lines of the charging Blood Demon army.

They poured out of the outer city and right into the defense's lines. Archers and mages on the walls or behind it fired repeatedly into their midst.

Repeaters fired continuously, leaving lines of explosive arrows that raked across the enemy's position.

Members of the Alvan army were firing and reloading their rifles or their M32s. They didn't have the numbers to give everyone the M32s but they were incredibly effective with the Blood Demon army charging through the streets and the rubble of the city. They were trained to stay together so that they could be protected by a barrier.

Now that there was no Mana barrier to cover under, it made them the perfect targets for the M32s.

There were Elites and Masters among the soldiers, using the weak for cover and advancing on the walls.

Even with the wealth of spells and firepower pouring into them, with their techniques and history of being in life-and-death situations before, the Blood Demon army was able to push forward.

Erik looked over as a section of the inner wall exploded outward. People were sent flying and rocks rained down on those behind the wall, littering the open ground behind the wall. Ranged fighters readied their weapons and faced the new breach as the Blood Demon army started to pour forward into the fresh breach.

Erik had called up the fighters still affected by the concoction to create a reserve force. Everyone else who wasn't showing signs of the concoction reducing their Strength was on the walls already.

Erik fired, killing a Master who reached the top of the still intact wall, trying to flank the defenders who were getting organized.

Rugrat's design on the new rifle worked well; Erik could work the bolt action of the gun, without needing to move his head out of the way and fire again.

Three more people dropped to the ground as Erik dumped the magazine.

"Reloading!"

He smacked a new one into place and pushed the action forward, continuing to fire.

"Movement!" He heard on the section of wall in front of him.

He kept back from the wall in a watchtower connected to it so he could see the battlefield. He wasn't right up against the barrier so that a stray spell or ranged attack within the barrier could get him.

The watchtower was also filled with repeaters that were firing down on the Blood Demon army, turning the streets and the blown-out buildings into a bloodbath.

Erik looked out as a group crossed the tombstone- and body-covered ground, making it to the wall. Attacks rained down on them, only leaving just a handful to cower under the edge for cover.

One pulled out a cannon and fired it into the wall.

The blast caused the wall to lose it's stability, the blood Demon soldiers raised their shields with their strength it was easy for them to deflect the falling rubble, ready to charge forwards once it had settled.

Another Blood Demon soldier used a spell scroll. The wall next to them distorted, becoming blocks and falling apart as another section exploded.

Another cannon went off, piercing the wall and continuing through to pierce the walls of the watchtower Erik stood in, making it shake.

Erik could see the Blood Demon army charging forth as people tried to angle their fire downward on the approaching foes but the resistance on the wall was sparse.

Erik took out his M32 and fired into one of the larger breaches filled with Blood Demon soldiers.

The repeaters on various watchtowers tracked over and concentrated on the breaches now, suppressing them, but more holes were opening up as new weaknesses were exposed.

"We need to leave," the Masters from the Blue Lotus and the Crafter's Association guarding Erik said as they fired arrows into the enemy.

If we fall back then we'll be fighting from the valley and they'll control the inner city, at that point it would be easy for them to grind down our forces into nothing with ranged attacks and keep us caged in the Valley, we could only retreat into the dungeon and fight it out there.

"No, we stay here. We hold this wall," Erik yelled as he called up Rugrat and Glosil directly.

"Glosil, I'm passing command to you. The enemy's spirit is broken if we can get their leadership or take out the Titans and Demons we can turn this around." Erik turned towards the inner wall, seeing undead charging into a breach and creating a new wall, waiting beyond the holes in the walls to kill anything that came through. They were strong but dumb, great for defending breaches. Nearly all of the defenders remaining Master-classed forces were fighting the Blood Demons and titans in the outer city so it was up to the undead to hold the line.

"We need to push our people up to the front line, reinforce the Tareng guards." Erik said.

"I understand," Glosil said, his voice grim. "Good luck."

"Luck? We don't need luck! We make our own!" Rugrat yelled, the wind distorting his words.

Erik could hear that he was talking while riding.

Another section of wall exploded. Erik looked over, his body tightening. It was where he had seen a section from Alva's army fighting.

He cut the channel and jogged across the wall to get a better vantage. "Cover the breach!"

Erik wanted to jump in and pull his people out, but he was a soldier first and a medic second.

Civilians that had volunteered were rushed forward to pull out the wounded and evacuate them to the healers and alchemists to the rear.

Erik turned back to the battlefield and pulled out his M32, ejecting the grenade casings into his storage ring. He reloaded it, snapped it closed, and aimed at one breach, firing past it and on to the area on the other side. He adjusted his aim, doing the same for the two other breaches. It might or might not kill anyone but it would put the fear of explosives into them.

Mortars and long-range spells were being called in, no longer into the outer city, but just over the wall to seal off breaches and to keep others from entering. It was like putting gum on a hole in a dam. It slowed the amount of people going through, but eventually they would make breaches in enough places that the indirect fire wouldn't be able to cover them all and they could flood in.

A demon made it to the inner wall. It swung its fist, smashing the wall apart as people hosed it with fire. Its head opened, even while being hit with different attacks.

A pillar of chaotic Mana tore down the side of the wall, killing an untold amount of people and melting the wall.

Blood Demon soldiers rushed from behind to where the demon was as it hit the wall, breaking it and entering the city. Masters at its feet rushed forward in a flood as the demon fired out

Mana blasts from different parts of its body. When it stepped on corpses, their bodies were added to its mass, repairing it and allowing it to grow bigger.

Tens of ballistas filled the sky and struck the demon, making it stagger under the weight of fire. A few of the Masters were killed by ballistas that missed the large demon.

Rugrat rushed forward, part of the quick reaction ground force as they fired their ballistas and used spell scrolls at the fresh breach caused by the demon.

Attacks rained down on the demon and the Masters around it, slowing and killing them.

Another spell scroll created an outline over a large section of broken walls. The rocks covering the ground flew up and returned to the wall, repairing it as if the wall had never been broken. Those who had rushed past the wall in to kill the defenders now had nowhere to retreat as their backs were against the walls.

They were slaughtered as defenders tried to get back on the walls and hold out.

That fight was only on a small section of the wall. Erik reloaded and fired into the breaches that hadn't been repaired and watched as more sections of the wall were turned into flying stone and dust.

The members of the Alva Army that had been acting as medics now put down their stretchers. They had the coordination, they had the cultivation and they had the levels added with their impressive weaponry. It was the first time the people of Tareng had seen the Alva Army go all out.

Sections coordinated with one another, laying down a base of fire and advancing. Titans challenged them as they used spell scrolls freely, not caring about their loss. Grenadiers pasted destruction across the lines.

They plugged breaches and forced back the Blood Demon Sect.

If it was three months ago then we wouldn't have stood a chance. Coming to the fourth realm had removed any excess that they had before and focused their minds and their actions. With their firm foundations in tactics their increased strength had a multiplicative effect when fighting alongside one another.

Erik assessed his bodyguards turned combatants supporting from afar. Suddenly, several Masters appeared in a breach to the northwest of Erik, slaughtering their way in.

Erik changed to his rifle as he fired on them, killing a few, but it wasn't doing enough. Like throowing rocks into a stream hoping to stop it. The breaches were under pressure all along the line as the defenders moved from the walls to the ground to hold their positions.

Erik advanced, taking out a Defender's Might pill and chewing it. He felt strength fill his body.

He knelt and fired his rifle, again and again, but it seemed that the Blood Demon army had sensed a great weakness as they all rushed the breach next to where Erik and his Alvan soldiers were.

"Calling in fire support, grid Four eight, seven three, Three two one nine, confrim!" Erik called up the mortars. They had based the grid system off of the main castle and added it to their maps.

"Understood, fire support mission on grid, four eigh seven three, three two one nine Confirmed! Clear to fire?"

"Clear to fire."

"Sergeant Drumm, keep your people back, mortars coming down on the other side of the wall!" Erik switched to another channel.

"Understood!" The section got into what cover they could find, the masters gathering on the other side for the push.

Erik dropped behind the wall on the roof he was observing from as someone started firing at him. He stayed down and scooted away.

"Never seen a battle commander on his hands and knees?" Erik barked as he saw the stunned looking guards with him as he pulled out a scroll and tucked it into his vest, ready to use it if needed.

Whistling could be heard from above as Erik pulled out his heavy repeater, putting his back against the wall.

The mortars rained down on the other side of the breach as the mortars landed.

Erik stood up and turned, putting his repeater on the wall as he released Gilly, she let out a yell, stretching as the guards looked at her in surprise.

The mortars stopped firing as Erik saw through the dust, he fired with his repeater, the other Alvans joining in, nothing made it through that breach as they advanced, the breach had turned into a slaughter, the Blood Demon Soldiers trying to flee as masters, experts and normal members were shredded.

"Gilly repair the wall!" Erik said.

Brown runes that were hidden in her skin glowed as the ground started to push up dragging the sonte back together and fusing it together with dirt.

A Blood Demon appeared like a runaway train and slammed through the wall, sending the parts that Gilly had repaired, everywhere, the Alva soldiers had to dive for cover as the rocks rained down.

Gilly let out an enraged roar, her squeaky tone taking on a deeper noise as mana billowed around her and a spell formation appeared in front of her mouth. Water attribute mana in the area collected as she released an attack that looked like high speed rain drops piercing through the Blood Demon. It was shredded, not knowing how it died as it dropped backwards into the breach.

Erik looked at Gilly in surprise.

She let out a satisfied snort as the wall started to form again, the blood demon being crushed inside it.

The Two sections grouped up and moved to another area that was understrength and needed help.

Erik was studying his map, checking the information that had been passed to him through different recon and intelliegnce methods.

"It looks like they've committed their forces to the push, they've got evertyhing coming for us, their command element is at the rear and we have a good idea where they are," Erik talked to himself as he used his communication device.

"Glosil!"

"Erik!"

"I don't think that we're going to get a better chance to use Rising Coffin," Erik yelled through the communication device.

Glosil took a moment, checking his own information.

"If we wait much longer we won't have a wall between us and them."

"Send out the word, I'll activate operation Rising Coffin in three minutes!"

"Got it!" They cut the connection as Erik used his connection to the Dungeon core to send orders to the undead, getting them ready.

Glosil contaced him just a few minutes later.

"I sent the word."

"Good, Activating Rising Coffin," Erik said, his sound transmission device passing the message to Glosil who passed it to the rest of the defenders.

"You got mounts?" Erik asked the guards.

"Yes sir!"

"Alright mount up," Erik jumped onto Gilly's back, petting her neck, there hadn't been many opportunities for her to fight in the last couple of weeks which had left her annoyed as she had just transported him from one observation post to another unable to assist.

She was a lot calmer now that she had been able to show off her strength and defeat the Blood Demon all by herself.

"Good Girl," Erik said.

She started off, jumping off of the roof and moving through the streets, the Crafter's guards following closely behind on their own beasts.

Chapter: Rising Coffin

The ground shook as a hand of bones appeared. The glowing eyes of the undead were revealed as they climbed out onto the battlefields that they had once fought on and were soon to fight on again.

They carried their weapons in skeletal hands, silently moving forward, marching on the Blood Demon army, who were forcing their entrance into the city.

Thousands of undead had moved through the tunnels that were under the city, hiding just a few feet below the ground, ready to be called upon.

Once the undead were all freed from the ground, the cavalry grouped up, stepping onto their mounts, and started to move forward. Their mounts gained speed as those on their feet turned from a walk into a jog. The rangers jogged behind the foot soldiers, but at a slower pace, allowing a distance to be created between them as the mages at the back gathered power from the dungeon core.

***

General Ulalas looked at the walls of Vuzgal as another section exploded, rocks flying everywhere. Her forces rushed into the inner city as soon as the dust had cleared but there were flashes of light and explosions.

"Who are these people?" One of the remaining commanders hissed, their eyes dark and cruel.

"Who knows," Ulalas said, she hadn't seen weapons like theirs before or their tactics which kept them at range from their attackers.

If someone was fast enough then they could deflect the attacks but some would explode upon contact, making it hard to defend against.

Then there was the coordinated strikes from the whistling thunder.

"We have broken into the inner city through multiple breaches. Though the enemy is holding onto their positions and engaing us directly. We have pushed all of our forces forward, we don't have anyone else to commit," an aide said.

Ulalas nodded, feeling relieved, soon it would be all over.

"Chase them. We have the advantage. We're finally in the city—we can kill them all," Ulalas said.

Suddenly several spell formations appeared in the sky and on the ground. Spells landed on the defenders as their strength, defenses and speed increased.

"Buffing spell scrolls! Use everything that we have left!" Ulalas yelled, seeing another trump card come out as repairing spell scrolls were activated, the walls and the buildings around it starting to recover.

"Just how many spell scrolls do they have!" A general asked with a trembling voice as spell scrolls were activated and used as a primary method of attack against the Blood Demon Sect.

There was a yell from the rear of the formation. Ulalas looked over and her eyes widened as she saw an army of undead coming out of the darkness. There were no illumination rounds in the sky but the lights from the battle in Vuzgal was enough to flicker off their white bones.

The mounted undead ran through the healers, cutting them down. There had to be thousands as they appeared through the city, cutting into the Blood Demon's rear. They were impervious to pain and with every attack they reaped lives, undead that weren't mounted followed behind them, cutting through the ranks.

Undead were swraming through the city, hitting the rear of the forces that were up against the walls, the undead had them backed up against the wall as powerful spell scrolls were activated, falling on the Blood Demon Army, they lost hundreds in just minutes.

Ulalas had her sword out as a mounted undead clashed with her, she defending against the blow and was sent glying back.

They have to be Masters with the strength they are showing—undead Masters!

"Use holy blessings and smite! Hit them with magical attacks and weapons!" Ulalas yelled. She knew how slim it would be for them to have any holy spells. They were called the Blood Demon Sect, after all—they were more aligned with chaos than with purity.

"Recall the ten nearest Master and Elite units to fight the undead," she grabbed an aide and said to them.

"Yes, General!"

Ulalas never looked at them once, her attention now focused on the undead chewing through her back ranks.

She touched her bracer and pressed her thumb against the paper inside. Two different spell scrolls—one to create an illusion, the other to teleport—were her insurance. She needed to make this the biggest fight possible; then she needed to fake her death and escape.

Only then would people never look for her, thinking that she had died on the battlefield.

She had been promised a wedding with the man she had loved for years. He wasn't a fighter but a powerful tailor who made strong armors and clothes.

Then, months ago, she had been told by the sect that they were looking to increase their ties with another group and wanted to marry her off to that other sect. As if all of her previous achievements were worth nothing more than the fact that she was a woman. That her marriage agreement could be thrown away because the sect didn't find it convenient anymore.

She saw the Blood Demon Sect's true face then. She had known it before, but she had been blinded to their coldness. She had had her own hopes and desires, to marry and to flee the Fourth Realm, to head to higher or lower in the realms—it didn't matter to her as long as she was able to live a life without being away from the one she loved all the time.

She had wanted to go and find him to run away, but the city he was in was attacked. They hid the matter well, but they sent the man she loved into the battle. They knew full well that he was a tailor and not a fighter. She knew it was an order from on high to get her to forget about him and to come back to the sect and do their bidding after her beloved died.

She was nothing more than their dog to them. If she didn't do what they wanted, then they would get rid of her and replace her with the other dogs that were trying to get their attention and her position.

So she went to the people who were Blood Demon Sect's biggest rivals and offered them an opportunity that few would be able to.

She had the measures in her bracer to save her life but she didn't really care; she didn't have anything to live for anymore.

Instead of charging forward to fake her death, she organized her army to try to hold back the undead army. She pulled Masters who were waiting to enter the city to deal with the undead army behind them.

The undead cut a path through her lines to the mobile Mana barriers, breaking them down. The undead that were falling apart from damage charged forward and detonated the Mana within their bodies. They were all Master level enemies and the power that they could hold in their bodies was vast.

No living person would so willingly detonate the Mana in their body. The undead weren't people, and used detonating their body as if it was a calculation, like one would think about how they would aim their arrow, the spells to use—they thought of how to use their Mana detonations to the best effect.

The undead killed the mobile Mana barrier formations one after another. Some others got new ones up, but others were focusing on the undead that were plowing through the back of their army.

Untold Mana barrier formations were destroyed before the Masters and Elites called back by Ulalas showed up, charging into the fight.

She heard a flapping noise above her. Undead flying beasts appeared out of the sky and landed among the army. They were the same beasts that the aerial mages had rode. They had been hiding on top of the main city pillar, but now they reappeared again.

She was about to yell out when the winged undead beasts exploded. They had been level sixty and seventy mounts, but they caused the gigantic amount of Mana within their bodies to detonate.

Four-hundred-meter areas were flattened as tens of people were killed in each blast.

Ulalas's blood ran cold as she was tossed through the air by one of the detonations. She rolled a few times and got to her feet.

The undead army wasn't deterred by their comrades explosions, the archers firing on the defenseless on the ground. The mages cast their spells as the skeletal mounts trampled people underfoot and their riders continued on their bloodbath, their armor was covered with the blood of their enemy.

Ulalas was thankful that her army was spread out. If they had been all packed together, then the mounts suicide blasts could have destroyed most of her army in one shot.

The undead continued to carve a path through her forces and then detonate once they were weakened. She had her people spread out so that as few as possible of them would die from the Mana detonations and it would also take the undead longer to move through them.

The Blood Demon Masters ran into the fight, and although they were able to actually win against the undead instead of simply swarm them, if they didn't kill the undead quickly enough then it would detonate and take the master down with it.

She gritted her teeth and took the losses. She couldn't help but acknowledge that the enemies leader, although he was a sadist, was a commander who never stopped scheming or making advantages where he could.

Just how long had he buried the undead in the battlefield just so he could use them to attack our rear when we reached the inner city?

Her expression became guarded as she looked at the walls of Vuzgal. Instead of looking defeated, they seemed to be mocking her as the unwanted next thoughts filled her mind.

If he planned for them to come in while we were attacking the walls, did it also mean he planned for us entering the city? Just what are our casualties like?

She snorted and laughed. *Fitting end for them all.* Her cold eyes moved over the rest of the army—puppets that played according to her whims. Puppets that had obeyed her, as she had obeyed the Blood Demon sect, their oaths binding them to her service and making it impossible for them to go against her orders.

Suddenly the pain from before—the anger—turned into amusement. After all, wouldn't this be the death knell for the Blood Demon Sect? With the Blue Lotus and Crafter's Association leading the charge?

She thought that only if they got reinforcements would the people from Tareng have a chance of surviving this fight.

Her blood ran cold. This was not a war like she had dealt with before. When taking the city, she had thought the battle was half over. Now she knew the truth: this was no simple city. This was a city of death.

***

Erik looked at the fighting happening on the other side of the wall. The undead were pressing the Blood Demon Sect against the wall, the Titans and Blood Demons were falling as the attacking groups took them down. The rear of the army was in a mess.

Erik took out a sound amplifying device.

"Your leader is dead and you will be soon! The Blue Lotus and the Crafter's association knows of your crimes they're coming to hunt you down! We have the head of your General Ulalas!" Erik continued on. Glosil's plan to yell at the enemy striking fear into their minds as they were sleeping resonated with Erik. He made sure that there was space for them to escape It happened slowly as word was passed and then suddenly the tide of the Blood Demon Sect Army changed.

The Blood Demon Sect Army, hearing that their generals were dead, started to flee. They seemed to be relieved hearing Erik's words.

They were pitiful, having been used as nothing more than pawns as they ran in every direction, fleeing Vuzgal, heading to the East or West.

If they had mounts they rode, if they couldn't then they would run.

Erik was surprised with their actions but it was only their oaths holding them there, once they thought that their oath wasn't effective anymore than they ran.

Chapter: Two Pillars' Might

Across the Fourth Realm, the neutral cities watched armored men and women marching out of the Blue Lotus and the Crafter's Association buildings, heading to the totems in their cities.

Elder Lu stood at his window in the top of the Blue Lotus headquarters building. His eyes were on the totem and the blue and black armored legion that surrounded it, so thickly packed that one was unable to see the ground.

Elder Lu got a message from Cui Chin.

"We have confirmed that it is not a plague, but a concoction," Cui Chin said.

"Advance." Elder Lu ordered as he cut the channel.

The totems glowed in neutral cities across the Fourth Realm.

Hundreds of warriors disappeared.

The next groups marched forward as one and then turned to face outward, disappearing again.

Thousands were moving, all of them ranked Master by the measure of the Fourth Realm.

Across the Hang-Nim Alliance, they appeared in cities. People watched as they marched out of the totems and into the streets, advancing. They seemed to be exiting the city but waited as they got to the gates.

Their forces continued to build up as time went on. The totems stopped sending people, but instead of leaving, the Blue Lotus and Crafter's Association guards turned and faced the city. People looked on in confusion.

"The Nezzar and Red Sword sects colluded together to attack the Crafter's Association and Blue Lotus. Surrender or be put to the sword. Stay in your homes and do not venture out!"

People were confused and outraged, but they knew that these two powerhouses wouldn't lie about something such as this.

The elders and people of these sects were struck by fear. Some sent their guards to fight off the two armies that were already inside their walls. Some simply gave up.

Most of them had no idea what their sects had been thinking, but those who knew used whatever escape routes they had to try to get away.

Others captured their friends, to use them as bartering chips to reduce their own sentence. In the Fourth Realm, one couldn't simply survive by being a nice person.

***

As soon as the order was given to advance, Lei Huo and her elite force of level sixty guards and departed through the totem.

They all followed her lead, as they had arranged. The street out of the city was cleared. As they reached the empty land beyond, she looked at the three-hundred-strong fighting force.

They didn't have many numbers, but they were all old Masters who taught the Masters of the Fourth Realm. Most of them were level seventy and above.

There were even five level eighties that Lei Huo didn't know about.

She used the scroll that Elder Lu had given her. A vast formation appeared on the ground and in the sky before they disappeared in a flash of light as if they had never been there in the first place.

Sounds of fighting filled Lei Huo's ears as they arrived in the dead land between the outer walls and the Blood Demon army's temporary camp in the woods.

There were people from the Blood Demon Sect Army that were fleeing in every direction, seeing the Blue Lotus and Crafter's association forces, they turned and tried to flee in another direction.

They paid these fleeing soliders no attention as they charged forward into the city, seeing the signs of battle. They followed the roads that the Blood Demon army had needed to fight through block by block.

Lei Huo saw the signs of recent battle and increased her speed. The battle had not gone well. She had been getting reports but hearing and seeing what had happened were very different.

The defenders Mana barrier over the inner city was still there but Lei Huo could see signs of close combat at their base. Dead were eveywhere, as well as undead that had been brought down. There were few Blood Demon Sect Army Soldiers that were unlucky to run into them, being cut down before they could surrender.

She saw a massive snake wrap around one of the titans and sink its teeth into it.

The titan struggled but it was unable to do anything before they both crashed to the ground, sending up a pillar of dust.

The top soldiers of the Blue Lotus didn't yell out as they charged forward. When they saw people from the Blood Demon army, they cut them down, without sparing any more effort than necessary. They passed enemy lines like the wind as they rushed forward.

They slowed their pace as they saw that the fighting had msotly ceased with what remained of the Blood Demon Sect Army Fleeing.

"Search for their commanders," Lei Huo ordered, half of the force split up into groups and searched.

The rest continued to follow her towards the inner city

***

One of the titans had been able to make it to the inner walls, breaking inside, and was attacking the defenders.

Rugrat had been sent forward with the reserve to assist as Masters and the Blood Demon army had poured in with it.

They weren't even able to hold in any place; they were just trying to pull back the wounded as fast as possible.

The Blood Demon army had claimed this plot of land. Rugrat and the mounted forces had attacked those defending the titan but they'd been unable to hinder them greatly.

The Crafter's Association members continued to charge through from multiple directions, making the Blood Demon army clump together, which was great for the Alvan army fighters.

Rugrat aimed out of a window with an M32 and fired rapidly at a group of soldiers packed in together. He finished firing and ran off, reloading his weapon as he went. Arrows slammed into the window he had fired from, followed by a spell that blew out a section of the wall.

He jumped down into a courtyard and ran across a street. He made it to another house and jumped up to a good perch when he saw a two-man fireteam inside, calling in mortar fire.

"Don't miss!" he yelled and ran for another building. He could hear shooting off to the side as an army section had taken up residence in a large tower with its own Mana barrier and were hammering the new arrivals with repeaters and M32s as fast as they could reload.

Marksmen were taking out the leaders that they could see in the mess around the titan.

The Alvan fighting style was an odd idea for the other fighters. Seeing them kneel or lie down and still fighting.

Rugrat had seen people die too many times when someone was standing and sending out spells or firing a bow. It was hard to fire a bow from anything but standing; kneeling was possible but difficult.

Though, with the repeaters and rifles, the Alvan army could lie down and make themselves small targets. They could do a lot of damage in a short time period before moving to a new firing position so they didn't die from returning fire.

The defense of the outer city was traps; the inner city was filled with firing positions that Rugrat had checked out and prepared. Each with enough ammunition and good cover that someone from the Alvan army could make the enemies life a living hell.

George and the mounted beasts of the army were with the mounted forces of the Crafter's Association. They appeared as a group, made it onto a street and mowed the enemy down. They smashed through on their powerful beasts that clawed and slashed at the Blood Demon army before they disappeared into the side streets once again.

Rugrat pulled out his rifle and sighted on a leader ordering the army forward, pushing Elites and soldiers up front.

"That's not very nice." Rugrat stroked the trigger. The commander dropped and fell backward.

Rugrat changed aim onto a mage and was rewarded with a red bloom as he moved to his next target.

He got three more before someone seemed to get wise to his position.

Rugrat pulled out the M32 and fired into groups he'd spotted while shooting and ran. He pulled out the fired grenade casings as he heard spells, arrows, and anything launchable peppering the house he was just in.

Then it started to go quiet and people started to yell. Rugrat moved to a new firing position as he saw that there was a commotion behind the Blood Demon army.

Finally, he saw the source. The Blue Lotus reinforcements were here. They charged through the back of the Blood Demon forces, with their shields up and their blades ready.

Arrows cut into the enemies backs as they marched forward, not fast or slow, maintaining pace as they met the thinned-out Blood Demon army. Their swords flashed as blood appeared and their shields created a steel wall. The Masters from the Blood Demon army even tried attacking the new threat but they were quickly dealt with.

Three people appeared in the sky as they looked at the titan that had dared breach the inner city.

Two cast spells. Magical circles were usually only one or two circles and lines with runes in them. But these—these were a dozen circles and shapes linked together as the Mana in the atmosphere was excited.

Two golden beams appeared from the spell, hitting the titan that was turning around. The titans left leg and stomach disappeared and its head and right shoulder disappeared at the same time. There was no noise, just complete silence and bright golden light from the attacks as they hit the ground beyond, killing anyone there. The beams left behind only ruined high-Journeyman-level equipment as holes, ten meters deep, appeared.

The third person in the sky dropped to the ground. They moved through the Blue Lotus' arrow rain with ease as they placed their hand on their sword hilt.

There was a flash of light as the person stood there but a circular wave attack of some kind had killed and sliced apart everything that was within one hundred meters of the fighter.

It was only a split second but they had somehow executed a technique, just once with their blade, and sheathed it again in that blinding flash.

Rugrat grabbed his sound transmission device.

"The reinforcements have arrived!" he said, not really believing his own words.

Chapter: Losses

Glosil looked over it all. At the end, they hadn't even held back the reserve from the fight and they'd had civilians carrying the wounded back to be treated.

He moved to the side as another stretcher went by—someone who had been finally recovered, maybe from under a fallen wall, or were in the outer city fighting the Blood Demon titans or demons.

Smoke created a smog over the city as afternoon approached.

Glosil reached a building that had been hit with spells, taking down the house and sections of the walls. He wandered through the rubble on the floor.

"Sir." A corporal nodded to him as they watched the hallway he had walked through.

Glosil nodded to him as if he had seen him and walked back into the sunlight, seeing an Alvan army section or two. They were sitting down, covered in grime, leaning against the walls, eating food, drinking water, seeing to their gear's needs and then their own.

Glosil could feel the tension in the air, the kindling waiting for the spark. They were all coming down from the fighting. They had been running and gunning for a week and a half straight, then three days of close quarters combat with barely any sleep.

Some of them let out short laughs, but there was a heavy atmosphere that stopped anyone from cracking out a big laugh. Their eyes had a hidden darkness to it. For others, the pressure they made might make them feel awkward, make them feel out of place. For Glosil, he felt comfortable in it as he looked to those he knew personally. He didn't need to voice his questions, just look at them and get an answer.

"Sir." Domonos stood. He had a recently sewn-up breastplate, from being hit in the chest with an attack. He had recovered with healing and health potions, leaving a patch of clean skin and body armor that needed to be repaired.

"Sit," Glosil said as the sergeants started to rise up. Glosil put his repeater in his storage ring and sat down on the fountain that they were using as a perch.

"Tareng is being cleared out right now. There was only a small group there. People who did this got what they deserved. Crafters and Lotus sent in their armies, took over the perpetrators cities, and basically set in motion the end of another sect. People are heading out of Vuzgal for other destinations, mostly back to Tareng.

"Erik and Rugrat are going to a meeting with some head honchos. See what will happen with this place. I've got Yui and his people over with the supplies that we were able to secure, as well as Fred and his group. We'll collect our people and head to the supplies, ready to move to the totem if anything goes bad," Glosil said.

Domonos and the others nodded. They had fought beside the people of Tareng, but they were from different organizations. If they turned their sights onto the Alvan army, then they at least had plans in place if things did go that badly; thankfully, they still had seven thousand undead on their side.

"See to your people—pass the word," Domonos said.

The sergeants nodded and headed off.

"How many?" Glosil asked.

Domonos let out a sigh as his officer mask was pushed to the side and the human underneath was revealed. "Five." Domonos's eyes moved from the ground to Glosil. "What about overall?"

Glosil could tell he wanted to know but also didn't. Glosil took out a list. "Add the names."

Domonos grit his teeth and put down five names, his lower jaw working as he finished, reading over the names. Glosil knew what was on that piece of paper; he knew the weight on his chest and his heart.

Domonos looked up from the list, blinking to clear his eyes. He let out a sigh and passed it back to Glosil, reasserting his training and pushing it to the side.

Thirteen members of the Alvan army who had come with them through training, who they had known for either most of their lives, or who they had known only for a few months. Now they would go no further than the Fourth Realm.

Glosil didn't blame Erik or Rugrat. He knew their reasoning and if he was in their shoes, he hoped he had the balls to do it as well.

But some of these people—he had seen them grow up, he had seen them come in as nothing but kids, excited to go start a new village in the wilderness with their parents. He had protected them as they turned into young men and women; he had been there with them when they faced the beast horde and stood side by side, defending Alva village.

He'd seen them jump at the possibilities that Alva Dungeon opened up, how they had joined the military to look after those they cared about.

That was the hardest part, knowing how young they were, knowing that there was just so much more that they could have done in life.

Some had family; some might have not even dated yet and there was just no way that they would be able to experience that. There was no way that they would be able to see just what Alva Dungeon would become because of them.

Glosil took the piece of paper. Tt was simple, light. Not unlike any other piece of paper that he used to remind himself what to do tomorrow or used to send as a piece of mail.

This paper in particular, had a great weight to it. He carefully folded it up and put it in his breast pocket.

He wiped his grime-covered forehead as he let out a grunt, pushing himself to his feet.

**

Hiao Xen entered Elder Lu's residence. The residence was on the back mountain where the Blue Lotus members lived, but the mana concentration here was much higher.

Cultivating here would be like cultivating for four days outside.

He came to a garden where Elder Lu was sitting and reading a report. Hiao Xen made to bow when Elder Lu waved him to the seat beside him and finished with the report.

"You know Erik and Rugrat some?" Elder Lu asked.

"I know them well enough," Hiao Xen said, confused at why the leader of the Blue Lotus in the Fourth Realm was asking about them specifically.

"They and their people put their lives on the line for us. They could have killed our scout and then hidden in their city. Instead, they offered their aid. They revealed a city that we could take from them. Even when the commander of our forces lashed out at the enemy, leading tens of our masters to their deaths despite Erik's orders, they kept on fighting for us. They protected our people and our vassals. Yes, they may have gained levels, but they haven't asked for any kind of reward other than to get us to acknowledge the existence of Vuzgal as a neutral city and it remaining under their command." Elder Lu trailed off.

"The Blue Lotus owes them a great debt, one that we will find hard to fill."

His words were simple but Hiao Xen knew the deep meaning behind them. Erik and Rugrat had supported the Crafter's Association and the Blue Lotus in a time of need and hadn't taken advantage of them. Their actions were simple but there were few in the ten realms that would do the same as them.

"What can we give them as thanks?" Elder Lu asked, looking at Hiao Xen.

He felt the weight of that stare and didn't give an answer lightly.

"I don't think that we should give them anything," Hiao Xen saw the lines starting to appear on Elder Lu's forehead. "Erik, Rugrat and their people did what they did out of a sense of duty, according to their own honor and what they believe in. Yes, they lost people. I talked to some of them about it. While they make sure that the dead soldiers family is supported, they look to remember their fallen. They are a small but tight knit group. It is how they're able to show much strength on the battlefield. Monetary items will not appease them, it will only make them angry. Remembering their people's loss, sending your condolences, fulfilling the bargain promised and *showing* that we are thankful, that is much more powerful to them than just getting rewards. If they wanted materials and money, then they could easily demand it from us."

Hiao Xen held his breath as he watched Elder Lu. In the Ten Realms it was normal to give gifts in gratitude, especially when someone died from another group to help yours. Building people to experts cost a lot of materials and resources. The people of the Ten Realms needed more of these items in order to raise new members to secure the lost positions.

"They are not what I expected," Elder Lu said.

Hiao Xen looked out a short laugh.

"They're not what anyone expected."

***

Erik used his Clean spell, getting the blood and grime off his body and his equipment. He took the time to down another Stamina potion. His overclock had taken a heavy toll on his body. Only his healing skills and his concoctions combined with his powerful natural healing ability kept him on his feet. He had been looking after the wounded with other medics from the Alvan army after the main fight had been won.

People were surprised with the Alvan healing speed and the way that they healed people, and more had been brought to their tents than the other casualty collection points.

Rugrat had gone and checked on the rest of the army while Erik healed, collecting those who were dead while Glosil checked on the living.

Fred, William, Gilga, and Elizabeth stayed outside of the casualty collection point where Erik worked while Racquel, Reaper, and Dromm followed Rugrat and George.

Rugrat and Erik had both gotten messages from Hiao Xen. People from the headquarters had come through the totem and wished to talk to them.

Erik and the medics' work was coming to a close and there were other healers and alchemists to deal with the remaining issues of the wounded.

Erik sent the medics to meet up with the rest of the army as Rugrat met up with him.

"Thank you for the help," Erik said to Fred and his people again.

"You saved us and we have saved you. I wish we were able to help more." Fred frowned. He had come to know the people of Alva and made some close ties to them as they had talked about books and information on Alchemy. It had opened his eyes to the world beyond their valley. Losing these people—it was the first time he had to deal with something like it.

He wasn't even sure of his own emotions and seemed confused.

Erik nodded, seeing that he was having his own issues.

"What do you think that they want from us?" Rugrat asked.

"I'm not sure, but we should be ready to run. You check out the remote site?" Erik said in a low voice.

"It is complete. The Ten Realms accepted the deal. When some grows upstairs, more will grow down below. Sounds weird," Rugrat said.

Erik nodded and kept on walking. They made their way to the totem, where the group was waiting for them with carriages.

Erik and Rugrat boarded, they passed through the totem and appeared in a new city, the headquarters of the Blue Lotus in the fourth realm.

It rested atop a mount, the entire city looked like a blooming Lotus flower with the totem hidden at the base.

They arrived at the center of the city and then took formation enhanced elevators up, they passed through the different petals. They reached an are at the center of the lotuts, looking out of the windows one would be able to see the curving petals all around them.

"Damn I wonder how long that took them" Rugrat said.

"I'm going to bet a while, though it is easier to build here," Erik replied.

They moved forward as the doors were opened to a large room. Hiao Xen and Xue Lin stood behind an older-looking man.

The head of the Crafter's Association from Tareng, Daniels, stood behind a middle-aged woman.

Both the man and the woman sitting at the table had a deep aura, making it impossible to get a read on just how powerful they were.

The Blue Lotus man stood, the woman following.

"I am Elder Lu of the Blue Lotus and this is Elder Redding of the Crafter's Association," he said. The woman tilted her head as Erik and Rugrat cupped their fists and bowed their heads to the two of them. The motion had become more natural with their time in the Ten Realms.

"I'm Erik West and this is Rugrat. What would you like to discuss?" Erik asked.

Elder Lu raised an eyebrow while the corner of Redding's mouth twitched upward. Elder Lu was momentarily at a loss for words but he quickly recovered, giving Hiao Xen a quick side-eye.

"I was told that you were more forward. We want to thank you for your assistance. If it was not for your help, then the situation could only have been worse. I am sorry for your losses, and wish that this meeting had a lighter manner as we wish to discuss Vuzgal and your plans for it?" Elder Lu asked.

"I would like to know what is happening with the Blood Demon Sect and the Hang-Nim Alliance," Erik asked.

"The Nezzar and Red Sword sects will no longer exist in the Fourth Realm. Their root and branch guilds will have sanctions placed upon them, forcing them to turn to other sects or to dissolve with time. All of their higher-ups will be slaughtered. The Blood Demon army here has been mostly killed off. Their general and some other powerful figures will remain under our care to be an example to others of the fate that comes from crossing the Blue Lotus and Crafter's Association. The Blood Demon Sect will be slowly choked out economically with few of the other associations and neutral parties willing to trade with them," Elder

Lu's voice was like a brewing storm as the members of the two association in the room had to take a moment to hide their anger.

Erik nodded, understanding their anger and knowing it wasn't directed at him. The Blue Lotus and Crafter's Association could not let this go. They would rather set a bloody example and remind people why they didn't cross them than be too tame and called weak.

"Why do you ask of the situation in Vuzgal?" Erik asked.

"Elder Lu, if I may?" Elder Redding asked.

He waved for her to continue.

"Vuzgal is a massive city and it is centrally located, connecting the eastern Chaotic Lands, the northern mountain ranges and the central plains. It was a booming trade route in the past and it can be so again in the future. We are wondering if you are willing to turn Vuzgal into a neutral trading city as you initially requested?

"We would pay a tax to you based on the transactions within Vuzgal, build Blue Lotus and Crafter's Association buildings here and assist in the security of the city. We can assist in the administration of the city as well." She smiled.

"We would remain as the leaders of Vuzgal and you are looking for a place to do business within the city?" Erik asked.

Vuzgal was a prime piece of meat but it was simply too large for Erik and Alva to take a bite of. It was probably one hundred or a thousand times bigger than the current Alva Dungeon's first floor, which they hadn't even filled up completely. If they had the support of others and could leverage their strength, it wasn't impossible and the could build up their strength taking complete control over the capital with time.

"Essentially we also want to invest in you and your Capital Vuzgal," she said.

Erik looked to Rugrat, who shrugged.

Erik found it hard to not roll his eyes at Rugrat. It wasn't what she had said but what she had left unsaid that Erik found interesting.

They will leave Vuzgal to us and they will establish buildings and their presence there. This shows our deep connection with them, few others would want to attack us and possibly piss off these two powers. If I can rope in the Alchemist association as well? The valley is a perfect place for grwoing herbs. If we can rebuild the city, start building crafting buyildings. Invite the fighter's association to raid the dungeon. We'll need to act quickly to build up Vuzgal and turn it into a real Capital once again. We'll need to power level people in Alva and hire outsiders to bolster our numbers and train up a larger military to secure Vuzgal's position. Alva has grown in strenght but we only really control Vermire. If we can get a city in the fourth realm with the support of the associations, and the crafting dungeon changes. Erik forced himself to remain calm, bering the ruler of a city, one as powerful as Vuzgal and with all of the possibilities that came with it, it made his blood boi.

There was just one problem they were just soldiers at the end of the day. Running a city, one as big as Vuzgal, was not something that they could do easily, if at all.

"What about the other associations and groups?" Rugrat asked.

"That would be up to you," Elder Redding said.

They're trying to get first dibs on Vuzgal, be in a position of power over the others. The best way to control them and make sure that things don't get imbalanced is to spread that power around.

"I will need to talk to my teacher first before I come to an agreement," Erik said. He wanted to agree right away and not let this opportunity pass but he had to make the most of this deal, it was a rare opportunity.

"The Crafter's Association is willing to wait. Though, I do have one more question." She looked at Erik and Rugrat, as if seeing right through them. "In the records, there is supposed to be one very powerful dungeon located in the valley, sealed off by the city. Have you visited it?"

"We have," Erik said, without any hesitation.

She studied them closer and sat back in her chair, pulling out a contract. "This is what we are willing to agree to." She held it out and the oath lawyer with them took it, putting it in front of Erik and Rugrat. Elder Lu pulled out another contract as well.

"Three percent of all transactions held within Vuzgal. Twenty percent discount for yourselves and the rest of your army on our goods. A guard force of four thousand paid for by us. We desire a plot of land inside the city. Our tax rate will not increase and a council will be made of the powerful figures within the city. You will have at least thirty percent voting power of said council at all times. Adding a new member to the council will have to be agreed by all other members of the council. We also ask to have exploration rights of the dungeon."

"Exploration rights?" Erik asked.

"We can freely enter and exit the dungeon as we desire," she said.

"The dungeon will be open freely to all but it will cost one Earth Mana stone or a talisman to enter," Erik said.

"Talisman?" Elder Lu asked.

"There is a recess in the entrance for a talisman. I'm not sure what it will do, but the dungeons come from the Ten Realms—I don't want to mess with it," Erik lied.

Elder Lu and Redding shared a look.

"It is good that we don't stand in the way of the Ten Realms," Redding finally said. "An Earth-grade Mana stone is expensive, though."

"We can come to an agreement about Vuzgal first and then discuss the dungeon later on," Erik said.

"In that case, we will reduce our guards to two thousand and ten percent discount with only two percent of transactions," Redding negotiated.

"Five percent discount and three percent of transactions," Erik countered.

Redding looked at Erik's face before she nodded. "Very well."

"And there will be no council. Rugrat and I will be the City Lords of Vuzgal, we will not interfere in the running of the associations and we ask that you do not interefer in the running of the capital."

Elder Lu and Redding looked at one another.

"I will only allow a small branch be built there then," Elder Redding said.

"That is fine, it can be built up over time, we are not in a rush," Erik said.

I wonder if you'll kick yourselves once you find out what kind of dungeon we have?

The contract actually changed before Erik's eyes, amended to what they had said.

"It is a unilateral agreement. We don't easily move into a new city and call it a neutral trading city," she said, seeing the look on his face.

"The Blue Lotus will agree to the same terms."

Erik and Rugrat read them over, checking the information contained within.

Rugrat pulled out a piece of paper and an ink brush. He copied down the information on the contract. It was special spell scroll paper but it wasn't like the glowing contracts that the others had put forward.

With Rugrat using crushed reactive ingredients and imbuing them with his Mana, they glowed as he wrote out the contract.

"Looks good," Erik said as they passed it to Xue Lin and Daniels.

They took it back to the two elders.

Rugrat's printing wasn't the cleanest, but it had gotten better with his carving out formations. Though they were still far from the elegance and refined script of the contracts the elders had offered.

"We haven't dealt with those contracts before, but these should do just fine," Erik said. *This way we can make sure that you haven't hidden something in the contracts.*

They reviewed the contracts and signed them. The contracts were covered in a golden glow as the Ten Realms verified the contracts between them. Now, even if the contracts were torn up, the Ten Realms oversaw the contract binding them to one another.

"I will go and report to the headquarters now." Redding announced as she took her leave and Daniels followed after her.

The door closed and Elder Lu seemed to transform as his face relaxed and he stood up.

"For what you did, for the sacrifices that you and your people made, even when one of our number went against you. The Blue Lotus owes you a great debt. One that we may never be able to repay, but one that the Blue Lotus will remember. You saved a city of people and a great number of my colleagues," Elder Lu cupped his hands and bowed to them both.

Hiao Xen's eyes went wide as Erik and Rugrat were a little stunned.

"Thank you," Elder Lu said.

"We were just doing the right thing," Erik said, his voice softening.

Elder Lu stood up and smiled.

"The Blue Lotus and the Crafter's Association are lucky that you were there. I have applied to the higher realms for a special medallion and honor," Elder Lu personally pulled out a box and opened it.

It was filled with emblems of the Blue Lotus.

"These medallions mark you as honorary elders of the Blue Lotus. You and your people will be allowed into any Blue Lotus. You can pay what the Blue Lotus members pay for items we offer. You will be respected as an elder. We will not interfere with your life and you will not need to deal with the inner runnings of the Blue Lotus. In the last one hundred years, there have only been sixteen of these given out," Elder Lu intoned, his voice heavy as they looked at the one hundred and seven medallions. "For those that stood with us, when in our time of need."

He offered the box and Erik took it. Seeing those medallions, his mind went to those that wouldn't be going home. He questioned his decision still, he knew it was the right thing, but he would never stop thinking about what would have happened if he did a few things differently.

"Thank you," Rugrat said.

Erik nodded as well.

Elder Lu cupped his hands to them.

"No, I thank you," Elder Lu said. "If you are ever in need, do not hesitate to contact me. The Blue Lotus has all kinds of people. I am sorry about what happened."

"Shit happens and Olivia was only doing what she felt was right and best for her people. In the heat of it all I was harsh, I wanted to shock her and I wanted a clear line of command. She meant well. Don't punish her too hard," Erik said in a humble voice.

"I'll look into it personally. She will have to be tested before she can take on another powerful position like the one she had. Sometimes being unable to do anything can be much worse than being able to do anything."

"Have you got another contract paper?" Erik asked Rugrat.

"Here," Rugrat said, passing him the paper and a brush.

Erik pulled out a ripped contract and copied out the information within its two halves onto the new contract and passed the rough paper to Elder Lu.

"This is the agreement for the use of the Age Rejuvenation concoctions. Taking them away from people that need them isn't fair," Erik said.

Elder Lu was deeply moved as he took the contract from Erik's hands.

"Thank you," Elder Lu said.

Erik felt that something was amiss but he only nodded.

"We've taken enough of your time, please feel free to come to Vuzgal when you like. It's not much now but hopefully we can change that in the future," Erik offered.

"I'll take you up on that sometime," Elder Lu smiled.

He personally saw them out of the Blue Lotus headquarters. People talked to one another looking at Erik and Rugrat who were wearing their rough cloaks. They didn't look noteworthy but from the way Elder Lu acted around them, others made sure to not approach and recorded their appearance.

"Now, what do you want to do with the rest of the army?" Rugrat asked as they left the main headquarters building, crossing the city towards the totem that would return them to Vuzgal.

"I want to recover our disabled undead, start to rebuild the city with them working around the clock. I want you to take a team back down, install the totem, and take our heroes home." Erik looked over to Rugrat.

"I'll watch over it personally," Rugrat promised.

"We'll have a ceremony tomorrow and you depart the next day, if possible. I will contact different people to try to garner interest or at least knowledge of Vuzgal and send messages to the other associations and the like. If we have more of the different associations in the capital, then we can reduce their individual power and get a greater say."

"Will they all come over?" Rugrat asked.

"Maybe not, but we field them the option. Those who come over at first will get the same contract as the Blue Lotus and the Crafter's Association. We test the waters and then we open up the dungeon to people. With that, anyone who comes afterward must take on a new contract. Those who came before will agree because they want an early advantage over them. And they will agree if they want to enter the dungeon. Once you have the totem up, we can start to transport materials to Alva. With Vuzgal, we should be able to increase our knowledge and pass it onto the schools. We have built up a lot of momentum to this point. It's time that Alva shined."

Chapter: Head Home

Erik knelt in front of each of the totems for the fallen, cracking a smile as he joked or talked about something that they had shared, his eyes unfocused. He had to look up to the sky frequently to stop the tears from falling.

He took a shaky breath and stood. He walked away from the totems before he turned back. His face was like a piece of stone as he snapped off a salute. In his eyes, he saw the faces of those who he would never see again—memories of him training them, seeing them in trouble, seeing them laughing. Scenes that warmed his heart now and cut it like a knife at the same time.

Erik wandered back as he headed to the inner city castle.

The Alvan army had taken over the castle as their own once again.

Erik laid back on his bed, his body tired. He had not slept in a long time.

His notifications screamed at him angrily.

==========

Skill: Throwables

==========

Level: 46 (Apprentice)

==========

Your throws gain 5% power

==========

==========

Skill: Marksman

==========

Level: 65 (Journeyman)

==========

Long-range weapons are familiar in your hands. When aiming, you can zoom in x2. 0. 15% increased chance for critical hit.

==========

==========

Skill: Hand-to-Hand

==========

Level: 61 (Journeyman)

==========

Attacks cost 20% less Stamina. Agility is increased by 10%.

==========

==========

Skill: Stealth

==========

Level: 49 (Apprentice)

==========

When in stealth, your senses are sharpened by 5%

==========

My marksman was a result of me being able to use firearms and combining it with the new skills and abilities in the realms. While I was fighting, I was able to understand more about fighting hand-to-hand and incorporating fighting with several styles.

==========

Event

==========

You have successfully defended Vuzgal.
Rewards:
700,000 EXP
+10% defensive bonus to Vuzgal defenders.

==========

==========

Event

==========

You have saved the people of Tareng.

==========

Rewards:

120,000,000 EXP

Vuzgal gains the Title: Protector.

==========

==========

City Title: Protector

==========

Vuzgal forces and their allies receive a 10% overall buff when fighting within the Capital's territory. Enemies are debuffed 5% while in territory

==========

Erik let out a low whistle as Erik and the other members of the Alva military were covered in the golden glow of experience and the territory around Vuzgal was altered by the ten realms.

==========

You have reached Level 57

==========

When you sleep next, you will be able to increase your attributes by: 15 points.

==========

==========

35,877,377/56,900,000EXP till you reach Level 58

==========

His fighting ability had increased but right now he just wanted to get away from even thinking about combat. But he knew that he would be dragged right back in, he always did. He had faced losses before, but he kept fighting.

He sat up and pulled out a notepad and a pen. He took a breath and started writing letters to the fallen's families.

It looked as though it might be some time before he slept again.

Light started to creep in the next morning as Erik looked at the letters he had written. Paper littered his storage rings from his failed writings.

Still, those simple letters didn't seem like enough but they were all he could do. He met up with Rugrat in the morning, letters in hand.

"Everything ready?" Erik asked.

"Ready. And I pulled the people coming with me, closest to them and the like," Rugrat said.

They fell into silence.

"Get some sleep. We need you in your best condition," Rugrat said.

"I can do it later. I'm going to check on the dungeon," Erik said.

"Don't get caught. And I'm serious about the sleep."

"I will later." Erik headed into the castle after handing off the letters with shaking hands. With the dungeon core interface, he was able to see under the city. Moving the ground underneath the city allowed them to see everything, 'claiming' it as part of the dungeon.

They had found all types of hidden areas around Vuzgal. It allowed them to locate loot in a number of caches.

Erik used one of these tunnels to head out from the castle and into the valley, coming out of a cave in the mountains with towering peaks to either side.

It didn't take him long to enter the Bala Dungeon.

He accessed the plans of the dungeon and walked around. The new crafting areas had been completed. There was the original entrance that went into the fighting dungeon, but now there were new stairs down from a different entrance that reached a landing that had six corridors. Above each different hallway, there was a marker to show what kind of craft was practiced beyond.

These corridors spread out, ringing the main dungeon with crafting areas.

The first floor was for the Novices, then as the floors descended it went the Apprentices, then the Journeyman and finally the Experts. From the hallway transitions of Apprentice to Journeyman, there were areas filled with ingredients one could use for their craft. If the crafter were able to create an Expert level item, they would be randomly gifted a powerful item related to their craft.

After finishing, the crafting trial tester would get a token based on which level they had completed, allowing them to bypass the other earlier skill level floors on special staircases. If more than one person went down the stairs without a token, the door at the bottom wouldn't open to allow them into the testing areas.

One could only take the crafting trial once per month normally if they had a talisman they could enter an additional two times a month, for a total of three times as long as there was space.

Erik didn't really understand how, but the Ten Realms somehow took the power of the Mana that the dungeon core had refined as well as the different attributed Mana and created growing fields, mines, trees, raw leather, as well as ingredients as per their agreement.

Erik took his time walking the dungeon. It was the first time that he had been able to find peace in recent days.

There was a noise behind him. He looked to see a small, cute-looking Gilga rapidly expanding and becoming bigger.

"Didn't I tell you to stay in the city?" Erik admonished.

She cocked her head to the side and made a keening noise.

Erik could feel her care for him through their bond. He snorted, unable to get angry with her as he patted her side and scratched her scales as she made happy noises. Erik had forgotten how much comfort one could find with their animal friends.

Erik took some time, collecting himself before he got a call from Rugrat.

"Fred and his people have made some decisions," Rugrat said. "Meet us at their cottages?"

"On my way." Erik headed out of the dungeon and moved toward the cottages. He found the demi-human group standing there.

Elizabeth was hiding in William's chest as Racquel was talking to Rugrat, kissing him on the cheek before heading over to stand with the others.

Fred stepped forward to greet Erik.

"We wish to travel the Fourth Realm. Now that there is no threat, we'll head out. I hope that our paths will cross again," Fred held out his hand.

Erik nodded. "Thank you for your help. I hope we will be able to meet again." Erik and Fred shared an awkward handshake, Fred only recently having learned of the human custom.

"As do I," Fred said.

They said their goodbyes. Fred used a spell to help Old Xern. They stepped into the sky and quickly headed away. It was abrupt, but they didn't care for social norms and their straightforward actions were refreshing.

"Well, you should get packed up. We'll be heading to Alva in six hours," Rugrat said.

Time passed quickly as Erik sent out messages through Hiao Xen to the other associations about Vuzgal. He surveyed the damage to the city himself and put the Alvan army to work, re-building the capital and recovering the undead.

Some of their undead were destroyed beyond repair, while others simply needed more magical power. They were creatures of the dungeon, so they could be reformed. They didn't have a blueprint like some creatures that allowed them to be built with just a few reactants and the power of the dungeon core. Once they were completely destroyed, then they were gone and repairing them was incredibly power-intensive. But Erik put a priority on it. After all, they had plenty of power stored up in the main pillar.

People from Tareng had left in a flood already. The Vuzgal totem had worked all night and day, with people heading back home. Some had asked about buying a plot of land in Vuzgal.

Erik quoted them prices that one might have to pay in one of the much larger neutral trading cities that had at least three associations in it.

Not many had been willing to spend that kind of money.

Although the Blue Lotus and the Crafter's Association had put down their claim, there were only a few people who had arrived to survey the area and start building. Erik saw that there was a great interest in Vuzgal. Although it might grow in the coming years, it would need time to do so.

Erik had a plan to deal with that, but it would take time.

"Make sure to send Matt and others along as soon as you can. We have an opportunity to build out Vuzgal. I want to make sure that it is the best that we can do," Erik reminded Rugrat.

"I've got the list. Are you sure you don't want to go and deal with the council and their meeting about the future of Alva?" Rugrat asked, sounding incredibly close to pleading.

"You know I need to stay here," Erik said. "Don't worry, just—you know, try to think before you say anything?"

"Thanks for the pep talk," Rugrat said sarcastically.

"See you on the other side." Erik raised his fist.

"You know it, brother." Rugrat bumped his fist and turned toward the totem.

The rest of the group—around thirty from the Alvan army—headed to the totem with him. A flash covered them after a few moments of menu scrolling, headed back to the First Realm with totem parts in tow.

"All right, let's see if we can't make a barbecue out of this and lift the no-drinking ban," Erik said to Glosil, who was a little farther away from the totem, his voice loud enough that the others heard him.

They smiled and a few cheered as they headed back to the castle.

Even with the fire, food, drink, and company, the soldiers from Alva's army were all subdued. They were starting to recover from the losses—well, recover was one way to put it. They were learning how to bury the pain so that they could keep on going.

Erik and Rugrat had talked about the effects of post-traumatic stress disorder and how it affected people. Erik knew that there would be those among them who were affected and others who were able to deal with their issues and could continue to be in the military.

He was determined that even if they had PTSD or other psychological issues, he wouldn't abandon them or push them to the side as happened with the militaries back on Earth. It was easier to overcome it if they were still in, if that was what they wanted. Alva would see it as their duty to care for them as they had been willing to put down their lives; that was the agreement that they made serving in the military.

Seeing them together, it allowed them to decompress some and realize that the fighting had stopped, at least for now.

They talked about the people they had lost, or about things they had seen. War was no longer some foreign concept as the theories and information crammed into their brains by Erik and Rugrat had turned into reactions and tactics to be used to keep them alive.

I wish that tactics and training were enough to keep them all alive.

That night Erik increased his stats again, the gains they had made in the fourth realm had been immense, increasing the strength of the military to the point that they could enter the sixth realm freely.

We'll have to focus on our cultivation in the coming months, as we go higher, levels become secondary, skills, weapons, armor and cultivation have a much larger impact.

He closed his eyes.

==========

You have 15 attribute points to use.

==========

Three to Agility, should keep the trend going, three into mana regeneration and stamina regeneration, then six into mana pool. I really need to start increasing my mana cultivation. I can't let Rugrat get too far ahead.

==========

Name: Erik West

==========

Level: 57

==========

Race: Human

==========

Titles:

From the Grave II

Mana Emperor

Dungeon Master III
Reverse Alchemist
Poison Body
Fire Body
City Lord
==========
Strength: (Base 36) +41
==========
770
==========
Agility: (Base 29) +72
==========
555
==========
Stamina: (Base 39) +23
==========
930
==========
Mana: (Base 8) +79
==========
870
==========
Mana Regeneration (Base 10) +58
35. 00/s
==========
Stamina Regeneration: (Base 41) +59
21. 00/s
==========

Chapter: Heroes Return

Rugrat and the people of the Alvan army crossed the familiar Beast Mountain Range. Their mounts were much faster than before and it didn't take them much time to cross the ground.

They had sent word ahead; as they got to the valley, the cave entrance into Alva Dungeon appeared ahead of them. They dismounted from their mounts. They took out carts. On each of the carts, there were two coffins. On each of them was the symbol of Alva's army: a blue flame in the background with a crossbow and a sword crossed over it, with the words *Serve, Protect, Defend*, and *Loyal* carved into the circular emblem.

The Adventurer's Guild members and the policing force that had been caring for Alva stood at the checkpoints. They stood like statues as the mounts pulling the carts and the army marched into Alva.

"Heroes, salute!" a commander called out. The people at the first checkpoint slammed their fists against their chest as one, making the heroes' guard stand taller as they escorted their friends home.

They passed the first checkpoint and reached the next, the same scene being carried out as people saluted their heroes on their return.

They passed through the final checkpoint, entering Alva. People lined up on the main pathway from the checkpoint to the barracks.

Family members held onto one another, crying as they looked at the guard as they marched forward, not stopping. Some, even as they tried to fight it, let tears fall down their cheeks. Regardless of reactions, they didn't break their march. They didn't dare to wipe their tears—this was their friends' day.

"Hero escort, halt!" Rugrat ordered as they came to the barracks, its gates sealed.

"Who goes there?" Blaze asked from the barracks wall.

"Lily Ershman! Douglas Sorrez, Zhi Smith." Rugrat went through the names of the fallen, bringing new tears from the families. The rest of the guards stood there with their mounts, looking onward.

"Alva welcomes home her sons and daughters once more," Blaze intoned.

The doors to the barracks opened. Inside, there were men and women of the merchant factions, from the farms, from the academies, from the Adventurer's Guild—men and women who had all served in Alva's army, welcoming home their heroes.

"To Alva's heroes! Salute!" Blaze's voice bellowed through the barracks as these people who had been across the Ten Realms and that had rushed back to Alva for this ceremony all snapped off a salute.

"Heroes escort, for-ward!"

They marched into the barracks.

They were finally home.

Chapter: Alva's Determination

After Rugrat finished his duty and the fallen were placed into a hall for the families to see, he headed to the dungeon core. He called Egbert and Delilah as he took a collection of storage devices on a string with him.

Egbert was there and Delilah didn't take long to arrive.

"This is a Ten Realms totem. I don't know how many people we can get to work in the short term but this is our number-one priority. We need to get this up and running to create a link to Vuzgal so we can facilitate the movement of supplies to Alva. I don't know if it will even work, a city totem in a dungeon, but we need to try. You will have all of the automatons at your command to build it and you're allowed to use all the power that you need," Rugrat said. "I will assist you in building it, and the defenses around it. We need to be ready for anything."

He turned to face Delilah. "People who are related to the deceased will be allowed five days off to deal with their losses. Others will be allowed the day of the funeral off. The council meeting will proceed as planned. I will be heading it with you. We will honor our heroes and that means that Alva will continue on."

"Understood," Delilah said.

"Get me Matt, and those in the blueprint office and the construction department. I want them to look at Vuzgal and its construction. We only have a limited period of time that we can build the foundation that others will build upon. We need to look at the different people we will need to run Vuzgal. Thankfully, we will be basically just the central government and as long as we don't encroach on the contracts with the associations, what we say will be. We've got little time until the other associations gain interest, so we need to get everything in place now," Rugrat said. "Now it is time that we consolidate our gains. We need to carry out some small actions across the Fourth Realm to make sure we don't draw attention to ourselves and then we can look to Alva instead of external matters."

"Understood," Delilah said.

"We have a lot of work to do." Rugrat turned to Egbert and they headed out of the dungeon headquarters as Delilah started to send messages. There were people living in different cities who would relay the messages through to those in the other realms who could relay the message on through the Adventurer's Guild, the merchants, or the network of Alvans across the realms.

It only took a few hours until Matt got a message and started his trip back to Alva.

People went back to work, filled with a new determination. The funeral would be in a few days.

Seeing their heroes return, those who had come to Alva recently felt a greater connection to it. Those who already thought of themselves as Alvans, were filled with a sense of pride and loss that they didn't think possible. It had been their boys and girls who had died out there, for their dream, for Alva to grow.

They weren't going to let them down; for those who had sacrificed their tomorrow, they would work to build Alva today.

Those who had left Alva on different trips came back. The city filled with people from across the realms.

Rugrat visited the families of the fallen, passing them letters from the commanders who hadn't been able to come.

The families read the words from Glosil and Erik. New tears came forward, but there was not only a sense of loss in their cries, but also pride, proud of their loved ones and what they had been able to do.

A location was picked out for the totem, opposite the teleportation pad. To the north lay the totem, to the south the teleportation pad, to the west the barracks and the entrance to the dungeon. The east was all farmland.

Workers piled in, all taking construction jobs. Rugrat acted as the foreman, Egbert his assistant as the construction workers and the automatons worked together, building the totem day and night with the parts that had been carried from Vuzgal.

The people of Alva threw themselves into work. The cafeteria became livelier as people came together to talk and to meet one another. Bars and tea shops did a brisk business as people from the other realms met up with their friends and family.

***

Elan Silaz had gone back and forth from Vermire to Alva repeatedly. He had purchased a Mana gathering formation from Qin. The reason that he was able to sell Mana stones was because he had been able to get a Mortal Mana cornerstone. He had found out that allowing the Mana cornerstone to consume the power of a monster core could allow it to grow Mana stones. Monster cores were useful for increasing one's level or being used in different crafts, but combined with a spell he had learned, he could contain more of the monster core's power and force it into the cornerstone, greatly increasing its yield and multiplying the value of the monster cores.

With the Mana gathering and Mana storing formations, he could just put the monster cores in and they would be consumed, automatically filling the cornerstone with energy. Mana stone mines usually got smaller as they grew larger because the Mana in a large area would be sucked dry. With him supplying the monster cores and isolating the Mana cornerstone with formations, Mana stones could grow much faster.

He had looked at the Mana formation up on the ceiling of Alva Dungeon multiple times in jealousy. He could see the Mana stones that only got larger each time he returned.

He had learned that Yui was coming back and rushed back to Alva. He had seen the procession entering Alva and then the barracks. He recognized his emotions and his thoughts. He wanted to become a part of Alva, to be someone to share that burden. He wanted to pay homage to those who passed.

Like for many others, a barrier crumbled. He had seen Yui, Domonos, and Qin as people using Alva for their abilities. Now, seeing Yui and Qin in front of him, he knew that they were not using Alva: they were part of Alva, its beating heart. They believed in it in a way he found hard to understand.

"Yui, I need yours and Domonos's help to boost me," Qin said suddenly.

Elan and Yui looked at her. She no longer looked like a young princess but a woman of power. Her voice was calm and level, filled with a level of authority Elan had only recognized recently as he saw her dealing with her duties as a department head.

"What for?" Yui asked. There was a new depth to his eyes. He didn't just see her as his younger sister anymore.

"Formations. The Crafter's Association has formation schools in the Fourth Realm. In the Third Realm, there are sects, but formations are still a closely guarded secret. In the Fourth, they're much more widespread. I have been fumbling around with formations. We've put them together and upgraded a few. Even a beast can put together a few pieces of the puzzle, but they don't know the overall picture that the puzzle pieces make," Qin said.

"You'll need to do as we say and you'll have to have some more training before we take you to the Fourth Realm," Yui said, not denying her.

"The Fourth Realm is a land of death and destruction and you want to walk into it to learn about formations?" Elan scoffed, his voice harsh as he thought of the dangers that they would be walking into.

"Father," Qin eye's narrowed as she looked at him.

Elan grimaced and looked away, grinding his teeth. His children were much stronger than him, but that didn't change the fact that they were still his children. He cared and feared for them. Since he had learned that Yui and Domonos were in the Fourth Realm, he hadn't been able to sleep well and he had thought that it might have been a joke. He knew his boys were good fighters, but he never saw them as people to go to the Fourth Realm. He glanced at Yui, his sons Strength was now so high he couldn't even get anything close to a read on his levels.

Going to the Fourth Realm to learn about formations and I am here, thinking about growing a few Mana stones.

A flash of light appeared in his eyes as he nodded to himself. *It's time that I got serious. I might not be skilled in crafting, but I am a trader and a fighter. The loan I can apply for is sizable. If I was able to liquidate some of my assets in the First Realm and push into the higher realms... Will I just remain in the First Realm as they head higher? I will open up new trade routes and recruit people to Alva's side.*

He was normally a calm man, but now a determined look appeared on his face as he started to see a new future. He had been thinking about retiring, about slowing down, but as his thoughts grew, a new path appeared. He felt his blood boiling and his aura started to fluctuate powerfully.

"Father?" Yui hadn't seen his father lose control of his emotions this much other than when he and his siblings had been bleeding.

"All right, let's see just how far we can go," Elan Silaz said. "You charge ahead and I will come behind. From now on, the headquarters of the Silaz trading house will be in Alva."

His voice was not loud but both Yui and Qin had stunned looks as they saw their father's gaze before they looked at each other. All of them were looking toward a new future, a future that they never thought possible before.

Loss in the ten realms was normal, with everyone struggling to gain more power more strength. There were bound to be those that lost, those that died along the path.

The strength of Alva's people had increased drastically, it was a time to celebrate their new position. Instead of breaking out the food and wine to celebrate.

The people of Alva recognized those that had fallen. With their new position their strength would grow in leaps and bounds. People would remember the sacrifices that were made today for them to grow.

Thirteen men and women gave their lives for this opportunity. It shouldn't be taken for granted and they would forever need to prove that they were worthy of those young men and women's lives.

Chapter: Dust to Dust

Blaze looked out at Alva from the headquarters building. It had been months since he had last been in Alva. He was back for the meeting of the council with Elise.

The number of Alvan residents had increased to two thousand. Nearly a fifth of that outside of the dungeon, working as traders, students to different Masters, wandering the realms, or adventurers forging their own path.

Newly styled apartment buildings were being made. They took up the area of five houses but they reached up into the sky. There was talk of them reaching to the top of the dungeon.

His eyes traced the Ten Realms Totem that was being built up.

He took a deep breath and turned to the rest of the room. All of the members of the council were there. Elise leaned back in her chair, rocking slightly. Blaze stood, facing outward. Egbert sat down with a pen in hand as Elise, Delilah, Jia Feng, Glosil, Blaze, and Rugrat grabbed bits from the refreshments table. Having a late meal together just as they had back in Alva when they were defending their village. Now with the addition of Delilah and Egbert who was simply sitting there and talking to them.

"All right," Rugrat said. People moved back to their seats as Rugrat took one of the two seats at the head of the table. On the left there was Egbert; on the right, Delilah.

"We'll go around the table. What I want from you is what have you been doing, what went successfully, current operations and operations that failed." Rugrat looked to Delilah first.

"Alva has grown to a population of two thousand. We have more people coming in from across the realms, including people now from the Second Realm. The unclaimed land in Alva has been turned into farmland. The iron mines are thinning out, so we are looking for other veins of materials in the mountain range and have sought out trading partners discreetly for different materials." Delilah looked to Elise and nodded to her.

"The water treatment plant had to be increased in size with more people living in Alva. We have replaced needing to use spells with a series of formations that act like alchemical and cooking filters to clean the water for consumption once again. Building projects are underway to create taller buildings, like the Sky Reaching Restaurant in the Third Realm, so we aren't taking up farmland needlessly. This report details the loan and saving situation within Alva." Delilah pulled out a piece of paper and handed it to Rugrat.

"Otherwise, we have had people apply to join the military, but we have placed them with the policing force to at least give them some training. We have also started to stockpile the required materials needed for us to build tier-four buildings minus the funds needed as they are used with the banking system.

"The banking system has set up branches in the Sky Reaching Restaurant in the Third Realm and the headquarters of the Adventurer's Guild in Kaeju, with regional branches in other Adventurer's Guild branches. These are run by the Adventurer's Guild members but managed by the Alva Bank," Delilah reported.

"We are currently developing the Alchemy garden and the farmlands, increasing their growth speed. We are managing the space given over to farming and to residences and making sure that buildings are built according to the codes Matt has created. We are issuing multiple loans to encourage business within and outside of Alva. Elan Silaz was able to track down information about us, so I am having the policing forces look into ways to cover our tracks more. Possibly have more locations for the Alva

Healing House but I wanted to see what your thoughts were," Delilah said.

"Have Lord Aditya admit to a few people here and there that the Alva Healing House owes him a favor. Have the healing house corroborate his story. What about the other nations and groups around the Beast Mountain Range? Have they done much these last couple of months?"

"They have been busy with the collapse of the Zatan Confederation. The lost cities have been recovered and they are re-establishing their rule. The other groups in the area see Vermire as a neutral location to carry out their business. Vermire is expanding, nearly doubling its size to accommodate all of the new trade. There is one issue there—the fact that the animals of the Beast Mountain Range have been killed off by us. It has had an impact on the hunters. They are talking about the low amount of beasts in the area."

"Have the beast tamers and the alchemists work together to add concoctions to bodies of water and cultivate different ingredients that the beasts would consume, to increase their virility and their Strength. It would not be bad if there were a number of powerful beasts that make people in the First Realm not want to come close to us. A screen of creatures that would be hard for others to pass," Rugrat said.

Delilah nodded and made a number of notes. "That is all I have to say."

Rugrat looked to Jia Feng.

"We have changed the name of the tailoring department to the clothier department as they are not dealing with just forming clothes. They are looking at creating different weaves from sourcing their materials to giving someone a final product. There are five hundred people who have graduated from the elementary courses; there are forty children from five to thirteen who are being taught elementary courses and skills. They are allowed to specify which skill they want to do after they graduate and will get one year of free skill teaching from whatever department they desire. After that, they should be able to make items to pay for their later schooling. Adults are taking the accelerated courses, at night or on the weekends, but they do not get the free term afterward and have to pay for it. But with increased student loans, anyone who wants to can take a course.

"All of the different departments' main buildings have reached the third tier; this is a sheet detailing the Journeymen-level personnel. We have made a new program for people who are not students of the academy to rent out different workshops. The merchants have also started to create their own workshops and assembly lines. We have a number of people who are heading to the higher realms if they have the required level, such as the Third Realm to do cooking, or going to Vermire to deal in healing. Others are traveling the realms in search of inspiration and information on their craft.

"Without people heading to the battlefield dungeon, we have not been able to get more information books, but already the library's reserves of information are large. Though there is book learning and physical learning. Even with all of the books, getting subject matter Experts greatly increases the speed that one can advance their skill. Tan Xue is an Expert smith and having crossed the skill bottlenecks, she can help out the other smiths. It is part of the reason that they have the most Journeyman-level smiths. While one muyst have a firm understanding of the basics, they need more detailed and higher level information so that they can continue to advance. We have been promoting the students to test out their ideas and it has revealed interesting paths of development. It's just much slower. Books are one thing and information is great, but I want to put forward that we should be looking to recruit Journeyman and Experts as a priority. These people can affect a much greater change than just information," Jia Feng said.

Rugrat smiled a bit before letting out a deep breath. "Getting one Expert is already rare. Erik's teacher Old Man Hei is an Expert in the Third Realm, one of *three*. While they are much more common in the fourth realm, they only appear in large numbers in the Fifth Realm and are considered not common. But you could have more than a handful of them in one city in the Sixth Realm. With our inroads to the Fourth Realm, we can try to entice these crafters to assist us and create an academy in Vuzgal to train our people secretly.

"There are Crafter's Association locations across the Fourth Realm. They are insular, but with them just being there, there are people trying to join them. They can be considered subject matter Experts. Although the Crafter's Association might not take some applicants, they might be valuable to our Alva. If they can grow here, then it would give us powerful Experts without poaching from the Crafter's Association.

"Also, Erik and I plan to make the different groups that come to Vuzgal share some of their teachings. We hope to entice people who are visiting the city or the dungeon to join them in knowledge sharing, and to teach the people in the city, increasing its strength. If our people can attend these lectures and gain new ways to pursue information, it wouldn't be so hard as it has been in the past. That said, finding compatible Experts and Masters will be the goal of the traders and all of Alva's different groups.

"The one thing I haven't mentioned is that we can get recordings of everything happening in the crafting dungeon, so we can watch Journeyman- and Expert-level crafters without any fee. And we will be building a crafter's trial here in Alva as well, though we will need to increase the dungeon core's power so that it reaches farther."

Jia Feng quickly wrote down notes as the others on the council looked at Rugrat.

"The academy will be excited to learn this news." Her eyes shining as she gave a wide smile.

Rugrat let out a slight chuckle at her expression.

"Another sixty people graduated from the academy, and there are three hundred people as part of advanced education learning different skills currently. We are just losing too many people who are going other places to learn," Jia Feng.

"I wouldn't consider this a failing. They are people of Alva, in the end, and although they learned from here, they paid their fees and then they made items that were used by Alva. If we start trying to force them to stay, then fewer people will join us. Some may return of their free will, others might not. We aren't a sect," Rugrat said.

"I have erred," Jia Feng apologized.

"It is understandable. Alva's greatest strength comes from its people," Rugrat said.

Jia Feng nodded. Her eyes had been opened to the wide world. Being in Alva, where Journeymen were common, she thought it would be easy to bring in Experts and to grow the people that they had.

Blaze was next as he cleared his throat and looked at his notes.

"The Adventurer's Guild has headed into the Second and, to a limited degree, the Third Realm. With our head location in Kaeju, we've also established fifteen secondary branches in different cities around it, with trade routes run by the Trader's Association. All of the revenue of the Adventurer's Guild that has not been used to pay people for their services has been put back into the associations, building new facilities. We have about eight hundred adventurers, three hundred of which are people from Alva. We have about two or three thousand who are trying to join the Adventurer's Guild but we're not expanding rapidly—we want to maintain the quality of our people.

"Traders already have our teams in large demand and there are a number of private contracts to clear out beasts that have entered someone's land or there is a dangerous area that some researchers want to go in, that kind of thing. We believe that the Adventurer's Guild could eventually grow to eighty or one hundred thousand trained adventurers. We are looking at people to bring over to Alva, but it will take time for us to weed out those people that would be a good fit. We want to make sure that they don't have any alternative alliances or motives.

"Since we heard about the Fighter's Association in the Fourth Realm, we have been looking into that in greater detail. It looks like we are in direct competition in many ways. Though, they don't go to the lower realms. If we are able to reach into the higher realms, we need to look at how we would act on that. Do we keep separate from the Fighter's Association, do we pursue trying to become a root association—"

"A root association?" Delilah interrupted.

"Different places that cross realms can be broken down into roots and branches. The roots are the smaller places in the lower realms that feed up into the larger sects. These sects band together to survive, in say the fourth realm. Some of these sects reach higher, as they reach higher they create branches, smaller powerful groups that act as a hidden strength and deterrant behind the main combined sects.

With associations, they have their roots in the lower realms and don't band together but instead specialize. As people reach a higher strength they focus on their talents. Take the fighter's association. In the higher realms, there are specific classes and academies within the association that teach just Fire mages, just abjuration or illusion mages, fighters who use poison or those who use crossbows or sabers. If we become a root for the Fighter's Association, then we can't allow people from Alva to join. Once becoming a member of the Fighter's Association, then they are not allowed to be part of any other society. They could accept the oath, but then if asked about Alva, the two oaths would conflict and they would die.

"People who are external to the Adventurer's Guild could move into the Fighter's Association with no problem, but not those that have been accepted into Alva. So we're going to have to be very careful about who we want to become people of Alva and we have to look at what we're going to do once we encounter the Fighter's Association. We're a small player now, but say we get into a conflict or something—then we can have a big problem on our hands," Blaze said.

The others seemed to agree, but Blaze only really saw understanding in Rugrat and Elise's eyes. They had been to the other realms and been out of Alva the longest; they had been able to see the differences in the realms. "We have had different people try to enter our association who are spies from other groups. We have denied them all at this time, but we're getting attention."

"If we know who the spies are, there is no problem having them enter. They can feed their people wrong information and make us look better. The spies we know of are fine—the ones we don't are the problem. As people get to higher ranks and we take them in more, their contracts should become more restrictive, not allowing them to turn on us," Rugrat said.

"If they don't want to agree to these contracts?" Blaze asked.

"We don't force them but it means that they will stay at their current stage. Take it slow. It would be nice to have hundreds of thousands of people in the association, but quality over quantity. What about training?" Rugrat asked.

"That has been our bottleneck. We're paying our current members who are good for teaching a massive amount to do that instead of actually being adventurers." Blaze sighed.

"Don't force them all, or else the quality of the fighters will start to decrease because their training staff don't want to be there. Like we've done here—only the strongest can be the teachers, and they get the greatest benefit. Others get a solid salary for teaching, testing, and training the new people. If they truly want to be someone of the Adventurer's Guild, they will wait. If they don't—well, it doesn't really matter. Slow and steady—we have expanded rapidly in many different directions. It's time we consolidate our gains and take our time. If we race now, then the foundation of these new areas might falter."

"Understood," Blaze said, surprised by Rugrat's words. He had always thought of Erik as the leader. Rugrat might goof around and he was an idiot at times, but when it was important, he took his time to look through all the information before he came to a decision.

Blaze remembered when he had been hunting in Alva, Rugrat had been watching over him and his group.

There was a wolf that had charged him but an arrow that seemed to have eyes moved around his body, hitting the wolf. It was an incredible shot. He thought it had been lucky and it took him some time to find out that it had been Rugrat to hit the wolf. If it wasn't for him, then he would have been badly wounded at best.

He was happy to keep up the appearance that he was a simple redneck, but the truth was much more complicated. Otherwise, how would he have been able to make firearms, mortars, sockets, and more?

"We have people coming to us, trying to purchase weapons and gear from us directly in different places where their gear isn't that good. We've made it mandatory for people to be part of the association to purchase from us, that way the weapons are being used to increase our strength instead of competing against us. We have also been looking at moneylending and sending money through the branches. There are competitors in the area and I would prefer to keep it limited to just our people and those in the associations and their families before we can challenge these other groups. Even if we don't mean it in that way, they're sure to take it like that."

"Understood. It will be a good way to bring funds to the traders to increase the amount we can loan out, but if a short-term gain leads to long-term instability..." Rugrat tilted his hand, leaving the rest unsaid.

"Agreed," Bkaze nodded.

"Anything else?"

"That is all I have." Blaze sat back in his seat as he looked at Elise, who sat forward.

"This is going to be a long one," she warned Rugrat. Blaze snorted as he got comfortable. He knew most of what she was going to say; he had been there for most of it.

Elise glared at Blaze as he just smiled sweetly.

She narrowed her eyes at him. *Looks like I'll be in trouble later.* His smile only grew wider.

"Well thankfully I'm comfortable, small words please?" Rugrat said with a smile.

Elise shook her head and started talking.

"Our trade routes crisscross most of the continent Alva resides on in the First Realm. We trade mainly food items for raw resources that we sell to Alva to be refined or trained with. Low end goods are taken to the Second realm, and sold there for whatever is good. Industry has started to take root there with most of the trading conglomerates.

Food is taken to the third realm as well as high quality items. Trading in the third realm is hard as most people already have set trade routes. The first and second realms are the money makers for Alva. Looking at the fourth realm our outlook is better than ever.

Plenty of traders will want to move in, we have a large stock of high quality weapons, armors, concoctions, medical supplies, cultivation resources. Not because we didn't have a market but the only people we could trade with were the associations. The people of the lower realms didn't have the money to make moving and selling the products to them, worth it."

Elise finished her piece as Rugrat was still writing down notes. It was some time before he was done.

"How should we develop Vuzgal to increase trade? As a Neutral city it would be stupid to not capitalize."

"I would put forward that we should have our own auction house. If we have crafters there, we have stores to sell their goods directly or get commissions. We will need to look at the structure for traders and crafters that are coming from outside."

"Why the auction house, doesn't the Blue Lotus do a good job?"

"They do, but they sell the best items, people don't need the best items all the time, just rare items sometimes. We should also create a trading platform between people. We hold items for a fee and then sell them on their behalf, people are busy and if we can increase the population and trading even for a small holding fee and taxation we could earn a slow but steady income."

Rugrat was impressed.

"I'll need a report detailing these different plans."

Elise pulled out a few folders and put them on the desk.

"I'll grab those afterwards." Rugrat took a breath expelling it with his first word.

"*Now* Vuzgal. We have the Blue Lotus and the Crafter's Association building in the city, more out of thanks than business at this point. It gives us protection from would be agressors. They do not know about the crafting dungeon yet that I sent you all information on. Erik wants to tell the various other associations and pillar groups about Vuzgal, in an attempt to interest them, then rebuild Vuzgal how we want it to be. We plan to invite navigators over from across the Fourth Realm, people who cross through the totems, to have access to Vuzgal and bring in traffic and customers.

"We have created a dungeon that targets crafters. Erik and I- if you have another opinion please tell us- are thinking of making Vuzgal focus on crafting. Replicate the facilities that we have here. Create an Academy to recruit talents, workshops inside the city to bring in more people and trade. We add in Sky Reaching Resturants and Wayside inns-which will be palces people can rent and stay in for periods of time instead of buying housing. Erik is looking to invite the Alchemist Association to work the valley. With time we hope ti turn Vuzgal into a hub of trade and training. Concurrently," Rugrat took a breath, "Glosil will coordinate the expansion of the Alva military, it's reorganization and reclaiming the remaining floors of Alva Dungeon."

Blaze sat forward. It wasn't that the other parts weren't alarming, but they would need to hide things and tiptoe around. The other things would be just complicated and annoying to deal with. The other floors of Alva Dungeon were still an intriguing mystery from the day they entered Alva. He wanted to know just what was lurking in the depths below.

"We get that totem put up and then we can start moving materials and people around with greater freedom. If some power level it won't be long until they can make it into the fourth realm" Rugrat said. "Alva must be stronger than it was yesterday. We have a duty not only to those who water the ground with their blood, but for the people who are living. We need to press the advantage while we have it and grow faster than ever before."

"What about the resources stockpiled in Vuzgal, Alva and the other branches?" Delilah asked.

"With the new totem, everything should be gathered in Alva. The items should be evaluated. What to be reserved for the academies and to grow Vuzgal and Alva, then what should be sold. Elise you will need to break down what should be sold to our traders, what should be sold in Vuzgal for the greatest profits."

"Do you have an idea of what items were recovered?" Elise asked.

"Kind of," Rugrat said and took out a piece of paper, it went around the table to Elise.

"Assorted jewlery, gems, gold silvers and worked high value items, Four thousand eight hundred and fifty items. Crafting materials two hundred and five different kinds, varying amounts. Crafted items. Thirty-five thousand one hundred and thirty seven. High level apprentice and above in quality, with multiples. Salvaged miscellanious items deemed possibly valuable, written works, or unable to categorize, twenty-eight thousand Seven hundred and twelve items with multiples," Elise read out the different categories.

"Well you really did loot an entire city," Egbert said, with a note of approval.

"Didn't even leave the floor tiles in some places," Rugrat said with pride. "Using good metal like that is a waste of coin!"

"Did you leave anything in the city?" Elise asked.

"Well we weren't able torecord everything, just gathered it up and grouped it together to ship it down. That's probably about a third, maybe a half?" Rugrat thought aloud.

"

***

Rugrat was in his office as Delilah entered.

"I haven't submitted myself to this much paperwork, ever, I think," Rugrat complained as way of greeting. George let out a bored snort from his place under his feet.

Delilah pulled out a chunk of meat and George's eyes opened. His expression changed as he stood and moved to Delilah.

Just like the other soldiers and Rugrat, George had gone through a change while he had been gone. He was much more powerful than before, but still he was the same person.

George made to nip at it when Rugrat clicked his tongue.

George lowered his head, knowing he had done wrong.

"Sit!" Delilah said.

George quickly sat down, looking up at her.

"Lie down," she said.

He got on his paws as fast as possible, his wide eyes focused on her and the steak.

She put the steak on the ground, stood back up and went to the seat in front of Rugrat. "Eat!" she said as she got to the chair.

George eagerly latched onto the steak as Rugrat nodded in approval of his discipline.

"What did you ask for me for? What can I do for you?" she asked Rugrat.

"How are the people of Alva?" Rugrat asked.

"They're okay..." Delilah felt as though she were missing something—they had just had a meeting on how the people of Alva were.

"I mean, what is the sentiment of the people? With this kind of tragedy, it has a chance to break a group."

Delilah thought about the people she had seen, and all the meetings. "It seems their identity as people of Alva has grown stronger. They have their history as people outside of it, but many of them are referring to themselves as Alvans now. Some people are complaining about taking Vuzgal and helping these other groups that aren't part of Alva. They don't see why we need to help them. Others are sticking up for you and Erik, saying that it's what Alva does; they stand together and they do what is right, even if it is hard. People will not like everything, and there will always be naysayers, but the people of Alva are no longer a group of wandering villagers. They don't know what your plans are for Vuzgal, but they and I trust you and Erik completely," Delilah explained.

"That's good, and nice that they're not following us blindly," Rugrat said with a tension relieving breath.

Delilah cocked her head to the side.

"Having the power to do as we want is good at times. At others, we want to hear suggestions. It's like how you have implemented a great number of changes in Alva, but you didn't need to have us say yes to everything," Rugrat offered.

Delilah nodded hesitantly. She didn't get it all but she was thankful for the praise.

"Now, one thing I want you to focus on is increasing the policing force. We have three people watching over Alva. I want to increase that to fifteen and then one cop for every fifty residents. It's not that I don't trust the residents, but if the Alvan army is out as they are now, then I want to have a reserve militia type force in place. Egbert is powerful but he is one person. The "Adventurer's Guild is also strong but they're all over the place. With the policing force, they can be trained to specifically defend Alva until reinforcements arrive. Also, it gives people who like the military, or the Adventurer's Guild, a place to be while remaining in Alva. There should be a military in Alva, but they will focus on external operations and might be called away. Our military is small but it is getting immensely powerful."

"We have been building up a police force but there isn't much for them to do. Alva is rather peaceful." Delilah said.

"I hope it stays that way, but we've what gout four times the amount of residents now?"

"Close to three thousand Alvans that live within the dungeon, another two thousand that are in the realms, trading, part of the adventurer's association or pursuing a craft or their own path," Delilah said.

"I hope that the police never have to do anything, but we still need them. If we can't enforce our laws, then there is no need for them. What have they been doing with the extra time?"

"They are training in the battlefield Dungeon, they are reading up on the fighting manuals, they havve regular sparring and fitness tests. They have some of their people in the higher realms increasing their levels and assisting people. Actually, there is something that I wanted to bring up on behalf of them," Delilah crossed her hands.

Rugrat leaned forward, interested.

"We have nearly half of our people roaming the realms, the police force has asked if they might be given the power to randomly check on the differen groups we control. Report on the Traders, the Adventurer's and so on?"

Rugrat sunk into thought. "I like it, but I don't want them to be in the shadows, Elan and Egbert watch over our people to see what they're doing in the dark. The Police force will act in a more offical way. Have them go to these different groups and audit them. They check their goods, they ride along with them and then report back to their overseers what they've seen. How is the court system?"

"We have it prepared but we haven't used it for much other than disputes between traders and fines for people that didn't obey certain rules of Alva," Delilah read off a piece of paper on her note pad.

"Okay, we need to make sure that the system remains neutral. There might be people with concerns or don't think that things are above board. Elan and his people will be watching the police force closer than anyone else as they have an incredible amount of power," Rugrat said.

"Okay, so allow them to audit different groups and go to the other realms, but create an oversight with Elan so that they can't step out of bounds," Delilah wrote down her notes as Rugrat let out a small laugh and sat back in his seat.

Delilah looked at him with a curious look.

"Sorry, just, well I didn't realize how much Alva has matured. Seeing how you react to a big task as if its nothing much."

"Well," Delilah seemed at a loss for words, as she frowned.

"That, right there," Rugrat pointed at her expression. "That shows me that you've made the position yours. Inside you don't think that it's much, but let me tell you it is. Erik and I are good soldiers, but neither of us are great leaders. We can train troops, we can teach 'em how to fight. We can be devious bastards. Control an army in the thousands and get them to fight effectively? There was a reason that we mainly left the Tareng forces to control the defense."

"But," Delilah seemed to have a hard time putting her thoughts into words. "You're Erik and Rugrat!"

"Thank you dear, I was forgetting my name for a bit there," Rugrat winked and laughed at Delilah's eye rolling.

"We're two people, *people*, not some all powerful mighty greek gods that can do everything and anything and fart hawaiian breeze. We might have started Alva, but you and the people of Alva, those on the council. You've taken our foundations and built a city upon it. We grow enough food in three months to supply us for a year. You're constantly changing and upgrading the school system, children are coming out with an education that only sect members could enjoy in the third realm. Eighty percent of the population is an apprentice in at least two crafts. Twenty to Thirty percent have reached Journeyman in at least on craft, three percent have reached mid Journeyman level in at least one craft. That is one hundred and fifty Journeyman level crafters! That is no small thing," Rugrat said, giving her a look that tried to impress upon her all that she and Alva had achieved.

She looked down, taking in his words, deeply affected by them.

"There was a lady who came from Vermire a few weeks ago, she was older, forty or so. She had run away from home and an arranged marriage, she was barely making ends meet but she worked hard in taverns, she worked hard but she was stepped on her entire life. She applied for a position with Vermire. She went through the screening and arrived here in Alva. She was scared, didn't know what was going on, she had taken a jump and she didn't know where she would fall. Her future a mystery.

I saw her as she arrived and then she went on to the classes, to learn more about Alva, to learn about the academy. Didn't hear from her for weeks. Then the other day she came to my office. She was working at one of the bars and learning in the academy's night classes. She came in, this woman hardened against the world and started crying in that very chair.

"She hadn't eaten in two days, she didn't have the money for it, she had been sleeping outside. When she arrived here, she was able to get a warm meal, able to drink clean water, to sleep in a bed."

Delilah held out her fingers, as she repeated herself. "Water, food and a roof over her head. Just for these three acts of kindness changed her world. She was then checked over and healed by the doctors, she found a job and gained a loan and a small apartment. She is debt, sure, but she has a life here, food, water and shelter. Those things aren't as common as many think."

They sat there for a minute as Rugrat shifted awkwardly, not sure what to say or do.

"And you know what, I might only have about one to three people per group send me a message, or meet me. They've come through their own trials, but Alva has given them a harbor from the world. All of them want to thank you and Erik. You might have only founded Alva, but you have set a direction for us and you could have run away but you keep coming back, pouring out all of your wealth and materials to help us grow. The libraries are filled with books you and Erik have gathered. Traders come back and donate more books for free. You know why?"

"Why?" Rugrat asked, having to clear his throat.

"When you and Erik came back you always had books with you, they keep that tradition alive. Quietly passing books to Egbert, growing Alva's knoweldge and strengthening younger generations. When you took Vuzgal, you started to ship back mountains of resources, trusting in us to organize them, to sell, to sell to our students and upgrade the city with. That is not how the ten realms works. Leaders hoard everything that they can, only giving out scraps to others. You take little for yourselves and give all you can. Why are you racing to increase your strenght, the strength of the army?"

"Well, so they can protect Alva if we can't, and to get more to help Alva, and it's people. To see more, we just want to grow you know, we're not completely selfless," Rugrat rebutted.

"Yes, I am *acutely* aware of how human you are, remember I was there when you had food poisoning," Delilah said in a peturbed voice.

"Ahhh, damn," Rugrat chuckled.

"The thing is, you are both increasing your strength as a challenge to one another, but as you do, you pull Alva up with you. Look at our forces, you could have taken the lions share of the experience. Instead you raised our army's strength so that they would be an elite fighting force even in the sixth realm."

Rugrat didn't know what to say, he felt as if he was boxed in by her words.

"Thank you," Rugrat said, looking to Delilah.

"Sometime it's hard for us to realize what we've done and who we've affected without someone telling us."

"Yeah," Rugrat murmured.

There was a knock at the door, disrupting their conversation. Rugrat cleared up his notes and George licked his chops and paws.

"Come in," Rugrat said.

The door opened as Elan Silaz entered the room.

"George, get out of the way, will you?" Rugrat asked, seeing the wolf lying in the middle of the floor.

George wandered back to his bed in the corner as Elan made to bow.

Rugrat waved his hand. "Never been one for bowing, so no need to do it here." Rugrat indicated to the open seat and Elan sat down next to Delilah.

"Welcome to Alva. I might be a bit late in saying that but I know your boys and Qin are happy to have you here. Just things got busy, and well, you found us on your own. Now I need you to find something else for us," Rugrat announced.

"Erik and I come from a place called Earth. We're transcenders, or people from outside of the Ten Realms. You've probably heard of the myths and legends and how empires usually burn after the arrival of transcenders from other places. Don't worry—we're not here to make that much chaos. Though, there are more people out there who are from Earth. I know that your network is vast. Alva is willing to invest into the Silaz trading house to make sure that it increases in size. On the outside, you will be a trader of weapons, armors, clothing, etc. for monster cores and Mana stones. Under that, I want you to recruit people from across the realms for Alva. People who are hard workers and who want to build a new life, much like the people that you have brought to Vermire. I also want you to go and search for people from Earth. Where Erik and I come from."

Elan, to his credit, didn't show much of a change in expression. "At first, I thought you came from some greater power in the higher realms. Then I thought that you were hiding out in the First Realm to make a comeback. Then I found out that you had built *this*. Actually learning that you're not from the Ten Realms makes it a bit easier to deal with all of the surprises," Elan explained and then laughed.

Rugrat smiled and continued. "It's not something that we've revealed to many, but if you are looking for people from Earth, ask them if they've ever bathed in mangos, sat on the United States of America or went up under to Australia. That should get their attention. The sentences make no sense, Australia and the United States are countries while mangos are a fruit. People from the realms won't know what you're talking about. People from Earth will look at you as if you're insane," Rugrat said. "Make sure to be discreet. There are probably quite a few who have made a stir. Even if there is only information of them heading to the higher realms, let Delilah know. So, would you be willing to retire?" Rugrat asked.

"What?" Elan asked, caught off guard as Delilah looked at Rugrat.

"You've got a good ability to gather information. We've been doing it with the traders, but they're traders at the end of the day. Although they gather information, it is likely connected to the trades happening in the area. What I want is for you to become an intelligence officer, someone in charge of gathering information," Rugrat said.

"What would the specifics be?" Elan asked.

"You would bribe, cultivate, and create sources across the realms. Your goal would be to root out the dangers that lie ahead of Alva. Find out who is looking at Alva, let us know if there is anyone trying to mess with our assets. Figure out what our enemies are doing. Get us information on the higher realms and their conflicts. We were able to get some information on the Fourth Realm and it allowed us to make a split second decision when we got there, to react and move. If we did not gather that previous information, we might have been drafted by the army of the city of Aberdeen, where we arrived in originally. There is an organization in the Fourth Realm called the Fighter's Association—basically people who are nuts about getting stronger. They've got people all over the place, but they only take in the strongest one percent of any group. They're the overlords of the fighting world. Arrogant, too. That is something that Blaze has to be ready and plan for if he advances into the Fourth Realm with the Adventurer's Guild. We need information you can gather to be ready for that."

"What about the business?" he asked in mild irritation.

"Well that is the decision. Wren is a good lad, if you take this position then you will not be allowed to control any trading company, well unless it is a cover for your people."

"What if I refuse?"

"Then you would still be a person from Alva, you would be able to trade as you want, eventually rise in levels and strenght. You might even become the trading council leader if you really go for it. Though I would need to find a different intelligence officer. Someone to find out the dangers that lie in Domonos and Yui's path," Rugrat said.

It is cruel, to involve his sons but he isn't lying.

"Are you threatening them?" Elan asked, his voice chilling.

"Threaten them?" Rugrat frowned. "Domonos and Yui control the Tiger and Dragon Platoon, their authority within the military is second only to Glosil. I have trained with them for months, I have shed blood with them and fought beside them. I would never threaten them," Rugrat's words left no room for buts, what's and ifs.

"Your daughter teaches me about formations and is one of the chief designers of weapon systems in Alva. They have come under my command, they have become Alvans and I will wage a war against any that wrongfully kills one of our people. On that you have my word."

Delilah felt a thrill run through her body as she looked at Elan.

"I am sorry for being rash, they are worth more to me than all of the wealth or power in the world," Elan said.

"I understand, this is a lot to take in. It would be a lot of work as well. You could recruit from the policing force and other areas of Alva, train them to create information networks, pull together our current information networks and organize them. On this point Erik and I can give you some pointers. It is because of your children's positions and their loyalty that we are offering you this position," Rugrat didn't hide anything.

"If you want me to gather informaiton from the other realms doesn't that mean I'll need to be a higher level?"

"Yes it does, though we can power level you with resources and attaching you to some of our fighting forces to increase your level rapidly," Rugrat said.

Elan fell silent for some time but his eyes seemed to glow brighter each second.

"Okay, I'll do it," Elan said.

"Why?" Rugrat asked.

"I have been running my business for years, Wren has gained back some of his humilty and I have been giving him more control recently. I want to see what he can do by himself. As you said Yui and Domonos are travelling through the realms and putting themselves in danger, if I can help them I will. I have wanted to see the realms, and this is one way to do it. I have been bored with business, but being able to know what is really happening, that still gives me a thrill. Now to see what is happening across the realms. To be part of a group that few knows about but has considerable power. I, well I'm excited. I don't think that it will be easy, I think that it will be incredibly difficult, a number of sleepless nights lay ahead of me, but I would be the first person to do it. That has some power to it."

"You will be a secret aide to Delilah in the future. You will only report to Erik and myself. You will need to report to Delilah and Egbert and you will need to swear to a highly restrictive oath. You will have great power but if you abuse it..." The room grew cold as the air stilled. The Mana didn't circulate, falling under Rugrat's complete control. "We will have a problem."

"I understand. I will not let down the Silaz name."

Delilah felt that Alva was shifting. It was no longer a village, or just some secret group. They spanned over realms, had crafters of multiple professions, agreements with the Blue Lotus, Alchemist Association, traders and their chambers of commerce, Crafter's Association, and possibly more in the future. They were small but the power on her shoulders seemed to grow heavier.

Chapter: Crafter Dungeons

Erik, Roska, Gong Jin, and Niemm were alone in the meeting room inside their castle in Vuzgal.

Erik pulled out files and folders with locations and information filled inside them. "These are locations where I want you to create crafter trial feeder dungeons. I have included a set of plans for the feeder dungeons that you can use on the dungeon and the dungeon will build them for you.

"I'm being watched by the Blue Lotus and the Crafter's Association closely right now. I have listed down safe locations in each of the folders. When you are out making these feeder trials, gather information about other dungeons in different and remote locations. Check the situation in the cities controlling the dungeons. Check the difficulty of the dungeon and see if you can enter them for a fee. If the dungeons meet those criteria, upgrade them to feeders. I want you to all return to Alva in three weeks time. Set the crafter dungeons to finish up in five weeks, or when they're complete after that if the dungeons need more time. You'll probably be tailed initially. Jump through the locations listed in those documents. With inviting the navigators over, we've been able to confirm that these locations, although they might not be the best, they're safe enough to use the totem to get in and out of. Use navigators to do multiple jumps and switch navigators up so you make it hard to be trailed if they're questioned. Once you're clear of observation, start getting to work on the dungeons. Questions?"

"When do we head out?" Roska asked.

"Over the next two days," Erik said.

"Do we get funds?" Niemm asked.

Erik pulled out three storage rings and tossed them over. "There should be plenty in there to help you."

Niemm checked inside and nodded. "I'm thinking of splitting the team, Storbon and I are the only one with the dungeon master asbilities so we are the only ones that can call up the dungeon core."

"Agreed, though there might be people that control the dungeons, if someone else does, leave them alone," Erik said.

Niemm seemed to have more questions.

"We have the ability there have to be others, the Alchemist Association use a dungeon as their garden, who knows about up here in the higher realms?"

Niemm made a noise of agreement as Erik stood.

"Oh, one thing I forgot to add. If you find any dungeons that people don't know about, see if you can take them down and take the core. If we can upgrade and repair Alva's dungeon core, that would be for the best. Even better if we can increase its size."

The others all made notes before Erik rapped the desk with a knuckle. "Good hunting!"

Erik went off to his next meeting. He headed out of the castle and to the Blue Lotus building. He was meeting with the overseeing head of the Blue Lotus Vuzgal location, a man by the name of Darius Tan.

"I need to make a request. I'm not sure who to make it to." Erik said as sipped his tea once the meeting started.

"What kind of request?" Darius Tan questioned as he smiled.

"I wish to employ Hiao Xen for a period of time to manage this city," Erik explained.

Darius frowned and fell into thought as Erik sat there, watching his expressions.

Hiao Xen had proved himself to be trustworthy. He was also good at managing people. Erik wanted to make Vuzgal a success and although he had his plans in place, he didn't know how to run and operate the city to its full capacity. He needed someone to do that for him.

"I can certainly make the request to my seniors. He would need to agree with the request. I'm not sure if they would be willing to release him so easily from the Blue Lotus."

"I'm not asking for him to be released from the Blue Lotus, just to manage this place. But he would need to make an oath to be neutral in all dealings and that he could not reveal information I give him or on the dealings he has with me. I will not make him break faith or go against the rules of the Blue Lotus either," Erik said.

"I certainly haven't heard of anything like that before, but given your position, again, I can only make the request," Darius said apologetically.

"That will be enough. Don't worry, Vuzgal will soon get busy!"

***

Egbert looked at the Ten Realms Totem that reached up into the upper reaches of the dungeon. It nearly touched his dungeon's ceiling as it stood at the north point of the city.

A number of people stood around; they had come to see the creation event. Even in just the one week since Rugrat had returned, there were more people coming to join Alva.

He might be undead but it didn't make him unfeeling. He found it hard to watch as the twenty-three members of the Alvan army were put to rest. He had been accepted into Alva as much as he had accepted them.

"How we looking, Ivory?" Rugrat asked as he walked up.

"Not bad, Hillbilly," Egbert fired back, making Rugrat frown at the quick snipe.

"Feeling all elbows and knees?" Rugrat asked.

"You! When did you change my hips and my upper arms around! No wonder I felt like I got shorter and I was having troubles moving my arms! I only took a short time to recharge last night!"

"These dungeons have eyes," Rugrat chuckled.

"Come on, just a bit more," Egbert muttered, as he shifted his hands in his robe as he tried to pull his upper arm out of his hip joint to discreetly rearrange himself. "That's not right," he muttered. He jumped around on one leg, juggling some leg bones, some vertebrae and an upper arm bone.

"Uh?" Rugrat grunted.

Egbert looked up as everyone caught him in a rather suggestive pose: his hands inside his robe, with his upper arm bone poking at the lower part of his robe as he hopped around on one foot. The area around him turned quiet at his display.

"This isn't what it looks like. I'm just rearranging myself," Egbert explained in a rushed voice.

"Thought that you at least had to see a doctor to do that," Rugrat quipped.

"Shut up, will you?"

"Well, you have that spell to rearrange, right?" Rugrat asked.

"Yes, but I need to be in parts to do that, so—"

"I can help with that!"

Egbert felt a breeze beside him and he sensed Rugrat had moved. "Huh?"

"Super slam!" Rugrat had his elbow out as he launched himself at Egbert, the elbow drop turning him into a pile of flying bones.

"I can see my house from here," Egbert's head said as it bounced up into the sky. He cast his spell; his bones went back together, reforming his body as his robe wrapped around him in a dignified manner.

Blaze coughed from the side. Elise stood beside him.

"Shall we start this thing?" he asked, looking at the totem that had been assembled section by section.

"Egbert?" Rugrat said, regaining some control over his voice."Please let me know what you think of the books. Duty calls!"

Egbert followed Rugrat as they went to the totem.

They reached the bottom of the totem, people falling silent.

"Egbert?" Rugrat asked, worried he had gone too far.

Egbert cast the final fusing spell.

The totem's last sections were fused together. The runes on the totem lit up with power from the dungeon core.

==========

You have added a special building: Ten Realms Totem

==========

==========

Ten Realms Totem

==========

With this building, you can cross the realms. People heading to higher realms for the first time will not have to pay a fee but will be sent randomly to locations in the higher realms they are eligible to join. One can travel from this totem to other totems they have used before. Costs are paid in Mana stones or monster cores as well as gold, silver, and copper.

As the city owner, you will get 10% of the fee that one needs to pay to use the totem.

==========

"Well, I think that it works." Rugrat pushed the notification away.

"Looks good to me too," Egbert confirmed as he snapped the last loose bone into place.

Rugrat pulled out an Earth Mana stone and selected the menu before anyone was able to say anything. He disappeared one second, then reappeared a few seconds later.

"Well, folks, it looks like we've got a working totem!" Rugrat declared.

People who had been stunned came out of it and others cheered.

Having a totem was quite the achievement.

The high tier workshops the common citizen didn't really understand; they hadn't seen them before. But they knew the strength that a Ten Realms Totem meant. It turned a village or town into a proper city. Only a place with a proper totem could be called a city and with it, a cities prosperity and wealth would grow by leaps and bounds.

Chapter: The Great Trade

Erik suddenly got a message when Rugrat appeared through the totem and then disappeared again.

He smiled as he looked at the message: "Totem works, Egbert wants more lewdness"

Erik rolled his eyes and smiled. With the totem, one of his biggest concerns was removed. Going through the totems of other cities in the First Realm was bound to alert some people to their presence. Now that they had a totem, their people could move easily from location to location across the realms without drawing suspicion. If there was a threat in one of the various realms, they could move people faster. Transportation was any power's lifeblood, from Earth to the Ten Realms.

"Now we need to power level some people. One group to collect the resources from the hidden dungeon when they're needed; other groups to start trading and establish our own hold over Vuzgal. Once people find out about the hidden part of Bala Dungeon things are going to start to pick up. We have just two weeks to get ready for it."

Erik also got a response from the Blue Lotus. It seemed that the position of Honorary Elder wasn't just all words, they would allow Hiao Xen to assist him for five years, if he agreed. Erik sent Hiao Xen a message and requested a meeting.

***

Hiao Xen had heard some rumors from different friends, about how people in the higher parts of the Blue Lotus had been discussing him in connection with Vuzgal and Erik.

He had ignored it but then Erik had requested a meeting. He also got a message from his friends saying that the Blue Lotus had approved Hiao Xen to cancel some of his obligations to the Blue Lotus.

He was confused, but he trusted Erik and headed off to the meeting as soon as he could.

Erik sat on a stump in a courtyard, reading over reports as people from the Alvan army moved carriages out of the houses to around the totem and teleported them away.

"Erik." Hiao Xen made to bow.

"Don't worry about that," Erik said. Even with his position in the eyes of the Blue Lotus, he still saw Hiao Xen as a friend, which made him feel closer to Erik. Many people upon getting a higher position would look down on the people they were once friends with.

"I have a request to make of you. Would you like to be the lord of Vuzgal? I have talked to the Blue Lotus and they said that they would be able to agree to this, though only for a short period. If you call five years short. I wouldn't make you go against them—well, unless they were pulling some shit and then I would deal with them. You would just have to treat everyone who is a resident or person of Vuzgal fairly," Erik said.

"I—"

"Here is the contract. You don't need to make a decision now. Take some time to look it over," Erik offered.

It will take time for this place to be built up. Erik could take his time, retire here. Though the Erik I know would want to keep on going. Sure, he would use this place as a stop but he wouldn't see it as his primary responsibility. If he did, then he would have settled down in Taeman city, where he could have used our relationship to gain a high position. Though if he wants to keep this place, just what is his long term goal?

"What is your goal? These prices rival what one would need to pay in the larger neutral cities but you are only selling about five percent of the available housing, why so little? There is war going on to the East and the Chaotic lands will need more than just a new place to trade with. You need a population, more traders, incentives, there aren't many here," Hiao Xen said, pushing past his normal reserved façade.

"We only have a certain amount of land, if we sell it all now and then it increases in price later, wouldn't we be the idiots? We are selling only two percent of the land and three percent will be rented. We are looking to create an industry of wandering inns that will house people that are visiting for a short period. The prices will be reasonable so that people can come, trade for a short period and then leave, making most of our population mobile. Though we can draw people in with the Sky Reaching Resturants and Bala Dungeon in the valley, it can offer Journey man level gear and even expert level items and we triggered an event that we triggered when we entered the dungeon. Something called a crafter trial. I'm not sure what it is, but we finished it. It says that it will take some time before our rewards are revealed. With just the dungeon able to give weapons and armor, including a powerful armor set, people will flood from all over. Vuzgal is on the rise."

"Crafter Trial?" Hiao Xen's brows pulled together as he held his chin. "Crafter trials have appeared in other dungeons, they are dungeons with crafting workshops, one creates items and then offeres it to the dungeon and then the dungeon once confirming the grade of the item will give them a prize and allow them to access higher grade workshops. These dungeons have started a new round of competition as some have the apprentice grade, others the Journeyman grade, while the crafters lose the item, the rewards can be many times greater, such as a higher grade blueprint, or training manual or rare resource."

Hiao Xen fell silent, Erik sitting there opposite.

"With the protection of the associations it means that there are few people that will try and challenge Vuzgal in the near future. If it is a crafter dungeon trial, what do you plan on doing?"

"Charge them one Earth grade mana stone to enter? Or talisman, there's a talisman thing on the wall," Erik said.

"Well that practically confirms it, there are talismans given to the crafters, some are using them as medallions to show off their ability. They can be used to bypass workshops. If someone has a journeyman level talisman then they can access Journeyman level workshops. Okay, that changes things. If we can use the neutrality of the city, motivate the Crafter's association to sell materials, advertise to others about requiring materials. There are a number of workshop areas in the city correct?"

"Yes."

"Good, if we can renovate those or combine those, do you have city planning?"

"We've looked at it some," Erik pulled out a map and passed it to Hiao Xen.

"You should widen these roads and put the city on a grid system, also I would own the stores beside the major roads, that way you can retake ownership and expand the roads as needed. With time you'll push to the North. The roads around the Totem need to be developed more, that will become our bottleneck until traders can start coming down the roads. There is a war going on to the West, the north road is in disrepair, the East road is still rough from your fight with the Blood Demon Sect. Roads and ease of access is the main problem of any city. We need to plan for a thousand years in the future, not tomorrow."

Hiao Xen was noting down information as Erik looked on, not wanting to break his though process.

"We're going to need to upgrade the sewage systems and the city's infastructure. What about on the military side of things?"

"We are looking to recruit more people and increase our strength quickly. Don't want to rely on the associations too much."

"Good, but remember if it is in their interest they'll send more resources over to affirm their position. Don't be arrogant, but remember, if it benefits you both then they'll probablu go for it. You can leverage these benefits, tying them closer to Vuzgal. Standing by youtself is only going to hurt in the future. Even the associations need one another from time to time."

"The valley around Bala Dungeon is also filled with Earth and Water attribute Mana, making it an ideal location to grow different alchemical ingredients. That, with the natural higher density of Mana in the Fourth Realm..." Erik shrugged.

"You are learning," Hiao Xen praised.

"Okay, so what about the house prices?"

Hiao Xen snorted and sat back.

"I'd say keep them the same," He waved the pencil in his hand as an idea hit him.

"Actually, I'd say that you hold an auction for them," Hiao Xen laughed.

"What?" Erik asked, lost.

"Well at the first few auctions, few if any people will buy anything, that gives us time, people will think that we think too much of ourselves. At the same time we talk and negotiate with the people of the assocaitions, get their backing, we build up these wandering inns for people to stay in, renovate the city and increase the military strength. Now what is your aim for the city?"

"I'm, not sure, crafting and trading?" Erik asked. "Why do I feel like I'm the person being sold on this idea?"

Hiao Xen paused for a moment. "Well, building a city, it's exciting no? And I'm just offering some friendly advice! Okay so, we're looking at crafting and trading, which I think plays to your strengths. I have also heard that there are people interested in your weapon technologies, that could be a good revenue generator," Hiao dropped his voice suggestively and then cleared his throat.

"So if you can rebuild those crafting workshops in the city, peole will just come for that, if there is really a crafting dungeon then we have that as well. Then with the Blue Lotus auctioning off items and then the Crafter's association people using the workshops, or buying and selling items. Add in the general merchants and we're looking good. You have already drawn in the Alchemist association as well. Damn, "Hiao Xen chuckled. "Then, well there are the dungeons, the sky reaching resturant, if you're neutral as well. High prices with entrance fee?"

"No, keep it low, more people coming and going," Erik said.

"Looks like you have been thinking ahead, tax rate?"

"Seven percent, less three than other cities, and then it can reach five percent for different groups, gives us room to barter."

"Good! Okay, so for construction? Your biggest flaw is really people."

"Well it would be your job to hire more people, for building, our troops and the undead can all work as laborers. A lot of them are apprentices and there are a few journeyman crafters among them," Erik smiled secretively.

"What?" Hiao Xen asked.

"Well we have the designs for an Expert level workshop.

"What kind of workshop?"

"All of them," Erik dragged out his words as Hiao Xen felt his blood boiling in excitement. He wanted to yell out his questions. *How did he get expert grade workshops blueprints? Why are his soldiers Journeyman level crafters?*

Hiao Xen calmed himself and took a deep breath, looking at the map, his notes, seeing an image in his mind. Thinking of the level of destruction in Vuzgal.

"I will need to talk to my family before I agree to anything," Hiao Xen said.

"That makes sense. Take your time," Erik said.

"Well, looks like you two are up to something." Rugrat said as he entered the courtyard in a teleporting flash with a man beside him with a beard and an odd-looking hat.

"Small projects, Erik?" the man asked in wonder as he looked around him.

"Hiao Xen, this is Matt Richardson. He's a friend of mine and the one who will be in charge of fixing this place up," Erik said.

"Ah, so you'll be the one managing this place once I'm gone. Sounds like you'll need all the luck that I can give." Matt reached out his hand.

"Rebuilding Vuzgal will be a hard task." Hiao Xen confirmed as he extended his hand.

"Thankfully, I've got blueprints already made up for a lot of what we'll need, so that should make it a bit easier. I get to set my own hours, which makes things a bit easier to manage. I'll focus on the inner city first and then the outer city. Though some of it will remain empty lots or basic rooms for guilds and associations to fill in." Matt let out a sigh. "A task from Erik is rarely easy."

"Good to see you, Hiao Xen. Hope that the family has been well," Rugrat said.

"They're both doing well. My son has applied to be a guard for the Blue Lotus and there is a high chance he will be accepted, though the attack mages have their eyes on him. He was able to open another two Mana gates since you last saw him," Hiao Xen said with some pride.

"I knew he had it in him!" Rugrat guffawed with a hearty laugh.

"Well, you have much to do and I need to go and discuss this with my wife. I hope you all have a good day." Hiao Xen said as he departed.

***

"Let's go to my office." Erik led Rugrat and Matt to the castle, giving command to Yui to organize the carriages of materials that were headed to Alva.

"How are things from lower?" Erik asked as they walked.

"Organized things—the leaders are all talking to one another, organizing, consolidating and such. We've expanded fast and furious style in the last couple of months. Got a bunch of new recruits across the board, more people than ever. Elan Silaz paid a visit. I talked to him about our plan to grow some eyes and ears more aggressively. Everything is going well. We don't have anything of immediate concern. How are things going here?" Rugrat explained.

"Everything is according to what we planned. We need to work on building up the city. Should take a few weeks to stabilize. Most of the people from Tareng have left, only a few have bought a piece of land. I'm talking to Hiao Xen about managing all of this. I sent word to Old Hei about Vuzgal.

"I talked to some farmers, showed them the valley and they drew up some plans on it with a few alchemists to see about working the land there."

Erik nodded as they fell silent.

Matt was looking around the city with a professional eye as there was a noise in the distance.

Erik and Rugrat saw George flying as an irate Gilga chased after him.

"Looks like George ruined her midday nap." Erik chuckled as he shook his head.

"Little devil," Rugrat sighed.

"So, what do you want me to do with the city?" Matt asked.

"Vuzgal was originally broken down into the inner and the outer city. The inner city holds most of the noble homes, the higher-classed crafting workspaces and upper markets.

"I want to focus on the inner city first, on cleaning up the streets. The castle is the central piece and the roads around it are like a wagon wheel with the spokes outward, with the intersections having watchtowers to watch over the area.

"I want to turn these intersections into places for markets. I want the waste and water system to be reworked to our standards through the whole city. I want to have Sky Reaching Restaurants located in the city, as well as Wayside Inns for people to rest in at a cheap fee. The inn's will be for adventurers and people who are visiting. It will be a cheap place to stay for a few weeks so people don't have to get homes. I aim to have a high amount of non-resident traffic moving through the city.

"Once the inner city is cleaned up, we'll plan the outer city. The outer walls will be turned from a circular wall into lines of bunkers and the streets will be in a grid form. The east, west and south gates will act as the basis of the grid system. Cut through what is left, put down water and waste systems and roads. People will be allowed to buy plots of land in the outer city, though we will break them up into sectors.

"To the east and west sides, where the roads come in, we will have merchant houses and warehouses. On the major roads of the entire city, I want to have storefronts but as the roads meet and head more south, we will have more crafting workshops. To the north, we will have the Fighter's Association and people coming to fight at the dungeon.

"There will be a major intersection ahead of the castle where the associations are located, then the castle and then roads that lead to the dungeon. These will have rich buyers and sellers of high-quality goods to tempt those going into the dungeon."

"So fighters in the north. Traders and warehouses east and west. From north moving south, there will be crafters, then the associations, then the castle, then high value traders, then the southern exit into the valley. Have Wayside Inns located at different key locations. Mark building zones the outer city but have people build their own homes. Need a planning office here to make sure that they build it up to code. The inner city will need to be repaired; need zoning for different places and jobs. Break up where businesses can buy land, so at least when starting there isn't a monopoly over the best trading spots.

"Fit in some residential areas inside of the warehouses and close to the crafting workshops. It will be crafters who want to stay inside of the city or the workers we need to commute to the government buildings. With the bunker systems, we will get a lot of ruck from the walls, but building the bunkers shouldn't be so complex. Basically need to make a modular design and then replicate it over and over again. These undead workers have the Fuse spell, right?"

"That's correct," Erik said, sensing that Matt was more throwing the question out than needing an answer as he was stuck in thought.

Matt pulled out his freshly updated map from Erik and looked at it. "Well, I can send these plans back to Alva and get people in the blueprint and city planning department to start breaking up the land and zoning it. Then I'll have them work on the Wayside Inns. As much as it looks like fun, I'll need to work a while on the bunker system. I would suggest that we have Qin up here to look it all over. She can maybe fit a formation to it all, increase our fighting strength."

"What about the barrier?" Erik asked.

"With a wall we're going to get that area underneath that the enemy will be inside the barrier. If we go with interlinked bunkers, have to talk to the formation masters, but being a big bubble I think that we can go right infront of the bunkers, gives ut cover and then only if the enemy is ontop of the bunkers will they be inside the barrier

"I'll need your help in designing the bunkers. They'll be pretty simple, but I'll make them so that people have bathrooms, underground medical facilities, air circulation, heating in the winter and cooling in the summer. Rugrat was talking earlier about formations to help mages defend. I can hide those in different open areas, turn them from courtyards and trading areas into mage casting areas."

"With the Mana cannons we can probably hook them up to the dungeon core for power." Rugrat added.

"Shouldn't be an issue," Matt shrugged. "Though might be good to ask some mages about different offensive spells can use so that we can try and fight back against them.

"You're speaking my language," Erik nodded in confirmation.

They reached the castle and Matt pulled out a map of Vuzgal. "Right now, order the undead to start cleaning up the streets. That will make construction easier in the future. I'll plan out the streets, then the waste and water systems, then power systems. I can just enlarge what plans I have already made from before, plug those in."

Erik and Rugrat led him into the main pillar and then through a secret door into the dungeon core.

Matt looked around at the glowing Mana stones. "Damn." Matt whistled. The Mana density was much higher in here, making one feel relaxed and temporarily forget their thoughts, before focusing them and removing the fatigue in their body.

"Could you give me access?" Matt inquired as he composed himself again.

Erik pulled up a screen, giving Matt the correct dungeon access.

Matt moved to the center of the room. The dungeon core was located underground, hidden from the eye but he was still able to access the building interface to see the city above them.

Matt pulled out pieces of paper, blueprints he had already designed.

Once he input a number of them into the Vuzgal dungeon interface, he pulled up the large three-dimensional map of Vuzgal.

Matt inputted all their previous plans into the dungeon interface and adjusted where needed or where conflicts arose.

The dungeon started to make changes underneath the city, firming up stone, creating basements, building new sewage lines. Changing the makeup of the ground so that the covering stone just needed to be placed down and fused. Work began on the first bunkers, hidden away from prying eyes.

He studied it for a second and then started to put down Sky Reaching Restaurant foundations. They were based off the same design of the original in the Third Realm. They were shorter in the outer city and grew taller and larger in the inner city. The tallest restaurant just a few blocks from the association and castle, commanding an incredible view over the city.

"What about the Wayside Inns?"

"Have some done up apartment-style, then others that are the one main hotel and then separate buildings. As larger groups come, they'll want to have an entire house to themselves. Vary the sizes so that even if a powerful group comes, they'll have a place for them and their guards to stay," Erik said.

Matt made some notes and moved the city display around a few times, expanding it on certain buildings.

"What are you doing?" Rugrat asked.

"Well, instead of designing them from the ground up, I'm finding buildings that suit my needs at least in part; then I'll use those parts, put them together, check the structure and then build them. Nice and simple—don't need to start from scratch either. Though that bunker system will be all new," Matt said.

"You put more thought into it?" Rugrat asked Erik.

"Yeah, we're on an incline to the various approaches so we slope the ground down further. Make a ramp up to the bunkers. The front-line bunkers will all have repeater fire bases and rifles. When we upgrade to machine guns, we can switch the repeaters for them."

"When we can get the ammunition issue sorted out, I need to revisit that," Rugrat sighed.

Erik continued talking as if he hadn't heard Rugrat.

"The second line of bunkers have cannons and observers. Have them in lines—create arcs of fire. Anything that comes from the ground, we make their life hell. Then we have heavy repeaters in batteries: one in the watchtowers in the inner city and the outer city. Bury explosives and formation traps in the ground, activate on our command.

"Have two lines for people to pull back to. When they do, the older sections of the line are mined and turned into a trap for the enemy to enter.

"As they cross the first line, then they can be fired on by the second line. We don't need much of a slope, but enough for each of the bunker lines to fire over the previous. And we only need the firing slit above the ground at ankle height."

"Make them a pain in the ass to hit, but we can see in any direction still. Nasty." Rugrat approved.

"Then resupply lines of tunnels throughout, making it easy to move ammunition up and wounded back. Though if someone attacks here, hopefully then they'll be dealing with the full might of the associations and not just us."

Chapter: Dungeon Dance

"I hate this place!" Yuli yelled as they ran through their latest dungeon. Behind them, a creature that looked to have the eyes of a snake, the body of a furry mammoth, and the face of a saber tooth tiger was chasing them.

"Shut up and keep running!" Niemm yelled as he threw another grenade at the wall. It landed next to a pillar, breaking the pillar in it's explosion and dropping the roof on the creature chasing them.

A group of beasts charged out of a side room, only to have Tian Cui slide underneath them, turn her body and jump at their backs by launching off the wall.

Her blades flashed as she beheaded one and stabbed another. The mole-looking creatures cried out as a red gas seeped from Tian Cui's body, creating a curse that rushed out to meet the others.

The mammoth shaped beast crawled out of the debris piled on top of him. His left eye was sealed shut and it's body was covered in wounds.

The mole creatures turned to attack Tian, only to see she had jumped free and was now following the party still running away from all of the creatures.

Niemm used a spell scroll, slowing them all, the rest of the special team getting away easily

"Lucinda?" Niemm called out.

"Up here to the right!" Lucinda responded.

They entered a large cave-like, the ground was uneven and slick with water puddles with stalatites hanging from the ceiling, water dropping from them to drop onto the rocks and water below.

There was a glow from above that settled on three chests on pedastals and a tiled floor, behind them there was a door.

"Hopefully that's the exit," Tian Cui ventured.

The stones between the three chests moved as if they were part of a Tetris game until a blue glow was revealed. Niemm and the others climbed up the steps, jumping up them as fast as they could.

The mammoth sized beast appeared from the doorway they had just exited, looking at the party running to the dungeon core. Its eyes widened, as if realizing something as it stomped toward the stairs.

Niemm reached out and touched the dungeon core. "Control!" he yelled as screens appeared in front of him.

The beast dropped to the ground and stopped moving. Now it was bowing to them, under their control.

"Shit!" Yuli exclaimed as she slumped down and sat on a chest.

"That's a mimic," Niemm said casually.

She jumped up, but the chest didn't change. "Sarge!" she complained.

Niemm waved his hand and the chest opened to reveal a mouth and its arms slurped out of the side and moved. The arms looked like planks of wood.

It waved at the group as Niemm pulled out a stack of blueprints and used the build function of the dungeon. It took him only a few seconds to add the blueprint and set the dungeon to work. Then he pulled out a Ten Realms contract and raised it above his head.

A golden glow fell on the contract and then on Niemm. A screen of accepting the changes appeared in front of him.

"One more dungeon sorted out," Niemm announced.

"We've only been able to capture five dungeons in the last two weeks," Lucinda complained.

"Well, we were tailed by the associations pretty heavily in the beginning." Niemm consoled as he added another set of instructions that would create a secondary dungeon, hidden from the first. It would hide the dungeon core and create a place for the people of Alva to resupply and restock at in case of emergency.

"I hope the others are doing better," Deni remarked.

***

"Covering!" Imani yelled.

"Fuck this!" Gong Jin shouted.

"Moving!" Simms exclaimed.

Han Wu covered the ground behind Gong Jin with explosives.

"Cultists, am I right?" Han Wu asked as another group of the charging cultists were cut down by the grenades.

"Covering!" Simms and Gong Jin yelled. They dropped to the ground and started shooting at the cultists, firing their heavy repeaters and cutting down the pursuing cultists.

"Moving!" Han Wu and Imani yelled, pulling back as they reloaded their weapons.

"Covering!" The low noise from Han Wu's grenade launcher sounded out again as Imani's rifle sounded as if it were automatic. One or two cultists dropped with every shot.

"I hate this job!" Simms yelled.

"The center is just behind them!" Gong Jin bellowed. "Simms, get that spell scroll ready!"

Simms and Gong Jin dropped to the ground, Gong Jin while shooting.

"Covering!"

"Moving!" Imani and Han Wu started to run again. Their Stamina and Strength was impressive, allowing them to cross a large distance. But the large hall they were running down only had one entry from behind them and hall in front was coming to an end.

The cultists were firing their bows furiously, but the special team members had only been left with a few bruises and scrapes.

The cultists spells were dangerous; although they'd get an A for effort, they were terrible at aiming. They were also not terribly good at organizing themselves when they were getting blown up and killed. Only their fanaticism kept them fighting and wanting to keep the location of their cult a secret.

"Weirdos!" Gong Jin fired his repeater from the ground with his right hand, giving them the middle finger with his left hand. His strength reached the point where the repeater didn't strain him at all.

"The Cult of Vaskala will claim the lives of the defilers!" a cultist yelled out.

"Covering!" Han Wu and Imani yelled Han Wu rebutted with fiery grenade launcher destruction

.

Han Wu's covering grenades went off. In the enclosed space the wall of noise Gong Jin couldn't hear anything as he worked his jaw. Simms yelled out a chant, while he held a spell scroll up and ran incredibly fast toward Imani and Han Wu.

"Moving?!" Gong Jin yelled but he couldn't hear anything that Simms was saying.

Gong Jin ran back only a little bit before he dropped to the ground again.

Three spell formations appeared on the ground. The Mana power in the room sucked into them as three summoned large boars appeared from the ground.

"Go!" Simms yelled, the boars charged forwards, spearing the cultists and forging a path through them. The charge rolled up the cultists. There was nowhere for them to run in the corridor.

The cultists forward momentum quickly turned into running away.

"Dungeon core?" Han Wu asked.

"WHAT?!" Gong Jin squawked, only barely hearing a noise.

"Dungeon core?" Han Wu asked, louder now.

"The fuck was in that grenade?! I can't hear!"

"Oh." Han Wu responded as he laughed dryly. Gong Jin might not be able to hear, but seeing the guilty look on Han Wu's face, his eyelid started to twitch and a vein popped out on his forehead.

***

Roska and the rest of her group appeared in a cave. A glowing light came from her hand as storage devices fell to the ground.

"Ugh, can we go somewhere warmer?" Yang Zan asked as the wind cut to the skin. He wrapped his cloak around him tighter.

"You didn't get frozen by that white yeti! I think my frostbite has frostbite," Davos muttered.

Tully shivered. "I'm not trying to stop cold attribute beasts again. All of their attacks are so damn cold. I'll need months of warmth to recover."

"We can go to the Linem Islands?" Roska half suggested, half asked as she looked sheepish.

"Hell to the yes." Xi tossed Roska the storage item he had picked up with the dungeon's core and its items.

***

Hiao Xen stood on his balcony, looking over Yeda city. It was the city that he had been promoted to just a few months ago.

"Are you still thinking about his offer?" Nuo Xen, his wife asked.

Hiao Xen only let out a heavy sigh.

"Take it," Nuo said suddenly.

"I thought that you said you wouldn't interfere with my work?" He looked at her.

"I meant when you weren't being an idiot. Look, is Erik a simple person?"

"No, but then what happens if I return to the Blue Lotus after the five years? I'm not even a hundred years old. I have plenty of more time I can give them and I haven't heard anything from the leaders of the Blue Lotus."

"What does that tell you?"

"That this is a test or a trap," he said in a sour voice.

"How?"

"They would tell me to take it if they wanted me to. They don't need to wait on my decision. I know that there is a reward from the Blue Lotus, but they haven't talked about it. So, either I stay in my position and accept their gift for assisting, or I take the position offered by Erik."

"Is there anything that you have to agree to that will break your relationship with the Blue Lotus completely?"

"No, but—"

"But you will be in command of a city," Nuo Xen reassured him.

"A city that only has builders, a few undead and guards who are contractually obligated to be there," Hiao Xen said.

Nuo clicked her tongue and shook her head. "Then why do you look so excited and I know that you're hiding more from me?"

Hiao Xen didn't answer a smile hanging off of his lips.

"So my mysterious husband when do we leave?"

"Who said that we were leaving? If we go then it could put our position in jeopardy," Hiao Xen.

"Erik is not a simple man, and you would be running a capital. Looking at you things are not so simple as they look on the surface. With time, it will grow stronger. You owe him, for our son. Do him this favor and you are right in both obligations—you have hundreds of more years afterwards to devote to the Blue Lotus. Who knows you might help one another and reach new hieghts. It is not often that one can do this." Hiao Xen sighed as his wife continued in a lower voice. "I have heard that Elder Lu is keeping updated on the situation there. Seems that others are expecting big things from Vuzgal."

"When did I get so lucky to have a wife like you?"

"You must've been a great humble man in your past life," She teased.

"You knew as soon as he asked what your answer would be," she whispered into his ear.

He looked at her, his mouth pressed together into a white line. "How come you know me this well?"

"I'm your wife you silly man." She kissed his cheek.

"All right, I'll announce my decision tomorrow."

"Good, so where will we be living?"

"In the castle," Hiao Xen smiled.

"A Capital Castle?"

"There is a whole district behind it with smaller palaces and buildings, in there," Hiao Xen said.

"A whole palace to redecorate," Nuo said a hungry look in her eyes.

I hope that relocation and renovation costs are included!

***

"Don't you think people will be suspicious?" Storbon asked as he followed Erik through a hallway inside Bala Dungeon. They passed through a doorway and went up some stairs.

The defend a point part of Bala Dungeon was laid out like a cross.

At the main intersection where the four arms met, there was a large second floor. There was also a tree in the middle of the room. It grew from the ambient Mana. There were trap doors around the tree, where chests would rise out of the ground.

"There are other defense dungeons in the realms. Here they have to defend a tree from the beasts that spawn in the dungeon for as long as possible, then they need to flee out one of the exits. There are plenty of exits available. If they clear five waves, then one of the chests rises up, filled with loot from the Ten Realms. As time goes on, then more beasts are spawned each wave. The Ten Realms will spawn beasts based off the Mana in the area, so with all the bloodshed around Vuzgal, then combined with the Earth and Water Mana in this valley it will feel perfectly normal for an addition to the dungeon to have appeared over the centuries," Erik said.

"Aren't you afraid people will abuse it?" Storbon asked.

"Oh, they will, for sure. But then our Bala Dungeon will grow much faster than others, with so much fighting and ambient attribute Mana around. It will be slow to start, but purifying that much mana, the dungeon core will grow, purifying more mana and using the excess to build more floors workshops, with some of that energy being stored up in a mana storing formation."

Erik checked on the construction progress of Bala Dungeon. It was still underway. It would take another couple of days to complete. The layout was incredibly simple to speed up making the new parts of the dungeon.

"The Original Bala Dungeon, then the crafter dungeon and then our own hidden dungeon underneath," Storbon said.

"Then the two extra dungeons."

"The Endless dungeon and the other regular dungeon?"

"Yeah," Erik said.

"Lots of building," Storbon paused.

"Cat got your tongue?"

"When would a cat cut out my tongue?" Storbon had a perplexed look on his face.

"Its- nevermind, what do you want to ask?"

"Well, I heard that we're going to be expanding the military."

"Yes," Erik said, working on the interface.

"Are we going to increase the saize of the special teams?"

"That is my aim eventually. Though Glosil will be in charge of that. Rugrat and I aren't good commanders for large groups, never trained for it, we could eventually, but it doesn't make sense. Glosil is the commander of Alva's military, about time we made it official instead of being micromanaging idiots," Erik smirked and looked at Storbon.

"Seems like there is something new each week," Storbon said.

"Keeps you on your toes," Erik chuckled.

"How are you?" Erik asked as he was working with the interface.

"Good, sir," Storbon said, becoming straighter.

"Cut the shit," Erik said, not looking away from his work.

Storbon bent, his body deflated like a balloon as the dark circles around his eyes appeared. "When I talked to people back in Alva, my old friends. They listened to what happened up here, they nodded like they got it, but they didn't. They didn't understand just what we did, how we lived, how we fought. How we put everything on the line—*everything*. It was like they thought we were playing some game. It was honorable; it was great—but they don't know what it really was. What it means to just be a soldier!" Storbon shook his head in frustration.

Erik waved the screen away and turned to Storbon. "It is something that very few people understand and fewer can relate to. When you become a soldier, when you see war, everything changes. You aren't the person from before. It's something that only other people who went through it can talk about." Erik put his hand on Storbon's shoulder.

Storbon looked up at him.

Erik had repaired his mis-developed body. He had given him a shot at a life larger than being a cripple. He'd taught him how to fight, led him at the defense of Alva Village and the war in the Fourth Realm.

To say Erik didn't feel responsible for Storbon was an understatement.

Erik knew that he was one of the few people Storbon could just unload his baggage to. It was hard, but as they would walk through hell for Erik, he would do the same for them and lead the way through the flames.

Chapter: Master and Student

Tan Xue looked at the pilfered Mana cannon. There were a few different types: one that was complete, another that had been broken down into parts, and a few other broken versions, broken by attacks or from overloading itself with power.

She had been wrapped up in smithing for the last couple of months, as if she had rediscovered smithing again. She held classes in the room, working and explaining what she was working on and why she was using different techniques.

The smiths were all of a peak Journeyman level, seeing her working and being able to ask her questions was enough to inspire them and send them off to work on their own projects.

Julilah waved her hands at the cannons, "Welcome to the leftovers."

"These are powerful pieces of magical engineering—formations and smithing working together to create such a powerful tool," Tan Xue marveled.

"Powerful but crude. They're just large machines to focus and fire out a Mana Blast. The mortars take less material and can fire faster, their damage isn't as high but with modifications to the tube in materials, ammunition and formation," Julilah scoffed, looking down on the siege equipment.

"The mortars might not be hard to make, but the ammunition takes time to build and ship. Their biggest issue wasn't the weapon system, but getting ammunition to the mortar teams. This cannon uses Mana from a person or from Mana stones. Although its rate of fire is low, its power isn't too bad," Tan Xue said.

"Correct!" Rugrat announced loudly as he entered the workshop, with Qin following him.

"I thought you just went back to Vuzgal?" Tan Xue asked, carrying somewhat of a scowl as she quickly checked to make sure Rugrat was wearing actual clothes.

"I went back and told Erik what is happening here. He needs to stay there. All eyes are on him, and I have work I want to do!"

"I was wondering why you didn't come and bug me before you left," she said.

"What did you get for becoming an Expert?" Rugrat grinned.

Tan Xue rolled her eyes but couldn't stop the corners of her mouth turning up. "You know, it is rude to ask someone what they got for increasing their skill level."

"A new hammer, maybe an anvil, tongs or books? Blueprint designs?" Rugrat's eyes shone.

She snorted and pulled out a book, tossing it to Rugrat.

He looked at the cover. "War axes smithing compendium?" He quickly opened the pages.

"No blueprints but it is a technical book on different ax-es—how to make them, techniques to use and that kind of thing. It goes from Novice to Mid-Expert level, though." Her last words were tempting and Rugrat smiled, looking up like he had when he had been given his first rifle.

Tan Xue laughed at the partial madness that was seen in his eyes; appearing her own eyes. Julilah backed away and Qin looked at the two smiths.

She raised her hand and looked at Julilah and mouthed, *"What happened to them?"*

Julilah shrugged with a worried expression.

"Weapons," Qin coughed before Rugrat was able to speak.

Rugrat looked to be internally debating something.

"We have our own skills to work on as well," she scoffed impatiently.

"I want you to repair these Mana cannons, and figure out how they work. Also, I might have an in with the Crafter's Association so you can go and talk to some formation masters. I found out that there are some people who, for a fee, will offer classes on formations. I know that you feel kind of lost. I was originally going to go to these lessons myself but I know a lot less than either of you two do. The classes are not cheap. One hundred Earth Mana stones each."

Qin let out a cold breath and Tan Xue raised an eyebrow.

"Formations are not cheap to make and lessons are hard to find, especially from someone in the Crafter's Association who has reached the low Journeyman level. A mid-Journeyman level formation master is worth the same amount as an Expert-level smith. Smithing is practical from the beginning but then it becomes more technical with time and then combining theories with technical. Though it still takes a formation master to inlay a formation on a weapon. A formations master needs expensive materials and needs to have a lot of knowledge, practice or formations to copy in order to increase their level. You have techniques to make formations and know how to make formations but are lacking in the basic building blocks. This will allow you to make up for that weakness," Rugrat said as he nodded in an attempt to be sagely.

Julilah and Qin looked at each other and then Rugrat, the greedy and intense look in their eyes not too different from the looks that Rugrat and Tan Xue had shared not a few minutes before.

"When can we go?" Julilah asked as she bounced on the balls of her feet.

"We would need to increase your level and then we could send you off to the classes. It would take three months for you to go through the classes. You can pay us back with work, or with mana stones, this investment that Alva places on you and you would need to venture into the battlefield dungeon to be boosted in level by the Alvan army. Also, you would get some training with fighting beforehand and you would get some Adventurer's Guild guards for the duration of your schooling," Rugrat said.

"Why are you spending so much on us?" Qin asked in trepidation.

"Really, a trader's daughter." Tan Xue nodded in approval.

"Formations are where we're the weakest. There are formations across the Ten Realms and they're used frequently. We only have about seven people who are competent in formations, meaning that you can copy out formations. As we are now, we're just taking and repeating formations. We need to build new formations that are not just copies but are powerful improvements on the old. Formations that are tailored to our needs, not machines adapted around them. Take this centrifuge," Rugrat said as he put it on a worktable.

"I had to go and find a formation blueprint for the formation that makes it spin. I had no idea how I could make a formation that could do such a simple action. Someone could have given me a formation that summons a demon—I wouldn't know. And I don't know now how I can improve it. Say I want it to use less power? I'm lost. Compare that to the weapons I make; to make the strongest weapon, I need to match the base material to the enhancers, the right weapon shape and formations to bring out the greatest power.

"Formations are half of our weapons. Right now, we're copying formations onto the weapons, copy and paste, not modifying them to bring out greater strengths of the weapons," Rugrat said.

Tan Xue nodded. "Whenever making a weapon, just putting a formation on it, instead of making a formation for the weapon," Tan Xue snapped her fingers, finding a way to relate it." It's like having a pair of boots that are made from exquisite animal hide and are well crafted, but are being held together with just string."

"I guess that works," Rugrat said, confused by the analogy.

"I agree," Julilah said.

"Me too," Qin said, finally understanding.

"Good. You both start tomorrow. Today, try to figure out how these cannons work and we can start repairing the ones that we have. Thankfully, we've got a bunch of them!" Rugrat cackled to himself.

"I have a few questions," Rugrat said to Tan Xue before she headed over to the cannon that had been laid out in disassembled parts that Qin and Julilah were currently looking over.

"Go ahead," Tan Xue sighed.

"As we continue to advance in the Ten Realms, we will need to improve our weapons at a faster rate. I wanted to see if you were willing to set up an Alvan army supply department. A department that would be under the Alvan army and part of the academy. The army would pay the people involved for their time but it would be their duty to make and improve the weapons and gear that the army uses, things like new breastplate armor or new rifles."

"I could do that." She nodded.

"Sweet! You find the different workers who we can rely on. Here are the different contracts." Rugrat passed her the contracts that showed what the pay and the benefits would be for joining the Alvan army supply department.

"The leader of the department will change once every year and they will be someone who has served in the army. There will be a few managers underneath them. They will propose changes to equipment. It will be your job to see if they are feasible and also carry out upgrades that will increase the fighting strength of the Alvan army."

"Okay," Tan Xue replied. "Though I do have a request."

"What is it?"

"Any Expert or higher level weapons and blueprints, would I be able to inspect them? I have become an Expert-level smith, but I still have a long way to go if I want to become a Master," she said in a solemn voice.

"Done. And we're actively looking for more ways to improve the strength of the crafters here in Alva, like lessons or artifacts or otherwise," Rugrat prattled on.

"Do you know when the crafter dungeon will be completed here?" Tan Xue asked.

"Should be only a few more days, why?"

"I might have an Expert-level crafting room in the black-smith department, but I heard that there is no restrictions on working in the Expert-level crafting room in the dungeon. As long as I show that I am of the Expert level, I can enter the rooms there and be able to smith to my heart's content. I would need supplies to work with but I can work from there, leaving an Expert-level workshop free in the blacksmith department. Which could greatly increase yours, Taran's, or another smith's speed at improving their own smithing skill."

"I'm still a long way off becoming an Expert."

"You going to let Taran beat you?"

Rugrat's eyes thinned as his competitive streak was revealed. "Like I'd let that old bastard beat me!"

***

"A message has come in from Erik," Old Hei's head of security Khasar said as he was tending to plants in his private garden.

"Pass it here please," Old Hei took the note with his dirt-covered hands, staining the paper's surface.

He let out a laugh and then folded the paper up. "Send word to our associates in the Fourth Realm. Tell them that I suggest that they visit Vuzgal and pay what they need to join the city. Tell them that if they do not, they will regret it in the future. Put my name on the recommendation."

One of his assistants started to send the message through their sound transmission device.

"It looks like Erik and Rugrat have taken over a city in the Fourth Realm." Old Hei tapped the letter against the palm of his hand.

"A city, in the Fourth Realm?" Khasar repeated, sounding alarmed.

"Didn't I tell you that they would surprise us?"

"But to establish an Alchemist Association there?"

"Erik revealed some interesting information to me about a growing land no weaker than our own gardens here, possibly even stronger."

"No wonder you recommended it."

***

Elder Lu was being updated on what had happened in Vuzgal. He didn't expect to get a report so soon. He looked up at Cui Chin, who put down a folder on his desk.

"The Alchemist Association have agreed to Mister West's terms and will be entering Vuzgal, even with a stricter contract than what we or the Trader's Association have. They have sent over some of their finest craftsmen and a great number of gardeners," Cui Chin reported.

"What happened?" Elder Lu asked.

"They went directly to Mister West and were led into the valley next to Vuzgal. They returned not ten minutes later with the contract already confirmed and people being gathered. We were able to gather word as there has been so many new people moved over to Vuzgal.

"It looks like they're still discussing something but it looks like something in the valley interested them greatly. Also, there is one more piece of news. Hiao Xen has agreed to the contract. He will assist Vuzgal as well as Erik West and Rugrat. He will remain neutral in all conflicts between the associations and in his treatment of the associations, unless it is beneficial to the association in question as well as Erik and Rugrat."

"If he shows his ability to bring Vuzgal to prosperity and manage it well, then it will pave his way with the Blue Lotus and it will show where his true allegiance lies." Elder Lu nodded. It was both a trap and a test, one that could go either way. It depended on Hiao Xen's ability and whether he was able to remain the same man while away from the Blue Lotus's control.

"Vuzgal is quickly being repaired. Roads are being pulled up inside the inner city and replaced. They have installed new infrastructure and are repairing all of the main facilities and are building large towers into the sky. These appear to be Sky Reaching Restaurants, a restaurant that is connected to Erik back in the Third Realm. Different tall structures are being constructed as well, seemingly as temporary residences fit for powerful families and sect managers or just for common travelers. They have been laying down roads in the outer city, but they are laid out in a grid, sometimes going right through original houses and buildings that are in the way. All of the streets have been made large to fit a great amount of traffic. It looks like they are preparing for the future in a big way. We do not know where the resources and items that they looted from the city and were able to obtain from the fighting have gone."

"It looks like they are thinking like we are and preparing for the long haul. It will take time for the fighting to settle down in the east and the people from lands to the west will arrive soon, but it will only be in small numbers and they won't be willing to pay the prices that have been posted in the city."

"They are also making an odd sort of defensive system that is built out of fused stone and then placed underground, leaving only a small section above the ground."

"They have some small secrets, but it looks like everything is going as we planned. Let me know if there is any other big matters but otherwise I think it would be wise to pass this to someone of a lower position to look after," Elder Lu concluded.

As Head of the Fourth Realm Blue Lotus, he worked with massive alliances. Now that they had dealt with the Blood Demon Sect and the Hang-Nim Alliance, Vuzgal looked to be stable—albeit erraticly with Erik West making confusing decisions. *If he was to decrease the price for someone to go to Vuzgal, he might have gotten more of the associations and people to head over. I thought he wouldn't have been so arrogant. But there must be something about the dungeon that interested the Alchemist Association or perhaps his standing of being the direct disciple of an Expert alchemist and a member of the Alchemist Association pushed them to agree to his terms.*

Cui Chin bowed and headed out of Elder Lu's office.

Elder Lu pushed the folder to the side and turned to a new report.

Chapter: Next Stage

Qin and Julilah stood in front of the totem in Alva Dungeon. It had only taken three days for Domonos and his group to boost their levels. There had been other people from Alva who had gone along with the Alvan army. The Alvan army was killing as many monsters as possible with their newly gained Strength. The more they killed in the battlefield dungeon, the less would be in the lower levels of the dungeon when they cleared the floors. Eventually there would be a point where they would kill all of the creatures from the lower levels and then the dungeon core would be spawning in random creatures under the Ten Realms. Though they wouldn't know when this happened unless they went to the lower levels of the dungeon and saw that there were no more creatures left. Based on their only foray into the first Metal floor, that point of clearing all the creatures seemed far away.

So the slaughter continued and people from Alva had their levels boosted. They had to pay the gold or Mana stones it cost to enter the battlefield dungeon and transfer the points to Egbert who could use them to purchase items for the dungeon as whole.

The soldiers did the hard work and after only killing a few beasts, they could increase someone who had been level ten their entire life to a level fifteen or twenty.

The army's power allowed them to take down most beasts in just two or three hits. They had to go through nearly twenty beasts before they started to reach creatures that were a challenge.

They accrued a massive amount of dungeon points but they continued to build up their points for rarer weapons, materials and books. The Battlefield dungeon had turned into a game for them. A place for them to simply grind for dungeon points instead of providing any real experience.

High Journeyman level weapons, cultivation manuals and pills. Anything that could increase their strength was picked up. If the fight with the Blood Demon Sect taught them anything, it was that there was always someone stronger.

People from across Alva paid high fees to join their groups, giving them their dungeon points to increase their level.

Paying money for levels there were few who wouldn't agree, increasing levels meant an increase in power and even how long someone could live for!

Qin had always heard about her brother's strength and his fighting ability, but he had put it on full display over the last couple of weeks.

Julilah and she had been raised to level thirty. Both girls were sad to say goodbye, but they were happy to finally be learning about their skill.

Tan Xue and Egbert looked rather emotional and even Qin felt her throat closing up as she waved good-bye to her father and Domonos.

There was a flash of light and Alva was replaced by a gray-looking town. The buildings were perfectly gray, with formations scribed all over the walls, adding colorful runes.

Such a waste of resources! she couldn't help but think, looking at the walls and the formations on them. They had been carved into the other spotless buildings as art, serving no other purpose.

"A formation on three different planes," Julilah said, seeing past the waste in resources and looking at the technical side of the formations.

"How do they make a formation work with it on three faces at ninety degrees to one another? Doesn't that make a weak point in it?" Qin said, her own thoughts kicking in.

They talked about the different formations as they followed Rugrat, who wore a robe that hid his identity. He might look like some mysterious Master to others, but knowing him, Qin and Julilah paid no attention to his solemn air, thinking it more comical than serious.

They entered the center of the city. There was a number of powerful associations or pillar organizations in the city.

Rugrat walked across the grounds. He reached the Formation Guild that would be Qin and Julilah's home for the next three months. The two of them looked at the building. It looked like a box that had multiple formations carved into it. One could see the power moving between the large formations' lines and runes.

"It's as difficult to make a large formation as it is to make a small one," Qin said.

"Defensive, attack?" Julilah asked, studying it.

Qin looked at it. "Both?"

Rugrat produced a token and the guard looked at it before nodding and allowing him to pass.

They entered the grounds. A formation covered the entire building, making it seem open, but they had a wall like the other associations. It was just theirs was hidden, using Mana instead of stone and building materials to exist.

They passed formations that glowed and distorted the air, moving square, spherical, and other formation-covered objects that rotated, rising and falling over one another.

"They're all floating, but none of them are touching even if they look chaotic," Julilah observed. "Formations in harmony so that the base formation and the formations on the objects don't interfere with one another."

Formations engraved in different rare materials were on display, making a thoroughfare to the main building. Formations appeared in mid-air, changing colors and form.

One's mind started to relax as they neared the main building. The Mana gathering formation was the best quality in the city. The Mana density had already shocked Qin and Julilah, who believed simple formations could run off just the ambient Mana in the Fourth Realm.

Their minds focused and they felt their concentration increase. Their thoughts became more concise as they looked at the parts of the formation instead of being interested in the effect it had.

Their eyes moved from the flashy designs to the ones on the buildings.

They entered the main building and Rugrat showed his token again. It didn't take them long until they reached a side room. Rugrat had to show his token so much he kept it out before they reached the final room.

He knocked on the door and it glowed with a formation, opening. A woman looked up from her book. Glowing letters rested in the air above her. She moved the books slightly and the words changed. It was a magnifying tool that also made a holographic projection. Although it looked simple, it used at least three or four different formations.

"Yes?" she asked, looking perturbed.

"These two are here for classes." Rugrat put down the token and took out two more necklaces.

She frowned and pulled out a metal plate. She inserted the token into it, reading some information before she checked the other tokens. She nodded and passed them back. "Miss Qin and Miss Julilah to learn basics of formation making with Journeyman Alexi."

She stood. "I can take them over there. They shall finish classes in three months," she said, dismissing Rugrat.

"See you two later. If you get into trouble, come to Vuzgal," Rugrat reminded them.

They both nodded, feeling at a loss all of a sudden.

"Your room and food has already been paid for, just in case you spend all of your money on formation equipment. Make sure you make use of the library, too. It's an adventure—go and discover!" He gave a hearty laugh.

He might sound funny and he was odd, but he meant well. Hearing his words, they felt better and started to look forward to their lessons.

Rugrat headed off.

They turned and saw the woman was already down the corridor. They ran after her, shooting glances at each other.

The woman knocked on a door that seemed to be in the darkest corner of the building. A voice that could be barely heard on the other side of the door paused and the door opened.

Julilah and Qin looked into the room, seeing fresh-faced teenagers and young adults all looking at them in interest.

Even though they were young, they were all level thirty. Qin had been feeling proud about her level, but to these people they were only on the same level. They also wore the clothes of the formation department of the Crafter's Association.

All of their emblems were copper in color, though.

The man at the front wore a gold emblem. He looked to be middle-aged, slightly balding, and had a lifeless, bored look in his eyes.

"These two are exterior students for your class," the woman announced.

"Oh, take your seats and don't interrupt class," the teacher said.

The woman turned and walked away as Qin and Julilah walked into the class, feeling everyone's eyes on them as they found two seats but they were forced to sit apart from each other.

They smiled awkwardly as they took their seats.

There was disdain in the others' eyes, looking down on their common clothes and their lack of medallion. They weren't one of them—just an outsider who thought they could learn formations.

"For you just joining, I am Teacher Alexi." He let out a cough and then tapped on the board.

"Formations, at their base, are a conduit for Mana, turning Mana from raw energy into something. Many call formations the physical form of a spell. They are not wrong. Anything that someone can cast, you can make a formation for. With more power, it can have a greater effect." His tone made him seem bored of his own content, but Qin and Julilah were spellbound, listening to him intently.

"Formations and spells have the same power ranking system as each other. There are formations that use Elemental Mana which is commonly stored within Gems. This is replaced by pure Mana stored in mana stones. Formations can draw on the surrounding mana to store power and amplify their effects. Higher levels of mana stones, Earth, Sky, Celestial and Divine power more powerful formations. There are legends about formations being so perfectly placed that they are in tune with the ten realms and the ten realms supply's the formation power. While the power of a formation is important, we look at the *effects* of a formation to determine it's ability!" Who can tell me about the diferent grades of formations!"

Someone raised their hand but Louche's eyes moved to Qin and Julilah.

"Well we have some new faces here, could you present the different abilities of formations to the class?" He asked with an innocent smile.

"Well if formations are following in the lines of spells then there are a few stages. A formation at it's basic level must have power function and direction to function properly, then there are the levels of power, using elemental mana, using pure mana from mana stones. After that, you've got using the surrounding mana to amplify your formation, to do that you need to have a formation in tune with nature around it so that one action is multiplied in force. So how an explosion will go off and the wave of pressure will be the thing that kills people, not the actual explosion. Domains are next where the formation controls an area completely, say an illusion formation it will be impossible for someone without the same skill or higher than the person who laid the formation to know that they are in an illusion formation. Then there are formations that can change the environment that they are in, then formations that change the mana around them, refining it or changing it into different affinities. Spatial realm is where the formation master can create a formation that hold's a separate space from the rest of the world which the creator is like a god, free to destroy or create. This is easier to do than with mages I would think who follow the same standards. They have to cast spells and supply power, the formation masters if they can keep it connected to the ten realms can power this new space without losing a portion of their power. Though the resources required would be massive," Qin shook her head as Professor Louche had an alarmed look on his face.

"I thought that there was only the domain stage and that had five stages within it already?" One of the student's asked his peers.

Professor Louche cleared his throat, taking control of the class once again.

"Very good, spatial storage is the pinnacle of formations, though it is possible to get smaller versions of it that are not as big as a city."

A student put up his hand with Louche pointing at him.

"If creating space is so hard, how come we have storage rings, Professor Louche?"

"Storage rings can use a number of tricks to store items. They can be hollowed out on the inside and there is a spell to reduce the size of the item and weight. These combined formations have been refined over time, spreading them across the realms. Though as more items need to be stored inside, then stronger formations are needed. If someone was to create a large enough space, they could store a small city inside and they would be able to live and breathe in there without issue. Now, back to the topic on hand. Formations are made up of lines, runes, and shapes on the outside. Inside they are Mana lines, sub-formations, and control parameters.

"A simple formation can be carved and filled in with one type of Mana medium, though a complex formation containing multiple formations can have different Mana mediums or reactants inside the formations. Why do we need different reactants? To control the power of the Mana, convert it, or alter it into a new attribute. Having the wrong reactant can lead to the formation failing. Even in some formations there can be different reactants used at the same time, depending on the complexity that you are dealing with.

"Lines contain the power of the Mana. They can guide power, act as a buffer or an overflow, regulating power. Shapes are usually sub-components of a formation, or sub-formations as they grow in complexity. Runes are speaking control to power.

Think of the lines and the shapes as the human body and its Mana system, but the runes are the words, motions, or thoughts that one might use to cast a spell. This is part of the reason there are limitless types of formations and it is not rare to be the first person to create a formation.

"Everyone has their own style in formation making. They learn from different Masters, they conceptualize formations differently or they want to hide the technical aspects of the formation from their competitors. This adds their own flair to their work and can make the formations incredibly confusing. Copying one's formations works, but you'll be just shooting into the dark. Each formation master needs to find their own path to formation making.

"What I would suggest is that you make your library of runes as simple and as small as possible. Otherwise you'll have to write out a ton of symbols and you might not have that much space. When making a formation, most will copy others or they will research the smallest runes that they can use and combine them all together, with the different shapes and connecting lines. Even if someone wanted to know what the formation did, they would need to have the different books a formation master used when researching how to make this formation. Otherwise, they would need to see it in action or be told what it does."

A shiver ran down Qin's back, just thinking about the information they would need to understand to realize what a formation could do.

***

Rugrat was working in one of the smithies in Vuzgal when he got a call from Erik.

"Special teams are back," Erik said.

Rugrat put down what he was working on and then headed off toward the castle.

Roska and Niemm were there. Gong Jin's half team was in Alva.

Erik was reading a group of messages as Rugrat entered.

"Have a fun trip?" Rugrat asked.

"Not really," Roska grumbled.

"Everyone okay?"

"Yeah." Niemm nodded.

Rugrat paused for a second before he nodded. Losing someone under your command was tough. Especially if you blamed yourself for it, or you were in a team as close as the special teams.

"We were able to turn around twenty dungeons into crafter dungeons all over the place. We captured two dungeon cores." Roska pulled out the dungeon cores and Rugrat held up his hand as she tossed them to him. He put them into his storage ring as Erik looked up from his not-so-light reading.

"The crafting trials should activate over the next several weeks," Niemm said.

"Any major complications that will come back on us?" Rugrat asked.

"No." Niemm shook his head and looked at Roska, who shook her head as well.

"All right, well, then you're on building duty starting tomorrow. We've got plenty to build in the city still."

Erik got a message through his sound transmission device and answered it.

"Good work. Get some rest," Rugrat concluded while Erik was on the device.

They both saluted. Rugrat returned the gesture in Erik's place as they headed out.

Erik finished the call a few minutes later.

"There are some people from the Alchemist Association here. They wish to talk. Looks like Old Hei got my message." Erik moved to the door. "Let me know what's in the reports."

Rugrat looked at the pile of reports. "I can show them around!" Rugrat yelled as he turned to look at where Erik had been but he'd run out of the room already.

"Dammit!"

Chapter: Overpriced Messenger

"Thankfully, we've got a lot of Earth-grade Mana stones combined with the two dungeon cores, all of the contributions from the Blue Lotus, the Crafter's Association and the Alchemist Association, I guess?" Rugrat walked out of the totem located in Alva and walked to the dungeon headquarters.

Better food in Alva, anyway. He went straight for the Alva Dungeon's core. He disabled the formations protecting the dungeon core and stepped into the central chamber, standing underneath the dungeon core. A Mana mist floated around in the bottom of the chamber, being drawn into the dungeon core, and a cable-thick line of Mana shot up into the Mana storing formation in the ceiling above.

Rugrat took out the two blue crystals. The Mana mist in the room started to be pulled in toward them as they floated upward, reaching up toward the main dungeon core there. The smaller dungeon cores stopped beneath the main core, a blue light started to come off them being drawn into the original dungeon core. They quickly dissolved, turning into streams of light that wrapped around the main dungeon core that started to spin and rotate faster. It was like watching someone wrapping up a ball of wool.

The two smaller dungeon cores were reduced to nothing as the main dungeon core took on a lighter blue color, with hints of purple showing in the dungeon core crystal.

The Mana density didn't change as much as it had the first time.

Rugrat frowned and started to circulate his Mana system. His Mana veins started to glow as he looked around the room, exerting his domain.

758

"The Mana density on this floor can be completely refined by the dungeon core," Rugrat said to himself. "The Mana density here doesn't push the dungeon core to its limit. The Affinity Mana in the surrounding area will start to be purified as the dungeon core pulls in more Mana. What about when we connect up the other levels, though?"

The dungeon core started to slow down its rotation, a precious crystal, commanding the Mana within the room and across the floor. The Mana density decreased slightly, but the purity of the Mana increased.

==========

Quest Completed: Dungeon Reborn

==========

Upgrade the dungeon core, returning it to its peak condition.

==========

Rewards:

+10,000,000 EXP

==========

==========

Title: Dungeon Master III

==========

Control over the Dungeon building interface.

Grade: Common Earth (Can be upgraded)

Ability: Dungeon Sense, 15km radius.

Cooldown: 12 hours per day

Increase all stats by +1

Able to bestow title Dungeon Hunter (2 remaining)

==========

"Not bad at all." Rugrat felt his Strength increasing.

The second dungeon core was absorbed as well, one of the notifications he had just received, changed.

==========
Title: Dungeon Master III
==========
Control over the Dungeon building interface.
Grade: Greater Earth (Can be upgraded)
Ability: Dungeon Sense, 30km radius. (Can be used 4 times a day
Increase all stats by +1
Able to bestow title Dungeon Hunter (4 remaining)
==========

==========
Quest: Dungeon Master
==========
You have returned your dungeon to its former glory. Advancement quests are unlocked. Grow your dungeon's power!
==========
Requirements:
Increase your dungeon core's grade to Sky Common
Increase the Strength of your minions (Complete)
==========
Rewards
40,000,000 EXP
Dungeon Master Title IV
==========

"Not bad, only need to increase the level of the dungeon core in the future. The cities get more options with a larger population," Rugrat thought aloud.

"With more dungeon hunters we can find more cores to add to our dungeons and expand them or create secondary bases. The experience is welcome as well," Rugrat looked up at the mana storing formation, as the dungeon increased in grade it was able to process more mana than ever before, purifying more than ever before. The mana density inside the dungeon increased in purity and density. It wouild passively help them grow as time went on. Increasing one's concentration, the mana cultivation speed and their recovery. Children born there would be more in tune with mana than other children in the Mortal realms that were not from a big clan or sect.

He left the headquarters and then went to the smithy. He did a round checking on others, trying to bide his time before he headed to his own smithy and threw some materials into the furnace.

"So how were their classes?" Egbert asked some time later as Rugrat was beating on metal, refining it from Mortal grade to Earth grade.

"Not sure, but they should be fine. If not, we'll tear the formation school apart," Rugrat said as he worked. "Anything change around here?"

"Not really. The medics have been competing against each other since you left, gone through five or so tester minions I summoned. I swear that they start shivering as soon as I animate them," Egbert said.

"They paying for the materials at least?" Rugrat finished on a lump of metal and put it to the side, letting it cool. He took out another red-hot ingot and hammered it out into a sheet, sprinkling Mana stone dust on it before he folded the metal. His arm was glowing and his hammer had blue veins in it. Blue and green Mana sparks shot out from where the hammer struck metal, injecting Mana into the metal's structure.

"Yes." Egbert sounded distracted.

"Something up?" Rugrat asked.

"Aren't you a high-class blacksmith? Shouldn't there be a bit, you know, *more*?"

"You don't always have good days filled with inspiration. Some days you just have to refine materials, check your enhancers and go research, or just bang out weapons and tools. Being a Master doesn't mean that you necessarily have inspiration every time you touch a hammer. Some days you just have to grind through it. Good and bad, even if you've had a boring time doing it, you'll pick up the tools of your trade the next day and the next. Doing it again and again until that moment of inspiration, that moment where something clicks, and then boom! You can shoot off for weeks just working on a single idea." Rugrat put the hammered metal to the side and pulled out another piece with his tongs. "And some days you're just wondering what to do, so you refine some more metal."

Egbert made a thoughtful noise, but didn't say anything.

Rugrat didn't pay attention. His annoyance and boredom from earlier had relaxed; his hands and body moved in the same familiar motions from before. He practiced his swings, tried out a few different techniques he had been thinking of or heard of. He was only refining metal, after all, so even if he messed up his strike, it didn't have a lasting impact.

It was the perfect time for him to practice his hammering techniques.

Time passed and his stomach seemed to make complaints and his body started to think of other things he needed to do.

He stopped some time later and put the last refined ingot off to the side. He had dozens of ingots off to the side. Once he had started, everything else had faded away. "Just have to start sometimes and it gets better, or you'll surprise yourself."

He stored the ingots away and headed out of the smithy. He took a look at the order board. People had requested items to be crafted; available smiths took on different jobs with variable skill requirements in the hope of gaining a skill point. The smithing teachers picked out items for the smiths to work on to also increase their skill or the smiths would take on extra jobs to earn some money. There were also smiths who weren't in school anymore who would take on private jobs or jobs that were left unfilled.

At all times of the night and day, the smithy was in operation, much like the rest of the academy. No matter the time, there was always at least a few people working, be it in the library or the different workshops.

"I need to see Rose." Rugrat let out a defeated sigh as he looked over to the main government office building that reached up towards the ceiling, hiding behind the remaining manor from the gnome's times.

It was still early in the day; with the time changes from Vuzgal and Alva, his day had been extended by another eight hours.

It wasn't long until he found himself in Rose's office.

"Hiya. I've come to make a deposit to the treasury," Rugrat said.

"In what amount?" Rose asked, sounding professional.

"About thirty thousand Mortal Mana stones and another thirty Earth Mana stones." Rugrat pulled out a square-looking storage device and put it on the table. It was unremarkable, only with a few formations on its surface.

Rose coughed violently, turning red as it kept on. Finally she took some water, coughing some more and wiping her hair out of her face. "Should I ask where this came from?"

"Well, we recovered thousands of Earth-grade Mana stones from Vuzgal, and thousands of Mortal-grade Mana stones. The former royal family might have used up their Mana stones to power the Mana barrier, but there were plenty of traders and nobles who didn't get the chance to do so, or kept their wealth hidden. The fight with the Blood Demons took thousands of Earth-grade Mana stones to power the mana barrier—the Blue Lotus and the Crafter's Association tossed in a bunch of Mana stones for us as well.

"The dungeon core in Vuzgal is still pouring power into the cornerstones and we've got the Mana gathering formations there now too, so it is even faster than before.

"With time, we'll recover all of the Mana stones that we used. In the meantime, we've got protection from some powerful people. So Erik and I agreed to take ten percent of what we had and put it into the treasury. The Mana stones will grow back with time, but if we give an injection of funds to the treasury, then we'll be able to upgrade the academy faster and increase the financial power of our traders," Rugrat confirmed, more trying to convince himself to give up the money than to explain it to Rose.

"Well, it is enough money to buy a kingdom in the First Realm—maybe a city in the Second." Her eyes moved to the box and then back to Rugrat.

"It won't bite," Rugrat said. "Though I'm interested—where will it go do you think?"

"The first thing will be an investment into the Sky Reaching Restaurants. They have turned into places where the cooks of Alva can test their skills and where they can recruit new, interesting talents. They are also information hubs as people from the various larger powers go to the Sky Reaching Restaurant for important meetings. They can also be locations for our traders to stay and get caught up on various messages.

"The second investment will be into the Adventurer's Guild. They are growing rapidly. With the increase in funds, they will be able to have others to deal with smaller issues and look to their core issues to become stronger.

"Then there are the traders. Money is another kind of strength. They can use these funds to overpower the people who are going against them and increase the size of their businesses. They are constantly getting our loans and most companies have several loans with us. They use the money they borrow from us to buy more or better items, selling them for a greater profit and then simply paying us the interest on the loan as they're earning much higher than before. Many will just increase the size of the loan instead of paying it all back in one go, acting as a large base for them to increase their revenue."

"What about the academy?"

"Well, the academy is kind of difficult. It is not something that we thought we would be upgrading in the near future. We would like to, but for one of the workshops to be upgraded another tier. It will cost ten Earth-grade Mana stones per building."

"I know that Erik and I would be willing to take Mana stones from Vuzgal in order to pay for the upgrades to the workshops. If Jia Feng agrees, then we'll upgrade the smithy to tier four."

***

Cui Chin looked at the latest information that had come in from Vuzgal.

He took it and headed to Elder Lu's office. It wasn't long until he was allowed in.

He presented the report and bowed. "The token force from the Alchemist Association isn't just going because of Expert Zen Hei. They sent along a high-Journeyman-ranked alchemist as the messenger. They were escorted by Erik into the valley just a week ago. They seemed to be close to Erik as he saw them off at the totem. There has since been people coming back and forth from the Alchemist Association and Vuzgal.

"Originally it looked like they would send a small group there as a sign of respect to Elder Zen Hei and his direct disciple. However it looks like that valley has a great draw for the Alchemist Association. A deal seems to have been agreed upon. The Alchemist Association started to pull out a number of powerful people from their association, including high-level gardeners from different gardener families who tend to Expert-level ingredients. They are building in the same area of Vuzgal as we are, but their building is much larger and the people working on it are some of their best craftsmen."

"Why have I not heard anything about this before?"

"I thought that they were visiting with regards to the fact he is the direct disciple of an Expert-level alchemist and a member of the Alchemist Association. They wouldn't be going this far if there wasn't more to it. Erik has also sent word out through the different navigators he invited into the city. He paid their fees to come to the city, housed them in the first Wayside Inns and fed them in the Sky Reaching Restaurants, letting them wander the city and take it in.

"The navigators are now spread across the Fourth Realm. Most of them want to head back soon, so they'll guide people heading to Vuzgal to enjoy the city once again. He has also sent messages to the Crafter's Association, to us, and to the other associations. Some from the Fighter's Association are already appearing in Vuzgal. Those from the east Chaotic Lands are on the move, with Erik letting them stay in the city for a week without paying a fee. With the normally high fees of the city and removing them for different people, it is gaining their interest. After all, something that was greatly expensive becoming cheaper is much more interesting than something that was cheap becoming free," Cui Chin said.

"It looks like he and Hiao Xen have been busy," Elder Lu observed.

"There is one more thing. Hiao Xen has been looking for information on different dungeons and places that have a high Earth content."

"High Earth content? He has reached Body Like Mortal Iron—is he trying to go for Body Like Earth Iron?"

"The information points to it," Cui Chin confirmed.

"Do we know where his people are going? Or where his special teams disappeared off to?"

"Not at this time." Cui Chin kept his voice neutral, but he was angry with himself for losing them.

"Increase the speed of transfer and the grade of the Blue Lotus in Vuzgal. We can't be left behind by the Alchemist Association too badly."

"Yes, Elder Lu." Cui Chin bowed, being dismissed.

***

"I was able to find one." Hiao Xen entered the room where Erik was working.

There were various alchemical ingredients around; Erik's face was purple with green spots. He shivered and managed to get out, "Urggh, feet, urrghh achk!"

Hiao Xen rushed forward and smacked Erik on the back, forcing him to spit out the ingredients he was chewing on.

Erik took out a poison recovery concoction and quickly quaffed it. Erik's hands started to unclench and his body started to relax.

"Ughh, I was nearly done figuring that one out." Erik shivered as he looked at the glob of roots on the ground. "I'll test it out more later on."

"You were testing it?" Hiao Xen asked, shaken up from the ordeal.

"I couldn't find anything on it in the books that I borrowed from the Alchemist Association here." Erik waved at the different books around his study. "Though I guess they only just started to move their library over, really. Well, did you have something that you wanted from me?"

"I—I—well, I was able to get information on a heavy Earth-attribute dungeon. It is a dungeon owned by the Stone Fist Sect. They are a group of several sects and families that focus on body tempering. They focus on dungeons that have to do with the various elements. I guess this is to go through the temperings they need to increase their Body Cultivation.

"They get into a lot of fights and they focus on fighting others for these dungeons. And there is a lot of infighting in the sect, families within trying to get more power. They also have some special constitutions within their ranks," Hiao Xen said.

"What's the condition of the Earth dungeon? Is it a dungeon I can pay to enter, a dungeon that only opens every so often?"

"It is one of the core dungeons that they control. You can only be invited in," Hiao Xen said. "If you were able to use some force politically, you could force their hand. They are a powerful sect, but they are very direct, making them easy to deal with but not the best traders. Using the Alchemist Association to get them to move might be possible."

"So again we need Strength to talk to them." Erik pondered for a second. "It shouldn't be long until we have the capital to request a visit to their dungeon. How is the plan going with the navigators?"

"They have all headed out across the Fourth Realm. All of them seemed excited to return, eager to bring more people here. I didn't think to use them as a way to influence people needing

a navigator. It was a powerful move. What did you do to interest
the Alchemist Association? I had some of them coming over today to talk about terms of renting out the valley?"

"I showed them the valley. With its shape, it hasn't allowed
the ambient Mana out much, creating a natural formation. Water
and Earth Mana have gathered in the area, turning it into a place
that would be ideal for high-level ingredients." Erik paused for a
moment.

"They rinsed me. I was able to get them to agree to give us
better prices on finished products. They will sell us ingredients at
market places. They will rent the valley to check the validity for
five years. Then they have the first right to purchase. They will
put in more guards, but it will be to close off the valley from the
paths that will be going to the different dungeons. They will upgrade their headquarters here, mainly to prepare and ship more
ingredients. I made the rent immediate, not thinking that they
can harvest all of the plants that are in there already. I was able to
get them to adhere to the five percent taxation on anything that
they sell within Vuzgal."

Erik sighed as Hiao Xen patted his shoulder.

"Their negotiators have been doing it for hundreds of years,"
Hiao Xen said. "You did better than I thought, it might be because of your identity as one of the Expert level master's disciple."

"Your pity isn't making me feel better in anyway," Erik complained.

"Well how much will they pay us?"

"Three Sky Mana stones per year," Erik looked at Hiao Xen.

"That's good right?"

"We've got people to act as guards for the dungeons and another powerful association supporting us," Hiao Xen.

"Crap," Erik deflated.

"Well my next piece of news isn't that good either. The Sha people that you sent me to search out. It looks like they are looking for you as well. Information has started to spread about the Blood Demon army being defeated by a group of people using Sha weapons. The Sha were initially proud of the news, but now they're finding out it's not someone from their clans. They're starting to look into it. It won't be long until they find out about Vuzgal."

"But they haven't yet?"

"Not yet. But they are a powerful force—it will only be a matter of time."

"Do you have a location where the Sha clans live?"

"Ra-Hie. It is one of the cities under Sha leadership. In the Seventh realm. Otherwise they control a large portion of the fourth realm, they haven't expanded in generations, maintaining their position and growing their strength in the seventh realm. Also related to weapons and the kind that your two groups use. I have had people asking if they can purchase the blueprints or completed weapons. Such as the repeaters, grenades, explosives, mortars and rifles."

Erik let out a heavy breath.

"Pause them I don't know if we want to start telling people about all of our military secrets. Hint that we will be willing to trade with the associations thata are allied with us. We will not give them blueprints but repeater weapons aren't out of the question.

"They'll be pleased to know, is there anything else you need from me?"

"I don't think so. Next time that someone wants to negotiate with me, can you go instead?"

Hiao Xen smiled and stood.

"That I can do. See you later," Hiao Xen headed out of the room.

"I hate having to expand my Alchemy Book," Erik grumbled as he tossed a plant into his mouth. There was a grisly popping noise.

Hiao Xen's skin formed goosebumps from the popping noises and Erik's wordless complaints of the ingredients' taste.

***

Qin rubbed her head as she let out a hiss.

"What the hell is happening, why does my skull feel like it's reversing!" Julilah was on the floor yelling.

"Shut up! You're so loud!" Qin shot back, dropping to her knees as she grunted in pain.

==========

Skill: Formation Master

==========

Level: 54 (Journeyman)

==========

When working on formations Stamina loss decreases by 20%. Able to read 15% faster.

==========

==========

Upon advancing into the Journeyman level of Hand-to-Hand, you have been rewarded with one randomly selected item related to this skill.

==========

You have received the book: A basic guide to rune design line placement

+100,000 EXP

==========

She saw the notifications but they were half forgotten as she felt like a wealth of information was at her fingertips.

"Journeyman skill book," Qin whispered, Tan Xue and the other Journeymen talked about the mysterious book.

The book was unlocked when someone was a Journeyman compiled all of the information in their mind into one book. Any information that they had learned about their craft or skill was held within these books. They weren't physical creations, just something created within one's mind.

It was like a cheat sheet, compiling all of their information together. They could record concepts or ideas, anything that they had learned about materials related to the skill, as well as spells and techniques.

When she started querying through information in her mind, she felt as if she had crossed a boundary, Alexi's words linking the runes to language with connected to effects the runes would cause.

When she thought of a potential action a formation could do, a stream of runes would appear in her mind. They would change and switch as she read and analyzed them, simplifying them down and becoming fewer letters.

She was left shaking. There were thousands of runes already in her mind. Although she knew that they were a key part of the formation creation process, it was only when Alexi told her of their importance in the language of creation that she was able to connect them directly to different effects.

There was still a lot she didn't understand.

I'll need to read more books to build up a full rune-based lexicon.

She dismissed the book, nodding as if understanding what Alexi was talking about as he continued to lecture. The person beside Qin let out a dismissive snort at her actions.

Qin didn't even look at them, leaning forward in her seat and focusing on Alexi's lecture completely.

She couldn't be bothered by their attitude, entranced by Alexi's words as the clouds that had seemed to cover her formation knowledge slowly started to clear.

Chapter: Uproar in the Fourth

Erik led the way, paying the fee as he led Gong Jin and his half special team through the gates of Ra-Hie. The Sha wore goggles and held front-loading weapons like blunderbusses, muskets, and short shotguns; pistols festooned their clothes like ornaments. The air smelled of burned carbon, like a firearms range.

There was a dull noise in the distance.

"Seems like something went off," Gong Jin said.

Han Wu was looking around. People stared at him and his bandolier of grenades.

"They look kind of like firearm peacocks," Erik said to Gong Jin.

Gong Jin sighed and his eyes went dull. He was already numb to Han Wu's actions.

"Don't worry Jin, Han Wu knows how to put himself back together fine now. Being in a city of other explosive idiots isn't such a good time for the rest of us though." Yang Zan sighed.

"What is a peacock?" Gong Jin asked.

"A colorful bird that likes to show off, I guess." Erik shrugged as they entered the city.

"I will wait at the tavern Glorious Flame." The navigator pointed out a location on Gong Jin's map and updated their maps with his own. It was really good having a navigator to go to new cities.

He waved them good-bye and headed to the tavern.

The group headed out. They went to a shop that sold weapons.

"No one but Sha is allowed in this shop," a guard said. He was short but he had a strong-looking blunderbuss with formations on it.

"What if someone has a Sha weapon but isn't a Sha?" Erik asked.

"Then we'll hunt them down. If they're lucky, they'll become a person of the Sha clan—or they, their friends, and six generations of their family will be killed."

"Bit drastic," Erik said.

They headed away. They saw a group of Sha at an outdoors range, shooting at targets. The weapons were powerful, much stronger than the old weapons of the same grade, but they were only muskets, rifles and pistols—front loaders at that. They hadn't moved on to cartridges; bolt action and semi-automatic weren't even a concept. Mortars or artillery were not used but they had grapeshot cannons, or load them with ball and buck, nasty shit and grenades were seen as a curse.

"Their powder is plenty powerful. I guess they've been working with it for longer. Their Alchemy formulas would be useful," Han Wu commented as he studied the pilfered powder.

"Yes, but they haven't advanced or innovated any further—I only see one design for the blunderbuss, the pistols, muskets and the rifles. I see some changes to the platform to enhance it, but no evolutions like we have. Seems they just use different base materials, formations and modified shapes to increase lethality. Not anything like how a bolt action reduces the power of the shot compared to a front loader, but then they increase things like the range and rate of fire. I wonder if they even have rifling for their barrels." Erik let out a sigh. "Let's go take a look at the guards of the different Sha clans."

They headed to the different clans, checking out the guards there. They wore different clothes so were easy to distinguish one from another.

Wait a minute, are those petticoats? Erik looked at the funky-looking shorts and pants with a second glance and then checked out the buttoned-up jackets.

"Let's head to the clan head residence," Erik said, feeling odd.

He stopped as he saw the guards who were marching around the clan's building.

"Pirate hats, petticoats, and those colors. French colors? Damn, they look like they're right out of the seventeen hundreds. Could it really be possible?" *Could the Sha actually come from Earth? They look French. I can't tell if someone is speaking French or not.*

Erik looked up at the gates where there was what looked like a motto carved into the gate.

"Mother fucker," Erik hissed. He turned around, his eyes catching the other people moving around: the wigs, the hats, the way people talked, the smoking pipes. Now that he thought about it, it was as if he were in a eighteenth-century camp, with people with muskets everywhere.

"Something wrong with the words in the gate?" Yang Zan muttered. "France will never fall? What does that mean?"

"Trouble," Erik said as they headed to the tavern.

The navigator saw them and stood. They headed out of the tavern and went right for the totem.

"When were the Sha clans created?" Erik asked the navigator.

"Oh, it has to be around two or three hundred years. They weren't much early on, but then with their rows of blue jackets and their lines of weapons fire, they were able to beat back others. The Commandant came out of nowhere and united several clans, together they called themselves the Sha clan, internally they call themselves the bourgeoisie."

"Haven't others got the blueprints for the Sha weapons?" Erik asked.

"They have them but the Sha will fight anyone who makes the weapons unless they make an oath to never make Sha weapons again or try to research them further."

"What about if a higher power gets them?"

"They can get them all right, but the Sha weapons aren't strong enough to fight with the people who are higher than the Sixth Realm. So to the higher powers, the Sha weapons are kind of useless. The Sha have solidified their position here in the Earth tier realms and they teach how to fight with their firearms and their bodies. The cost to make the weapons and their special ammunition is incredibly high. Also, it's only in the last few hundred years that they've focused on Mana Gathering or Body Cultivation. Instead, they focused on things like art and on food in the higher realms. They're some of the most highly paid artisans and are regularly pulled into different guilds that focus on the arts instead of fighting," the navigator explained.

"A French colony. Must be someone that came here three hundred years or so ago, so seventeen hundreds." *In the seventeen hundreds the French were fighting the settelers of the united states. Hopefully that won't be a problem. Or it could if they want to hold onto firearm technology. They must have ways to increase the lethality of their weapons, at that point they were still using swords, so shouldn't they be good with that as well?* Erik wanted to learn more, hoping that Elan would be able to develop his information gathering network faster and get him some concrete information.

"Alright, take us to somewhere with some good bars. I need a drink and something to eat."

"Can do!" The navigator grinned.

Erik got a notification he looked down, checking the information. *Looks like Rugrat added those dungeon cores.*

==========

Quest Completed: Dungeon Reborn

==========

Upgrade the dungeon core, returning it to its peak condition.

==========

Rewards:

+10,000,000 EXP

==========

==========

Title: Dungeon Master III

==========

Control over the Dungeon building interface.

Grade: Greater Earth (Can be upgraded)

Ability: Dungeon Sense, 30km radius. (Can be used 4 times a day

Increase all stats by +1

Able to bestow title Dungeon Hunter (4 remaining)

==========

==========

45,926,836/56,900,000EXP till you reach Level 58

==========

***

Mister Felix Diaz had been specially asked by Hiao Xen to assist him in surveying a piece of land. He was taking his time to map out the regions of the Fifth Realm, but the request came with an offer of money that would assist him in his studies, as well as lodging and the promise of his travel fees.

He hadn't been impressed with Vuzgal. It was large but in a state of construction.

Then he had seen the Wayside Inn and he had been surprised in their quality. The people there had been eager to help. The staff were all strong, but they and their families were working for the leadership of Vuzgal. They were getting reduced-cost housing that they were working towards buying and they were away from the fighting in the Fourth Realm. Most people were willing to drop their pride to bring that kind of safety to their families.

He had taken up the job of surveying, being joined by Journeyman alchemists from the Alchemist Association. They had smiled and treated him politely, there to observe as two people from Vuzgal watched and helped out.

He entered the valley and immediately knew that it was one of the holy growing grounds. The Mana inside was naturally balanced to increase the speed and strength of any plant that was raised within.

He surveyed the valley quickly and efficiently. He was there only to support his dream to map an entire continent in the Fifth Realm.

On the third day, he found that there was an odd stone structure with a conveniently placed door.

The guards around him all went on alert. The alchemist looked at the building in surprise.

The guards ventured in and then quickly returned, talking into their communication devices.

"What is it?" one of the alchemists asked.

"It's a dungeon. We have passed word. They will be sending people to investigate it. We're told to continue sear—uh—surveying," the guard said.

The other guard moved to Diaz. "I've been told that there is a considerable bounty for finding dungeons," the guard said in a low voice, sharing a look with Diaz.

Diaz smiled. A thrill ran through his body. He never dreamed of finding a dungeon.

On the night of the third day, he found a waterfall, but there was an entrance behind the falls. They passed behind the water and into a cave. There was a rune-covered doorway and a set of stairs leading down.

***

"You ready?" Barkwoodson looked at his brigade as they stood in front of Bala dungeon. They had paid a heavy fee to the Vuzgal guards to get a slot to enter the dungeon. There were a certain amount of people allowes into a dungeon per hour. Once one group entered then the dungeon floor would be blocked off to others until it was cleared. If one didn't clear the floor in the alloted time then they needed to leave, once they made it to the next floor the timer started all over again. The slots were to make sure that there weren't people just waiting outside the dungeon all the time. The slots were expensive to make people think about twice for buying them. They needed top clear the first floor to recover their losses, after that, everything that they were able to harvest or loot they could sell on or use.

The rewards they could earn from this would allow them to upgrade their weapons. They had been soldiers as part of a sect, but the sect had been destroyed and they had turned to being dungeon raiders. Fighting was the only thing that they knew. They had suffered defeat after defeat; now was their chance to turn it around.

They let out a cheer and he turned, raising his sword toward the dungeon.

How many times did I make the same gesture when we were moving in formation, going to attack someone else or to defend a line? Now we will make our own future!

They climbed down the stairs into the depths of the dungeon. It started to get darker. Then there was a floor that appeared before them. There were stairs leading down, but now there were several corridors leading away from where they were standing. There were plaques above the different corridors; each of them had a symbol: a cauldron for Alchemy, a formation, a hammer and anvil, clothes and a staff crossed with a bow.

"What is this?" someone asked.

"I ain't never heard of a dungeon like this before."

"What are all of these crafting symbols about?"

"Let's go and find out." Barkwoodson led the way down the path with the hammer and anvil.

The corridor was nicely illuminated and it seemed welcoming instead of threatening.

They all kept their guard up. Anything that was relaxing in a dungeon was bad.

They reached the end of the corridor and they found a smithy. With an actual anvil, fire source and tools strewn about.

Barkwoodson stepped into the smithy.

==========

You have entered the dungeon: Crafter's Trial

==========

Complete one smithed item of at least the Apprentice level to advance.

==========

You have 2 days to complete the item. [1:35:59:58]

==========

Barkwoodson stopped in his tracks. A shield appeared behind him. He backed out quickly.

==========

You have left the smithing area. You will have to wait one month to enter again.

==========

"Follow me!" He ran out to the corridor, then stood there. Nothing happened and he headed down a new corridor. The rest of the brigade looked at one another, not sure what he was doing.

==========

You have entered the dungeon: Crafter's Trial

==========

Complete one item of clothing of at least the Apprentice level to advance.

==========

You have 2 days to complete the item. [1:35:59:58]

==========

"This..." He shook in agitation and quickly pulled out his communication device. "Lila, you said that you knew someone at the Secrets Guild. I have something that I want to sell them!"

"Are you drunk again?"

"No! I'm in a dungeon!"

"I have work to do, though," she complained.

"I'll pay for your day of work. Just go to them, will you? I need to talk to them!"

***

"There were two more dungeons found in the valley next to Vuzgal. They are being investigated as we speak. Though they look like another classic dungeon and an endless dungeon. The Fighter's Association have more people there now," Cui Chin reported.

"Where is Erik?" Elder Lu inquired.

"He is in the city Sages Keep."

"Does he know of the new dungeons yet?"

"Probably not. Otherwise, he would have rushed back."

"It is Sages Keep—there is plenty to keep one entertained for a lifetime there," Elder Lu said in a dry voice.

Cui Chin smiled and nodded when he was interrupted with a message. Only a priority message could force a message into his vision.

"Someone has found a new dungeon. It is called Crafter's Trial. There are supposedly several different areas that crafters can use—Apprentice locations and one gets temporary bonuses to their skill from entering them. Someone created an Apprentice-level item and they entered a Journeyman-level workspace that is no less powerful than a tier-three Journeyman workspace." Cui Chin repeated the message as he listened to someone talking through his communication device.

"What?!" Elder Lu shot up. "Send out people to verify this information. Contact the Blue Lotus nearest to the newly discovered dungeon. Have them ready to receive people. If the dungeon is controlled by a group, prepare people to go over and start negotiations for entry," Elder Lu said to one of his aides.

Cui Chin stopped his current call, and there was immediately another.

"Elder Lu, it looks like there are more than one appearing. It looks like a mutation on the dungeons overall perhaps. Some are calling it a dungeon upgrade or a new type of dungeon."

"Mobilize all of our forces. Have them listen for more information and be ready to act as soon as they learn of new locations!" Elder Lu said to the aide, who had paused from their dash out.

They nodded and rushed off.

Elder Lu had not forgotten his promise to go and visit Vuzgal. He wanted to help out, his presence would draw others attention and assist their growth, but so far he had been unable to get away.

He idly touched one of his storage rings. Inside there were a number of rare materials and then one simple ingredient that was rare simply because people destroyed the plants as pests most of the time.

One thousand-year-old Lidel leaves.

If I could request Erik to make a more potent concoction, then I could give it to Janet. He wanted to ask Erik not as an Elder of the Blue Lotus but as a husband. He rubbed his face and let out a sigh, there was still work to do before he could leave.

Chapter: Vuzgal's Rise to Prominence

The inner and the outer city showed signs of development now. The roads were still under construction but the outer wall had been torn down and cleared away. The bunker system was the second priority after demolishing a path through the city for the new roads and rebuilding the roads inside the inner city.

With the Alchemist Association showing up, people had gained a greater interest in Vuzgal. The revelation about the two new dungeons drew in more. The Fourth Realm was in uproar about the new Crafter's Trial dungeons that had appeared in various places. Many of the crafting groups that had been interested in Vuzgal changed their aim towards the new dungeons but now most of the fighters from all over were looking at the city and its three dungeons in interest. The fees had been announced. For the main dungeon, it was one Earth-grade Mana stone to enter. For the waterfall regular dungeon, it would be one hundred Mortal-grade Mana stones. The endless dungeon would also be one Earth-grade Mana stone. People were eager to find out the rewards they could get from these dungeons. The Fighter's Association directly applied to join the city. They didn't build a large building, but they weren't ones for appearance, focusing on Strength instead.

The Wayside Inn's cheap prices, much cheaper than the residences in the city, brought people over. The people from the Alchemist Association who had heard about the Sky Reaching Restaurant from their friends in the Third Realm went to check them out. They found that their friends in the Third Realm had been understating the meals there. They were expensive, but each and every person agreed they were reasonable prices for the Fourth Realm, where it was rare to get delicacies and food. Most took concoctions or different plants to recover their Stamina.

Food was an expensive luxury in the Fourth Realm and concoctions were much cheaper and faster to use.

High quality luxurious food was hard to find anywhere that wasn't a neutral trading city.

Erik and the rest of the special team came back from Sages Keep.

The Alvan army had been rotating around, getting time off in Alva, or spending time back in the barracks and training in the academy.

Training programs were being set up for those who wanted to join the army under Rugrat's supervision. The newest round of weapon upgrades were being created: new heavy repeaters and bolt action rifles. Rugrat was focusing on ammunition, which had led him to working on semi-automatic weapons as a testbed for fully automatic weapons with easier to manufacture but still lethal rounds.

Mortars were being improved, with a few formations added and new shell types being tested.

Erik and the group looked around the city that had grown since they had been gone and wandered to the castle.

Erik stood in one of the recovered castle windows, looking out at the city while drinking some coffee when Hiao Xen came in with reports on the new crafter dungeons.

"Erik, if we were to reduce the price, give newcomers better prices and incentives... We have done it with the people already around here, what about the others? With these new crafter dungeons, it will be hard to attract people other than fighters," Hiao Xen pondered.

Erik turned from the window. "Compared to other capitals' prices, are our costs higher or lower for those wishing to come over?"

"They are less. But they are capitals—we are just a regular city, barely that in terms of population," Hiao Xen said.

"Agreed. But we have the land available; we have the location. Advertise the different creatures that are outside of the city—that is also another resource. We have three dungeons and a valley that will allow alchemists to create Expert-level ingredients. We have smithies already available; we have workshops up to the Journeyman level within the city. Now is the time that we start recruiting. Send out people to different cities as ambassadors. We are a neutral city, looking to raise crafters from all walks of life. If they want to learn join, they only need to be an Apprentice and pay, or pass our screening and become a sworn citizen of Vuzgal. We just need to see from them dedication to the job. We will offer materials and information. I want to turn Vuzgal into a city that builds people up."

Hiao Xen nodded.

"Make sure we hire quality, not quantity. We need people who are interested in growing and will be loyal to Vuzgal. It would be better to get those interested in the craft instead of monetary needs. Tell them that we will take care of their monetary issues towards perfecting their craft and they only need to worry about mastering their crafting techniques."

"It will be easier to do that."

"Even if the numbers are low, we will not reduce our standards," Erik warned.

Hiao Xen sighed. "It is sometimes better to bend rather than break," he warned.

"It is better to stand tall in the sun and grow while we can than bend in the sun and try to grow when it's not sunny." Erik smiled before putting his hand infront of his mouth. "Did that make any damn sense?"

"Kind of," Haio Xen tilted his hand back and forth. "Might want to work on the sayings."

"I'll add it to the list. Also, there will be a group coming in the future. They're part of the treasury bank. They can offer loans, investments, and the like. I have talked to them about giving people loans for houses, mainly for the people you have hired to run and maintain the city. It is also an opportunity for the traders to get a loan to increase their buying capacity. I will leave the lenders placement up to you. Twenty percent of all our revenue will be placed in to investments with them. There, it will give a shot of money to Vuzgal's economy and it will also gain interest for us over time."

"Are they really capable of handling such funds?" Hiao Xen asked. Banks weren't uncommon and the different associations had their own versions but they were only used in the higher realms due to the higher profits that they could earn. Sects and kingdoms also had their own types of banks that they would use to grow people and create investment and loan systems.

"They are," Erik confirmed. "Did the Alchemist Association drop off the stones?"

"Yes, they have paid for the first year, three Sky grade mana stones. They have begun constructing their gardens and erecting walls."

"Announce that today the dungeons will be opened. Make sure you tell the Alchemist Association first so there aren't any bad feelings. When the treasury comes, pass them the Sky stones, see what they can do with it."

"I will have a meeting with them personally before I let the rest of the city know. You know with those kinds of funds we could tempt a lot of people to join Vuzgal." Hiao Xen said.

"Keep one of them to recruit talents and support Vuzgal's finances," Erik said.

"That should be more than enough."

"Good. To a prosperous Vuzgal," Erik passed him a cup and poured some booze into it they tapped their cups and drank.

"Well I'll leave you to it, some of us have work to do," Hiao Xen ribbed.

"Go forth minion and impress my rule upon the fourth realm!" Erik said as if a drunk tyrant.

"Night," Hiao Xen said with a smile, stopping himself from bowing as he left the room.

Erik smiled. Hiao Xen had been working hard, but he had dealt with it and was in his element, handling everything with panache.

But it's just the calm before the storm.

Gilly who was lying in the corner got up and stretched letting out a noise.

"Sorry I'm not as interesting and George, you can play with him when he returns," Erik sighed.

She let out a snort refuting his words as Erik hid his smirk in his drink. Scratching her back as she pushed into his hand, her one leg hovering and kicking in mid-air.

***

Galaan stepped forward through the south gate. He and his team had combined their funds to pay the Mana stone fee, getting a token that the Alchemist Association guards checked before letting them pass. Beyond the gate was the domain of the Alchemist Association. Walls were being hurriedly built; there were more guards in the valley than they had brought into Vuzgal. They were rebuilding the defenses around the valley on the mountains and they were guarding the paths that had been made through the valley to the three dungeons.

Plants were being harvested and the ground was being designated for different ingredients to be grown there.

He hefted his heavy broadsword onto his back and waved his group forward. They were all from the Fighter's Association. They wore a mix of mid and high Journeyman gear. Hearing about the dungeon that would allow one to get up to Expert-level gear, they had been interested. They had arrived at the Fighters Association building, finding people looking for information on the dungeon. There weren't any complete maps and the association was paying for people to fill in the blanks. Other groups had made requests for different materials that reportedly could be found in the dungeons.

There were plenty of useful ingredients that could be found inside that would make it useful for even high-level groups to clear the dungeons, the items recovered worth much more than a single Earth Mana stone entry fee.

"I hope we can get a new pair of boots. These ones are getting worn out," Yellow Rabbit said.

"Probably from your stinky feet." Erin stretched and rolled her shoulders.

"Hopefully we get some high Journeyman-level gear. Be good to get new stuff. I heard that not only do our levels and numbers count, but the speed we clear the dungeon will change our rewards," Brian said, walking with his staff.

"What about you, boss? Is there anything you want?"

"Hoping we can get some of that Malcite ore to repair my sword," Galaan said.

It wasn't long until they reached the five floor dungeon. They cleared out the first floor and took the time to look around and search out every nook and cranny to make sure that they didn't leave anything behind.

"Well, we should be able to get at least a full map out of this," Brian said.

They had been able to get a pair of low Journeyman boots from the first floor, but searching the dungeon took time.

"We agreed that the first time would be to learn about the dungeon; the second to get gear," Erin reminded him.

They passed through the first three floors with ease. Then they reached the floor boss of the fourth level.

Yellow Rabbit fired an arrow into the water. It cut through and hit the hidden creature.

It rose out of the water and shot water out of its mouth. Yellow Rabbit dodged the attack as the water hit the wall behind him, leaving a perfect hole.

A domain settled over everyone, increasing the effect of Water-based magical attacks and reducing the power of all other kinds of magic.

"Use the binding scroll!" Galaan shouted.

Yellow Rabbit ran around as Erin charged forward. Her fists glowed with power; a tendril of power wrapped around her body. As her fist hit the creature, the tendril of energy was released. Scales were cut and a bloody gash was left on the creature's face as Galaan came in from the other side. His feet were glowing as he seemed to stand on the air, using a technique to get extra power and double jump before his sword turned a dazzling gold. He stabbed forward as five more golden sword images appeared around his blade. He struck out, stabbing into the beast.

The creature looked back at him with a sense of satisfaction. The air moved as the beast's tail, which had been hiding under the surface, struck out at Erin. She fell back from the attack. She didn't have a technique to move in the air like Galaan; she could only brace herself, being tossed back and hitting the wall.

Around Brian's staff, a magical circle appeared. Light shot out of the magical circles and struck the beast. It didn't cause much damage but it weakened its defense and decreased its Strength. The water domain started to weaken as Yellow Rabbit finished with the spell scroll he had been activating.

Black chains shot out of the ground, wrapping around the beast, pinning it in its pool as Galaan attacked it again and again. Quickly dropping the creatures health and leaving deep wounds. Erin charged forward; she had some wounds but her armor had protected her vitals. She kicked and punched. The confident beast now struggled against the chains restraining and binding it.

Yellow Rabbit pulled out his bow and started shooting arrow after arrow into the beast. A green glow covered them all as Brian gave them a group buff.

The beast activated its berserker skills. Its power grew and it broke through the chains. But the team was well practiced; their attacks had been laced with poisons, curses, and debuffs, decreasing its Strength.

The scaled creature charged toward Yellow Rabbit, who ran off while squeaking in minor panic. The others attacked from distance, with Galaan running in and cutting at its back.

The creature turned and hit Galaan with a Water attack, his armor left ringing by the impact of the water.

He dropped to the ground, stopping the blood from rising up in his throat. He threw a healing potion back.

Brian waved his staff, activating its attack. "Meteor's Light!"

Dozens of small formations appeared around him, turning the dark dungeon into day. They condensed and light beams shot out, tearing off scales and hitting the beast, leaving severe injuries.

It dropped to the ground as its health hit zero and a tombstone appeared.

Galaan walked over to the beast, nudging it with his foot as he undid the latches on his armor. The fresh dents made it hard to breathe and he could feel the bruises on his chest were fighting to form as the healing potion ran through his body.

Erin came over, grunting. She started to apply a cream to her arms, loosening up her joints.

"Damn, that one is strong," Yellow Rabbit said.

Erin grunted and spat out a tooth.

"That's going to itch regrowing," Galaan said.

She flipped him the bird as Brian sent them both ranged heals, making their bodies relax as they recovered.

"Tough beastie," Galaan said with approval.

Yellow Rabbit went over to the tombstone. "Good loot as well. Worth a few Mana stones at least."

The altar shone as a piece of chest armor was revealed.

It was copper colored, with runes down and around the sides.

"Well, easy replacement." Yellow Rabbit grabbed it and headed over to Galaan, passing it to him.

"Brian?" Galaan passed it to him.

Brian pulled out a monocle and put it over his eye. Runes along the rim activated as he inspected the goods.

An inspection skill or item was necessary for the Fighter's Association teams. When getting a piece of equipment, there were a lot of variables that most people wouldn't notice. Having someone who could find out the value and the abilities of the different gear or materials was invaluable. It also helped them to root out traps or cursed objects.

No trained Fighter's Association member would freely take a weapon or piece of gear in a dungeon and wear it without first checking just what its ability was. Otherwise, they could put on a piece of equipment and it might be a trap, or a mimic.

A blacksmith could also inspect smithed items in their ability level, but one usually needed to pay them to appraise the gear. It was worth it if the item was powerful, but if it wasn't that powerful, then they would just be throwing gold away.

Brian looked over the information on the armor and then passed it back. "High Journeyman, I would say. Has the ability to increase sneak and the power of sneak attacks. Decent defense and durability, better than your current gear. It also adds a wind element to attacks—should work with your sword. Though it is better when used with a bow. After we're done here, we can trade it."

"Okay." Galaan pulled off his armor and stored it and pulled the new armor on. He had replacement armor in his storage ring, but they were all weaker than the armor he had before and weaker than this new breastplate. Even if it was meant for a different class and weapon user.

They headed down to the next level.

There was a large boar waiting for them. It controlled metal. Its skin was so hard that it took two hits from Galaan in the same spot to pierce its hide.

They advanced and entered the different rooms. There was a snake that hid in the roof and released poison into the room and then sneak-attacked in the low-lighting marsh land-like room. Then a water elemental that could compete with Erin for Strength and was much stronger than Brian's spell casting ability. Then an Earth elemental that would move through the ground like a person could move above it.

Then they came to the final room. The floors above had been tough, but the fifth floor had been a real challenge for their team. They took their time to heal up and prepare after each fight.

They reached a room with a tree that looked like the one above the dungeon. There were other trees in the room, but they were much smaller.

They didn't advance into the room as others had gone before them through this dungeon and they had learned the secret of this floor.

Erin and Galaan covered Yellow Rabbit and Brian as they pulled out powerful spell scrolls that had red runes carved into them. The runes seemed as if they would set fire to the page as they started calling out the activation phrase.

Nothing happened until they finished activating the spell scrolls.

Spell formations appeared and two fire domains overlapped each other, creating a sea of fire.

The small trees started to wail, coming alive as they were being burned by the flames.

The main tree shook in anger but it was unable to move, instead smacking the ground with its branches that extended, nearing the attackers. But with the distance, they jumped away from the impact and used their long-range attacks, such as darts, spells, and arrows to fight back. They had to watch their feet as roots shot up out of the ground, trying to impale them or trip them up.

They used another spell scroll and continued attacking, wearing down the grove and its main tree.

"Good idea with the fire scrolls, Erin," Brian commented as they stepped across the ground. There were tombstones all over the place, but Yellow Rabbit was directly bagging up the tree corpses. There was a bounty out on them, after all, and they could sell them through the Fighter's Association to those who were interested. Being burnt might reduce their price, but they should still get a fair price.

They reached the final altar; it was a set of boots. They stored it away, learning its stats wouldn't be of any use to them right now as the boots were too small to fit any of their feet.

They exited the dungeon, riding the platform to the surface being greeted by they sky once again. They stepped off of the platform now in the valley.

The Alchemist Association guards watched them as they took the path from the platform exit and circled to the entrance of the dungeon, presenting their second pass. They'd paid two Earth Mana stones to enter the dungeon, one time after another. It was a larger cost and they needed more gear for it, but then they would get twice the payoff.

They limbered up before heading back in.

"All right, one more time and we're free for the day. Let's see just how fast we can get through it this time," Galaan said.

"With the complete map, we won't need to wander around aimlessly!" Yellow Rabbit chirped.

"Who was complaining about it taking too long?" Erin asked.

Yellow Rabbit grumbled but he didn't say anything else as they headed down into the dungeon again.

"This is different." Galaan cautioned, they were halfway down the as he looked around at the new floor. There were still the stairs leading down, but now the corridors had symbols above them.

"Don't tell me it is one of those Crafter's Trial dungeons as well," Brian whined.

They had all heard about the new Crafter's Trial Dungeons.

"Let's go and check out the different corridors. If we can bring this layout back and sell complete maps for everything, we should be able to get a nice finder's fee," Galaan said.

They headed down one corridor together.

"There are places for people to use tokens on the normal crafting rooms but then there are also ones over there." Yellow Rabbit pointed to sealed doorways to the side of the workshops.

"There must be close to one hundred Apprentice-level workshops here." Brian marveled as he went over to what Yellow Rabbit was looking at.

"Expert?" he said out loud, his voice breaking slightly.

"Hmm?" Galaan said, but Brian was looking up at the doors with a look of shock.

He read the two plaques above: "Passage to Journeyman-level workshops. Passage to Expert-level workshops." His voice slowed to a halt as he read the information on the second doorway.

"We need to go back to the association right now and report this!" A new dungeon was one thing, but having the possibility for Expert-level workshops—he would be negligent if he didn't report this as soon as possible.

***

"The other associations have all started to show interest in coming to Vuzgal," one of Hiao Xen's aides said as they were inspecting the new road that had been laid down in the inner city.

"All of them?" he asked.

"All of them."

"Stall them and find out just what is happening. Something must have changed their minds. See if there was anything strange happening in Vuzgal or the surrounding area as soon as possible," Hiao Xen urged.

Another aide stepped up. "There are a number of people coming through the totem and seeking residence or to purchase property in Vuzgal."

"What kind of people?"

"They're mostly crafters connected to the various associations."

"I just got a message that the Crafter's Association is planning to upgrade their building and that there are Journeyman-level crafters coming through to start on the project. Others are applying to head to the main dungeon," the first aide said suddenly, sounding shaken.

"Since the arrival of the Crafter's Trial dungeons, the associations have been focusing on building up their locations nearest these trials. But now they're sending over their highest level workers to build here. All of the associations are coming over and they're wanting to access the main Bala Dungeon. Send someone to the main dungeon and have them report on if anything has changed!" he snapped off as he turned toward the castle and the mounted convoy waiting for them.

"Let's head back," he said to the guards as he got into the carriage. The people from the Alvan army led the convoy back toward the castle as more information came in.

"One of the teams went into the dungeon," the second aide said and looked up at Hiao Xen. "They're saying that there is now a Crafter's Trial dungeon attached, but there is passageways to a Expert-level workshops inside it and it is much larger than the other reported trials."

Is this part of the event that Erik said that they triggered? Were they the reason that the crafting dungeons appeared? Is that why he was confident?

Hiao Xen contacted Erik and reported everything to him.

"Increase prices to normal capital standards. I will have a new agreement for the associations to complete. We asked them before and they looked down on us; we need to instill that we are the rulers of this city. They will all be presented with the same contract. If they do not sign it within three days I will have a second contract ready for them," Erik said.

"Did you know this would happen?" Hiao Xen asked.

"Well, after talking to you, seemed that it would happen eventually. It seems that you're breaking up sorry, losing connection. *Schrrak* You're going to have a lot of work to do! *schrrak* Good luck!" Erik cut the call.

Hiao Xen looked at his sound transmission device and then looked out at the city passing by outside his carriage. Things were sure to change quickly now.

"Why was he making all that noise?" Hiaso Xen sighed. "Looks like it's going to be an eventful few days.

***

Erik put down the call as he looked at the men and women arranged on the parade square. The barracks and training facilities were large enough to house and train an army of ten to twenty thousand.

Erik's plans weren't that big, yet. Instead, there were just one hundred new and nervous recruits standing in the training square beyond the castle window. They were looking around nervously as sergeants, corporals, and lance corporals marched up and down the ranks. It reminded Erik of months ago when he had stood in front of the original Alva military and turned them into a fighting army.

Now it was time to do it all again. They would train them on tactics in Vuzgal, then increase their levels with the dungeon, their body and mana cultivation with classes with assistance from the medics and teachers. It wouldn't be cheap and they needed people that would remain loyal even as they grew stronger.

It wouldn't be a fast process but Erik knew that these things weren't to be rushed. Ranks didn't matter as long as they had strength. After all, hadn't he been able to stop an army of thousands from advancing smoothly with just fifty or so members of the Alvan army? With the new rifles, repeaters and Rugrat already talking about upgrading mortars, it was time that they used their momentum to secure their position in the Ten Realms.

"We've got Vermire, four dungeons and a city. The outpost needs to expand, we need to clear the floors of Alva Dungeon and make it completely ours and we've only just started with Vuzgal. We need to recruit more people into Alva. We've been racing ahead in levels, power leveling people, but then our basic skills and techniques haven't developed as quickly." Erik let out a laugh and rubbed the back of his head. He could talk freely with the security formations that had been added to the office.

"What are your orders?" Glosil asked.

Erik turned to Glosil.

"It's time that Rugrat and I took a step backwards, you are the leader of the Alva Military. So, my question to you would be, what do you think that we should do?"

Glosil didn't answer right away but took a few moments.

"Oragnize, build strengthen," Glosil finally said. "We need to organize our forces better. Units to defend, units to attack, units of engineers to create paths, medics to heal, Scouts to search ahead, weapon courses to master weapon systems. Artillery and ranged units to support from the rear. Supply and repair units, to create and repair weapons and armor, to craft the supplies needed by the other units. Ammunition, bandages, food and so on. Build, if we want to hold Vuzgal then we need the numbers to do so. Which brings up questions of, do we let them all know about Alva or only select groups, which goes to organization again, units that know and those that don't. Then Strengthen, we send the specialized units to learn in the academies. We make the regular soldiers masters of their weapon systems and have an understanding of other roles. We have a small military we need quality to over come quantity. It will take more resources and time.

"Though regular soldiers instead of just waiting on the engineers can start to prepare an area ahead of them. If there are wounded they can render aid that can save lives and keep people stable until they get to the real medics. We teach people how to fight as a section, a platoon a company and higher levels. If we want to recreate the military strength of Vuzgal, we will need ten thousand to twenty thousand soldiers," Glosil warned.

"What is your plan?" Erik asked.

"Instead of racing to the fifth, we'll focus on strengthening our foundations. We will take time to learn of the higher realms and plot out a path. Elan needs time to establish his command and then develop it. While that is happening, we begin recruiting, we re-organize the military so as we grow we have a plan. We increase the strength of our people through training and levels. We now have the strength to take the lower floors of Alva Dungeon. With those floors open we can send people down there to increase their body cultivation. The military is one of the biggest expenses of Alva, if we can reduce those training costs and give back to Alva," Glosil left the rest unsaid.

Erik studied Glosil. His plan sounded simple, but the changes it would have on the military would be as big as the training they had gone through before they entered the fourth realm. It would also deal with the threat of the lower floors that had been a worry in the back of Erik's mind.

"Firm up our foundations and grow while we can," Erik crossed his arms, looking at the floor and letting out a breath through his nose.

"Instead of focusing on charging forward, lets increase our strength now." Erik said, coming to a decision, he had felt ready to make another breakthrough with his mana gates, as well as his body cultivation. His Alchemy and healing skills had fallen to the wayside as he focused on his combat strength. He still needed to adjust to his new power.

If we don't fully digest Vuzgal and use our gains to increase our strength then we will only regret it later, we can't let the victory here blind us.

***

Cui Chin, like the other information leaders of the different associations, had gotten word on the Crafter's Trial dungeon that was located in Vuzgal. They'd immediately sent over more people to increase the grade of the Blue Lotus building there.

They'd dispatched a higher ranked manager as well.

"Vuzgal has given us a number of surprises. It is good that we got the original contract." Elder Lu looked at the new contracts that were being given out to the new associations that had yet to join Vuzgal and the contracts that were being handed out to people who wanted to join the city as residents or workers. "This new contract is expensive but they will pay it."

Cui Chin nodded. Vuzgal had turned into something of a gem in the Fourth Realm. "Do you think that they are dungeon masters?" Cui Chin asked suddenly.

Elder Lu put down the contracts. "I would say that I doubt it, but there was those people of Erik's disappearing and we don't know where Rugrat is off to and where his different 'special teams' went. Though, to have multiple dungeon masters, that would be difficult to do. They've probably seen a few dungeons, but if they were dungeon masters, wouldn't they try to keep them to themselves? Instead of telling others and allowing them entrance?"

Cui Chin and Elder Lu fell silent, thinking on it.

"Dungeon masters are only common in the Seventh Realm. It is hard for one to become a dungeon master and is passed down to their subordinates who become their vassals. They have the power to alter dungeons but keep the information to themselves. Even we have only found out a few clues about the clans with dungeon masters. Most of them remain underground, allowing people to fight and train in their dungeons for a fee. One has to have the luck of the heavens to become a dungeon master unlike city lords that can be created as long as one establishes a city and is recognized by the ten realms. Even if Erik and Rugrat have dungeon masters, they haven't done anything against us. How have the different design teams found the new crafting dungeons?" Elder Lu asked.

"We are still getting a complete copy of the dungeons' blueprints, but we should be able to have a copy soon enough to start converting a few of our dungeons to have crafter trials as well."

"Good, but we don't want to spread them too widely. Otherwise it could create instability," Elder Lu said in warning.

"I have been watching over this personally and using only those I trust. There shouldn't be a leak in information," Cui Chin said.

"Good, well I should go and inspect the progress of the Blue Lotus location there," Elder Lu said.

Cui Chin was a little stunned.

"What, can't I go and inspect a Blue Lotus location?" Elder Lu asked with a raised eyebrow.

"I didn't mean any disrespect, Elder Lu," Cui Chin said bowing quickly.

Elder Lu laughed, waving to Cui Chin.

"Don't worry I know what you're thinking. They helped us in a time of need, now there is a high level crafter dungeon attached to their city. People are going to look at Vuzgal and want to take it from Erik and Rugrat. If I go there, it shows that we are close. It will make others think twice about attacking and dissuade many."

"Do we want to do that?" Cui Chin asked in a strained voice. Elder Lu frowned slightly.

"I know that it is your job to be skeptical of others. They saved Tareng and were made honorable Elders, that is no simple honor. I think that we should place some more trust in them and try to help out."

"I will see to the arrangements. Should I let others who have designs on Vuzgal know our attitude?" Cui Chin asked.

"That would be for the best," Elder Lu's voice held a note of approval. Cui Chin usually worked in the shadows, he knew of just what Erik, Rugrat and their people had been through. Internally, Cui Chin felt that helping them out only felt right.

Chapter: Invitation

Erik watched the twenty or so recruits working in the barracks. The Alvan army were going all out on their training. They hadn't even touched firearms yet, just working on the basics.

The gates to the barracks opened as a convoy entered. Erik looked over. People stood at the doors, looking in. They were from various families and groups; all of them were looking to talk to Erik and create closer connections. A number had tried to bribe the different members of the Alvan army, or the people who worked for Erik, for personal access. Those who took the bribes were immediately fired. None of the Alvan army had even looked at the money.

Erik had put out rules that people of Vuzgal's administration would not take in bribes and listed it with the other rules in the city.

He also had every person who did trade with the city make an oath that basically made them not be violent, or try to steal within the city walls.

People wanted to fight back against his rules, but Erik held the cards and he had the support of the different associations now. All of the associations had crafters of some kind in their ranks and the Expert-level crafter dungeon trial was a massive draw. The other dungeons were also powerful and enticed a number of people over from the other established cities.

Vuzgal's crime rate was incredibly low so far. The inner and outer city was filled with the sounds and sights of construction. In the Ten Realms, buildings were built much faster, taking what would be months or years on Earth, just a few weeks or days to complete.

The associations' buildings had been completed, creating the association circle around the central castle.

Crafters worked on repairing the castle, under Matt's guidance. The undead, which had scared people at first, were now seen as an attraction as they were a low cost and untiring labor force, moving materials around as needed.

The outer defenses were completed and manned by the mixed units from the associations and the Alvan army.

Trading market stalls had cropped up as they were easier to build. The Wayside Inns and Sky Reaching Restaurants were packed with people. In a night, thousands of Earth-grade Mana stones were changing hands throughout Vuzgal.

The convoy cleared the barracks gates and the gates closed behind them as the convoy moved through the training areas of the various units. People who thought it was just another guard position either got their act together and pushed on, or they left through the gates. The units grew smaller and smaller, allowing new training programs to be started.

It was better to train someone who hadn't been a fighter before than a fighter. The fighters already thought they knew what to do, while those who didn't have any training picked it up easily and took everything said to them as gospel.

Erik and Glosil had started to work on the new outline of the units.

At the base there would be Fireteams made up of Four privates and one Corporal, three fireteams would be combined under a sergeant's command to create a rifle squad. Three rifle squads, a scout squad and a Mixed support squad with a fireteam of Battle Mages, a fireteam of medics and a fireteam of Engineers each led by their own corporals who reported directly to the Staff Sergeant who was the second in command. A senior sergeant assisted the Staff Sergeant who got their orders from the Second Lieutenant, altogether, these eighty-two people formed a Rifle Platoon. So far they only had enough people to form one

Rifle Platoon. They still had to work on the organization for the support and artillery platoons, followed with a combat company's makeup.

The convoy stopped and Hiao Xen got out, talking to his aides. He was busy with all the people going to him because they couldn't get to Erik.

"Is there still people trying to get you to give them slots to enter the crafter trials?" Erik asked.

"Yes, but I kept on telling them what you told me," Hiao Xen said. "They have been trying to bully others into not going at all in protest but I put an end to that as well by preparing to evict them if they went against our policies."

"Good. They're testing us now, want to see if we'll bend to their whims. We just keep on acting on the level, don't change our policies and enforce them all equally—we'll be fine." Erik nodded. "So what are you here for then?"

"Well, I thought that you would like to know that I was able to get that invitation that you've been looking for." Hiao Xen pulled out a letter and gave it to Erik.

Erik quickly read it. "Well, looks like it's as you said. The Stone Fist Sect has sent me an invitation. Looks like they want to get closer to us. Strength really comes in different ways—they've even offered to clear out the dungeon for me. I think they've seen through the reason I want to go there—they're even offering help with healers." Erik laughed lightly. "They are a sect that deals with hand-to-hand combat and tempering the body, so it makes sense that they would put the dots together."

"They have asked for a reply," Hiao Xen mentioned.

"I'll head out there in three days with one of the special teams. I should find out soon enough if it works or not for me. How are things on your side?"

"There is roughly one Sky Mana stone changing hands every-day or every other day in Vuzgal. That rate will continue to increase as time passes. The people from the eastern Chaotic Lands have arrived and there are people fleeing the war from the west who are coming into the city as well. We have been able to fill about eighty percent of the cities service jobs. I am having an internal review conducted to make sure that they are following Vuzgal's rules completely.

"The crafting stations in Vuzgal have remained under our control but we are leasing them out to different people, allowing companies and the regular people to get access to them. I have brought some crafters to our side with lucrative incentives. They will watch over the crafting workshops and look at hiring more potential crafters to our ranks. There are people clearing out the surrounding forest of beasts with the spare time between accessing the dungeons.

"Raw materials are coming in from all over the Fourth Realm and other realms. I've had several people seeking out information on you, about your relationship status. Some might be eyeing you to see about pairing you off with someone in their family," Hiao Xen said with a hint of a smile.

Erik laughed. He would be lying if he said he wasn't interested, but he didn't want to be forced into a relationship. He didn't need another ex-wife, and one who could wield a sword or fireballs sounded suitably terrifying.

"The associations have sent over gifts, as well as the other people of power. I have told them that we are not interested in bribes and they will not be reciprocated. They all answered that they were fine with that and to keep the gifts. I think that some of them really think that we will be interested by the items."

"Well, crafting materials store away, Mana stones put into the bank, techniques and information books, I'll review them.

Expert level items, I'll keep. Everything else, get over to the Blue Lotus to be auctioned off," Erik said.

"And in the future, do you want me to repeat these instructions?"

"Please, unless you think that there is an item that I will be particularly interested in."

"Okay."

"Through my contacts I have heard that there are a few groups that are now looking at Vuzgal with eyes of hunger."

"They're welcome to try and take it from us," Erik growled. They had paid in blood for Vuzgal he would no longer let it go without a fight.

Hiao Xen had an awkward expression on his face when he got a sound transmission.

His eyes widened in alarm.

"What is it?" Erik asked, touching his storage ring, ready to fight.

"Elder Lu has come to inspect the Blue Lotus location here. He has requested a meeting with you and Rugrat," Hiao Xen reported, sounding stunned by the message.

"Okay?"

"Sorry, it is just Elder Lu doesn't really go anywhere. He invites people to the Blue Lotus Headquarters. To put it in perspective, he has level Seventy and Eighty guards around him so that no one gets ideas. They're enough to level any city. He has more power than the leaders of the sects in the Fourth Realm."

"So, kind of like having the president leaving the country and going to another and then asking the country politely if they'll talk with him?"

"What is a president? Is that like a sect or clan head?"

"Uhh, not really but I guess it is the closest thing that people have to in the Ten Realms, or maybe association head would be closer."

"Okay, but yes, it would be like that."

"Alright, sure," Erik nodded to himself, he had a decent impression of Elder Lu. Meeting him wouldn't be bad.

"Also, it might solve some of the issues that have appeared. It shows that the Blue Lotus is interested in Vuzgal and with the Head having a close relationship with Vuzgal's city leaders, some of the other powers will think twice before acting on their greed," Hiao Xen said, looking at Erik.

"Do you think that he did this knowing that?"

"If I know it, he definitely does. I wouldn't be qualified to attend him with my current position in the association."

"Huh, okay," Erik pondered the possibilities as he walked towards the meeting.

***

Elder Lu entered Erik's office. He could tell that it wasn't used frequently.

Erik looked up from his papers, quickly standing up. He looked at the guards of Elder Lu. Even seeing them and feeling their deadly pressure he was relaxed.

The guards moved into the room as Elder Lu coughed.

The guards looked at Elder Lu, an awkward expression on their faces.

"I'm sorry, they're a little alarmist," Elder Lu apologized.

"No worries, I've been in their shoes before. Feel free to check the room. There is a balcony that way, bathroom over there, only entrance and exit to this office is the one you came through. I'd post a few people on the balcony," Erik said, feeling for the guards.

The guards looked from Erik to Elder Lu.

Elder Lu studied Erik one more time and cupped his hands. "Thank you, sorry again."

"Better safe than sorry," Erik confirmed, moving to greet him properly. "Thank you for coming all this way."

"It's hardly far with a totem," Elder Lu said with a small smile.

Erik smiled and the two of them moved to the couches in the room.

"Still, your actions have sent a warning to the people that were starting to look at Vuzgal like it was prey. For that I am grateful."

Elder Lu studied Erik.

He is straight forward, dealing with both those that threaten him and those that support him. Based on his words and what he did when faced with the Blood Demon Sect, he'll die to uphold his beliefs if he has to.

Elder Lu was moved by this novel approach. It was different from what most others would do in the Ten Realms.

"It is just a visit," Elder Lu downplayed.

"Mhmm," Erik said, clearly he saw further to Elder Lu's real reasons. "Well, I am sorry that there is not more to see here. Tea?"

"Please, and I have no worries that Vuzgal will become a gem in the future."

Erik pulled out three cups and served Elder Lu, his nearest guard and then himself. "I hope that we can all benefit from it."

He's an alchemist and serving me tea, so of course my guards are going to be nervous. Diffusing their suspicions upfront. Others would take it as a slight to their honor.

Erik looked to the guard and the cup.

"So is there anything that I can help you with?" Erik asked, not making anything out of the guard taking the cup and drinking from it.

After the first sip he finished it all and cupped his hands to Erik, he might be a lower level but he'd gained the respect and thanks of the guards.

Erik smiled and nodded to them. He then refilled the guards cup and switched it with cup in front of Elder Lu. In response to the raised eyebrows he shrugged and said, "In case the poison was in the cup and not the tea."

The guards were initially alarmed and then embarrassed at their oversight, yet still internally grateful to Erik.

He seems more at ease with people that fight and kill.

Elder Lu took the tea and raised it to Erik.

They both took their cups and sipped, Elder Lu was surprised as he felt his mind calm and he was able to put down some of the worries that had been plaguing his mind.

"Good tea," He said as he sipped from it again, it combined medicinal ingredients with regular ingredients, adding a greater depth of flavor and benefits.

"I would like to take credit for it, but thankfully I got it from the cooks of the Sky Reaching Restaurant," Erik said.

"Ahh, the restaurant that you started in the Third Realm," Elder Lu said.

Erik nodded with a smile.

"You did your research."

Elder Lu's eyes crinkled as he shrugged slightly. It had been part of the information on Erik.

"But yes, they made it," Erik freely admitted. "We're looking to bring more of our people up here and develop some more restaurants. Too many people focus on Stamina concoctions, while a good cook can make a meal that will recover the same Stamina and taste good."

"I look forward to it," Elder Lu responded, intrigued by the idea. He raised his cup to Erik again and took another sip.

"I do have something I want to ask you, not as the head of the Blue Lotus in the Fourth Realm, but as a man." Elder Lu knew very well that Erik could take advantage of him. It was, in a way, a test for Erik to see if he would try and blackmail him.

"I was wondering if you would be able to make a rejuvenation concoction?"

"You have the formulas for those already."

"Yes, but I was wondering if you could make a stronger concoction. I, of course, have the materials for it and would be willing to pay according to the Alchemy Association's rules."

Erik looked into the distance, he seemed to be calculating something. Elder Lu watched his expression, looking peaceful on the surface yet he wanted to drag an answer out of Erik forcefully underneath.

"What ingredients do you have?" Erik asked.

Elder Lu passed him a list.

Erik looked at it and then closed his eyes. He opened them with a difficult expression.

"My Alchemy ability is not yet high enough for me to make a stronger concoction. I don't like to take advantage of people who are in pain if I can help. I will need more Lidel leaves to refine my Mana control, in order to create a more potent end product. It will take me time to do so."

"Okay, that is understandable," Elder Lu said, feeling relieved.

"Sorry that I can't help you right away. I will need to talk with my teacher. I have let my crafting abilities slip."

"It is not a problem. I will give you these items and see if I can procure more One Thousand Year Lidel leaves," Elder Lu said, taking out a storage device from his robe and passing it to Erik.

"Thank you," Erik said.

They talked on simple matters after that, about Vuzgal, about the situation in the Fourth Realm.

Erik saw Elder Lu out, heading to the totem. The two of them cupped their hands to one another, showing to all that Elder Lu saw Erik on the same level as himself.

Elder Lu was impressed with the man's foresight.

Still, it is early days. We'll have to wait and see what he does.

Chapter: Larger Horizons

Julilah and Qin were sitting in the library. The two of them, like they had done countless times before, reading each other's books and sharing notes. The two of them were on very different trains of thought, but they would ask each other questions randomly to grow their own knowledge.

"Line positioning theory?" Qin asked.

"Straight, curved, or angled?" Julilah didn't look up from her book.

"Straight."

Julilah picked up a book, checked the cover and put it in front of Qin. "Midway to the back, The chapter talks about line art. They talk about how they pushed the formations to their limits, finding out the limits of the line positioning by accident." Julilah said, giving key points as she continued to read her own book.

Qin opened the book and flipped through.

Hmm She said, finding the section as the half sentences from Julilah started to make sense. She was just getting into it, filling in more information in her Formation Skill Book when a voice interrupted her thoughts.

"Look at these two rats, spending their time in here reading and studying. Not even sleeping or taking the time to eat outside."

Qin looked up to find Ilyana and her group moving toward hers and Julilah's hidden table in the back of the library.

"What do you want?" Qin asked with narrowed eyes.

"I need to make sure that you rats aren't dirtying the books of my Formation Guild," Ilyana said in a righteous voice. A sneer covered her lackeys' faces as they looked down at the duo and the books around them.

"Childish." Qin shook her head and continued to flip through the book as if they weren't even there.

"Too scared, trying to hide in these books? As if you rats could learn anything about formations in the few months you have here!" Ilyana hissed, incensed by their disregard toward her.

"The dumbest dogs bark the loudest," Julilah said simply as she flipped the pages in her book.

Qin found the section on the line positioning.

"Oops!" One of Ilyana's friends 'fell' forward and dropped a drink on the books and on Qin.

"Librarian! There is someone defacing books!" Ilyana yelled out, a gloating look in her eyes as the girl dropped the cup into Qin's lap.

It wasn't a few moments later that a librarian appeared.

Qin didn't have time to do anything before they appeared. *Ilyana and her friends must have seen when Mister Herric was walking around in this area and timed doing this so that I wouldn't be able to cover it up.*

He saw the book covered in the drink and the drink on Qin and the floor.

"You!" He rushed over and grabbed the book from her hands, horrified. The books were the lifeblood of the Formation Guild. Other crafters might have different materials as they were more physically inclined, but the Formation Guild was all based on theory. To them, books were the backbone of their craft and their guild.

He waved his hand and stored all of the books on the table. "You are banned from this library!" he yelled, his beard trembling in anger.

Julilah looked at her hands where the book in them had been ripped away.

She got up calmly as Qin used the Clean spell, her face turning red in anger.

"I challenge all of you to a formation duel. The loser will be kicked out of the Formation Guild, never to return or use their items!" Qin declared.

"You defaced a book and now you're challenging me to a duel? You have guts!" Ilyana snarled.

Herric let out a indignant sound. He might be neutral, but at the end of it, they were outsiders and Ilyana was a member of a clan that had been formation masters for generations.

Qin said nothing back.

"I'll take your duel! The person who loses will also have to be the other's slave." Ilyana cackled in glee at the thought.

"Despicable," Julilah commented as she stood.

"Fine, one hour from now we will have our duel. I don't have time to waste on you." Qin turned and started walking away. Julilah followed her out.

"If you run, my Mao clan will hunt you down!" Ilyana shouted to their backs.

"Your clan?" Qin looked back at Ilyana with a smile on her face. She had been hearing about Vuzgal even without trying to. She also knew that Erik was ruling the city while Rugrat was in Alva.

From the standing of Vuzgal, she knew that the power of Alva was much greater than she ever thought. They now had direct alliances with most of the associations and lifetime binding contracts.

"Maybe it is time that we changed schools," Julilah said to Qin.

"This one is getting noisy," Qin agreed, forgetting Ilyana and the others as she kept walking.

"I've nearly spent most of my funds on materials," Qin said awkwardly as they turned the corner, not seeing the victorious smile on Ilyana's face.

Herric left, going to report the duel and to repair the book.

"Me too," Julilah said with a dry laugh. "Rugrat did say to contact Vuzgal if we needed to. Isn't your brother there?"

"Yeah, but he'll make fun of me," Qin pouted.

**

Elder Mao Yahui was working in his private workshop when there was a knock on the door. He frowned but finished off his last rune. He deactivated the isolation formation and used another formation to open the door.

"I am sorry to disturb dear Elder, but your granddaughter Mao Ilyana has challenged an outsider to a formation duel," the servant said quickly, bowing to Elder Mao.

He was a teacher in the Fourth Realm, his Strength enough to allow him to the Sixth Realm. But in the Fourth, he could recruit new talents into the clan's faction. Although it might look harmonious on the outside, all of the associations had several factions internally, whether they be political, regional groups or families that were interwoven into the fabric of the associations. He could also offer help to the younger generation of the Mao clan that had come from root families or were sent down to experience the lower realms and temper their minds while teaching here.

"What for?" Elder Mao knew his granddaughter was an arrogant woman, coming from the Fifth Realm. The family hoped to change her thoughts and make her stronger through the schools learning experience. She had created her own group within the students and influenced those in the same skill level as her. It showed good management skills, but she had a petty streak in her still that was quite unseemly.

"There are two outsiders who are taking the basic formation classes with her. She is using them as an example to increase her influence," the servant said. They had seen enough of these games to know what was on the surface and of course the idiotic thoughts behind it.

"Using the outsiders, she instills the thought she is trying to preserve the strength and purity of the Formation Guild and make her a hero in the eyes of her generation. It is a good move. Do we know this person's background?" Elder Mao asked.

"No," the servant said quickly.

Elder Mao looked over at them. The weight of his gaze made the servant bow.

"Not even the head of the school knows where they came from. They were simply given tokens and admitted."

Elder Mao stood. The Journeyman level badge on his chest showed two lines through it as the formation glowed through. "What is the bet for?" he asked, feeling uneasy.

"To be dismissed from the Formation Guild and become the other's servant," the servant said.

"Let us go and take a look," Elder Mao sighed.

***

"Seems like it must be a boring day," Julilah said as Qin was jotting down notes. The two of them sat in the dueling arena. It was an oval building with raised seats around it. The stage was an ovaloid, split in the middle.

"Hmm." Qin responded as she read over the rules of the arena.

"Have you found anything useful?" Julilah stopped looking at the people who were coming in from across the school.

Formation duels weren't common and in a place where book study was the primary way to increase one's knowledge, seeing two people clash with formations was an interesting change of pace.

"Well, there are a few kinds of duels. There are formation quality duels. We have a third party officiate and we make formations in a certain period of time—the highest quality or grade formation wins. There is formation disassembly: the two people look at each other's formations, saying what they are, what their function is, their strengths and weaknesses. The person who gets the most things correct about their opponents formation wins. The third is fighting formations. The two formation masters use formations to attack each other. They can only use formations that they have made while in the arena. The last one is only used if the problem can't be resolved in any other way."

"Do you know which one Ilyana will choose?" Julilah asked.

"Nope!" Qin said, a smile on her face.

"You know, you're bullying her."

"Didn't you run around making mischief and trying to peek into Tan Xue's smithy all the time? Now you're all adverse to danger?"

"One gets more mature with time," Julilah said with a sniff and upturned nose.

Qin snorted and shook her head.

People piled into the stadium, even from the higher classes. There was a great number of Novices from the classes that Qin and Julilah were in. Though there were also low and mid-Apprentice students who showed off their emblems proudly, looking down on the duel area as if adults watching children squabbling.

"I heard that Ilyana is actually closer to forty years, but with her higher levels she looks like our age," Julilah said.

"She must be either a bad or a lazy study—we haven't made it to twenty yet." Qin frowned.

"Remember our standards in Alva are skewed to other places. She might have a number of tricks up her sleeve, so be careful."

"Should be exciting, shouldn't it?" Qin grinned.

"I was wondering why you didn't get the teachers to deal with her. You *wanted* to have a formation duel."

"They sound like fun," Qin defended.

Julilah smiled a bit. "Yeah, they do. But now I won't be able to have one because of you. Do you think that I could get one of the higher ranked formation masters to fight me?" Julilah's calm voice turned excited as she grabbed Qin's hands.

"What about being calm, collected and adult-like?"

"Sod that! I want to have some fun as well. I've only been messing around with books all this time. I'm sooo bored and then I was trying to be all cold like I've heard of ice princesses in those books, the kind that people don't get close to. They sound so cool! A beauty like me must protect her character!"

"I knew you were hiding one of your own trashy books inside the formation books so that the librarians wouldn't catch you!"

Julilah shrugged, but didn't admit nor deny it.

Ilyana appeared at the other end of the dueling stadium. A few people started to clap. She nodded to them, a determined look on her face, but there was a gloating look in her eyes as she saw Julilah looking as though she were comforting Qin by holding her hands.

***

Ilyana stepped up to the stage.

"What will you do once she becomes your slave?" one asked.

"Well, I have been in need of a new seat and there is the fact that I have always needed someone to run various errands across the cities and the realms. Thankfully, she should have some funds to carry out these jobs. Then I should sell her onto the slave traders. I heard the dark market has a number of people interested in young-looking women who have fallen from grace."

"For someone who dared to treat our Formation Guild like her own, she should be treated like the bottom feeder she is!" one said, a vicious look in her eyes as she looked over at Qin and Julilah.

They had been in the Fourth Realm for a long time. There were no means that were seen as too far, only too little. One needed to remove the obstacles in their way through any means necessary.

A judge appeared some time later, waving Qin and Ilyana forward. "Miss Qin has initiated the challenge, so Miss Mao, you will have to pick the type of duel," he said.

"Fighting formations," she said in a grave voice.

The judge was stunned for a moment before asking in a deep voice, "Are you sure?"

"Yes."

"Miss Qin, are you okay with this duel?"

"Yes."

"Okay." He activated protective formations around the arena so that the attacks wouldn't spill out onto the people in the arena. "You will only be allowed to use formations that you create here to attack each other. Any use of a previously fully prepared formation will mean immediate disqualification and forfeit. The first person to be thrown off the dueling platform, admit defeat, or go unconscious will lose. If the fight ends in a tie, then I will judge the winner based on the formations used. Do you understand these rules?"

"Yes."

"Yes." Qin's fists opened and closed.

Ilyana had a look of disdain on her face, but her face froze as she saw the excited smile on Qin's face.

She's probably trying to throw me off. Look at how nervous she is, moving her hands. This contest seems simple from the start—just two people who need to create formations and fighting each other with them. But it is a contest about preparing. If one has formation plates with formations already traced out, then they only need to carve into the pre-traced lines. If they have the reactants ready, someone can save precious minutes, allowing them to attack first. The person who strikes first will be the winner in this match, that will be me!

She stretched her hands. She had a number of formations traced and ready. With the resources of the Mao clan and her training, she was always prepared for confrontations.

She had spent the last hour amassing traced formations and preparing reactants to give her that extra edge. She didn't want to win; she wanted to dominate Qin. It would showcase her power, raising her standing, and it would firm her position in the academy.

Killing the chickens to warn the monkeys.

"Ready! Begin!" the judge yelled.

Ilyana grabbed a formation plate from her storage ring and she pulled out a carving tool. Her hands started to blur as she carved out the formation, following the traced lines.

A Mana blade appeared on Qin's boot. She used her hand as a pivot, carving out a circle in the ground. She used her blade to cut out a rudimentary formation in the ground.

Ilyana was working on her formation and walking around so it would be harder to target her. She saw the formation on the ground. It was as basic as possible: a simple Mana barrier, a tier-one formation, in the Novice level. Ilyana's confidence soared as she focused on her formation.

Qin threw out jewels that slotted into the formation, activating it and creating a Mana barrier.

"A tier-one Mana barrier—it won't be able to hold out for long with repeated attacks," a member of the crowd said. "Using the ground and the jewels she has to create the formation, it was quickly done, but it is rough and simple. Ilyana comes from the Mao clan—they have formations that easily surpass other formations of the same grade."

"What is she doing now?" another asked as a formation plate was pulled out and then carved into; she slotted gems into it and tossed it down. The formation grew stronger.

"A tier-two Mana barrier?" someone asked.

"Tier two? But she made that second sub-formation afterward?"

"It is formation layering." An Apprentice-level formation master sat forward, his disinterest from before turning into intrigue.

"Formation layering?"

"Using a basic, easily made formation and then adding in secondary formations that increase its strength," he said.

"Isn't that cheating?" someone asked.

"Cheating?" The Apprentice could only shake his head with a wry smile. "Creating a formation as one whole is much easier. You can review everything about the formation before activating it. With the layering, you need to know the first formation perfectly. Then you must place down the following formations so that they perfectly resonate with the first, or else instead of reinforcing the formation, the formation will fail."

Qin tossed down another formation. The Mana barrier that had been hazy turned crystal-clear, standing proud as the jewels now shone.

Ilyana injected power into her formation with a flourish and tossed the formation out. It hit the ground and the wind whistled as the formation's runes turned green and then blue and white. A tornado of green appeared above the formation plate, sending out air blades that struck Qin's Mana barrier.

"A tier-two attack formation," Qin said with a note of approval, while she worked on her own formation.

Seeing Qin's formation wasn't failing, Ilyana frowned and started to carve another pre-traced formation.

Qin tossed down another formation and the Mana barrier stabilized as Ilyana was halfway through the second formation.

Ilyana finished her formation. The formation activated and spun as flames appeared from the runes, wrapping around the formation plate, until a firecloud tiger appeared.

The tiger roared at the heavens and charged forward. Ilyana nodded in approval and started to carve another formation.

Qin smiled as the tiger hit her Mana barrier. As a beast of magical power, it couldn't cross her Mana barrier at all. She finished the formation in her hand, but it didn't look complete.

"Is that a third-tier formation?" an Apprentice asked her fellow peer.

"I'm not sure. I can't understand it. It looks broken to me," he replied with a frown.

"Maybe she was too rushed, being under attack," the first said.

Qin grabbed the formation and pulled out a shard from a Mortal Mana stone. Its power filled the formation. She raised it in her hand and pointed it at Ilyana.

The wind tornado's power weakened a bit as it continued to thrash against Qin's barrier. The firecloud tiger fought harder, its power quickly being consumed, making it turn dimmer.

"This is the end," Qin said.

Since the Metal floor, she had realized just how weak she was and reliant she had become on her special mana channels. So she'd looked at using formations to increase her Strength, though this was the first time she had tried it out.

The formation she held in her hand wasn't complete. It would have been a tier-four formation if it was completed. As she cast a spell, the wind turned chaotic her hair flying behind her as she looked like a war goddess riding a war chariot as the air in front of her hand shook as a spell formation appeared in sections, snapping together. Her spells were even shaped like formations now. Her spell was like a key for the formation as it trembled, the stage shaking.

A larger spell formation appeared in front of Qin's spell, the two spells rotated until they lined up perfectly. Qin cast her spell Mana was turned into crystals shooting out of the large formation, the space between the two mirrored formations was empty.

The gem like shards of mana struck the tiger and the tornado.

Explosions rocked the stage as Qin stood there, her face expressionless as the tornadoes and formations were blown away while Ilyana let out a yell and raised her hands to defend herself. The talismans and formations in her clothes and jewelry activated.

The blasts hit her, weakened by destroying her formations.

Ilyana was still tossed back from the stage and tumbled across the arena grounds. Dirt stained her clothes and her hair turned ragged. The blast caused the tiles of the arena to shake and the Mana barrier around the arena took the remainder of the impact.

Qin lowered her hand as the blast dissipated. She nodded, as if everything was to her satisfaction. People looked at the silent arena as Qin started to clean up her formations, putting them away.

With my mana channels I can compact the mana to a higher degree and purity, even forming attribute crystals of different mana. I should thank Ilyana for giving me a stage to test out part of my strength. Now I know how to use it better. If I combined the crystals say when making a formation then wouldn't it change the attribute of the formation more, so that it would require less mana to activate?

The judge coughed, remembering where he was. "For this match, Miss Qin wins!"

People were still numb, not knowing whether to clap or to boo.

***

"No—no," Ilyana cried. Her world felt as if it were falling down around her ears as she heard the determination of the judge. "She has to have cheated! How?!"

"There was no cheating." The judge's voice turned heavy, as she was putting his honor into question.

"I did not mean it that way." She had the presence of mind to bow to the judge as she clasped her hands to him. "She must have been hiding her age or her abilities!"

"Well, shouldn't you have looked that up before you had your flunky pour hot tea on me and the book I was reading?! I was working on a new design! Do you know how precious those books are?!" Qin screamed, starting to get angry again as she remembered the episode.

"For hiding her age and ability, this should be a draw, no?" a voice called from the stands.

People turned to the powerful voice.

"Elder Mao is here!" someone whispered in the crowd.

"Isn't Ilyana his granddaughter?"

"He is the strength of the Mao clan in the academy. The Mao clan will not allow this to stand." Another sighed.

"The power of the formation clans is substantial indeed," another agreed.

"How did I hide my Strength?" Qin demanded.

"You have no pin and you are attending a beginner's class. What other reason would you have to attend other than to humiliate the people of my Formation Guild?" he said calmly.

The crowd started to nod and looked at Qin and Julilah with eyes of suspicion.

Qin rolled her eyes. "We don't have a basic knowledge of formations. We only had some ideas about it. I don't see why I have to convince you. Also, we don't have those badges like you do. We're not part of the Formation Guild."

"But hiding your age—shouldn't you be ashamed?" Elder Mao said. "The older generation fighting the younger generation—isn't it bullying?"

"Yes, yes it is. So, are you willing to have a duel?" Julilah asked, doing her best to act innocent. All eyes turned to her. She smiled as she looked at Elder Mao, like a wolf would look at a cornered prey.

Elder Mao flicked his robe, his agitation showing on his face. "Very well!" he exclaimed. "If I win, you will both leave my Formation Guild!"

"If I win, I want you both to apologize and Ilyana must, under oath, tell the truth of what happened," Julilah said sweetly.

The crowd's opinion swayed.

"The truth under oath—if she means that, then could Ilyana really be targeting them?" someone asked.

"It looks like there is more to be seen here!"

"Two formation duels and with Elder Mao a mid-Journeyman formation master! I would pay money and lose years off my life for this opportunity!"

"Wait till I tell my family—they will go green with jealousy, this should be most fun!"

The crowd's excitement built up as Elder Mao nodded. With just a few words, she had been able to turn his words and the sentiment of the crowd around.

He thought it would be a silly fight. Qin had showed some ability, but it wasn't earth-shattering. It was bullying for him to go up against Julilah but he had to defeat her completely. This was now a matter of honor for the Mao clan.

He jumped from where he was and fell into the arena, settling on the ground.

"Elder Mao." The judge bowed to him.

"I thank you for your time and your fair judgements," Elder Mao said, discreetly acknowledging the judge's previous call that Mao Ilyana had lost.

The judge bowed deeper. "It is merely my duty as a member of the Formation Guild."

Elder Mao didn't miss the hidden meaning. These were outsiders and they couldn't have their faces dragged through the dirt with their actions. Elder Mao would need to redeem their Formation Guild.

He stepped up to the stage; Qin talked to Julilah before high-fiving her and heading off the stage.

Julilah stood there as the judge stepped forward as well.

Qin pulled out a sound transmission talisman and used it on her sound transmission device.

Elder Mao didn't pay attention to it. There wasn't anything that could shake the match.

"Elder Mao has created the challenge, so Miss Julilah, what kind of duel do you wish to have?"

"Formation building," Julilah said without pausing.

The audience calmed down and quieted.

"Formation building? She wants to go up against Elder Mao in formation building?"

"Well, being a Journeyman formation master, he has unlocked his Formation Book. His information is probably vast with his age. Being in the Fourth Realm, he has probably had to face life-and-death trials, meaning the fighting with formations will be difficult," another thought aloud.

"Seems she is not taking him lightly!"

"Do you think she would win in any of the challenges? It just might not be as bad of a result as some of the others." Another chuckled.

"Truly, some people are just at the bottom of a well," someone else said.

***

Yui was running a briefing on the training groups for Erik when he got a call. "Sorry, it's from Qin."

"Answer it," Erik said.

"Qin, I'm in the middle of something and I don't have Mana stones to lend you," Yui said.

"Julilah and I might be in some trouble. It started with a girl, Ilyana, making me challenge her to a duel, but now Julilah is fighting an elder."

"Tell me everything from the beginning." Yui had matured, not charging into action. He was a leader of one of Alva's platoons; he couldn't simply charge out to fight for his sister now.

She reported everything to him and Yui was left with a difficult expression on his face.

"Something happen?" Erik asked.

Yui quickly relayed the situation to Erik.

"Tell her to send us a message if anything else happens." Erik raised his sound transmission device to his mouth and sent a message.

"Erik is looking into it. If anything happens, don't hesitate to send a message," Yui said.

"Okay," Qin said.

"Promise me," Yui begged.

"I promise. I'll hold a sound talisman to send a message."

"Good. We'll get this sorted out soon." Yui ended the talk as Erik finished with his call.

"I talked to the head of the Formation Guild here. They will send a message to the head over there. Niemm, you and your team are on me. Yui, I need to know you'll follow my orders to the letter," Erik said.

"Yes, sir." Yui saluted.

"Okay, you can come as well. We'll head off right now. If it is resolved, we'll leave, but if something goes wrong, we can intervene." Erik stood.

Niemm started sending messages and pulled out his armor, putting it on.

"Are you sure, sir?"

"Qin isn't one to overreact and we need to show that we will not be bullied. Strength is all that the people of the Ten Realms know, so we have to show it once in a while," Erik said in confirmation.

***

Academy Head Yan Zemin lived a comfortable life. She was a peak Journeyman formation master, with half a foot in the Expert level. She had achieved her position later in life and although it was possible for her to reach Expert level in formations, she was much later than those geniuses so she didn't get the resources or attention of others.

She was made the head of the academy and carried out her tasks faithfully, not showing favor to one group or another. She largely ran the academy from afar, taking time to take in the sights and discover art across the Ten Realms.

She was sitting and having tea in her garden, looking over the perfect scene. Formations to gather Mana were set up, allowing plants from across the Ten Realms to bloom, filling the air with their refreshing scents.

If one was to look carefully, they would see that the plants were in a formation of their own, everything perfectly laid out and measured.

She was interrupted by someone entering the garden. She knew it by the change in Mana flow. She sighed and looked over as a messenger hurried over.

"Word from Vuzgal, Formation Guildmaster." He dropped to his knees.

"Go on." Seeing how fast he had arrived, she felt something was wrong.

"Two students, a Miss Qin and a Miss Julilah, are patrons of the Vuzgal lord. He called in a personal favor to have the two attend basic formation classes. He has sent word about a possible issue and hopes that we can make sure that any conflicts don't escalate," the messenger said.

"Speak plainly," she said, not willing to try to figure out the hidden meaning in his words.

"Miss Qin and Miss Julilah are dueling right now; they must have gotten word. They are fine with the duels and will agree to the results, but they don't want the two ladies to be hurt. They went up against Mao Ilyana, and Elder Mao stepped in to try to save face for the Formation Guild."

"Ilyana, she is a good prospect, but she is nearly two times the duo's age. Did they fight her at the same time or help each other?"

"No, Miss Qin used layering formations and then an enhancing formation to defeat Ilyana."

Yan Zemin's brows creased. "I will go over there myself." She sighed and pulled out a formation-covered pendant. She put it on her robes. The formations glowed as two phantom wings appeared on her back. She took off and headed toward the dueling platform, only dust left behind where she had been standing.

***

Two tables had been brought to the arena. Elder Mao and Julilah had their materials and items laid out on the tables.

The judge looked at them both. "Please begin," he said.

Julilah grabbed a formation plate and started to carve into it.

Elder Mao checked his equipment once more and then picked up a carving tool. He started to carve into the formation plate, his motions fluid from years of practice.

"Every movement of Elder Mao seems to be in harmony with the formation plate. He only needs to carve a line or rune once, without any need for revisions," an Apprentice said, stunned.

A few Journeyman-level formation masters had joined; seeing Elder Mao's work could be said to be a lucky chance for them.

Julilah didn't take long to finish with her formation plate. It was set up with lines connecting five holes in the outer formation and one in the center.

She went to the next formation plate and then frowned. She appeared to be looking through a book—many missed it, but the judge saw her actions and focused on her.

Elder Mao didn't know what was going on with Julilah. He was focused on making his formation. Even if he was going up against a junior, he wouldn't create a sub-par formation.

He knew that Ilyana's freedom relied on him. He had removed those distractions from his thoughts. Formations needed to be made with utmost focus.

He finished carving the formation and moved to an ink slab and a selection of reactants in a tray of bottles. He combined the reactants into a solution on the ink slab. He took out his brush and dabbed it into the reactants and started to trace out the formation with the reactants.

He finished some time later and looked up at Julilah. Now, all that was left to do was introduce power into his formation.

His eyes were deep and controlled but his eyes turned alarmed as he saw her sitting in her chair. But her eyes were up in the sky; she made motions with her head.

To others, it would look bizarre, but to a Journeyman-level crafter, they would know what it looked like when one was looking through their skill-related book.

She's of the Journeyman level? He was a bit shocked to say the least. He thought she might be older than Ilyana, but based on the level of low thirties and her appearance, he didn't think she was that much older. *If she is already in the Journeyman realm, then isn't she some kind of genius?* Elder Mao racked his head, before he calmed himself down. He had been a Journeyman for a long time and his skills were strong for the realm.

Still, it could create problems even if she is kicked out. She and Qin are close. I will have to get Ilyana to agree to release Qin from being a slave. There might be a bigger background to them. If I win a victory over one, then I can annull the agreement between Ilyana and this Qin.

***

Julilah had been studying formations for nearly two years now. Coming to the academy run by the Formation Guild, she felt that finally a lot of things had snapped into place. With the lectures, although they were basic, they built up the roots of one's formation knowledge and ability.

Still, she had been researching most of her time here. Finding out something new was exciting and she and Qin competed against each other all the time. It was unknown whether Qin would be able to keep her position as the department head in a few years with Julilah neck and neck with her.

Qin had taken to studying combat formations, including ways to make formations during battle so she could fight with them.

Julilah had gone a different route, looking to enchant items. With the socket formations that Rugrat had created, she had altered her own techniques and worked on them for months so her own knowledge of formation sockets was even greater than Rugrat's now.

She had then taken up compartmentalization, similar to Qin's way of making different parts of a formation and building them up with the systems that were needed to achieve the desired result. She had broken formations into several components; if she messed up one formation, then she could take it out and replace it if needed rather than losing the formation as a whole.

She sighed and put away the formation she had been working on and took out a fresh formation plate. She could feel the seconds ticking down and the eyes of everyone on her as she double-checked the information in her skill book to make sure she was carving the formation out properly.

She kept on working; her competitive side ignited as she dared to make the strongest formation that she knew of. A formation that she had not actually fully built before.

She knew it was risky, but the thrill of it all invigorated her. She had been acting all cold and emulating being an adult to try to get people to leave her to study, but now her younger side drove her to take risks and put it all on the line.

***

Yan Zemin looked at the formations on the tables. She was up in one of the higher rooms around the arena. Quite a few of the teachers had come out to see what had made Elder Mao enter the arena against a student.

Still, she was able to find an empty room to view the competition.

Elder Mao's formation was done with traditional methods and was a high-quality mid-Journeyman level formation: a defensive Mana barrier formation that all Journeyman formations masters had done before.

"He didn't believe his opponent would be that much trouble." Yan Zemin whispered as she looked at the formation in front of Julilah. She had seen formations like it before, but it was usually used by high-Journeyman-level formation crafters or Experts in order to save materials; if one part of the formation didn't work, then it wasn't all destroyed and become a wasted effort.

From her actions, Julilah showed that she had entered the Journeyman level already.

Yan Zemin pulled out a thin scroll and opened it.

It was the orders she had got from the Vuzgal Formation Guild about them entering her school and they were to be treated like any other student. Their background and their skill level wasn't known. When they had to fill out information sheets, they didn't put down their last names; the only thing she gained from it was their age.

Both of them were still teenagers.

"Vuzgal is becoming a new jewel of the Fourth Realm. Its lord is mysterious, training up fighters who use ways similar to the Sha to fight. He is a member of the Alchemist Association and a healer as well as a fighter. He even has a Blue Lotus head controlling the city." Yan Zemin tapped her armrest in thought.

A part of me wants to try to recruit them, but we just got a partnership with Vuzgal. Poaching his people would only anger him for sure. If there is a possible way to leverage a spot in the crafter's dungeon trial ahead of the lines...

Julilah used a Mana stone, imbuing the formation with power. The reactants started to glow, the formations ready to be activated at a moment's notice.

She checked it once and looked over to the judge. "I am done."

Everyone looked as the judge took the two formations to a testing table of his own. He checked the formations over—their line work, the runes, and reactants.

The more he studied the formations, the more wrinkles appeared on his brow.

Yan Zemin sent him a message. "Teacher Lin, do you require assistance?"

"Head Yan Zemin, I am indeed in over my head. I can make a proper evaluation on Elder Mao's formation but not on Student Julilah's."

Yan Zemin didn't miss how his address toward Julilah had changed. Miss created a greater distance, while Student acknowledged that she was someone who had learned formations.

"I will be down." Yan Zemin exited her room and used her flying formation, descending from the skies and into the arena.

"Who is that?"

"Head Yan Zemin!" someone yelled out.

"I only saw her once at my brother's graduation ceremony but it must be her!"

The students and the teachers bowed to her as she appeared on the stage next to the judge, Teacher Lin.

Elder Mao bowed to her; Qin and Julilah cupped their hands and gave small bows, their eyes filled with suspicion. Yan Zemin's eyes didn't miss the sound transmission talisman on Qin's hands.

She turned to the two formations and looked at them. The original evaluation of Elder Mao's formation was right on. He had made so many of them that there were only a few flaws in its creation.

She looked at the other formation. There were a number of flaws that showed with someone who was still trying to figure out the formation.

Her impassive face showed a hint of a smile. She tapped her lips before nodding to herself.

"It is close, but Student Julilah wins," Yan Zemin proclaimed.

Everyone wanted to deny this result.

Julilah let out a laugh and Qin grabbed her in a fierce hug. The two of them jumped up and down in excitement.

"Though I must say that I don't agree with these bets." Yan Zemin's voice turned colder.

Qin and Julilah stilled their exultations. Elder Mao and Ilyana looked up to Yan Zemin as if she were a savior.

"Elder Mao, being closed up seems to have made it harder for you to see the goings-on in the outside world. You will be taking up a teaching position for the next ten years," she said in a grave tone. "Mao Ilyana, your actions have shamed the Formation Guild and my academy."

Ilyana paled.

Yan Zemin already had her suspicions of what had really happened and she would investigate it all. She turned to Qin and Julilah. "I am sorry for this request and I know it is an awkward one to make. Will you allow Ilyana to remain within the academy? I still need to investigate the matters around this but you already made a bet."

"It was fun to use our skills somewhere other than the classroom. I'll leave her punishment up to you, Head Yan." Qin bowed respectfully.

Yan Zemin had seen many people. With their Strength, they weren't being arrogant and trying to shame the Formation Guild any more than they needed to.

"From now on, I believe I speak for the staff when I say that you have graduated the Novice and Apprentice classes. You can pick whichever classes you want to attend up to the Journeyman level and browse all of our libraries, other than the sections above Journeyman and the restricted areas," Yan Zemin announced.

Julilah and Qin bowed to her.

"I declare these contests at a close." Yan Zemin clapped her hands together.

The crowds stood up and clapped, some with mixed feelings. But none of them could deny the exciting show they had just seen.

"A student beating an elder, and what technique did she make?"

"That formation—I have never seen it before. There are multiple formations inside one another. How don't they burn out?"

"Was that your first attempt?" Yan Zemin asked Julilah, using a spell so others couldn't see or hear her talking.

Julilah nodded as Yan Zemin's smile grew.

"Bring Qin and visit my garden in two days." Yan Zemin looked around, seeing over a dozen people wearing cloaks with a dangerous aura.

Her eyes thinned as she looked at the two strongest. She didn't know when they had arrived, the competition grounds were public for people to see the strength of the Formation Association and bring in money.

The men turned back towards her, they seemed to notice her eyes on them.

They wore strange armor under their cloaks and she saw a strange crest on their chests, there was a spire standing above a castle with a V underneath.

"Vuzgal?" She muttered to herself.

She swore one of the men smiled, he touched the brim of his cloak hood in salute and they turned away again, walking down the corridor.

She looked at Qin and Julilah before she rose into the skies, leaving the arena behind.

***

Erik and the special, left the formation academy, people moved away from the cloaked group, they didn't try to restrain their complete auras. After all strength was respected across all of the Ten Realms and getting stuck in foot traffic kind of sucked.

Yui relaxed and the rest of the group did as well.

"Looks like they even got access to more classes and books. Seems like they're running off to a library now." Yui let out a laugh, filled with tension as he relaxed.

Erik stood and smacked his shoulder.

"Thank you, sir," Yui said.

"We protect our own—it just happened to be your sister. But we would do it for anyone from Alva or from those who have asked for our help," Erik said. "Though it is good to not be needed sometimes!"

They had serious expressions on their faces as they continued towards the totem.

Chapter: Stone Fist Sect

Erik had been training people during the day, increasing the number of people within the army. Their numbers were growing faster the longer they went on. Hiao Xen had filled all of Vuzgal's administrative positions. With the review boards, the people who had come expecting a free ride or had been using their power to allow others to skirt the law had been removed or forced to work for Vuzgal as their prisoners.

The roads to the east had been cleaned up and there was traffic moving every day. Expert crafters from across the realms came and visited the city for the chance to use the Expert crafting rooms.

The Sky Reaching Restaurants had been built, but the chefs, cooks, and staff still needed to be trained up. People from the Division Headquarters in the Third Realm were moving to Vuzgal to reduce the burden on staff.

The Wayside Inns and the bank were doing a big business with financing people; Mana stones passed hands constantly.

The Blue Lotus had weekly auctions with items that could normally only be found in the other capitals. The Alchemist Association had the biggest presence after the Crafter's Association.

If one needed anything to be crafted, they could find it in Vuzgal.

The inner city had been revitalized and the large noble manors were now being upgraded with additional floors.

Stores had gone up what seemed like overnight, with taverns and tea houses following quickly on their heels. The associations buildings all sat at the associations circle, standing up proud and tall.

The warehouse district had people coming in and out at all times, with materials moving to the crafter's workshops that constantly churned out high quality products. The crafter workshops were being upgraded as well. Hiao Xen had bought plans, upgrading them straight from tier one to tier three. In the cities, unlike dungeons, one could purchase the plans, but then they needed to build everything themselves.

As soon as funds came in, they were spent: on the military's expenditures, put into the bank, or used to purchase materials from the surrounding areas. They had also started the city libraries; depending on one's contributions to the city, being a resident for a long time, or helping out the city, one could access the library, finding all kinds of information on many subjects. It was a new idea and a costly one but Vuzgal had the money to spend. Hundreds of people came just to study in the library and hopefully be able to start crafting.

Vuzgal was advertised as a city of traders and crafters, but the fighters also had a large presence. The three combat dungeons gave ample rewards worth up to ten times the admittance fee and the possibility to level up as well.

In a day, three Sky Mana stones' worth of money were moving through the city in trade. Just in taxes, Vuzgal earned one hundred and fifty Earth Mana stones per day. With the dungeons, Sky Reaching Restaurants, Wayside Inns, rent, and the totem's revenue being piled up on top of that. Erik had taken over the old Alchemy lab that was hidden in the castle. Now that he had the time, he took out a pile of ingredients and used his Reverse Alchemist abilities to increase the amount of knowledge he had on Alchemy and the ingredients that could be found in the Ten Realms.

He went to the Alchemist Association in Vuzgal at times, looking up information on available pills for Mana Gathering Cultivation and Body Cultivation.

He had bought a new pill called the Earth Tempering pill. It was supposed to temper one's body with the Earth attribute over time. The problem was that although they weren't that hard to create, you would need to start with one pill per day on the first week, two on the second, and this would increase for ten weeks. If one forgot for one day, they would need to increase the amount of pills they consumed by another one each day.

It would end up being tens of pills and the reasonably costed pills turned into a large cost, especially if one just missed the time period to take the pill just a few times.

Erik stored the last ingredient he had tested out. Information filled out the pages of his Alchemy Book on the ingredients he had just worked with.

He stood and then grabbed the chair as he felt his legs were numb. "Crap!" He used a healing spell on his legs, restoring their function.

"Everything okay?" Roska asked from the door.

"Yup! Just some minor difficulties! Come on, you damn legs." Erik tried to shake them out and get them back alive. He finally half stumbled and fell his way to the door.

Roska was on the other side, giving him an odd look as he started to humanize. "You ready?"

"Maybe?" Erik shrugged as they kept walking. The rest of Special Team Two waited for them near the castle's exit. With the Mana stones they were pulling in each day, going between the realms was no longer an issue with the Alvan army rotating in and out to train and to rest.

They wore cloaks to hide their identity as they left the city.

They passed through the totem; the mid-morning turned into nighttime as they arrived in the Stone Fist Sect's city.

The city had all kinds of healers and alchemists around, as well as stalls selling items that were said to help with tempering one's body. Body Cultivation ruled this city without a doubt.

People wandering all over the place with weapons at the ready.

It took them nearly an hour to reach the main headquarters of the Stone Fist Sect. People were lined up to enter the hall.

Erik and the others joined the line.

"Well, looks like there are a lot of people here," Han Wu observed.

"Thank you, Captain Obvious," Yang Zan chipped in.

"They wanted to bring us in to share in the festivities—seems that someone is getting married and there will be most of the Stone Fist Sect around," Erik said.

"So...best behavior—Han Wu," Roska warned.

Han Wu made a mocked hurt face as they moved with the rest of the line.

Erik passed over the invitation that he had been issued.

The person at the front door bowed as they entered.

"Lord of Vuzgal, Erik West!" someone announced.

"Well, there goes staying under the radar," Erik muttered to Roska.

They pulled off their cloaks as they headed into the room.

The people all watched them coming in.

An older man with a husky build walked over to them with a wide smile. "Lord West, I am glad to see you! I'm Lord Morraine!"

"It is good to meet you, Lord Morraine," Erik said. The people around them both started to move over to him.

They had a brief conversation, with Lord Morraine hinting at getting some personal concessions. Thankfully, he didn't push it too much and he left Erik alone after some time.

Others moved in to make their introductions and to greet Erik. He met with them throughout the evening. His face muscles hurt from forcing a smile for such a long time.

"From the Elsi clan, Mira Elsi!" the announcer called out.

A woman walked out. All eyes were drawn to her as she walked in with a green and purple dress. She had an impassive face, as if she couldn't hear the comments below as people talked among themselves.

"Mira Elsi—she is the betrothed to the Young Master Perkins. She might be beautiful but she sullied herself with a beast from the lower realms."

"It is only because of her special constitution that someone like Young Master Perkins would be even willing to look at her."

"Young Master Perkins is a lecherous fellow, with three wives and more than ten times that in concubines!"

"His father is a man of power, so none are willing to step in his way."

"I heard she even had two children. She and Young Master Perkins are well suited!"

Erik heard their conversations and looked up at the lady, frowning.

"Mira? I've heard that name before I think...some time ago now." He felt that the information was on the tip of his tongue but he couldn't figure it out in the end.

"Do you know her?" Roska asked.

"I'm not sure but something sounds familiar," Erik said.

The festivities went into the night. Erik drank and ate, entertaining the different members of the Stone Fist Sect and those who walked up to him.

It wasn't until much later he escaped to a residence that had been prepared for him. He didn't do much other than read books and hang out with the special team as they waited until the next day.

Through the servants, he was able to request to see Lady Mira Elsi. He felt that if they were in the same room, he would remember what he felt was so familiar about her.

Lord Morraine appeared once again and took them off to the dungeon located in the outskirts of the city.

They left the city in carriages. The trip did not take long at all and they soon arrived at what could be called a small town onto itself. The walled town surrounded the dungeon, supplying the dungeon explorers with all the items they might need.

Here the streets were filled with just those from the Stone Fist Sect.

People came out to see the lord of Vuzgal, a city that was making a name for itself in the Fourth Realm.

"Sorry about all of this, but hearing someone as storied as yourself, others can't help but be excited. I know that the Stone Fist Sect truly values your time and your presence." Morraine chuckled, studying Erik out of the corner of his eye.

"Thank you for your kind words." Erik had gotten better at this doublespeak that most powerful people in the Ten Realms seemed to do with ease.

"The dungeon has been cleared out before but when going in, you will find a heavy pressure upon yourself, compressing your entire body. Break this token and we will send in someone to assist if you are in danger," Lord Morraine said in a grave voice, handing Erik a plain stone token in the shape of a large coin.

"Thank you." Erik turned to the members of Special Team Two. "See you lot in a bit. Don't touch anything."

He walked down the stairs of the dungeon. The air seemed to be damp and musky. It smelled wonderful, like freshly tilled soil. Erik found that he was out of breath as he walked, taking a few minutes.

"The pressure has increased, though it's not like high altitude or even being underwater. Is this higher gravity?" He looked around. "Tempering body with Earth attribute—does it mean withstanding the pressure?"

Erik continued on, taking breaks periodically to recover. It took him a few hours to pass through the dungeon. As he got closer to the dungeon core the gravity steadily increased, making every action harder.

He took out Wraith's Touch salve and put it on his neck, using it to numb his nerves so he wouldn't feel the gravity building up on his body.

Using his Simple Organic Scan, he looked to see whether there were any changes in his body. His body was slowly compressing and compacting.

He used Simple Heal, allowing his body to recover but now, instead of rebounding and going back to the way it was, his bones, his skin, his muscles, and the rest of his body regrew and compressed his Fire tempering and the Fire Mana that had become a part of his body appeared.

"Iron body—I get it now," Erik muttered. He continued forward, his pace now at only a few steps a minute, the gravity climbing. He had to take breaks, getting used to the gravity forces and then keep on moving. Like iron, Erik's body was the raw material, the Fire energy already inside him the heat, and the Earth energy the hammer. Only with the two of them could they reform Erik's body—removing the impurities and bringing out a raw hidden material, just as iron was refined. With his compressed system, threads of the yellow Earth Mana seeped through his pores and bathed his body. With each compression, there was more power stored up in his body.

A faint yellow fog appeared in his Mana channels. Erik had to stop, finding it hard to breathe. Each step was now torture. He had to stand there, letting his body adjust.

He had learned from Rugrat, taking his time instead of trying to force his cultivation.

He took hours to take even a few steps. His foundation was strong, all of his work was adding to his original strength.

Though, with his foundation, it was harder for him to temper his body.

"This is a lot harder than what I read about in the books from the different associations," Erik said through his teeth, using the words to rally his body. He fell to his knees and had to crawl forward.

He went up to his limit, holding on as long as he could before his Mana started to dry up.

He tried to drag himself back but had to use the token, breaking it. He heard people approaching. Two disciples from the Stone Fist Sect who had already gone through the Earth tempering grabbed him and carried him back. Erik felt his entire body becoming lighter and lighter as if it were nothing. He passed out in relief.

In his body, yellow Earth Affinity energy and Fire energy circled each other like dragons passing through his body.

***

Erik woke up in the residence they had stayed in the night before. He felt as if he were in a new skin; as if he had taken a weight off for the first time in months and it almost felt foreign being so light and free.

Erik got out of bed, controlling his Strength like when he leveled up a few times and dumped stat points into his different attributes.

Still, his notifications hadn't showed any changes and he felt as though there were still some way to go before he could fully temper his body with the Earth Affinity energy.

Well, the way I see it, there are two ways to do it: be exposed to high Earth Mana Affinity and slowly integrate it into my body, compressing and regrowing, or to subject myself to rapid bursts of Earth energy, letting it run rampant in my body. For the first, if I am doing it without aid, it could take months or years. If I was to do it the second way, I would need to have someone watching me. Though I can at least confirm what happens and what I need to do. If we can open up the Earth floor of Alva Dungeon, there must be a way to concentrate that energy. If it was possible to concentrate the attributes on every floor in Alva Dungeon, then we could temper people that way, instead of having to make expensive and wasteful concoctions.

He went to the door, quickly getting used to the changes in his body. He reached the door, finding the special team waiting outside.

"How are you feeling?" Yang Zan asked as he stood up from a card game.

"A bit compressed." Erik smiled as Yang Zan indulged him with a smile.

"Mind if I check you out with a Simple Organic Scan?"

"Go for it."

Yang Zan walked over and put his hand on Erik. Using Simple Organic Scan, he checked Erik over quickly.

"Mira Elsi agreed to the meeting. She is waiting on us," Roska said.

"Anything happen?"

"Haven't got any messages."

"We good?" Erik asked Yang Zan, who had finished with his Simple Organic Scan.

"Looking fine to me." Yang Zan nodded.

Chapter: Return to the First Realm

Mira Elsi stomped around the room.

"First, I'm being sold off to a lecherous man who wants nothing more than my body. Now I need to wait on every man who comes through to our sect." The Mana in her body circulated furiously before she was able to get herself under control.

Doing the family's bidding is the only way that I can protect Feng, Felicity, and Chonglu.

The fight seemed to go out of her and she deflated. She had ways to stop the lecherous Young Master Perkin's advances, but she wouldn't be able to find everyone's weaknesses and use it against them.

"Lord West is on his way over," a servant said.

She let out her frustration in a long exhale. All of her servants were loyal to her and handpicked. They didn't dare to speak up as she raged around the room.

It wasn't long until the door opened and Lord West walked in.

"Hello, I was wondering if you could answer a question for me," Lord West said as some of his guards moved out behind him.

"What is it?" Mira asked in a cold tone, annoyed with his direct manner.

"Do you know a Chonglu?"

How does he know that name? Does he want to use them against me? Her body shook in anger, as cold fear filled her.

"No?"

"If you want to use them against me..." Mira started.

"Use them against you? I think you have me wrong," Erik crossed his arms, frowning as he closed his eyes, remembering the worsd from back then.

"Their father said that his wife was from a powerful clan that lives in the Earth realm. She was adventuring in the Second Realm when they met up. They adventured together for some time before going to the First Realm and establishing themselves here, looking to settle in and have a family.

Erik saw that he had the attention of the entire room, as the Ice Empress truly looked like an ice statue as he started walking and talking, back and forth to jog his memory.

"Little did he know that her family had other plans. They sent people down from the Fourth Realm to deal with them. Dragging away his wife without letting her say goodbye. While telling me that they would never allow the spawn that I had desecrated Her Holiness with, to survive.

Erik didn't miss the chill in the air, or the wrath in her eyes that were focused on Erik completely. If he said one thing that was wrong she would strike him down. He continued, not paying her anger any heed.

"They left and he didn't think much of their words, he was lonely but he had his children to live for. It was cut short as both the girl and the boy were affected with a nasty poison.

Erik paused his steps and looked at the Ice Empress, feeling hisbody shaking slightly in rage as a twisted smile, formed from pain and anger filled his face.

"They were *toddlers*." His rage escaped for a second, anyone that killed children without care or remorse, or because of some stupid system they believed in. He didn't care what damn excuses they came up with. If he found them, he would make them suffer.

He composed himself and kept walking, unable to look at anyone for fear that his emotions would take a hold.

"It seeped into their bone marrow and took root. For two years they lived off of healing concoctions, in a comatose state, nearly dead. Their father shut himself off from the world, cared for them, focused only on them.

"Thankfully they recovered, do you know what the names of the twins were?" Erik looked to the Ice Empress who looked to be a chaotic mess of emotions, her eyes filled with tears, her fists balled in rage and her body shaking from an emotional backlash that was more powerful than any physical attack.

"Felicity and Feng," Erik's words were light as he looked her in the eyes.

She lowered her head, forcing herslef to keep her composure.

"Thank you for telling me your story I am sorry but I won't be able to see you out," She said in a hoarse voice, looking to the floor.

"I hope you have a good day my lady," Erik tilted his head and left the room quickly.

As the door closed Mira raised her head as ice formed around her.

"I am going to see the contract hall!" she said savagely.

None of her attendants dared to stop her as she turned and stormed out of the room.

***

Erik and the special team said their goodbyes to Lord Morraine.

"Are you sure you don't want to stay longer? One will need to go into the Earth-attribute dungeon multiple times in order to complete the temperings."

"Thank you for your hospitality, but I have some other things that I need to attend to," Erik said.

"Ah, it is a shame. Very well." Lord Morraine sighed, but he saw that there was no changing Erik's stance.

Erik went to the totem and nudged Gong Jin. "Take us all the way down," Erik said.

Gong Jin and Erik shared a look as he nodded and used the totem interface.

Earth-grade Mana stones disappeared from their hands and they disappeared in a flash of light.

Noise greeted them as Erik smiled freely for the first time in a long time.

"It is good to be home!" He laughed as he looked out over Alva Dungeon his eyes falling on the teleportation array. With the resources from Vuzgal and the newfound strength of the Alvan army, the limits on all of their growth were coming to an end. It was time that they reclaimed the other floors and grew the strength of Alva, not just their military.

It was time to cultivate, to grow their skills and increase their crafting levels, it was time to build Vuzgal, Alva, Vermire, their branches and prepare to head to the fifth realm.

Vuzgal's time had only started.

Thank you for your support and taking the time to read **The Fourth Realm**.

The Ten Realms will continue in the **Fifth Realm.**

Please, if you have some time, leave a review or rating, they help to spread the word about the book!

You can check out my other books, what I'm working on and upcoming releases through the following means:

Website: http://michaelchatfield. com/[1]

Twitter: @chatfieldsbooks[2]

Facebook: Michael Chatfield[3]

Goodreads: Goodreads. com/michaelchatfield[4]

---

1. http://michaelchatfield.com/

2. https://twitter.com/chatfieldsbooks

3. https://www.facebook.com/michaelchatfieldsbooks/?ref=hl

4. https://www.goodreads.com/author/show/14055550.Michael_Chatfield

Patreon (you can get sneak peeks about what I'm working on, signed books, swag and access to contests): https://www. patreon. com/michaelchatfieldwrites[5]

Thanks again for reading! ☺

Interested in more LitRPG? Check out https://www. facebook. com/groups/LitRPGsociety/[6]

---

5.   https://www.patreon.com/michaelchatfieldwrites

6.   https://www.facebook.com/groups/LitRPGsociety/

Don't miss out!

Visit the website below and you can sign up to receive emails whenever Michael Chatfield publishes a new book. There's no charge and no obligation.

https://books2read.com/r/B-A-MXIG-ZWAY

BOOKS 2 READ

Connecting independent readers to independent writers.

Also by Michael Chatfield

Printed in the USA
CPSIA information can be obtained
at www.ICGtesting.com
LVHW051920031123
762582LV00077B/15